I0788552

The Steve Williams Series I

By

J.E. Taylor

The Steve Williams Series I © March 2024 by
J.E. Taylor

Cover Art by Cora Graphics
www.coragraphics.it

The Steve Williams Series

Special Agent Steve Williams excels at his job, catching the most heinous of monsters walking the earth.

Serial killers.

When his job brings him face to face with a psychic, he struggles to accept her gifts in his neat little black and white world. Armed with her visions, along with his skills as an FBI agent, he hunts the worst of the worst, but will he catch the killer before they set their sights on him?

Unstoppable, breath stealing, and terrifying all at once.
Gripping, rich and magnificent!

The Steve Williams Series mixes compelling crime thrillers with supernatural forces that will grip the reader from page one. This six-book series takes you through some of Steve Williams' darkest cases in his FBI career.

The STEVE WILLIAMS SERIES I hard-cover edition includes Dark Reckoning, Vengeance, and Hunting Season.

Dark Reckoning
Chapter 1

THE INSTRUCTIONS FLUTTERED ON the ground under a new rubber mallet, ignored.

She tugged on the hem of his shirt. "Daddy, you promised."

"Just a minute." He lifted his hands from the canvas. Poles swayed and metal scraped. Before he could catch it, the tent imploded. Again. Muttering a few choice words, he picked up the fabric and the aluminum frame.

"But Daddy, you said we'd take a walk when Mommy went to the store."

"Can't you see I'm busy?" Amy's father glared sideways at her and tugged on the canvas again. "Just stay out of my way until I get this up." He turned his back and continued to fiddle with the tent poles, swearing under his breath.

Amy slipped to the edge of the campsite, blinking back tears at her father's harsh words. "Stupid tent." She glanced in her father's direction.

He yanked the canvas over the unstable rods yet again, cursing as the tent tilted this way and that.

She stepped into the woods, swallowed by the forest.

That had been hours ago. Now she stumbled through the underbrush, sobbing, searching for the campsite, wishing she had stayed by her father's side.

She turned in frantic circles, but dense brushwood blocked her path in every direction. Blueberry bushes, barberries and prickly thistles pulled at her clothing and scratched her legs. Evergreens reached high, mingled with century old maples and oaks, dimming the last of the evening light.

Amy's hoarse voice persisted, yelling, "Daddy!" over and over and over. Her cries fell on the deaf ears of the New Hampshire forest.

Fighting through a thick clump of bayberry, she fell onto crunchy dried moss in a clearing bordering a small pond. She scrambled to her feet. The still black water rippled, and Amy froze, her eyes glued to the malignant form rising from the surface.

What climbed out of the water was far worse than any Pokémon she'd ever seen, and fear locked down her ability to function.

She couldn't move.

She couldn't breathe.

She couldn't scream.

The staccato beat of her heart thrummed like the wings of a hummingbird and she shivered despite the summer heat, her sweaty tie-dyed t-shirt not enough to keep her warm in the damp clearing.

When it stepped onto the shore, the ground sizzled and the stench of burning moss and rotting flesh blanketed the cove.

Her paralysis broke. A shrill cry of terror, like a lamb at slaughter, barreled from her throat and she turned, fleeing through the woods.

She ran as fast as her little Keds would take her.

But it wasn't fast enough.

THE SEARCH PARTY COMBED through the dense forest, each member clutching a picture and calling Amy's name.

The young FBI agent halted, the child's name swan-diving from his lips in a silent rush of air. The earth in front of him was painted reddish-brown with pieces of cloth, flesh, bone, and blood-streaked hair scattered through the red sludge. But the sneaker caught his attention.

A single, blood-splattered Keds.

He took a step back, his gaze bouncing between the photograph in his hand and the carnage before him, trying to reconcile the bloody remains on the ground with the happy child in the picture.

Bile rose in his throat and he gulped, forcing it down his already burning esophagus, willing his churning stomach to settle.

He looked down, surprised to see the snapshot crumpled in his clenched fist.

His eyes were drawn back to the gruesome scene, scanning the massacre and snapping back to the bloody sneaker.

"I swear I'll find you, you son of a bitch," he promised.

He pushed the button on the radio clipped to his shirt, his voice rumbling in his tight chest. "I think I found her."

Dark Reckoning
Chapter 2

THE APARTMENT DOOR SWUNG open. Afternoon sun bleached the picture window, streaking the room with slivers of light.

Jennifer Curtis scanned the expansive living room from the rich mahogany bar to the oversized entertainment center and everything in between. Her jaw dropped, and pressure built on the back of her eyes. "Oh, my God, this is fantastic!"

She set the carton down on the tile entry and walked through the living room, sliding her hand over the deep brown velour chairs, relishing the lush fabric against her fingertips, mesmerized. Kneeling on the couch, she glanced at the balcony and the magnificent view of Mirror Lake beyond.

"I thought you might like it."

She turned and smiled at her best friend, running her hand through her ebony hair. "I had no idea this is what you meant when you said a nice little apartment."

Tracy added her carton to the building pile of boxes in the entry and brushed her honey-colored bangs out of her gray eyes. "Daddy bought the building this summer, and it took some convincing, but he finally crumbled and gave me the penthouse for the year. This is our dream place." Tracy's eyes danced with childish joy. Her hair shimmered in the sunlight. "Look around," she said over her shoulder, and disappeared from view.

Jennifer wandered through the apartment. Besides the sprawling living room, a kitchen that could only be categorized as a chef's dream sat to the right of the entry, and monogrammed nameplates adorned the bedrooms in the hallway on the left. At the end of the hall stood a common dressing room, and a bathroom torn right from the pages of Architectural Digest.

She ran her fingers over her gold monogram and a chill crawled up her spine. Her vision transitioned to a shaded red, like blood dripping over the lens of a camera. She shuddered, shaking the bizarre hallucination away, and blinked at the glimmering script that mocked her sudden wave of fear.

Drawing a deep breath, she closed her eyes and swung the door open. Jennifer let her breath out slowly and stepped inside, opening her eyes.

Definitely over the top. Smooth cherry furniture, canopy bed, satin and silk in shades of powdered blue adorned the bedroom, sprinkled with accents of pink here and there, including light sheer curtains billowing gently in the breeze of the open windows along the back wall.

She crossed to the door in the far corner, opening it with curiosity. Cedar drifted from the large walk-in closet, enveloping her, reminding her of the woods in northern Maine.

Thick and fragrant and dangerous.

Icy fingers tickled the base of her neck, sending tingly sensations over her skull. She swung the door closed and a red flicker in the far corner caught her eye.

What the hell was that?

She yanked the door wide, her eyes scanning the closet again, but she couldn't locate the source of the flare. The air shifted, sending a cool draft into her room. She closed the door and rubbed the newly formed bumps on her forearms, chalking up the nip in the air to an over-active air-conditioner.

She glanced out the window. Brooksfield University and the surrounding mountains filled her vision and a slow smile spread across her lips. *God, it's good to be back at school.* She tossed herself onto the bed with her arms spread across the lush fabric.

"Nice view." Tracy leaned against the doorway.

"The best." She propped herself on her elbows. "This is really ours?"

"Yup. After we finish bringing our things up, I'll show you my room."

"I gather that's a hint?"

Tracy nodded and turned, walking out of the room.

Jennifer followed her to the foyer. A dozen moving boxes lined the path to the door. "Have I really been gawking this long?"

Tracy grinned over her shoulder and pushed the button to the elevator.

An unsettling vision gnawed at the edges of Jennifer's mind, but it was lost the moment the elevators opened. "This is going to be a fantastic year."

The whir of the descending elevator lulled them in the silence and they both watched the numbers on the display.

"How's Billy?" Jennifer looked away from the bright digits crawling through their countdown.

Tracy's face lit up. "Billy is wonderful!" She grinned like the mad hatter. "And we've got someone we want you to meet."

Jennifer rolled her eyes. "Come on, Tracy, you know I hate it when you play matchmaker." Jennifer stepped off the elevator and pushed through the lobby doors, heading toward her car.

"This wasn't my idea, it was Billy's." Tracy caught up with her with eyes wide and sincere. "He's really a nice guy."

Jennifer grabbed one of the two remaining boxes and started back toward the building. The trunk slammed, and Tracy's hurried footfalls followed her into the lobby and the waiting elevator.

"Jen?" Tracy broke the silence as the doors closed.

"I'm not ready yet. I know it's been almost two years since Tom died, but..." The engagement ring he gave her the night he died still sat in the little velvet box on her bureau at home. Open, dust ridden, like a shrine. "Not yet." Tears filled her eyes, and she blinked them away.

"You can't keep mourning him forever. Tom wouldn't want that."

"I know." Jennifer edged around the clutter in the apartment's entrance. "Are you going to show me your room, or what?" She changed the subject to something Tracy would latch onto like a fighting bulldog.

Tracy beamed and led her down the hall. "Ready?" She swung the door open. "Tah-dah!"

The room was decorated in soft shades of yellow and lavender and, apart from the colors, it was a mirror image of Jennifer's—with one exception. The view.

Jennifer crossed to the window.

The mountains stared back neutrally.

"Mirror Lake," she whispered. When she turned, Tracy's arms were laced with goose bumps, and her face was a peculiar shade of pale. "Are you okay?" Jennifer asked, and in a blink, the room disappeared.

A little girl chased a butterfly and stood perfectly still when it landed on her outstretched hand. She looked up and her smile disappeared. Her eyes darted at the thick woods surrounding her and she slowly turned, searching for the path she had followed. She bit her lower lip, and the butterfly took off. She followed, mistaking a clearing for their campsite. When she stepped from the thicket, soft moss cushioned her feet and the butterfly fluttered into the open sky.

Water shimmered, reflecting the butterfly's winged journey against the clouds above. The small cove was lush and fragrant with spring flowers lining the edge of the pristine pond.

Curious, she wandered to a flat rock resembling a clover, crawling until she was peering over the edge at her mirror image.

The reflection altered, aging from the six-year-old to that of a young adult. A beautiful woman with honey blonde hair and gray eyes smiled back at the child on the rock.

Blinking, her mind came back to the present and her gaze landed on Tracy, the spitting image of the reflection in the water. Jennifer's hand shot to her mouth, covering the short gasp of air. She pretended to yawn, covering up the initial shock of her vision. Usually her visions were unpleasant, but this one had held the carefreeness of a child.

Tracy dragged her eyes away from the lake, her face still pale.

"Are you okay?" she asked again.

Tracy nodded, and the color crept back into her cheeks. Her eyes looked too bright, too intense. Her gaze drifted toward the window again. "The lake is haunted."

Jennifer burst out laughing, but it quickly dispelled with an 'I'm-not-kidding' look from Tracy. "Really?" She parked herself on the bed, ready for another convoluted story, one that would explain her vision.

"There's an old Abinaqui Indian legend about a rock that hangs over the water in Paradise Cove. They say if you kneel on it and look at the surface, you can see your future."

"No shit!" Jennifer folded her leg under her.

Dimples appeared briefly on Tracy's cheek, and she pressed on. "That part of the lake is practically impossible to get to and has been for as long as I can remember."

"Then how'd you get there?"

Tracy's forehead creased. "What?" Her smoky gray eyes shielded something behind them.

"Never mind." Jennifer waved away the question. "Tell me more about the cove."

Tracy glanced at the lake and the edges of her lips dragged into a frown. "The legend says if you touch the water while it's showing you the future, the mirror breaks, and you see beneath it."

"And?" When Tracy didn't answer, she asked the nagging question, "What's beneath the surface?"

Shaded by her bangs, Tracy's eyes flashed to the window and back. With an inhale of air, the words tumbled in a rush. "There are all sorts of stories. From the boogeyman to the devil himself, but the Abinaqui legend says people see a glimpse of their own death." She paused and chewed on her bottom lip for a second. "The legend also mentions a beast that will wreak havoc on the town if it isn't given an annual sacrifice. Maybe that's what's happening lately. Why some folks have disappeared, and others have been found in pieces."

Chills caressed Jennifer, blooming into visible bumps over her exposed skin, and she shivered. She read the papers. She knew about the violent deaths near the lake this summer. "Now you're just trying to creep me out." She crossed her arms.

Tracy's lips twitched into the kind of smile earmarked for psychopaths. "Come on, we've got a lot of stuff to put away." She left the room.

Jennifer looked at the lake. Ever since they were thirteen, Tracy enjoyed freaking her out. The girl was truly warped.

She walked into the living room, finding Tracy busy putting CDs and DVDs in the entertainment cabinet.

"Is there really a legend, or was this just another elaborate story of yours to scare the shit out of me?"

"There really is a legend. Google it." She put the last of the DVDs away and tossed the empty box toward the entry hall.

"Just out of curiosity, how do you know so much about Paradise Cove?" *And why haven't you ever told me about it before?*

"My father grew up here. Enough about the lake. Let's finish unpacking."

She studied Tracy. Her eyes darted everywhere in the room except to meet Jennifer's, and she kept repetitively rubbing her palms on her hips.

"You've been there," Jennifer said.

Tracy looked away toward the lake. "No."

In the distance, evil laughter mingled with the wind. A metallic taste filled Jennifer's mouth, and she ground her teeth against the sudden swell of fear.

Tracy headed for the kitchen. Her steps hurried, as if fleeing from the questions in Jennifer's eyes.

"We need to put the food away before Billy gets here," Tracy mumbled with a frazzled edge.

Jennifer stared at the lake, wondering why Tracy had just lied.

Dark Reckoning
Chapter 3

THEY WORKED TOGETHER STOCKING the freezer and refrigerator. Once all the cold items were stashed away, they started filling the cabinets. A knock at the door interrupted the silence and Tracy exchanged a glance with Jennifer.

With a grin, she grabbed Jennifer's wrist and pulled her into the living room.

Tracy dropped Jennifer's wrist and swung the door open. "Billy!" She flew into his arms.

At least a foot taller than Tracy, Bill picked her up, twirling her around in a big bear hug, their lips locked in a more than friendly greeting.

His hair was lighter than Jennifer remembered, but then again, he had worked all summer as a lifeguard. He smiled at her with his soft brown eyes and put Tracy down. "Hey, Jenny."

"Hey." Her gaze dropped to the man standing behind Bill. Warmth spread in her belly, and she had to suppress a grin. Dark hair shaded the piercing blue eyes she remembered from her youth, but the rough stubble was new, and it gave him a rugged bad-boy look. He leaned on the doorjamb and crossed his arms. He stood just shy of six feet and the tight powder blue t-shirt accented the well-defined muscles of his chest and abdomen. The slow, easy smile spreading across his lips formed perfect crescent dimples at the very edges. The heat in her belly turned to a tingling chill.

His smile alone could charm the pants off Mother Teresa. Her cheeks bloomed with fiery crimson flames, and she smiled back.

"Jenny, this is Steve Williams. Steve, this is Jenny Curtis." Bill walked into the living room.

"Hi," they both said, shaking hands as if they had never met before this moment. A hint of humor reached his eyes, and then it disappeared.

When his skin touched hers, the chills his smile created turned to molten lava in her veins, and she took a deep breath to quell the inferno before it devoured her. Instead, she focused on his grip, firm and solid. Disappointment flooded her when he pulled away and walked past her into the living room.

"Want a beer?" Tracy asked. Both Bill and Steve nodded, and Tracy grabbed a couple of cans from behind the bar.

"Thanks." Steve glanced around the room. "This sure beats the frat house." He headed onto the balcony and leaned against the railing, studying the view. He popped open the beer and glanced back at them. "Great view."

Jennifer stood at the sliders, taking in his full-grown form, wondering at the wisdom of their game. When Tracy pushed her gently from behind, she shut down her doubts and glared over her shoulder.

Jennifer stepped onto the terrace. "So, you're in the same fraternity as Bill."

"Yes." Steve glanced at her.

"Hey, want to go swimming?" Bill asked from behind them.

Jennifer turned. "Isn't the lake closed for the season?"

"No, it's open until the end of September," Steve said, drawing her attention back to him. He drained his beer. "I'm up for it if everyone else is."

"Come on, Jen. It'll be fun!" Tracy said, her voice filled with a whining plea.

"The lake is beautiful this time of year." Steve leaned against the balcony, looking back at Jennifer. "And I won't bite." He flashed a winning grin. "I promise."

Jennifer's resolve melted. "I guess we're going swimming." She headed back toward her room with Tracy in tow.

"Well?" Tracy whispered.

Jennifer met Tracy's inquisitive gaze with a sharp glare and shut the door on any further conversation. She leaned against the door and closed her eyes. She hadn't been prepared for his overwhelming presence or the feelings she had locked away for ten years. He still left her tongue tied with her heart palpitating in her chest like a runaway train.

She changed and took a deep breath, getting back into character before heading out to the living room where they all waited for her. When she stepped into the foyer, Steve raised an eyebrow. His slow, obvious survey made her nervous, and his lips curved into a smile the moment their eyes met.

Jennifer's heart skipped a beat. "Let's go."

They waited in awkward silence for the elevator.

"What are you studying?" she asked Steve when the doors opened.

"Criminal Law."

Jennifer clamped her lips together in a smirk and offered a derogatory huff.

"What?" Steve asked.

"You look more like a criminal than a lawyer."

Steve smiled, stepping out of the lobby into the bright sunset. "I never said I was going to be a lawyer."

"Jen, do you mind driving with Steve?" Tracy didn't wait for an answer. She pulled Bill toward her shiny, souped-up Jaguar, handing him the keys.

"I guess not," Jennifer replied under her breath. Turning to Steve, she offered a half-hearted smile.

"Really, I won't bite," Steve said, and led her to a beautiful BMW roadster, opening the door for her.

Jennifer slid into the passenger seat and glanced up at the sky. The first hint of starlight sparkled against the deep blue canvas. Fifteen minutes later, they pulled into the beach parking lot next to Tracy and Bill and it was showtime.

Jennifer bolted before the car completely stopped. "You arrogant son of a bitch!" She clenched her fists and stalked off toward the water, creating small sand sprays with each stomp.

STEVE WATCHED HER FROM the car, amused at her little display. He wiped the smile from his lips and stepped out of the car. Tracy and Bill stood with slack-jawed stares.

"What'd you do?" Bill's glance moved from Steve to Jennifer standing on the beach, shifting from foot to foot and muttering loud enough to be heard from the parking lot.

"I said a few things about her, ah, career choice," he explained, selectively choosing the words.

Tracy rolled her eyes and headed in Jennifer's direction.

"What are you, a fucking idiot?" Bill snapped.

"Acting," Steve grunted.

"Dude, she's a hell of an actress." Bill shot a sideways glance in Steve's direction.

Steve shrugged like he didn't have his own opinion of her very convincing skills. He really didn't give a damn what Bill's opinion was, not with his incessant insistence on playing matchmaker. "She has quite a temper." Steve attempted to suppress his smile.

"Oh, yeah," Bill said, as the two of them watched the girls on the beach.

"JEN, ARE YOU OKAY?" Tracy asked.

"That jerk had the nerve to laugh at me because I want to be an actress." She glared at Tracy. "Nice! You said he was a nice guy. He's an asshole!"

"Shush," Tracy whispered, looking over her shoulder.

"I don't care if he hears me. You're an asshole!" she yelled over her shoulder. She closed her eyes, calming herself.

"Sorry, Jen, just forget it. Let's go swimming."

Jennifer peeled her shorts off, dropping them on top of her flip-flops. "I guess in his arrogant way, he paid me a compliment." She waded into the water behind Tracy. "He said I have a pretty face and a decent body."

Tracy laughed.

Steve and Bill headed toward the water. Bill dove in and came up next to Tracy, wrapping his arms around her, and whispered something in her ear. She smiled and nodded.

Jennifer sent a cross glance in Steve's direction when he approached. Dimples flashed before he glanced away.

"I'm sorry," he said, scanning the lake.

"Look at me when you apologize," Jennifer snapped, her tone yanking his attention back to her.

He blinked and his baby blue gaze met hers. "I, ah, I said I was sorry."

"Fine." She dove under the water to stop the grin from forming.

Tracy and Bill retreated, leaving Jennifer and Steve alone.

Steve pressed his lips together in a thin line, watching Tracy and Bill disappear into the woods. When they were out of hearing range, he turned toward Jennifer and clapped, his scowl turning into a genuine smile. "Outstanding performance, Jen."

Jennifer stifled a laugh under her hand. "God, Steve, they're going to kill us when they find out."

"I had to call you when Bill told me who he wanted to set me up with."

"I'm so glad you did," Jennifer said. "I didn't even know you were coming to Brooksfield. I thought you already graduated."

"Well, we kind of lost touch there for a while," he said, his intense gaze captivating her.

Jennifer's smile faded. "I'm sorry about that."

"I'm sorry about what happened to Tom."

Her throat tightened at the sincerity in his eyes. She nodded and dunked under the water to get her bearings. When she surfaced, movement on the shore switched on her acting skills. She pressed her lips together and crossed her arms, sending a sideways glare at Steve.

Steve smiled with his back to the shoreline, but he got the hint. He swam to the raft and hoisted himself up onto the surface.

Jennifer turned towards Tracy as she approached.

"Would you mind going home with Steve?" Tracy eyed him on the raft. "We want to go to that new place down the road... unless you want to come dancing with us?"

"I'll pass on dancing."

"Then would you mind catching a ride back to the apartment with him?" She waved her hand toward the raft.

Jennifer glanced over her shoulder. He was lying on the raft on his back, looking up at the sky. She tightened the muscles in her jaw, letting a beat of silence descend before she turned her head back in Tracy's direction. Instead of meeting her pleading stare, she opted to focus on her hand, making slow trails in the water.

"Please?"

Jennifer huffed and raised her eyes to Tracy. "Fine, but you owe me."

"I promise I'll make it up to you." Tracy dragged herself from the water and joined Bill on the beach. She waved just before she ducked into the passenger seat of the car.

Jennifer waited until Tracy's car pulled away and then swam to the raft.

Steve rolled on his side, propping his head up on his hand.

"Why criminal law if you don't want to be a lawyer?" she said, climbing the old iron ladder and folding herself Indian-style in the small space between Steve and the outer edge of the raft. She tried to ignore the heat that seemed to develop in the space between them.

He shrugged, the setting sun reflected in his eyes and his lips curved into a sexy smile that she remembered from their youth.

"Stop grinning at me like that and answer my question."

"Law enforcement."

"That's much more believable than you being a lawyer."

His eyebrow rose, and he pushed her off the raft.

"You bastard," she said when she broke the surface. She skimmed her palm on the water, sending a wave over the raft, drenching him.

Steve stood and launched into the air. He arched over her in a perfect dive, spearing into the water a few feet beyond her, his entrance clean enough to produce almost no splash.

Seconds later, a tug on her ankle closed the water over her head, cutting off her sudden yelp.

Steve wrapped his arm around her waist, pulled her against him, and surfaced. His laughter rang out over the lake, creating a musical echo filling her ringing ears. He grabbed the side of the raft to stabilize them in the water and met her gaze.

The flash in his bright blue eyes made her heart skip a beat and, being this close to him lit a fire in her that had been dormant for the past two years. Whatever witty, scathing response had been ready to come out as they surfaced faded away into oblivion. The urge to close the distance and taste his mouth took hold. Jennifer licked her lips.

"I'm hungry." He released her and started toward the shore.

The moment he pulled away, disappointment flooded her, weighing her down, and for a second, she thought she'd be dragged under the surface again. She reached out, clinging to the side of the raft. He sliced through the water, his strokes powerful and full of grace. Sighing, she followed the path he cut before her.

He walked up on the sand and ran his hands through his wet hair, sending water down his well sculpted back. He glanced back at her with a playful smile.

Staring at his gorgeous profile, Jennifer felt the breath leave her lungs in a silent rush. The sunset played off the droplets on his body, his muscles glistening as he turned toward her. The intensity of his stare made her knees weak, and she almost stumbled onto the sand.

HIS SMILE FALTERED. WATCHING the water slip off her body stirred a long latent heat within him, and his gaze lingered on her ample curves above and below her tiny waistline before taking in her shapely legs, the entire ensemble enough to make any man drool.

"Ten years," he whispered, stepping closer. "God, you grew up to be a beauty." Gently, he wiped the wet hair away from her cheeks, his fingertips throbbing with the sensation of her skin. Steve squashed the urge to take her face in his hands and kiss her beautiful lips.

This can't happen.

He retreated and looked out over the water, trying to put some distance between him and Jennifer's powerful magnetic pull.

JENNIFER STOOD STILL. HER cheek still burned where his fingers had touched, and her hand rose, swiping the same warm path. Blowing a slow stream of air, she reached down and grabbed her shorts and flip-flops, slipping them on. His profile remained distant and unattainable, and she slowed her approach, wondering what exactly was going through his ruggedly handsome mind. The muscles in his arms flexed, and he glanced in her direction, but his eyes never left the sand near her feet.

"What's wrong?" She cautiously stepping closer.

He met her gaze. "Nothing's wrong. Where do you want to go?"

"I don't think we're exactly dressed for a sit-down meal." Jennifer spread her arms.

"What are you in the mood for?"

Her eyes swept over him, and she smiled, imagining being skin-to-skin in a more compromising situation than out by the raft. She stopped short of fanning herself to cool the inferno that bloomed in her belly. "Chinese sounds good."

"Works for me." He headed toward the car, tossing her a towel and grabbed one for himself. He folded it on the driver's seat and Jennifer followed his lead.

"Last I knew, you were supposed to be getting married. What happened?"

Any trace of a smile on his face disappeared. "She killed herself the day before the wedding."

His answer shocked her into silence. "I'm so sorry," she said once her damn mind-stall ended.

He kept his eyes on the road as he drove. The muscles in his jaw jumped, and he sucked his lower lip between his teeth like he was contemplating what to say.

After he shut the car off in the parking lot, he turned to her. "I haven't been able to let it go. I never finished school. I put my focus into restoring this car and when I finished, I decided I'd shut myself off from the world long enough." He ran his hand over the dashboard. "This car kept me sane."

She studied his profile, torn between throwing her arms around him and asking the flurry of questions assaulting her mind. He was five years older, so he should have graduated long before two years ago. She tilted her head, taking a closer look, but all she saw were layers of pain and anguish.

"And here we are." He reached to grab his t-shirt on the floor in front of her. "You don't have a shirt, do you?"

"No."

"So, to go, then. What do you want?"

"Spicy chicken with fried rice." She looked into his eyes. The hurt was still there under the surface, and more than ever, she wanted to wrap her arms around him and make it disappear.

Steve's lips pressed together, and fire filled his eyes. "Don't look at me like that, Jen. I'm not a charity case." He slammed the driver's door and headed into the restaurant without waiting for a response.

At the door, he stopped and glanced over his shoulder. Their gaze locked and warmth spread through her. She sank down in the seat, closed her eyes, and drifted back ten years.

She hugged herself on the front stoop as he waved goodbye from the back seat of his parent's car. Salty tears slid into the corners of her lips and she flicked them with her tongue. A hollow feeling grew in the pit of her stomach with each yard the car traveled. By the time they drove out of sight, her chest had constricted with sobs.

He had promised he would write. And every day she checked the mailbox. When that first letter arrived, her heart beat so hard that her hands shook. She ripped open the letter, devouring every word.

He wrote often at first, and then the excitement turned to sour disappointment when nothing arrived for weeks on end. As time wore on, his letters became more sporadic and then non-existent.

By the time she got to high school, her boy next door had become just a precious memory.

Jennifer opened her eyes and stared at the man who had made such an impression on her as a child.

Steve dug his wallet from his back pocket and peeled off the cash. Handing it to the cashier, he grabbed the bag and trotted back to the car.

"I didn't know how much I missed you until I saw you today," Jennifer said.

This time, the smile touched his eyes. He handed her the bag, started the car, and glanced over his shoulder as he backed out of the parking spot. The heat from his arm's proximity to Jennifer's shoulder gave her a peculiar tickle in her stomach.

"I still remember how cute you looked in that little yellow dress, like you got all decked out just for me," he said.

"I did." The heat bloomed in her cheeks.

He took a deep breath and pulled to a stop in front of the apartment building. His eyes scanned her briefly, and then he turned away.

Jennifer noticed his quick inspection, and it reminded her of the way Tom used to look at her when they had a block of alone time. "What were you thinking just then?"

"How green your eyes are." He opened the car door and took the bag of food from her.

She bit her lower lip while they waited for the elevator. Standing close was like being an inch away from an electrical fence, the current between them alive and twisting and dangerously close to ignition.

The elevator started its climb to the penthouse. They let the silence fill the space between them until they were in the apartment. "This really is a nice place." He headed onto the balcony with the food.

Jennifer followed and sat on the lounge chair next to him, watching as he arranged the boxes on the table between them. Their fingers brushed when he handed her a pair of chopsticks, and his slow, lazy smile made her heart flutter. *Oh, what I wouldn't give for a taste of those lips.*

"I still can't believe Tracy's father did this for her." She glanced back at the apartment.

Steve nodded. "The benefits of money."

She plucked the spicy chicken from the white box using the chopsticks and slid it into her mouth.

"You're pretty good with these things." He held up his own chopsticks and awkwardly grasped a piece of chicken from the same box. Halfway to his lips, the chicken shot from between the sticks, bounced on the balcony, and rolled off. He glanced between the chopsticks in his hand and the edge of the balcony with raised eyebrows before he slid his gaze her way. "Oops. I hope no one was walking into the building."

Jennifer giggled. "I can't wait to see what you do with the rice."

Steve reached into the bag and pulled out a plastic fork with a grin. "Yeah. That's not happening." He put the chopsticks down and ate with the fork.

Jennifer roared. She held her stomach with one hand and covered her mouth with the other, trying not to let the food spout with the laughter.

"Stop laughing at me." His smirk was enough to keep her giggling.

She swallowed. "I can't help it," she said, winding down. "That was too damn funny not to laugh." When she took a healthy portion of rice on her chopsticks and put it in her mouth without dropping any, she giggled again.

"Now you're just showing off."

She nodded and swallowed. "You want a beer?"

"That'd be great," he said, and put another fork full in his mouth.

AFTER SHE RETREATED INSIDE, he let his eyes drift to the magnificent scenery. A three-quarter moon rose over the mountains, reflecting on the surface of the lake below. By the end of the week, the moon would be full, and the view would be breathtaking.

Music blared in the living room, and he jumped, spilling rice all over the table. His gaze shot from the scenery to the room behind him. Jennifer frantically turned knobs, her profile screamed panic, and he chuckled. Not one of her attempts decreased the volume and Steve stood, stepping inside to lend a hand.

"I don't know how to turn this down," she said over the music.

Steve crossed the room and scanned the hardware in front of him. After a few seconds, he reached down and turned a knob. The music lowered to a respectable level. "That was... interesting." He headed back toward the balcony. On his way out, he grabbed the beer Jennifer had left on the bar.

The entire day had been interesting so far, and he laughed under his breath. "You're about as good with that as I am with these." He pointed to the stereo and the chopsticks, respectively.

Jennifer blushed and sat, opening her wine cooler. After they finished eating, she leaned back in the lounge chair, looking out over the moon-drenched lake. "The lake is beautiful."

"Mhm," Steve agreed, glancing at her profile. *Not as beautiful as you are.* "I like your choice of music." He leaned back in his chair as Nickelback piped onto the terrace.

"When do you think we should tell them?"

"Let them sweat it out for a while." Steve took a sip of the beer. "I don't like being set up, and what they pulled tonight pissed me off. You don't pull that kind of shit on a friend. Not after the fight we staged. I sure as hell wouldn't have left my best friend in that situation. That was just shitty." He took another swig.

"She hadn't seen him for a couple of weeks," Jennifer said.

Steve huffed. "You're actually making excuses for their behavior?"

Jennifer shifted in the seat and shrugged.

"Let them sweat for a while."

"I'm not sure I can keep this up for very long."

Steve smiled. "You're the best actress I've ever seen. You'll do just fine. I'd be more worried about me." He returned his attention to the scenery. *Yeah, I don't know how long I'll be able to keep my hands off you.*

A blush crept into her cheeks, and she stood. "I'm going to change." She tilted her head and tapped her lips with her finger, her eyes drifting over him. "I think I may have a pair of shorts that will fit you if you want to get out of your wet clothes," she offered with a sheepish grin.

"You have something that would fit me?" He raised an eyebrow.

"I might."

"Okay." Now he was curious to see what she brought out for him.

She returned in dry clothes and hesitantly extended a pair of faded cut-offs to him.

Steve stood, reading the melancholy expression in her eyes and the slight tension in her arm as if second-guessing the offer. "These were Tom's, weren't they?" When she nodded, he took them from her outstretched hand. "Are you sure?"

"Yes," she said. Her eyes met his. "I'm sure. The bathroom is at the end of the hall."

He walked away, turning once to look at her before he disappeared around the corner.

Steve inspected the soft, well-worn fabric and then his reflection in the mirror. *I can't believe she did this.* His thoughts drifted to Peggy and the full closet at the cottage. *If the situation were reversed, could I do the same?* He didn't have an answer, at least one he'd admit to, and he shrugged the questions out of his head. Stripping out of his wet suit, he slid the shorts on and raised an eyebrow. They fit.

He picked up his wet swim trunks and walked into the living room. "What should I do with this?"

Jennifer had her damp clothes in her hands already. "I'll take that." She stared at him. "They fit." She took his wet shorts, turning and heading toward the kitchen.

"Why are you going into the kitchen with wet clothes?"

"I'm going to put these in the oven." She smiled sweetly, holding the wet clothes up and hesitating in the doorway.

His mouth dropped for a split second. His mind going blank for a response.

"Seriously, our laundry room is off the kitchen." She disappeared, and then the dryer turned on.

She got you, dude!

Her sense of humor was still a little warped, even after all these years. He chuckled dryly. When she stepped through the kitchen door, he said, "I thought...well, never mind. You got me."

She laughed.

The musical tenor of her laughter set him into action, and he crossed the distance, sweeping her into his arms. Her eyes widened and her laugh teetered into a gasp. The line of her body arched into his touch. As one hand tangled in her long damp hair, the other planted in the curve of her back, just itching to go lower, but he held it in place. Staring into her jade eyes, he forced a ragged breath and slowly leaned toward her luscious, parted lips, wanting to taste the sweetness of her mouth.

This cannot happen!

It was as if someone tazed him. He jerked away, startled by his silent admonishment. Her eyes were still closed, her lips poised in expectation. His breath caught in his throat, and he fought against every fiber of his being, forcing his arms to loosen. He stepped away.

Her eyes shot open, and a crease appeared between her eyebrows. Questions filled her eyes, along with hurt. Her arms circled around herself as his rejection settled in.

He cursed under his breath. His heart thumped in his chest, and his breath matched the electrifying experience. He focused on taking long, slow breaths, trying to regain control over his wild libido.

"I have to go." He took another step away from her. Two years of not feeling anything, in contrast to the overwhelming tornado of emotions, was too much for him to cope with. He turned and headed for the door.

Jennifer caught his arm. "Steve."

He didn't look at her. "You aren't ready for this, Jen." He opened the door.

"How do you know?" she whispered.

He met her gaze. "Because I saw the way you looked at me when I came out in these shorts." He removed her hand from his arm. "It was good to see you again."

"But?"

He gave her a little smile. "I'm not ready for you either." His voice was soft and gentle, and he turned, walking to the elevator, refusing to look back because if he did, he wouldn't be able to leave. When the elevator doors closed, he rested his forehead against them, welcoming the cool metal.

He closed his eyes and for the first time in two years, the face he saw etched onto his eyelids was not Peggy's.

Dark Reckoning
Chapter 4

JENNIFER STARED AT THE elevator for almost a full minute, thinking he would change his mind and come back. Hope fizzled with each second that passed. When he didn't, she closed the door and inhaled, trying to ease the sting of his rejection.

She crossed to the balcony in time to see his car disappear. Her chest constricted with emptiness. She thought she had read the same things in his eyes that she had experienced. A current living between the two of them, pulling her to him from the moment she saw him at the door, it had grabbed hold of her.

It couldn't be just one sided. Could it?

On the heels of the question, guilt reared up. She had lent him Tom's shorts, and he knew the magnitude of that gesture.

"Damn him," she muttered with genuine frustration.

Her gaze dropped to the mess on the table and she started cleaning up. Her mind drifted, analyzing every look, every move to understand why he pulled away.

Guilt singed the edges of her mind, and the answer came with along with the buzz of the dryer. He had said as much in the car. He hadn't let go. Neither had she, if she was being honest with herself.

God help her, she had to let Tom go because the way Steve held her had felt like coming home.

With a sigh, she gathered the containers and dumped them in the garbage, taking the bag to the dumpster and destroying any evidence he had been at the apartment. When the dryer buzzed again, she retrieved the clothes, folded them neatly, and tucked them away on the top shelf of her closet.

Something in the back of the closet rustled, and Jennifer jumped, spinning toward the disturbance. Cold air engulfed her, and the hair on the back of her neck bristled. Fear wrapped around her heart in a tight fist, constricting the sudden pounding in her chest. Air pulled from her lungs. Wheezing, she drew a thin breath and shivered. She shot out of the closet and slammed the door, but it did nothing to eradicate the feeling she wasn't alone.

She backed away slowly, wishing Steve had stayed a little longer. With her eyes glued to the closet door, she changed into her nightshirt and grabbed her bathrobe. She retreated to the living room, slipping the floor length chenille around her as tightly as it would go.

HANDS SHOOK HER.

"Jen, wake up," Tracy demanded.

Her eyes fluttered opened trying to place where she was. She looked up at her friend and it all came back to her. "What time is it?"

"Around two," Tracy answered. "How did it go?"

"How'd what go?" she mumbled and sat up, still half asleep.

"Steve. Did he come up?"

She shook her head, awake enough to slip into the role. "He's an asshole." Jennifer got up and headed to her room. "Night." She closed her bedroom door on Tracy's questioning eyes, crawled into bed, and instantly fell asleep.

DURING THE NIGHT, THE closet door popped open, and a pair of red shimmering eyes peered out. Jennifer shivered in her sleep and pulled the blankets tight.

Dark Reckoning
Chapter 5

JENNIFER WOKE AT EIGHT and wandered into the shower. She let the pulsating jets wash away the edges of sleep. Lingering, she enjoyed the massage on her back and legs. After what seemed like an eternity, she reluctantly shut the water off and wrapped herself in a towel. Her brow furrowed as fragments of a dream drifted into her consciousness—blood, pain, and fear.

She shivered at the image and shoved it down into her subconscious where it belonged, then flipped on the hairdryer to take the chill out of her wet locks.

Tracy strolled in and yawned, wiping her eyes. "God, what a night."

"Mhm." Jennifer glanced at her roommate.

"You ought to give Steve another chance."

"Why?" Jennifer turned off the hairdryer.

"He's really not an asshole," Tracy began. "I still think you're perfect for each other." She headed into the shower.

If you only knew, Jennifer thought and turned on the hairdryer again.

Thirty minutes later, they stood waiting for the elevator.

"I still don't understand you," Tracy grumbled. "He's a nice guy."

"Then you go out with him."

"You're impossible." Tracy threw her hands in the air.

"Let it go, Tracy." Jennifer knew better. Tracy would never let this go.

"But..."

"—But nothing. Leave it alone, I don't like the guy."

Tracy pouted the rest of the way in the elevator, playing with her keys. She let the silence build between them until they stepped into the bright morning sunshine. "Couldn't you give him a chance?"

Jennifer groaned. "I want nothing to do with him."

Tracy sat in the driver's seat of the Jaguar and turned the ignition. Jennifer slipped into the passenger seat.

"What did you do last night?" Jennifer asked, focusing the conversation on Tracy.

"We danced and drank, and you know." Her cheeks turned pink. "We had fun."

"I'll bet." Steve's smile came to mind, making her insides feel like a pile of warm, silly putty. She didn't hear a word Tracy uttered. Her mind was miles away until Tracy turned onto Fraternity Row. "Where are you going?"

"Sorry, Jen, I promised Billy I'd pick him up this morning. His car is on the fritz again. He said you could ride with Steve."

Jennifer looked at her. "I wish you would have told me at the apartment. I could have driven myself. Besides, why can't he ride with Steve?"

Tracy pulled up to the curb. "I need to bring him to the shop before we go to get our schedules."

"Great fucking friend you are," Jennifer said under her breath as she got out of the car.

Bill and Steve sat on the front porch of the frat house. Bill's lips pressed into a thin white line, and he shot to his feet, scrambling down the stairs at the first sign of Tracy's car.

"Thanks for understanding, Jen." He slipped into the passenger seat the minute she vacated it.

"I guess you need a lift." Steve approached her.

"Apparently." She glared at Tracy's car as it pulled away from the curb.

"Car's this way." He turned, heading toward the parking lot. She followed Steve and sat in the passenger seat when he held the door for her. "Sorry about last night." He shut the door and walked around the car, slipping into the driver's seat.

"No apology necessary," Jennifer said. "How'd you hook up with the frat boys?" She gestured at the house.

"I was in the same fraternity at Yale. I figured it was probably better than off campus. At least I'd feel like I was a part of something again." He looked up at the house. "Now I'm wondering if that had been a good idea or not. There isn't much privacy here." He turned over the ignition, but he didn't put the car in gear right away.

A STORM OF EMOTION swirled within him and being this close to her just increased the velocity. He stared at his hands, gripping the steering wheel before letting his eyes wander in her direction, taking in the tan legs and the hem of her white skirt, slowly taking her in until their eyes met. Electrifying heat took hold. With a deep breath, he dragged his eyes away and backed the car out of the parking spot.

"Are you all right?" she asked, her voice tentative, like she felt the torment rolling off him.

He nodded, but didn't look her way.

"Stop the car."

Her sharp outburst caused him to swerve. Steve jerked the steering wheel back in line, correcting the car's trajectory and settling back on the proper side of the road. "Why?"

"I don't want to ride with you if you're going to shut me out." The anger in her voice matched the spark in her eyes.

He glanced in the rearview mirror to see if Bill and Tracy were in view, but no one he recognized shared the road with them. "Are you acting right now?" he asked cautiously, not knowing where this aggravation sprouted from.

"Stop the damn car."

He pulled to the curb, and she shot out onto the sidewalk. He slammed the gears into first, set the brake, and ripped the keys from the ignition. He ran after her, grabbed her arm, and spun her around. "What are you doing?"

"Leaving you alone." Jennifer yanked her arm from his grasp.

Steve grabbed her again and pulled her close. "Maybe that's not what I want."

"What exactly do you want, Steve?" She shot up at him, her eyes fiery and frustrated.

Without thinking it through, he kissed her hard and pulled away. "You." He let her go and stormed back to the car, breathless and aggravated that he actually gave in despite every warning in the back of his mind.

"You sure have a funny way of showing it," she called after him.

The car rolled away, leaving her standing on the sidewalk. He parked less than a block away, taking a deep breath to quell the storm. "Get in," he said when she marched by the car, heading toward the school.

"No," she snapped over her shoulder.

"What the hell do you want from me?" he growled.

SHE STOPPED AND TURNED. The rightness of being with him hit her like a physical blow, silencing her because everything she wanted to say just wasn't enough. His blue eyes locked with hers, knocking her senseless and fueled her, making her feel alive and vital.

He pulled the car up next to her. "What do you want, Jen?" he asked, softer this time.

A powerful combination of fear and wanting flashed in his eyes, making him seem vulnerable and sexy.

"You're not ready for what I want."

"Then tell me, what the hell do we do now?" He kept her intense stare. "What do we do?" He threw the car in neutral and ran his hands through his hair.

His tousled, frazzled look yanked at her heartstrings. She glanced down the road and then opened the passenger door. "I don't know." She sat and took a deep breath before meeting his gaze. "But next time you kiss me, you better make it last a hell of a lot longer than that."

He blinked and then a slow, sexy smile spread over his lips, making her shiver and impossibly hot at the same time.

Steve slid the car into gear.

"You'd better wipe that grin off your face before either Tracy or Bill see it. That's a dead giveaway."

He obliged and put on his moody expression. "Better?"

"Yes, and no." She suppressed a grin of her own. "I like the sexy smile."

"Ah," he replied. "I'll have to remember that."

Jennifer was quiet for a few minutes. "Tracy isn't going to let this go. She really thinks we are perfect for each other. She wants me to give you a second chance."

Steve glanced sideways. "Bill said I was a fool."

They pulled into the student center, and he put his game face back on. He opened the car door for her. His expression looked tight, annoyed, but his eyes surveyed the parking lot before they landed back on her.

"You're quite the actor, you know," Jennifer said, studying him.

"I have to be in my line of work." His eyes went a little wide, and then he spun towards the student center.

"And what line is that?" she asked, stepping onto the asphalt next to him.

"I'm a law student." He headed into the student center without waiting for her.

He studied his surroundings with sharp eyes, drinking in every detail, and it hit her. He's not here to study law, he is the law.

Jesus, he's here because of the murders.

Oh my god, he's a cop?

She ran up to him and caught his arm. "Are you working now?" The steady glare he gave her made her drop her hand and step back.

"I'm going to pick up my schedule." He opened the door, ignoring her question. His eyes never stopped moving.

"Are you?"

"That is none of your concern, Jen. I'm enrolled as a student here," he answered, and breezed past her.

She stopped in her tracks.

Steve approached the desk and retrieved his schedule. He studied it as he strolled in her direction. "Start acting, babe." He walked out the doors, leaving her with a thousand questions.

Jennifer shook off the momentary shock and approached the desk. Moments later, she had her schedule and wandered out in the same direction Steve had gone. She found him sitting on a bench, reviewing his schedule.

Steve squinted up at her with a scowl. He motioned for her to sit down next to him. "I can't discuss this with you." He kept his eyes on his schedule.

"Steve." When he glanced at her, her heart skipped a beat.

"I can't."

"Okay. I won't ask." Perplexed, she took a deep breath and leaned back. "I don't have any classes today," she replied, handing him her schedule. Her Tuesdays and Thursdays were loaded, and except for a couple of Wednesday classes, the rest of her schedule was blank.

Steve handed it back. "Bitch." He tilted his schedule so she could see. "I've got classes every day starting at eight."

"Aww," Jennifer said without sympathy. She saw his lips curve at the edges and watched in amazement as he suppressed it again.

"Here they come," he said under his breath.

Jennifer stood and hurried toward Tracy. "I can't believe you did that to me!"

"Was it really that bad?" Steve asked.

Jennifer glared at him, and he met her eyes with the same ferocity. "As a matter of fact..."

"It wasn't all that pleasant for me either," Steve barked at her. "You are a bitch." He stood and walked away.

Jennifer watched him, her mouth open in surprise.

Bill took off after Steve, grabbing his arm and swinging him around. "You need to apologize to her."

"Fuck you." Steve yanked his arm from Bill's grasp and stormed away, disappearing around the rear of the student center.

Bill's jaw went slack, and he headed back to where Jennifer stood.

"What the hell were you two thinking?" Jennifer snapped when Bill returned to Tracy's side. "He's an asshole."

Bill looked away. "He didn't seem like one when I met him over the summer. I thought you two would be perfect together. You both know what it's like to lose someone and I thought..." He trailed off.

His words burned through every other thought, and her eyes narrowed. "That was the qualification for setting us up?"

"Jen." Tracy sighed.

"That is such a bullshit reason!" She walked away, and Bill caught her arm. "Let go!" She glared at him.

"Don't be mad at Tracy. This was all my idea, not hers."

"Bullshit. She pushed me just as much as you pushed him."

"I'm sorry, Jen. I thought you two would hit it off." Tracy wouldn't meet Jennifer's gaze. "Do you want a ride back to the apartment?"

Jennifer took a deep breath. "No, not right now. There are a few people I want to say hello to. I'll walk back later."

"It's a haul, Jen," Bill said.

"Then I'll swing by the frat house. Someone there can bring me home, right?"

Bill shrugged. "True."

Jennifer walked away.

"Are you mad at me?" Tracy asked.

Jennifer turned and fluttered her hand back and forth. "A little, but I'll get over it."

"You know I love you, right?"

"Yeah, I know."

Dark Reckoning
Chapter 6

JENNIFER WALKED AROUND THE corner of the student center and was yanked behind the trees. She yelped in surprise.

Steve rammed her against a gigantic oak out of sight from the walking path. His eyes sparkled. "Sorry I scared you." He leaned in to kiss her and stopped inches from her lips, staring into her eyes. "I'm not so sure you really know what you want." He pulled back a little and the edges of his mouth curve upwards.

Jennifer's heart raced. She couldn't move and couldn't speak, lost in his intense stare. "I... I," she sputtered as the shock gave way to irritation.

"You what?" His breath smelled like cinnamon.

Jennifer moved swiftly, stepping closer and sweeping his foot out from under him at the same time she pushed, knocking him flat on his back in a perfect Osoto Gari. "Don't corner me like that ever again."

Steve stared up at her with wide eyes. "Damn girl."

Jennifer put her hands on her hips. "My dad thought I should learn to defend myself. I'm a black belt."

"I'll have to spar with you sometime." He picked himself up and brushed the dirt off his shorts.

"You would lose."

He laughed, musical and full. "Next time, you'll be on the ground."

"Want to bet?"

He snorted and walked away. Jennifer lunged for him, and the world spun. Within a blink, she was on the ground with his arm across her chest. He was infinitely faster and more powerful than she imagined. Her breath caught in her chest as humor sparkled in his eyes.

"So, what did I win?" He barely concealed a smirk, masking it with a devilish grin.

A thousand thoughts flew through her mind, but the one that slipped through her lips almost made her laugh. "The right to protect me any time you want."

He lifted his eyebrows. "That's a given." He stood and helped her up, attempting to brush the dirt off the back of her skirt. "You're going to need to change."

She arched, trying to look at the back of her skirt, but only saw the edges of dirt. "Can you take me back?"

Steve glanced at his watch. "Sure. I've got a little time."

They walked to his car, keeping an eye on the parking lot and the student center for Bill and Tracy. Fortune ran with them. No one they knew saw them slide into Steve's car.

"Who do you work for?" she asked after a few miles of silence.

"I'm not discussing this with you."

His voice carried a warning, but she plowed forward, undeterred. "Local police? State police? What?"

"Let it go." He gave her a sideways look before focusing back on the road. "Please."

Jennifer's mind filtered through all the possibilities. One stuck, triggering a vague memory, and she tilted her head, glancing at him. When they were little, he told her his grandfather was an undercover agent with some government agency. She blinked and glanced down at her hands, pulling the memory from the recess of her mind. She bit the inside of her lip, concentrating.

The full memory formed. "FBI!" she blurted loud enough to startle him.

The car swerved, and Steve sucked the air in. "Jesus, Jenn." He glared at her for a moment and then turned into the apartment parking lot. He pulled in front of the building and shifted the car in neutral. "Look, I am not discussing this with you," he said, meeting her gaze. "Someday I will, but I can't right now. Okay?"

Jennifer nodded, but she knew she was right just by the caution flaring in his eyes. However, his inability to confide in her rubbed her raw. She opened the car door to get out.

"Jen?"

His soft voice pulled her around. And she studied his profile. He stared ahead of him and shifted in the seat before he glanced at her.

"I need to go somewhere, and I'd really like company."

His smile didn't reach his eyes. Instead, she saw trepidation in his irises, and that made her decision easy.

"Oh. Okay. Just give me a couple of minutes to change." She trotted inside, wondering what exactly they were going to see that made him look so vulnerable.

HER DIRTY SKIRT SWAYED with her stride, and Steve sighed. He closed his eyes and tilted his head back against the headrest while he waited for her to return.

He had been doing field operations for close to five years, recruited right out of high school because of his grandfather's request. He graduated at the top in his class from the academy and received a commendation for his first undercover assignment at Yale, nailing a serial rapist.

He met Peggy while he was at the academy. She went everywhere with him, and after his first collar, he asked her to marry him. The relationship had been a quiet one, no tension, no fighting, just simple adoration. There were no warning signals hinting at her unbalanced state. After re-examining their life together, over and over and over, every day since she killed herself, he still didn't see any clear-cut sign.

After she died, he turned reckless with his career and his private life, requesting the most dangerous assignments, and bedding every hot babe he came across despite his boss' reproach. He had no fear, no remorse, no passion. He was just a cold shell driven by a boiling anger.

This assignment was a little slower paced than the rat race of drugs and mafia games he chased over the last couple of years. When undercurrents of bizarre hazing rituals found its way into the bureau, they pulled him from a job in the city. His boss wanted him here, wanted his insight, and wanted his ability to blend in.

At first, the assignment aggravated him. It was too slow, too safe. But ever since he found the carnage in the woods, catching the son of a bitch was no longer a choice. It was a need motivated by fury.

He opened his eyes and looked at the apartment building.

Jennifer was a complication he didn't expect. When Bill mentioned her name, he caved under Bill's matchmaking harassment. Memories of her standing on her front stoop waving goodbye flooded back. She was so damn young then, but they had some sort of connection, otherwise he never would have been so excited about each of her letters.

Talking to her on the phone this summer had been nice, but actually seeing her, man, that knocked him on his ass.

On cue, Jennifer walked out of the building in shorts and a t-shirt, making the casual outfit look like designer threads. She would look good in a paper sack. He smiled and pulled out onto the road.

"Thanks," he said, heading toward the lake. His smile faded as the task ahead haunted him.

"Where are we going?"

"To my grandfather's place."

"I get to meet your grandfather?"

Steve shook his head. "He died a few years ago. The property is mine, but I haven't been at the cottage in a little over two years."

"Oh." She watched the scenery pass in silence.

He ground his teeth together to quell the rising unease. And when he took the turn onto the unpaved road that led to his grandfather's place, the unease turned to something that sat in his stomach like an acid bomb.

Steve stopped the car, his knuckles turned white on the steering wheel, his grip making his hands ache. Taking a deep breath, he moved his hand onto the stick shift, put the car in first gear, and released the clutch slowly. His heartbeat pulsed in his ears as the woods closed in. The car eased around one of the sharp turns in the driveway.

"I'm not sure I can do this." He slammed his foot on the brake, stopping, floundering.

"Why?"

Her soft question broke through his paralysis. "The last time I was here I found Peg." He glanced at Jennifer, then back at the rambling driveway.

Jennifer placed her hand on his. "You don't have to do this."

"I need to face my demons." He glanced at her hand. It was warm and soft on top of his and gave him the strength to roll forward again. He took a deep breath and rounded the last curve. The neglected cabin stood out among the trees. An overgrown expanse of lawn surrounded the cottage bordered by the shimmering lake. Steve let out a little grunt of surprise.

"What?"

"The landscaping company hasn't been out here yet. I called a couple of weeks ago." He parked the car and shut it off, but didn't make a move to get out. He stared at the last place he'd seen Peg alive and let his eyes wander to the gazebo at the water's edge. They were supposed to get married in the gazebo. The benches lining the makeshift aisle were still sitting on the lawn in the same position they had been two years before. Pain seared through him.

Jennifer followed his gaze and put her hand to her mouth. "Oh, Steve."

Steve got out of the car. The sympathy in her voice brought the anger back and, with it, the nerve to move. "Apparently, I wasn't what she wanted." He slammed the car door.

JENNIFER DIDN'T RESPOND. FIRE flared in his eyes—the sadness and hurt overlaid by anger and ferocity she didn't think he was capable of. She got out of the car and slipped to his side, never taking her eyes off him.

"Stop looking at me like that," he said without looking her way.

"Like what?"

"Like I'm gonna explode into a million pieces and take everything in my wake with me."

Jennifer huffed at the analogy until he shot his eyes to her. "Sorry."

He nodded and headed to the door, digging the key out of his pocket. He put his forehead to the old wood.

Hesitantly, she touched his shoulder.

"I'm sorry I snapped at you, but this is hard for me."

"If it wasn't hard, I'd think there was something wrong with you."

"I knew I brought you for a reason." He met her gaze. "You always made me feel stronger than I really was." He flipped the lock and pushed the door open.

Jennifer ran her fingers down his arm and clasped his hand in hers. He took it and squeezed. Together, they stepped into the cottage.

The cottage was neater than she expected. But everything was covered with a thick layer of dust that stirred in the gentle breeze, tickling her nose.

Jennifer sneezed.

The smell of mold and rotting wood drifted around them, and she swore there was an underlying scent of death.

Steve gripped her hand tighter as he walked toward the bathroom. "I found her in here." He reached for the doorknob and hesitated, bringing his hand away. A derisive grumble came from his chest, and he grasped the doorknob again and turned it.

The slow creak gave Jennifer goose bumps, and she clamped her jaw against the shiver that threatened. Steve threw open the door and the moment Jennifer stepped into the bathroom; the room changed. She gasped, and her grip tightened, clamping down on his hand like a vise.

Candles flickered around the tub. A pretty blonde sat in the water, glancing at the array of items she had lined up on the shelf. She reached for the prescription pills and emptied the bottle, downing the pills with the glass of wine sitting on the edge.

The woman closed her eyes. "I can't do this to him," she whispered, looking out the window toward the lake. "I just can't."

She reached for the shiny razor blade and deliberately slit from wrist to mid-forearm. Deep crimson red flowed from the open wound.

"Jennifer!"

His voice cut through the vision like the razorblade slicing through the woman's wrist, and she blinked back in the dusty baron bathroom. "I smell lavender and red wine." And then the room went black.

STEVE CAUGHT HER AND looked around frantically. "Wake up." He softly tapped her cheeks. "Come on, baby, wake up." Repeating the words he said two years ago drove panic into his voice. He glanced at the tub and back at Jennifer. "Jesus, wake up!" He shook her more violently than he intended.

Jennifer snapped her eyes open. "I'm awake," she said as he wrapped his arms around her, squeezing her against him. "I'm awake. But you're crushing me."

Steve pulled away. He touched her face and sat back against the doorjamb. "What was that?" he asked when he was certain his voice wouldn't shake.

"I saw her," she said.

"What are you talking about?"

"There were candles, and she had a glass of wine." She glanced at him. "Lavender scented candles and a bottle of prescription pills. She emptied it with the wine." Jennifer looked at the tub. "It was filled, so the water was over her body, but not to the rim. There was a good four to five inches between the waterline and the lip of the tub." She took a deep breath and looked at her wrists, tracing the path of the razor blade. "She cut her wrists the long way and put the razor on the edge of the tub." Jennifer closed her eyes. "And she was crying."

Every single word from her mouth cut as deep as the blade that shredded Peggy's wrists. Steve stood and drifted away from Jennifer. She painted the exact picture right down to the little

details, as if she has been present when his
fiancée took her life.

A high-pitched whine drowned the sound of
his breathing and he reached for the doorjamb,
the air sharp, suffocating. He needed fresh air,
and he turned and walked out the door.

He wanted to believe something otherworldly
just happened, he really did, but his life was
based on fact and tangible evidence, and this
was as far from tangible as it got.

He stopped at the end of the dock, staring out
over the lake as his body burned with conflicting
emotions.

Jennifer followed him.

When she stepped into his peripheral vision,
anger shot to the surface. He glared at her.
"What the hell are you doing? Do you think this
will make me feel better?"

Jennifer stepped back.

"This isn't a joke." He grabbed her, digging
his fingers into her arm. He jutted his chin
toward the cottage. "It isn't something to mock
like you just did."

"Let go!" Anger flashed in her eyes. "I saw
what I saw. Now let go!" She shoved him away.

His foot slipped on the edge of the dock, and
he lost his balance, falling into the lake,
dragging her with him. The chill in the water
slapped him back in control, and he hauled
himself onto the end of the dock, his wet
clothing clinging to him, wringing an icy shiver
from his bones.

Jennifer swam to the edge, and he offered her
his hand, but she slapped it away. "I can get out
by myself." She pulled herself up next to him.

A few minutes of strained silence went by,
and then Steve chuckled at the absurdity of the

situation. Hysterics took hold. He gripped the edge of the deck, shaking as the laughter belted out of him.

Jennifer looked at the sparkling water.

"What are you, a fucking clairvoyant?" he asked when his laughter finally subsided.

Jennifer shrugged. "I guess you could call it that."

"I don't know if I believe you." His doubt returned.

"It happens from time to time. I usually don't pass out, though," she explained, avoiding eye contact. "I rarely see things in the past; it's usually present or future." She paused and sighed, meeting his gaze. "That was completely disturbing."

"No shit. You had no color in your face and your eyes... You scared the hell out of me."

"She kept saying she couldn't do this to you," Jennifer said.

"Well, she fucking did." Anger clawed at his belly. "There is no excuse for suicide, none. If she didn't want to marry me, she should have just told me. Instead..." He clamped his lips together against the obvious.

Jennifer nodded and pulled her wet shirt away from her skin. Thlwup.

The sound knocked his frustration down, replacing it with a much-needed moment of levity. She blushed self-consciously.

Steve inhaled and scanned her wet form, acutely aware of how close she was sitting. Distance. He needed some distance from this brewing cocktail in his blood. He stood, slipped off his sneakers off, peeled his wet shirt and dropped his shorts without so much as a glance in her direction.

He dove into the water, letting the chill strip whatever heat still clung to him. He swam out a few feet and turned, treading water.

"You are welcome to join me if you'd like," he said. Conflicting emotions gripped him as soon as the words spilled from his lips. Having her nearly naked in the water wouldn't help his need for distance, but he so very much wanted to feel her body against his, despite her chilling display in the cottage.

She raised her eyebrows. "I'm not exactly in a swimsuit."

"Neither am I, in case you didn't notice."

"Oh, I noticed." She made no attempt to move, but the smirk on her face sent his pulse racing.

"Be adventurous." He faced the other direction. "I won't even look." He waited patiently and, when she didn't slip into the water, he turned back toward the dock. She was now on the steps with his wet clothing piled beside her.

"You be adventurous." A hint of a smile played on her lips.

Steve hauled himself out of the water and walked steadily toward her.

HE REALLY IS A fine specimen of a man, she thought, sliding her gaze over him. He swept her up in his arms and carried her back down to the end of the dock. For a moment, she thought he wasn't going to follow through, but his dimples appeared just before he jumped in the water.

When they surfaced, she splashed him, and he yanked her close, wrapping an arm around her waist and planting a kiss that was neither gentle nor sweet. It was insistent and demanding and hot as hell, stealing her breath with its intensity. It stopped time and clouded her logic, mesmerizing her.

He pulled away and searched her eyes, his breath as ragged as hers. And then he let her go, swimming away from her like the kiss had no effect on him.

She stripped her wet shirt and tossed it on the dock, where it slapped the wood with a wet flop. Steve climbed up on a rock at least fifty yards away and leaned back, staring at the afternoon sky. His expression was plaintive.

She swam out to him and climbed up next to him. The water lapped the waistline of her shorts and she let the silence stretch between them.

He nodded with his chin toward the cottage, the gazebo, and the long-since forgotten benches. "I think I'll tear the cottage down and build a house."

Jennifer looked back at the little cottage and sighed. "But it's charming."

Steve shrugged. "It lost its charm a long time ago. It's time to move on."

Jennifer met his gaze. His words sinking in slowly. "Are you talking about the house or..." She couldn't quite articulate the thoughts swirling in her head, but her voice held the hope that had crawled under her skin.

He kept his gaze on the shoreline. "You scare me."

A chill turned her arms into a raised relief map, and she rubbed them. "You? Scared?"

He chuckled and glanced at her with a shrug. "This detachment I've had since Peg died. Not giving a shit about anyone or anything. It's saved my ass more than once."

Her heart started drumming in her chest, challenging the hope riding her blood as she anticipated his next words.

"So yes. To finally feel something again freaks me out. Not to mention whatever happened to you in there..." He waved at the cottage and glanced at her. "And the conclusion you came to in the car doesn't help. It puts me in a tough spot."

Jennifer opened her mouth, and he raised his hand, stopping her from speaking.

"Look, even when we were kids, you could read me. I guess I figured you would have grown out of that by now. I didn't expect you being able to put the pieces together so quickly. Hell, I didn't expect you at all into my neat little equation." He ran his hands through his hair and exhaled. "You've totally messed with my black and white, unemotional state of mind." His laugh echoed off the lake.

She crossed her arms tighter over her chest. This little pep talk of his wasn't making her feel any better about anything that had happened since they arrived here.

"You were right. I do work for the FBI and I could get fired for admitting that to you."

"Why could you get fired?"

"Because I'm *supposed* to be undercover."

Jennifer glanced at his profile, at the hard set of his eyes as he scanned his land. "You think the fraternity is involved?"

His jaw jumped, and goosebumps traveled over his shoulders. He didn't acknowledge her question.

She knew everyone in that fraternity. There is no way they were connected to the murders in

Brooksfield. "Steve, you're looking in the wrong place."

Steve huffed. "Should I be looking at you?" His eyes drifted over her in a way that sparked the heat in her core. "Are you hiding twenty lost souls somewhere?" His blue eyes shimmered. He slid his hand up her thigh and the smile spread. "I think I'm going to have to subject you to a strip search." He dragged her into the water with him, standing on a lower rock she couldn't quite reach. His hands wandered, his touch igniting her. His hand slipped between her legs.

"Seriously." She pushed his hand away.

"Resisting arrest? That's a very serious charge." He pulled her close and kissed her neck.

Jennifer tried to break his grasp.

She felt him teeter and catch himself in the water, pushing her gently against the side of the large rock they had been sitting on. "Handcuffs might be interesting," she said, her lips grazing his.

He chuckled and moved to her earlobe, nibbling until she squealed.

She slipped out of his grasp and headed to shore. She climbed up on the dock and scratched her head as she looked around.

"What's wrong?" Steve asked after he climbed up and pulled his shorts on.

"I thought I threw my shirt up here."

Steve laughed. "It's probably all the way to Paradise Cove by now. Or stuck on the reef."

He had her attention. "Paradise Cove?"

"Yes." Steve pointed to the line of trees at the edge of his property. "It's right over there. Why?"

Her gaze jumped to where he pointed. "Tracy told me about the legend."

"Legend?" He raised an eyebrow like she was daft or something.

"Yes. The legend." The quizzical look remained on his face. "I thought your grandfather would have told you about it."

"What? That Paradise Cove has the best bass in the lake?"

"You've been there?"

"Technically, it's part of my property, so yes. I've been there. More times than I can count. There's a path through the woods right there." He pointed to a hint of an overgrown path. "I'll show you sometime when you have sneakers or hiking shoes on."

Jennifer stared at the path, trying to reconcile the conversation she had with Tracy with these additional facts. "But..." Tracy's words echoed in her ear. *That part of the lake is practically impossible to get to.* She shook her head and chuckled. "Tracy really got me." A chill in the air grazed her spine, and she shivered.

"Let me get you a t-shirt." He turned and headed into the cottage.

She rubbed her arms and followed him. She waited in the living room while he rummaged in the bedroom. When he stepped out, he tossed her a gray Brooksfield University t-shirt. She slid it over her shoulders. The V dipped farther down than she was used to, and the hem came down to her mid-thigh, but it was comfortable, and above everything else, dry.

"It's not as hot out today as it was yesterday," he said as he locked the cottage.

"Oh, it was plenty hot out there," Jennifer said, catching his attention.

He grinned. "Tell me about this so-called legend." He opened the passenger side door for her.

She sat and waited until he had himself situated in the driver's seat.

"Tracy said it has something to do with the Abinaqui Indians. I guess there's a certain rock in Paradise Cove. It's shaped like a clover. They say if you sit on the rock and look into the water, you can see your future. She also said there's a reef blocking it from the rest of the lake and that it's nearly impossible to get to by land."

"There is some truth in what she said. There is a rock like that in the cove and there is a row of rocks blocking any water entrance. I've seen a few drunken idiots tear up their boats trying. The only land access I'm aware of is the path in my yard. The other side is thick woods and pretty nasty underbrush. But in all the time I've sat on that rock with my grandfather, I have never seen my future in the water."

Jennifer shrugged. "She said that if you touch the water while it's showing you the future, you see your own death."

Steve chuckled.

"Stop laughing at me," she said, her mouth curling at the edges despite her best efforts to stop her smile. "She also mentioned something about if a beast isn't given an annual sacrifice, it will go hog wild tearing up the town."

"Really?" He glanced at her and then back at the road.

"She was trying to creep me out, saying that was the reason for the disappearances and mutilations."

"I never heard that story before. I think if there was any grain of truth to it, my grandfather would have said something."

"Tracy said everyone in town knows about it."

"And how would Tracy know that?"

"Her father grew up in Brooksfield."

He chewed on his lower lip and turned the car on. "Where to?"

She reached over and turned the radio down before she reached into her pocketbook. "Hang on a second." She smiled at Steve as she dialed Tracy.

"Hey Jenn. I am so sorry for earlier…"

"Yeah, well, we can talk about that later. Are you at the apartment?"

"Yes. Why?"

"Think you could pick me up at the student center?"

"Sure. I'll be right over."

Jennifer closed the phone. "You can take me to the apartment, please."

Steve let out a gloriously full laugh. And Jennifer mentally made a note to make him laugh more because it just tickled the right spot inside her.

He chuckled and turned up the radio as he navigated the dirt driveway back to the main road. "You are an evil woman."

She held her forefinger and thumb slightly apart. "Just a wee bit."

His smile faded. "Can I ask a personal question?"

"Shoot."

"Has there been anyone since Tom?" Steve shifted the gears, making quick work of the drive to her apartment.

"No." She watched the trees before looking back at him. "You?"

He let out a little laugh. "You don't want to know."

She stared at him, and when he glanced at her; she raised an eyebrow. She really wanted to know, otherwise she wouldn't have asked.

"Let's just say I got around." He glanced at her. "But no one had my attention like you do." He looked back at the road and his cheeks turned red. "Not even Peggy."

His admission stunned her into silence, especially since he had been the one to pull away both times things got heated. The entire afternoon left her aching for much more than a sizzling kiss.

When he pulled up in front of the apartment building, he ran a hand through his hair and took a deep breath. "What I told you today has to stay between us."

She rolled her eyes.

"I'm serious, Jenn."

"I would never betray your confidence." She reached out and squeezed his hand.

"Not even to your best friend?" He cocked his head and glanced up at the apartment building.

"No. Not even to Tracy."

His shoulders relaxed. "So, how long are we going to keep up this charade?"

"They set us up because we both had someone we love die."

Steve's jaw dropped and eyebrows rose at the admission.

"I kid you not." She lifted her hands in an oath. "So, I'm apt to let them sweat for a few more days." She backed away toward the apartment door.

"Works for me. I'll see you later." He waited until she entered the building and then focused on everything that went unsaid today.

62

Dark Reckoning
Chapter 7

STEVE'S HEART POUNDED IN his chest as he drove back to the fraternity. Jennifer's little story about the legend gave him some credible information that he hadn't had before. He felt like he just won the lottery. He nodded at his fraternity brothers as he vaulted up the steps and closed and locked his door. He found the desk key on his keyring and unlocked the top drawer, pulling out a notebook and a special cell phone.

He jotted down every part of the conversation, and then just stared at his notes. "Legend my ass," he muttered under his breath. His grandfather had never mentioned a legend, and Steve was damn sure that he would have, considering they had Abinaqui blood in their heritage.

He flipped open his cell and punched in a four-digit code and waited for the message tone. "Hey Jack, I think I might have a lead. Can you find out everything about Tracy Sheehan and her family, particularly her father? I believe he's from Brooksfield. Thanks."

He closed the phone and lay back on his bed, pondering the day. Jennifer was quite the actress and his smile slowly faded. *Could she be that good?* He closed his eyes and swore. "Shit." She had gotten him to admit what he did and why he was here so easily, like slicing through butter on a hot day.

He stood, feeling foolish and angry. Every important detail about Peg's death was in the public record, and the rest of it could have been made up. The only thing that didn't add up was the way she had looked right before she passed out. Color drained from her, leaving her looking more like an aged corpse than a living, breathing soul. That couldn't be faked. Could it? Doubt filled him.

He shook his head in frustration. A part of him didn't want to believe. A part of him didn't want to care. A part of him didn't want this kind of complication. His self-doubt saved his life over the past two years, keeping everyone at arm's length and giving him a cold, clear perspective on those he observed. He'd lost his edge with Jennifer, and he knew it.

He locked the notebook and cell phone away and stormed out of the room. Right into Bill.

Bill grabbed Steve and slammed him into the wall. "You called my friend a bitch."

Steve glared back. He was in no mood for this right now. "Back off." He shoved Bill away.

"You are such a fucking idiot. You are going to come with me and apologize."

"The hell I am." Steve stood his ground. "She is a bitch."

Bill swung and caught Steve square in the eye.

Steve slammed back into the wall with the force of the punch. His eye pulsed from the shock of the impact, swelling shut. "What the fuck did you do that for?" he snapped, covering the hot space Bill's fist left.

"I swear I'll kick your ass if you don't apologize to her." Bill towered over Steve.

Steve stared back, tempted to take him down, but kept his boiling temper in check. "No." He watched as Bill balled his hand into a fist. "And if you try to hit me again, I'll put your head through the wall."

Bill hesitated and backed off, taking a step away. "I thought you were a decent guy. If I'd known what a prick you were, I would never have tried to set you up with her."

"She's arrogant."

"No, she isn't," Bill said. "She is probably one of the most pure-hearted, loving people I know. She doesn't have an arrogant bone in her body."

Pure. That definitely described her to the core. Still, he was surprised Bill zeroed in on that particular word. "That's not what I saw."

"You insulted her career choice. What'd you expect?"

Steve shook his head. His eye hurt along with his pride. This was the second time someone got a drop on him today. "I don't know," he said. "I guess I expected Peggy." He turned to walk away.

"You know what? You really don't deserve her, but you bet your ass you're going to apologize."

Steve stopped and kept his back to Bill, considering the comment. "Fine, but if she gives me grief, I'm leaving." He shot a warning glance over at Bill. "And if you try to stop me, you'll find yourself on your ass."

Bill smiled. "I'll give Tracy a call."

Dark Reckoning
Chapter 8

*S*HE RAN THROUGH THE *woods, her heart racing in her chest, branches whipping and tearing her exposed skin. Pitch black, not even the moon penetrated the cover of the trees to give her any light. She had to get away, get back to safety, but had no clue of where she was running.*

His scream put on the brakes and she skidded on the damp leaves, whirling in her tracks. His voice, laced with pain and panic, propelled her in the direction she had fled. She broke through the underbrush into the small clearing, shaking and terrified. On his knees, he struggled to stand. Jagged cuts on his face and chest oozed red, saturating his bare skin with thick blood.

Something sharp sailed through the air towards him.

"No!" she screamed.

She shot up in the chair, the scream escaping from her mouth.

Tracy burst onto the terrace, out of breath. "What happened?"

"Nightmare." Jennifer looked around, her gaze falling on the lake. She shivered.

A knock on the door interrupted them.

Tracy disappeared to get the door.

"Where's Jen?" Bill asked, stepping into the apartment.

"On the terrace. She just woke up from a nap."

Jennifer glanced at Bill when he stepped onto the terrace. She wiped the sleep from her eyes. Her gaze shifted, falling on Steve standing behind Bill. That woke her up with a start and her mouth dropped for a fraction of a second. Steve had a hell of a shiner. Her mouth popped closed, and she pressed her lips together, narrowing her eyes at Bill. "Did you hit him?"

Bill shrugged and stepped back inside. "I'll leave you two to talk." He shuffled Tracy out the door and Steve leaned over the balcony, waiting until they had left the building.

"I'm supposed to apologize to you," he said, watching them drive away. He finally turned towards her.

Jennifer crossed to him. "Does it hurt?" She touched his eye, and he winced.

"Not as much as my pride. That's the second time someone got the drop on me today, and the first was a woman. Can you believe it?"

With the dream still fresh in her mind; his joke was lost on her.

"What's wrong?"

"Nightmare."

"I hope I wasn't the cause." He looked down at the parking lot before she could answer. "Where do you think they went?"

"Probably to grab some food." It was almost dinnertime.

He nodded and headed inside, grabbed a beer out of the refrigerator behind the bar, and took a seat on the overstuffed chair in the living room.

He reached for the remote and began aimlessly flipping through the channels.

Jennifer followed him in. His cavalier attitude grated on her. "You seem mighty comfortable here."

STEVE RAISED HIS EYES to her and glanced back at the television, struggling with the same doubts he had earlier. He met her gaze when she sat on the couch. "Are you acting with me?"

Jennifer recoiled under his direct, intense stare. Her green eyes flashed, and she shot to her feet. "Get out." She pointed to the door, shaking with barely contained anger.

Steve didn't move from the chair. "Sit down, Jen." He recognized the nuance of genuine emotion in her eyes. Her expression differed from when she acted angry—so much so he was surprised Tracy fell for it. He waited until she sat down, still glaring at him. "I had to be sure."

"Sure of what?" She crossed her arms.

"That trusting you wouldn't get me killed."

Jennifer's jaw dropped, and her arms fell to her sides. "You had to ask after today?"

"Especially after today." He leaned forward. "You got me to admit things I never should have. Things that could burn me, Jen. This isn't a game. People have disappeared, and I have to assume the worst." He did not fill her in on those who had been found.

"But you know me." Hurt filled her voice.

He shook his head. "No. I knew an eleven-year-old girl. Things can change drastically in ten years." He scanned her. "Things have changed drastically," he said, his eyes returning to hers. He leaned back slowly and switched gears. "Technically, I could bust you for having alcohol here. Tracy's a minor."

Jennifer's eyes narrowed. "Were you acting with me?"

Steve laughed. "If I were acting, I would have fucked you on the dock."

Her mouth dropped open.

"Yeah. I can be kind of a dick," he said to the shock on her face and climbed to his feet. He crossed and stood looking down at her, running his fingers over her cheek and into her hair before he planted a soft kiss. "See, as much as I want to keep my distance from you, I just can't. As much as I want to taste every goddamned inch of you..." He shut his eyes. "You aren't just someone I met on the street."

"What the hell is that supposed to mean?"

He smiled. "It means that I care about you."

"You have a funny way of showing it." She stepped away. "The fact you doubted me hurts."

Steve shrugged. To him, it was a matter of self-preservation and training. "I question everything, Jen. It keeps me alive."

Jennifer studied him and her arms slowly dropped to her sides. "You look tired."

He nodded and huffed a small laugh. "This emotional shit is exhausting."

Jennifer cracked a smile. "Have you ever been shot at?"

"Yes, and it isn't fun."

Her face paled at his answer. "Have you ever shot someone?"

Steve shook his head. He stood and went out onto the balcony. When she stepped next to him, he said, "Do you really think you can handle that part of my life?"

Jennifer quietly gnawed on her lip. "It doesn't thrill me," she said. "I don't like the idea of you in harm's way... I don't like that at all." She shivered next to him.

"I can't change who I am. I enjoy putting the bad guys behind bars."

Jennifer smiled. "You always loved playing cowboys and Indians when we were younger."

Steve laughed. "I guess." He always made her play the Indian, and she looked ridiculous as she'd hopped around, pounding her palm to her lips, making funky Indian chants. The memory warmed his heart.

"So, can you?" he asked, still smiling at the memory.

"I can handle it. But I still don't like it."

Steve glanced at the parking lot again and the road beyond. There was still no sign of Bill and Tracy, so he leaned over and stole a kiss. "How about dinner to make up for my less than gallant behavior?"

She blushed and smiled.

"Can you remember how to get to my grandfather's place?"

She nodded. "I think so."

He looked at his watch, calculating the time it would take him to get to the fraternity house, clean up, and get to the cottage. "Then I'll see you there in an hour?"

"Sure, but it's like five miles to fraternity row."

"That's just a warmup." He kissed her cheek. "I'll meet you at my grandfather's. Wear something nice." He closed the door behind him and headed out.

Steve sprinted the first few miles, hoping he wouldn't run into them while he was running flat out. He wanted to be far enough along to make the timeframe realistic without looking like a complete idiot. When he'd crossed half the distance, he settled into a moderate jog, forcing his wheezing breath back into a natural rhythm.

They passed a few minutes later, and he raised his hand in a wave to their matching wide-eyed, slack jaw stares. He wiped the sweat off his face and laughed, continuing his exercise regimen back to the fraternity house.

Dark Reckoning
Chapter 9

JENNIFER WATCHED HIM TEAR out of the building. He was fast, and she wondered just how long he could run at that insane pace. Laughing, she sat back down in the lounge chair and closed her eyes.

Fifteen minutes later, Tracy and Bill came into the apartment.

"Jen?" Tracy called.

"Yeah?" she answered from the balcony and stepped into character. Tracy and Bill came out holding a bag of Chinese food and it took everything Jennifer had not to smile. She looked up at them.

"We saw Steve jogging towards fraternity row. What happened?" Bill asked.

"He apologized." Jennifer closed her eyes again.

"Why didn't he stay?" Tracy asked.

Jennifer opened her eyes. "He doesn't like me very much," she replied. "And the feeling is mutual." She got up and headed toward her room.

"Jen?" Tracy whined from the hallway.

"What?" Jennifer swung around. "What were you thinking?" She slammed the bathroom door behind her, shutting off any further commentary and any possibility of her slipping up.

Dark Reckoning
Chapter 10

JENNIFER STEPPED INTO THE shower at the same time Steve turned onto Fraternity Row. Out of breath, he bound up the steps to his room. He glanced at his watch. "Not bad."

The five-mile trek only took him a little over thirty minutes. He grabbed a towel and headed to the bathroom to clean up. Twenty minutes later, he was on the road.

Steve paced by his car, clad in gray dress pants with a light blue button-down shirt. The swelling had receded, but the skin around his right eye was still tight, and it stung when he wiped a stray hair off his forehead. He glanced at his watch again.

Headlights came around the corner, blinding him, and the tenseness in his back loosened as she stopped next to his car. When she stepped out of the car, he stopped pacing and stared at her casual attire. There was no way the restaurant he made reservations at would let her in with the shorts and t-shirt she wore, no matter how good it looked on her. "You consider that nice?" He waved his hand at her.

"Give me a little credit. I couldn't just walk out of the apartment dressed to kill, that would have dredged up way too many questions."

She had a point.

"I figured I'd change when I got here. Do you mind?" She carried her bag to the door and waited for him.

"Sure." He reached into his car and pulled the keys from the ignition.

"You look nice," she said when he slid the keys into the lock next to her. "Very nice."

"Thanks. We have reservations in fifteen minutes." He leaned against the wall by the door, waiting. Peg used to take at least a half hour to get ready, so he resigned himself to being late, which was one of his major pet peeves. The bureau pounded punctuality into his head, more so than his parents had, and he shifted from foot-to-foot, uneasy with the inevitable.

"How far is it to the restaurant?" Jennifer peeled off her shirt in the middle of the living room and reached into her bag, pulling out a sexy little black dress.

"Uh, about fifteen minutes." Steve straightened, watching the silky fabric drape over her skin. She smoothed it over her body and slipped her shorts off, revealing a hint of black underwear before the fabric of the dress fell over her thighs again. She quickly slid the black high heel sandals on and then turned to him, unclipping her hair.

The transformation took less than a minute and left him breathless.

"Better?" She stuffed her clothes, flip-flops, and hair clip back in her bag and then ran her hands through her hair.

He didn't respond with words. He moved across the room and took her in his arms, kissing her deeply.

When he pulled away, she ran her hands over his clean-shaven face. "I'll take that as a yes."

"That definitely was a yes." He led her out of the cottage to his car. He leaned in and plucked the single rose off the seat, opening the door for her as he handed her the rose. "For you."

Jennifer took the rose with a smile. "Thank you."

Steve focused on navigating the winding driveway. "How'd it go with Bill and Tracy?" He pulled onto the road.

"Uneventful. I didn't say much. Just that you didn't like me very much, and the feeling is mutual."

"That must have killed them." In the little time he'd been exposed to Tracy, he picked up that she had to know everything that was going on or she wasn't happy. "Tracy's a journalism major, right?"

"Yeah, why?"

He shrugged. "I bet she'll end up doing entertainment news."

"Why do you say that?"

"She's a busybody. Has to have her hand on the pulse of everything and the juicier the information, the more she gets off on it." He paused. "Regular news just isn't that glamorous."

Jennifer laughed.

"What made you choose acting?" He glanced over at her.

"I got the bug when I did a high school play my sophomore year. I loved to dance in the recitals, but this was different. I was so scared I actually threw up before my first performance, but when I stepped on the stage, everything changed. It was such a rush, having all eyes on me, having people hanging on my every word or note I sang, and at the end, the applause. Steve, the applause is like a drug. It put me in a different state of being and I crave that feeling."

"You mean I'm falling for an applause junkie?"

Jennifer looked over at him with her jaw askew. "What did you just say?"

"You're an applause junkie?" He hadn't meant to say that out loud.

"That's not what you said." She crossed her arms and stared at him, her lips forming an adorable pout, and he turned his attention back to the road without comment.

"Did you mean it?"

Steve didn't respond until he had parked the car in the parking lot of the restaurant. "I should bring you with me the next time I interrogate someone. You seem to be able to get the most intriguing information without trying."

"WHAT DO YOU WANT, Steve?" She swirled the wine in her glass and took a sip, looking over the rim at him.

He sighed and sat back. "I can't think beyond the job right now. I need to concentrate on what I was sent here to do." He took a sip of his drink. "Before someone else disappears."

He was pulling away again. "So today…"

"Today was the best day I've had in over two years," he replied. "Minus getting hit in the face." He smiled a little.

"But?"

"But I can't focus on you." He scanned her again. "As much as I'd like to..." He took another sip of his wine. "Pledge week ends Thursday and initiation is on Friday. Over the last four years, more than half of the disappearances occurred during pledge week. I'm running out of time."

"I still think you're looking in the wrong place."

"I don't think so, Jen." He paused as the waitress approached and he ordered for both of them in flawless French. Steve continued after the waitress left. "I'm not off base on this. Trust me."

"You want me to trust you?" Jennifer asked with her head tilted slightly, looking at him over her wineglass.

"Yes."

"Then tell me what you said in the car."

Steve chuckled and leaned forward and kissed her on the cheek. "You know what I said," he whispered in her ear and sat back down.

Jennifer froze and everything in front of her line of vision disappeared.

A young girl dressed in shorts and a t-shirt stood in the same clearing from Jennifer's nightmare. Dread wrapped around her chest and her heart fluttered.

The water rippled, and a black form rose from the depths of the pond. Jennifer wanted to scream, wanted to tell the little girl to run and run fast, but her voice locked in her mouth. All she could do was stare at the beast in silent horror.

When it stepped onto the moss, the girl found her voice. A shrill cry, a cry of panic, of fear, of terror belted from her lips. And she ran into the woods, still wailing. The thing followed, agile and fast. The sharp siren cut off moments later and the sudden silence was broken only by wet sounds of flesh being stripped from bone.

A sharp pain in Jennifer's hand brought her back to the restaurant, and she looked down. A shard of the broken wine glass stuck out of the meaty part of her palm near her thumb. The numbness subsided enough to make her stomach roll. She swallowed the bile that clawed up her throat.

Steve took her hand and gently removed the glass. His gaze was focused on her wound, but his cheeks were a shade paler than when they walked in. He grabbed his napkin, poured ice water on it, and wrapped it around her palm. Pressing gently to stop the flow of blood, he raised his wary gaze.

"Are you okay?" he asked. The restaurant staff hustled around to clean up the glass, issuing apologies.

No, I'm not okay. Instead of voicing her thought, she shrugged.

She allowed the manager to escort them to the office, where he inspected the cut. The blood was already clotting, but the manager pulled out a first aid kit just in case. Steve took over and cleaned the wound, putting a band-aid over it.

He glanced up at her. "Can you give us a minute?" Steve asked the manager as he stood.

The manager nodded and said they would have another table ready in a moment.

"Thank you," Steve said. The manager left the office and then Steve turned his attention back to her.

Jennifer stared at the bandage on her trembling hand.

"You broke the glass."

"I got that much." Jennifer took a quick glance at him.

He stared at her, waiting for her like a parent waits for a child to admit she broke a treasured vase.

"A... a little girl around ni... nine or ten, reddish blonde hair and a... a tie-dyed t-shirt... was there a child like that on the missing per... persons list?"

"No, why?"

Jennifer lifted her eyes to his just as the shakes took over her entire body. "There will be," she said.

HER EYES TILTED BACK in her head, exposing just the whites.

Steve moved, catching her. She slumped against him, and he shuddered, reliving her transition at the table. Losing color from both her cheeks and lips and the death-like quality that shrouded her eyes freaked him out. He shook off the shock and reached for the first aid kit. He grabbed a smelling salt, broke it between his index finger and thumb, and waved it under her nose.

Jennifer moved her head violently away from the foul smell and came around. "Dear god, what is that?" She pushed his hand away.

"Smelling salts." Steve dropped it into the garbage. He ran a hand through his hair before he closed the door. Instinct took over, and he picked up the pen and pad on the desk, pulling the manager's chair in front of hers.

"Tell me what you saw."

Each word, each description that fell from Jennifer's lips, brought a fresh wave of dread through Steve, tightening his chest. She described the scene, right down to the little girl's dirt laden Keds. He jumped when the manager knocked on the door and called out to them in French.

"Un moment, s'il vous plaît." Steve's eyes locked with Jennifer's. He glanced at the notes and ripped the sheet off the pad, folded and stuffed it in his pocket. He put the pad and pen back on the desk and opened the door.

"Sorry, she got a little shaky there. I think we should get our order to go." He glanced at Jennifer.

She nodded with tear-filled eyes.

The manager stepped away, returning a few moments later with a bag of food packaged for them.

Steve reached for his wallet.

"No, monsieur, this is on us." The manager put his hands up.

Steve hesitated and then slid his wallet into his back pocket. "Merci beaucoup." He took the bag and put his arm around Jennifer's waist, leading her to the car.

They drove in silence back to the cottage. His mind swirled. They had kept the details of Amy's death out of the press, but there had been pictures of the manhunt for the lost child. It didn't add up.

He needed answers, and his training took over, his mind on autopilot. He parked and headed inside with the bag of food. Darkness shrouded them. "Damnit," he muttered and handed her the bag. He rummaged around the kitchen until he found a pack of matches and lit the hurricane lamp on the table.

Soft light pierced the room and Jennifer approached with the bag. He took it from her.

"The electricity isn't being turned on until later this week."

She sat in the chair across from him, still quiet. But her gaze tracked his movements as he set the contents of their meal out on the table and rummaged through the drawers for silverware. He pulled a bottle of wine out of the bag. "I guess they really didn't want a lawsuit."

Once glasses were set and the wine poured, he took a seat and brought his gaze to her. "What really happened back there?"

"I'm not really sure." She picked at the food in the to-go container, taking a small bite despite her total lack of hunger. "This is delicious." She pointed her fork at her dinner.

He took a bite, but he didn't taste the food. Just going through the motions of a friendly dinner was difficult.

"I freaked you out."

He downed his glass of wine and reached to refill it again. He laughed. "And I'm not easily unnerved."

"I'm sorry for ruining the evening." Jennifer returned her attention to the meal.

"I actually like this better than the restaurant." He smiled at her. "But I have more questions for you." He slung his arm over the back of the chair, swirling the wine in his other hand, and studied her reaction.

Her gaze shot up to his, and her eyes narrowed.

"What happened at the restaurant, Jennifer?"

REALIZATION SET IN AND irritation crept over her skin. The calm smooth cadence of his voice was marred by the sharp suspicious interest in his eyes. He was drilling her for information—as if she was a suspect.

What the fuck?

"You're interrogating me?" She pushed the chair back to leave.

"Sit down!" Steve slammed the wineglass on the table. Fury blazed in his eyes, transforming his rugged features into a frightening mask of anger.

Jennifer stood and headed toward the door, hell-bent on getting away from him and his enraged glare.

His hand landed on her shoulder and spun her around. She reacted to his sudden and less than gentle manner, but he easily sidestepped her Osoto Gari. She found herself face down on the floor with her hands clasped behind her back. Cold metal ensnared her wrist, followed by the click of the handcuffs, and panic set in. "What are you doing?"

Steve hauled her onto the kitchen chair, threading the cuffs through the back spindles and fastening them around her free wrist he held. He stormed out of the room and came back a few seconds later with two photographs and slammed them on the table in front of her.

"She wasn't among the missing—she was one we found. Her name was Amy, and she disappeared a month ago. She wandered away from her parents' campsite and was found a few days later."

Jennifer's wide, shocked eyes gaped at the photographs, twitching from the picture of the smiling girl to the second of something torn to pieces, bloody and mangled. She didn't understand. She didn't understand at all until her eyes landed on the bloody discarded sneaker. Her gaze shot up to Steve in horror.

"Oh god, oh god, oh god," Jennifer repeated over and over. Trembling. All the heat in her face drained, and she pushed the chair away from the table with her feet.

"How could you know so much detail, Jennifer?"

Jennifer stared at him, and hot tears cascaded down her cheeks. *He thinks I did this.* "I wasn't in Brooksfield last month. I was in New York."

Steve stepped back, blinking rapidly. His gaze bounced between her and pictures on the table.

The tears continued. "How could you possibly think I could do that?" She sobbed and hung her head.

He pulled open his cell phone. "I need you to verify the whereabouts of someone from July fifteenth to August fifteenth. Jennifer Curtis, date of birth July 16, 1986. Permanent address, 174 Evergreen Lane, Norwalk, Connecticut. Call me back when you have the information." His eyes, narrowed and questioning, never left her. She continued to sob.

"How could you think that?" She raised her tear-stained face to meet his suspicious glare.

DOUBT AS STRONG AS an arrow to his heart knocked him back another step.

The phone rang, and he answered it. "That was quick," he said, and listened. Steve stepped forward, took the pictures off the table, and left the room. He tucked them away in his briefcase in the bedroom and closed his eyes.

"What about Tracy Sheehan or her father?" he asked softly. "I asked you to check into them for me. Were they in Brooksfield during that time?" He waited on the line this time. He got an answer, although it wasn't what he expected. He closed the phone slowly. They were in New York at the same time as Jennifer.

He hung his head. "Shit." He slid the phone back into his pocket and glanced toward the kitchen, pondering what this really meant. Twice today she described details that were impossible for anyone to know unless they were there at the time of the incidents. Twice he doubted her.

"Damn it all to hell." He crossed into the kitchen.

He pulled a chair over to where Jennifer sat, unwilling to let her out of the restraints just yet. He studied his hands and when he raised his eyes, she returned his gaze, the tears still slowly trailed down her cheeks. He flinched at the pain in her eyes.

"I'm sorry," he whispered.

"Un-cuff me. I want to go."

He shook his head. "Not yet."

"Now!" The anger kicked in full force, stopping the flow of tears.

If he let her go now, he would never see her again. His chest constricted at the thought. "You described her in detail. What the hell was I supposed to think?" He couldn't help the plea in his voice.

Jennifer started to say something; then closed her mouth. She took a deep breath and exhaled, her gaze softening. "I see things. I told you that earlier."

Steve closed his eyes and lowered his head, trying to comprehend these new intangible facts. "I am at a loss here," he admitted. "Things are black and white for me and this... this is a shade of gray I have never run into before. It's not tangible, so it's hard for me to accept." He leaned back, glancing at her. "You have visions of what happened?"

"Glimpses."

"Can you describe who did this?"

Jennifer slowly shook her head. "I don't know what I saw." She chewed on her lip and her eyes stared right through him, like she was looking at something far in the distance. She blinked and met his gaze. "It has to be some manifestation of my imagination. Some personification of evil because I can't begin to describe, let alone comprehend, what my mind is showing me. It's black as night and has a form like a man, but I don't know what it is." Her brow creased. "It's the same thing I saw in my nightmare earlier today."

"Tell me about the nightmare." He put his hands on his knees and paid attention to her tells. He caught no sign that she was trying to yank his chain. What he saw was brutal honesty, and it twisted his gut.

"It was hurting you," Jennifer said.

Steve sat back, blinked and digested what she said as well as how she said it. She was not comfortable with him getting hurt. That much was clear in both her tone and her gaze. "You keep referring to the killer as it."

Jennifer nodded.

"Why?"

"What I saw wasn't human. And I'm not entirely sure my imagination could conjure such an evil thing."

"There were no animal tracks. We checked." He refrained from telling her there were no tracks at all.

Jennifer sighed. "I don't know what it is." Her brow creased with uncertainty. "How could you think it was me?" Pain reflected in her gaze.

"It's my job to think that way."

"Your job sucks," Jennifer replied.

Steve smiled. "Sometimes it does." He stood and went behind her, releasing the handcuffs. He stepped around and took the seat again, putting the cuffs on the corner of the table.

Jennifer rubbed her wrists but didn't move. "How can you think you're falling in love with me and at the same time think I am capable of murder?"

He leaned back and ran his hands through his hair. It was a contradiction he couldn't explain to her. "My job demands I look at all possibilities, however remote and unlikely. The facts you presented me with at the restaurant warranted my actions." He knew it wasn't the explanation she wanted, but it was all he had.

Jennifer swallowed hard. "Are you really falling in love with me?"

Her breathy question broke through the barricade surrounding his heart, and he nodded. "I don't want to."

"Why not?"

"Because I just fucked up any chance I had with you." He stood and left the cottage, crossing to the dock steps. Sitting, he scanned the water and the mountains beyond. "Stupid idiot."

He should have known she was a force of nature meant to bow him over. She had when he was sixteen and she was only eleven, whether he wanted to admit it. But back then, the age difference seemed insurmountable. And then his parents had taken jobs states away. He wondered what would have happened had they not moved.

Jennifer took a seat next to him a few minutes later, and he raised an eyebrow in surprise.

Neither of them spoke. Time passed, and they looked out at the lake.

Steve finally looked at her. "Why are you still here?"

She sighed, keeping her gaze on the water. "Because I'm in the same boat you are."

He gently took her hand, but didn't dare look at her. He could feel the electricity flowing between them and if he looked, he would act. "It's only been two days." He was going to say they could cut their losses, but the words wouldn't come.

"Yeah." Her reply was barely a whisper, and then she said five words that changed everything. "But I can't leave now."

His grip on her hand tightened, and he turned his head, ripping his gaze away from the lake to look at her. The same need swept through every fiber of his being reflected in her eyes, and he reached for her. His mouth found hers and all else was forgotten. The lake watched neutrally as he carried her back to the cottage.

Dark Reckoning
Chapter 11

HE LAID HER ON the bed and his blue eyes were unsure as he stretched over her. His hesitancy was as endearing as it was frustrating, and Jennifer pulled him to her lips. The kiss was slow and soft, tender and sweet, not at all what she expected.

He pulled away and his gaze traveled over their surroundings.

Jennifer swallowed hard. They were laying on the bed he had once shared with Peg. Letting him borrow Tom's shorts was nothing compared to the magnitude of what this meant.

"We don't have to do anything here if it bothers you," she said softly, conflicted between the desire in her bones and the sorrow piercing her chest.

He stared at her. His gaze was intense as it moved from hers to her lips. Instead of speaking, or even acknowledging her offer, he dipped his mouth to hers. This time, the kiss transitioned from sweet to searing. This was the kind of kiss love stories were written about.

His hand slid up her side and cupped her breast. His thumb circled her nipple through the fabric of her dress. His touched blanketed her with heat, unlocking the passion that she had tabled for the last two years.

Need as sharp as claws raked over her skin, and she nearly tore his shirt off. They couldn't strip fast enough for her, and the ripping of fabric resounded in the room.

Steve jerked up and stared down at his torn shirt. Dimples appeared as he stripped the fabric off.

"Sorry," Jennifer muttered as her lips nipped his throat.

"I've got more." He smiled down at her and shimmied out of his pants.

She pulled her dress the rest of the way off, and with it came her unclasped bra. She tossed it aside and her gaze landed on his chiseled chest. The muscles rippled as he peeled off her underwear.

His gaze drifted over her like a sweet caress, and when his eyes finally met hers, the need she saw matched that which flamed over her skin. His lips crushed hers with his first thrust.

He filled her, stretching her with pleasure so intense, she gasped under his kiss. The sudden presence of him took her breath away in one instant and ignited her soul in the next.

He broke the kiss and stared down into her eyes, keeping his body still. The way his gaze searched hers melted any hurt she had experienced earlier in the evening. There was such adoration in his eyes that her heart expanded, filling her chest with more than just raw lust.

The moment passed, and his expression turned carnal. He moved his hips slowly, exploring her neck and chest with his mouth.

Each swipe of his tongue drew more heat in her belly.

She reveled in the passion, the oneness she felt with him as she matched his rhythm. The intensity increased, driving his fevered thrusts harder and deeper until she peaked, diving over the wave that nearly drowned her with its toe-curling power. She gasped his name, nearly blind from the ecstasy.

He kissed her, silencing her moan, along with his own groaning climax. The kiss lingered until his weight sagged on her. He propped up on his elbows and studied her face. Jennifer breathed in the scent of sex and pine on the air as she tried to get her heartbeat to even out.

"Holy god." He traced her cheeks with his fingers.

"No kidding." Her voice was still raspy with aftershocks.

He rolled off her and pulled her into the nook of his arm, surprising her with a snuggle. She would have never pegged him for the type of man that liked to hold his woman after sex. Tom certainly hadn't. Then again, what she had experienced with Tom didn't even come close to the sensations Steve created.

It was as if she had never truly made love before this moment.

THUNDER RUMBLED IN THE distance as they lay spent on his bed. He closed his eyes and suddenly sat up in the bed, startling Jennifer.

"What's wrong?"

"Rain," he answered as he pulled his pants on. "Where are your keys? I'll put your windows up."

"In the kitchen, in my bag."

"Be right back." He bolted out of the house, feeling the first raindrop as he started his car, pushing the button to retract the convertible top back in place. He secured it and rolled the windows up. He trotted over to her car and slid the keys in the ignition, putting the windows up just as the sky opened, dumping buckets on him as he fled for cover. Steve laughed, walking back inside, soaked to the bone.

"I'm okay; I just got caught in the rain. The movie was good. I'll head out just as soon as this downpour stops. Don't wait up for me." Jennifer turned off her phone, smiling at his dripping form. "You got there just in time."

She had dressed in the shorts and t-shirt she had arrived in, much to his chagrin. "Yeah. Who was that?" He ran his fingers through his hair, approaching her.

"Tracy called. She was worried. I told her I went to grab some food and ended up going to a movie."

Steve pulled her to him, getting her clothing soaked. "Stay." He kissed her.

"I should go." She tried to push away, but he was insistent.

"Stay long enough to watch the storm with me."

His heart thumped under the hand she placed on his wet, bare chest. She looked into his eyes, his wet hair dangling, sending droplets of misplaced rain onto her upturned face.

"Stay," he implored, and slowly bent down. His lips grazed hers lightly. "Please," he said against them. He pulled away just as slowly.

Jennifer's cheeks glistened with the water from his hair, and she flushed, her irises expanding with the connection between them.

He smiled at all the physical signs of affection, the ones she couldn't control. Ones he was sure he mirrored.

She nodded.

He stepped away and headed into the bedroom, grabbing his torn shirt. He slipped it on and stepped out, holding the shredding hem. "I can't believe you ripped my shirt."

Jennifer turned crimson. "You weren't moving fast enough."

With a smile, he took her hand, leading her to the bench under the picture window. When he settled on the seat, she scooted between his legs, leaning against him, and he wrapped her in his arms.

The lightning storm brewed over the lake.

"I love thunderstorms." He kissed the back of her head.

"Me, too."

Lightning danced on the lake.

Thunder cracked overhead, and Jennifer jumped. Steve chuckled and squeezed a little tighter. She relaxed again.

"What are we going to do about your roommate?"

"I can't pretend anymore," Jennifer replied under the rumble.

Steve nodded. "Do we just tell them outright?"

"Where's the fun in that?"

Steve looked at her reflection in the window and smiled. She was looking at him, not the storm. He shifted his gaze back outside. A lightning bolt split a big oak in the yard and his smile faltered. The half of the tree that faced the lake slowly bent into the water, like an elegant ballet. The other side of the oak stood fast.

"I'll have to cut that down eventually," he said.

"Mhm." She closed her eyes, drifting to sleep on his chest.

Steve alternated between watching the storm and watching her face in the window's reflection.

What am I going to do with you?

He sighed and kissed the back of her head before glancing outside again.

Jennifer snored. A light feathery sound that reminded him of waves gently lapping the shore. He closed his eyes, leaning his head back against the wall.

Dark Reckoning
Chapter 12

THE RINGING OF A cell phone brought both of them out of a sound sleep. Steve groaned. His leg had fallen numb, and he almost crumpled to the floor when he stood. Jennifer was on her feet, alert but confused. She looked around the cottage, her eyes landing on the bright scene outside the window. The sun was out.

"Shit." She bolted to answer her phone and Tracy's voice rang through the small cottage.

"Where are you?" Tracy asked.

Steve clamped his mouth shut, hopping around the tiny cottage, trying to wake up his useless leg. He bit his lip at the amused expression on Jennifer's face, turning away as she answered her roommate.

"I headed out early."

"I didn't hear you come in last night," Tracy replied.

"I'm sorry. It was very late, and I assumed you were with Billy. I'll talk to you after classes," Jennifer said.

Steve turned back to her, shaking his leg and allowing a smirk to grace his lips at her answer.

"I have to go." She hung up without waiting for an answer and crossed her legs, pointing toward the bathroom. "Does the plumbing work?"

Steve nodded. "It should." He continued limping around the cottage, his leg hurting from the pins and needles prickling through his waking skin. He glanced at his watch and his eyes went wide. "Oh, shit!" He stumbled toward the bathroom. "Jen, it's after nine," he said to the closed door.

The door flew open seconds later. "What time did you say it was?" Her eyes were wide.

"It's nine-thirty." He slid past her, closing the door behind him.

Steve came out a few minutes later. His clothing was disheveled, and he looked around the room. "I missed my first class." He gathered his things.

"I don't have my schedule with me." Jennifer looked at him as she hand combed her hair.

"Neither do I."

They stopped frantically running around the cabin and looked at each other. He started laughing first, and then she joined in.

"No, you don't understand," he said through the laughter. "My boss is teaching the eight o'clock class."

Her eyebrows went up as she continued to laugh. "Oooo, you're in trouble," she taunted.

He shot across the room and wrapped his arms around her. "It was worth it, waking up with you." He kissed her and took her hand as he led her out of the cabin. "But I am going to get reamed, truly reamed," he added, as he locked the door.

"The food?"

"I'll clean up later. I have to shoot over to the frat house and get my damn schedule." He slid into his car and took off like a bat out of hell, leaving a dust cloud in his wake.

Dark Reckoning
Chapter 13

STEVE SKIDDED TO A halt in front of the fraternity house and ran in. Quickly changing into a pair of shorts and a t-shirt, he reached for his schedule and a notebook, and flew back out. His cell rang as he turned the key in the ignition. He answered and put it on speaker. "What?"

"It's Professor Murphy. You missed my class this morning."

"I overslept," Steve grumbled, shifting gears. Late for his third class of the day—so much for being the model college student.

"Please tell me you at least have more information for me than you did yesterday," Agent Murphy snapped into the phone.

"No." Steve slid into a spot in the student parking lot. "I have to go. I'm late for my next class." He heard his superior curse under his breath. "Pledging starts this week," he added as he closed the door. "I'm sure I'll have some more information for you before the end of the week." He ended the call, consulted his schedule, and headed in the general direction of the lecture hall. Many of the people he passed stopped and stared at him. Entering the building, he glanced down at his shirt and almost laughed aloud. It was inside out. Veering into the bathroom, he stripped and slipped the shirt on the right way and glanced in the mirror. His eye and cheek were purple with blue around the edges and his hair disheveled to the point of unruly. *No wonder everyone was staring.* He wet his hands and smoothed his hair back, combing it into place. Satisfied, he slipped out and into the back row of the lecture hall, hoping he'd go unnoticed.

"Good of you to join us. Mr. Williams, I presume?" The professor turned and stared him down.

Steve smiled awkwardly. "Sorry," he mumbled. Every eye in the class turned in his direction.

"If you can't make it in time for my class, you'd better drop out now because I will not tolerate tardiness. This is your one and only warning." He turned back and continued where he had left off.

Steve opened his notebook and glanced around. Everyone had turned his or her attention back to the professor. Glancing at his schedule, he grimaced. He had public relations next. *That must be a mistake.* He closed his eyes for a moment and took a deep breath, trying to concentrate on the lecture, but his mind was restless. It kept wandering back to Jennifer.

"Are we boring you, Mr. Williams?"

Steve's eyes flew open. "No, I listen better with my eyes closed."

The professor pursed his lips. "If that is the case, what was I just discussing?"

"The Miranda rights and the effect they have on the interrogation process."

The professor's face turned red. With a nod of satisfaction, he continued the lecture.

Steve glanced at the student next to him and shrugged. He focused his attention on the lecture and closed his eyes again, leaning back in the seat. As he half listened, his mind rattled off everything he learned the last couple of days.

A nagging feeling gnawed in the pit of his stomach, masked by the pangs of hunger. *Damn it, I'm missing something significant here.* He leaned forward, doodling in his notebook.

He needed to get back in the good graces of his fraternity brothers in the next couple of days. He had alienated Bill, and that wasn't a wise thing to do—after all, he was the president of the fraternity.

Click.

Steve looked up.

How was it that the president of his fraternity wasn't dating a sorority girl?

He leaned back in the seat and pretended to focus on the professor. He couldn't play this game with Jennifer anymore, not if he wanted to remain close to Bill Tyler. He closed his eyes at the next thought, his head dipping. *I'm going to need to use my relationship with Jennifer.* He let out a silent huff. *Sometimes this job sucks.*

Steve checked his watch. He still had a few minutes until class was over. He took the syllabus out. Damn, he'd have to do some work this semester if he couldn't crack the case before long. He sighed, looking back at his notebook. He stared at the paper. His eyes darted around the room and back down at his doodling. He blinked and looked again. Scrawled across the middle of the paper in red were words that stunned him.

She is mine.

The handwriting definitely wasn't his. He had written Jennifer's name several times on the paper, and they all had the crisp sharp edges of the blue ballpoint pen he held. Those fuzzy edged words like a felt-tip pen on a paper towel hadn't been there when he opened the notebook. He flipped the page and then flipped through all the pages. The deep red scrawl reminding him of blood graced every single page in the composition booklet. He slammed the notebook closed, gaining the attention of the room once again.

"Is there a problem, Mr. Williams?" The professor asked, obviously annoyed at the interruption.

Steve fumbled this time. He looked down at his notebook and back up again, trying not to shiver noticeably. "I... ah... no. No problem."

The professor studied him and then looked around. "That concludes today's lecture."

Steve bolted out of the room before the professor could get another barb in. He staggered out of the building and toward the adjacent lecture hall where his next class was. Preoccupied with the crimson scribbles in his notebook, he nearly plowed someone over. "Sorry," he mumbled absently, without really seeing the person he had almost flattened.

"Steve?"

Her voice brought him back, and he snapped his head toward her, still haunted by what he had seen.

"Are you okay?" Jennifer asked.

He hadn't even noticed her. He had noticed no one. "I... ah..." His eyes shot between her and the notebook. "I don't know."

"What's wrong?"

He glanced at the notebook, afraid to open it.

"What happened?"

He shook his head and looked around. "Something really weird. It doesn't fit in my black and white world."

Jennifer raised her eyebrows.

He took a breath and held it while opening the notebook. The words glared out among the doodles.

She is mine.

He flipped through the pages, showing her the bleed-through letters gracing each sheet. "It wasn't there when I opened the notebook."

Jennifer stared at his doodles, then up at him in confusion. "You wrote my name several times."

Steve blinked and stepped back. He looked from the page to her. He flipped to a page he hadn't doodled on and held it up for her to see.

"It's blank," she replied, looking at him like he was just shy of a full deck.

"You can't see that?" He stepped back again.

"See what?"

He scanned the paper and then raised his eyes to her as an urge took hold. He leaned over and planted a kiss. As he pulled away, he held up the notebook.

He must die.

Jennifer's eyes went wide.

He closed the notebook. "Not very black and white, now is it?"

Jennifer shook her head. "He must die? What does that mean?"

Steve's brow creased. He flipped the notebook open. "It says *she is mine*."

Jennifer looked down. "I'm seeing *He must die* and it looks like the page is bleeding."

Jennifer's flesh broke out in goose bumps as Steve closed the notebook. He flipped his wrist to see the face of his watch. "I've got a class starting any minute."

"So do I."

Steve sighed, his gaze jumped between her and the notebook debating whether to go to class or take the time to analyze the problem.

"I missed my first class. I can't miss the next one," Jennifer said. "Neither can you."

Steve nodded. They walked without talking and when they both turned into the same lecture hall, Jennifer raised an eyebrow.

"Public relations?"

"I guess my boss thought I needed it." He took the seat next to her in the back row.

Jennifer put her hand over her mouth to stifle a laugh.

"Fuck you," he whispered. He looked at his notebook. "Do you have a piece of paper?" He didn't want to open the notebook again.

Jennifer ripped off a sheet from her pad and handed it to him.

The class surprised Steve. It was actually found it interesting. He slid the notes into the notebook without opening it and stood at the end of class. "That wasn't bad."

"Communications classes aren't all fun and games."

"Yes, they are," he said. He walked outside. "You should try criminal law sometime."

Jennifer hit him in the arm with her pad and stopped when Steve sent a glare her way.

"We have company. It's time to act, babe."

"You have got to be the cockiest son of a bitch that I've ever met," Jennifer said, loud enough to be heard by Tracy and Bill, who were now less than thirty feet from them.

Steve stopped and turned toward her. "Look who's talking." He took a threatening step toward her. "Princess." He spat the words at her. "You're just a pampered bitch."

Jennifer reached up to slap his face, and Steve caught her hand easily. Tracy and Bill sprinted to reach them.

Steve dropped his notebook and yanked her to him. He wrapped his arm around her waist and looked into her green eyes. "You should try a real man sometime." He planted a kiss on her, crushing her lips under his.

Jennifer's free hand slowly slid up his arm and around his neck.

HIS HEART BEAT AGAINST her as he kissed her in mock anger. He released her wrist and plunged his hand into her hair. The kiss deepened. Jen lost herself in the heat of it, forgetting she was supposed to be acting, forgetting the words she read in the notebook. She just melted into him.

Steve pulled away, and the edges of his lips curled into a smile as their eyes met. He stepped away and picked up the notebook.

Jennifer's face flushed, and her chest rose and fell noticeably. The urge to fly into his arms again overwhelmed her, but she resisted. Tracy and Bill misinterpreted the intensity of her stare, thinking she was livid, which played perfectly into their little game.

Bill reached to grab Steve. "Son of a bitch."

Steve reacted, knocking his arm away. "Don't even think about it," he warned Bill and glanced back at Jennifer.

"Fuck you," Jennifer blurted, her voice hoarse, her chest heaving a little less.

Steve raised his eyebrow and in two strides was standing over her again. "When?"

Jennifer saw Bill start toward Steve and raised her hand like a traffic cop stopping a line of cars. "Back off, Bill, I can handle this," she said, her eyes returned to Steve.

Steve winked down at her, and she had to suppress a smile. His back was towards Bill and Tracy, so he had the advantage in breaking character.

Bill stopped short and exchanged a look with Tracy.

"You couldn't handle it," she shot up at Steve.

"Want to bet?" he asked, his voice low and sultry, making her break out in shivers of anticipation.

"You aren't man enough."

"Oh, yes, I am." He took her in his arms and kissed her again. This time, it was slow and seductive. His hands sliding around her waist, pulling her close. "I can handle you any time I want," he said, pulling his lips away from hers. "Right, babe?" He smiled down at her.

"Like you did last night?" She smiled up at him and they turned to look at Bill and Tracy. They looked identical, arms hanging by their sides, mouths agape and eyes wide. She grinned at her roommate.

"You bitch," Tracy gasped, staring at Jennifer. "I was so worried about you last night."

Jennifer smiled at Steve. "I was in good hands."

"So, this was all a game?" Bill asked, gawking at Jennifer and Steve.

"Pretty much," Steve answered.

"You let me hit you?"

"I didn't see it coming; otherwise, you wouldn't have touched me." Steve looked down into Jennifer's eyes. He moved, so he stood next to her with one arm around her waist, facing Tracy and Bill.

Tracy kept swinging her gaze back and forth, blinking incessantly.

"I have half a mind to belt you again," Bill said. He put his arm around Tracy's shoulders.

"Look, we both were tired of people meddling in our lives, trying to set us up on blind dates. There were times I nearly took your head off, right until you said her last name." Steve shrugged and glanced down at her. "We were neighbors as kids and our parents kept in touch. I wasn't even sure it was the same Jennifer Curtis until I called her."

"You knew each other?" Tracy gasped.

"Yep," Jennifer said.

Tracy put her hand on her hip and narrowed her eyes. "So, you planned this all along?"

Jennifer just smiled.

Steve glanced at her. "Yes."

Jennifer looked up at him, knowing her fondness was visible in her eyes.

"So... we were right," Tracy said smugly.

"As much as I hate to admit it, yeah, you were right," Jennifer said.

Bill looked at his watch. "Trac, we have to boogie." He glanced at the two of them and shook his head. "I'll see you back at the frat house." He pointed at Steve with what looked like a forced smile that didn't quite erase the aggravation in his eyes.

Steve escorted Jennifer to his car, his arm firmly planted around her waist. "You do improv pretty well." He grinned as he opened the car door for her.

Jennifer hesitated. "My car is over there." She pointed.

"I know. Get in," he replied, and watched her slip into the passenger seat.

He drove back to the cottage. "I've got to clean up the mess from last night," he explained, turning off the car. "You can go down on the dock or whatever while I take care of the food, okay?"

"I can help, you know," Jennifer said.

"If you come inside with me, I won't do what I came here to do."

"So, you can't handle it." She smiled, daring him to shirk his duties.

Steve returned her salacious grin. "I can handle you just fine."

"Really?"

Steve looked at his watch and then up at her. "Really?" He headed to the door.

Jennifer followed, and he flipped the light switch. The light went on this time. He glanced over his shoulder at her. "I've got all the modern conveniences now."

Jennifer took a seat on the window bench while he headed into the kitchen to clean up the dinner they had never finished.

He grabbed a garbage bag and dropped the barely touched to-go containers in, tying it closed. The silverware and wine glasses went in the sink, and he corked the half-empty bottle of wine and put it by the refrigerator. It was all so... domesticated. Jennifer smiled.

As he walked out of the kitchen, he picked up the cuffs on the edge of the table, walking toward her with a wicked grin.

"What did you say about handcuffs yesterday?" He dangled them from his index finger.

The sun glinted on the steel, and she jumped to her feet, backing away from him, right into the entry of the bedroom. "Oh, no, you don't! I'm still aggravated with you for chaining me to the chair."

"You were adventurous enough to come inside." He lunged, catching her before she could spin away.

Her heart jumped in her chest and she laughed, but didn't fight him. A new curiosity filled her skin. The thought of being restrained by him sent a flush of heat over her.

Steve tossed the cuffs on the bed and stripped her shirt and bra off. Then he swept her off her feet and put her on the mattress. When he climbed on top of her and took her wrists, goose flesh broke out across her chest, hardening her nipples.

He slid the cuffs around one wrist, securing it in a much lighter grasp than last night. He threaded the cuff through the bars on the headboard and secured her free wrist, grinning down at her.

His blue eyes sparkled, and the smile on his face made her tremble. "Are you going to interrogate me?" Her voice shook with the idea.

He ran his hands gently from her wrists down her arms, slowly touching her skin with his fingertips. "Oh, yes." He leaned down to kiss her.

"Every inch of your lovely body." He kissed her neck and nibbled on her ear, chuckling.

A delicious shiver cascaded through her.

He ran the tip of his tongue down her neckline, gently stroking her breasts with his hands. Moving his mouth to her nipples, he ran his tongue around them playfully.

She squirmed in his grasp. He continued his interrogation of her body with his hands and mouth, loving her like she had never thought possible.

Wave after wave of ecstasy coursed through her, making her gasp and shiver, moan and climax, over and over until she begged for him.

He slid inside her, his eyes wild with passion, his face flushed, but he took his time, moving his hips slowly. She peaked again, this time calling his name. His eyes closed, and sped up, arching into her with his own climax with her name on his lips.

He trembled, his muscles shuddering as he lay on top of her.

"My god," he breathed and reached for the keys on the dresser, unlocking the cuffs.

Jennifer stretched languidly and then slid her arms around his neck. "Did you find what you were looking for?"

"Yes, exactly what I was looking for." Steve's slow, sexy smile formed, and he ran his fingers across her lips. "I want to hear you call out my name like that for the rest of my life." His gaze lingered on her lips before they locked with her eyes.

Jennifer's eyes widened at the admission and the underlying commitment he was offering. The thought cascaded a waterfall of emotions, elation and a fear she couldn't fathom.

Steve closed his eyes and rested his forehead on her shoulder. He gave her a squeeze and pulled away. "I need a shower." He rolled off the bed. He glanced at her and headed into the bathroom.

Jennifer pulled on her clothes and headed out to explore the yard. She glanced at the lake and around the property; her gaze falling on the path in the woods. The flip-flops she wore were not the ideal footwear for the woods, but she went for a hike, anyway. Following the meandering overgrown path wasn't as difficult as she thought it would be. When the woods gave way to the cove, her breath caught in her throat. The sun shone down on the most glorious inlet, making it sparkle like diamonds. Wildflowers grew on the edges of the water, the sweet smell drifted on the gentle breeze. The large, flat, clover-shaped rock jutted out over the water.

"Paradise Cove."

A gentle field of lush moss covered the ground surrounding the water, and she slipped her shoes off and stepped onto it. She was rewarded with the sensation of stepping on a cloud.

She chewed her lip as she stared at the rock, wondering if the legend was true. It would be quite a change to see her future instead of those around her. Tentatively, she stepped onto the rock and took in the mirror-like water.

Her reflection stared back, and she laughed at the wonder in her eyes. A bug landed on the water, causing a rippling effect, and she watched with interest as the ripples caused the image of her face to change.

"Pretty, isn't it?" Steve asked, making her jump.

Jennifer turned. "Yes, it is."

Steve stepped onto the rock behind her and wrapped his arms around her waist.

Jennifer glanced at the rippling reflection of the two of them in the water. His gaze was glued to hers. "What are you thinking about?"

"The future." He smiled. "Maybe there is a bit of truth to that old legend after all."

She turned in his grasp, meeting his sincere gaze. "You think?"

He gave her a shrug and glanced at his watch. "I have to go. We have a meeting at the fraternity tonight."

"I have a class from seven to ten, anyway."

Steve frowned. "Come by afterwards, all right?"

"Sure." She smiled up at him. "Have you ever walked on that moss with your bare feet?"

"Yes, feels like you're walking on a cloud."

Jennifer laughed. "Those were my exact thoughts when I took my shoes off."

He took her hand and waited while she slipped her shoes on.

"Where does that go?" She pointed to a narrow path of running water heading into the thicket, out of sight.

"Nowhere." He led her back towards the cottage.

"It has to go somewhere," she said, following him.

He paused. "My grandfather said it goes nowhere. It dries up in the bed of Black Cove."

"Black Cove?"

"Yes, it's just a big sink hole deep in the woods." He pulled her along.

"Have you ever seen it?"

"No, there's too much undergrowth in the forest to get back there." He turned and smiled. "I tried several times as a kid but couldn't get through. My grandfather blew a gasket when he found out."

Jennifer drew her eyebrows together.

"The state forest starts back there and if I had gotten lost..." Steve trailed off. "Well, let's just say he wasn't thrilled with me."

"Where did they find that little girl?" Jennifer asked.

"In the state forest."

The hairs on the back of her neck twitched. "We never talked about the notebook," she said as he led her across the lawn.

"I know. We made love, instead." He looked back at her as a crease formed between his eyes. He glanced at the cottage and stopped as soon as they were on the lawn. "I never asked..." He bit his lip and met her gaze.

"Asked what?"

He ran his hand down his face. "Birth control?"

Those two words widened her eyes. She shook her head and a lead ball dropped into her stomach. "I didn't even think about it." She covered her mouth.

His face paled, and he glanced at the lake as if fighting some internal demon. "I didn't either." He closed his eyes and sighed.

Her mouth went dry. She wasn't prepared to be a mother, and the thought terrified her. "What if..."

His gaze jumped back to hers and the tilt of his smile warmed her. "Well, then I guess we'll just have to deal with it."

"I'll make sure I'm prepared next time." He kissed her cheek.

"Are you always this reckless?"

"In my job, yes, in my private life, no." He looked back at her.

"Somehow, that doesn't make me feel any better."

He disappeared into the house and when he came out; he had the garbage bag in his left hand and his gun, cuffs and keys in the other. He threw the bag in the trunk and shuffled the gun to his right hand, slipping into the car.

"Why do you have that?"

Steve laughed. "Don't worry, the safety's on." He put it in the holster attached to the bottom of the seat.

"Why do you have that?" she repeated, recoiling a little in the seat.

"Jennifer, I'm a cop," he reminded her as he dropped the cuffs into the glove box and locked it. He started the car, meeting her gaze.

His light-hearted smile faded as he studied her, and she was sure every one of her misgivings screamed from the depth of her eyes.

"This isn't a game, is it?"

"No, it isn't. And if I'm wrong about you, I'm a dead man." He shrugged and then raised his eyebrows. "But after the last two days, I guess I can die happy because I've already had a small taste of heaven." He smiled without looking at her.

"You're not wrong about me, Steve." She put her hand on his.

Steve glanced at the floor by her feet. The notebook was still there. "Open that please." He pointed his chin at the notebook. Jennifer leaned over and grabbed it, flipping it open at the center.

She is mine. He must die.

"It changed," she said, almost tossing the notebook away.

Steve glanced at the bloody words and took a deep breath. "Close it."

She did, tossing it back to the floor.

Steve glanced at the discarded notebook and then back at the road. His brow furrowed. He glanced at Jennifer and then back at the road as he pulled into the student center parking lot and slid into the spot next to her car, pulling the keys out of the ignition. Leaning back in the seat, he ran his hands over his face. "Hand me the notebook."

Jennifer picked it up between her thumb and forefinger like a dirty tissue and held it out for him. She gripped the door with her other hand while he opened it again. The words stared back.

"Who must die?" he asked, like he was trying to solve the riddle in his mind.

You.

Jennifer gasped. Her face and hands went cold.

His brow creased as he looked from the page to her and back. "The words are the same."

She shook her head.

"What does it say?"

Her chin trembled and her vision blurred. "You," she whispered. "It says You."

Steve closed the notebook. "I ain't dying," he said harshly, tossing the notebook behind her seat. "Neither are you. Not till we're old and gray and our grandchildren are grown with kids of their own." He grabbed the garbage from the trunk and crossed to the dumpster, tossing it inside.

HE STARED AT THE ground in front of the dumpster. His mind fogged with aggravation. Bloody words in a notebook wasn't something he knew how to chase down. *Are you fucking kidding me?*

He turned and stopped, gazing at her tightly wrapped arms around her torso. "Damn." He could see the toll this freaky experience was having on her.

Nothing is going to hurt you. Not as long as I'm breathing. He promised himself.

Approaching her, he took her face in his hands. "No matter what that says, we will both have long and happy lives. I promise."

Jennifer's chin continued to quiver, and her eyes filled with tears. "Don't make me promises you might not be able to keep." She put her head against his chest.

He started to say he would, but he just kissed the top of her head instead. She was right—in the line of work he was in, he couldn't make those kinds of promises. "I promise I'll be careful."

She nodded into his chest.

He glanced at his watch. "I don't know about you, but I haven't had anything substantial to eat since yesterday afternoon. Do you want to grab a bite at the pub?"

"Why don't we go back to my apartment?" Jennifer wiped her face. She fished through her pocketbook for her car keys. "I really don't want to be around a bunch of people right now."

"I can't. I've got to grab something quick and head back to the frat house." Taking her hand, he said, "Come on." He tilted his head toward the buildings and pulled her along. "You have to eat," he said, making a valid argument, and her stomach responded with a loud rumbling. "See?"

"Okay." She caved.

They went in and sat down. The pub wasn't crowded, and the waitress came right over to take their order. They each got a bacon cheeseburger, fries, and soda.

Steve scanned the nearly empty room, in a matter of seconds sizing up each person who came within his line of sight. No one in the room posed a threat, and he returned his gaze to Jennifer.

"Do you do that everywhere you go?" Jennifer asked and twirled her finger.

"Yes," he answered, his focus falling back on her.

Jennifer laughed. "It's a little unnerving."

He smiled. "I guess we're even."

"What do you mean?"

"Your visions or glimpses or whatever you call them unnerve me." He took a sip of water. "Did you ever have any other visions like you had about that girl?"

Jennifer chewed on her lower lip. "I've had some nightmares. Always people I don't recognize, but the dark figure is the same. I always woke up before…"

"Before what?"

"Before it killed them." She sipped her water. "At least I assume it killed them."

Steve leaned back in the chair, debating on asking the next question.

"What?"

"If I showed you pictures of the missing people, do you think you'd recognize them?" The paling of her cheeks made him regret asking the question.

"I don't know."

The waitress interrupted with their plates.

"Can you pinpoint when you had the visions?" he asked after the waitress had left.

Jennifer looked down at her food. "I had three yesterday. One that happened two years ago, one that happened a month ago and one that hasn't happened yet." She pushed her plate back.

"You have to eat."

"I'm not hungry."

"We have had nothing to eat. You need to eat. Trust me." Then he basically inhaled his burger before Jennifer even took a bite. "It's good." He licked the juice off his fingers and wiped them with a napkin before picking at his fries.

Jennifer took a bite. Her eyes widened, and she attacked the meal with the same zest as he had. He let her finish the burger before he resumed the conversation.

"Tell me about the nightmare yesterday." He dipped a fry in ketchup and plopped it into his mouth.

"No." Jennifer pushed her plate away and picked up her soda.

"Ignoring it won't make it go away."

When she raised her eyes, they were almost a glowing green, and he moved back in his seat.

"You were hurt and bleeding and calling for me. It had you when I ran back into the clearing. And it laughed."

His appetite vanished. He dropped the French fry back onto his plate. "Describe the clearing."

Jennifer tilted her head and narrowed her eyes. "It was dark, and the brush was doing a good job of tearing me up as I ran. It seemed worse heading back, thicker, like the place had miraculously regenerated and refortified around the opening. It felt like the universe didn't want me to get to you." She shivered and rubbed her arms. "The clearing itself was ugly and desolate. An exact opposite of Paradise Cove's lush beauty." Her eyes seemed to focus on him again. "I'd rather think about something else right now."

Steve nodded and signaled for the waitress to bring the bill and left the money on the table. He had heard enough for one day, too.

Jennifer was quiet as they walked to the cars.

"What's on your mind?" Steve asked, seeing the crease between her eyes.

"Nothing really."

"You certainly look like you're thinking about something."

Jennifer leaned against the driver's side door of her car and her cheeks turned crimson.

Amused at her all out blush, Steve asked, "What?"

Jennifer rolled her eyes. "Today," she began, and looked at her hands. "Had you ever done that before?" She glanced at him sideways.

He raised his eyebrows, questioning her silently.

"The, um, interrogation?" Her entire face was crimson now.

Steve laughed. "No. I've never used the handcuffs for... for pleasure." He grinned and shifted on his feet, a hint of heat creeped into his cheeks. "And I've never so thoroughly interrogated anyone." He glanced around the parking lot. "Have you had the pleasure of that kind of inspection before?"

"No, never," she said. "Tom wasn't as creative as you are."

He smiled in response. He kept forgetting how inexperienced she really was. "I have to go," he replied, and stepped toward her. "And this conversation isn't making it any easier." He leaned down and kissed her gently. "I'll see you tonight?"

"I'll swing by on my way back to the apartment." She unlocked her door and Steve opened it for her.

"Bye, babe." As she pulled out of sight, his smile faded.

He reached into his car, pulled out the notebook, locked his beamer, and headed towards the library. He had Indian folklore to research. There were plenty of books on Abinaqui Indian tribes. Hell, his grandfather had a few in the study at the cabin, but there were damn few about their folklore. After exhausting every book on the shelf, he took a seat at the computer, logged in with his student ID, and plugged in the tribe's name. He scanned the results, stopping on an interesting passage. When he clicked, the story filled the screen, and he read it, digesting, before reading it again.

Palawion, the chief of the Abinaqui tribe in the early 1700s, and Steve's very distant relative, died in a massacre near Mirror Lake.

But that wasn't the interesting part. The Indian chief was said to be a master of black magic and conjuring spirits. After his death, any white man broaching the area either disappeared, or was found rambling and bleeding, swearing a monster in the woods attacked them. A monster summoned by Palawion with his dying breath.

He leaned back in the seat, rubbing his eyes, and glanced at the notebook. He flipped it open and the bloody words still graced the page. Steve grunted, slammed the notebook closed, and logged off the computer.

He headed to the law building, hoping to find his boss.

He was no longer sure a human being caused the disappearances.

Dark Reckoning
Chapter 14

STEVE WALKED INTO THE small academic office and closed the door, turning toward his boss.

"What the hell happened to you?" Special Agent Jack Murphy asked, removing his glasses as he rose to his feet. His salt and pepper hair was cut in a close cropped military style screaming Fed, yet, when paired with the corduroy patched jacket, it added a scholarly air, allowing him to blend with the rest of the pretentious professor crowd.

Steve's hand shot up to the side of his face, and he winced. *Crap, I forgot all about my eye.*

"Someone got the drop on me. Don't worry—it had nothing to do with the job," he said, quickly neutralizing the concern flashing in Murphy's eyes. He sat in the chair and opened the notebook in the middle. The bloody words leaped out at him. "Murph, can you see anything on this page?" He held the notebook up.

Murphy looked from the blank page to Steve's face. "Is this a joke?"

"No. Is this page blank?"

"Yes, what's your issue?"

Steve closed the notebook and leaned back in the chair, shaking his head. "I'm not sure that the fraternity is the origin of our problem."

"What do you think is?" He leaned forward.

Steve cocked his head to the side. "I'm not sure." He kept eye contact with Murphy. "That girl was torn to pieces, Murph."

"I know. I was there."

"I still can't fathom a person doing that." He glanced at the notebook again. "What if it isn't human?" he asked, meeting Murphy's eyes.

"We ruled that out. There were no animal tracks, no sign of droppings, and none of the victims found had signs of being eaten. Animals don't kill for sport. Only men do."

Steve tilted his head. "That's what I keep going back to. The freshest kill we found was Amy, yet there was no sign of the body having been foraged by animals. They put her death something like two days before we found her. These forests are full of scavengers. Why didn't they touch her?" He leaned forward. "Or any of the others that were found?"

Murphy leaned back with his brow scrunched.

Steve took a deep breath, venturing ahead with his train of thought. "What if it isn't human... and isn't an animal?"

"What else is there?"

Steve shrugged. "Nothing that I would have considered before today. Did you know I have a touch of Abinaqui blood?"

"Your grandfather mentioned your heritage."

"Well, I just spent the last two hours at the library researching the slaughter of the Abinaqui tribe, and there's a damn legend about a monster in this area that the tribal chief conjured just before he died?”

Murphy leaned forward and studied Steve. “What the hell are you mumbling about?”

“Black magic.” Steve opened the notebook again and stared at the words. “You see a blank page. I see blood red words in the center of every page. It makes no sense. I’m not the only one who can see it either; otherwise, I would be checking myself into the psych ward.” He flipped the notebook closed and tapped it absently with his fingers. “I’m not sure what we’re dealing with.”

Murphy sank back slowly. “Maybe you should take some time off.”

Steve glared at him. “I’m not crazy,” he growled low.

“I never said you were,” Murphy answered. “But you haven’t had a break since Peg died.”

“I’m fine.” He stood and began pacing. “But between a girl with visions and a notebook that bleeds words, I’m not so sure what is behind the disappearances.”

Murphy’s eyebrows rose, and he pushed back in the chair. “Visions?”

“Yes.” Steve stopped pacing. He saw the doubt in Murphy’s eyes, but he didn’t explain further. Instead, he waited for the flurry of questions.

“Visions of what?”

“She described in detail what Amy wore that day.”

“And you didn’t haul her ass in?” Murphy’s eyes widened, and little blotchy splotches of burgundy broke out on his cheeks.

“You said she was in New York at the time of Amy’s death,” Steve said, and started pacing again. "Believe me; I grilled her before I called you."

"She knows who you are?" Murphy shot to his feet, flew around the side of the desk, and stepped into Steve's pacing path. The color in Murphy's cheeks spread to cover his entire face in an explosive plum.

Oh, shit. Steve stopped and shoved his hands in his pocket. He looked sheepishly through his bangs at Murphy and nodded. The color transitioned from plum to red and Steve swore Murphy's head was going to explode from the pressure.

"Where is she now?"

"On her way back to her apartment."

"Please tell me she isn't a student at Brooksfield," he growled.

Steve shrugged and smiled a little. "She won't say anything, trust me."

"You slept with her?"

Steve couldn't help but smile. "Well?" he cringed and gulped the sudden dryness from his mouth.

"Please tell me she is at least of age," Murphy barked. Steve nodded. "I want her brought in right now," he ordered.

"Can't do that," Steve replied. "Her roommate is the fraternity president's girlfriend."

"Are you out of your fucking mind?" Murphy grabbed Steve by the shirt.

"She won't say anything," Steve said.

"And why not?"

"Because I'm dating her." Steve kept eye contact, calmly meeting Murphy's angry glare.

Murphy slowly let go. "You're what?"

"We're dating."

Murphy blinked rapidly and sank onto the desk, the color abating a little from his face. "How long?"

"How long what?"

"How long have you been involved with someone related to this case?"

Steve's face suddenly grew hot, and he turned away, mumbling, "Three days."

"Did you just say *three days*?"

He turned back, and Murphy's jaw was clenched so tight Steve could see the tendons jumping in his neck and the veins throbbing at his temple. "I grew up with her, but I hadn't seen her for ten years until three days ago. I didn't expect this. I didn't expect her to be so goddamn beautiful that I'd have a hard time breathing around her. I didn't expect to see her, and I certainly didn't expect to sleep with her, but it happened, okay?" The words tumbled out in a flurry, trying to mitigate the explosion he knew was coming.

"Is she the other person who can see the words?" Murphy asked, as one eyebrow rose in suspicion.

"Yes, but..."

Murphy grabbed him by the arm and pushed him toward the back of the office. "Drug test— now!" he barked. "And until I get the results, you are not to see her, or I'll have your badge."

"Bullshit! I'll gladly do the drug test, but I won't stop seeing her. That would completely fuck up my cover, and Bill Tyler will go ballistic on me again." He pointed at his eye. "I got this because he defended her honor."

"Drug test." Murphy pointed toward the bathroom. "Under the sink."

Steve found the containers and complied. He walked out a few minutes later and handed Murphy the sealed container full of urine. "Bill is your chief suspect. Do you want me close to him or not?" Steve watched Murphy slide the container into an envelope and put it in his bottom drawer. "If I'm with her, I'm with them. Jen does not know Bill is on our radar."

"Let me see if I get this straight," Murphy started, "first you get yourself into the fraternity of the chief suspect, second you date the roommate of his girlfriend." He paused. "That was the perfect cover." He shook his head and paced, the anger radiating off him. "But you didn't stop there. You put your identity at risk by blowing your cover with the girl. An entire summer of undercover work fucked up in just three days because you couldn't keep your dick in your pants." He stopped and glared at Steve.

Steve shrugged. "She will not say anything."

"I don't give a flying fuck what you believe. Bring her in!" The glass on the door rattled under the volume and timber of his bellow.

Steve shook his head.

"I should take your badge right now. I'm ordering you to bring her in."

"I can't do that," Steve said, knowing the ramifications of disobeying an order. "I need her, and she won't say a thing."

"How can you be so sure?" The octaves lowered a fraction, and so did the crimson shine in Murphy's cheeks.

"Intuition," Steve shot back. "You know damn well I don't trust anyone off the bat. I knew this girl growing up. We were close."

"You said you hadn't seen her in ten years. A lot can change in ten years." Murphy mirrored Steve's exact words the day before.

"I know. I all but outright accused her of killing that girl last night. I didn't take her word for it. I checked out the facts before I backed off. I risked losing the best thing that ever walked into my life because of this fucking job." He turned his back on Murphy, his fists in tight balls, and he inhaled a deep breath, gaining control. He unclenched his hands.

Silence settled on the room. "I know it's crazy, but I'm in love with her, and she's right smack in the middle of this thing." He faced Murphy.

"You can't be objective anymore," Murphy said.

"Yes, I can. Just don't ask me to bring her in. She isn't drugging me, Murph, and neither is anyone else. Maybe her visions, or whatever they are, can help us catch the son of a bitch faster."

"This goes against the book, Williams."

"I know, sir."

Murphy looked out the window and eased down on the edge of the desk, crossing his arms. "I knew your grandfather, you know." He brought his gaze back to Steve. "He was the best field agent the FBI ever had and until today, you were following a close second." He gripped the desk. "God damn it, Williams!"

Steve shifted under the angry stare, and his heart leaped into his throat. *He's going to fire me. Shit.* Instead of pleading his case, he remained quiet and held the stare.

Strained silence filled the room, and neither man spoke for the length of ten heartbeats.

Murphy inhaled, and his tight lips parted. "I'm going to go out on a limb here, but I want to meet her. Have her in the pub tomorrow at noon."

"She has class tomorrow at noon. Can we do it Friday instead?"

Murphy glared at Steve, his lips turning into a thin white line. "I've got to be out of my fucking mind. Fine, but if you're not there with her on Friday, I'm bringing you both in. Now get out of my office."

"Thank you, sir." Steve picked up the notebook and left before Murphy could change his mind.

He headed back to his car, glancing at the clock on the dashboard as he slid into the driver's seat. He had close to five hours before he would see her again. He started the car and headed to the frat house.

Bill sat on the steps, his face formed in an angry scowl. He nodded acknowledgement when Steve approached.

"You hurt her, and I'll rip you to pieces," he said, and stormed into the house, leaving Steve stunned on the front stoop.

He looked up at the Beta Theta Pi flags flying over the entry of the frat house. The eyes of the red dragons watched and waited for their next victim. Steve shivered as their glance passed over him with a ripple from the wind. He shook his head. *At least it isn't the skull and crossbones like Phi Kappa Sigma down the block.*

He headed inside.

Dark Reckoning
Chapter 15

JENNIFER WALKED INTO THE apartment, smiling.

"You didn't have to pull that on us, Jen," Tracy called from out on the balcony.

"Yes, I did. Do you realize how many bad dates you and Billy have set me up with since Tom died?"

Tracy crossed into the living room and flopped on the couch. "They weren't all bad."

Jennifer laughed. "Uh, yes, they were." She tossed her notepad on the coffee table and headed to the refrigerator for a soda. "You want a drink?" She turned toward Tracy.

"Sure." Tracy continued sulking on the couch.

"All they were interested in was getting into bed with me, nothing else." Jennifer handed Tracy the can of soda.

"Like Steve was any different."

"That's not all he wants, and that's where he differs from everyone else you have subjected me to."

Tracy tilted her head like an inquisitive puppy. "Did you sleep with him?"

Jennifer's face heated. "That's none of your business."

"Oh, my God!" Tracy shot to her feet. "You did!"

"I'm not going there with you Tracy," Jennifer said, but she could barely suppress her smirk.

Tracy grinned. "How was he?"

She wanted to tell Tracy it was none of her business, but all she could do was smile until her cheeks hurt.

"That good?" Tracy sat and put her feet on the coffee table, crossing her arms.

Jennifer laughed. "Yeah, that good. Like the earth moved."

"What made you say yes?"

Jennifer glanced outside, filtering through the events to figure out what she could and couldn't say about Steve, realizing that she couldn't reveal that he had a place of his own. That would screw up his cover big time.

"It just happened. One minute we were talking and the next..." She sighed and smiled. "Besides, he is one fine-looking man."

Tracy nodded. "Even with the black eye."

"Especially with the black eye. For some reason, that just makes him more..." Jennifer searched for the exact word.

"Sexy."

Jennifer laughed. "Do you have the hots for my boyfriend?"

Tracy raised her eyebrows. "No, not really. He's just sweet eye candy."

Jennifer giggled. "Don't tell him that. It'll just go to his head."

"So, we finally found the right one for you."

Jennifer's smile faded. "As much as I hate to admit it, yes. I think he may very well be the one."

Tracy's mouth dropped. "How can you be so sure?"

"I just know," Jen replied. "I can see forever with him." She took a sip of her drink. "Didn't you know with Billy?"

"I'm not sure he is the one. I love him to death, but forever? I just don't know about that."

"When did you come to that conclusion?"

Tracy shrugged. "I don't know, this summer I guess." She stood and walked onto the balcony. Jennifer followed, taking the spot next to her at the railing. "He doesn't want to leave New Hampshire," she continued. "This isn't what I want." She surveyed the view of Mirror Lake and the surrounding mountains. "It's wonderful for school or visiting during the summer, but living up here would drive me batty." She glanced at Jennifer. "I want New York or L.A., just like you do."

Jennifer nodded absently. "I wouldn't mind spending the summers on the lake," she said, more to herself than to Tracy.

Tracy turned to her. "You couldn't wait to get out of here last spring. What changed?"

Jennifer shrugged. "I don't know. It's peaceful up here and there are beautiful places around the lake." She took a sip of her soda. "Are you going to see Bill tonight?"

"No, he has some pledge stuff to do. They're deciding what the initiation ritual will be this year." She rolled her eyes. "Like it ever changes."

"You know what the ritual is?" Jennifer asked.

"Yes, but I was sworn to secrecy."

"Come on, I promise I won't tell." She made the sign of an X over her chest. "Cross my heart and all that stuff."

Tracy sighed and pulled open the tab on her soda, taking a sip. She stalled long enough for Jennifer to think she wasn't going to spill the secret.

"The fraternities and sororities that have been here a while all seem to do the same thing," Tracy began. "So, it's not really a big secret, but it's how far the pledge is willing to go that matters." She looked at Jennifer and shrugged. "Some chicken out and others, well, they drop out all together."

Jennifer's interest piqued. She'd never pledged a sorority. "What do they do?"

"They tell the pledges about the legend of Paradise Cove and send them there," Tracy said, picking at the tab on her soda can. "They're supposed to get a picture of their reflection. That's what's required to get in, but I guess there's a bonus as well. If you follow the stream and get a picture of where it ends, you don't have to pay dues." She looked up at Jennifer. "Didn't you ever wonder why I wasn't in a sorority?"

Jennifer shook her head. "No."

"Well, I wasn't willing to get the picture, and I certainly wouldn't follow that stream. You don't know what's back there." She took another sip of her drink. "Bill did it, and he must have chickened out on the second part because he still pays dues. Steve probably will have to go through initiation, but I'm not sure what they do with transfers. He came from Yale, right?"

"Yes. He took a break from school when his girlfriend died."

"Well, if they make him go through initiation, tell him not to go," she said.

"Don't be ridiculous." Jennifer took her last sip and heading to the kitchen sink.

"You have to tell him not to go," Tracy said, this time with more urgency.

"I'll mention it." Jennifer rinsed the empty can and dropped it in the recycle bin. She had no intention of telling Tracy he had already been there countless times, or that his house had the only access. She wiped her hands and looked at the clock. "I need to get ready for class."

She went to her bedroom, stripped, and stepped into the closet. Shuffling through her clothes, she tried to decide what to wear for Steve. The closet door closed behind her. The click of the latch startled Jennifer. She turned and the bulb above her popped, plunging her into darkness.

The temperature plummeted, and she shivered. Fumbling for the door, she suppressed her growing panic. Her breath hitched in short bursts from her chest.

"It's just a closet," she said, trying desperately to keep calm.

A hand reached out and grabbed the back of her neck. She yelped in surprise. She clawed at the door, missing the doorknob. The scream finally reached her vocal cords and barreled out, echoing in the darkness.

Tracy threw the door open, her eyes wide, and then Tracy's expression changed.

Tracy laughed, lightly at first, and wound until she folded on the floor, gasping for breath between the gales.

Jennifer glanced in the mirror and saw what had grabbed the back of her neck. It was one of her teddy bears that fell from the shelf. Heat crept into her cheeks, and she peeled the bear from her shoulders, flinging it to the back of the closet. She flipped the light switch on and off as the laughter simmered out of her. "The bulb must have blown."

"The bear got you!" Tracy pointed through the laughter.

"Do we have a light bulb?" she asked, still mortified.

Tracy nodded, her laughter calming. "You scared the daylights out of me when I heard you scream." She headed into the bathroom. In the pantry, she pulled a light bulb out and grabbed the stool.

"Sorry, I kind of freaked out. It was so dark and cold in there and when the bear fell, I guess it sent me over the edge." She laughed as she took the stool and stood on it while Tracy spotted her. Jennifer unscrewed the dead light bulb, handing it to Tracy in exchange for the good one. When she stepped off the stool and hit the light switch, bright light filled the closet.

"Thanks." She smiled and looked back at her clothes.

"I'd wear this." Tracy reached across and pulled out a blue sundress with spaghetti straps. She handed the dress to Jennifer and walked out with a smile.

Jennifer reached down and grabbed her flip-flops, slid them on, and stepped out of the closet. She flipped off the light and closed the door behind her. Out of the corner of her eyes, she saw a flash of red and opened the door again, peering into the darkness. There was nothing there but the damn draft drifting over her legs and making her shiver.

She shut the door.

Jennifer dressed, combed her hair, and freshened her makeup. She stood back in the dressing room and scanned herself with a critical eye.

"He's going to love that on you." Tracy glanced in at Jennifer. She had changed into a t-shirt and sweatpants, and carried her textbook for her Law of Libel and Communications class.

"Homework already?"

"I got my books today, and I figured this is the class that's going to be the most difficult and I'd better get a jump on it if I want to keep my GPA up there." She shrugged. "I'm going to park myself on the couch, watch some scary movies, and do a little studying tonight. I don't think Billy will be coming by." She took a breath. "Are you coming home tonight?"

"Yes. I'm not staying at the frat house," she said. She had done that once with Tom and didn't want a repeat of the morning awkwardness. Only one bathroom for a dozen guys was ludicrous. "Do you mind if Steve comes back with me?"

"Yum, eye candy." Tracy grinned, her eyes sparkled mischievously.

Jennifer chuckled. "He looks particularly good in the morning." She headed out, swiping her notebook, pocketbook, and keys off the hall table, and closed the front door behind her.

Dark Reckoning
Chapter 16

STEVE CAUGHT UP WITH Bill. "I don't intend to hurt her."

Bill stopped and turned toward him. "I hope not. Because she's special."

"I'm aware of how special she is."

Bill softened a little. "You know, I should kick your ass for what you pulled on Tracy and me." He crossed his arms and leaned on the entry wall.

Steve shrugged. "Yeah, well, blame that on the actress."

Bill raised an eyebrow. "You did some first class acting yourself." He looked at the bruise on Steve's face. "You should have told me." He walked away.

"Why?"

"Because I'm your fraternity brother," he said, facing Steve and taking a few steps backward before he turned away. "There are no secrets here," he said over his shoulder before disappearing around the corner.

Steve went to his room, threw the notebook on the desk, and collapsed face-first on the bed. He reached over and turned the radio on before he closed his eyes.

Just for a few, he thought and drifted to sleep, listening to the soft music and the distant conversations in the frat house.

Dark Reckoning
Chapter 17

A HAND GENTLY RAN over his back, startling him out of a sound sleep. He looked up into Jennifer's face, and then around the room in surprise. "What time is it?" he asked, his voice groggy with sleep.

"Twenty after ten."

Steve's head turned sharply to confirm what she had told him. The green numbers of his alarm clock read ten twenty-two. "Holy shit." He sat up straight. He hadn't even heard her come into his room. "I never sleep that soundly," he grumbled and looked around as he rubbed the sleep from his eyes.

"I guess I tired you out today."

"I'll be right back." Steve grabbed his toothbrush and toothpaste and headed towards the bathroom. Quiet permeated the fraternity, and he stopped, listening to the nothingness. His skin prickled, but he shook it off. He slipped into the bathroom and threw cold water on his face to wake himself up. He brushed his teeth, getting rid of the pasty taste he woke up with.

"Where is everybody?" he asked when he returned.

"I don't know. One of the pledges let me in and pointed me to your room."

Steve sat down next to her. "I haven't slept that soundly since I was in high school." He rubbed his face. "I didn't hear everyone leave or you come in either." He glanced at her. "That's not good."

"This is a little more organized than I expected. It's not like the organized chaos at the cabin." She looked back at him.

Steve smiled and leaned over, biting her earlobe. "I'm more organized in my job than in my private life," he whispered, his voice barely audible. He ran his lips over the corner of her jaw and turned her face toward him so he could kiss her.

Time stopped with the kiss. The world around them disappeared as they floated on the intensity of their shared emotion. Breathlessly, he pulled away, and the room came back into focus.

"What if I told you I wanted to run away to Vegas with you," he whispered, his voice husky from the heat rushing through him.

"And do what?"

"I was thinking about one of those cheesy wedding chapels," he answered, nipping at her neck. "You know, the ones where the justice of the peace is dressed like Elvis."

Jennifer giggled, and he pulled away from her neck and raised an eyebrow.

"Is that funny?" he asked.

"Yes, very."

"Why?" Irritation crawled up his spine.

"You don't remember?"

She'd stumped him, and he bit the side of his lip, wondering what she was referring to.

"When we were kids, you promised to marry me in Las Vegas when I turned twenty-five."

His eyebrows shot up, and the past flooded in like the tide. "Shit, that's right. I forgot about our little pact."

"And we sealed it with blood." She glanced at her finger.

His index finger tingled with the memory, and he smiled. "So, do you still want to?" He returned his lips to her neck, the question hanging on the air like a thick bank of fog, and his heart jumped into hyper drive, waiting for an answer.

The answer.

"We'll see," she said as his lips trailed down her neck.

Steve stopped. "You used to say that when we were kids," he said, pushing her away. "When you didn't really want to do something."

Jennifer shook her head. "No. I said it when I wasn't ready to decide."

Steve sat up, frustrated. "Do you feel the same way I do?"

"I'm reasonably sure I do," she answered, sitting up.

"Reasonably sure? That's like reasonable doubt. It's hardly the answer I wanted to hear." He stood and went to the window, looking out at the backyard of the fraternity house. His attention snapped to the expansive lawn.

"I want to be absolutely sure before I answer you, Steve," she said.

He stopped paying attention to her the moment he looked out the window. When she touched his arm, he jumped for the second time that evening.

"I'm sorry. What were you saying?" His eyes drifted back to the bizarre scene.

Jennifer followed his gaze. "What is that?"

The fraternity members wore black robes and stood in a pattern that was unrecognizable unless you were looking down on them like they were.

"It's a pentacle," Steve answered. "Pentagram," he corrected with a shake of his head.

Bill stood in the center, surrounded by a circle of candles. He was reading from an old leather-bound book; the members repeating his words. Steve recognized the language—Latin, although he had no clue of what was being said. At the end of the incantation, Bill reached into his pocket and pulled out an egg, cracking it into the challis at his feet.

Even from a distance, Steve and Jennifer saw blood run out of the eggshell. Steve pulled her away from the window. Away from the prying eyes of the fraternity when Bill looked up toward his window. He prayed no one saw them. He held her to him, pressing his back against the wall next to the window, trying to disappear into the shadows. "Jesus." He looked at her.

Footsteps of the Beta Theta Pi members filtered into the house.

Steve pushed her down on the bed, yanked the straps of her dress over her shoulders, and lay on top of her. He buried one hand in her hair and put the other one at her waist, tugging a little on the dress, kissing her. His heart hammered in his chest, praying this would be enough to keep the wolves from attacking.

Jennifer seemed to understand the moment his lips found hers, and wrapped one arm around his neck, tugging on his shirt until her hand found skin.

Seconds later, his door swung open. Bill stared at Steve and Jennifer and faltered. "Sorry." He closed the door on Steve and Jennifer's surprised faces looking at him from their compromising position.

Steve glanced back at Jennifer and put his finger to his lips. She closed her eyes and nodded.

"I think we need to go to your place," he said loud enough for anyone eavesdropping to hear.

They climbed out of the bed and Steve took her hand, leading her to the door. He inhaled, opened the door, and stepped into the hallway with Jennifer.

"Sorry about that," Bill said, awkwardly waving his hand toward Steve's room.

Jennifer blushed, looked down, and then over her shoulder at Steve.

Just the right amount of embarrassment, Steve thought as their eyes met. He glanced back at Bill. "Yeah, well, we're going to her place, where the doors have locks that work." He grinned and winked his good eye at Bill.

Bill's face fell as he looked between the two of them. The slackness in his features morphed into a hardness Steve recognized. His eyes narrowed as they landed on Steve.

"It's all right, Billy," Jennifer said, obviously mistaking the look for over-protectiveness.

Steve knew better. Bill wasn't being overprotective. He was angry, bordering on rage. He caught the way Bill stared at Jennifer when they walked out of the room.

Bill wanted his girl.

He put his arm around her, drawing her close—a protective reflex. All the while, his smile never faltered. "I'll catch you in the morning." He led Jennifer away.

Dark Reckoning
Chapter 18

BILL SENT IMAGINARY DAGGERS into Steve's back as they walked out of his sight. The sting of jealousy bloomed to something else altogether. He walked to his room and dialed the familiar number. "Hi Trac," he said when she picked up.

"Hey, hon," Tracy said. "You all done with your fraternity stuff?"

"Not quite. We still haven't finished discussing the initiation rite," he said. "We just took a quick break, and I thought I'd call you." He closed his eyes, feeling guilty for the lie. "I saw Steve and Jen a little while ago. Looks like they are heading your way."

"Will you be over later?" she asked.

"Nah, I think we're going to be late," he said, feeling a measure of relief. "I'll see you in the morning."

"Ok, I love you."

Out of habit, he returned the usual salutation and hung up the phone. He crossed the hall to Steve's room, looking around. There was nothing unusual about the room or his belongings. When he flipped open the notebook, Bill chuckled, amused to see Jennifer's name doodled all over the first page of the notebook. He flipped through the pages. Steve hadn't taken a single note from class in the notebook. He closed it and noticed a loose paper in the front. *Ah, he took notes*, Bill thought. He flipped through the empty notebook again.

Fanning the empty pages, he sighed. Just as he began to close it, he saw a small circle of red appear out of the corner of his eye. He opened the notebook again and almost dropped it.

Bring her to me

Bill closed the notebook and then opened it up again. The words were still there. He flipped through the pages and the words leaped from every sheet except the last. Instructions scrawled onto the page while he stared at it. Big, looping script, blood red, described the exact details of the initiation ceremony right down to the rules he was expected to play by.

He inhaled sharply as two names appeared, along with specific commands. This year, his marching orders were very different from the past, and he glanced out the window, thinking of the bloody egg.

Goose bumps traveled up his arms. He looked back at the notebook, reading the parameters for this year's sacrificial rite, shivering.

The penalty for not following through scrolled beneath the instructions and Bill dropped the notebook, stepping back. The air froze in his lungs and his hand flew to his mouth. He stared at the warning, understanding the ramifications if anything went wrong.

Snapping his eyes away from the meticulous description of his painful death, he scanned the rest of the instructions.

One particular caveat kept his attention, and he inhaled, nodding. He could do that. He definitely could do that, and so could everyone else in this fraternity.

Hell, they'd all be salivating over the thought.

"Ok, I'll do it."

A small smiley face scribed into the bottom of the page and Bill snorted.

The bastard's got such a fucked-up sense of humor.

Bill tore the page out, folded the paper, and stuffed it in his pocket. He closed the notebook, replacing it on the desk before he walked out of the room.

Dark Reckoning
Chapter 19

STEVE GLANCED AT JENNIFER as he pulled the car out of the parking lot, his hands tight on the wheel. His foot ached to floor the pedal and peel out, but he tempered his urge.

"What were they doing?"

Steve shook his head. "I have no idea, but it looked a little like some sort of witchcraft."

Jennifer laughed and stopped with a glare from him.

"Or devil-worship," he added, putting a sobering spin on everything.

"I can't believe that," Jennifer balked. "It could have just been a fraternity ritual."

Steve glanced at her, communicating his skepticism with his eyes. "If they were standing in any other pattern, I would agree with you, but a pentagram?" He shook his head and looked back at the road.

"Didn't the Masons use a pentacle as their symbol?"

Steve glanced at her. "Jen, they were performing a ritual in Latin that ended with the cracking of that egg. We both saw the blood come out of that shell. That has nothing to do with Masons." Bill's expression when the blood came out of the eggshell, followed by the look on his face when he saw Jennifer leaving the room, dug under Steve's skin like a parasite, festering.

He didn't like this recent development at all. He drove for a while, saying nothing.

"Tracy told me something before I went to class." She shifted in the seat.

Steve's stomach growled, and he pulled into Joe's, the local burger joint on the corner across from the university's main campus. He ordered a burger, fries, and a milkshake and looked over at Jennifer. "You want anything?"

Jennifer shrugged. "A chocolate shake?"

He ordered her a chocolate shake and drove up to the window to pay and collect their food. He handed the bag to her, pulled into one of the far parking spaces, and put the car in park. "Go ahead," he said as he took the food. "Tell me."

"Tracy said the initiation for the pledges is the same thing every year. They tell the pledges about the legend of Paradise Cove and send them there. They're supposed to get a picture of their reflection. That's all that is required to get in, but there is a bonus as well. If you follow the stream and get a picture of where it ends, you don't have to pay dues."

Steve processed this information. That could explain some disappearances, but it still didn't explain the girl they found this summer.

"Tracy told me to tell you not to do it if they make you go through initiation." She offered him a sip of her milkshake.

"If they ask, I'll go. It's part of the cover." He finished his burger and took a sip of the shake. "Was Tom in the fraternity?"

Jennifer nodded. "Yeah."

Steve offered her a French-fry, and she declined with a shake of her head. "So, he must have gone through the initiation."

"That's what Tracy said. I know Tom didn't do the second part because he bitched about the dues to me for two years. Billy still pays dues, according to Tracy." She looked back at Steve.

Steve nodded as he crumpled the empty fry container, dropped it in the takeout bag, and crumpled that as well. He pulled himself up and tossed it into the garbage barrel in front of the car, raising his arms in victory as it circled the rim and fell in. He grinned at Jennifer and started the car.

Jennifer finished the remainder of her milkshake, crumpled the cup, and tossed it at the barrel as he pulled forward. She turned and offered a smug grin as her garbage went in without hitting the rim. "Nothing but net."

Steve laughed. "You're something else."

THEY PULLED INTO THE apartment parking lot and Jennifer waited while he put the top up on the convertible.

"No more work." He escorted her in. "I'm done for the night."

Jennifer smiled. "No interrogations?" she teased as the elevator doors closed.

His slow, sexy smile appeared. "I didn't say that." He pulled her to him and kissed her. "I didn't say that at all." The doors opened, and he pulled away, stepping out of the elevator ahead of her, looking both ways.

"Looks like you're still working," Jennifer said to his less than casual inspection of the hallway.

"Old habits die hard." He shrugged. "And they keep me alive." He fit her keys into the door.

When the door opened, Tracy jumped from her perch on the couch. Jennifer led Steve inside and glanced at the television. *What Lies Beneath* played on the screen and Tracy sat alone in the dark.

Jennifer looked at the television and then back at Tracy. "You are one sick girl."

"You know I like scary movies." Tracy pouted.

"But alone in the dark?" Jennifer asked.

"That's the best way to watch them. Watch the rest with me?" she asked, glancing between Jennifer and Steve, her eyes lingering on him before returning to Jennifer.

Steve shook his head. "I've got an eight o'clock class." He scanned Jennifer with his eyes, conveying his desires.

"I think we'll pass," Jennifer said, leading Steve back to her room. She flipped on the light and closed the door behind her.

Steve looked around. An amused smirk found its way to his lips.

"What?" Jennifer said, following the path of his gaze.

"Girly," he remarked, and walked to the second door leading to the dressing room. Closing it, he flipped the lock, smiling back at Jennifer.

"Girly?" She looked around.

He nodded, approaching her. "Satin and lace." He stopped in front of her. "Silk and cream," he said, his voice smooth and raw at the same time, his eyes hungry for her. He ran his hands down her bare arms.

Jennifer tilted her head back and closed her eyes; his touch ignited her. Her breath quickened at the fire rising inside her, fanned by his hands running over her bare neck, dragging the straps of her dress off her shoulders.

Steve reached and flipped the light off, then moved her toward the bed. He kissed her and pulled away as he gently pulled the dress over her head.

"Reasonably sure?" he asked in a low, sexy voice. He kissed her neck, unhooked her bra, and dropped it on the floor. "Show me *reasonably sure*," he whispered, and flicked her ear with his tongue before finding her mouth again.

Jennifer ran her hands up his bare chest and around his neck as she kissed him, feeling his smooth skin against hers. "How would you like me to show you?" she asked against his lips as he leaned on the edge of the bed.

"With your sweet mouth." Steve licked her lips and took her hands. He put her index finger in his mouth and pulled it out slowly. "And your soft hands," he whispered, tilting his head and flashing a brief smile. He moved his hands lazily over her bare torso. "And your delectable body." He yanked her to him, crushing her with an insistent kiss.

Jennifer reached down and found the button on his shorts. Flipping it open, she unzipped slowly. The clicking of his zipper overpowered the brush of their skin. She smiled under the pressure of his lips, running her thumbs under the waistband of this underwear. She shifted away from his insistent mouth, running her tongue down the strong arch of his neck.

He leaned back against the bed, his chest rumbling, purring his approval as she kissed her way down his bare chest, slowly removing his shorts. He kicked the fabric aside and got lost in the feel of her.

STEVE BRUSHED THE HAIR away from her face as she lay on his chest, exhausted from their exertion. "I'm reasonably sure I'm in love with you." He closed his eyes.

Jennifer kissed his chest. "I love you, too." She drifted into a light sleep.

Steve's eyes went wide. He hadn't expected that. If he was being honest with himself, he hadn't expected any of these intense feelings. He couldn't ever remember feeling this protective over Peg. He couldn't ever remember feeling this raw desire, either. It shook him to the core anytime Jennifer smiled at him.

As he listened to her soft and even breathing, his mind drifted back to the case, analyzing the scene outside the fraternity.

He kept coming back to the way Bill looked at Jennifer.

He shivered, and she shifted, rolling off him and onto her side on the bed. Steve pulled his arm out from under her and found his underwear and shorts. Pulling them on, he wandered into the bathroom. When he came out of the toilet stall, Tracy was leaning against the door to the dressing room.

"You didn't waste any time, did you?" Tracy's eyes drifted over him, taking him in as he walked back toward Jennifer's room.

Steve stopped in his tracks, the surprise genuine at what he saw in Tracy's gaze.

Tracy laughed quietly as she stepped into the room, approaching him, batting her eyes and licking her lips in a way that sent an uncomfortable warning across his skin.

"Actually, it's really none of your business what I do with Jen."

Tracy tilted her head. "She didn't tell you? We share everything." She moved in front of him and put her hands on his bare chest. "Everything." She stepped closer, looking up into his eyes.

Steve removed her hands from his chest and stepped back. "Not everything."

He stepped around her and into Jennifer's room, shutting the door on Tracy. He stood with his back against the wood, looking at Jennifer sleeping peacefully on the bed, wondering how the hell he was going to tell her that her best friend came onto him.

Dark Reckoning
Chapter 20

SUNLIGHT BROKE THROUGH THE window and Jennifer squinted, turning her head into the pillow with a low groan. She glanced at the clock and the numbers blinked, changing. It was five fifty-six in the morning and she hadn't closed the mini-blinds last night like she usually did.

"Mhm," Steve mumbled, squeezing her tighter against him. "Morning sunshine."

"Morning," she answered, rolling towards him.

"I need to get moving." He glanced at the clock and sat up, rubbing his face. "By the way, we need to be in the student center pub at noon on Friday." He threw his legs over the side of the bed.

"Why?"

"My boss wants to meet you." He gathered the clothing on the floor. He hated to put her on the spot, but he knew Murphy. "I need you there at noon sharp. Otherwise, Murphy will haul both our asses in." He pulled his shirt on.

Jennifer sat on the edge of the bed and glanced over her shoulder at him. "You told your boss about me?"

"Yes, it's relevant to the case."

"Ah." She grabbed her bathrobe out of the closet. "I'll be right back." She headed to the bathroom, relieved herself, splashed water on her face, and then brushed her teeth. She searched the pantry on her way out and grabbed one of the extra unopened toothbrushes, and headed back to the bedroom. "Here," she said, handing it to Steve.

"Thanks." Steve plucked it out of her hand and headed to the bathroom. He came back a few minutes later and wrapped his arms around her, planting a minty kiss.

"Want some coffee?" Jennifer asked.

"That would be great." He let go and followed her into the kitchen.

Jennifer started a pot of coffee and tossed Steve an apple. She shined hers on her bathrobe and took a bite.

"I thought I smelled coffee," Tracy muttered, interrupting their quiet morning together.

Steve's gaze shot from Tracy to Jennifer, then down at the counter. He didn't seem to know where to look now that Tracy was in the room.

Jennifer noticed his sudden nervous energy and laughed.

Steve shot his gaze in her direction and his eyes said it all.

"Tracy, you didn't," Jennifer said, looking at her roommate.

"Yeah, I did. And he passed," she said, pulling a second cup down and putting it on the counter. She smiled and turned toward him. "Sorry, but I had to make sure you were for real."

Tracy grabbed an apple and tossed it in the air before she shined it on the lapel of her bathrobe. "You hurt her, and you will have to answer to me." She leaned against the counter, crossed her legs, and took a crisp bite of the granny smith apple. "Understand?"

Steve let out a laugh, looking between the two women. "You freaked me out last night," he said to Tracy.

"And yet you said nothing to Jen." She took another bite.

He didn't meet Jennifer's gaze right away. "Yeah, well, I couldn't figure out how to tell her that her best friend came on to me. If you had done it a second time, I would have said something."

Jennifer poured two cups of coffee, handing one to Tracy and bringing the other to him.

"How many have you done that to?" He hooked his thumb over his shoulder.

Tracy smiled. "Quite a few, including Tom. He was the only other one who passed the test." She sipped her coffee. "You see, I protect my friends."

Steve nodded. "You don't have to worry about Jen. I'll be there to protect her."

Tracy sipped her coffee. "You better."

"I will." He stared her down.

Tracy crumbled and turned to Jennifer. "He is hot, though. Eye candy." She smiled at him and headed out of the kitchen.

His cheeks reddened, and he studied his coffee. He took a quick glance at his watch. "I have to go, Jen. We can talk after class?"

Jennifer nodded and walked him to the door, kissing him and watching until the elevator closed. She shut the door and walked to Tracy's room. Without knocking, she threw the door open. "I can't believe you did that again."

"Don't worry; he didn't even give me a second look." Tracy peeked out of her closet carrying an outfit in her hand. "I had to make sure he wasn't just blowing smoke to get you into bed." She held up the dress and looked in the mirror. "Aren't you glad you know?"

"Tracy, I knew the moment I saw him. I didn't need you to do that."

Tracy turned. "But I needed to know. I needed to know he loved you enough..." she trailed off and looked out the window toward the lake. "Enough to protect you, no matter what." She looked back at Jennifer and headed into the bathroom to clean up.

Jennifer went into her bedroom, drew the shades, and lay back down in the darkened room. She didn't have to be anywhere until her eleven o'clock class. She drifted to sleep.

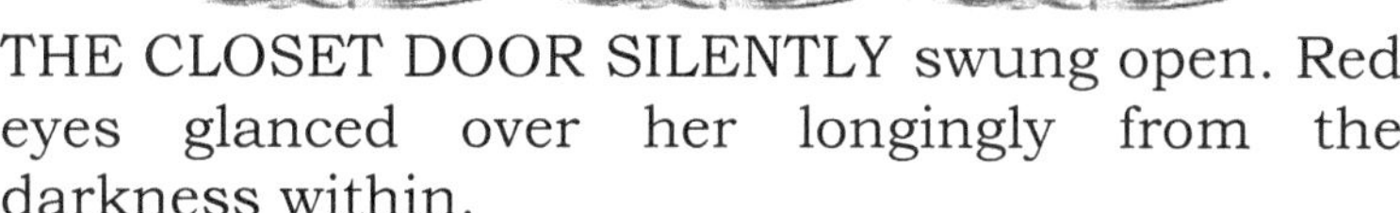

THE CLOSET DOOR SILENTLY swung open. Red eyes glanced over her longingly from the darkness within.

Dark Reckoning
Chapter 21

STEVE PULLED HIS CAR into the frat house lot and threw it in park, looking up at the building. He stretched before sliding out to head inside. He almost made it to his room before a hand grabbed him, spinning him into the wall.

"Who do you think you are?" Bill growled. His breath stank of beer and his eyes were glossed with bloodshot drunkenness.

"Let go, Bill."

"No!" Bill pushed his forearm harder against Steve's chest, holding him in place for the moment. "You stay away from Jen," he muttered belligerently.

"Last warning." His voice lowered as anger coiled, ready to strike.

"I'm gonna mess you up," Bill slurred. Balling his hand into a fist, he swung.

Bill's fist never connected. Steve blocked the punch, grabbed the arm holding him, and spun Bill around, making him trip before slamming him onto the floor with his arm bent behind him. Steve put a knee in the middle of his back and leaned over. "I warned you," he said in Bill's ear. "Are you going to cut the shit?" He pulled on

Bill's arm, causing Bill to let out a protest of pain.

"Are you?" Steve asked again.

Bill nodded.

He let go and stood, taking a couple of steps back as Bill slowly got off the floor. The bastard had the audacity to glare at him as he got up. Steve tensed, ready to inflict damage if Bill came at him again.

Bill leaned against the wall unsteadily.

"Bill, you're drunk. Go sleep it off."

"Stay away from her," Bill muttered and stumbled into his room, slamming the door.

Steve glanced at the few who had seen the altercation. "I don't get it. He's the one who set us up on a blind date," he said to the nearest fraternity brother.

"It's not the dating part that he's pissed about," Joe Dalton pointed out.

Steve raised his eyebrows in question.

"He's pissed that you're sleeping with her," Joe explained.

"That's really none of his business." Steve continued toward his room.

"It is his business," Joe interrupted. "He and Tom were best friends."

"And that has to do with this how?"

"He's been looking after Jenny since Tom died."

"And?" Steve pushed.

"And I'm not sure he expected Jenny to fall for you." Joe looked down the hall toward Bill's room. "I'm not sure he expected her to fall for anyone Tracy set her up with."

Steve followed Joe's gaze toward Bill's room. "He doesn't..." he trailed off and looked back at Joe. "But he's with Tracy."

Joe nodded and wandered away, leaving Steve dumbfounded in the hallway and looking at the other fraternity members. Steve shook his head and went to his room, grabbing a towel before heading off to take a shower. He let the water wash over him, praying he'd done a convincing acting job. He wanted everyone to think he had no clue until today that Bill wanted Jennifer. He finished cleaning up and put on clothing, glancing at his watch. He had a half hour before class and needed some food. The apple Jennifer had given him wasn't enough to keep him until noon.

When he walked into the kitchen, the room went silent. "What?"

"Everybody knows you don't mess with Jennifer," Adam said.

"Well, nobody told me that. He punched me because I didn't want to date her. Now he's going to punch me because I am?" Steve went to the refrigerator to see what was inside. Nothing appealed to him, and he turned his gaze toward the group at the tables.

"No. He's going to take you out because you slept with her." Adam took a sip of the coffee in front of him. "Was she worth it?"

Steve stiffened and swung a glare toward Adam. "Worth what?"

Joe shot a warning glance at Adam and shook his head. Most of the members of the fraternity were looking at Adam with wide, shocked eyes, their mouths hanging askew.

"Nothing, never mind." Adam recovered quickly and looked at his coffee.

Steve glanced around the room and decided this was not the place to eat breakfast.

He headed out of the kitchen and paused in the doorway. "If anyone else asks me anything related to sleeping with Jen, I'll kick your ass. Understand?"

He didn't wait for an answer.

Dark Reckoning
Chapter 22

ONCE STEVE'S CAR FADED into the distance, Joe glared at Adam.

"You stupid son of a bitch." He swatted the back of Adam's head.

"What?" Adam shrugged.

"Don't worry. You'll all get your turns with her, too." Bill appeared in the back entry to the kitchen. "She's the sacrifice this year," he slurred, stunning everyone.

Joe looked toward the front of the house and wondered what Steve would do if he knew his girlfriend had just days to live. He shook the thought out of his head and focused on what her skin would feel like against his.

The slow smile that spread across his lips was identical to that of every other fraternity member in the room.

Dark Reckoning
Chapter 23

JENNIFER WOKE AT QUARTER to ten and wandered into the shower. The hot water beat down on her, clearing out the cobwebs. Waking up with Steve had felt so right with his powerful arms around her, keeping her safe and warm. It certainly was something she could get used to.

Wrapped in a towel, she crossed to her closet; dropped the towel and stepped inside. She flipped through the clothing, debating on what to wear. A slow smile spread over her lips while her fingers ran over the fabric. Her eyes scanned each outfit before pushing it aside. She wanted to look perfect today. Her gaze landed on a pale pink sundress with dainty spaghetti straps and a fitted bodice. He'd love that.

She reached for the dress, and the closet door swung closed, catching on the towel. The light flickered, and Jennifer looked up, her brow furrowed in annoyance, her hand inches away from the garment.

I changed that damn thing yesterday.

Cool air drifted over her from the rear of the closet, and she shivered, casting a glance at the back wall. There was no air-conditioning duct she could identify.

Where is that draft coming from?

Goose bumps rolled up her arms, and she stripped the dress off the hanger, leaping back into her room. She flipped the light off and picked up the towel, closing the closet door. Her eyes never left the door while she dressed.

Jennifer walked back to the closet, her heart beating frantically in her chest, and she cursed under her breath. "God damn it, Jen, it's only a fucking closet."

The doorknob was cold enough to produce fog on the metal as she wrapped her hand around it. Sweat broke out on her brow, and she bit down on her lower lip, trying to keep the fear in check.

She yanked the door open, and her voice locked in her throat. Her breath seized in her lungs. Instead of her garment-filled closet, the view was replaced by the clearing from her dreams. The black water shimmered, glinting evil shards of light from the surface. Dried moss almost as black as the water surrounded the pond, fractured by a crude carving. With recognition came the shakes.

It was a pentacle.

The water moved, catching her attention. Red eyes surfaced, returning her terrified gaze. The chuckle that drifted over the clearing into her room broke her paralysis.

Jennifer slammed the door and took a few unsteady steps away from the closet. She couldn't speak, never mind scream. Her voice became completely nonexistent, and she fought to bring air into her lungs, wheezing as it scraped over her vocal cords.

Panic attack.

She frantically looked around the room. Her eyes landed on her pocketbook, and she lunged for it. Rummaging through, she found what she was looking for. She flipped her phone open and pressed the send button, scrolling frantically down the list of recent calls until the number she wanted was highlighted. She pressed the send button again and put the phone to her ear.

STEVE JUMPED WHEN HIS phone rang in his pocket. Everyone in the class looked at him, including Murphy. Steve dug the phone out and glanced quickly at the number. He stood up and walked out of the classroom to take the call. He only heard wheezing on the phone. "Jen?"

"Can't breathe."

Steve froze. "Where are you?"

"Apartment."

"I'm coming." He ran toward the car, digging the keys out of his pocket.

"Can't breathe," she repeated.

He knew what was happening—he'd heard that wheezing before and flashed back to the first time she had an asthma attack in his presence. He shook the memory away and focused.

"Okay, I'm in the car. What I want you to do is go into the shower, turn it on as hot as it will go, sit on the floor outside the stall so you don't get scalded, and close the door. Stay on the phone with me, all right?" Steve heard the creak of the door and the rush of water follow. "Now sit on the floor until I get there. Just stay on the line with me, okay?"

"Okay," she wheezed.

"My class was such a snoozer." He kept talking to keep her calm. "Murphy doesn't have a clue about how to keep a class full of college kids focused." He laughed, still hearing the wheezing on the line. It sounded a little less labored. "He's great in the field, though. I trust him with my life. He worked with my grandfather, you know." He could hear her getting some air now. "I'm almost there. You feeling a little better?"

"Yeah." She still wheezed, but it didn't sound as constricted.

"He wasn't too pleased that I got up and left his class. I'm sure I'll hear about it later." He pulled into the parking lot. The frantic look in his eyes reflected in the rear-view mirror didn't match the levity in his voice. The light conversational tone was a stark contrast to how fast he slammed into a parking spot and bolted from the car. "I'm in the parking lot now. Still with me?"

"Yeah." Her voice sounded a little stronger.

"You don't have an inhaler, do you?"

"A what?"

"Asthma medicine."

"No."

"I'm in the elevator now." He pushed the button. He counted the floors for her. "Fifteen," he said, and the elevator doors opened. "Think you can make it to the door?"

"Yeah."

He heard the water sound fade as she made her way down the hall. He closed the cell phone when she opened the front door.

Jennifer flew into his arms, tears streaking her cheeks. Steve led her back toward the shower, where the outer room was full of steam.

He sat her down and settled next to her with his arm around her shoulder. "Slow deep breaths." He breathed with her. "That's it."

"Steve..." she started, her eyes still frightened.

"No talking right now. Just breathe for me." He watched her, smiling and kissing her forehead. "That's right, just breathe." He leaned his head back against the tile and took a deep breath himself, letting the panic he felt melt away in the steam. "The last time I remember you having one of these, you were five or six." His eyes closed. "Scared the crap out of me then." He let out a quick laugh. "This time wasn't much different." He glanced over at her. "We were playing in those caves in the woods," he recalled. "You got freaked out by something and started that horrible wheezing." He shook his head at the memory. "I carried you all the way home and Sammy kept asking me if you were going to be all right." He looked over at her. "Your mom took you and did the same thing we're doing right now."

The tears spilled down her cheeks. "I saw what happened to Samantha." Jennifer's voice was stronger and her breathing was less restricted. "That's what caused it."

Steve looked over at her. "You saw my sister's death?"

"Yes. And it wasn't pretty."

"No, I imagine it wasn't." He closed his eyes. Samantha ran out in the road after a ball and had been mowed over by a speeding truck. After her death, they had leaned on each other. One had lost a best friend, the other a little sister, and together they got through it. "So, what set you off this time?" He glanced at her.

She tilted her head against the tile. Her hair, wet from the steam, clung to the damp skin of her face and neck. Her cheeks flushed, and she took slow, deep breaths. "I'm not sure what I saw," she finally said.

He let her breathe for a while and just held her. "What do you think you saw?" he asked as her breath became regular again.

"My closet... it wasn't my closet. I saw the clearing in my visions. And that thing, that thing was looking at me and laughing."

He kissed her forehead, but didn't know what to say. "Just breathe." He held her, leaning his head back as well. Droplets of water covered his hair, and his body became slick with sweat from the hot steam.

Steve's phone rang, making them both jump. "I've got to learn to put this thing on vibrate." He dug the phone out of his pocket.

"I've got your things. Is everything all right?" Murphy asked.

"Yes," he said. "I'll come get my stuff later."

As though he were irritated by Steve's calm manner, Murphy barked, "What happened?"

Steve looked over at Jennifer, clutching at her chest to regain a regular breath. "Jenny had an asthma attack. She'll be okay in a little while. She's just a bit shaken up right now."

"Your vision girl has asthma?" A brief laugh passed through the phone line.

"Fuck off, Murphy."

"Don't talk to your boss like that," Jennifer scolded, her breath laboring around the words.

Murphy must have overheard her in the background because he said, "I like her already."

Steve smiled and looked over at Jennifer. "I need to go."

"Check back in a little while," Murphy ordered.

"Will do." Steve ended the call.

Jennifer rubbed the steam off his watch. "I need to get to class."

He shook his head. "No, you need to breathe."

"I am breathing," she answered.

"But it's still not natural. You're still forcing it."

"What are you, my mother?"

"No, I'm the man you're going to marry."

"Says who?"

"Says me."

"I can't miss another class." She tried to get up.

"Yes, you can." He pulled her back down. "Just like I can."

"You're missing another one?"

He nodded. "You're worth it, babe." He kissed her gently.

"So, what do we do now?"

He leaned back, and the corners of his mouth curved up with the slow smile. He didn't answer her in words; just let the look on his face convey what he was thinking.

Jennifer hit him lightly on the chest with the back of her hand and started laughing.

"We're already hot and sweaty." He grinned and tilted his head on the tile to look at her.

"I don't know if my lungs could take that right now."

Steve looked toward the shower and then back at her, raising his eyebrow.

"You go right ahead. I'll just sit here if you don't mind." Jennifer waved him toward the shower.

Steve laughed. "I meant you in there with me."

"I know what you meant. I'm not that naïve."

"We both need a shower." The small room was as hot as a sauna and the droplets of liquid running down their skin weren't just from the steam. He slipped his shoes and socks off and stood, locking the door. Stripping, he tossed his clothes in a small pile on top of his sneakers. "Come on," he said, putting his hand out to help her up.

Jennifer sighed. She took his outstretched hand and let him help her to her feet.

Steve pulled the sundress up and over her head and dropped it on the accumulating pile of clothes. He peeled off his shorts and underwear, watching her do the same, and stepped into the stream of water. "Goddamn!" He danced out of the shower; reaching for the controls and turning the heat level down. His shoulder was red where the water scalded it.

"Duh," she said after he turned the water to a cooler setting.

Steve yanked her into the shower against him.

Jennifer reached over and flipped the jets on, and all three valves shot water against them besides the showerhead above.

"Oh, my god." Steve closed his eyes as the water pulsed against his body. "I'm never getting out of this shower," he said, holding her.

"That's what I said after the first time, too." She rested her head against his chest.

"Ah." Steve let out a small groan of pleasure as the water worked the stress from his body. His arms fell to his sides, relaxed.

Jennifer tried to move him to get in the path of the jets.

"Nanana," Steve protested. "I'm not done yet." With his head still tilted back and his eyes closed, he pulled her into his arms. "This is heaven."

"Yes, and I'd like a little of it, too," Jennifer replied.

Steve smiled and turned sideways, with Jennifer still in his arms. The side jets hit their backs. "Better?" His eyes were still closed. He opened them, looking down at her.

Jennifer nodded and flipped the back jet off, leaving the side jets working on each of their backs. She closed her eyes and let the water do its magic.

Steve ran his hands through her hair, watching her, aware that he shouldn't take advantage of the situation, but his resolve waned with her naked body in front of him. He removed his hands and stepped back, running them over his face. "All set?" he asked when her eyes opened.

Jennifer sighed and nodded. She reached up on her tiptoes and gently pressed her lips to his, wrapping her arms around his neck. Their tongues slowly intertwined in a kiss that took his breath away and seemed to fill her lungs again.

Steve flipped the streams of water off and they separated, each grabbing a towel and wrapping it around their soaked skin. Jennifer scooped up the steam-saturated clothing and dumped it in the washing machine off of the kitchen.

"Thank you for being here today." She led him out of the laundry room and into the kitchen.

"I'll always be there when you need me."

Jennifer blushed. "Promise?"

"I promise. Do you still have my bathing suit here?"

Jennifer nodded, and then the color in her face faded. "It's in the closet." She looked back toward her room.

Steve headed toward the bedroom.

"No, don't!" A wheezing panic filled her voice from behind him.

"It'll be fine," he said, walking into the room. The closet door was cracked.

"I closed the door, Steve." Her voice shook.

Steve glanced from her to the closet and pulled the door open. "Just a closet." He flipped on the light. "See?" He spotted the swim trunks. When he reached for them, he felt the cold draft drift along the back of his hand. He picked up his shorts and turned back toward her, slipping them on under the towel. He stepped out of the closet and closed the door. "There's a draft in the closet."

"There isn't an air-conditioning duct in there." Jennifer took his towel and tossed it over the chair at her desk.

"Hmm." Steve focused his attention back on her. "You hungry?"

Jennifer rummaged through her drawers and found some clothing. She slipped her underwear on and folded her towel on the back of the chair with his. She fidgeted with his obvious gaze on her. "Stop staring."

He grinned. "Sorry." He looked out the window. "Are you hungry?" he asked again.

"Yes," Jennifer answered once she zipped up her shorts and adjusted her shirt.

He glanced back. "Want me to make you something?"

Jennifer raised her eyebrows, amused. "You cook?"

"A man's got to eat." He swatted her on the behind as he walked past her.

Steve's cell phone rang. He grabbed it off the counter in the dressing room, checking the number before he opened it. "Hello?"

"Hey, Steve, it's Bill. I'm sorry about this morning."

"You were a little drunk."

Bill laughed. "A lot drunk," he said. "I just get protective of her. Tom was my best friend."

Steve was quiet. He traded a look with Jennifer and gave her a nod and a smile. "You sure that's all it is?"

"Yes," Bill said without hesitation.

Steve knew a lie when he heard one, and this was a whopper. "Apology accepted," he replied. "I have to go. Later." He flipped the phone shut and sauntered down to the kitchen.

"Who was that?" Jennifer asked.

"Bill," Steve answered, with no further explanation. "What are you in the mood for?" He opened the refrigerator.

"Surprise me." She sat at the counter.

Steve surveyed the contents of the refrigerator and glanced at the clock. It was a little after eleven. He hadn't had anything substantial for breakfast, so he decided brunch was in order and whipped up a vegetable omelet for the two of them. He rummaged through the drawers until he found the silverware and grabbed two forks and knives. Bringing the omelet over to Jennifer, he set it down between them.

Jennifer pulled the plate toward her. "What are you having?" she asked.

His smile disappeared. The omelet he made wasn't a single person meal.

She burst out laughing. "I'm kidding." She pushed the plate back between them. She cut a piece and put it in her mouth. "This is great."

Steve shrugged. "It's just an omelet." He looked around the kitchen again. "This is a great place to cook." He smiled. "I'd love to have a kitchen like this someday."

"I hate cooking. I burn just about everything."

Steve laughed. "Well, at least one of us likes to cook. Eating out gets expensive."

Jennifer nodded and took another bite, but her smile soon faded. "Why do you think I'm seeing that place in the closet?"

Steve paused. "I don't know."

"This was different. There was no one else in the vision. Just that thing; and I could have sworn it looked directly at me." She shivered and then something else triggered. "There was a pentacle carved into the moss."

Steve stopped, his food hanging on his fork halfway to his mouth. "A pentacle?" He put the fork back on the plate.

Jennifer stared at the half-eaten omelet. "I'm not sure it was a vision, either." She slowly raised her eyes. "I think it was happening right then and there." She took a deep breath. "It was laughing at me." She visibly shivered.

Steve picked up his fork without commenting. It was just a little too bizarre for him to believe. He continued eating in silence, dissecting her story in several ways. Every way he turned it in his mind, it always came back to the fact that she was the center point of what was going on.

"Jen, if I showed you those pictures," he began, without looking at her. He leaned back and pushed the almost empty plate away. Glancing at her, he walked out of the kitchen and onto the balcony.

Jennifer put the plate in the sink and followed him out. "Finish what you were going to say."

Steve shook his head. "I don't want to put you in the middle of this thing," he said, looking out at the lake. "I want you as far away from it as possible." He turned to her.

"I think I'm already in the middle somehow," she said, echoing his thoughts.

"I don't want you to be."

She ran her hand up his arm, and he covered it with his. "I'll do whatever you need me to."

Steve glanced over at her. "I've already used you enough." He looked back out at the lake.

"What are you talking about?" Jennifer removed her hand, stepping away.

Steve closed his eyes. "There you go again." He shook his head and laughed.

"How have you been using me?" The hurt in her voice made his eyes open.

He leveled with her. "You've kept me close to the primary suspect in our case." Jennifer took another step away and Steve grabbed her arm. "I'm in love with you, Jen." He didn't release her arm. "That isn't part of the job."

She tried to yank herself away, but he didn't let go. Instead, he stepped to her, wrapping his arms around her. Her furrowed brow and pouty lips, along with that spark in her green eyes, made him smile.

"You aren't the primary suspect, babe. You just happen to be roommates with his girlfriend."

Jennifer blinked. "Billy?"

Steve nodded. "Yes. And last night was just another indicator that I'm looking in the right place."

"I can't believe Billy is involved in this. I've known him for close to seven years now," she balked. "He and Tom were friends in high school."

"Most of the missing persons list were rush candidates or pledges of Beta Theta Pi, and Bill has been the fraternity president for the last two years." He took a deep breath. "Before he became president, the run rate was one or two missing persons a year, which, technically for a college town like this, is normal; however, those were also related to the fraternity."

He looked into her eyes. "That's where I come in. I look young enough to be a dropout trying to get my shit together after what happened with Peg. I gain the sympathy of the fraternity president because he can relate—he lost his best friend a few years before in what looks like a legitimate car accident." He shrugged. "Then the curve ball was thrown. Your name came across in the report." He lifted his hand to her face and ran his fingers down the line of her jaw, stopping under her chin. "And my God, what a curve ball you are."

He leaned over, tilting her face up, and kissed her. "Our little game was fun, but it put a strain on the friendship I had built with Bill over the summer. I was losing his trust and confidence."

He ran his thumb over her lips. "Little did I know putting an end to our game would blow up in my face."

Jennifer tried to move away, but he kept her against him. "What do you mean, blow up in your face?"

"Jenny, Bill wants you."

Jennifer raised her eyebrows as a surprised laugh escaped. "He's with Tracy."

Steve tilted his head with a shrug. "He may be with her, but he wants you. And that scares the shit out of me." He kept eye contact with her, his hand still on her face.

"Why does that scare you?"

He shook his head. Strong and pure emotions played in the depths of his heart. "I have no tangible reason, just a very uneasy feeling." He ran his thumb over her lips again. "And that instinct has never been wrong."

"You have nothing to be afraid of," Jennifer said, as though she thought he was scared she had the same feelings for Bill as he had for her.

Steve smiled. She really was sweet and naïve sometimes. "I'm not afraid of losing you to him. I'm afraid he's going to hurt you."

Jennifer laughed. "Billy would never hurt me," she said, pushing away gently.

Steve disagreed with her, but didn't argue. He glanced at the hot tub. "Want to change and try that out?" He pointed his thumb over his shoulder. "I'm already in swim trunks."

Jennifer disappeared into the apartment. She came back a few minutes later in her bathing suit and helped take the cover off. They slipped in the hot bubbly water.

"I really need to learn to keep my pants on and my mouth shut around you," Steve said. He threw his arm around her shoulders.

Jennifer glanced at him, furrowing her eyebrows. "Why?"

Steve inhaled. "Because information just tumbles out when I'm with you, and that really isn't good. You're not an agent with the bureau." He stopped and sighed, leaning his head back on one of the cushy headrests. "I'm not supposed to discuss the case with anyone but my boss." He tilted his head toward her. "By discussing it, I could compromise the case. What's worse, it could put you in danger."

"How so?"

"I never thought about the ramifications if you slip up." He pulled his arm from her shoulders and studied his hands. He shrugged and looked at her. "I know you wouldn't intentionally say anything, but..."

"Steve, I will not say a word to anyone."

"Not even Tracy?"

Jennifer shook her head. "No, not even to Tracy."

Steve kept her gaze. "But you told her we slept together."

Nodding, Jennifer said, "Yes, I did."

Steve raised his eyebrows. "Why?"

"Because she's my best friend and girls talk about that stuff."

Steve grinned and looked away.

"She knew you wanted to get me in bed," Jennifer smiled. "You weren't very conspicuous about checking me out."

"Yeah, well..." He shrugged.

"Jen?" Tracy's voice rang through the apartment.

"We're out here," Jennifer called.

Tracy and Bill stepped onto the balcony.

"Hey, I thought you had class," Tracy said to Jennifer.

"I did. But I had an asthma attack."

Tracy raised her eyebrows. "Another one?"

Jennifer shrugged; she hadn't had one since Tom's death. She looked over at Steve. "I called Steve, and he knew what to do."

Tracy shifted her gaze to Steve. "You're certainly handy to have around." She batted her eyelashes, bowing her back slightly to show off her frontal endowments. "What else can you do?"

"He can cook." Jennifer smiled.

Steve felt the heat rush to his cheeks. He didn't like this kind of attention.

"Mhm, at least I know you won't starve to death." Tracy glanced over at Bill. "I'm going to change and join them." She disappeared, leaving him looking after her.

Bill glanced at Steve and Jennifer, and without a word, he headed inside to find Tracy.

"See," Steve whispered in Jennifer's ear, nodding toward the door.

"See what?"

Before he could explain, Tracy popped out onto the balcony. "Do you like to cook?" Tracy asked as she slid into the hot tub opposite Jennifer and Steve.

Steve nodded. "Yeah. You?"

Tracy nodded. "But I hate to bake."

Steve chuckled and glanced at Jennifer. "I understand she's pretty inept in the kitchen."

Bill's laughter reached them, and he appeared in the doorway. "That's an understatement," he said, sliding into the water next to Tracy. "She once tried to cook for Tom and nearly set the kitchen on fire," he explained. "What were you trying to make?"

"French fries," Jennifer mumbled.

"Thank God your parents had that fire extinguisher in the kitchen," Bill laughed. "She tried to put out a grease fire with water. What a mess. Tom grabbed the extinguisher and put the fire out before the entire kitchen went up in flames."

Steve looked curiously over at her. "You didn't know water makes a grease fire spread?"

Jennifer shook her head, her face bright red from more than the steaming water. "I do now," she pointed out. "Thanks a lot, Bill."

Steve put his arm around her shoulder and planted a kiss on her lips. "I'll have to remember never to leave you in the kitchen unsupervised."

Jennifer smacked him lightly with the back of her hand. "Bite me."

Steve brought her hand up and placed it playfully between his teeth with a grin. She yanked it out, laughing. Steve stood up. "I'll be right back." He excused himself, stepped out of the hot tub, grabbed the towel she had brought out and dried off the best he could. He disappeared into the apartment.

TRACY LOOKED OVER AT Bill. "Are you hungry?" she asked.

"I'd love a sandwich and a beer."

Tracy stepped out, wrapping a towel around her before heading inside.

Bill turned toward Jennifer.

"I never got the chance to thank you," Jennifer said.

Bill's eyebrows shot up. "For what?"

"For setting me up with Steve."

Bill looked over his shoulder and then back at Jennifer. "I'm not so sure about him, Jen." His eyes drifted over her body.

Jennifer shifted uncomfortably under his gaze. "Why not?"

"He's been around."

Jennifer glanced in the apartment and then back at Bill. "So he told me."

"And you're okay with that?" Bill asked.

"I couldn't care less what he did before he met me."

"Okay." Bill said, but the thin press of his lips told her otherwise.

"How's pledge week going?" Jennifer asked, wanting to change the subject.

"We've got some pretty interesting characters this year."

"Are you camping again for initiation?" That had been a long-standing tradition of Beta Theta Pi.

Bill nodded. "Yep." His smile broadened, like a wolf just before it takes down its prey.

Dark Reckoning
Chapter 24

JENNIFER SMILED WITH RELIEF when Steve and Tracy stepped back out on the deck. For the first time in close to seven years, being with Bill had been awkward. Their conversation was stunted, and his leer was definitely disturbing.

Steve put a soda on the table between the lounge chairs and took a seat. "I put the laundry in the dryer."

Jennifer slid out of the hot tub, accepting the soda from his outstretched hand, and took the seat next to him.

Tracy joined Bill in the hot tub.

"Are you doing okay?"

Jennifer nodded, glancing toward Tracy and Bill. She glanced back at Steve. "Do you have any more classes today?"

Steve nodded. "But I'm going to miss them."

"They're here now. I'll be just fine."

"We can watch out for her," Bill piped in.

Steve shook his head. "I'll pass," he said. "You didn't see how bad she looked when I got here. I'd just as soon stay to make sure she's all right. But I appreciate the offer," he said. "Besides, my clothes aren't done yet and I don't think they'd approve of me coming into class like this."

Jennifer sighed. "I really don't need looking after."

"Yes, you do. You were barely breathing when you called me."

Jennifer glared at him. "I'm not a child."

"I never said you were. I'm not doing this for you. I'm doing it for me."

"Don't give him a hard time. He just wants to help," Tracy said, flipping off the jets to the hot tub and climbing out with Bill.

Bill looked at his watch. "I've got class in a little while, so I'm going to head out," he said, and disappeared.

Tracy followed him inside.

Jennifer and Steve exchanged a look.

"What?" Steve whispered.

"Nothing," Jennifer said, glancing inside as Bill kissed Tracy goodbye at the door. She wondered if her discomfort was a side effect of what Steve had insinuated earlier or if Steve was actually right.

"Feel like going for a ride once our clothes are dry?"

"Sure. Where?"

Steve shrugged. "Just out."

Tracy came out onto the balcony. "What are you doing for the rest of the day?"

"I figured we'd get out of here for a while," Steve answered.

"Where are we going?" Tracy asked.

"I figured I'd take Jennifer over to the shore for the day, a walk on the beach, and maybe a little dinner," Steve replied with a shrug. "You're welcome to come with us."

"I'm supposed to meet Billy for dinner."

Jennifer's face drained of heat and her breath hitched. The balcony dissolved, becoming the desolate cove once again.

Dusk settled over the water, elongating the already malevolent shadows.

Kids no more than sixteen or seventeen, preoccupied with tearing each other's clothing off, stumbled into the clearing, kissing and pawing at each other.

Neither one saw the beast rise out of the water, but Jennifer did.

"Run." The word came out in a rush of an exhale; her lungs screaming in protest at letting the last of her breath go.

The kids didn't notice until it was upon them. The screams cut off as soon as they began.

"Jenny!" Steve yelled, shaking her gently.

Her eyes refocused on him, darting between Tracy and Steve, her breath coming in tortured hitches in her chest.

"Breathe," Steve said calmly. "Just look at me and breathe." He kept eye contact with her. "Tracy, go get me a glass of water, please."

Tracy immediately obeyed.

"Two teenagers. It got them," she wheezed after Tracy disappeared into the kitchen.

"Breathe," Steve demanded.

Jennifer did as he instructed, staring into his concerned blue eyes. When Tracy returned with the water, Steve held it for Jennifer to drink.

"Jesus, Jen," Tracy said, setting a hand on her forehead.

Jennifer broke eye contact with Steve to look at Tracy. She shrugged and then looked back at Steve. Her breathing slowed to a normal pace. "I'm okay," she finally said. She wanted to run, to get away from the apartment, to get away from Brooksfield and the nightmares plaguing her. "I need to change if we're going to go." She slowly stood.

"You sure you want to go?" Steve asked.

Jennifer nodded.

"I got her from here," Tracy said, escorting Jennifer back toward their rooms. As soon as she was out of Steve's earshot, Tracy stopped Jennifer in the hall. "What did you see?"

Jennifer shook her head. "I'm not sure."

"Bull. The last time you did that, you saw Tom die." She scooted Jennifer into her room. "What did you see?" she asked again. A cold draft slipped out of the closet, making her shiver. She glanced at the open doorway and turned to see Jennifer staring with wide eyes.

"Get Steve," Jennifer wheezed.

"Don't be ridiculous." Tracy walked over, switching the light on inside. She looked back at Jennifer. "Nothing to worry about." Jennifer made no move to come closer, still struggling for air.

"What do you want to wear?" Tracy stepped inside.

"I don't know," Jennifer said, catching her breath again.

Tracy glanced at the clothing and pulled out another pretty spaghetti strap sundress, pale blue-green like the waters in the Caribbean. "I like this one." She grabbed the matching flip-flops on the floor.

Tracy left the closet, closing the door behind her and smiled at Jennifer, handing her the dress and shoes. Paleness overshadowed Tracy's face. The look of harried shock when she came out of the closet was replaced with the plastic expression she presently wore.

"See, nothing in your closet but the big stuffed bear that got you the other day."

"The closet freaked you out."

"It's cold in there," Tracy said. "I'll have my dad send someone up to look at the air-conditioning."

"There isn't an air-conditioning duct, I looked."

"I'll still have him send someone. There's got to be some sort of issue. You don't just get drafts like that from nothing." Tracy headed out of the room.

When Tracy came out, Jennifer was standing by Steve, twirling her car keys.

"I think I'm going to pass so I can make dinner with Bill," Tracy said.

"You sure?" Jennifer said.

"I'm positive. You two go, have fun, and I'll see you later."

The dryer sounded in the background. "You think the clothes are dry?"

"Go check," Jennifer said.

Steve disappeared. He came back a few minutes later in the clean, mostly dry clothes. "We don't need to stop," he said, pulling his shirt over his head.

"See you later," Tracy called after them as they stepped into the hallway.

"I need to make a quick stop at the mall to pick up a birthday gift for my mom," Steve said as they settled into his car. "I hope you don't mind."

"Not at all. I have to pick up some lotion anyway, so this is perfect," Jennifer said.

Steve nodded, although he would have preferred not to have her in the mall at the same time. "You can grab what you need while I pick up something for my mom and then I'll meet you in the food court."

"You don't want my help?"

He smiled. "I'm just going to get her a charm for her bracelet, but if you want to come with me, you can. I just thought if we separated, it would be much quicker, and I could get you down into the salt air sooner." He sent her a wink.

Jennifer smiled. "Fine, I'll go do my thing and meet you in the food court."

At the mall, Steve stood looking at the directory, wondering if he had truly lost his mind. Waking with her in his arms had clinched the deal in his mind. He wanted that for the next however many years he had on this earth. He just hoped she felt the same way. With Jennifer standing at his side, he calculated his window of opportunity. It would be tight, but he smiled and tapped the shop she was heading to. "You need to head upstairs, that way." He pointed to his left. "I'll meet you in the food court." He planted a quick kiss on her lips.

He waited until she was out of sight and took off to the right, to the jewelry store three spots down on the main floor. He walked inside, scanning the rings until his gaze fell on a set that all but screamed Jennifer. He swallowed and looked at the clerk, wondering what the hell he was doing.

"I'd like to see that set." He forged ahead, pointing to the pair of rings. He prayed his voice didn't shake with the bundle of nerves that attacked.

The clerk beamed and took the set out of the case and put them on the velvet holder for Steve to see. "These are exquisite. The center diamond is one carat and flawless. The clarity is a B, which is excellent. The smaller diamonds around the band total another carat, each being roughly a tenth of a carat itself, all packaged in twenty-four carat gold." He smiled. "The diamonds in your band are roughly an eighth of a carat each, for a total of a carat and a half. The pair is on sale today for six thousand dollars."

Steve nodded. "That wouldn't happen to be a size five and a half, would it?"

"Unfortunately, no. It will take a couple of weeks to resize the bands." The clerk took out the ring measure and measured Steve's ring finger. "I would need to resize yours as well."

His stomach dropped with disappointment, and he almost asked if they had one in the case in her size. But nothing else had appealed to him. Steve glanced at the mall and nodded. "Fine."

The clerk wrote each item up and took the credit card Steve handed him.

"You don't have student discounts on top of the sale?"

"Not on engagement rings," the clerk replied and scanned the card. "But with the sale, you saved twenty-five hundred dollars. The retail price for this set is eighty-five hundred."

Steve whistled and signed where the clerk pointed. He scribbled his cell phone number on the slip. "Let me know when it's in." He tucked the papers away in his wallet.

"Thank you, Mr. Williams. I would expect them to be ready in a week. We'll give you a call."

"Thanks." Steve found a bench facing the food court and sat, waiting for Jennifer. His stomach rumbled with nerves, and he took a deep breath. The romantic beach proposal he had envisioned would have to wait. He closed his eyes. "I must be insane." He opened his eyes. It was way too soon for him to pop the question, yet something was driving him in that direction.

He raised his eyes, meeting hers.

"What's up?" Jennifer asked, taking a seat next to him.

"They didn't have the charm I wanted. Looks like I'll have to get it online."

Steve glanced at the bag in Jennifer's hand and stood. "It looks like you were successful," he said, and escorted her out to the car. He opened the door for her and rounded to his side, hoping she wouldn't catch the nervous tension eating at his stomach.

Jennifer's head tilted, and her eyebrows drew together as she regarded him.

"What?" he said, backing the car out of the parking spot.

Jennifer laughed lightly. "You're too funny sometimes."

"What?" He smiled over at her. *Oh shit, she knows.*

"You really don't have a clue what that smile does to women, do you?"

A measure of relief loosened the knot in his stomach. "I couldn't care less what it does to others. I'm just interested in what it does to you." He grinned.

"It makes me want to rip your clothes off and do naughty things to you."

Steve chuckled. "That's an interesting reaction." He sent a sideways glance in her direction. "I'll have to take you up on that when we get to the beach."

Jennifer blushed and shifted in the seat. "Do you have any music we can listen to?"

Steve reached behind her seat, pulling out a case of CDs and handed them to her.

Jennifer flipped through and found a Nickelback CD. She popped it in and Far Away came crooning out of the speakers and Steve joined in, singing along as they drove through the winding roads down towards Portsmouth.

"You can hold a tune pretty well," she commented between choruses.

He shrugged. "Maybe a little, but it's nothing compared to your voice," he said. Her voice was pure and sultry at the same time. "Good choice of song." He reached over and took her hand, squeezing it before he returned his attention to the road.

With his surprise tabled for another week, his mind drifted back to the case and her most recent vision. He glanced in her direction, relishing the melody of her voice filling the car, and waited until they were closer to their destination before he would broach the subject. She deserved some relaxation, especially after the asthma attack.

They continued the drive, listening to the music. When the signs for Portsmouth appeared, he turned the volume down. "Tell me about the vision."

Her hand clenched in his grasp. "Were there two teenagers on the missing persons list?"

"No," Steve answered as they pulled onto the short stretch of highway leading to the Piscataqua River Bridge that would take them into Maine.

Jennifer paused, watching the sailboats on the water below. "Can we not talk about that right now?"

Steve sighed and nodded. "For now." He squeezed her hand. He pulled off before the tolls and took Route 1A toward York Beach.

Jennifer grinned at the small quaint town of York and when Steve pulled out of the residential area into the view of Long Sands Beach, Jennifer gasped in awe. The two-mile strip seemed endless.

Steve parked and shifted to neutral, cutting the engine. He slipped off his sneakers and socks and opened the ashtray, counting out quarters to feed the parking meter. Jennifer stepped onto the sidewalk, barefoot and still in awe of the view. Her eyes locked on the Nubble Light House standing at the far corner of the point. "Wow."

"You've never been here?"

"No." Jennifer allowed him to lead her onto the beach. "It's pretty."

"It's one of my favorite places. I love sitting on the rocks at high tide, listening to the waves sift through the pebbles when they pull back into the ocean. It's soothing." He walked down to the waterline, holding her hand.

The quiet intimacy they shared cast a peaceful, serene glow on Jennifer's cheeks. "I love you," she whispered.

Steve smiled and squeezed her hand gently, letting the silence fall between them. "I loved Peg, but it was nothing like this." He let out a light laugh. "We certainly have chemistry." He glanced over at her. "But it is much more than that." He kissed her hand as they passed in front of a beachside restaurant. "Being with you always felt right, even ten years ago when we were just kids." He stopped and turned, so he stood in front of her, bringing his hand to her cheek. "I loved waking with you in my arms and I can't imagine a future without you in it," he finished and kissed her. He took her hand and began to walk again without waiting for a response.

She just walked alongside him, silent, her hand clasped in his. "I can't either," she said.

Steve grinned and let the comfortable silence fill the space between them as they strolled, listening to the ocean lap the shore, enjoying the warm breeze that enveloped them with the salty smell of the sea.

"Are you hungry yet?" he asked when they changed directions, heading back toward the car.

"Getting there."

"You like lobster?"

"Who doesn't?"

"I'll take you to the place that serves the best lobster rolls in town." Once they settled into the car, he drove farther down 1A to the center of York Beach, parking in front of a small street-side seafood place. He smiled and brought her inside. The place was small, with old plastic booths and a few random tables with chairs. The smell of cooked lobsters hung in the air.

With two cups of lobster bisque and two lobster rolls in hand, he grabbed napkins and spoons and led her back to the car. Navigating the one-way roads, he looped through the center of town and crossed to the peninsula that led to the Nubble Light House. Luck worked in their favor, and he caught a front parking spot. He hopped out of the car with the meal and climbed down the massive rocks, finding a sheltered dry spot to sit.

Jennifer followed and took a seat next to him.

Steve handed her a cup, spoon and lobster roll and took his out, sliding the bag and napkins under his thigh so they wouldn't blow away.

"This is so peaceful." Jennifer took her first spoonful of soup. "And this is so good." She looked over at him.

"I told you they had the best seafood."

"But the place is a dive."

"No, it's not. It's a seafood market. They recently expanded to include a little cooking besides just boiling lobster for their clients." He smiled and took a bite of the lobster roll.

Jennifer set the soup aside and unwrapped hers. She made a little noise of pleasure as she took her first bite.

Steve finished his in three bites. He cracked open his soup and took a spoonful as they watched the waves crash into the rocks.

When they finished eating, Steve threw the trash away and cuddled next to her, watching the endless ebb of the tide.

"Tell me about the vision," he breathed in her ear, bringing her back to the reality of what was going on in a little town less than a hundred miles away. She tensed up, and he tightened his grip around her, kissing her neck.

"A couple of teenagers. Girl and boy, and they were, um, preoccupied with each other. They never saw it come out of the water. I did."

"What is it?"

Jennifer shook her head. "Something evil," she said, "with red eyes that glow brighter than embers of a fire."

Steve kissed her shoulder and put his forehead against it. "Do you think this thing in your vision is a manifestation of your imagination because you can't come to terms with a person doing the things you're seeing?"

The question surprised Jennifer, but because it came from Steve, she gave it the thought and consideration he deserved. Her dreams were one thing, but that thing in her closet was another. She shivered. "No. It isn't human," she said with certainty.

"If it isn't human, how do I stop it?"

"I don't think anything can stop it."

"If it can be hurt, it can be killed."

They listened to the waves in silence.

Steve slowly opened his eyes and sighed. "Something changed over the last couple of years in Brooksfield. Something set off this chain of events."

"Tom and Peg died."

Steve nodded. Both their lives changed drastically two years ago. The disappearances had stepped up two years ago, and he wondered if there was a connection.

"Do you think there's a connection?"

"Hmm?" He pulled to the side so he could look at her face.

"You and me. A connection. Two years ago, both of our lives were turned upside down."

Steve glanced back at the water and squeezed her tighter. "I doubt it." He kissed her cheek. "Come on." He stood and helped her up.

"Where are we going?"

"Back to Brooksfield," he said, and let out a sigh. Jennifer's vision stoked his need to get back on the case, to prevent another disaster, another Amy, but the peace of the Maine shoreline pulled at him, offering him a reprieve from the horror attacking Brooksfield.

"I don't really want to go back."

His gaze met hers. "Neither do I, but I have a class in the morning." He opened the car door for her.

"We could get up really early?"

Steve laughed, tempted. He slipped into the driver's seat and glanced at the ocean, lulling him. "I can't," he said. "I shouldn't have taken this drive with everything going on, but you needed a little distance." He backtracked past Long Sands and the little harbor, heading toward the highway.

The buzzing of a cell phone filled the car and Steve dug his phone from his pocket and glanced at the display before bringing the receiver to his ear. "Hey, Murphy."

"We've gotten word of a couple of missing kids..." Murphy said on the other line.

"Let me guess. Two teenagers, a boy and a girl?"

The silence on the other end confirmed his question. Steve sent a glance in Jennifer's direction and took a deep breath. "I should be back in Brooksfield in a little over an hour."

"Where the hell are you?"

"I took Jennifer to York, Maine. I thought the salt air would help ease the asthma," he said. "Where do you want me when I get back?" he asked, hoping his boss would say the apartment.

"Meet me at your lake house and then I want you at that fraternity tonight," Murphy snapped. "I need you to find out what the hell is going on."

"Yes, sir," Steve said with no enthusiasm. "I'll be back as fast as I can." He flipped the phone closed and as soon as he merged onto the highway, his driving catapulted past aggressive to downright insane, and Jennifer gripped the door as he weaved through traffic. "Sorry." He offered a shrug.

"Was it two teenagers?"

"Yes," Steve answered. "And I can't stay with you tonight. Murphy wants me at the frat house."

"I could stay with you."

"I'll think about it," he said, even though he'd just assume hell would freeze over before allowing her at the fraternity, not with the way Bill leered at her at the apartment. Something was happening, darkening the landscape, poisoning everything it came in contact with.

They drove the rest of the way in silence. Steve held her hand and let the facts flow through his mind, the legends, the cove, the ritual. They all had to be connected, and he decided another internet search was in order. Even with his mind saturated with the case, his mood worsened the closer he got to Brooksfield.

The closer the town came, the more the deaths of two more kids ate at the lining of his stomach, turning the delectable meal into a roiling mass weighing him down. He glanced at Jennifer, her lips forming the perfect, kissable pout, and he flicked his gaze back at the road. Irritation snaked over his skin. "I'm sorry."

Jennifer squeezed his hand. "I know. Do you mind if I come with you to the frat house?"

Steve took a deep breath. "I can't do my job with you there."

"I don't want to be alone."

Steve glanced at her again, moving his hand onto the steering wheel. "I'll stay over tomorrow night."

"And if the thing in the closet comes back?"

"Sleep in the living room."

"You can be a son of a bitch sometimes."

Steve swerved to the side of the road and slammed on the brakes. He gripped the steering wheel, hard enough for his knuckles to ache, knowing his anger was misplaced. She didn't deserve it; the killer did, so he opted to keep his mouth closed. After counting to ten and reining his fury in, he shifted into gear.

Jen grabbed his hand off the gearshift. "No, say what you were going to say."

Steve closed his eyes. "Jenny, it's my job." He didn't look at her. He just leaned his head back and rubbed his face. "I'd rather be with you than looking for two dead teenagers." *Hell, I'd rather take you a million miles away from Brooksfield, where I'd know you're safe.* "I can't do this tonight." He was quiet for a second, and then put the car in gear and slowly pulled back on the road. He glanced in her direction. "And I don't think it's safe for you at the frat house." Silence settled in the car.

"I'm sorry," Jennifer said after the 'Welcome to Brooksfield' sign passed.

"So am I." Steve glanced at her. "I didn't mean to snap." The apartment complex loomed in the distance and when he finally parked in front of the entrance, he turned to her, yanking the keys from the ignition. "I'll walk you up."

The few extra minutes with her did little to lift his somber mood. In the elevator, he turned towards her, reaching out to graze her cheek with his fingers. "I wish I could stay with you tonight, but…" he said as the elevators opened up on the penthouse floor.

"You have to work." She finished his sentence and dug in her pocketbook for the apartment key. She slid it into the lock and opened the door.

An eerie quiet within the apartment unsettled his nerves and kicked his intuition up a notch. "Wait here," he said, and stepped past her with senses on high alert. Steve did a quick walk-through of the apartment, stopping in her bedroom. He shivered from the cold draft wafting from the closet, and he shut the door. When nothing else caught his attention, he headed back to the foyer. "Tracy's not here and you really have to have her look at the air-conditioning in your closet, because I could feel the chill when I stepped into your room."

"Tracy said there isn't a duct in there."

Steve raised an eyebrow. "Then there's a leak of some sort in the air ducts, which isn't good."

She wrapped her arms over her chest and bit her lip. Fear registered in her eyes as her gaze flicked to the hallway and back to him.

"Do you want me to get clothes out of your closet for tomorrow, so you don't have to?" he asked.

Jennifer's eyes sparkled with unshed tears, and she nodded.

He followed her to the bedroom and swung the door open. The temperature in the room plummeted, and he hesitated at the entrance, scanning the clothing. The sweet scent of cedar wafted from the opening, along with something that left an underlying taste in his mouth. He wondered if there was a Freon leak somewhere that triggered her asthma. It was a much more logical explanation than an imaginary monster.

Refocusing on the clothes, he turned to Jennifer. "What would you like?"

"The jean skirt and blue shirt back there." She pointed toward the back wall.

Steve grabbed the hangers, handing them to her and stepping out of the closet. He closed the door behind him, jamming the desk chair under the knob, making it impossible for the door to unlatch and open by itself.

"Thank you." Jennifer laid the clothes on the chair.

"Anytime. I just wish I could stay; maybe I'll be able to hang here tomorrow night." He kissed her goodbye and headed to the elevator.

Rubbing his face, he watched the numbers descend, a silent countdown like the one in the back of his mind, ticking off the seconds like a time bomb.

Dark Reckoning
Chapter 25

STEVE PULLED INTO THE fraternity and took a deep breath, shoving his foul mood out of sight where it festered under his skin. He walked inside, offering a "hey" and a smile to the group in the living room before heading up to his room. He changed into his jogging shorts and t-shirt and headed out for a run. A half hour later, he turned down the driveway to his grandfather's cabin. He slowed as he approached the police barricade.

"I'm sorry, son, this is private property," the officer guarding the driveway entrance said.

"I know. I own the property. Please tell Agent Murphy that Steve Williams is here," he said, jogging in place.

The officer's eyebrows lowered, and his eyes narrowed as he studied Steve. "Do you have ID?"

Steve pulled out his Brooksfield University student ID. "My badge is in the cabin," he said, still jogging in place.

The officer looked between the ID and Steve and finally handed it back. "Agent Murphy is expecting you." He stepped aside so Steve could pass.

Steve jogged the rest of the way up the driveway, approaching the cabin and the chaos outside. A search and rescue headquarters sat near the side of the cabin and the benches near the gazebo were filled with Brooksfield police and fire and rescue personnel under the makeshift canopy. Something about the callous way Murphy took over the property set his nerves on edge and Steve paced, allowing both his body and his temper to cool.

Agent Murphy left his post and crossed the expanse of lawn.

"You could have asked my permission," Steve said, his breath a little labored from the run.

"Look, this is the perfect spot to coordinate a search and rescue. It's containable," he said. "I didn't think you'd have an issue with it."

Steve bit down on the response. He had worked with Murphy long enough to know he took advantage of the best available opportunities and, as incensed as he was, if he were in Murphy's place, he would have done the same thing. "Fine." He stopped moving and wiped the sweat off his face with his shirt. "What do you need from me?" he asked.

"I need you to be at the fraternity acting like one of them and see if they drop any hints about this."

Steve took a deep breath. "I think that's the wrong place for me to be."

Murphy glared at Steve. "What are you talking about?"

"Jennifer had another vision," he said. "She's been with me for the entire day, Jack. I haven't left her side until about an hour ago when I dropped her off."

Murphy turned away, but Steve caught the skepticism in his eyes.

"I know how far-fetched this sounds, but Jennifer has some sort of weird psychic connection to this." He walked toward the dock and sat down on the steps.

Murphy followed and sat next to him. "Okay, let's say she does. How can we use that to catch the son of a bitch?"

Steve smiled a little. "I'm not sure. There's no rhyme or reason to when they show up and she thinks some monster is causing the deaths."

"She's right."

"No, Jack, she doesn't believe it's human."

Murphy laughed, and Steve shot a glare in his direction.

"What if it isn't?" Steve asked, "What if she's right?"

Jack looked out at the lake while he formulated his response. "Steve, I've seen some pretty sick shit in my life, all of which resulted from a human being," he said. "This is no different."

"Humor me. What if we are dealing with something outside the realm of the norm?" Steve glanced at his boss. "Just for a second, think as if it's a real possibility."

Murphy let the sounds of the task force fill the space between them before he spoke. "If it isn't human…" He gnawed on that statement for a while along with his lower lip. "I don't know, Steve. I just don't know."

Steve didn't think Murphy could take that leap, and he nodded and stood. "I need to get back. Can I catch a ride in a marked police car? That ought to get the conversation kick started."

Murphy laughed. "No way."

"Yes, Murph. I can use that. I'll tell them the jogging paths around this side of the lake are blocked by police, and a search and rescue effort is going on for some fools who got lost in the woods." He shrugged. "Otherwise, it'll be a bitch to work missing people into a conversation."

Murphy agreed and picked up his radio as they walked toward the driveway. "I need Agent Williams taken back to the fraternity in a marked Brooksfield police car."

The car pulled up and Steve slipped inside.

"I'll see you in class tomorrow," Murphy said.

Steve sent a quick nod in his direction before he closed the door and settled back in the seat, explaining what he expected of the officer when they got to the fraternity.

The police car parked in front of the frat house a few minutes later. Several of the members were sitting out on the porch. When the officer opened the back door and Steve stepped out, he shot a smirk in their direction and swiveled his gaze to the officer.

"Next time, you may want to heed the park closed signs, son." The officer slid back into the cruiser.

Steve nodded and walked up to the members of the frat house. He glanced over his shoulder as the cop pulled away. "God damn cops," he muttered as he lumbered up the stairs. "Ruined a perfectly good run."

"What happened?" Adam asked.

"I was running down one of the jogging paths around the lake and I ignored the no trespassing signs. Looks like some idiots got lost in the woods. There are cops everywhere." He shook his head. "They gave me a hell of a time for being in the park after six."

"What do you mean, cops everywhere?" Adam asked.

"They're all over the woods on the other side of the lake."

"Where?"

"Pretty much across from the public beach and down the length of the lake."

Adam and Joe exchanged glances. "Think they'll be gone by Friday night?" Adam asked.

Steve shrugged. "Beats me. It depends if they find the idiots who got lost. Why?"

"We camp over that way for initiation," Adam said, giving away nothing that Steve didn't already know.

"You may have to find another spot," Steve said.

Panic settled in Adam's eyes, and he snapped his head in Joe's direction.

"I'm sure they'll find them before then," Joe smiled.

Steve looked between the two of them. "I need a shower." He headed inside.

JOE STEPPED INSIDE AND waited until the shower turned on. He walked back onto the porch and smacked Adam on the back of the head. "Bill said not to clue him in on the initiation."

"What's Bill going to do with him during initiation?"

"I have no idea," Joe lied as easily as he breathed.

Bill had explained the initiation plans to him and asked for a few items. Joe had scored what Bill requested with surprising ease. As the next in line for the fraternity president spot, he had a special role to play this year. He wondered whether he could stomach it, but he didn't want to entertain not following through for even a second.

Joe looked up at the second floor. If he thought his role pushed the limitations of sanity, Steve's role was downright morbid.

He would bear witness to the entire event, even Jennifer's death.

Of course, that presumed the beast didn't just tear him to pieces on sight.

Dark Reckoning
Chapter 26

JENNIFER FOUND A MOVIE she loved and put down the clicker, curling up on the couch. She drifted off into a light sleep with Nicholas Cage navigating The City of Angels.

Jennifer kneeled in the middle of a dark room with candles decorating the walls all around her. The pentacle on the floor glowed with a fiery hue, yet the temperature plummeted, and she shivered. Ice-cold hands pushed her forward, burning her shoulders, and she screamed.

Jennifer awoke, bolting upright in the living room, shaking, her scream echoing in her ears. Her breath labored, and she told herself to calm down in a silent repetitive mantra while her heart leaped into overdrive with panic and fear.

"Only a dream," she repeated under her breath, wrapping the blanket tighter around her until she had control over her breathing. Her chest ached, and she leaned her head back against the soft cushion of the couch and took a deep breath.

She glanced at the clock, surprised to see it was still early, and she reached for the phone, dialing the now familiar number.

Dark Reckoning
Chapter 27

STEVE WALKED INTO HIS room with a towel around his waist when his phone rang. He flipped it open, closing the door behind him.

"Hey."

"We found them near where we found that little girl," Murphy said, and his voice betrayed his anger and disgust.

"Same condition?"

"Worse. Parts were missing this time."

Steve sat down. His other line buzzed, and he ignored it. "What parts?"

Murphy hesitated. "Both heads and his privates. Sheared clean off."

This was a new development, very different from the others, and he wondered why. "Do you need me out there?"

"I need you where you are."

Steve took a deep breath. "Any tracks?"

"No, and no signs of animals, either. We have the forensic team here now. What's going on there?"

"They're worried about the camping trip they are doing for their initiation ceremony on Friday night. That's the only thing I could get from them when I got back. I think Bill is with Jen's roommate tonight. Do you want me here or there?" he asked, hoping for the latter.

"I want you at the fraternity," Murphy said. "You may be able to get a hint of something while he isn't there in control."

"Okay. Gotta go." Steve hung up without waiting for further instructions. He looked at the caller ID to see who had called a few minutes before and hit redial.

"Hello?" Jennifer answered, breathless.

"What's up?" he asked.

"Nothing," she said, her voice that throaty sound that accompanied physical stress.

"Were you working out?"

"No, I had another nightmare," she said.

The slight tremble in her voice now made sense. "The teenagers?" he asked, his mind still logically on the case.

"No, and this time, it wasn't in that awful clearing. It was in something made of concrete."

"What happened?"

"When it touched me, my skin burned. It hurt worse than anything I've ever felt. It was like my soul was being raped."

Steve flopped back on his bed. All he wanted to do was go hold her in his arms, but he'd been given orders. "Awe, babe," he said, closing his eyes.

"Can I come over?" she asked, sounding a little like she was begging.

Steve inhaled but didn't speak.

"Please."

"Are Tracy and Bill there?"

"No, they haven't come in yet."

He understood her hesitancy to be at the apartment alone after having a disturbing nightmare, and he sighed. "Okay," he said, giving in to her plea. He hung up and stared at the ceiling, beating himself up for allowing her to come there. But he had no choice. He couldn't leave tonight, and he couldn't say no to her. He dragged a pair of jeans and a crisp blue oxford, leaving it unbuttoned. He hand-combed his hair back and went downstairs, grabbed a beer, and joined the guys on the front porch.

"You smell a hell of a lot better," Joe remarked as Steve took the chair next to him.

Steve smiled easily. "Imagine what the back of that cruiser smelled like." He raised the beer and took a swig while Joe let out a laugh. "So, what's up with the initiation? Do I have to do it?" he asked, looking over at Joe.

Joe shifted, like he was uncomfortable with the question. "Ask Bill."

"I'm asking you," Steve said, taking another sip.

"I'm not sure."

Steve nodded. "I'm not really into camping. Think I can skip it and hang with my girlfriend?" He drained the rest of the beer and let out a belch. He watched Joe out of the corner of his eye and did not like his reaction.

Joe broke out in a quick, knowing smile before he suppressed it and spoke. "I'm not sure. It's up to Bill—he's the president of the fraternity. You want another beer?" Joe asked, pointing at the empty bottle.

"Sure." Steve handed him the empty. He glanced back at the street, expecting to see Jennifer's car any minute. Joe came out with the second beer. At the same time, Jennifer pulled into the parking lot.

The smile that spread over Steve's face prompted Joe to look over his shoulder. Steve stood and walked down the steps with a grin plastered on his face.

Jennifer followed suit. She stepped out of the car with her winning smile. "I figured I'd surprise you," she said, playing the part beautifully.

"I like surprises," he said as he wrapped his arm around her waist and planted a kiss on her lips. "You want a beer?"

"Sure."

He escorted her up the stairs, pointed to the seat next to his, and handed her his beer. "I'll be right back." He trotted into the house to get another beer for himself, hating to leave her on the porch with all the rest of the fraternity members leering at her.

"HEY JEN," ADAM SAID behind a crooked smile.

"Hi," Jennifer said, shifting in her seat. Their stares set her skin crawling, as if every one of them was mentally undressing her. She crossed her arms and legs, unconsciously blocking their continued inspection.

Relief flooded through her when Steve stepped outside again and she took a sip of her beer, meeting his gaze and silently transmitting her discomfort.

Steve put his hand on her thigh, conveying his ownership to all on the porch. His meaning was clear, and he gazed around, marking his territory. Most of the guys filtered inside, but Joe lingered.

"It's been a while," Joe said. He glanced nervously at Steve, then back at her.

"Yeah, it has," Jennifer said.

"It's good to see you again."

"You, too, Joe."

He made his way inside.

Steve looked at her with a smile. He leaned over and kissed her cheek. "Not here, okay?"

Jennifer smiled in return, but it felt foreign and forced. Not natural, and certainly not the way she felt when she was acting. She tried a moment of levity instead of caving into the pressure building in her chest. "I'm hungry. Want me to cook you something?"

Steve sprayed his beer out in a laugh that caught both of them off guard. He coughed and laughed, wiping his mouth with the back of his hand. "French fries?" he sputtered, trying to dislodge what little beer had gone down the wrong pipe.

This time, the smile felt more natural, and a measure of relief lifted the weight, trying to constrict her lungs. "I'm serious about being hungry."

Steve nodded. "I'll be right back." He left her alone on the porch again.

A couple of minutes later, he came back with his shirt buttoned and his car keys in his hand. "Let's grab something quick at Joe's Grill," he said, leading her to his car.

The minute they were out of view of the fraternity, he took her hand. "I'm sorry, babe."

"That was weird."

Steve huffed and nodded.

"They were looking at me like I was their next meal." Jennifer shivered.

"I noticed," Steve said, taking a deep breath. "You can't stay with me tonight."

"What better way to let them know I'm yours?"

"I'm not playing games with you," he said. "That wasn't normal, Jen. All of them looked at you that way, not just one or two."

"They always took notice of me."

Steve turned his hard gaze toward her. "Taking notice is one thing, but that was anticipation." He looked back at the road.

"Anticipation?"

"Think about it. Think about the way I looked at you that day in the cabin just before we screwed around. That's the look each and every one of those fuckers had," he snarled.

Jennifer saw the fury in his eyes, and she sank into the seat, wringing her hands in her lap. He was right, and it chilled her to the bone.

"I don't want you anywhere near that fraternity."

"I really don't want to be alone tonight."

FURY RAGED IN HIS blood, pumping hot pulses through his skin. "Do you know what Adam asked me the other day?" Steve stopped behind the line of cars at the drive-thru. "He asked me if you were worth it. Do you have any idea how much it took not to knock his lights out?" He closed his eyes and took a deep, cleansing breath. "I can take down more than a few people at a time, but I'm not sure I can take out a whole fraternity and that's what I'd be up against if you stay with me," he said pulling up to the takeout speaker. He rattled off his order and turned to her. "What do you want?"

"French fries and a milkshake."

He placed her order, got the total, and dug in his wallet for money.

"Are you sure you can't stay with me?" Jennifer asked.

"I can't tonight. I promise I'll stay tomorrow night." He leaned back in the seat; the demands of his job took a toll on his emotions. Anger wasn't the only thing tainting his blood—icy fear played a part as well, and the behavior of his fraternity brothers was at the heart of his discord.

He'd like nothing more than to hold her all night, every night, but an order was an order and Jack wanted him at the frat house. He collected their dinner and pulled into a parking spot overlooking the valley.

As if reading his mind, she said, "I don't see why you can't just say screw it and stay with me."

The conflict within him boiled over and he exploded, "God damn it, Jennifer. This is my fucking job!" He got out of the car and whipped his shake at the garbage can. It smashed against the inside, spraying the garbage can and a few feet beyond with the chocolate drink. He stood leaning against the front of the car with his back to her, his arms crossed.

The muscles in the back of his neck and shoulders tensed with the creak of the passenger door and he grated his teeth together as she stepped into view. After a sharp inhale, he let the hardness in his muscles soften. "I know you're scared, and a little freaked out about your closet, but I can't protect you at the fraternity." He let the silence fall between them.

She offered him her milkshake, and he shook his head.

The gesture melted the layer of ice that formed around his heart, and he sighed, wiping a stay hair out of her face. Just the touch of her skin stirred him, and he shifted gears away from his feelings back to the case. "They found the teenagers, by the way."

Jennifer raised her eyebrows and her expression crumbled. "Oh, God."

"So, I've got my hands full right now. You can't stay with me, and I can't stay at the apartment." He took a breath. "Please stop making this more difficult than it already is."

"Oh." She stepped back, looking shell-shocked. Her eyes teared up, and her lips trembled. "Okay." She took a seat in the car, looking out the passenger window.

Steve saw the sting in her face as his words tumbled out, and he dropped his arms, looking up at the sky. "A little help," he said to the clouds in exasperation. Another deep breath and he turned, sliding back into the driver's seat.

"Jenny," he said, and waited. She didn't turn. "Please look at me." When she did, he cursed under his breath. Tears rolled down her cheeks, cutting a path through her makeup and leaving streaks in their wake. "You need to understand where I'm coming from," he began, holding up his hand to stop her impending interruption. "Please let me finish. I'd take a bullet for you in a heartbeat, and it's not just because it's my job, it's because I'm in love with you. I think I always have been, but that doesn't matter right now. What matters is stopping this thing before someone else dies. As you so eloquently pointed out today, we may be connected to everything that is going on." He turned the car on again and sat back. "The fraternity is caught up in it, too." He looked over at her. "I would like to keep you and the fraternity separate because I can't do my job if I'm scared shitless that something's going to happen to you." He put the car in gear.

"At least, at the apartment, I know nothing bad can happen."

"What about the thing in my closet?"

"It's only a vision, or nightmare. It can't hurt you like those men can," he said, bringing his point home. "Now, I'm going to let you finish your fries and drink with me on the porch. I'm going to walk you to your car and kiss you goodnight. You are going to drive back to the apartment and call me when you get there. Understand?"

"Fine," she said, causing him to look over at her. "You can be a royal SOB"

"Love me anyway?" he asked as he pulled into the parking lot and slid in next to her car.

"Yes," Jennifer said, grabbing her shake and the remaining fries.

Steve took the seat next to her on the porch. "I've got some homework to do," he said.

Jennifer slurped up the last of her drink and smiled. "Do you really have to do homework right now?"

Steve smiled back at her. "Yes, I do." He grabbed her empty containers and brought them into the house, coming back empty-handed. "I'll walk you to your car," he said, taking her hand. At the driver's side of the car, he took her face in his hands. "I love you, Jennifer Ann Curtis." He looked into her green eyes before he kissed her, running one of his hands down her arm and around her waist, pulling her against him.

Jennifer laughed under his lips.

Steve broke the kiss. "What's so funny?"

"My initials if we ever get married," she said, grinning like a fool. "I'm keeping my middle name."

Steve smiled. "JAW." He kissed her gently and stepped away with the same smile on his face. "If?"

She rolled her eyes. "Is when better?"

"What do you think?" he tossed back, although her little clarification just made his day.

He watched her pull out and waved, turning to climb up the steps.

"Is she strictly a pussy fuck or does she like it up her ass?" Adam asked. He leaned against the post, his gaze following Jennifer's car.

Like a light switch, Steve's mood changed. He barreled up the steps, stopping when he was toe-to-toe with Adam. "You want to lose your front teeth?" He tightened his fist, flexing his arm, and Adam flinched. "I didn't think so." Steve stepped toward the door.

"I've always wanted to bend her over this rail and fuck that pristine cunt until she screamed. Is she a screamer, Steve?" Adam asked, pushing beyond Steve's limits.

He stopped in his tracks.

JOE SAW STEVE'S FACE flush red from inside the house. He moved quickly, running outside in time to catch Steve's arm as he threw it back in a punch. Joe slammed Steve against the house. "You don't want to do that," he said. "I know Adam can be crude, rude, and obnoxious, but you don't want to hit him."

"The hell I don't!" Steve roared, and pushed Joe off. He swung and connected with Adam's jaw, sending him flying off the porch and onto the lawn on his back. He turned on Joe. "I don't want to hear anyone talk about my girlfriend like that," he growled and stormed into the house.

Joe waited until he heard the slam of a door, and he turned a glare in Adam's direction. "You stupid fuck," he said, and turned, heading up to Steve's room, softly knocking on the door.

"What?" Steve snapped.

"It's Joe, can I come in?"

His question was met with silence.

A moment later, the door opened, and Steve went back to lying on his bed with his law book opened. "I've got studying to do."

"Adam doesn't mean any harm," Joe began, but the look on Steve's face cut him off. "He's had a thing for Jenny ever since he met her."

Steve rolled toward Joe. "That doesn't make it right." He looked back at his book.

"He's pissed that you got the brass ring and you've only known her for what, four days?"

Steve sat up, glancing at Joe and biting his lip like he was debating whether to admit a secret. "I was Jen's neighbor until she was eleven. She and my kid sister were best friends before we moved out of town."

"You're kidding?" When Steve shook his head, Joe let a little laugh escape. "Really, wow, I didn't know that." He shifted and glanced down the hall before returning his attention back to Steve. "I didn't even know you had a sister?" He wondered what else about this guy they didn't know—not that it would matter when all was said and done.

Steve shook his head. "She died." He stretched back down, staring blankly into his book.

"I'm sorry, man." Joe wondered if Bill knew any of this.

STEVE NODDED AND LOOKED back at Joe. "Shit happens," he said, and went back to studying. He heard the door close as Joe left.

The phone rang, and he flipped it open.

"I'm home," Jennifer said. "Still no sign of Bill and Tracy."

"Thanks for calling." Steve closed his book. He had to get on the computer and do some more research into the town history and any lore he could find about the lake and Paradise Cove. If Jennifer was right and this thing wasn't human, he needed to know what it was and how to stop it.

"I'm sorry about earlier."

"You know how hard that was for me?"

"Yes. As hard as it was for me to drive away. I almost turned around a couple of times."

Steve inhaled, letting the last of the aggravation go. "I'll see you tomorrow. We've got that public relations class again, then we can go back to your place, and I'll make you lunch."

"You sure you don't want me to cook?"

"No, you live in such a nice place. I'd hate to see you burn it down."

"I can boil noodles."

He chuckled. "I'm sure you can. Goodnight, angel."

"GOOD NIGHT." SHE HUNG up. She smiled and held the phone to her chest when Bill and Tracy came stumbling in.

"What'r you doin' here?" Tracy slurred and stumbled forward. Bill caught her before she crashed into the wall.

Jennifer shrugged and waved toward the television. "Watching a movie."

Bill leered at her with the same expression as the guys at the fraternity.

"Where's Steve?" he asked, looking around.

"At the frat house. He had some homework to do." She shrugged.

"Ah," Tracy said, and stumbled again. Bill caught her with ease. He picked her up and disappeared down the hall.

Jennifer could hear Tracy giggling, which led to other noises she didn't want to hear. She turned up the television volume and curled up on the couch. She had a tough time keeping her eyes open, drifting to sleep before the next commercial.

Dark Reckoning
Chapter 28

JENNIFER WOKE UP AND stretched, smiling at the wetness between her legs and the gratified ache in her muscles. Her wet dream still colored her mind. *Steve can even satisfy me in a dream.* She turned the television off and headed to bed.

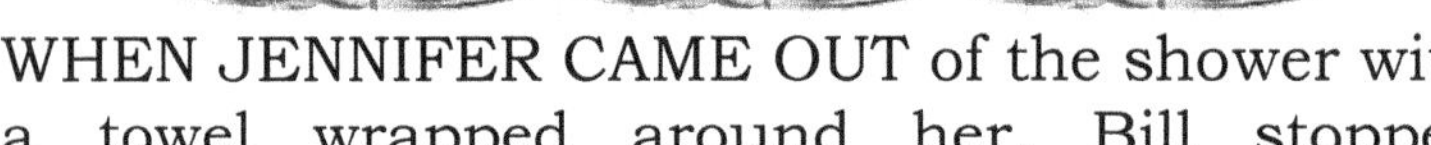

WHEN JENNIFER CAME OUT of the shower with a towel wrapped around her, Bill stopped halfway through the dressing room. He stared at her.

"Oh, hey, Bill," Jennifer said, brushing her long locks. "How's Tracy this morning?"

"Hangover from hell. I'm not far behind either." He scurried out of the room.

Bill drained a glass of orange juice in the kitchen as Jennifer walked in. He smiled at the exceptionally hot combination of the white miniskirt and blue shirt she wore with her wet hair flowing over her shoulders. "Steve's a lucky guy," he said, and he put the glass in the sink.

"Stop looking at me like that."

Bill raised his eyebrows. "Huh?"

"I don't like it when you check me out."

"Since when?"

"What do you mean, since when?"

"I've always checked you out. You didn't seem to mind it for all these years." He walked over to her and lifted her chin, so she looked at his face. "Why does it bother you now?"

Jennifer floundered and stepped away from him. "Because the way you look at me is different now. It's no longer just appreciation."

"Then what exactly is it you see?" he asked, curious to hear her answer.

"Anticipation," she spat.

Bill let out a laugh. "Your little episode yesterday must have messed with your mind more than you realize," he said, but his eyes betrayed him as they grazed her again.

"It's never going to happen." She stepped away and walked out of the apartment, leaving him watching after her.

"That's what you think." He slipped on his shoes by the door. He let himself out and entered the lobby as she drove by in her car. "In less than thirty-six hours, to be exact." He stepped out of the building and into the warm September sunshine. "Anticipation," he laughed.

She'd hit that one dead on.

Dark Reckoning
Chapter 29

STEVE ROLLED OUT OF bed, grumpy without Jennifer next to him. It seemed unnatural, and he marveled at how quickly the need stirred in him. He missed her and vowed this would be the last time he ever woke up without her by his side.

He scoured the internet for most of the night and came up with some interesting lore, but it didn't enlighten him as to how to stop the horrors happening in Brooksfield.

The urban legends provided the most interesting information. According to some obscure sources, the curse spewed forth from a dying Palawion who called a dark demon from the depths of hell to ravage any white man found on his sacred land could only be broken by the blood of his descendants. For years following his death, the area became a much bigger legend than the Bermuda Triangle. No white man dared to step onto Abinaqui territory.

Decades later, settlers came into the area with a witch doctor who swindled a deal with the demon, promising an annual sacrifice in return for reprieve in the attacks. When the demon took the deal, the lore said he was bound to the contract, which chained him to a small area of the forest as long as the sacrificial rites continued.

If the ritual was not performed to the demon's satisfaction, he would be free of the bonds that kept him contained, allowing him to wreak havoc on the white man's territory.

His mind wandered to the notebook and the implied meaning in relation to what he read, and he shook his head. "No way. The girl is mine," he whispered, yanking clothes out of his drawer. He headed toward the shower.

He made it to his eight o'clock class on time. Murphy looked like hell with dark bags under his eyes. Even his short military haircut looked disheveled. Steve wondered if they found any of the missing parts.

He didn't pay much attention to class. His mind kept returning to two things—the way the frat boys looked at Jennifer, and the words in the notebook. The initiation ceremony gnawed at his conscience. What did it really entail?

Visions of Jennifer falling prey to satanic rituals preyed on his mind—teeth tearing at her in cannibalistic sacrament, rape, torture, and blood sacrifices made to a dark god.

He shivered, shaking his head to lose the morbid nightmare rolling behind his eyes. He doodled on the page of his notebook, prompting more questions than answers. Bloody letters soaked into the fabric of the paper again.

Stay away, she is mine!

"Bullshit," Steve said aloud.

"Mr. Williams, do you have something to share with the class?" Murphy asked.

Steve stared at the paper, and then up at the classroom and shook his head. He exchanged a glance with Murphy and then lowered his eyes to the page. "No. Sorry for the interruption."

"Please see me after class." Murphy continued the lecture.

MURPHY CLIMBED THE STEPS and sat on the edge of the table in front of Steve. "What the hell is the matter with you?" he snapped as the door closed behind the last student.

Steve slowly turned the notebook. "Remember that leap I asked you to take yesterday? Try again and look at the center of the page."

Murphy did. He saw a blank page. As he turned away from the notebook, red caught his attention out of the corner of his eye. He snapped his attention back to the paper in awe as the words appeared in his peripheral view. When he moved his gaze directly to the page, it was still blank. "What the..." he trailed off and unfocused his eyes. He saw the fuzzy letters.

"Should have seen my reaction the first time they appeared."

"I must be overtired." Murphy rubbed his eyes.

"Tell me what you see."

"Stay away. She is mine," Murphy replied. "Looks like it's written in blood from the way the letters seep into the page."

"Bingo." Steve closed the notebook. "Still think it's human?" He stood.

Murphy looked at him, dumbfounded.

"It wants Jennifer." Steve pointed to the unassuming composition book lying on the desk. "It isn't going to get her." He swept the notebook off the desk and spun towards the door.

"It still could be a person. There are such rare things as projecting thoughts onto paper." He rubbed his eyes. "I've never seen it, but others in the bureau studying psychic activity have."

"There's a part of the bureau that studies paranormal events?" Steve asked. It was his turn to be dumbfounded, and he fell back into his chair.

"A small unit." Murphy pinched the bridge of his nose.

"Like the X Files?"

Murphy laughed. "No, not like the X Files."

Steve chuckled. "Well, I'll be damned." He traded a glance from the notebook back to Murphy, shaking his head. "You need to be clear of the woods before tomorrow afternoon." Steve stood again. "The initiation ceremony is supposedly taking place tomorrow night, and it's under the cover of a camping trip."

"I'll make sure of it," Murphy said. "Don't forget, lunch tomorrow. I want to meet her and if she doesn't show, I'm hauling you both in."

"I know. We'll be there." Steve left the room. He trotted to his next class, slipping through the door a few minutes late again.

The professor turned, staring at him. "Mr. Williams, you are late yet again," he said, drawing the attention of the room to Steve.

"My professor wanted a word with me after my eight o'clock class."

"I don't care. I thought I was clear on Tuesday—I give one and only one chance to be late. As of right now, the highest grade you can get in this class is a C." He turned back toward the board.

"I disagree," Steve replied. An argumentative mood scraped over his skin like rough sandpaper. He stood and trotted down the steps to the floor near the professor, gazing into the open lesson book. "I could teach this class more accurately than you and be entertaining in the process instead of making everyone fall asleep."

The professor's entire face went red, and he didn't speak.

"Don't have a coronary," Steve said, picking up the lesson book. "If I can accurately teach the class today, will you waive my being late?"

The entire classroom watched with slack jaws.

"Get out of my classroom," the professor sputtered when he found his voice.

"Law is all about negotiation, professor. I'm negotiating for an A. Aren't you the least bit curious whether I can do this or not? Whether I know your material well enough?"

"You were late. I only give one warning." The professor stood fast.

Steve closed the book, handed it to the professor, and walked out; grabbing his notebook on the way past his desk, leaving stunned silence in his wake.

Steve sat on the bench in the warm sun, frustrated.

He flipped open his phone and pressed the speed dial.

"I just pissed off Professor Lang," he said to Murphy.

"What happened?" Murphy sighed into the phone.

"I told him I could teach the material better than he did and he threw me out. I guess I'm dropping the class," Steve said, looking out at the campus. He had less than an hour before his next class. "And by the way, what the hell am I doing in a public relations class?"

"You have to ask after what you just pulled?"

Steve laughed. "Okay, I guess I deserved that. I'll check in later."

"Don't piss off any other faculty members today."

"I'll do my best." Steve folded the phone up. He walked over to the building where his PR class was and stretched out on a stone bench, waiting for the hour to go by.

"What are you doing here so early?" Jennifer walked up to him.

"I got kicked out of class." He tilted his head back so he could look at her.

"What?" She took a seat next to him when he sat up on the bench.

"I'm very good at pissing people off. And I think I pushed my last professor over the edge." He relayed what he had done, including his exiting statements.

Jennifer sat with her hand over her mouth, eyes wide in surprise.

"That's what everybody in the class looked like." He laughed, pointing at her.

"Steve, that was just rude," she said after the shock wore off.

"I didn't wake up with you in my arms, so I'm a little pissy today. It won't happen again."

"What, you being pissy?"

"No, not waking with you in my arms," he said, and the smile that graced her face made it worth it. "I missed you." He didn't tell her about the information he found online or the message in his notebook. He didn't want to ruin the lighthearted mood.

"I dreamed about you," Jennifer said, and her cheeks budded into tiny rosy spots.

"Really?"

Jennifer nodded. "Really."

"How was I?" he asked, perpetuating the humor.

"Almost as good as the real thing." She looked at him sideways.

He laughed. "Well, after class, I'll remind you just how good the real thing is." He bumped her gently with his shoulder.

"I'd like that." The blush took on a crimson tone.

"How would you like it today?" He grinned, prolonging the conversation just to see what color her cheeks would turn next.

"I don't know."

"Sure you do." He bumped her with his shoulder again. "Do you want control, or do you want me in control?"

Jennifer thought about it. "I'm not sure. Maybe a little of both." She raised her eyebrow at him.

He grinned and looked around, then back at her. "Have I told you lately that I love you?"

Dark Reckoning
Chapter 30

"CAN I HAVE A piece of paper?" Steve asked when they sat down in the classroom.

Jennifer looked at the notebook and back at Steve. The smile on her face faded away. She slowly ripped a page off her pad and hand it to him. "What'd it say today?" she asked, motioning toward his notebook.

He glanced at her sideways. "You know, I'd rather just forget it for today."

Jennifer was curious. "What did it say?"

Steve sighed and opened the book.

I am going to kill him.

Jennifer gasped and looked at Steve, her eyes wide with fright. *I'll be damned if I let that happen.*

He closed the notebook. "It said something different for you, didn't it?" He scanned the filling classroom before returning his gaze to her. "For me it said Stay away, she's mine. Like that's going to happen." He rolled his eyes.

Jennifer glanced toward the front of the class and saw nothing. Her heart raced, drumming a beat in her chest like the quick tempo stanzas in Queen's Bohemian Rhapsody. "No, mine didn't say that," she whispered, willing her lungs to relax. A distinct wheeze emanated from her, despite her efforts to control her breathing, and she focused on the instructor, tapping his pencil on the podium to gain the attention of the class.

"You should have let me just forget it today," he grumbled.

Jennifer reached over and took his hand, giving it a squeeze and letting go. She turned her full attention to the instructor.

STEVE STARED AT HIS hand and then moved his eyes, taking her in. The gesture was simple, yet it moved him. He didn't want to be in the classroom and fidgeted in his chair, tapping his pen on the desk until Jennifer shot him a warning. He doodled on the paper and kept stealing glances at her. So adorable, concentrating on what the teacher was saying and diligently taking notes, he wrote three words on the paper and slid it across the desk to her.

Jennifer glanced at the note and blushed. It was pretty crude, but she nodded, grinning at him, handing it back.

Steve sat back in the chair and folded the paper, a smile still on his face. He glanced at the table in front of him and almost tumbled over in the chair when his legs involuntarily pushed away from the counter. Blood pumped out of the notebook all over the desk. It spilled over the edge, and he slid further back, shooting a glance at Jennifer. Her wide eyes were glued to the red stain spreading over the countertop.

The blood ran off the front edge, onto the student sitting in the next row. He didn't seem to notice the gooey liquid dripping into his hair and oozing onto the collar of his shirt. Jennifer glanced around the room, catching a glare from the girl sitting next to her.

Jennifer turned back to Steve. He shook his head and put his hand out. She took it and grabbed her books. He yanked her out of the classroom, leaving the seeping notebook on the desk and the instructor irritated at their abrupt departure.

"The notebook was fucking hemorrhaging. What the hell was that?" he cried when they hit the fresh air.

"It obviously doesn't want us together." Jennifer's voice shook. "I think your note triggered it."

"It didn't like 'fuck me later?'"

"Imagine if you'd said 'fuck me now?'"

What a ridiculous time for humor, but it worked. He laughed aloud. "This can't be really happening. Notebooks don't fucking bleed." He practically dragged her across campus toward the parking lot.

"Can you slow down a little?"

He glanced at her and then scanned their surroundings. "Sorry," he said, slowing his pace. "I'm just a little freaked out right now." He flipped open his phone and pressed a number. "Is anyone at the cabin?" he asked. "Okay." He flipped the phone closed. "Looks like it's your place." He glanced over at her.

Jennifer scanned the parking lot. "Where's your car?"

"I walked to campus this morning. If you drop me at the frat house, I'll follow you."

"Sure."

"What did you see in the notebook?"

Jennifer started the car without speaking. "It doesn't matter because it will not happen."

"What did it say?"

Jennifer glanced at him. "It said it was going to kill you." She looked back at the road.

"I am not dying, and neither are you," Steve said. "I told you that the other day." He looked out the window and gripped the door handle like it was the last rung on a crumbling ladder.

Jennifer glanced at his pale white knuckles. "You have a problem with my driving?"

"No."

"Then why do you have a death grip on the door?"

"I don't like being a passenger in any car. Lack of control thing."

"Control freak?"

"Why do you think I'm a cop?"

"I don't know. I just thought you liked handcuffs."

His smirk morphed into a grin.

Jennifer pulled into the fraternity parking lot next to his car. "Can we just forget about all this for the rest of today?"

"Fine by me. I'll be right behind you." He hopped out of her car and dug the keys out of his pocket. He pressed the play button on the CD player and spun his wheels, peeling out behind her. The music filled the car, and he sang while navigating the streets back to the apartment, trying to let the tune relax the tension wiring his entire body.

Jennifer might be able to forget for a while, but there was no way he would get that vision out of his head, and he doubted anything short of a drinking binge would wipe it away. He pulled in next to her, hesitant to shut off the car and face reality. She approached his open door, and the way she stared at him woke up his libido and he grinned, finishing the song before shutting the car off.

He offered her his hand and the moment her skin met his, the fire in his heart bloomed. There was no way he'd stand by and let harm come to her, and he made a silent vow to protect her at all costs.

"You could sing that song to me every day of my life and it still wouldn't be enough," she said, opening the door to her apartment and stepping aside so he could enter.

Steve grinned and put his arm around her waist, swinging the door closed. He sang the chorus of Far Away, twirling her around the entry. "I'll sing every day if you promise to always look at me like that." He didn't wait for an answer. Yanking her close, he crushed her lips under his, his tongue slipped in her mouth, mingling with hers and blocking the vision of the bleeding notebook.

When the kiss broke, his mind drifted back to the case, and the levity disappeared. "I know you didn't want to think about what happened today, but after what happened yesterday, I want to take you out of Brooksfield." He wiped the hair away from her face. "I don't think it's safe for you here."

"You're the one it threatened."

"I'm a big boy, Jen. I can take care of myself. Besides, based on my research, whoever is doing this may be mimicking that old legend you told me about."

Her eyebrows shot up. "You still think it's a human after today?"

"Humans are capable of horrifying things, Jen," he said. "And Murphy tells me there are some out there with the mental power to induce hallucinations like we saw today."

She peeled herself out of his grip, grabbed her book bag, and took a seat on the cushy couch, sending him an exasperated look.

"Human or not, based on the notes I'm seeing, it is setting its sights on you, and I'm just in the way."

"I need to study," she said, opening the book in her lap. "And I really don't want to talk about this."

"I want you out of Brooksfield."

Her gaze shot to his. "For how long?"

"For however long it takes to catch this guy," Steve answered.

"I can't just drop out of school because someone's terrorizing the town."

Frustration soured his mouth, and he ran his hand through his hair. "Then why don't you stay at my place?"

"Oh, yeah, alone in the woods. That's just where I want to be." She rolled her eyes and dropped her gaze to the book on her lap.

"Can you just leave town for the weekend, then?" Every nerve ending in his body shouted to haul her away against her will, but he knew the second he turned his back, she'd find a way to come back into the hot zone.

She sighed and met his gaze. "Where do you want me to go?"

"I'll see if Murphy can arrange a safe house for you for the weekend."

"You're really serious about this," she said, putting her book on the table.

"Yes, I'm dead serious. After we meet him for lunch, I'll have him take you into protective custody for the weekend and I'll pick you up on Sunday."

"What am I going to tell Tracy?"

"I don't know. Tell her you're meeting your parents for the weekend."

She bit her lip and nodded. "Fine. But I'm not running off and hiding every time you think I might be in danger, understand?"

He couldn't help the smirk that surfaced. In twenty-four hours, he'd be able to breathe and concentrate on the case without worrying about her every waking moment.

"Don't you have homework?"

"You're kidding, right?"

"No. We have some stuff for the Public Relations class. Did you even look at the syllabus he handed out on Tuesday?"

Steve laughed.

"I may be dating you and willing to surrender into protective custody for you, but I am not doing your homework."

"I would never dream of asking you to do that."

"Bullshit."

He grinned. "Well, maybe."

"If you're here at the school, you've got to do the work." She dropped her notebook on the table and rummaged for a pen.

He crossed behind her and laid his hands on her shoulder. Leaning close, he kissed her neck. "Maybe I'll just make love to you for the next twenty-four hours."

"Tempting as that may sound, I really have to get some work done," she said over her shoulder, and broke away from his playful grip. "I am actually a student, remember?" She disappeared into her room, coming out a few minutes later with the rest of her books and a laptop computer.

Steve hooked his thumb over his shoulder. "I'm going to go take a nap on the balcony."

Jennifer watched him for a while and then went back to reading the textbook. By the time the clock read three, she had finished most of her work.

Tracy waltzed in from her classes, lugging her backpack and juggling extra textbooks. "Where's Steve?" she asked, looking around. "I saw his car."

"Out here," he called.

"I'm studying. He's relaxing." Jennifer rolled her eyes.

"Must be nice," Tracy replied.

Steve walked into the living room and grabbed a soda from the refrigerator behind the bar. "I'm cooking dinner tonight. Is Bill coming over?" he asked.

"You're cooking?" Tracy asked, blinking.

"Yes. Is Bill coming over?" he asked again.

"Nah, he has prep to do for initiation tomorrow night." She shrugged. "I'm surprised you're here with all that going on."

Steve glanced at Jennifer. "I'd much rather be here with Jen."

"Ah, if only I could find a love like that," Tracy said in a mocking tone. "He cooks, he dotes on you, and my, my, my, he is just delicious to look at."

Steve laughed. "So, it's just the three of us."

"Ménage à trois?" Tracy asked, raising an eyebrow and licking her lips suggestively.

"No, thanks," Steve replied before Jennifer could admonish her friend.

"I thought that was every man's fantasy."

"I've only got one fantasy, and she's sitting right there." Steve pointed at Jennifer.

"God, Jen, he is just too good to be true." Tracy plopped herself on the couch and flipped the television on.

"Soap opera?" Steve gawked at the television as Jennifer closed her books and leaned back to watch the program. He grumbled and went back out onto the balcony.

Jennifer exchanged a grin with Tracy.

"He isn't perfect after all."

"Close to it, though," Jennifer said, and glanced over her shoulder. "And I am going to marry him someday."

Tracy grinned. "Will I be the maid of honor?"

"Absolutely. I promise to pick out the most hideous bridesmaid dress just for you."

Tracy giggled. "Teal... or, better yet, pumpkin-colored, right?"

"Oh, don't make me gag," Jennifer giggled along with her friend.

Jennifer and Tracy settled in to watch the soap opera and Steve disappeared into the kitchen to begin preparations for dinner.

Delectable scents wafted from the kitchen and Jennifer and Tracy exchanged a look, both hopping to their feet and heading into the kitchen. A red sauce bubbled on the stove and the scent of fresh roasted garlic filled the air along with warm Italian bread.

"Out." He shooed them away. "I'll call you when it's ready." He closed the door on both of their questioning eyes.

Jennifer stared at the kitchen door, surprised. "How am I supposed to learn to cook?" She turned her arched eyebrows in Tracy's direction.

"Why would you want to, with a man like him?" Tracy grabbed two wine coolers from the bar, handing one to Jennifer before heading onto the balcony. She took a long draw on the drink, draining half of it. "Seriously, Jen. He is really wonderful."

"You don't know the half of it." Jennifer took a liberal sip of the cooler. "I'm so in love with that man, I can't think straight when he's around."

"Is he as good in bed as he is with everything else?"

Jennifer blushed. "Tracy…"

"Well?"

Jennifer tried not to smile. "Come on," she let out a little laugh.

"Is he?"

"Yes, amazing, now stop."

"You have to give me details," Tracy said, finishing her drink.

"That's just crude."

"I want to live vicariously through you at this moment, so give me details."

"No. Besides, you have Billy."

Tracy let out a sarcastic humph.

"You have Billy, right?"

"I don't know, Jen. He's been acting downright weird lately. First, he doesn't seem interested, then he's all over me and back again. I'm getting sick of his hot and cold behavior. Nothing is going to ever come out of the relationship, anyway. We never talked about marriage, ever. I'm just an easy lay for him," Tracy said, getting up and disappearing. Seconds later, she returned with two more wine coolers. "And he's just a substitute for a vibrator for me at this point. And a bad one at that." She opened the cooler.

"I'm sorry," Jennifer said, cracking her second drink open.

"Don't be. At least I realized he was a shmuck now." She looked at Jennifer. "So, tell me about him." She pointed her thumb toward the kitchen.

"He can make me hot just with a look," Jennifer admitted. "And when he touches me, oh my God Tracy, it's like my skin's on fire."

"His smile could make any woman hot."

"Yeah, well, getting that caught up isn't always a good thing. We both have forgotten protection more than once."

"Forgotten?"

"Haven't you ever been that swept away?"

She shook her head. "Never."

"It's kind of scary," Jennifer said, glancing over at the kitchen entry. "I'd sell my soul to be in his arms for the rest of my life."

Tracy shivered and shot a glance at the lake. "You don't mean that."

"Yes, I do." Jennifer finished the rest of the first cooler and started the second one. "Will you be our children's godmother?" Jennifer asked, looking out at the lake.

"I would be honored," Tracy said.

They sat in comfortable silence and drained their drinks.

Steve stepped onto the balcony a little while later and gave Jennifer a kiss. "Dinner will be ready in about twenty minutes," he said. He glanced at Tracy. "Where's the wine?"

Tracy got up and went into the kitchen with Steve, leaving Jennifer on the balcony to dissect the conversation. Tracy and Bill were having issues, which could explain his sudden intense interest. She huffed at the thought. It was much more than that, and she knew it.

She couldn't wait to be out of this town this weekend, but she'd never admit that to Steve. Just like him, she thought there was a connection and time was ticking.

Tracy stepped back onto the deck. "How come you always get the good ones?" she mumbled and sat next to Jennifer.

"You'll meet Mr. Right someday."

"I hope so," Tracy said, finishing her drink.

Steve poked his head out. "Dinner is served." He bowed graciously and led them into the kitchen, helping them with their chairs before taking the seat at the head of the table.

The presentation of the meal was restaurant quality. A chicken parmesan cutlet sat in the center of each plate, surrounded by angel hair pasta drizzled in sauce. In the center of each cutlet was a small sprig of parsley. Even the salad was fancy, with sliced tomatoes, shredded carrots and fancy cut cucumber in the shape of a rose in the center of the bed of mixed greens. The loaf of toasted Italian bread graced the center of the table, surrounded with roasted garlic halves strategically placed around the slices.

"I'm impressed." Tracy looked at the spread before her. "Very impressed."

He filled each of their glasses with the wine, graciously accepting the praise. "Thanks," he said, placing the bottle on the table.

Jennifer took a bite. "This is delicious!"

Tracy swallowed her first bite. "Oh, my God, this is heaven."

Steve smiled. "Glad you like it."

"If you don't marry him, I will," Tracy said to Jennifer.

Steve laughed and dug into his food.

"You're a law major, right?" Tracy asked as she washed down her food with the wine.

Steve nodded, glancing at Jennifer. "Yes."

"What's your concentration?"

"Criminal law."

"Defense attorney?" she asked curiously.

Steve shook his head. "No, I want to put criminals away." Dimples appeared in his left cheek as a partial smile surfaced.

Tracy glanced at him. "Really?"

"Yes," Steve said, shooting a quick smile Tracy's way.

"Have you ever broken the law?" Tracy asked.

Jennifer laughed, and both pairs of eyes swung in her direction.

"As a matter of fact, I did when I was younger, quite a few times," he replied, keeping eye contact with Jennifer.

"What'd you do?" Jennifer asked, surprised that he had had any trouble with the law.

He grinned and leaned back with his wine. "I never said I got caught."

Tracy laughed. "Oooo, and he has a dark side, too," she said to Jennifer.

"What did you do that was against the law?" Jennifer asked.

"I wasn't a saint in high school."

"What'd you do?" Tracy asked.

Steve shrugged, but kept quiet.

"Come on, you can tell us," Tracy pried.

Steve narrowed his eyes and tilted his head. "Aren't you on the school paper?"

"Yeah, why?"

"I'm not telling a reporter about my indiscretions." He grinned. "I can just see the headline now."

Tracy laughed. "Off the record, then."

Steve shook his head. "All you have on me is that I admitted to breaking the law a time or two. Hell, pouring that wine for you is against the law. You're underage."

Tracy raised her glass, swirled the wine around, and downed it. "More please?" She smiled sweetly.

Steve slid the bottle in her direction, but made no attempt to pour her another glass. His dimples deepened with his barely suppressed grin, making both Tracy and Jennifer laugh.

"So, have you spoken to any firms about an internship?" Tracy asked, continuing the line of questions.

"I never said I was going to be a lawyer," Steve said, finishing his dinner and refilling his glass.

"But your concentration is criminal law?"

Steve nodded and sipped his wine.

"What else is there?" she asked.

"Law enforcement," he said, putting his glass down. "That interests me more than show boating in a courtroom."

"But there's no glamor in law enforcement."

"I'm not interested in glamor or fame. I'm interested in justice."

Tracy tilted her head, studying Steve. "You really are a white knight."

"I wouldn't say that."

"Ever shoot a gun?" Tracy asked, causing both Jennifer and Steve to blink in her direction.

"Yeah. My grandfather was a cop. He taught me to use a gun," he replied. "You?" he asked Tracy.

"A hunting rifle," she replied. "My dad took me on a hunting trip once. Holding a weapon that could kill in an instant was scary and thrilling at the same time." She shrugged. "But I couldn't shoot Bambi."

Steve seemed to size her up at that moment. "You don't scare easily, do you?"

"Not particularly," Tracy replied. "I enjoy watching scary movies when I'm alone."

"So, what scares you?" Steve turned the tables, digging.

"Things I can't control," she replied without hesitation.

"Doesn't seem like there are a hell of a lot of things that would fall under that category? Be more specific," he said, stroking her ego and questioning her at the same time.

"You know... things..." Tracy said, shifting uncomfortably.

Steve glanced over his wine. "No, I don't know. What things?" He took a sip without breaking eye contact.

Tracy smiled. "Things that go bump in the night."

Steve laughed and glanced at Jennifer. She sent him the evil eye, willing him to stop, hoping the warning was clear. He took the cue and backed off. "I'll have to remember that if I get up in the middle of the night."

Tracy laughed. She took the last bite of the meal and stood, clearing the plates. "I'll clean up." She smiled over her shoulder. "You two go relax."

"You sure?" Jennifer asked, bringing her plate to the sink.

"Yes. Go relax," Tracy said.

Steve put his plate in the sink. "Thanks, Tracy." He pulled Jennifer into the living room and onto the balcony, wrapping his arms around her. "What was the warning glance all about?" he whispered in her ear before sucking her ear lobe.

"You were interrogating her."

"So? She was interviewing me."

"She isn't a suspect. Don't treat her like one." Jennifer kissed him before he could argue.

"All right," Steve said after their kiss broke. He glanced at the panoramic view and sighed. "Isn't Thursday party night here?"

"Yes. We usually go dancing."

Steve raised his eyebrows. "Then I think we should."

Jennifer laughed.

"You don't think I can dance?"

Jennifer shook her head, still laughing.

"I got moves, baby." He twirled her around.

"I know that, but can you dance?"

Tracy appeared, wiping her hands on a cloth. "What's so funny?"

"Steve wants to go dancing." Jennifer laughed.

"I'm in," Tracy said. "Assuming I'm invited," she added as an afterthought.

"It's Thursday night, and I figured some of the fraternity brothers would be out before the big night," Steve said with a shrug. "And Jennifer here thinks the idea of me dancing is the funniest thing she's heard today."

Tracy looked him over. "Oh, yeah, I bet you smoke on the dance floor."

"Tell her that." He pointed to Jennifer, who was in hysterics at this point.

"It's not nice to laugh at your boyfriend," Tracy said. "Especially when he's in the room with us."

"I'm sorry, I just can't see it," Jennifer said, winding down.

"Are you ready to go, or do I have to wait until you two get all decked out?"

"Five minutes," they said at the same time and ran down the hall.

Jennifer threw opened her closet and stepped in, flipping on the light. She grabbed a Maya blue dress with a flare skirt and fitted top. When she leaned down to grab the matching shoes, she saw a flash of red at the back of the closet. She jumped out of the closet with both the dress and shoes in her hands, slamming the door as quickly as she had opened it. Staring at the door, she tentatively reached out, her fingers grazing the icy doorknob.

"You almost ready?" Tracy called from the bathroom.

Jennifer turned away from the closet, peeling off her clothing. She threw the dress on and hustled into the changing room.

Tracy was touching up her makeup and glanced at Jennifer. "Nice choice."

Jennifer put on a little makeup and lipstick, ignoring the sensation of being watched. She sat on the stool and ran a brush through her hair while slipping her shoes on with one hand. Standing, she glanced in Tracy's direction. "Ready?"

"Yep," she said, pressing her lips together to blot the lipstick.

They walked out of the bathroom, grabbing their IDs from their bedrooms, and met in the hall, walking out to meet Steve.

Steve turned when he heard them coming, and his jaw dropped. A slow, wicked smile crossed his lips. "I'm going to be the envy of every man in that place." He put his elbows out.

THE ATMOSPHERE PULSED WITH a hip-hop beat. Even though it was early in the evening, the dance floor was already crowded.

"You ready for this?" Steve grinned at the two of them and waved at the tequila shots he brought to the table.

Tracy took the shot and sniffed. She tilted her head and raised her eyebrows. "This smells better than Jose Cuervo."

"That's 'cause it is. I upgraded to Tequilame."

Jennifer tentatively picked up her shot, looking at the two of them.

Steve started the tequila procession by licking the skin between his forefinger and thumb, pouring a small mound of salt onto the wet skin. He licked the salt, downed the shot and pressed a lemon slice between his lips, sucking away the bitter taste in his mouth, and replaced it with the tartness of the lemon. He dropped the lemon back on the tray and smacked his lips together with a shudder. "Your turn," he said, and the two of them followed suit.

Tracy threw back her head and let out a whoop as she set the shot glass upside down on the tray.

The slow heat of the shot relaxed the tense muscles in his shoulders, and he stood, putting his hand out to Jennifer. "You ready to own that dance floor?"

Jennifer took his hand.

"You coming?" Steve asked Tracy.

Tracy looked up at him, raising her eyebrows.

"I can handle you both. Besides, I'm not leaving you stranded out here alone." He glanced around the bar, scanning the crowd and cataloguing each face, each possible threat, before glancing back at Tracy.

Tracy stood and took his other hand.

He led them out onto the dance floor and let loose, smiling at the stunned expression on Jennifer's face. She really hadn't believed he could dance, but the years of karate training gave him the grace of motion that most of the other guys lacked. When the fast beat turned slow, he put his hands around Jennifer's waist and pulled her to him and her breath caught in her chest.

He glanced over at Tracy, and she nodded, slipping through the crowd back to their table.

"You certainly have the moves," Jennifer said, breathless from more than dancing.

Steve scanned the room again, then gazed at her. "I haven't done this in years," he admitted. Leaning over, he gently grazed her lips. "It feels good."

"IT SUITS YOU." JENNIFER looked up at him. He looked radiant, his face flushed from both the heat and alcohol and the edges of his hair wet with perspiration. He smelled like a spiced summer breeze mixed with an undertone of sweat, which made her heart flutter.

Steve laughed. "No, you suit me. I wouldn't be doing this if it wasn't for you," he said in her ear. As the song ended, he twirled her around, dipping her low. He led her back to the table.

"Another round?" he asked. They nodded. He disappeared through the gathering crowd at the bar, retrieving another round of tequila shots.

Tracy watched him walk away. "Is it wrong to envy you?" she asked, scanning the bar.

"Not at all." Jennifer reached out, squeezing Tracy's hand. "Thank you for setting us up."

Tracy smiled and nodded.

The rest of the evening was a blur of drinking and dancing, and they stumbled into the apartment a little after midnight. Steve twirled them both down the hall toward the bedrooms and bowed to Tracy before escorting Jennifer into her room.

"Night, Tracy." He closed the bedroom door.

"You." He turned toward Jennifer and twirled her around again and then tugged her tightly to him and licked her neck. "You taste salty." He fumbled with the back of her dress. "You know, I almost undressed you in the taxi," he said, nibbling on her ear. "It took way too long to get home."

"Probably wouldn't have gone over well with either Tracy or the driver." Jennifer tilted her head back, spreading her arms wide as he swung her around again. "You are so sexy," she uttered while he licked her neck again, ending with a kiss on her jawline. "Hot." She lost her balance.

Steve grabbed her close, and they stumbled onto the bed, laughing. "I am going to be so hung over tomorrow morning," he chuckled. "Murph is going to blow a gasket."

Jennifer giggled, yanking his shirt off. "I can sleep in tomorrow."

"That's so not fair." He kissed her harder than he intended, knocking their teeth together.

"Ouch." He touched his lips and checked his fingertip for blood. It was clear, and he offered her a drunken smile. "Sorry."

"You're the rocket scientist that chose tequila," she said.

"Yeah, but seeing you suck a lemon was so worth it." He grinned down at her.

"Ah, you had ulterior motives."

Steve nodded and felt in the pockets of his shorts. His smile disappeared. "I have nothing with me tonight." He kissed her gently and rolled onto his back, squashing his desires.

"Shit," Jennifer said.

"My sentiments exactly." He glanced at her. "I guess I just get to hold you tonight."

Jennifer giggled. "The one time you get me drunk, you don't take advantage of that?"

He raised his eyebrow, considering the possibility as his eyes scanned her. "Naughty girl," he whispered. The dress came off seconds later, and he kissed her body, moving his way down between her legs. He made her moan and writhe on the bed, calling his name over and over and over, making love to her with his mouth and hands. He ached to be inside her, but refrained. When she took him in her mouth, he wasn't able to contain himself any longer, arching into the explosion.

Shifting on the bed, Steve wrapped his arms around her and buried his face in her hair, spooning her.

"I love you, Jenny."

"I love you, too, Steve."

Sleep was immediate and dreamless for both of them.

NEITHER STEVE NOR JENNIFER stirred when the closet door unlatched and glaring red eyes peered out at them from within the darkness.

250

Dark Reckoning
Chapter 31

JENNIFER'S ALARM CLOCK WENT off at seven and they both moaned at the noise. Steve reached over and hit the snooze button, falling back on her.

The alarm went off ten minutes later. This time, Steve turned it off and sat up. "Oh, Jesus," he whispered. The imaginary vice tightening on his temples sent bolts of pain through his cranium and into his eye sockets. He held his head for a moment, thinking that would keep his brain from exploding through his skull. "Do you have any painkillers?"

Jennifer rolled toward the sound of his voice. "Bathroom medicine cabinet. Bring me some on your way back."

Steve got out of the bed on unsteady legs and let out a laugh. His underwear was backwards. He shifted his undergarments the right way, slid on his shorts, and headed in search of painkillers and bladder relief. He grabbed the toothbrush he'd used the other day and wiped out the horrible taste in his mouth. The medicine cabinet indeed had painkillers, a choice between acetaminophen, ibuprofen, and some prescription medication under Tracy's name. He chose the acetaminophen and filled a cup with water, downed three and put three more in his hand, refilling the cup for Jennifer.

Tracy walked out of the shower as he crossed the dressing room. "Morning," she said, seemingly unaffected by their night of partying.

Steve grunted at her and ducked into Jennifer's room. He handed her the cup and the pills and grabbed his shirt off the floor, sliding it on while she downed the medicine.

"I'll be right back." Jennifer turned a little green as she headed to the bathroom.

Steve closed the closet door and stood when she returned to the bedroom.

"You don't look so good," she said.

"I forgot what a killer hangover tequila gives me." He closed his eyes.

Jennifer gave him a kiss. "I'm going back to bed," she said, and crawled under the covers.

"Bitch," he whispered.

When he let a slight curve grace his lips, she offered him a smile in return. "Bite me," she whispered back.

"Later," he said. "Don't forget noon today at the pub."

"I won't. I love you," she replied and closed her eyes.

Steve looked at her for a moment and then leaned over, kissing her cheek. "See you later, babe."

"Bye."

Steve left her bedroom, closing the door behind him. The smell of coffee drifted from the kitchen, and he followed it. Two cups were set on the counter. Tracy was bringing sugar and creamer to the island. "I figured you could use some."

"How come you're so chipper this morning?" Steve asked. Even his eyes hurt.

"I took aspirin before I went to bed last night."

"Smart girl." Steve picked up the coffee and drank it black.

"You really do love her," Tracy said, studying him.

"Yes," he said, glancing in her direction. "I always have. I just didn't know how much until I saw her again."

"I'm glad. She deserves the best." She sipped her coffee. "And you definitely fit the bill."

"I appreciate that Tracy," he said, rubbing his eyes. "I'll see you later. I have to clean up before class."

"Be careful," Tracy said, causing Steve's eyes to clear a fraction. He tilted his head and furrowed his brow. "Driving home," she said. "You still look a little under the influence."

"Ah." The confusion cleared from his mind and Steve smiled, shrugging. "Just hung over." He set the cup down in the sink and took off.

"Still, be careful."

Dark Reckoning
Chapter 32

JENNIFER WOKE TO A silent apartment. She stretched, glancing at the clock—it blinked eight minutes after ten. She needed to get moving, and she rolled off the bed, stepping into the closet, and flipping the light on to peruse the clothing for something more appropriate to wear to meet Steve's boss. The door swung closed, and she jumped, spinning toward the solid wood and reaching for the handle. The light flickered and went out.

Chilling air surrounded her, and the landscape of the closet changed. Crunchy moss scratched the soles of her feet. As she glanced over her shoulder, water glimmered in the distance. But everything else was black. Panic as thick as the darkness surrounding her pressed on her chest, constricting, binding, debilitating. She let out a small noise, reaching, fingertips grazing against the wood grain in front of her.

Hands pushed her against the door, both ice cold and burning hot scorching her skin, caressing her. Jennifer wheezed, her gasps creating a fog in the freezing air. Her hands clawed at the door, desperately seeking the doorknob as the thing in the closet pressed against her. The stench of fire and rotting flesh filled the air. The rank breath of the demon from her nightmares tickled her shoulder. It grabbed her wrists, searing the skin and bringing her arms over her head. "I promise you will scream for all eternity." It hissed and a scream mixing pain with terror shot from Jennifer's restricted lungs.

Jennifer sat up, shaking and dripping with sweat. The dream hung on like a frightened child. She glanced over at the closet and shivered at the wide-open door. Her foggy, hung-over mind clenched, and she blinked a few times, just staring at the door. Wasn't it closed this morning?

She bit her lip, swearing Steve had closed it before he left.

Didn't he?

Unsure of which parts of her memory were real and which were dreams, she stared at that opening.

"He closed it," she said to the empty room. Reluctantly, she tore her eyes away from the gaping closet and glanced at the clock. It was almost ten. She swung her legs out of the bed, giving the closet a wide berth. She opened the shades, spilling light into the room.

"Come on," she said, stubbornly shaking her head. "It was only a dream." She took a tentative step toward the closet. Like Flash Gordon, she reached in and flipped on the light.

Only clothes and shoes, see?

She scanned the rack from the safety of the bedroom. Her focus zoomed in on an outfit and again she shot in, ripped the outfit off the hanger, and hopped out.

255

Chuckling at her skittishness, she turned the light off, closing the closet door.

In the changing room, she caught a quick glance of herself in the mirror and stopped. Her heart hammered against the walls of her chest, and her reflection paled. Burn marks in the shape of fingers wrapped around both her wrists. The clothes dropped to the floor and her lungs started their slow restriction, strangling the breath from her. The world tilted to slow motion and her hand rose to move her hair away from her shoulder, the other picking up the vanity mirror. Jennifer turned, holding the looking glass so she could see the reflection of her back. Forcing her eyes to stay glued to the image, she moved the hair away. Her hand squeezed the handle of the mirror tight, and her eyes grew wide. The wheeze coming from her lungs now whistled in quick panting beats.

Red welts. Red welts in the shape of hands. Red welts exactly where it had touched her in the dream.

"Jesus."

Shaking, she receded into the shower, locking the door behind her and letting the hot steam clear her lungs. She ran the soap over her skin. The cucumber and melon scent drifted on the air, mingling with her fear, and her eyes never left the locked shower door. When she finished shampooing her hair, she turned the water off and wrapped a towel around herself, tentatively stepping out of the steam and into the cool room.

Jennifer dressed quickly and ran a brush through her hair. All the while, her heart rattled against her rib cage like a fluttering bird caught in an unfamiliar house.

She expected the thing to come bursting through the door at any moment and couldn't get out of the apartment fast enough. Hurrying down the hall, she grabbed her keys and slid the flip-flops by the door on her feet. She ripped open the door and let out a surprised yelp.

Bill stood with his fist inches from the wood, getting ready to knock. "Just the person I was looking for." He stepped into the doorway.

"Billy, I'm going to be late for my lunch date." She tried to scoot past him.

"Yes, you are." He closed the door behind him, blocking her escape.

"What the..." Jennifer began.

Bill punched her in the temple, and she went down cold.

The ritual had begun.

Dark Reckoning
Chapter 33

BILL SMILED AT HIS handiwork and glanced over his shoulder at the closed doors of the crypt Adam and Joe guarded. Until the moment he had Jennifer in the trunk of his car, he wasn't sure he'd be able to pull this off. Now, in the tomb's darkness, anticipation boiled in his blood. Goosebumps covered his skin at the sight of her laid out on the altar, unconscious, naked, helpless.

When he ran his fingertips over her bound body, she shivered under his touch. He stepped back, studying her. A frown crossed his lips. He moved closer, lifting her head and fanned her hair out on the gray stone.

Better.

Satisfied, he crossed into the shadows, letting the vision of her fill his eyes. Need swelled in him, and he reached for the small square package in his back pocket. Twirling it between his thumb and forefinger, he waited.

Jennifer's moan echoed in the chamber. Her head tilted away from the bright sun that spilled through the stained-glass windows, shading the room in a collage of colors. Her hand stopped short of her face, the shackle chain rattling and scraping against the stone. Her eyes fluttered open. Deep creases appeared in her forehead as her eyes darted from the mosaic painting of Paradise Cove in the ceiling to the painted window. When she lifted her head, another groan escaped her lips and her head bounced back on the stone with a thud. The swelling in her right temple had abated, but the ugly purple bruise stood out against her tanned skin.

"Lay back, Jen," Bill said, bringing her attention to him. He stepped out of the shadows, restlessly twirling the package in his hand.

"Where am I?" She glanced at her right hand, staring at the metal shackle around her wrist. Her head jerked to her restrained left hand, and her eyes went wide, falling back on Bill and the condom he held.

"In a mausoleum in the cemetery," Bill answered. Approaching her, he ran his hand up the inside of Jennifer's exposed thigh. "Anticipation—what an odd choice of words for you to home in on, yet such an accurate description." He stroked her.

Jennifer tried to jerk away from him, her breath hitching in her chest. "Don't."

Ignoring her plea, he continued stroking her with the back of his knuckles. "You are the annual sacrifice this year."

"What? What sacrifice?" she asked, turning her head to the right, taking in the rest of the mausoleum. Hanging from the wall were several bones in the shape of pentacles and on the floor was a large pentacle painted in red. Her tear-filled eyes landed back on Bill. "Please don't do this," she said.

He smiled and scanned her naked form. Lust clouded his mind, and he slid his finger inside her dry path, hard enough to make her breath hitch.

"You weren't supposed to fall for him, Jen, and you certainly weren't supposed to fuck him," he said, letting the anger and jealousy take over. He continued to slam his fingers inside her, the frustration growing. He glared at her, grinding his teeth. "Why's your cunt so dry today, Jen? The other night it was dripping wet."

A wrinkle appeared between her confused eyes.

"On the couch, you came for me. I wanted to bury my face in your pussy and suck the cum out of you." His eyes met her horrified glare. "Tracy would never have known—she was passed out drunk in the bedroom."

Jennifer's lower lip quivered, and the tears slid down her cheeks. She shook her head, unable to speak.

Bill sighed. "Instead, I went and fucked her. I didn't care that she was unconscious. It was better than screwing this up. But now, now that I've got you here." Leaning over, he parted her with his hands and ran his tongue inside her, tasting her. At the same time, he ran his hand up her trembling stomach until he reached the soft mounds of her chest. He squeezed, pinching her nipples until tears sprang from her eyes.

"Billy, please don't do this!"

Standing, he licked his lips and pulled his hand away, laughing at the dying hope that flared in her eyes. "Ever since the day we met I've wanted to fuck you, and you were dead wrong about it never happening." He waved the condom pack. "As much as I want to slip this on and fuck you right now, I will have to wait until the ritual begins." He tossed the condom package onto her bare stomach. "Tonight, we all get to fuck you."

"No!" Jennifer screamed.

Bill laughed, meeting her fiery gaze and reveling in her fear. He gave a curt nod. "You're Beta Theta Pi's whore now."

"You son of a bitch!" Jennifer screamed, struggling to get free. "Steve is going to kill you."

Bill laughed. "Not if I kill him first," he said, and knocked on the door. "We'll be back tonight for the main event." He smiled over his shoulder at her as the doors opened, filtering light in.

Jennifer let out a shriek that carried out the door with Bill.

THE DOORS TO THE crypt closed, leaving her sobbing on the cold stone, with a cold certainty that she would never see the light of day again.

Dark Reckoning
Chapter 34

STEVE SAT IN THE student center pub, looking from his watch to the door and back. Murphy waited, impatiently drumming his fingers on the tabletop.

"Where is she?" Murphy asked, looking up at the clock. It was a quarter after twelve.

Steve shook his head. "I don't know. She said she'd be here." He pulled out his cell phone and dialed her number. It rang and dumped into voicemail. "Hey, babe, waiting for you in the pub." He snapped the phone shut. The uneasiness got the best of him. He called the apartment and listened as Tracy's and Jennifer's voices announced they couldn't come to the phone right now. He hung up in frustration, glancing over at Murphy.

"Do I need to put out an APB?" Murphy asked.

"She might just be fashionably late," he said, even though his gut told him otherwise. "You've got the safe house ready, right?"

"Yes. Are you all set for tonight?"

Steve nodded. "I still don't know the details, though." He glanced at his watch again and opened the phone, scrolling through the numbers. He pressed the call button and put the phone to his ear. "Hey, Tracy, Jen was supposed to meet me for lunch. Do you know where she might be?" He closed his eyes. "Okay, I'll try her cell again." He shook his head. "She doesn't know where Jen is," he said to Murphy and got up, dropping a twenty on the table. His insides knotted. Coiled rattlers struck, their sharp fangs piercing his stomach, their rancid poison burning. That burning sensation generated a certainty that something had gone terribly wrong.

His walk turned into a run as he made a beeline out of the student center toward his car. Murphy caught him by the arm, halting his progress. Steve yanked his arm away. Visions clouded his mind—visions of Jennifer lying in her room, unable to get to the phone, unable to get away from the sinister thing in her closet, unable to breathe.

"She was fine when I left her this morning." He continued toward his car.

Murphy grabbed his arm again. "I'm taking you off this case."

"The hell you are," Steve snapped, turning on Murphy. "She wouldn't just blow me off, Murph." He started toward the car again and stopped after a few steps. "You coming?"

Murphy shook his head, glancing at his watch. "I've got a conference call with my boss in fifteen minutes. As soon as you find her, let me know."

Steve got into his car and pulled out his gun, checked the clip, and slipped it back into place under the seat. He threw the car into gear, flying over to the apartment. Her car was still in the lot and his heart leaped into his throat. He jogged into the building and waited impatiently for the elevator.

"Come on, come on, come on." The numbers crawled, declining one by one as if time had stopped and restarted in jerking succession.

He closed his eyes. When the ascent began, his entire body tensed like a leopard ready to strike, and when the elevator opened on the top floor, he darted to the door. Knocking and pressing the doorbell in tandem, he closed his eyes, inhaling to calm his racing heart.

"Fuck it." He pulled out a credit card and slid it between the door and the jam. Closing his eyes, he felt for the curve of the handle. It took him a few minutes to finagle the lock, and then the door sailed open, banging against the wall. Steve stepped inside, yelling her name. He covered every inch of the apartment twice, including her closet.

She wasn't there.

Icy fingers wrapped around his heart, squeezing slowly.

"Damn, damn, damn," he repeated under his breath, turning in a circle in the living room.

He stepped into the hallway, surveying the ceiling until he found what he was looking for. He closed his eyes and hung his head for a moment. A fragment of relief flooded through him, tempering the chill in his heart.

Cameras, surveillance cameras. Thank god.

He needed those security tapes. He walked into the rental office on the first floor and realized he didn't have his badge. Instead of playing the FBI card, he improvised, smiling at the rental agent.

"Hi, I'm doing a story for the school paper about building security. Can you help me out and give me a tour of your security office and set up?" he asked, flashing his student ID. "Tammy," he added, glancing at her nametag.

"Sure. I've seen you around here a few times, haven't I?"

Steve flashed a brilliant smile and nodded. "My girlfriend lives in the penthouse—she's the one who suggested I talk to you. She said there are surveillance cameras all over the place in this building."

"It's standard these days to have cameras mounted in the hallways, elevators, and lobby, as well as in the parking lot, especially since the front doors aren't locked during the day."

Steve nodded, taking a small pad off the desk along with a pen, and jotted down notes regarding the camera locations. "What time do you lock the doors?" he asked as she motioned for him to follow her into the back hallway.

"We lock the doors from eight at night to eight in the morning." She smiled over her shoulder.

"How many cameras do you have in operation?" he asked as they went down a narrow stairwell and into a small room with six monitors.

"Six." She pointed, smiling at him. "We record video, but no audio."

"How long do you keep the recordings?" he asked.

"We have a rolling seven day recording process. Each disc represents a twenty-four-hour period."

"Do you ever review the tapes randomly?" he asked.

She blushed. "We sometimes spot check."

"Can you show me how it works?" He pointed to the recorder.

"I don't know." She bit her lip, looking from him to the control panel.

"Come on, we can check out what time I left the penthouse this morning."

She nodded and rewound the tape for the penthouse hallway. Something flashed across the screen quickly, then there was another flash, and finally she slowed the tape down. She found the spot on the tape where he'd left, slightly disheveled and hung over—a far cry from his current neat appearance.

"Can I try?" he asked.

Tammy hesitated, glancing between him and the monitor.

"I felt as bad as I looked." He pointed at the frozen picture. "We went to The Dean's Office last night."

She offered a knowing smile. "Ah. You recovered well." She ran her eyes over him and sighed. Nodding, she agreed, and Steve sat down at the control board.

He looked up at her for confirmation as he moved the controller back and forth, rewinding and forwarding the tape.

"That's right," she said. The buzzer went off, and she glanced at the monitor for the rental office camera. "I'm sorry. I have a customer in the office."

Steve turned. "Can I just write down the make and models of your cameras and system?" he asked. "I'll come right up when I'm done, I promise." He offered his irresistible smile.

Nodding, Tammy scurried out of the room.

Steve shook his head. *Security around here is pathetically loose.* He focused back on the video camera, fast-forwarding. Stopping, he rewound and played, watching Tracy leave the apartment a few minutes after he had. The second pass in fast forward. Another flash crossed the screen, and he rewound, stabbing the play button just before the anomaly.

His fists slowly closed into tight balls as he watched the screen. Bill stepped into the apartment, blocking Jennifer, and closed the door. The clock on the counter said it was eleven-thirty. Minutes later, he came walking out with Jennifer over his shoulder. She was out cold. "Fuck!" Steve popped the disc out, slipping it into a case, and slid it into the waistband of his shorts, pulling his shirt over it. He replaced it with a disc from a couple of days before, pressing record before he took the stairs three at a time. He closed his eyes at the landing, taking a deep breath to compose himself. With a smile plastered on his lips, he stepped into the office. "Thank you, Tammy," he said, putting her pad and pen back on the counter.

She smiled offhandedly at him and continued answering her customer's questions.

Steve walked out to his car and flipped the phone open. He stabbed the speed dial and waited.

"I'm on the other line," Murphy said.

"You need to subpoena the video surveillance at the apartment," he growled into the receiver. "Bill Tyler has Jennifer." He closed his eyes. "I've got the proof—the surveillance tape of him taking her is in my hands right now." He pulled the disc out and slipped it into the glove compartment. "It's in my car." He listened to Murphy swear. "Just get the damn subpoena so we can get the lobby and parking lot tapes."

"Where are you going?" Murphy asked.

"I'm going to get Jennifer." Steve glanced in his rearview mirror.

"It'll take me a couple of hours to get the subpoena, so don't do anything stupid."

"Why the fuck is there a tail on me?"

"To cover your ass," Murphy said.

"If he keeps following me, I'll shoot him." Steve hung up the phone. He swung out of the parking lot, shifting gears and outmaneuvering the tail. He took the twists and turns leading to his grandfather's place and slammed to a stop in front of the cabin. Jumping from the car, he lined his gun up to the last curve in the driveway, aiming where he expected the undercover FBI agent to pull into view. The sound of crunching gravel under the hum of an engine got closer, and Steve wasn't disappointed.

The agent's eyes widened, and he slammed on the brakes.

Steve stood down, setting the safety on the gun, and slid it into his beltline. Without another look at the shaken agent, he headed into the cottage.

He changed into a pair of loose jeans and clipped the gun to the inside of his right calf. The other calf sported his grandfather's hunting knife. His work boots covered the bulge when he stood, letting the pant legs fall. His handcuffs sat on the nightstand, and he opened the drawer, scooping up his badge before he swiped the handcuffs, tucking them both in the inside pocket of his brown suede jacket.

His jaw ached, and he took a deep breath, unclenching his teeth.

I swear if he's hurt you...

Steve looked at the ceiling of the cabin, stretched his fingers and cracked his neck, psyching himself into character. This had to be an academy award-winning performance. Otherwise, he'd never find out what happened to Jennifer.

Stepping out of the cabin, Steve stopped. The agent had been bold enough to park next to Steve's car. He leaned on his hood in the telltale FBI suit, his arms crossed, and his eyes shielded by the FBI issued shades.

"Murphy wants you to stay put until he gets here."

"Fuck you," Steve said, and walked past him.

The agent grabbed Steve's arm and Steve parried, twisting the agent's arm and forcing him face first on the hood of the car. Steve kept the agent pinned and leaned in. "I'm not backing off. Tell Murphy he can throw me to the wolves when this is done, but for now, he's going to have to trust me. He knows damn well we don't have an airtight case yet and I'm not waiting until we find my girlfriend's body to get the son of a bitch." He let go of the agent. "Tell him he can have my badge when this is through." Steve walked to his car and got in, reached into the glove compartment, and handed the disc to the agent. Then he peeled out of the yard.

Pulling up to the fraternity, Steve sat in his car, staring at the Greek insignia for a moment, reigning in the wild beast pounding on the doors of his soul. At least he didn't have to *act* like he was in a foul mood. He slammed the car door and stormed into the house, going straight to his room.

It only took a few minutes before knuckles rapped on his door and Steve closed his eyes, praying it wasn't Bill because he wasn't sure he could pull this off. Not with the angry beast roiling in his gut.

"What?" Steve snapped and yanked open the door.

Joe stood in the hallway and blinked, trying to hide his discomfort with concern. "You okay?"

Steve shrugged, staring out the window at the cemetery beyond the expansive yard. "She stood me up. No one has ever stood me up."

"I'm sorry, dude. Women can be a little fickle."

"Fickle? She's not even answering my calls. I don't know what the hell I did." He crossed the room and sat on the bed. "Everything was fine when I left this morning." He looked up at Joe, wondering just how much he knew about what was going on.

"Come have a beer with us," Joe said. "We're talking to the pledges about the initiation ceremony."

"What do you do for initiation?" Steve stood and followed him down the stairs, bracing himself at the sight of Bill.

"Camping. There's an old creepy legend about a spot on the lake and we dare them to go take a picture. They've got to show us the Polaroid before we initiate them. Of course, that's after we've told them all the gory details of the legend. The idea is to spook them enough to weed out the skittish ones." He laughed as he rounded the corner and hopped down the stairs. "Let me grab you a beer." He disappeared into the kitchen and Steve sat down as far away from Bill as the room allowed.

A few minutes later, Joe came out with two Coronas, one with a lime stuck in the bottle's neck and the other with a lime already floating at the bottom of the bottle. Joe took a sip of the one with the already floating lime and plugged the top of the other with his thumb and turned it over. Once the lime drifted to the bottom, he turned it right side up and handed it to Steve.

Steve took a swig, tasting an underlying bitterness, and held the bottle out to look at it. Glancing at Joe, he tried to place the taste, but all that came to mind was witches and ancient taverns. "You sure this is okay?"

Joe nodded. "The limes are a little tart." He shrugged and downed his beer.

Following suit, Steve drained the beer and handed Joe the empty bottle. "I think I'm going to head back upstairs," he said. "I'm not really in the mood for a party." He stood, and his stomach did a small flip. It took a second for his brain to catch up. "Shit," he said, and the room tilted. His gaze landed on Bill's Cheshire grin just before his knees buckled.

"What the fuck did you give me?" Steve asked as the room slowly flowed in and out of focus like an amoeba and his muscles refused to listen to his mind's orders. The faces elongated and flowed into psychedelic colors. He blinked in slow motion; the back of his eyelids took forever to come back up.

"Combo of Peyote and LSD and a roofie just because I don't want a fight," Bill said. "It should wear off in time for you to take part in our little ritual."

"Son of a bitch," Steve mumbled. His muscles felt like someone hung a two-ton weight on each wrist to the point he couldn't lift his arms. A slow understanding took hold, and he did his best to keep the glare in his gaze. "What did you do with her?" he whispered, but no one caught his question.

They were too busy stripping his jacket and shirt and holding him steady while others blindfolded him. A cool wet substance brushed against his chest and face, and he was helpless to flinch away. Every muscle ignored his silent commands to fight, to strike out before it was too late, even when his wrists were bound behind his back.

His brain fogged, and the colors played on his eyelids, distracting him. Vague sensations on his skin dimmed, and numbness replaced it. Pink Floyd filled his head, and he blinked his eyes open against the blindfold before they fluttered closed again. The music took physical shapes under his eyelids, and he drifted, enamored with the colors and music.

BILL DRAGGED HIM OUT the back door, throwing him into the backseat of his car along with his coat and shirt. Joe slid into the passenger seat, and they headed to the crypt.

"This mother's heavy," Joe muttered as Bill unlocked the mausoleum, holding the door as Joe dragged Steve into the room. He dumped him on the ground.

"Please help me, Joe," Jennifer begged.

Joe traded a glance with Bill and walked out the door, ignoring her.

"What the hell did you do to him?" Jennifer screamed.

"Gave him a little cocktail," Bill said, tossing Steve's shirt and coat into the corner where her pocketbook lay. "And he will do just about anything we say once the initial paralysis wears off. See you in a few hours." He grinned and left with her tied to the rock with Steve unconscious on the floor.

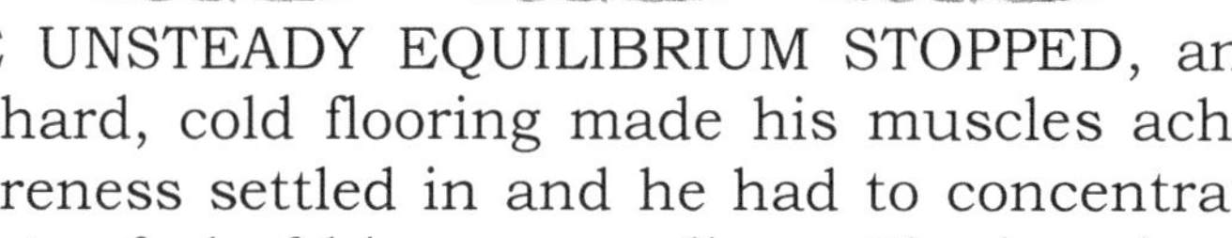

THE UNSTEADY EQUILIBRIUM STOPPED, and the hard, cold flooring made his muscles ache. Awareness settled in and he had to concentrate to get a feel of his surroundings. The imaginary colors still bloomed on his eyelids to the beat of the music, drowning out all cognitive thought. His mind jumped from one thing to the next as fluidly as an Olympic gymnast did until one word registered like a slap.

Jennifer.

A fucking roofie. Shit, how long does this last? If he was this bad off, there would be no stopping whatever those assholes had in mind. His breath grew harsh under the blaring music pumping in his ears. Focusing, he used the ground to dislodge the headphones, and with each movement, a new swell of disorientation took hold. *Roofies and LSD. Fuck.*

The headset fell from his ears, thumping on the floor behind him. Music still blared from the speakers, filling the small space, but he caught another noise in the room and tilted his head. Soft sobs sounded from behind him, and his heart hit an adrenalin high, pumping blood faster through his system. His arms and legs throbbed in time with his heartbeat.

He rolled toward the noise, pinning his bound arms under his back. "Jesus-fucking-Christ," he hissed and rolled back on his side, testing the bonds that held his wrists together. A measure of relief flooded him when he realized his wrists had some give, meaning it was rope or tape and not the metal of handcuffs.

"Jen, are we alone?" he asked, hoping he was right, and it was indeed her in the room.

"Yes."

Her sob sent both relief and fear through him, giving him a little more control over his faculties. He worked his wrists in small circles, forcing pressure against the bindings.

"What are you doing?"

"I'm trying to get some slack so I can get my hands in front of me."

"Why?"

"So, I can cut whatever they tied me with." *Assuming I still have my knife.* The thought produced a moment of panic and he put his forehead to the floor, breathing through the debilitating attack locking his muscles into painful knots.

"It's duct tape," Jennifer answered. "What the hell did they do to you?"

He sighed and continued the rolling of his wrists, stretching the tape. "They drugged me. I'm tripping on LSD, peyote and roofies. At least, that's what they told me before I blacked out."

"You're high?"

"As a fucking kite." He rolled onto his back, pulled his knees to his chest, and then attempted to slide his wrists under his ass. His wrists caught at the back of his hips, and he bellowed his frustration, pushing his seized muscles farther until he thought his shoulders were going to break. Just when he thought his arms wouldn't budge any farther, they jerked forward, slamming into the back of his folded knees.

The exertion exhausted him, and colors bloomed again, taking control of his concentration. He relaxed, laying his head back on the floor and just breathed. The colors swirled around him, adding a spin to their hypnotic quality, and his stomach followed suit, clenching and squeezing a moan from his throat.

"Are you okay?"

The concern in her voice cut through the fog, and he shook his head. "No," he said between clenched teeth, willing a lock-down on his stomach. When he was sure he wouldn't vomit, he curled, using his knees to push the blindfold up onto his forehead.

Light blinded him, and he clenched his eyes closed. Relaxing back on the floor and counting again. He blinked his eyes open, staring at a mural of Paradise Cove.

"Where are we?" His voice distorted in his own ears.

"In the cemetery," Jennifer sniffled. "In one of the mausoleums."

"That's fucking morbid." He ran his hands along his jeans, down his shins, and exhaled the breath he held in trepidation. His weapons were still there, and the release of tension put the room into a tailspin. "Oh, Jesus," he gagged, clamping his teeth together and swallowing the acid burning his esophagus.

When he closed his eyes this time, vivid visions of satanic rituals involving Jennifer danced across his eyelids, filling his entire form with a fear he couldn't contain. The demon from his research chuckled in his ear and then drew closer to Jennifer, harmful intent in his form, and Steve growled, lunging forward in the dream before being backhanded into blackness.

"Steve!"

Her scream cut through the hallucination, and he blinked his eyes open, disoriented. "God damn it," he muttered, admonishing himself until his gaze landed on the bones on the wall. He stared, shock waves rang through his head until her gentle sobs caught his attention.

He swung his head in the direction and all he could see was a wall of rock. "Jen?"

The scraping of chains filled the room and her face appeared briefly over the edge of the rock.

"What the hell?" He studied his surroundings a little closer. "Ah, fuck," he swore and rocked into a sitting position. He almost fell back over from the head rush. "Whoa," he whispered, trying to steady the sudden warp of the room. He glanced in her direction again, clearly making out the altar she was chained to.

He dropped his head to his knees, unable to consider the ramifications of their situation; instead, he concentrated on getting his pant leg up enough to access his hunting knife. Swirling colors in his peripheral vision kept distracting him from his goal, and he bit down on the insane urge to giggle.

"What are you doing now?"

"I've got a knife," Steve answered. The knife was now in view, and he pulled it out of the sheath. It immediately clattered to the floor. "Shit," he muttered and picked it back up.

"What..."

"Shush!" Steve interrupted. "I don't want to slice my wrist open, so be quiet." Ever so slowly, he ran the blade back and forth over the tape, intently concentrating. When the bindings finally gave, he closed his eyes and sat a moment, getting his bearings. Opening his eyes, he blew out a stream of air and tucked the knife back in the sheath, covering it with his pant leg again.

Steve stripped the tape from his wrists and stood.

The world of swirling colors tipped, and he lost his balance, side stepping until he slammed into the outer wall. He put his hand on the cool cement until the spinning stopped, and then he turned in her direction.

He was not prepared for the full view of her, and his knees buckled, dropping him to the floor as devastation crushed his chest. The room wobbled as tears filled his eyes. He stood, stumbling toward her. "Oh, baby." He picked up the chain holding her wrist, his dazed gaze transitioning from the bindings to her face and back.

Tears streamed down her cheeks. "He hurt me, Steve, and when they get back…" Her voice broke into choking sobs. "When they get back, he said they all get to…" Another sob. "He said I'm Beta Theta Pi's whore now."

Her words cut through the drugs, and Steve tensed, his hand clenching around the metal. His mind reeling, and the words surfaced, bringing her back into focus. "How did he hurt you?" His voice was low and deadly, matching the fury lining his cobalt eyes.

"He hit me and he…" She looked up at the ceiling, trying to find the right words.

"Did he rape you?"

"No, not the way you're thinking. He molested me here and told me he did the same thing the night I had the dream about you. He took advantage of me on the couch while I was asleep." Tears filled her eyes as she met his gaze. "But he's going to. They all are going to."

"Over my dead body," he growled, watching the slow track of tears leak from her eyes.

The full force of her words crashed down on him like a wrecking ball and his legs wobbled under him. The drugs crumbled what little composure he had, and he fell to the floor under the hurricane brewing in his heart and soul. Anger, devastation, fury, sorrow, rage, and grief alternated, sweeping through him at an unparalleled speed. His harsh sobs echoed in the chamber in between curses and vows of violence spewing from him, drowning out the music still pumping from the headset.

Shadows danced on the floor, catching his attention, and his sobs caught in his throat. "I'm sorry, Jen," he said, pulling himself to his feet and wiping his face.

Jennifer smiled a little. "It's okay," she said.

Steve shook his head. Even as high as he was, he knew it was definitely not okay. "It is as far away from okay as it gets. I need to sober up and get you out of here before it's too late." He scanned her naked form, unable to contemplate what would happen if he couldn't. "What time is it?" he asked, holding his watch out for her to look at.

"Almost seven," Jennifer answered. "It'll be dark in a couple of hours." She looked up at the stain glass window.

"Jesus, you're telling me I lost six and a half hours?" The room tilted.

"I thought you were dead when they first brought you in," she whispered, and her voice hitched.

He cradled her cheek in his hand. The mere touch sent tendrils of fire through him. "I told you, I'm not dying today, and neither are you." He scanned the room again and his gaze landed on his coat. He stumbled forward and stood over the crumpled material. He clean missed the fabric, jamming his fingers into the floor on his first attempt to pick up the coat. "Damn it," he muttered and tried again, this time fabric scrunched in his fist, and he fumbled with the coat, finding the zipped interior pocket. The zipper proved difficult, and the coat dropped from his grip.

A giggle caught his attention, and he glanced at her. "I know, I must be a walking comedy show right now," he smiled in her direction and then focused back on his jacket. This time he was successful, and he felt around in the pocket for his cell, but only his badge and wallet were still inside. "Fuck!"

He closed his eyes and focused, fumbling with the other pockets until his hand clamped down on a small square object. He yanked his cell out of the pocket and grinned, holding in the air like a prize. His euphoria vanished the moment he flipped the phone open. Nothing happened. He pushed the on button and the phone turned on, but immediately blinked off.

"Shit," he said, and looked at the phone again. "It's dead." He turned and kicked the headphones, sending them sailing across the room where they smashed into the wall and were silent.

"Check mine. It rang a few times earlier. It's in my pocketbook on the floor." She pointed her chin in the direction.

Steve picked up her purse and dumped it on the floor. He kneeled, staring at the swirling contents. Bright colors leaped out at him, capturing his attention.

"Steve!" she yelled sharply, catapulting him back to reality.

Steve nodded and reached for the cell phone. He missed and glanced at Jennifer. "I'm surprised the combination of drugs didn't kill me," he said, "Especially since I'm still having real problems after six hours." He tried again, and this time he succeeded in grasping the phone. "I can't see the numbers," he muttered and just pressed redial, holding the phone to his ear and hoping it wasn't calling his phone.

"Jen?" Tracy's voice filled the line.

"Hey, Tracy." Steve heard the shuffle of the phone.

"Hey, Steve, how's it going?" Bill asked.

Steve didn't react at first, but his blood pumped with poisonous venom. He stared at Jennifer. "I'm going to kill you, you son of a bitch," he growled into the phone.

"I see you found her. That's good." The phone muffled again as Bill put his hand over the receiver and asked Tracy to fix him a sandwich.

Steve saw red as he listened to the silence, imagining Tracy walking into the kitchen out of earshot. Moments later, a small chuckle came over the phone line.

"I can't wait to fuck her," Bill taunted.

Steve roared and pitched the phone across the room, where it shattered against the concrete. He paced like a caged lion, muttering ream after ream of curses. The fury radiated from him, filling the room with his echoing rant.

Dark Reckoning
Chapter 35

"WHO ARE YOU GOING to fuck?" Tracy asked, standing in the doorway to the kitchen.

Bill closed the phone, his smile fading. "What?" he asked, scrambling for an answer.

"You heard me—who are you going to fuck?"

Bill stormed inside and put his hand over her mouth. "Stop yelling," he snapped in disgust.

Tracy's eyes went wide, and her mouth dropped open under his hand.

He'd never treated her that way before, and confusion and fear filled her eyes. For a moment, he recoiled, dropping his hand. Then the nuance of change in her eyes, transitioning from fear to fury, fueled his ego, thrilling him as much as Jennifer's pleas had.

"Who?"

Bill tossed around whether to answer her and decided it would be worth it to see her reaction. "Jennifer."

"Jennifer who?" Tracy snapped.

"Your roommate," Bill grinned, and he actually saw the click in her eyes when everything fell into place. The shadow that passed over Tracy's features made him take a step backwards. The fear of the ritual going to hell and his resulting death clouded his brain like an adrenalin shot to the heart.

"Jennifer would never sleep with you. Ever."

He cocked his head in a silent dare. "That's what you think."

"What did you do with them?" She took a threatening step forward, and Bill took another step back.

"Nothing yet," Bill answered with a cold, calculating smile. "But that's going to change in about an hour."

"You can't do this, Bill. You can't!"

The last remnants of the man he used to be faded along with his humanity, shriveling up into a dry husk at the core of his being.

"I can and I will," Bill shot back, the excuses tumbling from his lips. "She was supposed to die two years ago. But no, Tom had to be the fucking white knight and trade his life for hers. This time, there's no one to make a bargain, and it wants both of them."

"I can't let you do that," Tracy said, advancing another step. "I won't."

Bill laughed at her, and she launched at him, a roar hissing from her mouth. He sidestepped, sticking his foot out, and she tripped, catapulting, spinning. The railing hit hip high and the force of the collision flipped her over the side. Her hands reached desperately for the railing and the sound of her nails scraping the metal gave him a start, like nails dragging down a chalkboard. Grinding his teeth, he watched her fall; her curses fading until her body hit the pavement with a wet slap, silencing her in a bloody bath.

Flipping open her phone, he dialed nine-one-one. "Someone just took a dive off the Brooksfield Heights apartment building." He hung up, wiped it, tossed it on the couch, and left the building by way of the back stairwell.

Dark Reckoning
Chapter 36

J ENNIFER CLOSED HER EYES as she listened to Steve ramble off expletive after expletive. Suddenly, the room shifted.

Tracy.

Tracy falling through the air with Bill's face smiling over the railing, getting farther and farther away.

Tracy screaming and then the scream cut off on impact, replaced by a silent black shroud.

"Oh god, oh god, oh god, oh god!" Her breath wheezed with each repetition.

Steve stopped pacing, swiped his jacked off the floor, and stepped to her side. He covered her with the coat and wiped her tears, staring at the wet droplets as they rolled over his fingers. He moved his gaze to hers. She still repeated the incantation, her entire body shaking. "What? What'd you see?"

"He killed Tracy."

Steve blinked. A crease appeared between his eyes. "No, Tracy was just on the phone." He shook his head, meeting her gaze.

Jennifer sobbed and nodded. "He threw her off the balcony. I saw it, Steve. I saw her die. Oh god, Steve, Tracy's dead."

Steve stepped back, shaking his head. "Uh-uh."

"They're going to kill us, too."

A slap wouldn't have been as effective as those six words, and Steve's jaw tightened. This time, he shook his head violently. "No, they aren't." He crossed the space between them and sat on the side of the altar next to her, placing his hand on her abdomen. "I won't let that happen. I promise." He touched her face and kissed her gently. "I promise no one will hurt you again."

"Don't make me promises you know you can't keep."

DESPAIR TOOK HOLD OF him, the drugs magnifying the emotion, and he closed his eyes, hanging his head.

Can I keep her safe?

In this condition?

Are you kidding me?

The trembling started in his hands and worked its way through his body. The truth was too much for him to bear and he turned away from her, clinging to the cold stone as silent tears trickled down his cheeks.

"Don't do this, Steve, please don't do this," Jennifer whispered, gaining his attention. "I need you."

Steve turned toward her, his gaze falling on the ugly bruise surrounding her eye, and his shaking fingers traced the black and blue pattern Bill had left earlier in the day. Beyond despair, his eyes met hers.

I should have followed my gut. I shouldn't have left you this morning. I should have taken you into custody to keep you safe.

"I'm so sorry." His voice shook. "Jenny, I am so, so sorry." He leaned forward, gently kissing each bruise, dropping hot tears on her skin.

"Please." Jennifer's voice trembled. "I need to know…" she trailed off and swallowed. "I need to know you love me. I need to know you will, no matter what happens tonight." The film of tears shone brightly in her eyes before the liquid spilled over, lining her cheeks and pooling in her ears.

"Ah, baby, I'll love you until I take my last breath." Steve kissed her with all the tenderness he could muster. He pulled away, her soulful eyes begged for a way out, and he sighed, resting his hands on her waist. The rightness of her burned under his skin and he silently vowed to get her out of this alive. Somehow. Someway.

"You still think a monster is at the heart of this?" he asked. He no longer believed in demons from hell—only demons pretending to be human beings.

"Yes," she answered and rolled, showing him her back.

His gaze landed on the scalded skin in the form of handprints, and he recoiled.

"I had another nightmare this morning and when I woke, the closet was open, and these were on my shoulders." She settled on her back on the stone again.

The lore leaped to the forefront of his mind, and he slumped on the stone next to her, picking up her wrist and inspecting the shackle. The keyhole drifted in and out of focus, and he cursed under his breath. "I could try to shoot the chains." He met her gaze. "But if I missed…"

"How many bullets are in your gun?"

"Six."

Her chin trembled. "In your condition, even if we were lucky enough to get me out of these with four shots, two bullets aren't enough to stop them."

He stood and paced until he stumbled. Working the lore, looking for weak points and ways out of this morbid ritual, they were hell bent on performing.

If the demon truly existed, there was only one thing Steve found that could damn him back to hell.

Spilling Abinaqui blood on sacred ground.

He glanced at Jennifer. "I know how to stop the demon."

Her eyes widened. "How?"

"Did you know that I've got Abinaqui blood in my lineage?"

Her eyebrows shot into confused arches.

He glanced at the door. "Heaven help anyone who touches you."

The last of the daylight faded, leaving them entombed in the dark.

Dark Reckoning
Chapter 37

BILL WALTZED INTO THE fraternity, whistling and carrying a bag with the last item they'd need. He looked up at the clock and then his gaze dropped to the senior members of the fraternity lounging in the living area. "We need to get the pledges out to the campsite and then the real games begin." Walking into the kitchen, he put the bag in the corner by the back door and scanned the eager pledges. "You all ready?" He smiled when each and every one of them nodded.

They filtered out, and all piled into the seniors' cars, following him as he drove onto an obscure dirt road that led to a small clearing where everyone parked. It was roughly a mile between Paradise Cove and Black Cove. He got out and pulled a couple of tents from his trunk.

Adam and Joe pulled tents out of their trunks and laid them out on the ground.

Bill set the groceries and the coolers near the tents. "Your mission tonight to complete your acceptance into Beta Theta Pi is to follow that path to Paradise Cove and get a picture of the reflection in the water with these Polaroid cameras. If you are daring, you can follow the small stream to Black Cove and bring us back a picture of that as well. If you bring a photo of Black Cove back, you'll never have to pay fraternity dues." He looked around the group. "We'll be back before midnight. Anyone with pictures will take part in the initiation ceremony. All those who don't return by then, well, you'll have to walk back to campus." He tilted his head and smiled. "Oh, and one more thing—each of you has to go alone." They all nodded. "You might want to pitch those tents and get a campfire going before you take off. There are hot dogs, beer, and stuff to make s'mores. I expect there will be some for us when we get here, right?"

The pledges nodded in agreement.

"We'll be back," he said.

The senior fraternity members retreated to their cars and headed out. They parked near the entrance of the dirt road and looked at each other while they waited just inside the woods, out of sight. A van slowed at the entrance and stopped just beyond the group. The side door slid open, and they piled in.

"Hey, Jake." Bill smiled at the driver. He was the former president of the fraternity and passed the torch to Bill when he left.

"Hey." Jake looked over as Bill took the passenger seat. "Who do we have this year?" he asked as the side door closed.

"Jenny," Bill said.

Jake swerved a little and looked at Bill. "She was off limits," he said. "Tom traded his life for hers."

Bill nodded. "That was two years ago. Things change."

"Jesus," Jake said, and glanced over at Bill. "Jesus." He slowly smiled and glanced in the rearview mirror. All the senior members were nodding.

"Yeah, man, we finally get to do everything we ever wanted with her." Adam smiled into the mirror.

"Speaking of that, did you stop and pick up the package by the back door?" Bill asked.

"Yeah, but I don't understand."

"That was the directive. She needs to be clean." He shrugged.

Jake looked at him for a moment and the next thought sent quivers down his spine. "You don't think..." he trailed off and physically shivered in the seat.

Bill laughed. "Yeah, well, everybody wants to fuck that piece of ass." He looked in back. "We also have someone else in the crypt."

Jake glanced over at Bill. "Who's that?"

"Jenny's boyfriend. But he's all doped up on Peyote and LSD. He won't feel a thing when we cut him."

"We aren't cutting her?" Jake asked. This was so different from the past sacrifices he'd been involved in. The girl was always used, and she was the one cut up.

"No," Bill said. "She's not to have a scratch on her," he replied. "Well, she'll be bruised." He grinned. "But that's acceptable."

Jake glanced at Bill, and then back at the ten other members of the fraternity as he pulled into the cemetery.

Dark Reckoning
Chapter 38

"STEVE?" SHE ASKED, HER eyes still scrunched in confusion.

He didn't want to burden her with the details of the plan forming in his mind. It meant he had to be alive and awake and get them as near to Mirror Lake as possible.

Now all his grandfather's warnings made sense. Although, if spilling their blood was a way to send this beast back to hell, then why didn't he or any of the others before him make the sacrifice?

He huffed. It was simple. None of them really believed in the lore. Superstitious, yes, but taking the leap to believing in a demon, no, none of them went that far.

Now it was up to him.

He reached down and un-holstered his gun, setting it on the side of the altar. Slipping off the rock, he leaned down and brushed her lips with his. "I need to get my shit together before they come. I'm going to take down as many as I can. Maybe I'll get lucky," he smiled. "But in case I'm not, I want you to know I love you and I tried."

Jennifer bit her lip, stifling the tears. "I know."

Stepping to the middle of the mausoleum, he did karate forms.

HIS BALANCE WAS OFF, but the forms were still beautiful to watch in the dim moonlight and her vision blurred. She didn't know what he had in mind, but the willingness to put himself between her and the hungry frat boys sent fear through her. What if he couldn't stop them?

She closed her eyes on all the what-ifs drifting in her head, and let the exhaustion yank her under.

He reeled into the clearing, sidestepping away from the black water as he snapped the picture. He laughed to himself and turned to head back the way he had come. A claw shot out of the dark, ripping through his flesh. He fell to his knees as the dark figure lifted his arm again.

Jennifer screamed and tried to sit up. "No, no, no, no." She sobbed in the dark.

"What's wrong?" Steve said, immediately standing next to her.

"It got someone else." The chains vibrated on the stone as she shook. "It just killed someone else."

Steve put his hand on her stomach. "I will not let it get you, Jen. I'll die before I let that happen."

That's exactly what she was afraid of.

The slam of a car door outside the crypt brought both of them to their present situation.

"Love you." He kissed her and stepped away with the gun in his hand, aimed at the door, unaware that he now stood in the middle of the pentacle.

Dark Reckoning
Chapter 39

THE DOORS SWUNG OPEN and the report of a gunshot made Bill spin from his perch in the van. Adam paused in the entrance, and a second shot sounded. This time Adam's head snapped with the force of the bullet, and he fell backwards, a hole smoking between his eyes.

Bill glanced at Jake and Joe, the fear pumping hot fuel through his blood. The rest of the brothers hugged the building walls outside the doors, their expressions mimicking both Joe and Jake. Horror, shock, fear, and all eyes landed on the van for further direction.

"He has a gun?" Jake asked, looking from one frat member to the next.

"Apparently." Bill glanced at Adam. "And he's either a damn good shot, or just lucky." He returned his gaze to Jake, and he swallowed the ball in his throat. "I'd rather take my chances with him than that thing..." he trailed off, thinking about the consequences if they didn't deliver Jennifer and Steve to Black Cove.

Both Joe and Jake nodded.

"So, what do we do?" Joe asked, his gaze glued to Adam.

"Storm the crypt. If we don't, we're just as dead as Adam," Jake said.

Bill waved the closer group to the van. "I want you three to get the gun away from that maniac," Bill said.

Three pairs of eyebrows arched.

"Why us?"

"Because you don't know the full ritual, and if we don't do it, we'll all be dead by the morning."

Their faces paled, and they exchanged glances before nodding. Before they could second-guess their decision, they spun and darted into the entrance. Three more rounds rocked the cemetery and then silence. A moment later, Kurt appeared and waved them inside.

Before the three of them entered the crypt, they hauled Adam into the van, covering him in the back. Bill wiped his hands on the robe he wore and grabbed the bag of condoms, his mind already mapping out his exact revenge for screwing up the night.

When he stepped inside, he paused, his gaze landing on Steve kneeling in the middle of the pentacle with the barrel of the gun planted on his temple. He even mustered up the courage to glare from behind dark bangs.

HE SILENLY CURSED HIS lack of accuracy. Adam was the only one who went down, but that's because he froze, and it gave Steve the time to guess at the right aim. The others were moving and with the drugs; he didn't have a prayer of picking them off. His ears still rang from the report of the gun in such a small space. When the rest of the brothers filtered in, he glared at them, ignoring the hot metal on his temple.

The firelight from the torches they carried cast reflections in the glasses of one of the fraternity members, and Steve got a quick glance at what they saw.

He looked like a demon himself, with glowing eyes amidst smeared paint on his face and a bloody pentacle stood out on his bare chest, along with two single red dots an inch from either clavicle. *Jesus, I'm a fucking mess.*

Refocusing his attention from the disturbing reflection back to the clan filtering in and closing the doors, his gaze never faltered, never diverted from the one bastard he wanted to see riding an electric chair. Bill smiled and took out the box of condoms, showing it to Steve, and then tossed it towards the altar.

Rage curled in a tight ball within him, itching to strike, but hands clamped on his shoulders, keeping him kneeling on the floor. "If you touch her, I will skin you alive," Steve growled low in his chest, staring at Bill.

Bill laughed and handed a challis to Joe before pointing the dagger at Steve. "You nearly ruined the entire ritual with your little shit fit with the gun. I'm going to enjoy fucking her while you watch."

Steve gritted his teeth. "I swear to God, you will die."

Bill laughed. "You're the one who's going to die."

"I'm not dying today," Steve snarled. "And neither is she." He flexed the muscles in his arm and the butt of the gun slammed down on his temple. He fell to his hands, bright lights blinded him, and he blinked, shaking them away. When he looked up, Bill wasn't in view and he got to his feet now that the gun wasn't planted against his head.

He turned toward the altar and his eyes widened. Dread filled every fiber of his soul at the sight of a knife held to the tender flesh of Jennifer's throat.

Steve locked eyes with her, and tears blurred his vision. He blinked them away, feeling the warm tracks slide down his cheeks. *Epic fail.* His internal voice chimed, and he exhaled, returning his attention to Bill.

He glanced around the room and his gaze landed on Joe. "What the fuck are you doing?" he asked, hoping to get through to someone.

Bill stepped to the altar, positioning himself between her bound legs. He grabbed the jacket covering her and flung it across the room. Leaving her exposed for all the men to see.

"She's the sacrifice this year," Jake explained. "The fraternity brothers get to do whatever they want with her and then we leave what's left for him."

Jennifer shook on the altar. "No!"

"You'll both get to see Tracy again," Bill said, and a bitter smile formed on his lips.

Steve still focused on the knife against Jennifer's throat, his heart racing, his mind turning over options for escape. Even if he could dodge the last bullet, he still wouldn't have the time needed to save her from that blade. His face scrunched in anguish, and he took a shaky breath. "Fucking bastards."

"Oh yeah, that little phone stunt this evening cost plenty," Bill said. "She took a dive off the balcony today."

Jennifer's chin trembled, and tears slid from the corners of her eyes.

"You killed her?" Steve asked, his attention now diverted one hundred percent to Bill and the full admission of murder.

"Had to—she would have caused problems," he said.

The expression on Steve's face changed. The entire room came into clear focus, and he slipped into automatic FBI gear. "William Tyler, I'm arresting you for the murder of Tracy Sheehan. You have the right to remain silent. Anything you say can and will be used against you in a court of law. You have the right to an attorney. If you cannot afford an attorney, one will be provided for you at interrogation time and at court. Do you understand these rights as I have read them?"

"What the fuck is this?" Bill asked, pointing the dagger in Steve's direction.

"You just admitted to murder. I need you and everyone else in here to understand your rights before I send you to jail for the rest of your life." Steve tilted his head with a smile.

Bill laughed.

"Look in the inside pocket of my jacket, Sherlock," he snapped.

"Charlie, take a look," Bill said.

"Oh shit," Charlie said, pulling out the badge and handcuffs. His gaze bounced between the badge and Steve. "Holy-fucking-shit," he repeated, and tossed it to Bill.

"Do you understand your rights?" Steve asked again.

Bill stared at the FBI emblem and Steve's picture below it. "Well, I'll be damned. You're a fucking FBI agent?" he chuckled. "Where's your backup?"

"They'll be here any moment. Do you understand your rights?"

"I think he's bluffing," Bill said, glancing at Jennifer for a moment and then back at Steve. "No one knows where you are."

Jake dragged the dagger away from her throat and gently traced her body with the tip.

Steve took a step toward them and stopped, his eyes betraying him as readily as the tense set of his shoulders.

"Are you willing to watch her die?" Jake asked as he put the tip of the dagger directly over her heart.

Steve shook his head.

"Then stand down," Jake said. "Or she dies."

Steve stepped back and put his arms down in submission. "Damn you," he whispered. "God damn you."

Charlie grabbed him from behind, pushing him down on his knees in the center of the pentacle.

"He's a cop," Joe said, looking between Steve and Jake and Bill. "I didn't sign up to kill a cop." He put his hands up in the air and took a step toward the door.

Bill leveled his gaze at Joe. "You want to run? Go ahead. You know the consequences." He moved his gaze around the room, landing back on Joe.

Joe inhaled sharply.

"What are the consequences?" Steve turned to Joe, hoping for an ally, but what he saw in Joe's eyes killed any hope, and the words that followed were like a mallet driving a nail into his coffin.

"A brutal, painful, prolonged death, one you can't run away from," Joe said, his eyes sliding away toward Jennifer and filling with the same anticipation the rest of the group had etched on their faces.

Joe licked his lips and nodded, meeting Bill's questioning stare. Steve noticed the bulge in the front of his robe, in front of all their robes, and despair chipped away at his humanity, replacing it with a cold craving for revenge.

"Cuff him," Bill said, throwing a rope that was behind the altar toward them. "And then tie that to his ankles."

Steve didn't move as they put the handcuffs on his wrists in front of him this time and then tied the rope from the cuffs to his ankle. Hanging his head, he shook, trying to contain his rage. He glanced toward the pledge with the gun and calculated his odds. He closed his eyes and despair wrung the life from his soul because he knew if he took that gamble, he'd lose.

The knowledge of what was about to happen didn't help his state of mind. It clouded everything and there wasn't a damn thing he could do to stop them. Unable to watch the brutality in front of him, he stared at the floor, hearing the box of condoms being ripped open and the shuffling sounds of a package opening.

Jennifer's uneven wheezing drowned out the remaining sounds and he closed his eyes, willing his ears to shut out her sobs. He wished he still had the blindfold and headphones on.

"I want him to watch."

Bill's voice penetrated his concentration and his eyes snapped open to the graceful arc of the pentagram painted on the floor.

Fingers snapped, and someone grabbed a handful of his hair, yanking his head back so he couldn't help but watch.

Bill loomed over Jennifer, his hands pushing her thighs wide. "We get to fuck her until the full moon fills the stained-glass window. I figure we have a little over three hours before that happens." He smiled and, with a violent thrust of his hips, buried his member in her, making her scream in pain.

"I'm going to kill you," Steve growled. "I swear." He looked at her face. Tears flowed, and her teeth clenched in pain as her green eyes locked with his.

"This is nothing compared to what he'll do to you," Bill said, pumping hard, his laughter filled the small space.

Steve mumbled under his breath, swearing vengeance, swearing he'd rip each of them apart. None of his whispered words were heard over Jennifer's cries, each painful sob punctuated with a grunt until Bill moaned and flopped on top of her.

He crawled off, stripping the used condom and dropped it to the floor before slipping his robe back on. Picking up the dagger as another fraternity member took his place, he headed in Steve's direction.

Steve struggled against the bonds and the hand holding his head in place.

Bill squatted in front of Steve. "Next time, maybe I'll fuck her up the ass in memory of Adam. That's what his plan was." He laughed and tapped the flat end of the blade on his lips, contemplatively raising an eyebrow. "Actually, that's on my list of to-dos as well."

Steve's guttural roar reverberated off the walls, scraping the lining of his throat, and he renewed his thrashing efforts. Sudden, blinding pain gripped his arm and Steve blinked, lowering his gaze to the dagger embedded in his flesh. Jennifer's protest brought his glance back to her in time for Bill to yank the blade out.

"No!" Jennifer yelled, focused on him instead of the animal assaulting her.

Steve didn't make a sound. He closed his eyes for a moment and then opened them back up when Bill yanked a handful of his hair. The drugs helped to keep the physical pain detached and surreal.

The mental anguish, on the other hand, was beyond his limitations.

The horror of their actions mixed with his own arousal sparked shame and fury to layer one after the other across his chest, pressing down on him until even drawing a breath hurt. Tears continued in a constant stream down his face as he watched the woman he loved raped and ravaged by his fraternity brothers.

Memorizing each depraved act, Steve swore they would never see the halls of justice.

When they'd each had a turn, Jake unchained her and pulled her to the edge of the altar, grasping a handful of her hair to keep her in place. The inside of her thighs and lower back sported ugly red and purple bruises from the repeated assaults.

Jennifer gagged, and her hand flew to her mouth, covering it.

"You throw up and he dies," Jake said, yanking her head back to make sure she had the full view of the next ritual. He nodded toward Bill.

Steve held her gaze, even when Bill placed the tip of the dagger in the middle of one of the round circles near his left clavicle. A calm layer of numbness settled over him, dulling the pain, dulling his physical senses and neutralizing his emotions. He'd do anything to protect her, even if it meant dying and as the dagger rose, that's exactly what he thought was coming.

"I love you." The dagger pierced his skin. Sharp pain followed, grinding and morphing as Bill pulled the blade out again, leaving a burning, bloody path. The room twisted, but Steve clung to consciousness, his jaw tight and his eyes blinking to keep focus.

"Get him off of there," Jake commanded.

Bill dragged Steve off the pentacle, relinquishing him to Joe.

During the transfer, the rope between Steve's hands and ankles snapped, and he blinked again, inhaling a deep breath at the turn of events. The dagger didn't hit any major organs. His lungs still worked, his heart still beat, and his vision cleared, sharper than before because of the pain, but he didn't emit a sound.

Bill traded the dagger for Jennifer, taking her by the hair and yanking her into the center of the pentacle. "On your knees," he said.

With the clarity of mind also came waves of murderous images and in each one, Bill played a significant role. His imaginary screams of pain brought a smile to Steve's lips. Knives and blood trailed in his vision path, blocking out the scene before him—the scene of Jennifer on her knees sucking Bill's dick while the fraternity brothers chanted an incantation in Latin. As Bill sped up, the incantation reached a crescendo, and he barely noticed the goblet pressed to his skin below his bloody wound.

Bill took a step back and Jake pulled the full challis away from Steve's skin.

<hr>

OF ALL THE EMOTIONS snaking in her skin, anger welled to the surface and Jennifer stood on shaky legs and punted. The top of her foot connected with Bill's balls, doubling him over. His high-pitched scream muffled when her knee slammed into his face, breaking his nose, and she let out a cry worthy of a warrior. Satisfaction, vindication, and adrenaline pumped through her veins, and she gathered herself for another blow. Her fist was formed in a tight ball and cocked back when Jake spoke.

"I wouldn't do that," he said calmly. Her gaze jumped from Bill's bloody face to Jake.

The rush in her veins fizzled, coating her skin with a cold sweat that sent shivers straight to her bones. Jake had the tip of the dagger to Steve's throat. Her fists dropped along with the welling shimmer of hope. When she turned back to Bill, the back of his hand smacked across her cheek and she spun, landing on her hands and knees on the cold floor. Her face throbbed with stinging heat from where he connected, and her vision blurred through the sudden layer of tears that sprang.

"Clean up that blood," Jake demanded, and motioned to the drops in the pentacle from Bill's nose.

Joe tossed her Steve's shirt, and she wiped up the few droplets of blood on the floor. Her eyes kept going back to the tip of the knife against Steve's throat. A small bead of blood slid down his skin from the sharp edge. She met his gaze and this time he was fully there, his soul penetrating hers. Pain and failure were inscribed in the blue of his irises, and she bit her lip, trying to convey to him that this wasn't his fault. The self-blame and responsibility in his eyes cut her deeper than anything else that had happened. She could deal with the physical abuse, the fear, the pain, even the thought of dying, but seeing the depth of his pain tore her apart.

"Good girl, now toss it out of the circle," Jake said, pulling her gaze away from Steve.

She tossed the shirt where he pointed.

With the blade still pressed to Steve's throat, Jake handed the cup to Bill and then pointed to the pentagram, directing Jennifer to the center. "Kneel in the center."

She shifted and kneeled where he told her to, her gaze flitting between the drop of blood slowly cascading down Steve's throat and his intense stare.

Bill handed the cup to her. "Drink."

Jennifer gawked at him, her mouth falling askew as her glance fell to the thick burgundy liquid sloshing in the challis. "You, uh, you want me to drink this?" Her voice carried the incredulous tone skittering through her, and she turned her head in Steve's direction. His wide eyes met hers. He glanced from the cup in her hand, back to her face.

"I don't believe I stuttered," Bill said. "Now drink."

She stared blankly at him, her mind misfiring. *Did he just say to drink Steve's blood?*

"Do you want to see him die right here, right now?" Bill asked, pointing at Steve.

Jennifer brought the cup to her lips. Her hands shook. Tipping the challis, she tasted his blood. It was warm and thick, and she forced both the sip and the gag down her throat. She let out a small sob, pulling the cup away from her mouth.

"All of it," Jake demanded. Bill pushed the cup back to her lips.

Jennifer looked at Steve as she drank, forcing herself to swallow the vile liquid. When she'd finished and dropped the cup, her hands flew to her mouth, covering it. Her entire body shook.

"Don't throw up, or we'll poke another hole in your boyfriend here," Jake said.

Bill picked up the cup. He turned it upside down and let the droplets fall onto Jennifer and the center of the pentacle.

Each droplet that touched the floor sizzled, producing steam that smelled like burning flesh.

Bill stepped away quickly and the outline of the pentacle glowed from a dull light to that of burning embers of a fire. Yet Jennifer shivered in the center, her breath coming in plumes of white fog. Cold wrapped around her, caressing her skin, chilling, and then the familiar burning touch of the thing in her closet clasped her shoulders, pushing her forward. This time it didn't stop there. Its icy member burned its way inside her and yanked out just as quickly.

Its scream echoed through the small chamber, drowning out hers and making everyone cover their ears. With her ears still ringing, the chill receded as quickly as it came. She sat back on her heels, her breath wheezing in her lungs. The pressure on her chest constricted, and she forced an inhale, dragging a minimal amount of oxygen in, enough to squeak out a shaky sob.

"Breathe."

His soft voice pulled her out of her panic, and she met his frightened, wide-eyed gaze. Concern layered over the fear and her lungs let up, allowing air to draw in with the smallest of wheezes. *Jesus.*

"What the hell just happened?" Bill asked Jake.

Jennifer slowly stood in the center of the pentacle, her head hanging low, her hair over her eyes, and realization suddenly gave her a new strength, a new hope. She gently moved the hair from her face so she could see Steve. "We hurt it," she said to him.

He blinked, clearly not understanding how that was possible, but she knew. She caught the anguish in the beast's cry. She caught the pain and reveled in it. Backing out of the pentacle, she stepped on Steve's discarded shirt and squatted, picked it up, and slipped it on. It fell to her thighs, and, despite the spots of tacky drying blood, it made her feel better to be covered up.

Bill glared at her. "You're just a common whore. We should have hunted you down two years ago. But no, Tom wouldn't stand for that! What an idiot."

Jennifer slowly turned to him. "What?"

"Tom wouldn't let us take you. He brought in some freshman instead and offered her along with his life in return for yours." Bill shook his head.

Jennifer's chin quivered, her illusions of her dead fiancé shattered to bits at her feet. "Tom did this?" She waved her hand toward the altar behind her.

"Yes," Jake answered. "Twice. The second year, he made the deal when you were chosen. He died a couple of weeks later." Jake exchanged a look with Bill. "He loved you," he added, and looked back at Jennifer.

Jennifer's face formed into a mask of anger. "Don't tell me he loved me," she shouted. "Anybody who does this doesn't have the faintest idea what love is." She shook again.

Bill looked up at the stained-glass window. "Time to go," he said, interrupting the conversation. He lumbered across the pentacle and reached for her.

No fucking way! She blocked him and sent a roundhouse kick into his ribs.

"Cut the shit!" Jake snapped.

Jennifer shot her gaze toward the voice and deflated. The edge of the blade dug into Steve's throat, tearing at the skin, and another thin trickle of blood ran down his neck. Bill grabbed her by the hair and threw her against the altar, knocking the wind out of her.

He retrieved a length of rope and the box of condoms from behind the stone, slamming the box down next to her. He grabbed her wrists and tied them behind her back, then pressed his body against her, pushing her farther onto the hard rock as he reached around and squeezed her breasts. "I could fuck you all night." He licked her cheek. "Maybe I'll have time for one more before I leave you to the beast."

He stepped back, pulling her to him and yanking the shirt higher around her waist. He forced his fingers between her legs. "Oh yeah, I'll definitely have another for the road."

She screamed and struggled in his grip. Bill twirled her around and a patch of duct tape

Jake pasted over her lips shut off the noise careening out of her mouth.

Jerked toward the now open doors of the crypt, and the van just beyond, the world swam before Jennifer's eyes, altering.

A young man, barely eighteen, walked into the clearing with a Polaroid camera. He was fairly good-looking, with blond hair and deep blue eyes. He snapped the picture nonchalantly and stepped back into the woods, waving the picture so it would dry. He looked at the print in his hand and froze. The claws ripped straight through his body, killing him instantly.

Jennifer screamed under the tape, her focus back inside the van. Her eyes darted frantically around until they landed on Steve. Her breath hitched in her chest as she struggled to breathe through her nose.

He leaned against her. "I'm here," he whispered, calming her a little. The men had shed the robes and put their clothing back on while Jennifer was trapped in her vision, and she was thankful.

"What the hell is wrong with you?" Bill snapped at her, and she stared back, concentrating on pulling enough air through her nose so she didn't pass out.

Steve glared at him as the van rocked over the uneven cemetery path to the lake. "Do you have any idea what the penalty is for killing a federal officer?" he asked and looked around the van.

No one spoke. They just glanced at each other. Jennifer watched their reaction, hoping Steve could find a chink in their armor.

"And New Hampshire does have the death penalty," Steve remarked.

"Shut up!" Bill roared and punched Steve in the mouth.

Steve fell back against the door, laughing and spitting blood from his mouth.

Bill rubbed his knuckles. "If they find any trace of either of you, it will be in pieces. And it won't trace back to us." He grinned. "It never does."

"Then why was I planted in your fraternity?" Steve asked, situating himself back on his knees next to Jennifer.

Bill chewed on his lip and looked around the van at the others, his fraternity brothers, partners in crime, and sighed. "Why did they place you undercover?" he finally asked. "Seems to me they sent you on a fishing trip. You have no evidence that directly relates to us."

Steve smiled. "I have plenty of evidence after today."

"You won't live to see the sun rise," Bill shot back. "So there goes your evidence."

"Did you know they have surveillance cameras in the apartment complex?" Steve tilted his head, playing his hand outright and Jennifer blinked.

She didn't even know they had surveillance cameras. That would place Bill at the apartment when Tracy died and show him abducting her. Under the tape, her lips spread into a smile. The bastard wouldn't get away with this.

Bill sat back. "Bullshit," he said without conviction.

Steve shrugged. "Think what you want. It is what it is."

This time, no one met his gaze when he looked around. He sat back against the opposite side of the van, silently assessing Steve. "Did you know he was a cop?" he asked her after a few minutes.

Jennifer didn't acknowledge his question. She didn't even look in his direction.

Bill grabbed her by the front of the shirt and hauled her across the van. "Did you know?" he asked when her face was directly in front of him.

She narrowed her eyes, meeting his angry glare.

"Leave her alone. She didn't know at first either," Steve answered.

"Did Tracy?" Bill asked Jennifer.

She shook her head, and Steve voiced her answer.

"No. She was just as clueless as you were."

"I wasn't talking to you." Bill glared over at Steve and then focused his attention back at her. "You realize Tracy is dead because of you?"

"Bastard!" she hissed behind the tape. Her eyes filled with tears because, at some level, she knew he spoke the truth.

"I told her I planned to fuck you," he said. "You should have seen how angry she got." He grabbed her breast through the shirt, squeezing.

Pain flared as he squeezed and twisted her nipple and she tried to yank away but couldn't. Bill grabbed her by the hair and let go of the shirt, moving his free hand up her leg. "It was funny," he said, slamming his fist into her stomach. "She knew you wouldn't let me touch you willingly." His hand went between her legs, entering her roughly. "Why is that?"

"Get your hands off her!" Steve yelled in vain.

"Fuck off," Bill shot over at Steve.

Each painful blow brought her closer to the edge of fury, and when he looked away, she slammed her head into his already-broken nose.

"You bitch," he yelled and slammed her down on the floor of the van, forcing his way between her legs.

Between Steve's curses and Bill's mutterings, Jennifer felt the van swerve to the right. In the chaos, she heard Jake yell, "Clean—he wants her clean!" But Bill's relentless thrusts tore her insides, forcing her breath through her nose and muffled screams from under the tape.

Charlie and Joe hauled him off her.

"Fucking bitch!" he yelled and scuttled away, zipping his jeans back up.

Jennifer rolled onto her side and looked at Steve. Tears blurred her vision, mixing with the wetness streaking his face, and he tilted his head. "I'm so sorry, baby," he whispered, and closed his eyes, taking a deep breath. When he opened his eyes, he glanced at Joe. "She's having a tough time breathing. Can you at least take the tape off her mouth?"

Joe looked in the rearview mirror at Jake.

"It doesn't matter. No one will hear her scream where we're going." He gave Joe a nod, and he reached forward, ripping the tape from her mouth.

Jennifer gasped, taking a great quantity of oxygen in with each breath drawn. Sobs mingled with each wheeze.

"You'll be dead before the sun comes up," Bill growled.

Jennifer turned her head away. Sobs ripped through her. She believed Bill—they would not see the sunrise.

Dark Reckoning
Chapter 40

THE VAN PULLED OFF the smooth surface onto a divot-filled dirt road, stopping a few hundred yards in. Steve traded a glance with Jennifer, and the group shuffled out the side of the van, leaving only Jake, Bill, and Joe in the back with them.

"Wait up, Stan," Bill called and shot a glare at Steve. "We're going to need you to stay with us."

Steve almost laughed at the nervous twitch those words had caused in the lanky sophomore. He moved his gaze back to Bill. "Where'd everyone go?"

"To the campsite," he said, and a smirk appeared. "We have to get her to Black Cove."

Before Steve could process the significance of the location, Bill grabbed Jennifer and held the dagger to her throat. "Cut his legs loose," he said to Joe and then turned his gaze to Steve. "If you so much as flinch, I'll kill her."

Joe flipped open a switchblade and cut the rope around Steve's feet.

Standing, he let out a hiss of pain, almost falling back down as his legs cramped. Slowly straightening, he flexed one foot and then the other, stretching the tight muscles in his calves, and glared at Bill. His mind swarmed with escape scenarios. The odds were more favorable with four of them, especially since the drugs had long since filtered through his system. The only problem was the knife against Jennifer's throat. His gaze locked on hers for the briefest instant before Jake grabbed her arm, pulling her away from Bill and the blade in one smooth move.

Steve got a glimpse of the gun tucked neatly in the back of Jake's waistband, and a flicker of hope flared. One bullet—that's all he would need to stop this madness.

Jake led the way, dragging Jennifer over the tree roots and sharp underbrush, ignoring her wincing complaints until she stopped and tried to yank away. Bill stepped to intervene, but Jake was quicker and flipped her over his shoulder, carrying her like a sack of concrete.

Even though he was sandwiched between Joe and Stan, Steve used her abrupt diversion to slide the key to his handcuffs out of his pocket, palming it before their attention returned to him. When the line moved forward, Steve said, "At least tell me why."

"It's been here since the dawn of time," Jake began.

Steve snorted. "What the fuck are you talking about?" he asked, certain they only knew half of the information he uncovered just by Jake's comment.

"The thing you saw in the crypt."

Steve was quiet for a few paces, sliding the key into the locking mechanism. "You don't know shit," he said, turning the key as he spoke to cover up the click of the cuffs' release.

Joe glanced back at Steve. "We know it requires a sacrifice each year in order to keep it within the confines of Black Cove."

"What a crock of shit," Steve said. He thought of the little girl found in the woods almost a half mile away from the area they were heading.

Bill spun around. He grabbed Steve by the throat, pulling him close.

"Chill, Bill. He'll find out soon enough," Stan said from behind Steve.

Bill let him go and turned back, passing Joe and continuing behind Jake.

Steve didn't follow immediately. He waited until both Bill and Joe were at least ten paces ahead and then took a couple of steps and stumbled, falling on his hands and knees. "Shit," he mumbled and shuffled to his feet, keeping an eye on Joe as he slid the knife out of his boot, palming it on the inside of his wrist, out of sight. Joe turned away from Steve, following Bill and Jake, chuckling. When Stan pushed him forward, Steve spun, twisting the blade in his grip and burying it through Stan's larynx and ripping through flesh and arteries in a violent tug. With his free hand, he covered Stan's mouth, quieting the gurgle. The gaping wound drenched Steve with blood, and he watched the shock in Stan's eyes transition to death. A quick glance over his shoulder revealed only darkness on the path before him, the curve hiding their presence. He laid Stan carefully on the ground, hurrying to catch up. Stumbling down the path in the direction they'd disappeared, he made enough noise to sound like two people.

It was dark enough that the group wouldn't have been able to make out Stan even if he'd been there, but it worked both ways. In his rush to catch up, he nearly collided with Joe. He pulled up at the last second when the shadow in front of him turned, revealing a pale face in the darkness.

"Nice trip?" Joe asked, his voice edged with sarcastic humor.

"Fuck you." Steve listened for the front of the pack. Their footfalls were farther along the path, a good ten to fifteen feet, and he focused back on Joe. "Why rape?" he asked.

"It's part of the initiation," Joe answered. "Fuck 'em any-which-way we can and then he gets her." His voice trembled, and Steve heard the distinct sound of a swallow. "When he's done, they're usually in pieces."

He could make out another bend in the path and knew it was now or never. He gripped the knife in both hands. Raising it high in the air, he plunged it into the back of Joe's neck, severing the spinal cord with a snap that could have been mistaken for a twig. He caught Joe's limp body before it hit the ground and quietly set him down. With a deep inhale, he yanked the knife from the body. His stomach lurched, but he pushed the sensation aside. He didn't have time to get sick, and he certainly didn't have time to mourn Joe or examine his actions. He knew that would come later, and he'd pay for it in spades, but for now, he had to get Jennifer away from Bill and Jake.

Hustling forward, he slid around the bend just in time to see Jake enter an opening in the woods. He quickly put his hands behind his back with the knife in his grip. He stopped at the opening, taking in the cove. *Jennifer was right—this is as desolate and cold as you can get.*

Jake threw Jennifer down in the center of the pentacle carved in dead moss, and turned towards the wood line. He pulled the dagger out, tossed it to Bill, and then kneeled, putting the sharp edge of his hunting knife to her throat.

"Where are Stan and Joe?" Bill asked, stepping closer to Jennifer.

Steve smiled. "Probably roasting in hell right about now," he answered, looking squarely at Jake.

Bill threw the dagger, and it hit Steve half an inch away from his open wound, sending him back a couple of steps. Pain gripped him, and he realized too late that his knife had come into full view, and he lost his element of surprise. "Fuck!"

"No!" Jennifer screamed.

"Do you want her to die right this second?" Jake shouted, gaining Steve's attention. "Drop the knife and get your ass over here."

He dropped the knife immediately and reached for the dagger, muttering under his breath.

"Don't touch that," Jake warned.

Steve put his hands back down and took a shaky step into the clearing. *I should have launched the knife at Bill the minute he stepped into the opening. Fucking idiot!*

With every step he took, he silently berated himself.

Bill stepped out of reach as Steve approached, and Jake pulled Jennifer back a few feet. "In the center." He pointed the knife and then brought it back to her throat.

Steve did as he was told, his eyes never leaving Jennifer's. *I promise I'll get you out of this, even if it's the last thing I do.*

"Kneel."

He kneeled.

Jake nodded for Bill. "If you make a move, I will kill her."

"That's getting old," Steve said, but kept his hands on his knees, digging his nails into the denim as Bill grasped the end of the dagger and yanked it out. Steve blinked, and the world spun. *Oh, shit,* was his last thought before the world went black.

"NO! STEVE!" JENNIFER'S SCREAM echoed on the water. Steve's limp body tilted backwards onto the moss, and she reached for him, but Jake yanked her back. Panic clouded her mind, and she struggled in Jake's grasp, screaming Steve's name over and over. "Get away from him, you bastard!" she spit when Bill collected blood from the wound.

Bill glared in her direction. "You're lucky I don't cut his fucking head off." He handed the cup to Jake and grabbed Steve's wrists, dragging him outside the circle surrounding the pentacle. "And while I'd love to do that, I think having him meet the beast is a much better choice. I imagine he'll do a lot of screaming before he dies."

She broke away from Jake, spinning and delivering an uppercut that snapped Jake's head back. He backhanded her, sending her sprawling on the moss. Before she could recover, Jake yanked a handful of her hair and dragged her back toward the center.

Jake ripped her shirt, and she swung, fury blinding her and the will to fight, to kill these bastards overrode common sense. She swept Jake's feet from under him, and he landed on his ass. She didn't wait for him to recover,

317

sending a kick into the side of his head, hoping to break his neck.

Arms grabbed her from behind and she twisted, reaching back and flipping Bill onto the ground at her feet. She stepped back and tripped over the challis, knocking it over. Steve's blood seeped into the ground and the horror on both Bill's and Jake's face made her laugh.

"Run, Jen."

Steve's labored voice made her spin, her gaze skimming over him, following his frightened gaze, and landing on the form in the water. Her nightmares flooded her muscles with fear, freezing her on the spot.

"Run," Steve said, his voice barely a whisper, his vocal cords strangled with fear. He took a deep breath, struggling to his feet. "Run!"

Dark Reckoning
Chapter 41

STEVE'S COMMAND LOOSENED HER paralysis and Jennifer bolted in the opposite direction; into the woods, flying within a few feet of where Bill had found his footing. Jake reached for her, but she knocked his hand away, fleeing from the beast from her nightmares.

The dream surrounded her, and she sobbed, the branches cutting her skin more deeply than the dagger had.

She slid to a stop, leaning over and vomiting the foul contents of her stomach on the dark forest floor. She spit and turned back toward the clearing, wiping her mouth with the back of her hand, her entire frame trembling.

She couldn't let him die; she had to stop that thing.

Dark Reckoning
Chapter 42

THE BEAST REACHED JAKE first and swatted him like a fly, his claws ripping through skin and bone like a master sword, separating his torso from his legs and sending his top half toward the wood line near Steve.

Steve's gaze landed on what was left of Jake and snapped to the metal object just short of the brush. He launched toward it, praying the thing wouldn't attack him next. When his hand swiped the gun from the ground, he spun, aiming in time to see Bill dart toward the path they came in.

The beast caught Bill before he left the crunchy moss. It toyed with him, raking a sharp claw over his back, and Bill screamed.

Its laugh cascaded over the cove, throaty, dark and full of menace. "I promised a painful death." The beast's voice scraped out of its throat and into Bill's ear, and then it tore his arm from his torso.

Bill's screams continued, and Steve stared at the carnage. His stomach dropped, and acid lined his throat when the beast disemboweled Bill. Intestines spilled out of the gash along with a torrent of blood. Bill's scream caught in a gag, bile and blood spewing from his mouth, encircling the now continuous scream. The beast sheared clean through Bill's leg, tossing the limb aside like a discontented child before dragging a still-screaming Bill under the black water.

Steve stumbled toward the path, but he only got as far as the center of the pentacle before the black shape rose out of the water again. Fear made his heart ram against his chest and each of his wounds throbbed in concert. Black like an oil slick and remotely in the shape of an enormous man, its eyes glowed, altering between red, orange, and yellow, just like the embers in a hot fire. Steve's mind reeled, and he pulled the trigger. The gun jammed, and he stared at it for a moment before his gaze snapped back to the thing approaching. "Shit!"

It reached out and hit him, sending him across the clearing. The gun fell onto the ground at the far edge of the wood line.

Steve scrambled to his feet, his eyes wide and darting around the cove until they fell on the dagger. He moved to retrieve it, wrapping his hand around the handle just as the beast came for him. He backed slowly away with the dagger in hand, and it stopped in the center of the pentacle.

"You." It pointed its claw. "You need to die." The ground shook as the words rumbled from its chest.

Steve blinked but didn't respond. The scent of fire and rotting meat radiated from the beast, filling Steve's nostrils from fifteen feet away.

This is NOT possible!

The temperature in the clearing plummeted to where he could see his ragged breath hanging in the air in front of him. He shivered, his teeth chattered uncontrollably. Yet the ground was singed with each step the beast took, filling the air with the stench of burned moss. He took an involuntary step backwards, his chest still oozing from both stab wounds. As he held the dagger in his hand, pointing it at the thing, his eyes darted between the blade and the beast's hands. It seemed like such an inadequate weapon against the razor-sharp claws at the end of the demon's fingers.

It changed its form, morphing, altering, solidifying.

Steve gaped at Peg. Peg with red eyes.

He blinked again, his mind unable to wrap itself around what he was seeing. He lowered the dagger a fraction of an inch. Sirens deep inside raged, and he brought the blade back up in response.

"You killed that little girl," Steve said.

"She was so sweet, innocent, and pure." It breathed and stepped forward, still taking the shape of his dead fiancé.

Steve could smell its breath. "You are not Peg," he said with conviction.

It took another step forward, and the outline of the pentacle glowed.

Steve stared at the ground and stepped forward, within the lines of the pentacle, bringing his gaze back to the demon, praying whatever the demon did, it would be quick, but the gleam in the beast's eyes promised otherwise.

It laughed and struck out, sending Steve flying to the far edge of the pentacle. The beast's claws left deep cuts along his face, neck, and chest, and burning agony ripped through his skin. He struggled to his feet and stepped back into the circle, the knife grasped in his hand. His throat closed in pain. His breath wheezed, and he took another step forward, allowing his blood to drip on the sacred ground.

"She's mine, not yours," Steve gasped, pointing the dagger in its direction.

The beast charged.

"Leave him alone," Jennifer's voice rang through the clearing and the beast spun in her direction.

JENNIFER GULPED, STARING DOWN the beast from her nightmares. It paused, lifted its nose in the air, and sniffed. A feral smile stretched across its face, revealing sharp, jagged teeth like a shark.

The beast stepped toward her. "I want to hear you scream for eternity," it said.

Jennifer froze and shook. *This thing was in my closet!*

It laughed. "Yes, I was there." It approached her.

"Don't touch her." Steve stumbled, dropping to his hands and knees.

Its smile faded. "She is mine." The beast reached out, grasping her wrist, and pulled her forward.

"I belong to Steve," she said, straightening her back and glaring at the beast despite the burning pain where it clasped her wrist.

"You were supposed to be mine two years ago," it growled and morphed into the form of Tom. "I died for you," it said.

Jennifer stared, her mouth dropped and the fear transitioning to shock as she stared into deep, dark eyes. Even his voice was accurate, but the stench of burning flesh and moss yanked her back to reality. She popped her mouth closed and leveled a glare, ripping her arm from his grip. She stepped forward, shoving the image in front of her.

Her hands burned. "I hate you!" she screamed in its face.

The beast roared, transitioning back into the black form, jerking away. In its fury, it picked her up and threw her across the clearing.

Her legs smashed into a tree trunk, whipping her around, and Jennifer yelped when she landed on the ground. Pain gripped her legs, and she didn't dare look at the damage. Her breath locked in her chest, and she struggled to bring air to her lungs. Her mind systematically shut down, and everything went fuzzy.

STEVE CLIMBED TO HIS feet and took a step in her direction. The pain etched in her features sent a surge of anger through him, overriding any sense of fear, and he turned on the demon, meeting its fiery glare.

"You tainted her," it said, pointing a claw in his direction.

"I guess drinking the blood of Palawion's descendant probably didn't help." He flipped the dagger, so he held the sharp edge, readying himself.

Its eyes narrowed, falling to the wounds traversing across Steve's chest and face and to the blood dripping on the ground. It took an unsteady step backwards.

Steve grinned. "Yes. I read up on you. On what could send you back into the bowels of hell." Steve pitched the dagger through the air and into the beast's chest. The dagger sank through the demon's skin, and it roared with fury, lumbering toward him.

Steve lost his balance, falling to his knees. In vain, he attempted to stand, but he crumbled to his hands and knees. The demon grabbed a fist full of hair, yanking him up and slowly ran its claws down his back, ripping the flesh open. Steve shrieked, his voice filled with pain and panic.

"You're coming to hell with me," it seethed. Letting go of his hair, it raised its arm to strike the final blow.

JENNIFER SAW THE GUN through the haze—it was the only thing clear in her line of sight. She picked it up and aimed at the beast. Clenching her teeth, she held on to consciousness with bitter determination, believing the bullet could kill the thing in the clearing. She said a silent prayer, asking God to make her shot true, and yelled, "Go to hell, you son of a bitch!"

When it turned toward her voice, she squeezed the trigger. The noise and light that filled the clearing astounded her.

The bullet cut through the dark, leaving a trail of white light in its path, piercing the beast where a human heart would be. The impact lifted it off its feet, sending it catapulting through the air into the center of the black water. White light seared the blackness as it hit the surface, sending waves of clear water in every direction, drenching Steve.

WHEN HE CRUMPLED TO the ground, the impact sent pain to every surface. He opened his eyes in time to see Jennifer's eyes roll up into her head and the gun slip out of her hand and onto the black moss.

Pulling himself to his feet, he stumbled to her. Picking her up in his arms, he headed toward Paradise Cove and his grandfather's cabin. When he stepped out of the perimeter of Black Cove, the water seeped into the basin, leaving a muddy, murky sinkhole. The remnants of a century's worth of the demon's carnage were visible for all to see.

Each step required Herculean effort. His arms burned from holding her, the torn skin of his chest and back screamed, threatening to drop him on the spot. He stumbled, caught his balance, and kept moving because he knew if he stopped, he'd die without knowing she was safe.

Please God, please God, please God.

He prayed with each step, and when he entered Paradise Cove; he began to cry. Great sobs fought the air for space in his ruined chest. The path to his grandfather's place seemed like an impossible feat, but when he stepped onto the lawn from the edge of the woods and saw the FBI lights and the central command station in the yard, he collapsed to his knees.

His last coherent thought before all went black, *Thank you, God.*

Dark Reckoning
Chapter 43

Murphy glanced toward the path again. The gunshot had come from that direction and the team was mobilizing.

He saw Steve stumble out of the woods with Jennifer in his arms.

The lights in the yard gave him a good look at his young protégé, and what he saw made his blood run cold.

Steve collapsed with her on the lawn and Murphy started running.

They were both unconscious and barely breathing when the ambulance pulled in to bring her to the hospital in Concord, and the Life Star Helicopter landed to take him to Boston.

Neither one of them saw the sunrise over Mirror Lake, just as Bill had predicted.

Dark Reckoning
Chapter 44

“**O**H, LORD, HELP ME get through today,” she whispered. Her voice echoed in the empty chapel. It was the first time Jennifer had been back to Brooksfield since that horrible day two months before.

She slowly pushed her wheelchair out of the small church. The cold, misty day slapped at her cheeks while her black hair hung in her eyes. She rolled toward the gravesite. A wilted rose lay in her lap.

Sighing, she stopped in front of the shiny new headstone, engraved with care. A tear rolled down her cheek and landed on the rose.

Picking up the flower, she tossed it onto Tracy’s grave. “I miss you,” she whispered to her best friend’s headstone. “I am so sorry.”

A hand descended on her shoulder, making her jerk in surprise. She turned and looked at him, eyes wide with shock. She hadn’t seen him in two months, since she killed that thing.

It had been a miracle that he’d been able to carry her for over a mile, and still another, that he was alive at all. Along with the broken arm resting in a sling, the only visible scar traversed his cheek and continued down his neck, stretching under his crisp white shirt.

The tailored black suit hid the bulk of his injuries. Bandages wrapped around his torso, immobilizing four broken ribs. Angry red scars from the beast's claws cut across his chest and back along with the multiple stab wounds, all hidden by the dark Armani knock-off. He'd cut his hair recently, shorter and cleaner than it had been in early September.

"It wasn't your fault, babe," he said, looking at Tracy's gravestone. *If I hadn't called her...*

"Murphy said you almost died."

Steve nodded. "They told me I did. It was touch and go for a while, I guess." He glanced back at her, and her tears started again. "But I was damned if I was going to die and never see you again."

"When did you get out of the hospital?" she asked through the tears.

"Last week. My parents have been taking care of me, and it really sucks." He offered her a hint of a smile. "This is the first time I've been in Brooksfield, though. I heard you were coming."

Jennifer nodded. "My folks drove me up."

Steve nodded. "I know. Your mom called." He took a deep breath. "Why didn't you come see me?"

Jennifer began to sob and shake her head. "I was afraid to."

Steve turned the wheelchair toward him and kneeled in front of her, trying not to wince. "Why?" he asked, his own eyes welled with tears. He had enough exposure to rape victims to know the answer, but he asked anyway.

"Because you saw, you saw everything."

Steve took her hands in his and put his head on her knees, grappling with the mental anguish. Hot tears burned the back of his throat. Yes, he saw everything, every nasty, vile thing they did to her, but it didn't alter the depth of his emotion. He loved her and failed her.

He shook his head slowly and looked up, the tears running hot tracks down his cheeks. "I'm sorry I couldn't stop them," he whispered. "That I couldn't protect you."

"You did the best you could under the circumstances." She pulled her hand out of his grasp and wiped her face.

Steve looked down at the ground. "I should have taken you into custody when I first realized you were in the middle of this. If..."

Jennifer cut him off. "Stop! There was nothing either of us could have done differently. If we had, we would be dead right now and that thing would still be alive."

He knew she was right, but it didn't stop the nightmares or the feeling of responsibility over what happened to Tracy. Steve looked up at her. "Do you still love me?" he asked, deathly afraid of the answer.

Jennifer nodded, tears spilling from her eyes again, lining her cheeks. "Do you?"

"God, yes," he said, wiping the tears off his face. "You are what kept me alive." He removed a small box from his pocket and took her hand. "I never want to wake up again without you by my side. Ever." He looked at Tracy's headstone. "This isn't exactly the grand spectacle I'd originally planned, but I figure Tracy would appreciate being a part of it in some way." He looked back at Jennifer and slipped a ring on her finger. "Jennifer Ann Curtis, will you marry me?" he whispered, his eyes sparkling with tears.

Jennifer lowered her eyes to her hand and a ray of sunshine broke through the haze, hitting the diamond ring he had placed on her finger. A prism of light surrounded them in the lonely graveyard. She glanced into his eyes. Tears spilled down her cheeks, and her throat constricted from the wave of emotions crashing over her.

Overwhelmed, Jennifer couldn't utter a sound. She closed her eyes to gain control, sucking her bottom lip and taking a deep inhale through her nose.

"Jenny?" he asked, his voice laced with doubt.

"Yes," she whispered, and opened her eyes.

Steve let a slow smile form on his lips. He kissed her gently and stood, pushing her wheelchair into the chapel. "How about right now?" he whispered in her ear, pushing her up the aisle.

His parents stood at the front of the chapel, along with Murphy and a priest. And for the briefest instant, Jennifer thought she saw Tracy, standing by the altar in a hideous pumpkin bridesmaid dress with a Cheshire-cat grin on her face. With a blink of her eyes, the apparition was gone.

Jennifer laughed softly. "Right now is as good a time as any." She looked up at him with the first genuine smile she'd felt since the night the three of them binged on tequila and dancing.

The End

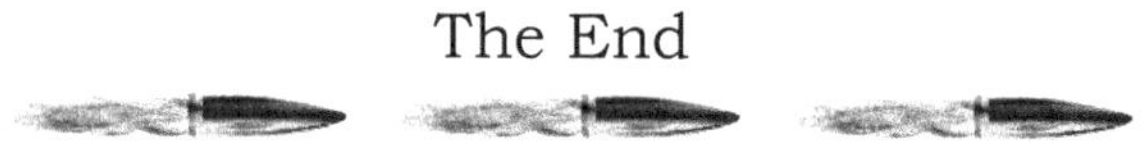

Continue The Steve Williams Series on the next
page with VENGEANCE.

332

Vengeance
Chapter 1

Part One
Charlie and the Cocaine Factory

STEVE WILLIAMS STOOD AT the printer, scanning financial records. The light bled from beneath the cover, creating the only beacon in the otherwise dark office.

"Come on, come on." He shifted from foot to foot, his eyes darting between the copier and the door, intently listening for any sound beyond the swish of the machine. When the paper spit out, he propped open the lid and flipped the ledger to the last page. As he hit the copy button, the cell phone in his pocket vibrated.

"Shit." He flipped the phone open. "Hey, Jen."

"Where are you?" Her groggy voice asked.

"The office. Why?"

"You need to come home."

"I have to finish this." He yanked the copies from the tray and turned off the machine.

"I had another vision."

Steve took a deep breath, calming his nerves. He really didn't have time to discuss her vision; he needed to get out of the building before someone saw him. "Another dream?" he asked, anyway.

Silence.

He stuffed the papers into his attaché case. "When?"

"I don't know. A couple of hours?"

He slid the ledger back into the file cabinet and looked around the office one last time before he crossed to the door. "I'm on my way now." He closed the phone, opting for the stairs instead of the elevator.

Rapidly, he descended the stairway. The dim lights popped and flickered, sending shadows into the far corners of each landing. His eyes darted from shadow to shadow, and he cast a quick glance over his shoulder when he reached the entrance leading to the parking garage. He yanked the door open, turning his head toward the garage, and nearly plowed over the man blocking the exit.

Charlie Wisnowski stepped back, putting his hands up to stop him. "Whoa! What are you doing here?"

Steve halted, meeting the hard, gray eyes of his boss. "I, uh, got into an argument with my girlfriend and needed some breathing room." He swallowed and shifted the briefcase strap on his shoulder. "I figured I'd cool my jets here and look at those service contracts."

Charlie crossed his arms. His gaze landed on the briefcase. "Contracts?"

"Yeah. The ones you gave me this afternoon."

"Right." Charlie didn't budge from his spot, blocking Steve's escape route.

Skirting around Charlie, he took a backward step toward his car, every muscle in his body tense and ready for flight if Charlie reached for the briefcase.

"How do the contracts look?"

"A couple of things need tightening up." Sweat trickled down the small of his back, tickling his skin, and he squashed the urge to itch.

"Like what?"

"There's a gap in the service agreement. We need a better rate than triple time for off hour service," Steve began, thankful he had reviewed the documents before leaving earlier. "Especially since they consider regular hours between nine in the morning and three in the afternoon."

"You're shitting me?" Charlie's arms fell to his sides.

He smiled and shook his head. "No offense, Charlie, but I'd be loving life with hours like that."

Charlie scoffed and turned toward the building entrance. "Go home and screw your girlfriend," he said over his shoulder.

The door swung closed behind him, leaving Steve staring at the heavy steel. Glancing at the cameras mounted in the corners, he strolled to the car. When he was clear of the garage, he took a deep breath and tilted his head back against the headrest, letting the relief melt into his taut muscles. "Ho-ly shit."

He navigated the late-night streets from Manhattan to Brooklyn until he reached the parking garage across from his apartment complex. He pulled into a parking space, grabbed the bag, and crossed the street as he glanced at the brownstone building. All their lights were on, which meant he'd have to deal with the vision tonight.

He tossed the briefcase under the table by the door and crossed the loft to where Jennifer stood, drying her hands. "Are you all right?" he asked.

"You should wake me up before you sneak out in the middle of the night."

The touch of anger in her tone took Steve by surprise. He raised his eyebrows. "Excuse me?"

"I'm your wife, damn it." She stepped around him.

He reached out, pulled her close, and met her angry glare. "I didn't want you to worry."

Jennifer laughed. "And you think waking up to an empty bed will not freak me out? Especially when I've had one of my visions?"

Tilting his head, he looked at the floor before raising his eyes to hers. "I'm sorry, babe." He offered the crooked smile that always disarmed her. This time was no different.

Holding his gaze, she let a sigh escape before leaning in to kiss him.

Her lips were soft and inviting, with a faint flavor of cinnamon. Running his hands down her back to the hem of her baby-doll nightgown, Steve momentarily forgot about the close call with Charlie and led Jennifer to the bed in the far corner, his hands leaving her body only to flip off the lights.

Vengeance
Chapter 2

"WHAT WERE YOU REALLY doing here?" Charlie flicked the lights on, looking for anything out of place. He turned in a circle, surveying the desks and file cabinets throughout the work area.

Nothing was out of order, but a gnawing suspicion crawled under his skin, and he glanced toward his lawyer's office. Navigating the neat bullpen of desks, he crossed to the large window office opposite his and stepped inside. Spread over the desk were the annotated pages of the contract. Charlie picked up the top sheet, scanning the highlighted marks sprinkled over the document.

"Huh. Maybe the kid was telling the truth." He dropped the paper back on the desk, leaving Steve's office and heading into his own. Steve had done some damn fine contract negotiations for him over the last six months and set up some slick financing schemes to launder the money Charlie pumped through the organization. However, not once in all their conversations had Steve mentioned a girlfriend. That irked Charlie.

He shuffled through his file cabinet, pulling Steve's employee file and flipped it open, perusing the contents, he studied Steve's history, tapping his pen on the desk as he read. An only child, no living relatives to speak of, the last of whom were his parents, and they passed away when he was in high school, leaving him with next to nothing. He'd worked his ass off, taking two, sometimes three jobs at a time to keep afloat while going to Georgetown, and then finished his law degree at Yale.

Charlie chose Steve because he graduated at the top of his class, but more importantly, he was in debt up to his eyeballs. Now Charlie wondered what drove him to excel in the face of adversity, of such poverty.

What was his lawyer really made of?

Charlie hit the speed dial on his cell phone. "I need you to keep an eye on someone for a while," he said. "Steve Winchester, one of my staff lawyers." Charlie read off the address and flipped the file closed. "Report anything unusual to me."

He pocketed his cell phone and unlocked the top drawer of his desk. Stashed under a fake panel, a bag of his street product mocked him. His blow was dubbed the best in the city by his clientele. Dumping a small amount on the mirror, he meticulously cut the coke into three even lines. Charlie snorted the rows rapidly and sat back, sniffling. It took a few minutes for the rush to hit and then he locked the drawer and headed out in search of some action.

Vengeance
Chapter 3

JENNIFER SETTLED IN HIS arms, a small, satisfied smile on her lips.

"Tell me what you saw," Steve whispered in her ear, spooning her in the soft bed.

"A hunting knife covered in blood. It reminded me of the knife in the movie Rambo." She cuddled closer to him. "It was a blonde this time, and the bastard played with her before he killed her."

"Anything else?"

"There's something on his right wrist, but I couldn't make it out," she yawned. "I think it's a tattoo."

Silence filled the room. When her breathing evened out, he slid out of bed and booted up his computer. This was the third dream Jennifer had in the last few months involving a dead woman and a hunting knife.

Typing a special secure URL and his clearance code into the computer, the FBI logo appeared, giving way to the internal email system. Steve scanned his inbox before typing a new message to his boss.

Jenny had another one. Let me know if you find anything.

He looked between the message and Jennifer sleeping a few feet away, wondering if he was doing the right thing. He'd put her in the line of fire before, and that miscalculation almost got them killed. *But this is different.* He inhaled and pressed send before shutting the computer down.

Yawning, he crossed to the window and looked out at the street.

Someone was watching.

He stepped back into the darkness.

The car, in contrast, sat under the streetlight. Steve sat on the edge of the bed, his mind racing over the steps he took to cover his tracks tonight.

He must have missed something.

"Shit," he muttered and climbed under the covers next to Jennifer. "Shit!"

THE ALARM WENT OFF, startling Steve. He slammed the snooze button, stretched, and turned his attention toward the window. The car was still there.

He rolled toward Jennifer. "Jenny?"

"Mhm?" She turned away from the light filtering in the window.

"You need to leave."

It took a few minutes for his words to sink into her sleep-infested brain. She slowly turned her head toward him. "What did you just say?"

"I want you to go home to New Hampshire. It isn't safe here." He leaned over and flipped on the light.

"Steve." She sat up.

He put his hand up. "Please Jen. I ran into Charlie on the way out of the office and he apparently ordered someone to follow me." He hooked his thumb toward the window. "That car has been there all night."

"So?" She tried to look beyond Steve, and he shook his head, stopping her.

"He doesn't even know I'm married."

"What's the worst that could happen?"

Lowering his eyes to his hands, light bounced off the gold of his wedding band, which graced his right ring finger instead of his left. He twirled the band slowly and raised his eyes to hers, taking her in. Her dark rumpled hair framed her face, and her alert green eyes waited for his answer. Steve tilted his head, sighing. "If he finds out what I'm doing, he'll kill me, but before he does, he'll cut you into little pieces to make his point."

She shivered. "How can you stand being in the same office with that man?"

"It's my job and I want to take this son of a bitch down."

"I don't like your job."

"I know, but you knew what you were getting into when you married me." He reached out, wiping a stray hair out of her face. "We both know I can bullshit my way out of most anything, but if I'm worried about you, I might fuck up."

Jennifer bit her lip. "I don't want to go to New Hampshire."

He glanced down at her left hand. The diamond studded wedding band and solitaire engagement ring donned her left ring finger. "It's dangerous Jen."

"All the more reason for me to stay."

Closing his eyes, he hung his head, shaking it back and forth. "No," he said, meeting her gaze. "I don't have a good feeling about this and the last time I didn't listen to my gut where you're concerned, it almost got us killed."

"I can take care of myself."

"Jesus Christ!" Steve threw back the covers and hopped out of bed, storming across the little efficiency where he ripped open the closet and grabbed a suit before disappearing into the bathroom. The doorframe rattled with the force of his slam.

She swung the door open and stood with her arms folded. "Steve, it's my choice."

The toothpaste foamed under his angry brush strokes, and he spit before rinsing off the toothbrush and dropping it in the cup next to the sink. "No, it isn't." He swiped the back of his hand across his lips and turned in her direction. He had seen the photos of the poor souls Charlie had caught. The lucky ones got a single shot between the eyes. The rest, well; let's just say it wasn't pretty.

Jennifer pressed her lips together, her chest rising with the significant expansion of air in her lungs. "I just got the lead on Broadway."

"Off-Broadway." He reached in the shower, turning on the water to let it warm up.

"It's still the lead and I don't want to go home just yet. Not until we know for sure, okay?"

Steve closed his eyes and wiped his face with his hand. She had worked hard, going from audition to audition, getting rejection after rejection and then her luck changed, and she was offered the lead in *Vanities*. "Fine. Then you need to take the rings off." He stripped his boxers and shot her a glare.

Jennifer's eyebrows rose. "Why?"

"Because he doesn't know I'm married. He thinks I got into a fight with my girlfriend and landed at the office to get away from her."

She pressed her lips together in irritation. "You couldn't think of anything better than that?"

"I'm surprised I got that out. He scared the crap out of me." He sucked in his breath and opened the shower door. "Five minutes earlier and I'd be dead right now." He slipped under the water without further comment. He closed his eyes and let the stream cascade over his tired skin.

He just wanted to keep her safe. He didn't want a repeat of what happened in Brooksfield. He had gotten lucky, but not lucky enough to stop his fraternity brothers from raping Jennifer before attempting to offer her up as a sacrifice. Getting her clear before they finished the ritual hadn't been easy and just when he thought they were safe, something in the woods attacked, knocking his gun out of his grasp.

His chest and back still bore the claw marks from the struggle and the only reason he was alive today was Jennifer. She found his gun and killed the beast before she lost consciousness. To this day, he wondered which miracle was bigger: that her shot was accurate, or that he had the strength to carry her over a mile to safety without bleeding to death.

He never wanted to be that close to losing her again.

Dressing, he took his time forming his thoughts and when he entered the bedroom; he crossed to the bed, where she had settled under the sheets. He took a seat on the edge. "This is the first time either the bureau or the DEA has got someone this deep inside Charlie's operation."

"But why does it have to be you?"

"Because I am the best."

"You are a cocky son of a bitch." She sat up.

Steve shrugged, and he scanned his wife, smiling. "Yeah, but that's one of the reasons you love me." He glanced out the window and his smile faded. He returned his gaze to Jennifer. "Promise me something."

"What?"

"If I tell you to run, this time you run and keep running."

Vengeance
Chapter 4

STEVE SAT AT HIS DESK with the contract spread out in front of him and the electronic version on his computer, crafting the modifications needed in the service agreement. His mind kept circling around every step he took the prior night, trying to pinpoint a mistake. He came up empty every time.

Charlie cleared his throat.

Steve glanced toward the door. "Oh, sorry, I'm in the middle of updating the contract," he said, pointing toward the computer screen casually, but his heart now throbbed in his chest. Charlie stared at him, his teeth nibbling on his bottom lip in contemplation.

"Was she there?" he asked and shifted, leaning against the doorjamb.

It took Steve a moment to digest what Charlie asked, and Steve tilted his head to the side, sending a questioning glance in his direction.

"The girlfriend."

Like you don't already know. Play it cool. Steve nodded and took a deep breath, stretching his back and swiveling the chair toward the door. "She's moving in with me." He leaned back in the chair, rubbing his face.

"Really?" Charlie straightened up.

"Yeah, that's what the fight was about. She gave me an ultimatum." He gave a half shrug.

"Sucker."

"I guess." He pivoted toward his computer and returned his hands to the keyboard, hoping Charlie would leave without calling his bluff.

"I'm having a small get together at my place Friday night. I think you should bring her along."

Steve raised his eyes. Charlie rarely socialized with his employees, and this was the first personal invitation ever extended to him. The perfect opportunity to gain Charlie's trust was just thrown into the shitter because Jennifer wouldn't be there! Friday night, her play opened, and he promised he would be in the audience on opening night. Torn between his commitment to the job and the promise he made to his wife, Steve weighed the ramifications.

"I'd love to, but we can't. My girlfriend's play opens Friday and she'll kill me if I'm not there."

Charlie shifted and crossed his arms, his eyes darkening with doubt. "Your girlfriend's an actress?"

Steve nodded, wondering what Charlie would make of that. "She's starring in *Vanities,* down in Soho. It's her first lead."

"What's her name?"

"Jennifer Curtis."

"Maybe next time." He disappeared from view.

Steve stared at the now empty doorway and then returned his attention to the contract, silently swearing because Jennifer was now officially involved, not just some random girlfriend in Steve's life and not taking Charlie up on the invite might screw up his chances of gaining his trust. He was going to get reamed.

Royally reamed.

347

Vengeance
Chapter 5

CHARLIE CROSSED INTO HIS office, irritated with Steve for declining his invitation. None of his employees ever said no. They all clamored to be in his inner circle, but not Steve. "What the fuck is wrong with him?"

He realized he knew very little about his star lawyer outside of the outlined in his file. That would need to be rectified. The kid certainly seemed aloof, too distant and private, and getting any information from him was like pulling teeth. Today, he offered more than he had in the entire six months, almost as if he sensed Charlie's doubts. He swung his chair around and stared out the window at the surrounding buildings.

CW FOG Inc. provided the legitimate front to his illegal drug operations, as well as bringing in a decent amount of money on its own. Fiber optic glass had stepped up in demand and the creation and distribution for both the fiber optic business and his cocaine production occurred on the Brooklyn waterfront, miles away from his corporate headquarters in downtown Manhattan.

Steve had been privy to all aspects of the fiber optics business, but Charlie hadn't let him in on where the excess cash was coming from. He made it perfectly clear that all the money movements needed to be below the radar, citing tax avoidance as the primary reason for the creative financial schemes he asked Steve to devise.

His eyebrows scrunched together. Steve never once asked for further explanations, and that struck a chord. He swung back to his computer and searched for the Soho Theater. *Vanities* was indeed re-opening on Friday night. Staring at the monitor, he clicked on the cast link, shuffling through the pictures until Jennifer's came up.

He leaned forward, staring at the dark-haired beauty on his screen, and chuckled. "Now I know why you put up with her." On impulse, he bought a pair of tickets. He closed the web browser and stood, leaning on the window frame and flipping open the cell phone. "Anything?"

"No, he was with his girlfriend all night. His name's on the mailbox and it looks like she's moving in," the voice answered. "What's with this guy, anyway?"

"Just making sure he's legit," Charlie answered. He looked over his shoulder into the heart of the office.

"Do you want me following her or back on his tail?"

He debated and glanced at his watch. It was still early, and he expected Steve to be at the office until at least six. "Stay on her until lunchtime and then head this way." He flipped the phone closed and glanced at his calendar. He had a meeting with one of his distributors in an hour. Closing his laptop, he locked his office before heading out.

Vengeance
Chapter 6

THE CAR FOLLOWED STEVE out of sight, and she kicked into action. Suitcases came out and garments flew from the bureau into the open luggage as she tossed as much of her clothing as the two bags would hold. She unplugged the tiffany desk lamp and headed out to the garage, depositing the suitcases in the trunk of her car along with the lamp.

After seizing a box from the closet, she haphazardly threw some books and CDs into it, as well as a frying pan. Satisfied with the impression of a quick packing, she brought the box down to the car. She made one last trip up to the apartment and looked around. The decorative pillows on the couch caught her eye and on impulse, she snatched both the pillows and her make-up case on her way out the door.

Tucked out of sight on the far corner, she studied each car that pulled to the side of the road by their building. She didn't have to wait long before the man hired to watch her husband pulled into the same parking spot he had settled into the previous night. He leaned back in the seat, watching the entrance of her building.

Jennifer took her time, driving around Brooklyn, stopping to grab breakfast at a little café before she headed back to their apartment. She didn't have to be at the theater until later this afternoon, and the morning performance was much more critical because her husband's life was at stake. She had to make the man watching believe she was moving into their apartment.

She swung her car into the no-parking zone in front of the building and climbed out. She released the trunk before climbing out onto the sidewalk. With the first box balanced on her knee, she slammed the trunk closed.

A police officer stopped her halfway across the sidewalk.

"You can't park there," the heavyset officer said. Her gray hair curled around her cap, and she continued to point at Jennifer's car with each approaching step.

"Officer," she began, "I just have a few things to bring inside. I'll only be a couple of minutes. I promise." She took another step toward the apartment.

The officer flipped the page and wrote out a ticket.

"Please don't give me a ticket. I'm moving in today and I don't have any help."

The officer raised her beady, narrow eyes. "You can't park here."

Her arms were burning from the weight of the box. "Just let me bring this up and I'll move the car," she pleaded.

The officer went back to writing the ticket.

She debated whether she should go upstairs or move the car. "Screw it." She turned, entering the building, and headed to the elevator. The officer slipped the ticket under her wiper just before the elevator doors closed on the view. "Shit."

Returning a few minutes later, she ripped the ticket off the windshield and dropped it in the trunk, retrieving the two suitcases. Out of the corner of her eye, she saw the tail staring at her. She paid no attention to him and slammed the trunk closed.

Jennifer deposited the suitcases inside and locked up before heading down once more. This time, she slid into the driver's seat and pulled the car into the garage across from the building. She made a spectacle of herself juggling the throw pillows and tiffany lamp as she crossed the street, muttering under her breath and clutching the parking ticket in her hand.

The apartment door closed behind her, and she exhaled. The encounter with the officer had been annoying, but it also was a good diversion. It gave her a chance to get a better look at their stalker. Dark hair pulled tight into a ponytail, tinted glasses and a scar on the side of his Latino cheek. Based on the number of cigarettes on the ground outside his car window, he was also a chain smoker.

She made the point of going over to the curtains and throwing them wide to let in the morning sunshine before she unpacked her clothes and placed the lamp on the desk where she had grabbed it. When she finished, she headed into the bathroom and ducked into the shower, letting the water dissolve the tension from her muscles.

"Please God, let that be convincing enough," she whispered as she poured shampoo into her hand.

Vengeance
Chapter 7

THE CELL PHONE VIBRATED in his pocket, and Steve checked the display. A text message appeared with instructions. He waited a half hour, then locked his computer and walked out of the office, heading to the Starbucks down the street.

He scanned the busy crowd for a tail before stepping inside. The scent of muffins and coffee filled the small shop. His stomach growled, and mouth watered from the conditioned reflex of hundreds of Starbucks visits.

"Large vanilla latte," he said to the bubbly girl behind the counter and slid his Bluetooth into his ear. "And a blueberry muffin." He handed over a twenty, taking his change and his order, and headed to a corner table by the window where he opened the newspaper left behind.

A napkin fell out and Steve slowly crumpled it after reading the message scribbled on the thin paper. He glanced at the story highlighted in the message. A blonde-haired woman looked accusingly from the page of the newspaper. Found dead in her apartment last night. The information paralleled Jennifer's dream. "Damn."

"No kidding," the older gentleman in the chair right behind him said. "How'd you know?"

Steve inhaled and glanced at the reflection in the window. His partner, Jerry Kasmur, stared into the glass, their eyes meeting briefly. Jack hadn't filled Jerry in on Jennifer's clairvoyant abilities, and he wasn't in the mood to get into the details of his wife's gifts in a busy Manhattan Starbucks. Hell, it had taken Jack almost a year to accept it; he couldn't expect Jerry to in five minutes. "Crystal balls, remember?"

Jerry choked on his coffee, sputtering it all over the table, and Steve stifled a grin, scanning the article in front of him again before he spoke next. "By the way, I almost got nailed last night." He sipped his coffee while his gaze surveyed the crowd inside the restaurant and outside on the street between glances at the newspaper in his hands.

Silence.

His phone vibrated, and he pressed the Bluetooth, connecting the call. He took another sip, glancing at the newspaper while peeling away the wax paper from the bottom of the muffin.

"What happened?"

"I got the last of the documents and should have time to review them over the weekend," he said into the phone. "I'm hoping I'll have the final contract by Monday."

"What happened?"

"I ran into him at the office on my way out." He and glanced back at the newspaper. "Jenny's involved." He took a bite of the muffin, swallowing the nervous lump that had formed in his throat. "I needed a reason to be there at that hour and invented a crazy girlfriend." He shot a sideways glance at the glass.

"Jack's not going to like that."

Steve uttered a short laugh. "That's the understatement of the year." Jack had been livid when he found out Jennifer was in New York with him. She wasn't part of the agency. She was a civilian, and he didn't care that they were married. This assignment was supposed to be deep cover and the dossier they built for him had no mention of a wife. While her identity had been kept under wraps after the situation in Brooksfield blew wide open, anyone with the type of connections Charlie had could dig deep enough to find out about Jennifer's past, and her connection to the FBI. Using her maiden name on the billing made it much easier for that connection to be uncovered.

Returning his gaze to the paper, he asked, "Is this the same guy?"

"Yes," Jerry said.

"Missing digit?"

"Yes." The confirmation came with the scraping of the chair as Jerry got up, heading toward the door. "We've arranged for our seats to be next to yours at the play Friday."

"Jenny ought to love that." Steve rolled his eyes. Taking another bite of the muffin, he listened to his partner's chuckle before the line went dead.

He finished his coffee while reading the paper. A cop in the seventh precinct survived the latest victim, and she came home to find her sister dead. He'd seen some of the crime scene photos from the Slasher's earlier victims, and if this was anything like the other murders, it was messy as hell.

He flipped to the business section and after reading three stories, painting doom and gloom in the financial sector; he closed the paper, collected his garbage, and dumped it in the trash on the way out the door.

STEVE STEPPED ON THE elevator and pressed the button for the fifth floor.

A hand shot between the doors, causing them to retract. The owner of the appendage stepped into the elevator. He gave Steve a nod and went to press the button for his floor, but pulled his hand back at the last moment. "Looks like we got the express."

Steve glanced at his elevator mate, offering a civil elevator smile, memorizing as much about him as he could. CW FOG covered the entire fifth floor, and he had never seen this joker before. Between 6'1" and 6'2" with white teeth that poked out from behind his dark beard. The Prada shades shielding his eyes hinted that the man was better off than he appeared. A New York Yankee baseball cap covered most of his unruly curls, but some still poked out around the edges. The color matched the deep brown of his beard. His jeans were torn at the knees, but his Nikes were spotless. The corduroy blazer had patches on the elbows, reminding him of the pompous professors at Yale, yet he carried a package and clipboard under his arm.

The contradictions intrigued Steve. There was a strange, almost bohemian flavor to the man, the scent of sweat and nicotine emanated from him, mixing with the sweet aroma of vanilla latte in the small space. Steve took a sip of the coffee and watched the floor count rise.

When the elevator opened, he held the door for the man, watching as he headed into the office, approaching the empty reception desk.

"Can I help you?" Steve asked.

The man checked his clipboard. "Is Mr. Wisnowski around?"

"Do you want me to sign for that?"

The man shook his head. "Says here to hand deliver to Mr. Wisnowski."

"Okay. I'll see if he's in the office." Steve stepped out of the reception area. Charlie's door was closed, and he rapped his knuckles on the mahogany wood, waiting. After a moment, he headed back into the lobby. "I'm sorry, but he isn't in the office right now. You sure you don't want me to sign?"

The man nodded and wrote a quick note. "Have him call me schedule a more convenient time." He handed him the paper and disappeared into a waiting elevator.

Steve opened the note as he walked into his office and stopped in the middle of the room, reading the scribbled script.

Got a package from Mr. B. Give me a yell and I'll bring it by.

His eyebrows creased as he refolded the note and tucked it into his shirt pocket.

THE PRINTER SPAT OUT copies of the contract, and Steve picked up the group of papers, scanning his notes, and suggested updates. Charlie entered the office and Steve grabbed the last page off the printer and intercepted him.

"Do you have a minute?"

"What's up?" Charlie swung his office door open.

"I wanted you to look over the changes to the contract before I send it out." He handed over the pages. "And a courier was here earlier. He needed your signature and said to call him set up another time." He pulled the note from his pocket and handed it to Charlie.

A small smile appeared on Charlie's lips as he read the scribbled note. He pocketed the paper and took a seat behind his desk, motioning for Steve to do the same. Charlie scanned the proposed changes Steve gave him.

He nodded when he agreed and chewed his lip when he had reservations.

Steve had defined a more reasonable deal, sighting normal hours as between eight in the morning and six at night, and triple time only applied between the hours of midnight and six in the morning. Everything else was double time.

"You think they'll go for this?" Charlie asked when he looked up from the annotated contact pages.

"I don't know. They were pretty skimpy on the timeframe for reasonable and customary rates." Steve raised his eyebrow, leaning forward to rest his elbows on the arms of the chair. He clasped his hands together. "I think they're going to push for a longer triple time window."

Charlie leaned back, drumming his fingers on the desk. "I'm not thrilled about paying triple for any time of day."

"I could change it to say off hour service is paid at double time," he said, "but they might tell you to go pound sand."

Charlie chuckled. "Change it and let's see what their reaction is. If they squawk, offer them this deal." He handed the papers back to Steve.

"Will do." He walked out of Charlie's office with no more of a clue as to what the messenger's note meant than before. After making the updates, he sent an electronic copy to Hammond Boilers and waited for their reaction.

Vengeance
Chapter 8

THE EMPTY APARTMENT GREETED him. He tossed both his briefcase and overcoat on the desk, and opted to fix a quick meal before he settled into his daily de-brief. With the scent of chicken alfredo drifting through the flat, Steve opened his laptop and signed on. He attended to dinner, stirring the sauce until it thickened and when it was finished, he prepared a plate for both Jennifer and himself. Hers he covered and placed into a warm oven and his took the place of his briefcase and coat on the desktop. Settling behind the screen, he alternated between typing and eating, not really tasting the delicious meal he'd cooked. Instead, his focus remained on detailing his day at the office and the odd courier visit.

When he finished his recap, he pulled Charlie's file, popping open a Corona before reading the information for the hundredth time. Charlie's parents died in a car accident shortly after his brother was born. Paul Wisnowski had been traveling too fast for the conditions when he hit an ice patch that spun him into the path of an eighteen-wheeler. Both he and his wife died on impact, leaving Charlie and his younger brother Kyle in the hands of the state.

Because Charlie was such a rebel, it was difficult to find folks willing to open their doors to the orphans for any length of time. So, he and his brother flowed from one foster family to the next. When Charlie turned sixteen, he took off, leaving his younger brother in the hands of the foster system until he died in a car accident five years later, at the age of sixteen.

Charlie's family doesn't seem to have luck with cars.

Steve drained the beer and read the accident report for Kyle. The teenager lost control of his car and slammed into a tree. The car exploded, leaving the body mostly charred by the time the firefighters arrived.

He raised his eyebrows.

Cars don't just explode... unless it was an old Pinto.

Cocking his head, he leaned forward, pulling up the make and model. The kid had a Trans-Am, not a Pinto. He popped the cap off another Corona and sat back, reviewing the eyewitness accounts. The car didn't explode on impact. They said it took a good ten seconds between hitting the tree and the explosion, which was powerful enough to send a couple of bystanders onto their asses, contributing to the chaos at the scene.

Just doesn't seem right.

He chewed the inside of his lip in time with the gnawing sensation in the pit of his stomach.

Jennifer walked in the door, interrupting his train of thought.

"I moved in today," she said.

He met her stare, and the crease between his eyebrows deepened.

Jennifer pointed to her ear and then twirled her finger at the ceiling.

Steve glanced around, catching her drift and kicking himself for not thinking of it before. He hadn't had a scan of the apartment for a couple of weeks, and it would be just like Charlie to bug the place now that he was on his radar. "So I see." He returned his gaze to her. "How'd rehearsal go?"

"Good. What'd you cook for dinner?" She caught a quick kiss before dumping her pocketbook and coat on the chair.

"Chicken alfredo. There's a covered plate in the oven." He sipped his beer and closed the connection, shutting off his computer. Swiveling the chair around, he studied the room. Nothing was out of order.

"My god, this is good," she said through a mouthful of chicken.

"Feel like grabbing a drink after?" he asked, still surveying the apartment. His eyes landed on a knick-knack that he hadn't noticed before and he crossed to the window, smiling as he shot a sideways glance in her direction and drew the shades.

"After what?" Jennifer understood, taking the bait and teasing him.

Steve's smile disappeared, and he turned his back on the covered window. "After we screw around." His voice carried a certain lightness not reflected in his knotted muscles. He crossed and pointed to the piece.

"Why don't we have a drink first?" She shook her head and shrugged, telling him it wasn't hers.

It certainly wasn't his. He examined the ceramic bunny and glanced over his shoulder with a shrug. "Why's that?"

Her light laughter filled the apartment. "Because if we get into that bed, we both know we won't be going out tonight."

"You've got a point." Steve leaned on the desk facing her, his eyes still scanning the room for places where listening devices could be planted. "You about ready, then?"

How long has Charlie been listening?

Every conversation over the last couple of weeks flowed through his mind and the only time he went off script was this morning.

Shit.

He glanced back at the shelves where the ceramic bunny sat. He didn't think it had been there, but he couldn't be sure. He swung his apprehensive gaze toward Jennifer.

"Sure. Let me finish this and I'll be all set." She took the last bite of her dinner and rinsed the dish before they headed out.

"Jesus," Steve whispered on the street.

"You really think there's a tap in our apartment?" Jennifer asked.

"Yes. He's got a tail on us, which means he's got some questions about me." He glanced sideways.

"That isn't good, is it?"

He shrugged and stopped at the corner when the *Do Not Cross* sign turned solid. The tail car drove down the block and stopped. A bus pulled through the intersection, temporarily blocking the view, and Steve turned, leading Jennifer down the street to the right and into a small bar on the far corner of the block before the tail could track them again. They took a seat in the back and ordered a beer.

"No, it isn't," he finally answered Jennifer. "It's just a matter of how long he's been listening. If he heard our conversation this morning..." He trailed off. "Please reconsider going home."

"I just landed the lead in the play. Besides, I'm not leaving you."

He took a deep breath. "Charlie invited me to a get together Friday."

She stiffened, and the unhappy set of her jaw caused him to shake his head.

"I turned him down."

Jennifer blinked and tilted her head. She opened her mouth and then closed it and looked into her beer. "I don't know whether to thank you or smack you," she commented after her first sip.

"I promised you I'd be there."

She leaned back in the seat, and a smile played on her lips. "You chose me over your job? I'm flattered."

"Yeah, well, don't be. Jerry arranged to have the seat next to mine."

The bell over the door of the bar jingled with the next patron.

"That's him." She glanced toward the door and back at Steve.

"I figured it wouldn't be long. Just don't look at him again," he said. "Are you ready for Friday?" He tipped the beer to his lips and glanced at the mirror behind the bar, catching their tail's reflection in the smoky glass before returning his gaze to Jennifer. She was talking.

"So, I got a little angry."

His eyebrows creased. "Why'd you get angry?"

"Are you even listening to me at all?" she yelled. "Or were you watching the ballgame?" She pointed at the television above the bar where the Knicks were taking on the Celtics.

"I, uh…" Steve glanced over his shoulder. Her outburst drew the attention of the entire bar. He turned back toward her, seeing the spark in her eyes. "I heard what you said," he recovered, getting into character.

"No, you didn't! You never listen!" Jennifer stood up and stormed out of the bar with everyone staring after her.

He hung his head and stood, heading out with a shrug to the other patrons. He caught up with her around the corner near their apartment, grabbed her arm, and stopped her. "What was that all about?"

"Roll with it." She yanked her arm out of his grip and stomped into the apartment building.

Steve put his hands on his hips, exasperated. He hated it when Jennifer took matters into her own hands—things usually got messier when she did that. He made his way into the building and caught sight of the tail as the elevator doors closed.

The ceramic figurine hit him in the temple when he closed the apartment door. It fell, smashing on the floor. Steve ducked under the next item thrown in his direction, the heel of his palm pressed to the spot where the first torpedo hit. "What the fuck are you doing?"

"You never listen!" she screamed and hurled another item from the shelves at Steve. She picked up yet another item and pulled her arm back to send it sailing in his direction. "You're always ignoring me and now that I have your attention…"

"Don't throw that!" he bellowed. Jennifer's hand wrapped around a paperweight his grandfather gave him. Embedded inside the crystal ball was the emblem of the Marine Corps unit his grandfather had served with before he became an FBI agent.

"Why the hell not?"

"My grandfather gave me that." Steve crossed the room, tearing it out of her hand. He slammed it back on the shelf and turned his attention to the shattered bits of items he wasn't able to save. "Damn it, Jenny!" He glared in her direction. "You broke the eagle Peg gave me." He pulled his hand away from his temple. It was covered in blood and a warm trickle slid down his face. "And I'm bleeding."

Storming into the bathroom, he slammed the door behind him and looked at his reflection. "Shit." He was bleeding all right. Snatching a washcloth off the rack, he turned on the cold water and soaked the fabric, wringing it before he pressed it to the gash. Anger engulfed him, and he yanked open the bathroom door.

Jennifer ran the broom over the floor, collecting the glass in a small pile. "I'm sorry," she said without turning. "I overreacted."

"Ya think?" He continued to hold the wet compress to his temple, watching her sweep the glass into a dustpan. "I need stitches."

Jennifer turned with wide eyes. "You deserve it!" she snapped and mouthed the words *I'm so sorry*. She looked back at the pile of rubble in the dustpan and picked out the microphone chip. "What's this?"

Steve stared at the wiretap she held and shrugged, in full view of their stalker.

"You don't trust me?" She dropped the dustpan, sending the glass bouncing off the pan over the floor, and she crossed to him, holding the microphone in front of her like a dead mouse.

Steve stepped away even though he knew the anger emanating was manufactured for their audience. "I've never seen that before in my life," he answered, his gaze bouncing between the wiretap and Jennifer's face. "What the hell is it?"

"A microphone." She inspected the item closely. "My ex tapped my phone once with something that looked like this." She raised her eyes, tossing it to him.

Steve caught the small electronic device. He tilted his head, gritting his teeth. "I didn't put this here."

"If you didn't, then who did?" Jennifer barked.

"Maybe *you* did." He spiked the microphone on the floor, grinding the heel of his shoe on the speaker, destroying it.

They stood staring at each other for a moment. Neither one was sure whether the microphone in the knick-knack was the only tap in the apartment.

"I didn't plant the wire," Jennifer said, keeping in character. She sat on the edge of the bed. "Maybe it *was* my ex."

Steve sighed and glanced at the mess on the floor. He sat down on the edge of the bed, wrapping his arm around her shoulder. "I'm not your ex," he said for the benefit of any live microphones, "and if that son of a bitch comes anywhere near you, I'll kill him." He pulled the cloth away from his temple, the blue fabric now purple from absorbing the blood. "I need to get to the hospital. Can you drive?"

Jennifer audibly sighed. "Yeah." She led him out of the apartment.

"ROLL WITH IT?" STEVE asked as he sat in the emergency waiting room.

Jennifer chuckled and shrugged. "I didn't mean to split your head open."

"Yeah, well, you also broke the eagle Peg gave me."

Her smile disappeared at the mention of his ex-fiancé's name, bringing her back to the initiation rite that almost killed them the year before, and all the tragic events leading up to it, including the death of her boyfriend. "If you noticed, I also smashed the ceramic cat Tom gave me."

He hadn't noticed; he was too busy dodging the projectiles. He leaned back in the chair and closed his eyes against the raging headache. "I'll need to sweep both cars and the rest of the apartment over the weekend to make sure there aren't any more bugs."

"Do you think that quantifies me as the crazy girlfriend?"

Steve burst out laughing. "I'd say so." He glanced over at her. "You can be pretty scary when you put your mind to it."

Their stalker walked through the emergency room entrance.

"And you can be a royal jackass at times," Jennifer said, slipping into character.

Steve's eyebrows creased. "I have half a mind to press charges," he muttered, sending a wink in her direction.

"You wouldn't dare!"

Steve allowed a brief smile to surface before suppressing it. "Assault with a deadly knick-knack."

She burst out laughing, covering her mouth to stifle the echo in the small waiting room.

Steve looked at the floor, the smile gaining traction on his lips until the snort escaped and the laughter took hold. He glanced sideways at her. "I'm still pissed at you," he said, still chuckling.

"I know." Jennifer patted him on the back. "You'll get over it."

Vengeance
Chapter 9

THE KNICK'S GUARD MISSED the shot and Charlie jumped to his feet, his beer bubbling up from the sudden lurch. "Come on!" he yelled at the large screen television. He had a lot riding on this game, and with the home team teetering on a loss, his mood turned foul.

He switched the bottle to his left hand and snapped his right wrist, sending a small spray of beer over the glass coffee table. Tipping the beer to his lips, he drained half the bottle in one pull and sat down, glaring at the television, willing the Knicks to win.

The phone interrupted his mental chant, and he snatched it off the cradle. "What?" he snapped, his eyes still glued to the television.

"They found the bug."

Charlie's attention snapped away from the basketball game. "Who?"

"Your star lawyer."

Irritation blazed under his skin, and he clenched his teeth. The Celtics just sunk a three pointer and drew a foul.

Fuck. First the Knicks, now this?

He muted the television. "How?"

"His girlfriend."

Blinking, he digested the comment. "His girlfriend?"

"Yeah, she is a crazy bitch. I'm talking certifiable. She freaked out on him at a bar because he was watching the Knicks game and then when they got home, she threw the ceramic figure I planted at him."

What were the odds?

Speechless, he caught his slack-jawed expression in the television's reflection and closed his mouth. "Was that the only item she threw?"

"No, she threw a bunch of shit and one of them caught him in the temple." He cleared his throat. "Charlie, she was the one that made the wire. He didn't know what the hell it was. The girl's wacked. She accused your lawyer of spying on her, and the bitch just moved in today."

Charlie let out a huff combined with a laugh. "How'd he handle that?"

"Pretty smooth, considering her colossal shit fit. He seemed less freaked by the wire than he was of her accusation, even turned the tables on her."

"Did he figure it out?"

"No. They think her ex bugged the place."

"Where are they now?"

"The hospital."

"Excuse me?"

"He's getting stitches as we speak."

"You're shitting me."

Chuckling came through the line. "No, sir. She drove him to the hospital."

Something didn't add up. Steve didn't seem like the kind of person who would take that kind of shit, especially not from a woman, but who knows? He chewed on the side of his lip for a moment. "Stay on him," he ordered, going on gut instinct. He suspected the loyalties of his star lawyer weren't in the right place. He hung up the phone and took the television off mute, but was no longer seeing what was playing out on the court. His mind was preoccupied with how he could test that loyalty to be sure.

Vengeance
Chapter 10

THE ALARM WENT OFF, sending the shrill buzz through his head. Steve moaned. His head felt like cymbals banged together an inch from his ear, the vibrations and high-pitched whine filled his brain. Wincing, he sat up and touched the bandage with his fingers, took a deep breath, and blew it out slowly to settle his rolling stomach.

He took a moment, steadying himself, and willed his stomach to settle before standing and heading to the bathroom.

The shower's warm water felt like heaven, and he stood, letting the jets pound the back of his neck for longer than normal. He opened one eye when Jennifer cracked the shower door.

"Are you okay?"

Steve closed his eye. "I will be," he said, his voice barely audible.

"I am so sorry." She stepped under the stream and wrapped her arms around his waist.

"Hell of a pitch." His lips found the nape of her neck and his arms wrapped around her body. Sucking the warm water off her skin, he moved his lips up the line of her neck to her earlobe and gently nibbled. He pulled away from her ear and looked down into her bright green eyes before crushing her lips. Hers parted and their tongues mingled, rolling, tasting each other, the passion diminishing his headache while his hands wandered over her wet skin.

He made love to his wife under the warm stream of water. Her moans were a crescendo in his ear as they peaked together.

Trembling, he set her down and leaned his forehead on hers. His heartbeat returned to normal, along with his breathing. "I love you." He kissed her and stepped out of the shower to get ready for work. His headache was now a dull thump instead of the earlier sharp roar.

He sat on the edge of the bed and slipped on his shoes, tying the thin laces. He looked up at her when she came out of the bathroom wrapped in only a towel. Scanning her voluptuous form, he smiled and stood. "What time does rehearsal end?"

"I'll be home late tonight."

"I'll have something here for you when you get in." He paused by her side and kissed her cheek. "Break a leg." Grinning, he left the apartment.

STEVE STOPPED AT THE Starbucks around the corner from the office, grabbing his normal latte and a muffin and taking his normal seat by the window. Turning over the script in his mind, the explanation for the stitches, for the conversation he knew Charlie was briefed on, he poked holes in it, revising until he had a more believable story, one even he'd buy. He just prayed the stupid knick-knack wasn't there yesterday morning—otherwise, he was a dead man.

Linda looked up from the reception desk when he walked off the elevator. Her eyes widened and her jaw dropped. "What happened to you?"

Steve's hand shot to the bandage. "Nothing."

"Doesn't look like nothing."

"I got in the way of a flying knick-knack." Steve crossed to his office, closing the door on the few inquisitive stares.

Charlie walked into his office a half hour later. "I heard you were a mess. What happened?" He took a seat on the opposite side of the desk.

Steve looked down at his hands. "Jenny got a little angry."

"And what, threw a bowling ball at your head?"

He broke out in a grin and raised his gaze. "No." He touched the bandage. "This was a ceramic bunny. I'm just glad it wasn't my American eagle. That would have broken my skull."

His smile faded. "She was trying to kill you?"

"No. She was just pissed off because I wasn't listening."

Charlie raised his eyebrows and crossed his arms. "Is she usually this...unstable?"

"Not usually." He took a deep breath. "She's always been a bit high maintenance, you know? But lately..." Steve shrugged. "She's been stressed."

Charlie scrutinized Steve with sharp eyes. "I never would have pegged you for someone who would let a woman walk all over you."

Clenching his jaw, he let a fraction of the anger he felt toward Charlie surface. "I don't let anyone walk over me." He pushed the chair back and started across the room toward the door.

Charlie swiveled the chair around. "I'm concerned about you."

Steve stopped at the door, turning toward his boss with his hand on the knob. "Well, don't be. I can take care of myself."

Charlie smiled and stood, crossing to him. "That's what my little brother used to say."

Steve stared at Charlie. *Careful now.* His heart hammered in his chest at the sudden breakthrough.

He put his hand up. "My little brother seemed to have a knack for landing in abusive relationships, too."

Steve raised his eyebrows and stepped back. "Abuse?" He started laughing. "Charlie, I'm not abused. I just didn't duck fast enough."

Charlie put his hand on his shoulder, and he shook it off.

"I'm fine, really. Jenny's just going through an emotional time. Her ex is driving her nuts, and she was kicked out of her apartment, and the play opens tomorrow. She's just wound really tight." He let a laugh escape, realizing he was babbling. "Her ex even bugged our apartment."

Charlie tilted his head. "Really?"

"Yeah, he knew we've been dating and knows where I live," he nodded, crossing back to his desk. "I don't know how the hell he got in, but I'm going to look at installing a deadbolt. The microphone was in one of the broken ceramic pieces." Taking a seat in his chair, Steve met his gaze. "Man, she was pissed! She thought I planted it. Can you believe that?" He shook his head, slowly taking a deep breath, unnerved by

Charlie's silence. He continued anyway. "That guy did such a number on her. If the bastard comes anywhere near her..." Steve trailed off and thought of Bill, re-living the hatred that flared in his soul when he saw Jennifer being raped. He swung his eyes toward Charlie. "If he comes near her, I'll kill him."

Charlie stiffened at the venom in his voice. "Chill there, buddy," he said. "By the way, I got tickets for your girlfriend's play. I'll be there tomorrow night and you can introduce us."

The curveball stunned him, and he blinked. "I, uh, I thought you were having a party?" He couldn't keep the stutter of surprise out of his voice.

"I changed my mind." Charlie disappeared, leaving Steve staring after him.

Shit! Jenny's going to be pissed!

He swiveled, looking at his computer screen, analyzing the breakthrough with Charlie and playing the last few minutes over in his mind. *Shit.* Steve rolled his head, trying to loosen the tight muscles in his neck, wondering just how much Charlie knew.

A message from the maintenance company blinked in his email box.

His eyebrows went up, and he leaned back in the chair. "I'll be damned." He stood and crossed to Charlie's office. "They accepted the contract changes," he said, leaning in the door.

Charlie gave Steve a thumbs-up and pointed to the phone.

"Sorry." Steve headed back to his office. He crafted the email response, stating they would look forward to receiving the signed contract for execution. He sent the email, copying Charlie, and sat back. There were no more contracts to negotiate at the moment, and no trusts to execute, and he found himself in the unusual circumstance of having nothing to do.

Edgy from the morning conversation and looking for some levity, he pulled the cell phone out and pressed speed dial.

He swung the chair back and forth, looking out at the busy office.

"HELLO?" JENNIFER ANSWERED THE phone. Blinking against the morning sunshine, she crossed her arm over her eyes to block the bright rays.

"Hi, babe," he said.

"Hey." She stretched lazily in the bed.

"Are you still in bed?"

"Mhm."

"Wake up!"

"Uh-uh."

"Lazy girl."

"What are you doing calling me in the middle of the morning?"

"Just wrapped up the latest contract negotiation and I find myself with nothing on my plate, so I figured…"

"You'd call and harass me." She finished his sentence.

"Exactly. That's the least I can do, considering the six stitches in my head."

Jennifer let out a snort.

"My boss is coming Friday," Steve said.

She lifted her arm from her eyes and sat up. "Say again?"

"Charlie is coming to the play on Friday. You'll get to meet him."

It's supposed to be my night. The thought leaped to the front of her mind, but she bit down on letting it escape from her lips. "Fine."

"Fine?"

"Did you just call to razz me?"

Steve chuckled. "Gotta run!"

Jennifer stared at the phone, the dial tone transitioning into the horrible beep, beep, beep of a phone off the hook. She slammed the phone in the cradle and rolled out of bed.

Her stomach lurched when she opened the refrigerator. The scent of leftover chicken made her bolt across the apartment. Sliding on the floor of the bathroom, she fell to her knees just as the sour contents of her stomach emptied into the bowl. She spit and brushed the vile taste from her mouth. Nausea had seeped in over the past couple of weeks but hadn't started vomiting. Jennifer closed her eyes, willing herself not to be sick, not tonight and definitely not tomorrow.

"I can't be sick." She opened her eyes. "I can't."

Vengeance
Chapter 11

STEVE TURNED OFF HIS computer for the night when Charlie knocked on the door.

"They caved, eh?"

"They certainly did." He zipped his briefcase and stood.

"I've been thinking about your situation."

"My situation?" *Shit, here it comes.*

"Your girlfriend's ex."

"What about him?" Steve asked, attempting to hide the surprise and doubt shifting through his muscles.

"I can help you with that." Charlie leaned against the doorjamb and crossed his arms.

Steve leaned on his desk, adopting the same stance. "How?"

"I've got a lot of influential friends, Steve. If I suggest someone needs to disappear, they disappear."

Steve digested this information and kept eye contact while deciding how to play this.

Gamble.

"You know, I've never once asked where all that extra money came from. Now I'm wondering." He raised his eyebrows. "What exactly am I involved in here?"

Charlie laughed. "What do you think you're involved in?"

Steve allowed a small smile. "I'm not sure." His heart raced, and he prayed the gamble wouldn't backfire. "You're offering to make a problem disappear. That gets me thinking perhaps there are some things we're doing that aren't within the confines of the law."

Charlie straightened up. "And if that's the case?"

Steve inhaled and allowed his shoulders to slump a fraction. He exhaled and uncrossed his arms, leaning his palms on the edge of the desk, taking time to formulate his thoughts. This was a critical juncture, and if he gave the wrong answer, he wouldn't make it out of the building alive. "Hypothetically?"

Charlie gave a slow nod.

Steve kept eye contact. "I'm not sure," he finally said. "On one hand, I want to know, but on the other..." He shrugged.

"On the other?"

"On the other, if you are involved in something illegal and I know nothing of the details, I would never be a liability if subpoenaed."

"You're my lawyer. What about attorney client privilege?"

"There are some boundaries there. If the communication is used in the commission of a crime, the privilege is inadmissible. There was a Supreme Court ruling on that recently."

Charlie's eyebrows went up. "You're shitting me?"

"No. I'm not kidding and I'm really not too keen on going to jail for contempt of court." Steve grabbed his briefcase off the desk, approaching Charlie and stopping when he was shoulder to shoulder with his boss.

Dice in hand, he rolled.

"So, the question is, hypothetically, of course, do you trust *me* enough to take that kind of gamble?" Steve went to take a step out of the office.

"I trust you enough to handle my money," Charlie answered, turning toward Steve. "And you're damn good at it."

Bingo!

"Trust accounts, S corporations, LLCs. It's just moving money from place to place, Charlie. A shell game, nothing more." Steve's adrenaline kicked into high gear as he charted the path through the dangerous minefield he just stepped in. Charlie's last lawyer had been found shot dead in the park. The police report tagged it as a robbery gone wrong, but Steve knew better. If he wasn't careful, he could end up with a similar fate.

Charlie laughed. "Yes, but what you've done is slick. In the years that I've been doing this, I've never had a lawyer quite as creative with my money." He leaned closer. "Who *didn't* skim a cent off the top."

"I'm not here to steal your money, Charlie. You pay better than most firms in this market."

"Come; let's celebrate the success of the contract." Charlie put his hand on Steve's back, leading him through the empty office.

Steve figured he either scored big or was being led to his death. He kept his game face on, not showing a hint of the apprehension pulsing through his muscles.

"You've got alcohol in your office?" he asked when they crossed the threshold.

"Not exactly." Charlie closed the door and flipped the lock. "Have a seat."

Steve tensed when the lock flipped, but took a seat on the couch as directed. His eyebrows creased. "If you don't have alcohol…" He trailed off, meeting Charlie's direct stare.

Charlie sat at the desk for a minute, a serious expression on his face. "Ever experiment with drugs, Steve?"

"Excuse me?" His already pounding heart nearly tripled its rate, and he swore Charlie could see his shirt move with each frantic beat.

Calm your ass down!

Sweat saturated his palms, and he wiped them on his trousers.

"Have you ever used drugs?"

Steve looked at the door and back at Charlie with his mouth hanging open, debating on how to answer. "Hasn't everyone, at least once?" He sent the question back after regaining composure.

Charlie smiled. "What have *you* tried?"

He looked at his hands. "The usual."

"Define usual."

"Marijuana. I tried it a few times in high school."

"Anything else?" Charlie pushed.

Steve stared at his boss for a moment and nodded. "I don't see why this is relevant. It was a long time ago."

"What else have you tried?"

"I'd rather not answer that." Steve shifted in the chair, doubting his chances of leaving the office alive. He took a deep breath, calming his nerves.

Charlie shook his head and reached under his desk, drawing the gun out and pointing it at Steve.

"Shit, Charlie, what the fuck are you doing?" Steve jumped to his feet.

Ah fuck, he knows!

"Are you a mole?"

"What? No." Steve shook his head. *How the hell do I play this?*

He stared down the barrel of the gun, and the blood rushed out of his face. He shifted his gaze to Charlie. The man was grinning at his reaction. "And this isn't funny."

Charlie raised his eyebrows. "At least you didn't piss your pants like my last lawyer." He pulled the hammer back. "Now tell me what other drugs you've experimented with."

Steve pressed his lips together and glared at Charlie. "Put the fucking gun away."

Charlie laughed and shot a round into the floor a couple of feet in front of Steve.

He jumped backwards. "Jesus!" He didn't have to manufacture any hint of fear. It was real and alive in his veins.

Charlie leaned back in the seat with the gun still pointed at him. He tilted his head. "I won't miss with the next round."

"Fine!" he yelled, putting his hands in front of him. "LSD. Okay? I did acid in high school." Steve's voice cracked. "And, and I tried peyote once. And in college, speed kept me awake cramming for exams."

"Really?" He released the hammer and flipped the safety on the gun, but still held it, pointing in Steve's direction. "That's it?"

Steve nodded.

"What was acid like?"

"What?" he asked, staring at the gun.

"What was acid like?"

Steve rolled his eyes. "It was surreal, all right?"

"That's not good enough, Steve." Charlie flipped the safety off the gun.

Steve tilted his head and let out a laugh. The sheer fact he wasn't dead was a positive sign. "You're fucked up."

"Maybe so, but considering the questions you've asked tonight, I figured you and I had better have this conversation. Now, you were saying?"

"I don't know how to describe it." Exasperated when Charlie leveled the gun at him again, he continued, "I thought I could see air molecules. Okay? Psychedelic colored air molecules that drifted around like amoebas and tracks of light, like the photographs of car taillights when the camera's shutter is held open. And there was a metallic taste in my mouth the whole time, like biting on tinfoil." He smiled for a second when Charlie visibly shivered at the analogy. "Nothing I did would get rid of the taste. It just had to wear off with the acid."

Charlie flipped the safety back on the gun. "What about cocaine?"

Steve shook his head. His heart hammered, and he swallowed despite his dry mouth.

"Why not?" Charlie leaned on his elbows. "You seemed to be adventurous enough to drop acid."

"I never warmed up to the idea of putting something up my nose."

He unlocked the top desk drawer and pulled out a few items, placing them on the desk without losing eye contact with Steve. He cocked the hammer back and slid the items to the far side. Charlie offered a smile and pointed toward the mirror, razor blade and baggie of white powder. "You're going to get over that pretty quickly or I'm going to plant a bullet in your brain."

He stared between the cocaine and Charlie. "Um, I'm not sure I want to work for you anymore."

Charlie laughed and lifted the gun. "Get over here." He stood and pointed the end of the gun at the paraphernalia on his desk.

Steve stiffly crossed the room and stood on the other side of the desk, his expression alternating between fear and anger, unsure of how to play the next bluff. He was still alive. Being resistant hadn't killed him yet, so he gambled again. "Why the hell are you doing this?"

"I'm protecting my investment. Now sit your ass down." Charlie pointed the gun at the chair.

He hesitated. "What if I refuse?"

"Then I'm going to lose the best financial lawyer I've ever had."

Charlie said it so calmly that goose bumps appeared on Steve's arms. He slowly sank into the chair and stared at the drugs. *I wish I had my fucking gun.* He glanced back at Charlie and said a silent prayer.

"If you liked speed, you'll like this," he said. "Open the bag and pour some on the mirror."

Steve followed Charlie's instructions, cutting the powder into a finer grain and arranging it into four even lines.

Charlie reached into his drawer and handed him a two-inch plastic straw. "That's all for you.

Put the straw in your nostril, plug the other one and inhale."

"At gunpoint?" Steve's voice cracked again. *Jenny's going to kill me.*

Charlie nodded.

"Fine," he snapped and leaned over. The first snort burned as it went up his nose, dripping into his throat, making his eyes water. He sat back, choking on a cough.

"Keep going."

"Just give me a sec." He glared at Charlie and sniffled, rubbing the side of his nose to stop the tickling sensation that had set in.

"Now," Charlie ordered.

Steve leaned over and inhaled the next line of potent cocaine. The burning was less prevalent this time. He switched nostrils and did the same, sucking up the last two lines in rapid succession. Sniffling, he threw the straw on the desk and stood, crossing to the window with his back to Charlie. "Happy now?" he said over his shoulder.

"Not quite."

The tapping of the razor blade filled the room. Steve didn't bother turning. He watched the thinning traffic on the street below. The cocaine kicked in and a thousand tiny pinpricks dance across the surface of his skin. Steve's anger magnified, and he turned, glaring at Charlie. Four more lines were laid out on the mirror.

Charlie pushed it toward the edge of the desk again.

"No." He headed toward the door.

"I don't think you fully understand the situation, Steve."

Spinning in Charlie's direction, he asked, "Why are you doing this?" He approached the desk, glaring at Charlie. "I played your little game, I tried your drugs, now let me the fuck out of here."

Charlie held the straw out.

Steve knocked it out of his hand. His entire body tingled.

Charlie stood and pressed the gun to Steve's forehead. He reached into his shirt pocket where he had stuck a couple of straws, plucked one, and held it out to Steve.

"Fuck you."

The click of the hammer cocking back filled the room, immediately followed by the ringing of Steve's cell phone. He held Charlie's gaze while he pulled the phone from his pocket and flipped it open. "What?"

"Steve?" Her voice shook.

"I'm a little busy right now."

"I had a, a, a nightmare."

The bustling background of the theater filtered into the phone, and he knew from her shaky tone she had another vision and he'd bet a year's salary that it probably mirrored his current situation. "You okay?" His voice softened, although the smell of gunpowder and oil radiated from the barrel pressing against his forehead. He still held Charlie's gaze.

"Yeah. You?"

"I'm sure you'll be just fine. Just grab something to drink and do it again," Steve said, ignoring the question. "I've gotta go. I'll see you when you get home."

"Be careful." Her words mingled with his exhale, and he snapped the phone closed.

Charlie held the straw in front of his line of sight again. "Last chance."

Steve growled in the back of his throat, muttering curses before he grabbed the straw and sat down, sucking the lines into his sinuses.

Charlie sat back down, staring at Steve. "Are you a cop?"

"Fuck no!" Steve snapped, rubbing his numb nose with his index finger, sniffling repeatedly. "But right now, I wish I was one."

"Why's that?"

"Because I'd shoot you." He sniffed and drew in his breath as the tickling in his nose increased. "Then I'd throw your ass in jail." A high-pitched sound caught his attention, and he swiveled in the chair, looking for the source. His foot tapped uncontrollably on the ground, his heart picked up the pace. "Hell, I'd just shoot you." He turned his attention back to Charlie.

"So, you're not an undercover cop?"

Steve shook his head. He creased his eyebrows and looked at Charlie. "Why do you keep asking that?"

Charlie lowered the gun. "Because I'm not sure I believe you."

Steve laughed. "If I was a cop, you'd be in jail by now for tax evasion."

Charlie inhaled. "You asked me exactly what you were involved in."

Steve nodded. *Ok, Williams, get a grip. It's time to put on an Emmy winning performance.* His eyes slowly went wide, dropping to the mirror and the bag of cocaine. He raised them, meeting Charlie's gaze, letting his jaw drop.

Charlie bought it. He flipped the gun's safety and set it on the desk. "This is a front for my cocaine business. You've been laundering the money for me for six months, which, if I'm not mistaken, makes you an accessory." He pulled the mirror back in front of him and cut up four more lines, snorting them himself. "It's the finest product on the street." He wiped the mirror and put it back in the hidden panel in the drawer, along with the baggie.

Steve tried not to smile, admonishing himself silently. *Look shocked, you idiot!* His heart pumped the drug to the far recesses of his body, and he couldn't stop tapping his foot. "How much did you give me? Am I going to have a heart attack? Is it hot in here?" He fired off the questions in quick succession, loosening his tie, the cocaine rush far outpaced his adrenaline.

"Puts speed in the dust, doesn't it?" Charlie slid the gun under the desk. "Let's go get a drink and celebrate that contract."

Steve raised his eyebrows and let a high-pitched laugh escape. "You're out of your fucking mind. I'm not going anywhere with you. As a matter of fact, I quit." His foot kept tapping on the floor.

Charlie leaned on the desk. "That bug in your apartment was mine."

Charlie's admission caught him by surprise, and Steve pushed the chair back. "What?"

"I've had someone following you and your pretty girlfriend, so if you think about going to the police with any of this, I'll have you both killed." Charlie straightened up. "I'll expect you in the office tomorrow morning at your regular time. Now, how about that drink?"

Steve blinked, staring at Charlie, his mind firing off in so many different directions he found it hard to concentrate.

Jenny, he just threatened Jenny.

The clarity in that one thought brought him back to the task-at-hand. He caught his reflection in the window behind Charlie and snapped his mouth shut, grinding his teeth together. After a moment, he narrowed his eyes and tilted his head. "What's in it for me?"

Charlie laughed.

Steve crossed his arms and sat back in the chair, giving the impression of seeing the possibilities. "Seriously, Charlie. What do I get out of this arrangement?" He leaned forward. "Since it looks like I've got no choice, I think you should give me more of an incentive here. I'm a damn good lawyer and as such, I'm thinking I *should* get something out of this beyond the fine salary you're paying me." He sniffled, his foot still tapping at an annoying pace. "I'm not getting greedy, but I've got some whopping bills hanging over my head, ya know?"

Charlie just stared at Steve, his arms crossed and eyes blazing with anger.

"I'd like to see those bills... disappear." Steve snapped his finger and smiled at the analogy, bringing them full circle in the conversation. "Much more than her ex." He stood.

"You don't have any leverage here," Charlie spat.

Steve shrugged. "I think I do. And I'm not asking for a cut. I'm just asking for my education bills to be paid. That's it and I'll keep doing what I've been doing for you. No questions asked. That way I can get my girlfriend some nice things and maybe she won't throw ceramics at me anymore."

Charlie broke out in a smile. "You're something else." He sighed and nodded. "Consider it done, but if you get greedy on me or start skimming off the top, we'll be taking a little ride that you won't come back from."

"I got it." Steve stepped closer to Charlie. Feeling invincible now, he stabbed Charlie in the chest with his index finger. "But if you ever point that gun at me again, I'll break your arm. Understand?"

Charlie shifted his gaze between Steve's finger and his eyes and he chuckled. "Let's go get a drink." He walked to the door, flipped the lock, and swung the heavy wood aside.

Vengeance
Chapter 12

JENNIFER PACED THE EMPTY apartment.

"Where the hell are you?" she muttered, trying his cell phone again. It was past eleven, and she was frantic. The vision of the barrel of a gun pressed to his forehead had been enough to throw her into a tizzy at the theater, and his reaction on the phone didn't help. He'd been too calm, too cold, almost as if he knew.

He didn't answer.

"Shit!" She slammed the phone into the cradle. The various scenarios filled her mind, all ending with him dead, and she finally gave in. She crossed to his desk and opened the side drawer. Taped on the bottom was Jack's emergency number, and she reached for the paper.

The rattle of the key in the lock caught her attention, and she ran to the door, throwing it open. Steve stared at her, wide-eyed, keys poised where the lock had been moments before.

He dropped his briefcase on the floor and stepped into the apartment, pulling her to him without a word. He swung the door closed and kissed her hungrily.

She tasted scotch and pushed him away. "Where the hell have you been?"

"Work." He scanned her with his eyes and smiled.

Jennifer knew that look and shook her head. "No." She was pissed at him, and sex was not in the cards at the moment.

Laughing, he reached for her. "Yes."

Her brow creased as his hand clamped down on her upper arm, pulling her back against him. She studied his glossy, dilated eyes, and she knew. "Shit, Steve, are you high?"

"Oh, yeah." He pressed his lips against hers, his tongue forcing its way into her protesting mouth.

Jennifer pushed him away. "You're high? I've been scared to death here and you, you're high?" She couldn't believe it. Her husband didn't do drugs. He was a federal officer, and this just didn't happen in her world. "You, you, you stupid son of a bitch!" She swung her open palm toward his face.

Steve grabbed her wrist, stopping the progress of the slap. He yanked her towards him, his arms like a vise holding her against him as his lips wandered down the curve of her neck. The low chuckle that escaped tickled her skin, and she shivered.

"Stop," she said, but the command lacked conviction and she allowed him to lead her across the loft. His hands wandered, tugging at her clothing, and she accepted his kiss. His hardness pressed against the fabric of his slacks, signaling that he was more than ready for her. A flurry of discarded clothing lined the path he cut through the apartment and when they reached the bed, they were both naked; reveling in each other's sculpted bodies.

Steve flicked his tongue into the curve of her ear, following it to her earlobe, creating a tingling throughout her skin. He sucked, and then bit down. The sudden pain caused her to gasp. He chuckled.

There was no tenderness in his touch, just an animal need. Finding her lips again, he pushed her onto the bed under him, his hands searching and finding the spots that drove her wild, his mouth soon following the trail blazed by his fingertips.

STEVE ROLLED OFF HER and ran his hands through his hair, staring at the ceiling, satiated. A small smile graced his lips. "Wow."

Jennifer sat up on the side of the bed with her back to him. "Son of a bitch," she said, but didn't turn.

His smile faded, and he reached for her, his fingertips grazing her back.

She swatted his hand away. "Don't you dare get all lovey-dovey with me. You're in deep shit. Just because we screwed around doesn't mean I'm not angry. If you *ever* come home stoned again, I'm out of here." She shot into the bathroom.

The lock on the door clicked and Steve slid into his underwear, crossed to the bathroom door, and rapped his knuckles gently on the wood. "Jenny?" The sound of her retching sent his heart into a Mexican jumping bean pace, thudding against his ribs. "Are you okay?"

"No!" The word broke out between heaves.

The toilet flushed, and the water turned on and off before the door finally opened. "I'm not okay." She sailed past him and threw herself face first on the bed, muffling sobs in the soft down of the pillow.

"I'm sorry," he whispered, running his fingers lightly over her bare shoulders.

"It's not you. I haven't been feeling that great the last couple of days." She sat up and wiped her face. "But I'm still pissed at you for being high." She sniffled and wiped her nose with a tissue. "I need something to eat."

"Want me to cook?"

"No, I want to go out."

They got dressed in silence and left the apartment. "Walk or drive?" Steve asked, holding the door open for her. The unseasonably frigid wind slapped at their faces, and they wrapped their coats tighter.

"I'll drive," Jennifer answered after a moment's hesitation.

Steve followed her to the car like a wounded puppy, his hands shoved deep in his coat pockets and his head bowed, more to fend off her occasional glare than the bitter wind. He slumped in the passenger seat, and she drove through the winding streets, taking quick corners without signaling.

Eventually, Jennifer lost the tail and pulled into a late-night steak house. She headed inside without glancing at Steve.

He followed, still apprehensive about broaching the subject of what happened at the office. "Can we have a seat in the back?" he asked the hostess.

As soon as they were seated, he ordered a drink, despite the disapproving look from Jennifer. When the scotch was delivered, Steve drained half of it in one gulp.

"What are you doing?"

When he set the glass down, his hand was shaking. "Tonight, I've been threatened, grilled, shot at, had a gun pressed to my forehead, and been forced to snort eight lines of cocaine. I'm having a drink. Back off." He downed the golden liquid and set the empty glass on the table.

Jennifer locked eyes with Steve, and her cheeks flushed an angry red. "I saw the gun to your head."

"I figured it was that or when he shot the floor in front of me to make his point. You have impeccable timing. You called right after he pressed the barrel to my forehead, and I told him to fuck off."

Her mouth dropped, and she rubbed her forearms. "Jesus."

Steve allowed a crooked smile. "You may very well have saved my life." He paused and signaled the waitress for another drink. In the meantime, he picked up his water glass.

"I'm pregnant."

The glass slid from his hand, bouncing and tipping over, sending ice water all over his lap. Steve shot to his feet, brushing the front of his pants, but his eyes never left Jennifer's. "You're pregnant?" The question seemed ludicrous, considering, but he couldn't form words to express what he was feeling. Joy and terror mixed in his veins, creating a substance more jolting than the cocaine.

Jennifer nodded. "I bought a pregnancy test on the way home and it came back positive."

"That's terrific!"

Jennifer tilted her head and her eyes narrowed. "How exactly is that terrific? Huh? You're working for a psycho drug dealer, and I don't know from day to day whether you're going to come home or be found dead in an alley somewhere!" She kept her voice low, but her face filled with anguish. "How do we bring a child into this?"

"I'll be fine, Jen," Steve said, blotting his pants with a napkin and taking his seat again. "He bought it all. He believes I'm just his lawyer and you're my girlfriend, which tells me that the bug wasn't there yesterday morning. Otherwise, you *would* be a widow right now. He even admitted to bugging the apartment and putting the tail on us." Steve scanned the restaurant and his eyes found what he was looking for at the bar. "Speak of the devil." He raised his nearly empty water glass and nodded acknowledgment.

Jennifer turned in her seat, searching the restaurant until her eyes landed on the Hispanic man at the bar. She faced Steve again. "So, we don't have to pretend to not notice him anymore?"

"Nope." He folded his wet napkin on the table. "I'll be right back." He disappeared toward the men's room, circling around to the front of the bar, weaving through the crowd until he stood right behind the man. He stared into the bar's reflective glass until the man looked away from their table, glancing into the mirror as he took a sip of his drink. The man's eyes went wide, and he swiveled in the chair.

"Charlie told me I had a tail. I'm surprised you found us with the way she drives." Steve tilted his chin in Jennifer's direction without breaking eye contact with the man. "The name's Steve." He put his hand out.

The man lowered his eyes to Steve's hand and slowly accepted the handshake. "Emanuel. Manny for short."

His accent, a mixture of Hispanic and Brooklyn, made Steve smile. "Well, Manny, I assume you're the one that was listening as well," he said, receiving a nod in response. "Would you like to have dinner with us?" He hooked his thumb toward the table.

Manny's jaw dropped.

His reaction amused Steve, and a satisfied grin surfaced. "We both work for Charlie and obviously we are going to run into each other a lot, especially if you're my shadow, so I figured we'd just cut to the chase."

Manny briefly smiled. "I'll pass. Your girlfriend scares me."

"Yeah, well, she scares the hell out of me, too." He turned to go. "Nice meeting you, Manny."

"Same here," Manny nodded acknowledgement.

"What'd you just do?" Jennifer asked as Steve slid into the seat across from her with the same grin on his face.

"I just introduced myself to our shadow."

Jennifer glanced over her shoulder and Manny raised his glass in their direction.

"He turned my dinner invitation down, though."

"I swear, Steve; you're out of your fucking mind."

He flashed his most sincere smile and leaned forward, taking her hands in his. "Jen, I love you and I *promise* I will come home to you every night."

"Promise?"

Steve nodded. "I promise."

"And you never make a promise you can't keep." Jennifer finally let the smile surface.

"Exactly." Steve leaned over the table and kissed her cheek. "I'm going to be a father!" he announced to the tables within earshot. Congratulations were mumbled and when their meal arrived, they ate in subdued euphoria.

Vengeance
Chapter 13

CHARLIE WALKED INTO HIS apartment with a bag of Chinese takeout and settled on his couch, opening the white container and digging in while staring at the drivel on the television. Hours ago, he traded his cocaine high for a light alcohol buzz and some meaningless conversation with Steve while his rush leveled off.

He assured the kid that it wasn't enough to kill him, but he also didn't want Steve to go into cardiac arrest from the immense jolt eight lines of almost pure cocaine could cause. Feeding him glass after glass of scotch, the alcohol counteracted that rush with each drink downed.

He chuckled. Steve had some real balls, and a definite survival instinct, but he wondered if his girlfriend hadn't called, would he have had to put a bullet in the stubborn jackass's brain?

He didn't know, and that irked him. His judge of character was always spot on, but with Steve Winchester, his inner messenger seemed to have his wires crossed. Steve became more complex and less predictable with each layer he peeled back.

In the past, with his CW FOG recruits, the minute he revealed his true business plan, the greedy bid for takeover began. He could read it in their faces, see it in their eyes, and even though they swore their allegiance, kissing his ass more and more with each passing day, they planned his demise.

Not one of them ever argued with him in the face of a loaded gun or put an ultimatum on the table. Not one of them would have the balls to answer his cell phone in the middle of a showdown and sound as if it was just a normal day at the office.

The ones who didn't kiss his ass, groveled and begged and pissed their pants and they were the ones that ultimately ended up mugged in Central Park or at the bottom of the Hudson. But, in all his years doing this, he never once had someone outright ask what's in it for him.

The spark in Steve's eyes worried him at first, but then, when the wheels had stopped turning, the request that followed surprised him. A reasonable request considering all the kid had done with his money laundering schemes. A shell game, yeah, he was right, but it was a shell game he did very effectively.

Despite the kid's sincerity, Charlie wondered if the lure of money would taint him and eat away his reluctant loyalty. When Steve said he didn't want a cut, another enigmatic first, Charlie believed him. His eyes, even though they held a dark fury itching to let loose, also held the honest truth.

Charlie recognized what a rare quality that was in his business, and hoped like hell Steve would show at the office in the morning. Otherwise, they'd meet again and this time,

Steve wouldn't make it home to his pretty girlfriend.

Vengeance
Chapter 14

STEVE SAT IN HIS office, staring at the computer, not seeing anything. He was tired. Sleep eluded him, and he poured over all that happened during the day and evening. Jennifer's pregnancy wore on him during the night, along with his current career choice.

He raised his eyes, meeting Charlie's blatant stare. "How long have you been standing there?"

"Long enough. You look like hell."

"I feel about the same." He rubbed his eyes.

"Manny informed me you made him, and actually introduced yourself. That's pretty ballsy."

Steve uttered a laugh. "Putting a tail on me is pretty ballsy."

Charlie stepped inside the office and closed the door. "I'm glad you came in today. I wasn't sure you would, and frankly, I wasn't thrilled about knocking you off."

"Well, that makes two of us." He glowered.

Charlie took a seat across from Steve and pulled a check out of his pocket, placing it on the desk before sitting back in the chair.

"What's that?" He nodded toward the paper.

"That should cover your school debts."

Picking up the check, he studied it. It was made out for $73,642.78. His exact made-up college loans. He looked over the edge of the paper at Charlie and nodded, slipping it into the top drawer of his desk. "You didn't have to pull that shit on me, Charlie."

"It wasn't personal. I'm in a business where trusting the wrong person can be disastrous. Look at it from my point of view."

Steve sighed and nodded. "Yeah, well, it still sucked, and Jennifer was pissed."

"Flying ceramics?"

He laughed despite himself. "No, no flying ceramics."

Charlie stood to leave.

"Have you ever had a mole in the organization?"

"No, not one that lasted."

Steve gave a slight nod and looked at his computer screen. He brought his gaze back to Charlie. "Think there might be one here now?" he asked, creasing his eyebrows.

"One never knows." Charlie looked out the window facing the office staff. "But moles have a way of screwing up. That's when we catch them." He smiled over his shoulder.

"What should I be looking for?"

Charlie considered the question and turned toward Steve. "People who ask too many or too few questions." He nodded toward Steve. "You didn't ask enough questions. That's why I thought you were one."

"Ah. I'll remember to be a nosy SOB in the future."

Charlie burst out laughing and reached for the door.

"By the way, I found out why my girlfriend's been a little more psycho lately." He waited until Charlie turned back to face him. "She's pregnant."

He chuckled. "Your week just gets better and better, doesn't it?"

"Yeah, well..."

"What are you going to do?"

"I haven't thought that far ahead," he answered. "I'll probably marry her. I don't want my kid to grow up without both of us around." He raised his gaze to Charlie. "I've been there. It sucks."

"You lost your parents?"

He tilted his head and narrowed his eyes. "Like you didn't already know that."

Charlie tried to suppress a grin and couldn't. He shrugged. "I know you were orphaned in high school, but I don't know the particulars."

Leaning back in the chair, he studied Charlie, his hands pressed in a steeple, index fingers tapping together.

"I make sure I know as much about my employees as possible."

He kept silent, still thrumming his fingers. "I'm not sure I like that," he finally admitted. "I'm not sure I *like* any of this."

"Tough shit. How'd your parents die?"

Steve pressed his lips together, letting silence filter between them again before he spoke. "My dad died of cancer when I was ten. My mother was a nurse at the local hospital and was coming home from a double shift when she fell asleep at the wheel." He looked at his hands now gripping the soft leather arms of his chair. "It was tough, but I got through it." He swiveled toward the computer.

"My parents died when I was eleven."

Steve shot his gaze at Charlie, mustering up the right amount of surprise.

Holy fucking shit, the dude's opening up to me.

Why?

"And my little brother died about ten years ago. He was only sixteen. He'd be about your age now if he'd lived. So, I understand where you're coming from."

He narrowed his eyes. "Why are you telling me this?"

Charlie looked out the window. "Because we seem to have a great deal in common." He returned his gaze to Steve. "Which was another reason I thought you might be a plant in my organization."

He stared at Charlie and allowed a visible shiver. "That's just too fucking creepy."

Vengeance
Chapter 15

JENNIFER'S NERVES WERE A jumbled mess, and she took a deep breath, trying to keep her stomach in check as the pancake make-up spread like butter across her cheek. The funky play-dough scent made her gag, and she pulled the sponge away from her skin. Closing her eyes, she willed the sour taste in the back of her throat to disappear. Her system obliged, settling down enough for her to finish applying the stark stage make-up.

"Hey, Jenny, is this your guy?"

She turned. "Yep, he's mine." Smiling, she went back to finishing her make-up. The tantalizing smell of Chinese food drifted up from the bag he set on the corner of the vanity.

"How are you feeling?" Steve leaned over and kissed the top of her head.

"Eh," she said, touching up the bright blush on her cheeks. "How about you?" She glanced in his direction.

He shrugged. "I'm not the one who's pregnant."

His slow smile sent shivers up her spine. She returned his smile and shot a glance at the mirror to make sure the thick make-up didn't crack under the curve of her lips. She touched up a few spots and folded up her compact, focusing on the bag of food sitting on the corner of her make-up dresser.

"White rice with beef and broccoli," Steve said before she could ask what he had gotten her. "I figured spicy was not the way to go tonight."

"Thanks, spicy would have been a disaster." She pulled out the box of rice and chopsticks and took a few bites. "Aren't you eating?"

He shook his head. "I already ate." He leaned back in the chair. "You've got enough make-up on to compete with the streetwalkers."

A few pieces of rice flew out of her mouth, along with a belt of laughter. She glanced at him and wiped her lips. "It has to be thick in order to see it on stage."

"Ah." He glanced around.

"You've never been backstage before," Jennifer said as Steve's attention bounced between her and the controlled chaos surrounding them. Make-up artists and costume designers flitted from actor to actor, making sure all was in place. The stage manager barked orders to the gaffers, making sure the stage was set properly for the opening scene and the backdrops were in the proper order, along with the stage props.

"No. It's a little chaotic."

"This is calm. You should see it in a half hour, right before the curtain opens."

Steve swung his gaze back at Jennifer. "You're kidding."

"Nope." She plucked a piece of beef from the cardboard container and put it in her mouth. "Thank you." She pointed to the takeout he had brought.

"Anytime." He stood. "I'll see you after the play." He kissed her lips, careful not to smudge her make-up. "Break a leg, babe."

Jennifer smiled and nodded, focusing again on wolfing her food down before the make-up artist interrupted with the finishing touches.

With both Steve and her food gone, Jennifer took a deep breath, studying her reflection and getting into the frame of mind to play Kathy, the captain of the cheerleading squad and a control freak throughout the stages of her life until she learns to let go. She allowed a brief smile at her reflection, mulling over the similarities to her own life. When the bell rang, calling the cast to the stage, she was ready.

Vengeance
Chapter 16

A LINE HAD ALREADY formed at the entrance to the theater and Steve took the next spot, shifting from foot to foot and blowing air in his fists to keep warm. A hand grabbed his shoulder, startling him, and he spun toward the owner, exhaling. "Don't do that!" He turned away from Jerry, scanning the growing crowd. "Charlie's scheduled to be here tonight, too."

"You're kidding me?"

"Nope," Steve said over his shoulder. "So, you don't know me." He caught Jerry's gaze before moving his on to the crowd behind them. Charlie wasn't there yet, and he turned forward again.

"What happened?"

Steve glanced over his shoulder again, meeting Jerry's quizzical gaze. "Too much to discuss here." He scanned the crowd. "Showtime," he mumbled, catching Charlie stepping into line. He made eye contact and sent a nod in Charlie's direction just as the doors opened.

He took the aisle seat in the third-row center, letting Jerry and his wife slide into the row next to him. Steve offered an awkward smile and glanced around as the crowd filtered in. Finally, he caught sight of Charlie in the balcony behind him and turned, focusing on the stage. "Upper back balcony," he said without turning his head. He opened the program and flipped through the pages, stopping on Jennifer's picture. "She's pregnant." He glanced sideways at Jerry.

Jerry's eyebrows went up. He flipped open the program.

Steve pointed at the page, turning toward Jerry. "That's her," he said for the sake of the audience above watching him like a hawk. "And Charlie knows," he added.

"Shit," Jerry said, leaning toward his wife and pointing toward the picture and then Steve. "Why is he here?"

"Because I turned down an invitation to his house, and I had to give an excuse. So here we are." He leaned back in the chair, staring at the closed curtain.

Jerry glanced at Steve and then down at the picture in his hand. "Jack's going to have your head." He closed the program.

"I'm aware of that," he said. "I'll be right back." Steve stood and headed into the lobby to hit the bathroom before the show began. As he headed back, Charlie intercepted him.

"How's your girlfriend?"

"Unusually calm. Go figure." The lights in the lobby dimmed and brightened, signaling the show was about to begin. "I should get in there. If the curtain rises and she doesn't see me, who knows what she'll throw at me next?"

Charlie laughed, and Steve walked away.

He slid into his chair and the curtains opened. The lights rose, and Jennifer's voice filled the auditorium, making him forgot about his job, his partner, and everything around him.

Awed, he watched her perform the part flawlessly. All those nights of reading lines with her paid off in spades.

CHARIE RETURNED TO HIS seat. He looked down at Jennifer's picture in his own program. Damn, she was beautiful. The seeds of envy blossomed.

"Hot number," the man sitting next to him said.

Charlie glanced at his companion. "She's my lawyer's girlfriend, so don't even think about messing with her."

Kyle Winslow raised his eyebrows. "Moi?"

Charlie nodded. "Yeah, you."

The auditorium went black.

"Damn," both Charlie and Kyle whispered in unison as the lights came up and Jennifer stood, turning toward the crowd. They exchanged a look and returned their focus to the fox on stage.

Charlie couldn't remember being so captivated by anyone or anything, and the knowledge that she carried Steve's child didn't matter. He wanted her, wanted to own that voice, that body, that face.

Kyle leaned over. "You sure you don't want me to take out the lawyer?"

Charlie tilted his head, studying Jennifer, measuring her worth against Steve's, and he sighed. "Yeah, I'm sure," he answered after the opening song finished. "His skills are a little more valuable than hers." He traded a glance with Kyle. "But not by much."

Kyle smiled and nodded.

They watched the rest of the play in silence.

Vengeance
Chapter 17

THE CURTAINS OPENED TO a standing ovation, and Jennifer took a bow. The applause tingled all over and she scanned the crowd, quickly finding Steve. Their eyes locked and his smile, his smile, was as intoxicating as the applause.

The curtain closed, and the cast stood waiting for the second curtain call, the applause rocking the house enough to make the wooden stage vibrate. When the curtains opened again, the theater disappeared.

He was on her in an instant, his free hand wrapped around her neck, slamming her into the wall and burying the knife in her abdomen.

She gasped for air, stunned by the pain in her side. He lifted her off her feet, throwing her toward the bed, where she landed face down on the cotton bedspread with her legs sprawled wide. She clamored to her hands and knees, trying to scramble away, but he was faster, grabbing her by the hair.

Gagging and crying, she scratched his arm, trying to loosen his grip.

Frustration filled him. This one was all fight, and that just wasn't satisfying. He buried the knife in her belly again. "Shut the fuck up!"

Her cries got weaker with each slice until she could no longer fight against him, going slack under his grasp.

He brought the knife to her throat and sliced the tender flesh clear through to the spine. The blood didn't plume like usual, it just oozed, and he dropped her dead body on the bed. Fury filled him, and he slammed the knife into the small of her back. "Bitch!"

Jennifer blinked and was back on stage, the applause continuing, shocking her. *Holy Shit, holy shit, holy shit.* The thought repeated over and over until she saw Steve. He was no longer smiling. He must know she just saw another murder. She looked away and put on a smile for the crowd, bowing as the curtain closed again.

Her heart thundered in her chest, and she made her way backstage with the rest of the cast. She barely made it to the bathroom in time for her dinner to rocket out of her stomach into the toilet. She sat back on her heels and wiped her mouth with toilet paper, still trembling, the vision replaying behind her closed eyelids.

STEVE WAS IN MOTION before the crowd had time to disband. He grabbed the bouquet of roses at his feet and slipped through the side door leading backstage. He was immediately stopped by a large guard.

"Sir, the exit is that way." The guard pointed over Steve's shoulder.

"Jennifer Curtis is my girlfriend." He tried to navigate around the man but couldn't.

"Wrong," the guard said.

Steve stopped and looked into the eyes of the guard. "Get out of my way."

The guard shook his head. "I'm afraid I'm going to have to ask you to leave." He went to grab Steve's arm.

Steve parried and twisted the guard's wrist, sweeping his feet out from under him in a perfect *sante tachi waza* without crushing a single rose. He stepped over the stunned guard and into the chaos backstage.

"Jenny?" he called, his eyes darting around until they landed on her leaving the bathroom. Her face was still pale under the layers of make-up, and she curved her lips in a poor semblance of a smile until the guard got up off the floor behind Steve.

"What did you do?" Jennifer approached them, staring at Steve.

"Do you know this guy?" the guard asked from behind him.

"Yes. He's my husband."

Steve turned toward the guard. "We're not married yet." He looked back at Jennifer tilting his head. "You told everyone we're married?"

Jennifer nodded, and he saw the flash of irritation in her eyes.

Steve hesitated and then handed her the bouquet of roses. He shot an awkward smile over his shoulder and stepped farther into the chaos, leaning in to kiss her cheek. "You were great tonight," he said.

Jennifer led him to her dressing area and closed the curtain behind her. "Why did you have to do that? Now Gus thinks I'm a freak."

His smile disappeared. "Yeah, well, that's the cover."

She shot him a glare and yanked the costume off.

"You had another vision."

Jennifer stripped out of the clothing without answering Steve. She pulled on a pair of faded blue jeans and a sweater and sat at the vanity. "Yes." She wiped off the layers of make-up. "And now I have to meet your boss."

Steve took a deep breath. "Are you okay?"

She shook her head. "No, I'm not. I'm not okay." Her lower lip quivered. "I just had the performance of my life, and then the damn vision ruined it." She finished cleaning her face, balling up the wipes and tossing them into the garbage can under her counter. "Now I have to pretend to be interested in meeting your boss." A tear rolled down her cheek. "And all I want to do is throw up again."

"We can go home."

Jennifer wiped the tear off her cheek. "Really?"

He nodded. He wanted to find out about the vision, and Charlie could wait. "You don't look so good." He wiped the stray hair away from her face.

That was all she needed to open the floodgates.

Vengeance
Chapter 18

"YOU CAN TAKE OFF," Charlie said to Kyle as they waited outside the theater.

"You sure?"

He nodded. He didn't want to have to explain the man standing next to him, not tonight. Besides, he wanted to lavish Jennifer with praise for an exquisite job and having another testosterone-filled male volleying for her attention would dilute his chances of impressing her. And for some ungodly reason, he very much wanted to impress her.

He glanced at his watch as the staff trickled out from the show. "I'll catch up with you later in the week."

"Sure." Kyle wandered off.

Charlie returned his attention to the thinning crowd and flipped open his phone. "Steve, where the hell are you?"

"Sorry, she wasn't feeling so good, and I took her home," Steve said. "I'll introduce you some other time."

"How'd you get by me?"

"I didn't see you, otherwise I would have stopped. Sorry, but she's having a hard time, and I didn't want her to get sick on the sidewalk."

Charlie could hear the retching in the background. "Morning sickness?"

"I think so, at least I hope so."

"Tell her your boss thought she did a great job."

"I'll tell her. I gotta go. I need to get her to bed."

The dial tone filled the line, and he flipped the phone closed. Disappointment laced his blood, and he glanced at the picture in the program. Snapping the booklet closed, he took a deep breath, cleansing the growing irritation.

Surveying the crowd, he searched for something to spark his interest and on the second pass; he singled out someone and headed her way.

Vengeance
Chapter 19

JENNIFER CAME OUT OF the bathroom, wiping her mouth with the back of her hand. "Who was that?"

Steve folded the cell phone. "Charlie. He thought you were fantastic."

Jennifer shrugged. "I don't give a damn what your boss thinks. It's the critics that count." She pulled off her sweater and slid on a silky nightgown.

"I'll shoot 'em if they write a bad review."

She offered him a sickly smile. "That's sweet, but you can't shoot every critic in New York City."

"Yeah, I can." He pulled out a small box from his briefcase and set it on the shelf, flipping the switch on. A red light flashed, and the cube emitted a low hum.

"What's that?"

"It jams transmissions from leaving the apartment." Steve turned to her. "Renders bugs useless, but also does the same to cell phones and wireless connections. Now, tell me about the vision."

She inhaled, audibly sucking the air through her teeth. "Can you grab me a little ginger ale first?"

Steve poured half a can into a glass and brought it to her, taking a seat on the side of the bed.

She took a sip before she met Steve's inquisitive gaze. "This one was different."

"How?"

A crease appeared between her eyes, and she struggled to pinpoint the differences. "In the past, he seemed to be very much in control of the situation. This time he definitely wasn't." She studied her hands and took another sip of ginger ale before glancing up at Steve. "She fought back."

"Was it the same man?"

Jennifer nodded. "The same knife, and I'm sure there's a tattoo on his wrist. I just don't know what it is and I'm not sure if the color I saw was her blood or the tattoo."

"Red?"

"Yeah. It also looks like there's a hint of yellow, blue, and gray, but I get an overwhelming sense of red."

He pursed his lips. "Just on the wrist?"

Jennifer thought for a moment and then shook her head. "It goes up the forearm a little." She flopped back on the bed. "I wish I could get a clear picture of it."

So do I. Steve didn't voice the thought. "Anything else you can tell me about this guy?"

"Outside of the fact that he likes to kill?"

He raised his eyebrows and waited for her to continue.

She took a deep breath. "No. I've never seen his face. It's always in a shadow. But his eyes aren't. They're blue gray, leaning more on the gray side than blue." She shrugged. "Can't you identify him by his DNA?"

"It doesn't match any known criminal in our database. Believe me, we've checked. The DNA matches in all the murder cases, but it doesn't trace back to anyone." Steve tilted his head. "And you never told me about his eyes."

"I didn't?"

"No." He ran through everything she ever explained. "So far, I have a Caucasian male who is a little taller than I am, with gray-blue eyes and a tattoo on his right wrist. And he uses a Rambo knife to kill his victims."

"Yes. He rapes his victims while he kills them," she added.

He chewed his bottom lip. "Why do you think this one's different?"

Jennifer thought about her vision, about the growl in his voice, not the usual seductive purr. Each plunge of the knife accompanied a snarling hiss, and the last act before she snapped back to reality was that of rage. "He lost it, Steve. The guy was beyond angry. He was furious."

He paced, rolling it over in his mind. "And he's not in your other visions?"

"No. This is the first time I saw him lose control." She watched him pace and sipped her ginger ale.

"God damn, there's no rhyme or reason to his victims. There is no connection between them."

"Except for being murdered."

Steve shot a sideways look at her. "Outside of the cause of death." He flipped open his phone and pressed a sequence of numbers. When nothing happened, he rolled his eyes and put the phone back in his pocket.

Jennifer chuckled. "Forgot already?"

Grumbling, he nodded and took a seat on the side of the bed. "I need to give Jack a heads up and the sweeper won't be here until tomorrow."

"Well, you won't have to worry about talking to me anymore. I'm exhausted," she said, yawning the last word, drawing it out as she curled up into a ball.

Steve leaned over and kissed her. "I'll only be a little while." He crossed to the jamming device and turned it off before he settled behind his computer. He logged into the secure FBI site, opened his mailbox, and scanned the entries. Nothing urgent jumped out, and he opened a new email.

Jack, she had another vision. This one was different. Your unsub didn't act like he had in the past, leading to a completely different signature this time. She doesn't know what set him off, but she said he was angry. Dream girl insists it's the same man. So far, I have the following description: White male between six feet and six two and has gray-blue eyes. He also has some sort of tattoo on his right wrist that incorporates yellow, blue, gray and possibly red into the design.

Steve hit the send button and went back to his email box. Before he opened an email, a response came in.

Pick up the damn phone and call me. Now.

"Shit." Steve dug the phone out of his pocket.

"What's the matter?" Jennifer's eyes fluttered open.

"The Knicks lost again," he answered. He hooked his thumb toward the door and held up his cell phone. When she nodded, he plugged the blue tooth in his ear and left the apartment.

Steve hit the special sequence again and opened the door to the stairwell. "Hey, Jack." He trotted down the steps, his voice bouncing off the concrete.

"What the hell's going on?" Jack Murphy, the head of the Boston FBI office, snarled into the phone.

Steve emerged in the alley and started walking away from the front of the building. "On which front?"

"Your assignment?"

He was quiet.

"Steve?"

"I'm here. I'm just putting some distance between the apartment and this conversation," he answered. "I assume Jerry filled you in?"

"As much as he could, which wasn't a hell of a lot. He said Charlie showed up at Jennifer's opening."

"Yeah, well, the last couple of days have been real fun."

"Cut the crap, Williams, and tell me what's going on!"

Steve glanced over his shoulder to make sure he wasn't followed before finding a place to hunker down, sitting out of sight in a doorway. "Charlie caught me coming out of the office in the middle of the night on Monday." He heard his boss suck in his breath. "So, I gave him the crazy girlfriend excuse. He didn't buy it at the time and put a tail on us." He leaned back against the door. "That's where it got sticky. Jennifer staged moving in with me and going ballistic when we found a tap in the apartment."

"You found what?"

"A tap. It gets worse. Jennifer threw the ceramic figure at me, and I've got six stitches in

426

my forehead to show for that stunt, but she convinced our tail she was as mad as a hatter." Reaching up, he touched the bandage, listening to the silence on the other end of the line. "Charlie asked me to go to a thing at his house. It was for tonight and I couldn't blow Jen's opening off."

"Steve..."

"I know. I could have fucked up the entire operation," he snapped into the phone. "But Jack, I promised Jenny I'd be there."

"You don't have the luxury of making promises like that."

He closed his eyes and hung his head. "I'm not sure Charlie trusts me, even after the fucked-up test he put me through last night."

"What test?"

Steve could almost see the steam rising from the phone as his boss hissed the words through the line. "He put a gun to my head and made me do eight lines of coke. I'm surprised I didn't have a coronary."

Silence.

Steve said nothing more.

"Jesus."

"Yeah, I thought I was a dead man. I thought he knew."

"You are one lucky son of a bitch."

Steve laughed. "I'm not feeling very lucky, Jack. Jennifer is now involved, and Charlie doesn't know we're married. He thinks she's just my crazy girlfriend. And Jack, she's pregnant."

The air sucked in the phone as the information elicited another "Jesus" from Jack.

"She wasn't too happy with the development, either." He closed his eyes.

"Jennifer should leave the city."

"You try to get her to leave. I already had a crack at it, and she said no." He could feel the volatility in his boss over the phone line.

"She doesn't have a choice."

"How am I supposed to explain that, huh? Especially since Charlie knows she's pregnant."

"Charlie knows?"

"Yes. I told him this morning I really needed some viable reason for her volatility, and I took the facts and made them work for me. Charlie shocked the shit out of me. The dude opened up about his parents and his brother after I came clean about the pregnancy." He stood and stretched his back. "I need to get back to the apartment." He headed toward the building.

"She had another vision?"

"Yep. I'm sure no one missed the fear in her expression. At least it waited until the curtain call. She recovered and shook it off in time to take a bow, but man, she was pale for a moment there."

"That could be attributed to the pregnancy," Jack said.

"The paleness, yes, the change in her eyes, no. It's still god damn freaky to see that."

Jack let out a gruff harrumph on the other end of the line. "I can't believe I'm buying into this shit, but at this point I'll take stock in anything that brings us closer to nailing that son of a bitch."

"I hear you. Her visions still freak the shit out of me, but they've also saved my ass a couple of times. I just hope she can give us something concrete to go on." Steve used his key to slip into the stairwell, climbing to the fourth floor rapidly. "I have to bolt. I'll be looking over the financials this weekend and I'll record my findings Sunday night."

"Okay. I'll let you know if we find another victim."

"It won't be the exact M.O., so watch the wires for similarities."

"Will do." Jack hung up.

Steve walked back into the apartment, disconnecting the blue tooth and setting it on his desk. Jennifer was sound asleep, and Steve stripped, climbing into bed, and pulled her into his arms. "I love you," he whispered in her ear. She didn't stir, and he closed his eyes, drifting into a light sleep.

Vengeance
Chapter 20

THE DESK LOOKED LIKE the paper fairy vomited all over it, ledger sheets everywhere—including in and on the file cabinet behind Steve—as he poured over Charlie's financials. Jennifer emerged from the bathroom wrapped in a towel when a rap on the door interrupted their Saturday morning.

They exchanged a look, and he glanced through the peephole. He shot back. A sudden pounding cramped his throat, and he took a double take through the peephole before turning toward the desk. He went into action, scooping paper into the file cabinet, and pointed her to the door.

"Who is it?" she yelled, even though she had a reasonable guess from Steve's reaction.

"Charlie Wisnowski. Steve's boss."

She cracked the door; the chain preventing him from seeing anything other than her scantily clad body. "Steve's in the shower and, as you can see, I'm a little underdressed. Give me a minute." She smiled and closed the door.

He glanced at her, shook his head, and shrugged before he dropped the last of the papers in the file cabinet, locked it, and closed the laptop. He bolted past her into the bathroom, shutting the door quietly while she crossed to open the front door.

Jennifer took a deep breath, smoothing her shirt before she put on a smile. She opened the door. The first thing that hit her was his eyes, gray-blue and direct. Her smile faltered, and she ran her hand through her wet hair. "I'm sorry it took me so long to find something decent." She showed her disheveled attire with a flourish of her hand.

"No worries," he said. He scanned the open neckline of Steve's oxford she had on before he returned his gaze to hers.

"Steve didn't tell me he was expecting company today."

Charlie smiled and stepped into the apartment. "I didn't exactly tell him I was coming. Sorry for interrupting your morning."

A rogue sheet of paper drifted to the floor and Jennifer picked it up, stuffing it in the middle of the script sitting on the corner of the desk. "I'm sorry. Where are my manners? Please come in." She waved her hand toward the modest living area, heat flushing her face at the unmade bed.

Steve opened the bathroom door, hand combing his wet hair away from his face. He raised his eyebrows. "Charlie, what are you doing here?"

She was impressed with the performance. The surprise seemed genuine, and he wasn't the least bit ruffled like he'd been moments before.

"I figured I'd hand deliver these to Jennifer." He handed her a box of candy, along with a small bouquet. "Your performance last night was exceptional."

Flustered, she took the offerings. "Thank you." She looked up at his eyes and smiled, covering up the shiver that wanted to take hold. "Um, I'm sorry I wasn't able to meet you last night." She turned, crossing to find a vase for the pretty bouquet and setting them next to the dozen red roses Steve had given her.

She studied the floor, getting her nerves under control before turning and gazing at Charlie. The way he stared at her made her skin feel like an oily snake slithered across her flesh, leaving a trail of barely suppressed goose bumps. "I was a little sick after the show last night." She shrugged and walked to Steve. "He took good care of me." She hooked her arm around his. "He always takes good care of me." She laid her head on his shoulder to make her point.

HE CAST A SIDEWAYS glance at her. The clingy girlfriend routine gave him the willies, and he turned his attention to Charlie, peeling her off his arm. "Can I get you anything?"

Charlie shook his head. "No, thank you, I'm fine. I just wanted to swing by and drop off the flowers." He glanced at Jennifer again, scanning her with his eyes, interest flaring in his irises. He offered Steve a smile and a slight shrug.

"Thanks again for the flowers and the kind words." She sent her sweetest smile his way.

"You're welcome." Charlie stepped out. "I'll catch you Monday," he added and disappeared down the hall.

Steve closed the door and leaned his forehead against the wood.

Dear God, what the fuck was that all about?

Jennifer bolted into the bathroom.

He ran a shaky hand through his hair and sat at the desk, forcing a few long slow breaths reviewing the exchange. Every nuance, every unspoken word, every glance in her direction replayed, and his stomach burned. Fury filled his bones.

The bastard came to my apartment, and he has the hots for my wife.

He stood and crossed to the bathroom. "You have to leave."

Jennifer turned from the counter where she was brushing the acid taste out of her mouth. She spit in the sink. "I'm not leaving." She leaned against the counter, staring at Steve in the mirror.

"Jenny," he began, leaning against the doorjamb. He put his arm across the door, blocking her from leaving the bathroom. "This is dangerous." His low voice bore into her, along with his sharp eyes.

She pushed his wrist out of the way. "I'm aware of that, but I'm not leaving." Her eyes were just as steady as his were, and she walked into the living area and curled up on the couch.

Leaning his head back, he closed his eyes. "I can't do this with you here."

"Yes, you can." She turned on the television, flipping through the channels, and stopped on the local news station. Her eyes rose to his. "They found her."

He took a seat next to her, his eyes glued to the television. "Are you sure that's her?"

Jennifer nodded, and her breath hitched in her chest. "Charlie reminds me of the bastard who's doing this." She waved at the television and brought her hand to her throat.

Steve stared at her, processing the information. "How so?"

"His eyes, they're similar." She returned her gaze to the television. "Aimee," she whispered, and a tear slid down her cheek.

He put his arm around her shoulder and kissed her temple. "It isn't your fault."

"What good is having visions if I can't stop them?"

"I don't have an answer for you, but with each vision, you're able to tell us a little more about him. Eventually, Jack *will* catch him."

Vengeance
Chapter 21

HE DIDN'T BROACH THE subject right away. He was still a little gun shy from Charlie's visit and the news story that shook her up. He stood over the stove, cooking a Greek pot roast with a side dish of rotini noodles. "You staying here is really dangerous for both of us, Jen."

"Are you going to harp on this again?"

He turned, staring her down until interrupted by the buzzer. He drained the pasta and set it in a bowl before laying thinly carved slices of meat across the layer of curled noodles. He stirred the simmering wine sauce and flipped the stove off before pouring it over the top of the concoction. He set the dish down, grabbing the wine bottle and a single glass before he slid into the seat across from her. "Yes."

She licked her lips as the succulent scent drifted through the apartment and her eyes remained glued to the dinner. "Yes, what?"

"I'm going to harp again." The pop of the cork accented the glare she sent in his direction, and he ignored her in favor of filling his glass with the fine merlot.

"Steve, please, please don't do this. Tonight's the first time in a while that I haven't been nauseous and if you insist on pissing me off, I'm not sure what my stomach will do."

He shrugged and served a spoonful of meat, noodles, and sauce onto her plate and pushed the salad bowl in her direction. "I'm sorry Jen, but this isn't something I can just slough off, especially after he came here today."

"I know you were upset by him coming by, but if you think about it, it was kind of sweet."

Steve choked on the sip of wine, coughing and wheezing, his eyes tearing up as the alcohol burned the lining of his windpipe. "Sweet?" He squeaked the word out, wrapped in a harsh rasp.

"Yeah, the candy, the flowers, the concern. That was sweet."

He continued to cough and wheeze, wiping the corners of his eyes. Concern scrunched the flesh between her eyes.

"Are you okay?"

"Wrong pipe," he said when the coughing finally subsided, and he could draw a pain-free breath. He cleared his throat. "Charlie has the hots for you."

Laughter sputtered from her lips, along with a few stray pieces of noodles. "What the hell are you talking about?" She wiped her mouth with a napkin, meeting his direct stare. Amusement peppered her face, leaving a trace of a smile on her lips.

"I'm not kidding," he said. "Did you not see the way he looked at you?"

Jennifer rolled her eyes. "Oh, for the love of God, Steve, a lot of men look at me like that."

Steve's teeth clamped together. "I know, but they aren't Charlie Wisnowski, and they don't have mafia connections."

Raising her eyebrows, she took another bite of food and challenged him with her gaze.

She didn't get it. She had no idea how dangerous Charlie was. He had to find another way to get her to leave, another avenue, and it materialized in a clear train of thought. He dug into his food, contemplating exactly how to deliver the lines.

"Did it ever occur to you that he might decide you're worth more to him than me? Do you have any clue what would happen if he came to that conclusion?"

He didn't think Charlie would do anything of the kind. He was more apt to seduce her than to have him killed—especially with his greed for money and power. And Steve was the best financial wizard Charlie ever had. However, he wanted to bring the point home and if Jennifer thought her presence was a threat to his safety, she would be more apt to listen to reason.

"Huh?" She took a sip of her milk and swiped her lips with the napkin.

"You could kiss my ass goodbye."

She slammed her glass down and picked up her fork again, the aggravation claiming the set of her jaw. "You think I'd leave you for him?"

Steve scoffed. "Did it ever occur to you that he might decide to off me because he wants you?" He pointed his fork at her.

Her eyes blinked rapidly. "Wh-what?"

Steve raised his eyebrows and cocked his head. "That's the kind of guy Charlie is, hon."

"He'd try to kill you?"

He shrugged and took a sip of wine before attacking his meal.

She chewed slowly, digesting his words. She swallowed and her eyes narrowed. "You're just saying that, so I'll leave."

Fuck. She called my bluff. "Jen."

"No, Steve, that was low, even for you."

Steve threw his silverware on the table, followed by his napkin, and stormed across the room to the window. Anger, fear, jealousy all volleyed for dominance, and he concentrated on breathing. Breathing and counting. When he reached twenty, he turned back to the table. She continued picking at her food, taking a bite every so often, the bulk of her face concealed by her long hair.

"Jen?"

She glanced up, and he swore under his breath. Tears caught the light shimmering on her cheeks and he crossed the distance, dropping to his knee by her side.

"I know you don't want to leave. Hell, I don't want you to, either, but I also don't want you stepping in the line of fire. Now that you're on his radar, you're within reach of his wrath."

"What do you suggest I do?" More tears slid from the corners of her eyes. "Give up my career for yours?"

He hung his head. Anything he said in response to that question would land him in the doghouse. "Temporarily, yes," he finally said, without meeting her gaze.

The chair slid back, and she stomped across the room, slamming the bathroom door behind her. The sound of her retching reached his ears, and he stood, clearing the dinner dishes.

Suffocating silence hung on the air between them for the rest of the afternoon and when he went to kiss her goodbye, she turned her cheek instead. The rattle of the front door closing followed her rebuff.

Steve stared at the closed door.

Way to fuck up a perfectly good weekend.

SUNDAY WAS NOT BETTER. Jennifer ignored him, actually turning her back like an insolent child every time he tried to bring up the subject. He buried himself in Charlie's financials, plotting the money trail, but with all the aggravation, his concentration level landed in the shitter, and he only got about half of what he wanted done.

Monday morning, he stood in front of the door, his hand on the knob. "Damn it!" he muttered and dropped his briefcase on the floor, crossing to the bed and shaking her awake.

"What?" She blinked her eyes open.

"I didn't want to go to work with this still hanging between us." Steve sat on the edge of the bed.

"Then let it go," she said.

"I'm not comfortable with that, Jen. Actually, I'm not comfortable with any of this now that you're on his radar."

"I know." She exhaled. Sitting up, she wrapped her arms around him. "I'm not comfortable with you working undercover on this case."

He stiffened at her words, but for the first time since he insisted she leave, he had an inkling of how she must feel day after day, and he pressed his lips to the curve of her neck. "You know I love you."

She nodded. "I love you, too, and that's why I put up with all this."

He pulled away from her and stared into her sleepy green eyes. "Putting up with me doing my job is one thing; I'm paid to be in harm's way. You aren't."

She tilted her head, her eyes pleading for him to let it go, and he caved.

"All right, you win for now, but if I get any hint of things going south, I'm going to give the order for Jack to get you out of here."

Jennifer inhaled and nodded before offering a slight smile. "Have a good day."

He allowed his lips to curve into a smile and kissed her goodbye. The moment he slid into his car, his smile disappeared. His mind twirled around all the weekend information he uncovered in the finances, and he sighed. He wouldn't be able to finish the money trail timeline until next weekend. Jack would not be happy with him, but he'd just have to deal with it.

CHARLIE LEANED AGAINST HIS office door, waiting with a stern expression and a newspaper rolled up in one hand. Steve's heart lurched into his throat, but he kept his face neutral and offered a nod in Charlie's direction. He waved Steve into the office and stepped inside, closing the door and tossing the newspaper onto his desk.

Steve raised an eyebrow and hung up his coat before he crossed behind his desk and dropped his gaze to the paper. He sat and picked up the entertainment section, scanning the article Charlie circled.

A review.

A stellar review and a grin surfaced.

"Jenny's going to be walking on air after this." He glanced up at Charlie. "And let me tell you, she needs this." He set the paper on his desk and leaned back in his chair.

"Rough weekend?"

Steve offered a shrug. "She's been sick on and off, but she said it didn't hit her at the performances Saturday and Sunday like it did Friday night."

"Opening night jitters?"

"I guess." He broke into a yawn. "But beyond feeling sick, the stress of everything is draining for both of us."

"You need a little pick me up?" Charlie asked.

"I got my coffee."

A knowing smile surfaced, and Charlie reached into his pocket. "Try a hit of this. It'll be quicker than caffeine." He tossed a small vial and Steve caught it.

Studying the amber colored vial, he watched the powder shift against the sides as he rolled it through his fingers. He cocked his head to the right, returning his gaze to Charlie's.

"Every now and then, I need a pickup, too." He took a seat and pointed to the container. "Go ahead."

"I don't know..." He returned his focus to the cocaine and licked his lips, torn.

"Go ahead." This time, Charlie's tone was more demanding, much like when he drew the gun.

Steve put the vial down on his desk and glared at Charlie. "Maybe I'm not in the mood."

Charlie leaned forward. "Maybe we should take a long drive."

His sharp stare sent shivers down Steve's spine, but he crossed his arms and leaned back in his seat. "I'm not playing this game, Charlie. Either fire my ass, or cut the shit."

Charlie's musical laugh filled his office, but he was not amused. When he wound down, he sat back in the seat and studied Steve. "Boy, if I let you go—" he made quotes with his fingers "—you're not going to be out pounding the pavement for another job. I wouldn't be surprised if years from now, they found your remains somewhere *under* the pavement."

He clamped his teeth together and turned to his computer, flipping it on before he focused back on the drugs sitting there, mocking him. The sad truth was he wanted the rush; the sudden shot of adrenalin he knew would follow the first snort. Reaching for the vial, he met Charlie's gaze and unscrewed the cap. The cap had a tiny spoon attached, and he scooped a small amount of powder and brought it to his nose, inhaling the fine particles into his sinuses. The sudden sting brought tears to his eyes and before he completely lost his vision to the mist, he sucked a hit into his other nostril. "Happy?" he asked, screwing the cap back on and setting the small canister on the desk. He rubbed his numbing nose and sniffled a few times, blinking the burn from his eyes.

Charlie smiled and nodded. He stood and headed for the door.

"Hey, don't you want this?" He held the vial out to his boss.

"Nope, that's yours." He left Steve staring at the small jar of coke.

He swept it into his top drawer, welcoming the minor tingle and the thundering of his heartbeat in his ears. Charlie was right—it sure beat coffee. Hell, it left even the strongest European espresso in the dust.

His fingers flew across the keyboard working on the latest contract for CW FOG and his foot tapped, but his mind, his mind, kept circling on what Charlie was doing, what he was accomplishing with paying off the loan, with the coke. The bastard wanted him mortgaged up the wahzoo with no way out.

His fingers stopped, and he turned, staring at the paper, and a new thought dawned on him. He swiped the newspaper off his desk and crossed to Charlie's office, stepped inside and closed the door despite the fact Charlie was on the phone.

Crossing, he slid the paper on the desk and took a seat in the chair, ignoring Charlie's glare.

"Can I call you back?" he asked, and a moment later, the phone rested on the cradle. "What's up?"

Steve pointed to the paper. "You didn't have anything to do with that, did you?"

Charlie's lips thinned into a white line, and his eyes narrowed. "You don't think she earned that?"

Steve laughed. "Hell, yeah, she definitely earned a glowing review, but this," he started and waved the newspaper at him. "This puts her on the map. Big time and I don't know, I just have the feeling you might have pulled some strings."

Dimples appeared in Charlie's cheeks along with a smirk. "I called in some favors and had the right people go to the show on Saturday night."

"Did you pay them to write this?" Anger laced his tone and tingled across his skin along with the cocaine rush.

"No. I didn't. I merely suggested they take the time to see the play," he said, leaning forward. "But I didn't tell them why."

Steve chewed on the side of his cheek, his gaze bouncing from the paper to Charlie's face and back. "Why?"

"Because she's fantastic, and I thought getting a break would be a nice thing for her."

"Oh." Steve leaned back in the seat, his mind still firing off in different directions, none of which could reconcile with the decency of Charlie's act.

"I'm not a bad guy, Steve."

He exhaled and met Charlie's gaze. "Yeah, well, putting a gun to a guy's head brings forth some serious doubts where that's concerned."

Charlie chuckled and shrugged.

"Same with bugging my apartment and sticking a tail on me."

"It's not personal."

"Bullshit! It's very personal." He stood and crossed to the window. "It means you don't trust me. Not one bit, and out of everything that you've pulled on me in the past week, that's the thing that pisses me off the most." In the window's reflection, Charlie's eyebrows rose.

Steve turned and crossed to the door. "And I hate that this shit makes me so fucking talkative." He left the office with Charlie's laugh following him out.

Vengeance
Chapter 22

THE NEXT MORNING, STEVE slid behind his desk and opened his drawer, staring at the vial of coke. His gaze traveled from the Starbucks coffee cup back to the white powder and then to the office door. Licking his lips, he dropped the vial back in the drawer and closed it, turning to his computer and some new contracts instead.

His attention kept refocusing on the drawer, as if the cocaine was calling him, mocking, teasing, and finally he gave in.

Just one hit. That's what he told himself as he crossed to close his office door. The first hit stung, and the second hit numbed. He closed the container and tucked it away, sniffling and wiping his nose with the back of his hand.

When the rush came, he stood and crossed to the window, staring at the street for a moment before catching his reflection. He wiped away a smudge of white and returned to his seat, his fingers running over the keyboard at a faster pace than usual despite the self-loathing that raked his skin.

God damn it.

He glared at the drawer and then inhaled. This was exactly what Charlie wanted, what he planned, and Steve was walking straight into the trap.

If I'm not careful, I'll end up hooked on the fucking street product, and this craving will eat up my life. If I'm not careful, I'll fuck up everything and end up getting both of us killed.

He knew he was talking himself out of a losing situation. The craving already took hold yesterday, and he'd resisted until this morning, until he stared at the clear container.

"Fucking drugs," he muttered, snapping a glare at the door and back to his desk. The withdrawals from the pain medicine last year had been bad enough, but this, this was going to be infinitely worse, especially if this assignment took another six months.

He shuddered and turned his thoughts away from that to a more pressing issue. Jennifer. He needed to figure out what to do with her. He didn't want Charlie to think he had a shot, and with the flowers, the candy, and the glowing reviews, he was stacking the chips against him.

His fingers paused, and he stared beyond the screen.

Would Charlie contract a hit on him just to get Jennifer? If the tables were turned, would he?

HE RESISTED THE URGE to crack open the cocaine for the rest of the week, but the questions he asked himself still assaulted his mind, shading everything he did. When the weekend rolled around, he buried himself in tracking the money trail. He finally finished to the background cheers of the crowd in Mile High Stadium on the television.

Steve stood and stretched, cracking his knuckles, and stared at the document on his computer screen that outlined the trail of drug money from the time Charlie was a street runner to last week. Fifteen years of financial ledgers were excessive, but then again, everything Charlie did was excessive.

Steve sat and leaned back in the chair with the heels of his palms pressed to his eyes. The computer beeped, and he glanced at the screen confirmation that the report he promised Jack transferred. He shut the connection down, closing the laptop.

Lying on the couch, he stared at the ceiling, wondering if he'd be able to convince Jennifer to go. His thoughts wandered back to Charlie and the spark of interest he had seen in his eyes when Charlie looked at Jennifer. He was damned if he'd let Charlie think he had even the slightest chance. He would have to do something about that, but the question was what?

Steve sat up straight. "Ha!" He hit his palm on his forehead. "I am such an idiot." He jumped out of bed and crossed to their bureau, rummaging through the various boxes on the top until he found what he was looking for. He held up her engagement ring and smiled.

The jangle of keys caught his attention, and he yanked the door open before she could slip her keys into the lock. He grabbed her wrist and pulled her inside, slamming the door.

"Marry me!" he blurted.

"Are you on drugs?"

"No, I'm serious Jen," he dropped to his knee and held the ring out. "Marry me."

Jennifer looked between the ring and his face, her brow creased.

"If you insist on staying, you have to play this out," Steve said from his vantage point, still holding the ring out to her. "You'll get to plan the wedding of your dreams." He offered a smile.

"I already had the wedding of my dreams," Jennifer said, but she took the ring anyway, slipping it on her finger. "I guess this means we're engaged?"

Steve grinned and stood. "I guess." He wrapped his arms around her waist and kissed her. "I'm sorry for being a son of a bitch yesterday."

"Asshole is more appropriate."

"I'm sorry," he said. "But I just want you to be safe."

Jennifer sighed. "You keep forgetting I can take care of myself."

"And you seem to forget that it's not just you anymore."

Jennifer pushed him away and headed into the bathroom. "Asshole," she muttered and slammed the door behind her.

Steve waited until she came out. "If I really was an asshole, I'd have Jack take you into protective custody." He shoved his hands into his pockets, studying the floor before raising his eyes to hers. Shifting his weight and tilting his head, he spoke again. "But I don't think you'd ever forgive me if I did."

"You're probably right." The crooked smile that graced his lips shot straight to her heart. She crossed the room and slipped into his arms. "I'd still love you, anyway."

He kissed her, moving her toward the bed.

Vengeance
Chapter 23

ANOTHER STELLAR MORNING OF vomiting! Jennifer thought, running the toothbrush over her teeth and tongue to get rid of the acidic taste. She spit, and rinsed her mouth, wishing Steve could have played hooky this morning to take care of her. Sighing, she wiped her lips with a hand towel and headed back to bed.

She opened the bathroom door and froze. Her eyes bulged at the man with the knife. Ice filled her veins, stopping the breath in her lungs as her gaze locked with his hard, gray pupils before darting to his right wrist. Cold numbness slapped at her cheeks, the blood rushing away in full retreat, leaving her lightheaded. "Jesus," she wheezed and lunged toward the nightstand where the cell phone sat.

Oh God, please.

He moved quickly, but he wasn't fast enough. She reached the cell phone and pressed the speed dial before he reached her. He swung the blade.

Jennifer blocked the arch of the knife with the hand holding the phone and spun out of the way, ducking out of his reach and sending a kick into his kidney that sent him stumbling into the bed.

Steve answered on the first ring.

"Help me! He's here!" was all Jennifer got out before the man sent her crashing into the wall with a kick of his own. The phone flew from her grasp, sliding across the floor. A detached voice bellowed her name.

"You son of a bitch!" Jennifer spun out of the way. Adrenalin pumped, turning the liquid ice in her veins to fiery fuel. She threw a powerful kick when he lunged. Her foot caught his wrist, sending the knife sailing across the little apartment toward the door.

His face contorted with rage. When she tried to slide by, he threw a punch into her ribcage, sending her to the ground, dazed enough for him to get a grasp on her arm. He yanked her to her feet and slammed his fist into her face, splitting her lip. "Bitch!" He threw her toward the bed.

Oh God, oh God, oh God.

The silent mantra played on in her head and Jennifer twisted out of his grasp, lunging toward him. She used the inertia to execute a roundhouse kick that connected with his chest, sending him onto his back. She scrambled for the phone.

He reached out, grabbing her ankle.

She lost her footing, sprawling on the floor face-first, and he was on her.

"No!" The scream filled the apartment.

No, no, no, no, no!

Her mind kept the repetition, although her voice failed beyond the first scream. As she struggled underneath him, only harsh grunts came from her chest. She clawed at the floor, trying to get purchase to pull out from under his weight. Coherent thought ceased for her, replaced instead by the visceral will to survive.

He forced himself between her legs, pressing his full weight against her. Slamming his elbow into her shoulder, he stunned her while he fumbled with his zipper. His hand slid under her neck, squeezing, cutting the raspy grunts to a dull hiss.

Visions of the other murders clouded her mind.

I don't want to die! Not like this!

She clawed at his hand, trying to break his grip on her airway. When he slammed his hard shaft inside her, her entire body went rigid. Debilitating burning pain flared, pain like she'd never felt before. Even if his hand hadn't been crushing her airway, she wouldn't have had the ability to draw a breath. The second pump of his hips was no better, but she tried to buck him off, anyway.

"Bitch," he whispered, pressing his full weight into her in vicious, sodomizing thrusts.

Sirens in the distance stopped his assault, and he pulled away, scrambling to his feet and bolting. He snatched the knife off the floor and pivoted in Jennifer's direction.

"I'm not done with you." He slipped out the door, slamming it closed.

Vengeance
Chapter 24

STEVE SCANNED THROUGH HIS emails, and his cell vibrated in his pocket. He glanced at the number, flipping it open. "Hey, babe."

"Help me! He's here!" her panicked voice screamed. The thump of the phone against the floor came through the line.

"Jennifer!" he yelled, hearing the tussle on the other end. His mind reeled, trying to figure out what was happening, and then his train of thought snapped in place.

Dear God, the Slasher!

Already moving, he sprinted out of the office and down the stairs with the phone plastered to his ear.

The car peeled out of the garage, and he shot into the street, cutting off the traffic and dialing 911. "This is Special Agent Williams of the FBI. I need assistance at 1621 Broad Street apartment 4A. Rape in progress, and I believe it's the Slasher," he spouted, taking the turn onto the Brooklyn Bridge and dodging the morning traffic like an Indianapolis 500 driver. He swerved into any free spot regardless of the traffic direction, avoiding accidents with seconds to spare, navigating his souped-up BMW through the crowded streets.

"Sweet Jesus," he prayed, "please let me get there in time." His heart pounded, feeling like it would leap from his chest at any moment while the images of all the victims flashed before his eyes. "Not Jenny, please God, not her."

He slid in front of the building, reached under his seat, grabbed his gun, bolted into the building, and sprinted up the stairs. He barreled into the hallway, still at full tilt, throwing his shoulder into the door. The hinges shattered, and he fell inside the apartment, catching himself and swinging the gun into the room. His eyes darted to Jennifer lying face down on the floor, detecting the small rise and fall of her chest. She was breathing. His heart skipped in his chest, and he surveyed the rest of the apartment, his gun following the track of his eyes.

"He's not here."

Her voice brought his attention back to his wife. Jennifer slowly pushed herself to her hands and knees as he crossed to her, flipping the safety back on the gun before wrapping his arms around her shaking frame. Steve swallowed the lump of fear in his throat and blinked away the burning tears. "Jenny," he said, before her sobs filled the room.

"Freeze!" the voice bellowed from behind them.

Steve slowly raised his arms with the gun hanging on his index finger and the rest of his fingers spread out. "I live here," he answered, with Jennifer still clinging to him. "She's my girlfriend." He turned his head toward the officers converging on the entryway, their guns all pointed in his direction. "She called me."

"Step away from her slowly."

Steve took a step back, but Jennifer kept her grip on him, her face still buried in the fabric of his suit, muffling her sobs.

"Jenny, you have to let go," he said, lowering his free hand.

"Keep your hands up!"

Steve stiffened. "She's my girlfriend, and she's hurt!" He shot a glare at the officer and put his hand back in the air.

The officer came forward, still focusing his sights on Steve until he was within reach of his hand. He peeled the gun off his finger. "Is this man your boyfriend?"

"Yes." Jennifer nodded, turning her tear-stained face toward the officer.

"Is he the one who hurt you?"

"No!" Indignant by the officer's question, she pushed away from Steve, looking between her husband and the officer. "I called him."

Steve put his hands down, reaching for her face and tilting her chin up. "What happened?" A slight shake laced his voice, born from the slow fizzle of panic and adrenaline.

"You just missed him." She tried to steady her voice, but to no avail.

"Can you describe what he looks like?" Steve asked, moving Jennifer to the edge of the bed. The officer flipped his notebook open.

She winced when she sat, straightening up again. "Dark curly hair, stubble like he hasn't shaved in a couple of days. Expensive sunglasses. He was a couple of inches taller than you. I scratched his arm up pretty bad..."

Her words faded as his stare focused on the handprint around Jennifer's neck. His gaze fell to the bruises on her elbows and knees. "Did he..." He raised his eyes to hers, unable to finish the question.

"He had a tattoo on his right wrist. I think it's of a rose, but I can't be sure. The knife was just like the one in Rambo. I knocked it out of his hand, which is probably why I'm alive," Jennifer continued on autopilot, unable to look at Steve.

"Did he rape you?" the officer asked.

Jennifer nodded, staring at the floor.

The officer picked up his walkie-talkie and requested an ambulance.

"I can take her to the hospital," Steve answered.

The officer shook his head. "I would rather have the ambulance take her."

Steve looked at the badge on his uniform. "Officer Andrews, I can take my girlfriend to the hospital."

"We would much prefer to have her taken by ambulance, Mr. Winchester."

Steve swung toward the familiar voice.

"We'll take it from here," Jack said to Officer Andrews as the FBI converged on the apartment.

"What did he do to you?" Steve asked after the officer returned his gun.

"What he did to all his victims," she answered. She raised her eyes to meet Steve's.

Steve inhaled, biting the inside of his lip to keep from letting the emotion get the best of him. He hung his head, closing his eyes. The shakes gripped him, and he stepped back. Reaching for a kitchen chair, he slid into it before his legs gave out under him. Fury filled every cell, every fiber, every thought, causing a red veil to shroud his vision and his hands to clench so tightly his nails dug into his flesh.

Son of a bitch is dead.

Jennifer wrapped her arms around her chest and started to cry again. "He said he wasn't done with me."

Steve stood, pushed his anger aside, and crossed, taking her in his arms, holding her and whispering, "It's all right now, babe. He will not get the chance to hurt you again." He turned his gaze to Jack, meeting his boss's stare.

The medics arrived, and Jack gave instructions for a full rape work-up on Jennifer, while Steve held her and stroked her hair.

"You have to fix the door," she whispered, her eyes trained on the splintered wood hanging from a solitary hinge.

"Don't worry about that right now."

She pulled away, meeting his gaze. "I don't want him to be able to get in next time."

Her entire frame shook in his arms, and he nodded. "I'll fix it later, I promise."

Her chin trembled, and she buried her face in his shirt.

"Mr. Winchester, may I have a word with you?" Jack said before Steve could follow Jennifer out of the apartment with the attendant.

He hesitated and met Jennifer's gaze.

"It's okay. You can meet me at the hospital after you fix the door."

He raised his eyebrows. "Are you sure?"

She nodded.

"I'll be there as soon as I finish." Steve waited until she stepped on the elevator with the ambulance attendant before he turned back to the ruined door and his boss standing in the apartment. He knew her fixation with the door was a byproduct of shock, of feeling helpless, of needing something to cling to beyond what had happened to her. His stint at Yale taught him the bizarre things rape victims latched onto after being violated and even though he wanted to be with her, he knew the first thing to setting her mind at ease started with fixing the damn door.

Jack turned his attention to Steve after most of the personnel left.

Steve's cell phone rang, and he put his hand up, stopping Jack before he could speak. "Hi Charlie," he answered.

"Linda said you bolted out of here like the place was on fire. Everything okay?"

"No, everything is not okay. Jennifer was attacked at the apartment this morning."

"Jesus. Is she all right?"

"She's pretty banged up, but she's alive. I have to get to the hospital. I'll be in later."

"Take the day off," Charlie said.

"Thanks man, I appreciate it." Steve flipped the phone closed. He stared at the front door now, propped next to the gaping doorway. The hinges were bent and twisted, and the wood splintered from his entry.

"Sit your ass down," Jack ordered, pointing at the kitchen chair after the last of the forensic team left the apartment.

"What the fuck are you pissed about?" Steve snapped, ignoring the order. He grabbed a toolbox from the closet and dropped it by the door, pulling out a screwdriver before he looked at his boss. "Well?"

"You may well have blown your cover." He folded his arms, glaring at Steve.

"I don't give a shit. A regular 911 call wouldn't have dispatched as quickly as a call for backup." Steve jammed the screwdriver in and torqued it, loosening the screw until he could remove it with his fingertips. He pulled the first damaged hinge off the door, looking at the heavy metal in his hand before pitching it with all his might. It smashed the lamp on the nightstand.

"She'll be all right." Jack took a seat at the kitchen table.

Steve glanced over his shoulder. "If she had listened to me, none of this would have happened. I wanted her to go home until this case wrapped up. But no, she insisted." He chucked the next hinge with the same bravado as the first, letting the anger burn away any hint of fear in his heart. The third hinge embedded in the drywall between the bed and the bathroom and Steve stared at it. "If I had made her go, this wouldn't have happened."

"Steve, this isn't your fault."

He spun toward Jack, his jaw tight and his eyes narrow. "If..."

Jack cut him off. "Cut the shit, Steve. You can't be with her every hour of every day. This had nothing to do with your current assignment, so get over it and get your shit together."

Steve stared at his boss, dropping the screwdriver into his toolbox. "I need to go get a deadbolt and some hinges. Do you mind staying until I get back, seeing as I no longer *have* a front door?" He waved at the wood leaning against the wall.

Jack inhaled sharply. "Sure."

The trip to the hardware store only worsened his mood, and he slammed the bag on the desk, stripping his jacket and flinging it across the room. He wanted to be with Jennifer, not here fixing the fucking door.

Jack sat at the kitchen table with his eyebrows raised and a cup of coffee steaming in front of him.

"Are you going to help me?" Steve asked, peeling the first hinge out of the package.

Jack sighed. "Jennifer called."

Steve stopped and looked back at his boss. "And?"

"We talked. I'm sending a sketch artist over to the hospital, along with a psychologist."

The air went out of Steve's chest, and he gave a nod, returning his focus to the door.

"I suggest you speak with the psychologist, too."

Steve shot a glare back at his boss. "I don't think so." He returned his attention to fixing the door, screwing the hinges on. "Can you give me a hand with this?"

Jack crossed and held the door in place while Steve attached the hinges to the wall.

"I'll get the deadbolt later." Steve closed the door, leaning his forehead on it after it closed snug. He dropped the screwdriver on the floor. Curling his hand into a fist, he drew back and hit the door with everything he had. His guttural roar filled the apartment. He punched again, and again, and again, the rage growing with each brutal blow.

Jack grabbed his arm, stopping him. "Easy!"

He almost threw a punch at Jack, but stopped with his arm back. "I'm going to kill him!"

Jack let go of his forearm. "Easy."

"I'm going to kill him," Steve whispered, tears making tracks down his face. He dropped his arms, blood dripped from the knuckles of his right hand. He leaned his back against the door, fighting for control. His eyes planted on a single spot in the ceiling.

"You…"

"I'm fine, Jack." Steve shot his gaze to his boss, wiping his face on his sleeve. "I'm just pissed off. Rip shitting, ballistically, pissed off."

"Rip shitting, ballistically, pissed?" Jack couldn't help it; he chuckled and stepped away. "Is that a new technical term?"

Steve cracked a small smile. He glanced at his bloody knuckles. "This hurts like a bitch." He couldn't flex his hand without pain shooting up his arm. "I think I broke it."

Jack looked at the mangled mess. "I'm sure you broke it. Let's get you to the hospital."

Steve nodded, digging his car keys out of his pocket and handing them to Jack. He swept his coat off the floor and headed out of the apartment.

Vengeance
Chapter 25

JENNIFER SAT WRAPPED IN a blanket, humiliated from the rape exam. Pictures had been taken of the damage to her face, ribs and various bruises on her thighs, knees and elbows. She could have dealt with that, but the pictures of the entry wounds, the bleeding from her anal passage, were as demeaning as the rape itself.

All she wanted was Steve, but he hadn't arrived yet.

She hopped off the exam table and picked up her pocketbook, rifling through it. The cell phone wasn't there. Her breath hitched in her chest. It was probably still in the apartment on the floor somewhere.

"Excuse me," she said to the officer guarding the door. "Do you have a cell phone I can use?"

"Yes, ma'am." He reached into his pocket and produced the phone, handing it over to her with a nod.

"Thank you." She retreated into the room and dialed the apartment.

"Hello?"

Jennifer looked at the phone. It was her number, but the voice wasn't familiar. "Is Steve there?"

"Jennifer?"

"Who is this?"

"It's Jack. Steve went to get hinges and a deadbolt for the door."

She pressed her lips together and squeezed her eyes closed to keep the tears from leaking out. Steve was doing exactly what she asked him to do, and that solidified the lump in her throat. When she was sure she had control, she whispered, "Okay."

"Do you want to talk about what happened?"

Jennifer debated. This was the man who witnessed the destruction in Brooksfield and the best man at their wedding. She closed her eyes, inhaling and letting the emotions coiled up inside flow along with a fresh set of tears. "Jack, I was so scared," she began. "I kept imagining Steve's face when he found me dead, like all the other women that bastard killed. That's what kept me fighting." Her voice hitched, and she clamped her lips closed on the sob. Swallowing, she reigned in her emotions. "I couldn't let him find me like that. I got lucky and got to the phone before he knocked it out of my hand."

Jack's breathing filled the line as he listened.

"All I can say is thank god for karate. I got a couple of good licks in myself, so the bastard's sporting some serious bruises, too."

"Do you think you can give our sketch artist a description?"

"Yeah," she answered quietly. "I can do that."

"And I'm also going to send over someone you can talk to, all right?"

"I just want Steve."

"I'll bring him as soon as he gets back."

"Thank you, Jack."

"No problem, kiddo. We'll catch the bastard."

Hanging up, she wiped her face and brought the phone back to the officer. "Thank you."

"No problem, ma'am."

She climbed back on the hospital bed and wrapped the blanket tighter around her shoulders, curling up and shivering from more than just the chill in the air. When he had the death grip on her throat, raping her on the floor, she thought that was it. That was how her life was going to end. No matter how hard she fought, she wasn't going to win the battle.

The sound of the sirens had been distant, detached. Even his threat seemed fuzzy. But Steve knocking the door down was crystal clear. His wild-eyed expression coupled with the blotchy color on his face burned into her memory. He shook just as much as she did when he wrapped his arms around her, although she didn't think he was aware of it at all.

Jennifer closed her eyes, letting the drugs pull her into the darkness.

Vengeance
Chapter 26

THE HALLS ECHOED WITH footfalls, as Charlie's shiny Bruno Magli wingtip shoes clicked on the hard tile. With a bouquet in his hand, he approached the desk. "Can you tell me where I can find Jennifer Curtis?"

The nurse glanced up at him, taking in his finely tailored charcoal gray Armani suit and the flowers in his hand. She raised her arm, pointing down the hallway. "The room with the policeman stationed outside."

Charlie nodded and headed that way, wondering why there were police outside the door. The officer stood facing him as he approached.

"I'm a friend of the family," he said as he approached. "Is Jennifer okay?"

The officer gave him the once over and stepped aside.

He knocked lightly on the door and slipped inside without waiting for a response. Steve wasn't there, and Jennifer was sleeping in the bed. The blanket had shifted, giving him a view of her milky thighs. He licked his lips and reached out to touch her skin, stopping at the last second. His fingers hovered over her flesh, feeling the warmth radiating off her, and he pulled back, admonishing himself. Charlie took a step back and glanced at her bruised face as he cleared his throat.

✦ ✦ ✦

"STEVE?" JENNIFER'S EYES FLUTTERED at the sound in the room. When they cleared, she shot up to a sitting position, pulling the blanket around her. Her eyes pulsed in their sockets, and she stared at Charlie Wisnowski clad in a charcoal gray Armani suit, carrying a bouquet of flowers.

"I'm sorry if I startled you," he said. "Steve told me you were here." He offered a shrug and placed the flowers on the end of the bed. "Where is he?"

Her gaze darted between the door, the flowers, and the man in the finely tailored suit. *Where the hell was Steve, anyway?* "He had to fix the door."

"Are you okay?"

She wasn't about to get into anything with him, so she nodded. His eyes scanned her, and she shifted on the bed, straightening and tightening the sheets around her waist, trying to hide her discomfort. His eyes slid by her left hand and snapped back to the diamond ring adorning her finger. *Oh, shit.*

His brow creased, and he pointed at her left hand. "Did I miss something?"

Jennifer looked at the diamond. "Steve asked me to marry him this weekend." Charlie's eyebrows shot up and his mouth dropped open. The shock of the statement settled in, and he recovered his smooth demeanor before her eyes.

"That's fantastic."

"Why did you come here?"

"I just..." He stumbled over his answer, pointing at the flowers. "I was worried," he finally sputtered. "Steve didn't sound okay on the phone."

The way his eyes kept surveying her body and darting back to her face reminded her of the way the fraternity boys had looked at her a few days before they kidnapped and raped her. She shifted, pulling the blanket tighter, and her gaze dropped to his hands. A fraction of relief washed over her at the sight of his smooth and unscathed skin.

A knock on the door interrupted them. "Excuse me?" A woman poked her head through the door. "Ms. Curtis?"

Jennifer nodded.

"Do you mind if we come in?" She looked between Charlie and Jennifer.

"Please," she said.

The woman entered and took a seat, pulling out a sketchpad and pencil. She cast a glance in Charlie's direction.

Jack stepped into the room behind the sketch artist, his eyes flying between Charlie and Jennifer. His expression remained neutral even though he was meeting his target face-to-face. He nodded toward Jennifer. "Ms. Curtis, I see you have company, so I'll come back at a more convenient time."

"This is Mr. Wisnowski, my fiancé's boss. He came to see how we were doing," she said. "Charlie, this is Special Agent Murphy with the FBI."

"FBI?" He shot her a questioning stare.

Nodding, her hand fluttered to her face. "Apparently, the man who attacked me has done this before." She swallowed and looked at Jack. "Where's my fiancé?"

He hooked his thumb over his shoulder. "He's in the emergency room having his wrist looked at." Extending his hand to Charlie, he said, "Pleased to meet you, Mr. Wisnowski."

Charlie returned the handshake. "Likewise." He glanced back at Jennifer. "I'll go see if I can find Steve." He slipped out of the room.

Jennifer waited a moment before she turned her gaze to Jack. "What did Steve do to his wrist?"

"He had it out with your front door." He glanced at the sketch artist. "This is Special Agent Mary Stewart."

She extended her hand to Jennifer. "I am sorry to meet you under these circumstances." Her half-smile and slight tilt of her head brought home the reason they were there. "Now, can you describe any facial features of the man who attacked you?"

Vengeance
Chapter 27

STEVE SAT IN A chair holding his torn-up hand, watching the news on the television set. Movement at the corner of his eye caught his attention, and he looked toward the waiting room doorway. Charlie stood leaning on the frame with his arms crossed.

His eyes widened, and his jaw loosened, the surprise registering for an instant before he snapped his mouth shut.

Charlie slid into the seat next to him. "The FBI?"

He nodded.

"What the fuck?"

"Serial killer," he answered. With a stoic expression, he swiveled his gaze from the television to Charlie. "She's lucky to be alive."

"Jesus." He took a closer look at Steve's hand and pointed toward it with a silent question.

"I had a meltdown and beat the shit out of the door."

"Did they catch him?"

He shook his head. "No. Why are you here?"

"I stopped in to check on you."

Crock of shit! Steve threw a glare in Charlie's direction. "Don't worry, I will not rat you out."

"I never doubted that for a second."

Yeah right. He closed his eyes. "Sorry, I'm just a little stressed."

"Is there anything I can do to help?"

Turning, he stared at Charlie. "Find the bastard and kill him."

He shifted his gaze to Steve's hand and nodded. "I'll see what I can do." He stood to leave. "And congratulations on the engagement," he said before he left the waiting room.

Steve stared after Charlie, his mind grappling with the conversation. *How the hell did he know about the engagement? Shit, he must have seen Jenny.* The thought pissed him off more than he was already, and his hands curled into fists again. Shooting pain followed up his arm, and he winced. "Fuck," he muttered.

"Mr. Winchester?"

He looked up at the attendant.

"Please follow me." He led Steve into a room at the end of the hall. The doctor stood looking at his x-rays.

Crinkling his nose, he suppressed a sneeze as the smell of hot fiberglass and plaster filled the air. He took a seat on the table that the attendant pointed to. "Is it broken?"

The doctor removed his glasses and turned to Steve, nodding. "You've done quite a job on yourself. You've fractured the second and third metacarpal bones in your hand and you have a hairline fracture in your ulna. John's going to put you in a cast to limit the motion of those bones." He nodded to the technician. "Next time, you should think twice before taking on an oak door."

He glanced at his swollen hand. He wasn't sure he'd be able to get the dented wedding band off his ring finger, but he tried anyway, and with the help of some antibacterial soap, he was able to slide it off without too much damage to his knuckle. He slid the slimy, blood-ridden metal into his pocket.

With his wrist set in a blue fiberglass cast and already throbbing, he found Jennifer's room on the other side of the hospital.

The guard stopped him at the door, scanning him with skeptical eyes. Looking down at his blood-smeared shirt and back up at the officer, he pointed his new cast toward the door. "She's my fiancée."

The officer waved him through.

He stepped into the room. The moment Jennifer saw him, she burst into tears, and he shot to her side, wrapped his arms around her, and buried his face in her hair. Pulling away, he ran his left hand over her cheek, his thumb grazing her swollen lip lightly. "I'm here now."

Her teary green eyes lowered to the cast on his arm and back to his face.

"It's nothing," he said. "Stupid, really." He glanced at Jack, then back to Jennifer. "How's the baby?"

"The baby's fine," she said, sniffling.

The last hint of relief swept through him, and he exhaled. "Did you finish with the sketch?" he asked the agent sitting next to the bed. When she turned the rendering toward him, he stared at it, memorizing the likeness. His eyes narrowed, and he chewed on his lip. There was something vaguely familiar, but he couldn't put his finger on it right away. Then it all clicked into place, and he shot to his feet. "That's the fucking courier!"

"What courier?" Jack asked.

"The one who wouldn't leave the package for Charlie with me last week." The development was a physical blow. This meant there was a connection to his current assignment, to Charlie, or his organization at the very least, and he led her right into the middle of it. Again. He shook his head. "God damn it!"

Jennifer glanced from the picture to Steve. "You've seen him before?"

He nodded, trading a glance with Jack. Exhaling, he swung his gaze to her, pointing a splinted finger in her direction. "I want you out of the city tonight."

"Not tonight. I need you tonight."

"Jenny, I can't take the chance. He threatened you."

She looked between Jack and Mary. "Would you two mind if I talk to Steve alone?"

Mary packed up her things. "I'll get this on the wire." She left the room. Jack followed her out.

Jennifer's eyes filled with tears. "I'm *not* doing this pregnancy alone."

Steve sat on the side of the bed and took her hand, bringing it to his lips. "Jen, I can't take the risk of losing you."

She reached out, running her fingers over the rough fiberglass cast. "I don't want to be alone."

Steve racked his brain for options. He didn't want her in the city, not with what happened, but he also didn't want her too far away. "What about your parents?" He threw the question out there. Even though he and her father were at constant odds with each other, it was the most logical choice to keep Jennifer safe.

"You want me to go to my parent's house?"

"It's safer than being here with me. And it's not that far. I'll come by on the weekends."

"Can we find a different apartment instead?"

He didn't speak, but pressed his lips together. It had taken a few months for the bureau to obtain the apartment they were in, and he didn't have that kind of time right now. "I don't think that's possible." Slipping into the chair by the bed, he turned over his options. "I could have a bodyguard assigned when I'm not with you."

"I'm not sure I'd be comfortable with a strange man watching my every move." She shifted and met his gaze.

"Then it's your parents." He tried to cross his arms and couldn't comfortably manage it with the cast.

"A bodyguard or my parents—that's quite a morbid list of options."

"It's better than being dead."

Jack saved her from making a snide comment, walking into the room unannounced, followed by a nurse with scrubs for her to wear out of the hospital.

"What do you mean, the FBI doesn't have the resources?" Steve snapped at Jack. They stood in the hallway outside Jennifer's room while she dressed.

"The FBI doesn't have the manpower to put someone on her for that kind of time commitment," Jack answered. "I can have someone with her this week, and then I'm tapped."

"Jesus H. Christ!" He ran his good hand through his hair. The next thought that crossed his mind made his skin crawl, but it was the only other plausible option outside of her parents. "Fine, cover her this week and then we'll figure it out, but I want someone at the apartment before I leave, and they are to stay with her until I get home."

"Are you giving me orders?" Jack stepped toe-to-toe with him, glaring.

He didn't react to Jack's violation of personal space. Instead, he continued to level his cool, uncompromising stare at his boss.

Jack stepped away when Jennifer opened the door. He dug in his pocket, producing the keys to Steve's BMW. "I'll catch a cab."

He caught the keys in his left hand and looked at Jennifer. She was in no condition to drive, and neither was he. For the first time in his life, he wished he drove an automatic transmission. "Jack?" he called.

Jack turned halfway down the hallway.

"You need to drive Jen back. I'll take the cab." He tossed the keys to Jack and, with a nod; Jack went to get the car.

Steve walked Jennifer to the emergency entrance. "I arranged for an FBI bodyguard this week, so we don't have to decide right away." He saw her stiffen. "It's either that or your parents."

Jennifer didn't speak until she was sitting in the passenger seat, looking at him. "I'll see you at home?"

"Yes." He closed the door. Steve straightened his back, watching the car pull away, and then hailed a cab. After he rattled off the address, he settled into the seat and flipped open his cell phone.

"Charlie?"

"What's up Steve?"

He took a deep breath; hating himself for turning to the man he was sworn to take out. "The FBI doesn't have the resources to protect Jennifer while I'm at work. Do you?"

"What do you think?"

"I'm not playing games, Charlie. The bastard threatened to come back and finish the job, and I need to know if you've got someone who can protect her."

"Yes, I've got a few contacts. Do you want a male or a female watching over her?"

He hadn't considered gender, and the offer caught him by surprise. His initial reaction was to say a man, but based on what she had said at the hospital, he reconsidered. "A woman probably would be better under the circumstances."

"When do you want her to start?"

"How about Monday? I've got the FBI until the end of this week."

Silence blanketed the line. "I'm not sure I like the idea of you fraternizing with the FBI for any length of time. How about if I have her start Wednesday and you take tomorrow off to be with your girlfriend?"

Steve knew neither Jack nor Jennifer would like it, but he had to do what was best for his wife, and right now, that was making the alliance with Charlie. He exhaled audibly. "I was hoping you'd say something like that. I don't want them hanging around either, but I don't want my girl getting hurt, and it was the only option I had to make sure that didn't happen."

"Well, your options just changed," Charlie said. "I'll get on that right now."

"Thanks, man." He folded his phone and dug in his pocket for his wallet as the cab pulled up in front of the apartment complex. He fumbled to pull the cash out and traded a twenty for change before heading inside.

Formulating his thoughts, he knocked on the apartment door. He knew Jack wouldn't be pleased with the deal he just made with Charlie. Might as well have been a deal with the devil, but if it kept Jennifer safe, he didn't give a shit. He'd trade his life for hers in a heartbeat.

Jennifer came out of the bathroom with the back of her hand to her mouth. She traded a glance with him and stretched out on the bed on her stomach.

"I'm all set with a bodyguard," Steve directed at Jack. "We won't need the FBI's protection." He tore his jacket off, tossing it on the computer table.

"What the hell did you do?"

Jack's snarl was enough to make Jennifer roll to witness the conversation.

"I ensured my wife would be safe." He crossed the room and sat on the edge of the bed next to her, avoiding Jack's gaze.

"Steve, what did you do?" she asked.

"I pulled some strings."

Jennifer threw herself on her back and stared at the ceiling. "You asked Charlie."

He nodded and turned his head toward his boss. "He has the resources. We don't."

Jack pressed his lips into a thin line. "You stupid son of a bitch!"

Steve shot to his feet. "You couldn't guarantee her safety, so I took advantage of the resources that *I* have access to. I did what I had to do and honestly, it will put me in a better position than where I am right now. The last thing Charlie wants is for FBI involvement anywhere near one of his employees.”

“Don’t give me that as an excuse. You used the situation for your own personal gain.”

“You’re the one who put me on this case and you’re the one who couldn’t guarantee her protection.” He pointed his cast in Jennifer’s direction. “What would you have done if the tables were turned?”

“I would get my wife as far away from the city as humanly possible!”

Silence blanketed the room. He and Jack locked angry glares, neither one willing to back down first.

“This is going to be done my way,” he said. “Or you can kiss this ass goodbye.”

“Steve!” Jennifer gasped.

He shot her a quick glance before continuing. “I’m the one who’s knee deep in shit here. I’m calling the shots on how this goes down, not you and not Jerry.” He stood his ground, wondering if he had just screwed his career to the point of no return. “You’ve got enough information to lock him up for tax evasion, but you want to go for the drug charges on top of that. Well, this goes with the territory.” He spread his arms out. “Take it or leave it, Jack.”

Jack turned his back to Steve, his fists clenching and unclenching.

Steve cast a sideways glance at Jennifer. Her eyes darted between the two men, waiting for the floor to drop out from under them.

“Fine.” He swung around, pointing at Steve. “But so help me God, if you screw this case up...”

“I know. My ass is toast.”

Jack sucked in the air quickly. "More than that, Steve. I'll throw so many charges at you that you'll spend the better part of your life in a federal penitentiary."

He crossed his arms as best he could with the cast. "I'm a lawyer, remember?"

"You're a cop."

"With a law degree, so that pussy ass threat has no credence."

His face turned beet red.

"Don't blow a gasket, Jack. I'm good at my job and I want to take down Charlie as much as you do."

"Pussy ass threat? That's as good as ballistically, rip shitting pissed."

Steve broke out in a grin. "It's a legal term."

Jack burst out laughing. "One of these days, I'm going to have your badge."

He lifted his shoulders in an easy shrug.

"I only put up with your shit because you get the job done. The minute you fuck up, I'll yank your badge."

His smile faded, Jack's words itching under his skin. "You really think I'd fuck this up on purpose?"

Jack leveled his gaze. "I don't know, Steve. Money is a pretty seductive bitch, and Charlie is certainly throwing a shit load in your direction."

"Thanks for all your help today." He crossed to the door, opening it. "Now get out of my apartment."

Jack stopped when he was shoulder to shoulder with him. "Working undercover as a college student isn't in the same league that you're in now. Be careful to keep your priorities straight."

He slammed the door after Jack passed through into the hallway. His eyes landed on Jennifer's wide green ones. "What?"

"What's Charlie going to do? Assign that greasy thug to watch me? Thanks, Steve."

"He's getting you a female bodyguard. At my request."

Jennifer's eyebrows shot up into perfect arches. Her stunned expression was almost comical, but considering the current situation, he didn't react to the sudden urge to laugh.

Crossing to the bed, he lay down next to her, propping his arm up over his head. Throbbing immediately took over his limb, and he closed his eyes, breathing slowly to control the pain in his wrist. "It's more than you would have gotten from the FBI."

"Cut the sarcasm."

Steve sighed and looked at her. "You don't want to leave. I want you protected. And Jack was right. I capitalized on my situation and put myself into Charlie's debt."

She propped herself on her elbows and stared into his eyes.

"It was the smartest play I had. He would never have trusted me if the FBI was involved any further."

"But now I have to be on all the time."

"You could always go home, Jen. That's where I wanted you in the first place."

"Are you insinuating this is my fault?"

"No, I'm not. I'm just saying if your choice is to stay put, this is what you'll have to live with, because I'm not leaving you unprotected for a second." He rolled on his side and wiped a stray hair out of her face. "Not after today." *Never again.*

She nodded and curled into him, her back against his chest.

He ran his fingers through her hair, and they lay in the silence.

"You shouldn't have taken it out on the door," she said after a while.

Steve didn't answer her. His heart had found its way into his throat and a slow track of tears flowed from his eyes. The anger finally gave way to painful desperation as he ran through all the different outcomes the day could have resulted in if she hadn't been quick enough or strong enough to fight back. The image of her in the same position as all the bastard's other victims, raped, defiled, stabbed and dead, gave way to the memory of the gang rape in the crypt he had been forced to watch.

Never again.

Vengeance
Chapter 28

STEVE PUTTERED AROUND THE apartment after dropping Jennifer off at the theater for rehearsal and the evening performance.

He glanced at the clock. "What the hell am I going to do for seven hours?" It had been months since the last time he was alone for that chunk of time. The shooting range and gym were out because of the cast. Surfing the web had gotten old, and he'd already responded to all his emails from both CWFOG and the FBI before dropping her off. Pacing, he flipped through daytime television, which to him was as painful as having a root canal without Novocain.

"Fuck it." He tossed the remote onto the table and grabbed his coat. Twenty minutes later, he stepped off the subway across from the office. He walked into the reception area wearing jeans and a bomber jacket, looking much more casual than anyone else in the office.

Linda looked up and raised her eyebrows. Scanning him from head to toe, her eyes lingered on the blue cast poking out of his sleeve. "I thought you had today off."

"Daytime television sucks," he replied and walked into the heart of the office.

Charlie looked up from the copier, his head cocking to the side at the sight of him crossing the office. "What are you doing here?"

Steve stopped in the entry to his office, glancing at him. "Jenny insisted on going to the theater today. I was bored shitless at home after I dropped her off. So here I am." He offered a shrug to the multiple pairs of eyes staring at him and ducked into his office out of view.

Charlie walked in before he had a chance to take off his coat. "Desiree will be stopping by tonight to meet you and Jennifer."

"Desiree?"

"The bodyguard."

"A bodyguard named Desiree?" Steve repeated, not knowing whether to be slightly amused or aggravated.

Charlie cracked a smile. "Yes. She's a piece of work. Doesn't look like she could hurt a fly, but she can be as deadly as a six-five, three-hundred-pound thug. So, don't even think about testing her."

"Like that's going to happen." He raised his casted arm. "Besides, I'm not picking up Jennifer until after the show tonight."

He turned to leave and paused, glancing back at him with a thoughtful expression. "You feel like going for a ride?" he asked.

"Where to?"

"I think it's time I show you the operation."

Steve raised his eyebrows. *Careful now.* "I really don't want to know any more details than I already do, Charlie," he said, but remained standing and prayed he had an expression that crossed between apprehension and curiosity on his face. His heart was doubling down, sending adrenaline pumping through his skin. None of the others ever found out where Charlie's drug factory was, or if they knew, they didn't live long enough to report to their superiors. He shifted his weight and kept eye contact with Charlie.

Charlie closed the door. "Did the FBI have questions relating to me?"

Steve's muscles tensed at the question. "No. They were a little more concerned with catching the Slasher."

Ignored the snide remark, he asked, "What did they say when you turned their protection down?"

"They weren't thrilled, but Jennifer didn't want a stranger hanging around the apartment, even if he was FBI. That idea freaked her out, and considering what she's been through, they backed off. I saw a fed camped out on the street this morning, but he didn't follow me, so I think they're watching the apartment."

"They think he'll come back?"

"Yeah, he threatened to finish the job. We put a deadbolt on the apartment door as a precaution." He sat in his chair and closed his eyes. "If I ever get my hands on the bastard..." When he opened his eyes, Charlie shivered.

"You know, I'd actually feel sorry for that son of a bitch if you get hold of him."

Steve smiled. "If that happens, the fucker is going to experience a prolonged suffering death."

Charlie shifted in his seat and glanced away. "Come on." He stood and headed for the door. The request had come out in the snap of an order that Steve couldn't refuse.

Steve followed him to his SUV in the garage. He slid into the passenger seat and whistled. The vehicle was beautifully equipped with leather-heated seats, a sound system that most street punks would envy, and a GPS system in the dash, all hidden from view behind tinted windows. "Nice wheels."

"Not as sweet as your beemer."

"I restored it myself."

Charlie shot a wide-eyed glance at Steve. "Seriously?"

He nodded.

"You're just full of surprises."

"It took about a year to fix that baby up." He leaned back, memorizing the route. Taking a deep breath, he asked, "Why now?"

Charlie glanced at him with scrunched brows.

"Why trust me now?"

Navigating the streets from Manhattan into Brooklyn, he finally said, "Who says I trust you?"

Steve twitched in the seat and glanced at Charlie. "Where exactly are we going?"

He shot a glare in his direction. "Don't worry Steve—I'm not going to kill you." He tilted his head. "At least not today," he added, focusing back on the road.

"That makes me feel *so* much better."

Charlie laughed at the sarcasm-laced response. "I told you, I'm showing you the operation. I want you to help me run things both here and at the office."

"How so?"

"Manage the money and the traffic flow and the overhead."

Steve blew the air out of his chest audibly. He just hit the mother lode and how he played this was important. "That's a little out of my league."

"You're a sharp kid. You'll learn quickly enough. I'm looking for insight on how to be more productive. Maybe you can see different avenues of distribution that we haven't thought of."

He raised his eyebrows.

"I've got faith in you."

Faith? Where the hell had that come from? He shook his head and continued to stare out the window before swinging his gaze back at Charlie. "Why don't you get someone who really wants to do this?"

His smile disappeared. "Because anyone who *wants* to manage my business has delusions of taking it over—or worse, they're moles." He glanced at Steve. "Either way, anyone gung-ho on getting to this level is taken out. Besides, you've done a brilliant job with my finances, and I want that innovative spirit applied here."

"You kissing my ass?"

He burst out laughing. "Not in the least. This is business and you've got business savvy. I need that to get to the next level." He nodded toward the giant warehouse as he pulled over into a vacant parking spot along the sidewalk.

Steve's eyebrows creased. "This is the fiber optics plant." He had been out to this plant several times in the six months at CW FOGs, and while he noticed the warehouses on either side of the plant, he never really gave it a second thought. He'd miscalculated, thinking Charlie wouldn't dare have his cocaine operation next to his legitimate business.

Charlie pointed to the warehouse on the right of the fiber optics plant. "This one is, but the one next door isn't."

Steve surveyed the building, noting several cameras mounted under the roof's canopy. "Cameras?"

Charlie answered with a nod. "This place has a state-of-the-art security system. Cameras inside and out. That way we'll know if a sting is going down." He got out of the car and Steve followed suit. "On first glance, it just looks like a packing company, but behind the line of bubble wrap and cardboard boxes, there's a lab." He hesitated before punching in the access code. "You'll need to memorize this number." He pressed five, six, four, nine, seven, zero into the keypad.

"Five, six, four, nine, seven, zero?"

Charlie nodded and swung the door open.

"Any significance?"

"May sixth is the day my brother died. Four, nine, seventy is my birthday."

"You should never use your birthday as a security code," he replied. After a quick calculation, Steve said, "That makes you forty."

Charlie sent a glare in his direction and pointed to the inside of the door. "The entry is rigged with explosives and the trigger is in my office," he said. "If I ever see cops coming, I can set these puppies so when the door opens; anyone near them is blown to Timbuktu."

"That's a little extreme," he said, studying the explosives.

Charlie chuckled. "Not as extreme as the interior defenses."

Steve turned toward him, allowing the shock to register in his face.

"Come, I'll show you." He headed across the concrete floor to an open stairwell that ascended to an office overlooking the length of the warehouse.

His heart plummeted when he walked into the office. A bank of monitors showed all facets of the warehouse, inside and out. There were windows on three sides of the room, one looking out on the street with windows that reminded him of those you'd find in schools. They were long and pushed out once the heavy latch was disengaged. "All the windows are tinted?"

"And bulletproof."

Charlie's answer caused Steve to glance in his direction. "I'm impressed." He walked over to the bank of glass overlooking the warehouse and whistled. He had to give Charlie credit—this was one slick operation. The monitors showed the production facility, but the view from the glass only showed the packing facility. "Where is it?"

Charlie smiled and flipped a switch.

Steve's eyes nearly bugged out of his head as the silk screen slowly rose and the cocaine lab came into view. No one below so much as blinked when the curtain rose. He turned to Charlie in stunned silence. *Holy fucking shit.*

"Sweet set-up, eh?"

He nodded, returning his gaze out the window. *No wonder no one's been able to nail this bastard.* "Jesus." He took a deep breath and regained his composure.

"I move close to twenty-five kilos a year through this warehouse. My clientele is high end, not street punks," he explained, glancing at Steve.

Nodding, he tore his eyes away from the warehouse. "I can see why the doors are booby trapped."

Charlie smiled and walked over to a bank of switches. "These control the triggers on the door," he began, "and this activates the triggers for the explosives around and under the lab. I've got enough nitroglycerine and C-4 under this building to leave a crater the size of a city block."

Steve turned to the window overlooking the lab. "Where are the triggers for that?" His voice actually cracked, and he cleared his throat.

Charlie joined him at the window and pointed to doors along the fake wall separating the packing façade with the lab. "There are floor sensors under those doors. If the trigger is live, anyone stepping on the threshold won't know what hit him and everything in the building will disintegrate. Hell, everything for a couple of hundred yards will disintegrate."

"Even the fiber optics plant." Steve couldn't believe the precautions he had in place and shook his head a fraction.

"Yes."

"Well, that would be a pisser."

Charlie burst out laughing at the unexpected comment. "No shit." He turned and took a seat behind the large desk, opening the top drawer and pulling out a small bag of blow. "Sit down," he ordered.

He turned and stared at him. "Jennifer will kill me if I get high again."

Charlie reached under the desk and pulled out a nine-millimeter. "I'll kill you if you don't." He set the gun on the desk.

"Is this your plan? Show me the organization, get me hooked on coke, and make me your bitch?" He didn't move from the spot where he stood.

"Hadn't thought of making you my bitch." Charlie picked up the gun, swiveling the muzzle in his direction. He pushed the paraphernalia to the other side of the desk. "Just four lines today." He nodded toward the bag of cocaine. "Come on."

Steve crossed his arms awkwardly and held his ground. "Go ahead, shoot me." He saw a flash in Charlie's eyes and thought he was a goner, but he refused to move from the spot where he stood. He kept eye contact, praying he had played this hand right. "I'm nobody's bitch," he said after a moment of strained silence.

Cocking his head, Charlie flipped the safety on the gun, setting it down on the desk. He leaned back in the chair, crossing his arms. "But you are whipped."

He gave a huff and turned back toward the lab. "Do you distribute to the street at all?"

"No."

"Why not?"

"I don't want to get into gang turf. It's too volatile. Besides, the normal street addict couldn't afford this stuff. A gram of street coke goes for a little over a hundred. This goes for a grand."

"Why?"

"It's more refined than your average street blow."

"Ah, okay." He shrugged, giving the impression he had no clue of what that meant. "What's your profit per gram?"

"Fifty percent of the retail value."

Steve did the math. "You clear 12 million a year?"

Charlie snorted the lines he cut and nodded. "Yes," he said, but didn't expand on his links to the Bondino family, as Steve hoped he would.

"And you'd like to increase your profit." *Greedy son of a bitch is clearing twelve million a year and wants more? That's fucked up.* He crossed the office and sat down in the chair facing the desk. "And you're against branching out to the street?"

Charlie finished cutting four more lines and slid the mirror toward him with a clean straw. "Not if it means enlisting gangs to distribute, and the normal street junkie can't afford this." He pointed his chin toward the mirror.

Steve looked at the neat lines of powder. "How much does that represent?"

"A couple of hundred." Charlie waited, watching Steve stare at the powder.

"What do you cut it with?"

"Flour."

Steve raised his eyes and sighed. "Jennifer's going to kill me." He picked up the straw and inhaled all four lines, ignoring the sudden burning in his nostrils. *Not to mention Jack.* He sniffled and stood, crossing to the windows overlooking the road while Charlie stashed the mirror away. The rush was a fraction of what it had been the other night, settling into his skin like a dozen shots of espresso. "What if you cut more flour into a gram and lowered the price for street distribution?"

"I already thought about that route, but distribution on the street is more risky than the circles I deal in. It's not a viable avenue. Think of something else."

"What about pharmaceutical use?"

His eyebrows rose. "That's regulated by the government."

"Yeah, but I'm sure there's a way in."

"They only distribute pure cocaine."

He shrugged. "How pure is that?"

"Ninety percent—that's why it's so expensive."

"So, produce a small amount of pure cocaine and distribute through pharmacies."

Charlie leaned back in the seat, his fingertips resting together in a teepee as he mulled over his proposition. "I've got to admit, I'm impressed. That's an avenue that hasn't been mentioned before."

Steve offered another shrug. "Isn't that why you let me live? Because I'm... what'd you say?" He tapped his lip with his index finger, then pointed at him. "An innovative thinker?"

He nodded. "How do you propose we go about contact?"

The question threw him, and he didn't have an answer. "Do you have any contacts in your distribution circle that have an in on that front?"

Charlie's eyebrows rose again as he mentally scanned his client list. "Possibly."

"There you go." He glanced at his watch. It was almost five. "What time was Desiree supposed to show up at the apartment?" He scanned the bank of monitors and controls, memorizing the layout, before returning his gaze to Charlie.

"She said she'd swing by around seven." Charlie glanced at his own watch. "We'd better go. We'll take a ride tomorrow and I'll show you the lab." He grabbed a small vial of powder, handing it to him. "Don't use it all at once," he said as he flipped the control that brought the silk screen back into place, creating the illusion of only a packing company.

Steve pocketed the vial, watching the screen lower, and had to suppress the feeling of admiration that surfaced. It didn't matter how brilliantly conceived and executed this operation was; he was still a criminal. Jack's snide remark about money being a seductive bitch surfaced in his mind.

He wasn't kidding.

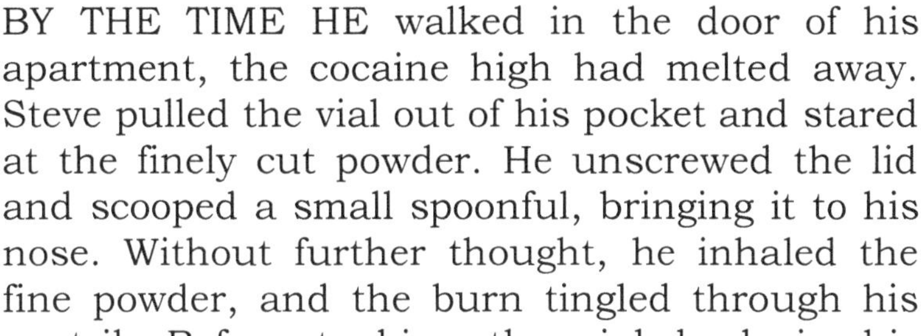

BY THE TIME HE walked in the door of his apartment, the cocaine high had melted away. Steve pulled the vial out of his pocket and stared at the finely cut powder. He unscrewed the lid and scooped a small spoonful, bringing it to his nose. Without further thought, he inhaled the fine powder, and the burn tingled through his nostril. Before tucking the vial back in his pocket, he repeated with the other nostril.

The rush hit and he paced, clicking through the different news stations, unable to sit still. When the soft rap on the wood filtered above the television, he pressed the mute button and tossed the remote on the couch before bounding to the door. He beheld the stunning blonde standing on his doorstep and his breath caught in his throat. "Desiree?"

Her luscious lips curved into a sexy smile that rivaled Jennifer's, producing instant heat within him. His gaze wandered down her lithe five-foot-ten frame as she stepped inside the apartment.

"You're a bodyguard?"

Desiree looked around the apartment. "Where's your girlfriend?"

"At work," he answered, still ogling. He tore his eyes away from her and glanced at the clock. "I'm heading over to pick her up in a couple of hours." He closed the door.

She studied him, her eyes falling on the cast on his arm. "What'd you do there?"

Steve glanced at his cast. "I punched the door." He let his eyes drift up her jean-clad legs

491

to the ample breasts pressing against the tight sweater and finally to her perfectly oval face. Her pale blue eyes peered at him curiously.

"Charlie hasn't told me a great deal about why I'm here. You want to fill me in?"

"Sure. Have you eaten?" He turned away from her and headed into the kitchen, mentally scolding himself for the inappropriate thoughts filling his head.

"Not yet. I was planning on grabbing something on my way out."

He opened the refrigerator, scanning the contents. He wasn't the least bit hungry, not for food at least, and every time he glanced at Desiree, his mind turned carnal. "I can throw something together if you'd like." He glanced back at her and stood straight, shocked that she was only a step away from him.

"I'd like that," she said, scanning the items in the refrigerator as well. "What'd you have in mind?"

When her eyes returned to his, he closed the refrigerator. "Um, maybe we should go out." Much to his chagrin, she stepped closer, putting her hand on his chest. He let out a nervous laugh and tried to sidestep her, but found himself cornered between the refrigerator and the kitchen sink.

Desiree grinned at his nervous response.

"Um, my girlfriend," he began.

She took his left hand and placed it on her breast, and her other hand slid down to his belt.

The sweater was chenille, soft and plush against his fingertips. He pulled his hand away despite the need fueled by cocaine. Again, he tried to sidestep, but her hand found its way down to the front of his jeans, rubbing suggestively.

"Um."

She cut him off with a kiss.

Steve's mouth opened, perhaps to protest, but her tongue playfully flicked against his. Stale coffee and cigarettes filled his mouth, and he pulled away in momentary disgust.

She unzipped his pants, finding his hard shaft and stroking him.

Dumbfounded at her bold advance, he blinked and opened his mouth to protest, but only a low rumble emitted from between his parted lips. The caress of her slender fingers disrupted all logical thought. It was only after she kneeled and slid his hard shaft into her mouth, sucking him with each sinuous stroke of her lips, that sensibility took over with one thought.

Jenny's going to kill me!

"I can't do this," he whispered, and pushed her away, awkwardly zipping up his pants before he crossed to the couch.

Desiree stood and raised a single eyebrow, wiping her smirking lips.

"Shit." He stared at her and ran his hand through his hair as the ramifications of what he allowed her to do raised their ugly heads. "What the hell were you thinking?"

She shrugged. "I had to be sure you were committed to your girlfriend."

It was his turn to raise his eyebrows, and he flopped onto the couch, rubbing his face with his hand. "And testing my commitment included giving me a blow job?"

She strolled to the couch and took a seat next to him, offering him another shrug in response. "I'm impressed. Most guys don't stop me."

A bark of a laugh escaped, and he scanned her again. "Yeah, well, you don't know my girlfriend. She'd kill me for not throwing you out the door at the first come on." *Never mind the fact I let it go as far as it did. Jesus, what the hell was I thinking?*

"Well, now that we have that out of the way," she began, smiling at him, "tell me why I'm looking after your girlfriend."

Steve blinked at the sudden change from sexy seductress to cool businesswoman. His mind still reeled from his colossal mistake, and he stumbled over words. "I, uh..."

"Mr. Winchester, are you okay?"

He laughed. "Don't you think you should call me Steve after that?" He hooked his thumb toward the kitchen.

Desiree smiled at him as if he was a simpleton. "I don't mix business with pleasure, Mr. Winchester. Now, please tell me what prompted you to request a bodyguard for your girlfriend?"

He hadn't caught up with her complete three-hundred-and-sixty-degree turn. Still shell-shocked by his own behavior, this only made it more surreal. He shook his head to clear the cobwebs. "Um, she was attacked here."

"Do you know who attacked her?"

"Yes, and no."

Desiree's head tilted, and her eyebrows drew together.

"It was the serial killer who's made the papers recently."

Her eyes closed, and she took a deep breath as the information seeped in. "The Slasher?" His nod confirmed her question. "From what I've read, she's lucky to be alive."

"He threatened to finish the job. That's why you're here." He scanned her with his eyes. "But I can't imagine you doing much in the way of stopping him." *Although sucking him dry could be an option.* He nearly laughed aloud at the thought.

"I'm a black belt in three separate arts— Karate, Tae Kwan Do and Judo—and I'm an expert shot." She stood and crossed to her pocketbook. "When I'm on the job, I carry this." She reached inside the purse and pulled out a Smith & Wesson nine-millimeter, showing it to him. "I also have hand-to-hand combat training, which I won an award for when I was in the military."

His eyebrows rose. "You were in the military?"

"I had two tours in the army. They paid for my college education, and I got to see a great deal of the world."

"How'd you hook up with Charlie?"

"Charlie and I have dated on and off for the past five years." She smiled sweetly. "He occasionally asks me to do an odd job or two."

Steve didn't know what to think. "Are you dating him now?"

The smile that surfaced made him shiver. Now he had another thing to worry about on top of Jennifer. What would Charlie do if he found out about her oral adventure?

Vengeance
Chapter 29

JENNIFER STOOD BACKSTAGE, CLINGING to the wall as the vision of another murder assaulted her.

"Jesus, no, Jesus, Jesus, no," she kept repeating, her voice getting louder and louder until the director, Raphael, shook her.

"Jennifer!"

Her vision blurred, and then everything went black.

In the blackness, she heard the low grumble come from his throat and the vision that materialized was worse than a kick in the gut. She welcomed the blackness when it wrapped around her a second time.

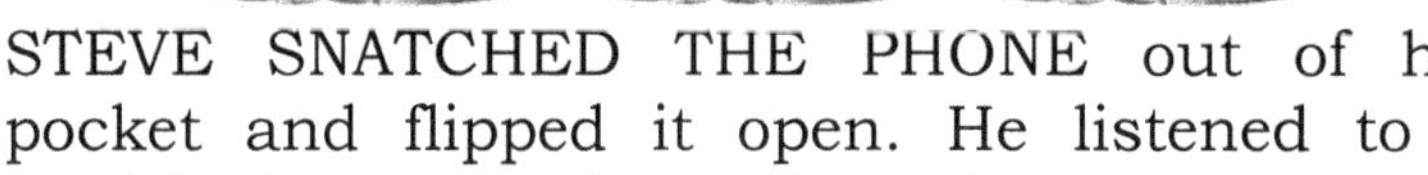

STEVE SNATCHED THE PHONE out of his pocket and flipped it open. He listened to a panicked Raphael. "What happened?" He signaled the waitress and traded a glance with Desiree.

"She was screaming, and her face was pale, and she passed out," Raphael rattled.

"I'm on my way." He folded the phone and stood, tossing money on the table. "You coming?"

Desiree stood and followed him to her car.

"How fast can you get to the Soho Theater?"

"On Vandam?"

"Yes."

"Get in. I'll get us there in ten minutes."

He didn't hesitate, and she was true to her word. Steve flew down the alley and pounded on the door. It opened just as she caught up with him.

Raphael was clearly frazzled. "She's in the back room. I put her on the couch."

"Is she conscious?"

"She wasn't when I left her, but she's breathing. Should I call 911?"

Steve shook his head. "Let me look first." He headed in the direction Raphael pointed, with Desiree close behind. He slid onto his knees next to the couch. A strong pulse met his fingertips when he pressed them to her throat. He exhaled, closing his eyes and the alarm abated. "Jenny?" He ran the back of his knuckles against her cheek. When her eyelids fluttered open, he relaxed. "Hey."

Jennifer's eyes went wide, and she shot into a sitting position, her eyes darting around the room until they landed on Desiree. They cleared and narrowed, and her gaze snapped back to his. Her jaw tightened. "I had a vision."

He sat back on his haunches under her sharp glare. *She knows.* "What did you see?" When her eyes rose to Desiree, his heart dropped.

"He killed again," she answered and swung her dagger like eyes back to him.

"What else did you see?" he asked, the dread bleeding into his voice.

Jennifer tilted her head. "Enough."

The ride back to the apartment was tense and silent. Desiree obviously didn't understand the dynamics between them until he leaned over and said two words. "She's pregnant." He glanced in the backseat and away from her glare. The color had returned to her face, but the anger was visible, at least to him.

"So, you're my bodyguard?" Jennifer asked from the backseat.

Desiree nodded and glanced in the rearview mirror. "I understand you were threatened."

"You could say that." She sent a glare in Steve's direction. "Didn't you tell her why you hired her?"

"He did. I just wanted to hear your side of the story."

"We talked," he said.

"Is that what they call it these days?"

Steve looked out the window, ignoring the barb. The fear gripping his heart was worse than when Charlie put the muzzle of the gun to his forehead. Without Jennifer, his life would fall apart. He couldn't bring himself to look at her for the remainder of the ride.

When Desiree pulled up to the building, she turned to face Jennifer. "I'll be here tomorrow around seven-thirty. That way I can settle in before Mr. Winchester leaves."

Jennifer nodded and slipped out of the car.

"Thanks," Steve mumbled, doing the same before following his angry wife into the building. He wasn't going to deny anything and when he shoved his hand into his pocket, he felt the vial, pausing and considering whether it would take the edge off the pending fight.

She slid her key in the lock and entered the apartment. Before he could step inside, she slammed the door in his face and flipped the deadbolt.

He heard the click and knocked on the solid wood. "Let me in, Jenny. I can explain."

The hysterical laugh that came through the door made his knees weak. He slid down the wall, wrapped his arms around his knees, and waited for her sobs to subside. He dug the vial out, staring at the powdery substance. His gaze traveled between the door and the vial. "Fuck it." He unscrewed the cap and took a hit before screwing the top back on. He sniffled and rubbed his nose, tilting his head back against the wall as the numbing drip started down his throat.

"Please open the door," he said, leaning his forehead against the wood.

"No!" The answer vibrated close enough for him to gather she was just on the other side.

"Please Jenny. It was a stupid mistake."

"You've been making a lot of stupid mistakes lately."

He looked at the half-empty vial of coke in his hands. "Yeah. I know." He closed his fist around it as the rush hit. "Please open the door."

"You're a jackass."

Steve laughed and scrambled to his feet as she threw the lock and yanked the door open.

"What are you laughing at?" Her bloodshot eyes glared at him, and she blocked the opening.

He pushed the door open, manhandling his way into the apartment, where he locked the deadbolt before turning back to her. "Because I am a jackass," he answered and slammed the vial on the desk in full sight. He stepped back, cocking his head in her direction as the drug pulsed in his veins. "I'm a jackass who hit gold today."

Jennifer stepped back as he advanced on her. His apologetic demeanor was replaced by that hungry look again. She looked at the vial on the desk and back at him. Her momentary shock and fear boiled into fury, and she swung her fist.

He blocked the punch with his cast, but he wasn't fast enough to block her kick. It hit him in the solar plexus, sending him back into the door and knocking the wind out of him. He struggled to get a breath even as she advanced again; her face a mask of fury. He moved quickly, wrapping his arms around her, pinning her arms to her sides. "Easy, Jen."

"Easy? You want me to take it easy?" She slammed her heel into his foot and her head into his nose.

"Jesus Christ!" he yelled as blood shot out of his nose. Blinking back stinging tears, he kept his arms tight, letting the blood run down his chin onto his shirt, and her hair. "I'm not letting go until you calm down."

"You're bleeding on me." She struggled to break loose from his grasp.

"Yes. Are you going to stop beating the shit out of me?"

Jennifer struggled in his arms. Her scream of frustration filled the apartment. It gave way to sobbing and Steve leaned over, pressing his lips to the back of her blood-splattered head. He sniffled again and released her, wiping the blood off his face with his sleeve as she turned to look at him.

"How could you?"

He didn't have an answer. At least not one she would ever understand. His eyes drifted to the vial on the desk. Before he knew it, she had it in her hand and pitched it with everything she had at the wall above the bed.

"No!" he yelled as it smashed, sending a puff of white dust raining down on the bed.

Jennifer stared at him. "How long have you been doing coke?"

Steve stared at the falling powder. "This is only the second week, but I've done it more than once today."

"Because you had to?"

He shook his head. "No, because I wanted to."

"Is that what happened here?" Tears flowed down her cheeks, and she pointed to the corner of the kitchen.

Steve glanced at her and nodded. "I was high, and I didn't say no right away." He walked into the bathroom and closed the door. Sitting on the toilet's lid, he put his head in his hands. Royally fucked up didn't describe what he had done, and he knew it.

Jennifer opened the door. "I'm calling Jack."

"The hell you are!" He shot to his feet.

"You're in over your head, Steve!" She stabbed her finger on the numbers.

"Bullshit!" He ripped the phone out of her hand and killed the connection. "Charlie showed me where the operation is. He showed me the fucking warehouse today. Whatever I'm doing, it's working!"

"In the meantime, you're becoming a junkie and cheating on me."

The air blew out of Steve's sails. "I'm doing my job." Lame as it was, that's what came out of his mouth, and he immediately regretted it.

"Getting a blow job in our kitchen constitutes doing your job?"

This time he didn't stop her swing, just closed his eyes and let her get her anger out. Her fist connected with his chin, driving him backwards, where he fell onto the toilet seat with a crash. "I'm sorry Jenny. I fucked up."

She glared at him. "Royally."

He reached for her, and she swatted his hand away.

"Don't even think about it. It's going to be a long time before I let you touch me again. A *long* time. Now get out. I need to clean up."

He left her in the bathroom, relief flooding through him at her last statement. It meant she wasn't walking out on him. He crossed to the kitchen sink and washed his face and neck where the blood had dried to a tacky film. Then he sat down at the computer to report on everything he learned today. He didn't bother looking up at Jennifer when she came out of the bathroom and snapped the covers off the bed, muttering about coke infested sheets.

Vengeance
Chapter 30

A KNOCK AT THE door woke Steve out of a sound sleep, and he glanced at the clock. "Shit!" He shot out of bed, grabbing a pair of sweatpants and slipping them on before he crossed to the door. He glanced over his shoulder at Jennifer. She hadn't stirred.

He undid the deadbolt and swung the door open.

Desiree stood outside the door, dressed in a similar outfit as the evening before, but the jacket was a bit more bulky, and she opened it, revealing the gun. Her eyes lowered to the scars on his chest and her eyebrows rose before her gaze returned to his.

"I need to get ready for work. Make yourself comfortable."

"What happened to your chest?"

"I was attacked by a wild animal a couple of years ago." He filtered through his drawers for underwear. Grabbing a suit out of the closet, he disappeared into the bathroom without another word.

When he came out, Jennifer was sitting at the table with a cup of juice, her usual sociable self nowhere to be seen, and she glowered at him. He crossed to her and kissed the top of her head. "I love you." He received a grunt in response and left without comment.

The subway ride to the office took twice as long during rush hour and he crossed the street toward the office rumpled from the crowded railcar. His cell buzzed, and he flipped it open, stopping outside the entrance. "Starbucks, now." The line cut, and he stared up at the building, pausing before heading toward the coffee shop around the corner. The headlines of the paper on his usual table caught his attention, and he closed his eyes and sat down. He never asked her more about the vision.

"Did you know about this?"

"I heard about it."

"He went ballistic on the victim and there was no semen."

Steve snorted, spitting out the sip of coffee he just took. "Wow, just what I wanted to talk about this morning." He wiped his face with a napkin. "Did you get my notes?"

"Yes. We want to take him down as soon as possible."

Steve glanced at the reflection.

"Jack wants you and Jennifer out of New York when it happens."

He turned in the chair. "Did you read the fucking notes?"

Jerry stood and shuffled away.

He stared at the headlines of the paper and flipped the page, reading the story, his blood already at the boiling point. If they went in half-cocked, Charlie would blow up the entire building. He couldn't let them do that.

Is that really your hesitation?

The thought crept up on him, causing him to look out at the street.

Is it, or are you hooked?

Steve's jaw tightened, and he focused on his reflection. "Hooked on what? That's the question." He folded the paper under his arm. Picking up his coffee, he headed to the office, lost in thought.

He slid behind his desk, turning on the computer but not really seeing it as he analyzed the mess he'd made. The rap on the doorjamb interrupted his thoughts. "Hey, Charlie."

"You ready to take that ride?"

Steve glanced at the few unopened email messages and nodded. He wanted to see the operation up close, and on a different level, he wanted another vial of white powder. His jaw tightened, and he glared at Charlie, breezing past him to the elevator.

"What the hell was that look for?" he snapped as they pulled out of the garage.

"Jennifer found the vial," Steve answered. "She was not happy and made me sleep on the couch."

"What'd she do with the vial?"

"She smashed it on the wall."

Charlie whistled. "She's a bit of a psycho that way." He glanced at Steve. "You sure you want to marry someone like that?"

He took a deep breath. "I'm sure. Life would be dull without her in it, even if that means dodging projectiles every once in a while." He allowed a small smile to surface. "Besides, she's carrying my child."

Charlie huffed.

"What?" Steve looked over at him.

"Nothing." He pulled into the same parking spot as before.

Steve got out of the car and walked with him to the keypad.

Charlie looked at him expectantly.

"Oh." He got the hint and punched the number in; stepping aside as the green light signaled the door was unlocked.

Instead of heading upstairs to the office, Charlie headed to the entrance of the lab. He punched in a different set of numbers and glanced at Steve. "You get that?"

"Five, four, three, two, one. Not very original," he replied.

"Yes, but it's easy for the staff to remember." He held the door open for Steve.

He stepped into the lab, which encompassed the equivalent of a city block and held a greenhouse with several thousand coca plants thriving in the warm, moist environment. Several processing stations harvested and broke down the leaves into the fine grains of cocaine Charlie distributed. As Charlie explained the process, pointing at the different stations in the greenhouse and outside of it, Steve listened in awe.

This lab had been operating successfully for fifteen years, growing and harvesting cocaine. The complex network of vats, tubes and substances was impressive, and again he had to remind himself that this was illegal, and he was sworn to take each and everyone in this room down.

"So, there's no direct access to the lab from the street."

"Correct. There's only one way in the building and one way out."

They crossed to a door on the ground floor under the office. Charlie slid his key in and flipped the light switch on before standing aside.

Steve thought the operation was impressive, but Charlie's arsenal was downright extraordinary. "What the hell are you expecting? The invasion at Normandy?" He walked in the room and scanned the multitudes of rifles, handguns, AK-47s and assault rifles. A majority of the items in the room were banned weapons. "Is that a Tommy Gun?" He pointed at a sub-machine gun with a round drum magazine attached.

Charlie smiled and nodded. "That's my favorite."

The weapons charge alone racked his brain, and he smiled, turning toward Charlie. "You've got quite the operation here." He stepped out of the artillery room, glancing at the packing company façade again.

Charlie shrugged as he locked up the gunroom. "I filter the chemicals through the fiber optics warehouse. Once a month, the supplies are re-routed here, where my girls sign for the orders." He pointed to the shipping office entrance on the far wall before climbing the steps to the office and holding the door open for Steve.

He collapsed in one of the overstuffed chairs across from the monitors—the entire operation at a glance. *Damn is right—this is fucking brilliant.* "I'm impressed," he said after a few minutes of silence. "I thought the fiber optics outfit was slick, but this, this is..." He trailed off, not able to articulate the awe.

Vengeance
Chapter 31

"DO YOU HAVE A problem with me?" Desiree asked from the couch.

"I don't like the fact that my husband had a bodyguard assigned," Jennifer answered from the kitchen table. She'd fought hard all morning to keep the orange juice down, and now that battle was on the cusp of being lost. She crossed quickly to the bathroom and slammed the door behind her. Making it to the commode just in time, she gagged on the acid as it flowed up her esophagus and into the toilet in a violent torrent.

A soft knock followed by, "Are you okay?" came through the door.

"Morning sickness," she called out over the flush of the toilet. She brushed her teeth and shuffled into the living area.

"Try this. My sister swears by it." She held a spoonful of organic honey out for Jennifer. "Trust me," she added when Jennifer scoffed.

She looked between the spoon and Desiree and then accepted the offer, swallowing hard, forcing the sweet lump down her throat. It felt like a bomb hit her stomach at first and she doubled over, thinking it was going to come up. Suddenly, the nausea disappeared, and she slowly straightened. Swallowing, she glanced at Desiree.

"My sister had a real tough time with her first child until someone suggested organic honey."

"Thank you." She didn't know what else to say. It was the first thing she'd tried that had worked.

Desiree smiled. "Your boyfriend said you were attacked in the apartment. Do you want to tell me about it?"

She opened her mouth to say something snide and thought twice. "My fiancé, and I'm not sure I want to really get into it right now."

"Okay. Maybe some other time."

Jennifer crossed the room, flopping onto the couch. She glanced up at Desiree. "He was in the apartment when I came out of the bathroom. If I'd been asleep or anywhere else in the room, I wouldn't be alive right now." She studied her hands. "I was able to call Steve before he knocked the phone away."

Desiree took a seat and reached out, placing her hand on top of Jennifer's. "You don't have to get into this now if you're not ready."

The softness of her voice and the genuine concern reflected in her eyes threw Jennifer. Her lower lip trembled. It had been a very long time since she had really talked with another woman. Ever since her best friend Tracy died, she hadn't connected with another female. Something about Desiree reminded her of Tracy, and her eyes welled with tears. She got a grip on her emotions and pulled her hands away. "I'm sorry," she said, wiping the tears off her face. "It's just been a hell of a week."

"You don't have to apologize to me."

Damn straight. The thought popped into her head, and she bit back from letting it escape her mouth. Desiree seemed to be genuinely concerned. "Why do you care?"

"Because all men are pigs and the ones who physically attack us should be castrated, hung on crosses in the desert, and left for the buzzards."

She sat in stunned silence, staring at Desiree. "You've got a little hostility there, haven't you?"

Desiree's laugh filled the apartment. "It comes from years of abuse and finally breaking free."

Jennifer cocked her head.

"My father abused me from the time I was ten. The minute I turned eighteen, I enlisted to get away from the bastard. The army gave me the wherewithal to tell him to drop dead, and then Charlie came along." Desiree's sarcastic smile softened at the mention of Charlie. "He took me in and made sure my father never got the chance to hurt anyone else. He throws me special details like this one to keep me living in the style I like without invading his space or feeling like I owe him something." She shrugged.

"We're talking about the same Charlie?" Jennifer couldn't help the question.

Desiree's brow creased.

"I'm sorry, but the man I've met just seems so... so..." She searched for the word, "superficial!"

"He is very materialistic, but he's got heart." She shifted on the couch, folding her leg under her so she could face Jennifer. "What happened here?"

"He tried to strangle me and... and..." She swallowed and drew a deep, steadying breath. "He tried to strangle me while he raped me. If I hadn't knocked his knife across the room, I'd be dead."

"Sounds like luck was with you that day."

Jennifer glared at her.

Desiree put her hands up. "Let me rephrase that. It sounds like there were several directions that the situation could have taken, and they all seemed to be in your favor. If just one of them had backfired, you wouldn't be here. To me, that says luck was in your court, even though you may not see it that way."

She softened. Whether she wanted to or not, she liked this woman. "Can I ask you something?"

Desiree nodded.

"Why'd you screw around with my fiancé?"

Desiree's eyes went wide. "Did he tell you?"

Jennifer nodded. "Yes." She sighed, and her gaze traveled to the corner of the kitchen and back. "If you're with Charlie, why'd you come on to Steve?"

Desiree's mouth opened and closed a few times, and then she shut it, looking down at her hands. Her cheeks turned crimson. "I'm sorry." She raised her eyes, meeting Jennifer's gaze. "He was just so..." Without finishing the sentence, she shrugged.

Jennifer inhaled deeply and nodded. "If you do it again..."

Desiree shook her head. "It was a onetime deal."

Her eyes narrowed. Something about how fast the statement came from her lips crawled under Jennifer's skin. "It better be, otherwise you'll be the one hanging in the desert." She stood and headed to clean up.

Why the hell had she seduced Steve?

Jennifer let the warm water cascade over her skin while the questions piled up in her mind. Desiree obviously cared about Charlie, so why do something that might blow up in her face?

Her eyes shot open. "Oh my God," she whispered. *Charlie.* Charlie set Steve up. First the cocaine, now the indiscretion. He probably had her tape it for some sort of blackmail. *But why?*

"To keep him in line." The answer was so simple she had to laugh. "Oh, Steve, what have you gotten yourself into?"

Vengeance
Chapter 32

STEVE ENTERED THE EMPTY apartment, scanning the room. There were no new knick-knacks or anything out of place, and he sat down at his computer and pulled out his cell phone. He punched in an access code and put the phone to his ear.

"Jack Murphy."

"You can't do anything, yet," Steve began without formally introducing himself. "I don't have the distribution channels, but I can get those, Jack. Just give me some time."

"How deep are you in this, Steve?"

The words tumbled out in rapid succession. "He gave me a walkthrough of the plant today and it is one of the slickest setups I've ever seen. Not that I've seen before, but you know what I mean. This blows any textbook case out of the water. I need to get those distributor lists before we bust the operation and you can't just barrel in there—he has the place wired. There is only one entrance into the building, and he has it rigged to explode if any unauthorized people enter the building. I'm sure if there is access from the roof, he's got that rigged as well. He's militant about security and has a secondary defense outside of the door. There's a trigger that stretches under the entrances to the lab and he said he has enough nitrous and C-four to blow up an entire city block. We have to get to him before he sets those triggers in his office, otherwise there will be a shitload of dead people."

Jack quietly digested the information.

"He also has enough weapons in the warehouse to assemble a small army."

He sighed. "Jennifer called."

"And?" Steve snapped, suddenly irritated.

"How deep are you into this, Steve?"

"What did she tell you?"

"That you've stepped over the line."

He bit back the response and stood, pacing.

"She said you've been using, voluntarily." When no response came, he continued, "And that you were manipulated into cheating on her."

Steve stopped. "We knew this was a possibility when you sent me undercover. He's a drug dealer. It stands to reason he would use his own product."

"He's manipulating you."

"I'm aware of what Charlie is doing. He wants so many hooks in me that I would never turn on him. The first step was clearing my debt. The second is getting me hooked on his product. I've got to give the impression that I'm moving down that path, otherwise he'll start having doubts about trusting me."

"You forgot the third piece of leverage," Jack pointed out.

"What's that?"

"The tape of what happened in your apartment."

Steve felt the blood drain from his face as he spun toward the kitchen. "What are you talking about?"

"Jennifer thinks Charlie set you up and has proof of your indiscretion to keep you in line."

He pulled out the desk chair and sat down heavily, his brain firing off in rapid succession. If Charlie did videotape the episode, he was hoping for more, but why the fuck would he do that? *Jennifer. Shit.*

"Does Charlie have leverage over you, Steve?"

"No, he doesn't. Jennifer already knows what happened."

"Okay, but if I get another call from your wife telling me things are out of hand, I'm pulling you from the case."

He smiled. The only way Jack would pull him from the case was if his cover was blown. And that was highly unlikely. "I'll keep that in mind."

"How long?"

"I don't know. He's hit me with a bunch of stuff the last couple of days, but his contact lists might take a while to flush out. I also need to see if I can get concrete proof of his connection to Bondino. I don't think that will be as easy."

"Be careful, Steve," Jack said. "On both the investigation front and with the cocaine. I don't want to have to pull your badge and throw you in detox when this is done."

Steve inhaled and looked at the vial of white powder Charlie had given him before he left the warehouse. "Me, neither," he said, slipping the vial into the desk drawer. "I'll watch my back."

Vengeance
Chapter 33

THE NEXT FEW WEEKS consisted of the same routine—the morning wake-up from Desiree, the evening pickup at the theater, and the cold shoulder in bed. Weekends were worse, and when the phone rang the Saturday afternoon before Thanksgiving, Jennifer snatched it off the hook after half a ring.

"Hello?" She folded the book she was reading. "Hi, Mom."

Steve's head swiveled in her direction and his jaw dropped. No one in the family was supposed to have the apartment number. *No one.* That had been the strict order of the FBI. Their cell numbers could be given out in case of emergencies, but not the landline.

She covered the mouthpiece. "I called them."

"Jesus, Jen!" He shot to his feet. "On the landline?"

"My cell was dead," she shot back and uncovered the phone. "Yes, everything is just fine. Thanksgiving?" She turned her back on him. "We'd love to come up for Thanksgiving. What time?"

Steve glared at her back with his hands on his hips. He couldn't believe her audacity, and now this. She knew they had been invited to Charlie's. She knew! "What the fuck are you doing?" he snapped when she hung up.

She turned and pointed at him. "You owe me. And I'm collecting. I haven't seen my parents for seven months and this is what I want."

"But Charlie?"

"I don't give a shit what you tell him, but neither of us will be there for Thanksgiving. Period."

He crossed the room until he towered over her. "I'll overlook the fact you used the land line even though we were expressly told not to. And I'll even blow Charlie off and spend Thanksgiving with your folks, but only on one condition."

"What's that?" she shot up at him.

"That you cut this cold shoulder attitude and forgive me."

"That's two."

He rolled his eyes. "Okay, two conditions."

Jennifer pursed her lips and stared into his eyes.

"I miss you," he admitted, lowering his gaze.

Those three words melted the hardness in her eyes, and she nodded. "You need to do one more thing for me, though."

Steve wrapped his arms around her. "What's that?"

"Promise me, no more cocaine."

He took a deep breath. "I can't promise that. Not until this case is wrapped up. Then I'll be as clean as a whistle."

"You better wrap up this case before the baby comes, otherwise you'll be living alone."

"I'll do my best." He wanted to be long gone by the time the baby arrived as well. Steve lifted his hand to her cheek, feeling the satin skin.

"I'm sorry for my lapse in judgment. I know it hurt."

"Don't ever do it again."

"I won't. I promise." He leaned forward, gently pressing his lips to hers. The sweet kiss turned insistent, and her lips parted, allowing his tongue access.

The pent-up passion that had been bottled for the past month erupted with the kiss, and Steve moved her toward the bed, stripping her clothes off along the way. He ran his hand over her once flat belly, feeling the slight roundness that hadn't been there before. Steve stepped back, his eyes scanning her from head to toe, noting a fullness in both her breasts and her hips that was new. "God, you're beautiful." With that, he pulled her onto the bed and made love to her slowly, savoring every kiss, every stroke, and every sound she made.

HE WALKED HER FROM the subway stop to the side door of the theater. "I'll be back at ten. Break a leg tonight." He had said the same thing every weekend night since the attack, but this time she leaned up and kissed him, a long, slow, lingering kiss that left him breathless as she disappeared through the door.

He sighed and turned, heading out to kill the next three hours. Steve flipped open the phone and dialed the now familiar number.

"Hey, Charlie, it's Steve."

"Just dropping Jen off?"

"Yeah, and I've got some bad news for you. We won't be there for Thanksgiving."

"Why's that?"

He could tell Charlie was not pleased. "Because Jen wants me to meet her parents before she starts to show."

"Oh. Okay."

"Yeah, that's going to be a fun experience. Hello Mr. and Mrs. Curtis, I'm the guy who knocked up your daughter."

Charlie burst out laughing. "Let's just hope they aren't as volatile as she is."

"No shit. And her father doesn't own a gun. Man, this is going to suck."

"Well, I'll give you that. You could still bail and come solo."

"Not if I want to live," Steve said as he slipped into a bar to grab a beer and watch the game. "I'll catch you Monday."

"Have a good one," Charlie replied.

The line went dead.

Steve folded his phone and slid into a seat at the bar, ordering a Corona and settling back to watch the Knicks game on the television. He was not happy about the prospects of spending any time with Jennifer's family. To say her father disliked him was an understatement. He was still pissed about her involvement in the case in Brooksfield, along with the fact they weren't there when their only daughter got married. If he had an inkling of what had happened last month or how dangerous it was for her to be in New York with Steve, he would blow a gasket.

Vengeance
Chapter 34

THE REST OF THE week crawled by, and Steve puttered at the office on Wednesday afternoon, dreading the night alone and having to hop in the car at eleven for the two-hour trip to her parents' house in Connecticut.

"You still here?" Charlie asked from the doorway.

He nodded. "I'll be wrapping up in a little while."

"Got your cast off, I see."

"Yep. They gave me a squeeze ball and some hand exercises to do, to build the strength back, but I'm damn glad to have that thing off." He curled his hand into a fist, then flexed it. "It feels kind of weird."

"Do you want some blow for the road?"

Steve looked up at Charlie and sighed. "That might not be such a bad idea." He had toyed with the thought on and off all day and hadn't been motivated to ask. It had been over a week since he ran out of the last vial Charlie had given him and he still craved the high.

Charlie tossed a vial to him. "Happy Thanksgiving." He headed out of the office.

"You, too!" He studied the vial, rolling it between his fingers as the powder slid slowly around. Steve closed his fist over the small canister and closed his eyes. Jennifer would not be pleased, but the alternative of dealing with her parents without some sort of chemical high was worse than the shit he'd get from his wife. He stood, pocketing the vial, and turned off his computer. It was after eight and he needed to get a bite to eat before he picked Jennifer up at the theater.

"ARE YOU OKAY?" JENNIFER asked as they crossed into Connecticut.

Steve glanced in her direction, then back at the road. "We can't discuss anything related to my job."

"I know."

"No matter how hard you father presses," he said.

"I understand. I'll talk about the play and the baby and that's it."

"Just so we're on the same page. I don't feel like catching shit from your father." He focused on the road and turned the radio up a fraction.

She turned the radio down and stared at his profile. The firm set of his jaw told her he was tenser than he had been in a while. She reached out, touching the hand that rested on the stick shift, lacing her fingers between them.

Steve offered her a slight smile before looking out at the dark highway. "I'm really not in the mood to deal with it if he starts up."

"I know. I'll try to run interference for you as much as I can. But you know Daddy."

"Pft!" he snorted. He gave Jennifer a sideways look.

521

STEVE WOKE TO AN empty bed and the scent of roasted turkey on the cool air. His eyebrows creased in momentary confusion at the unfamiliar surroundings. *Jennifer's parents' house.* The fleeting thought entered his mind before he turned his face into the pillow and drifted back to sleep.

"Steve?"

Her soft voice filled his ears, rocking him gently from sleep.

"Mhm," he grumbled and turned his head toward the sweet sound.

"It's almost noon."

Blinking, he glanced at her and then around the room. Bright sunlight streamed in the windows. "Holy shit!" He sat up, rubbing his face. "When's dinner?"

"Mom has everything set to go for one."

"I'll be down in a little while." He rummaged through the suitcase for clothes and his shaving kit and headed to clean up, still groggy from the sound sleep.

Thirty minutes later, after a hot shower and a hit of cocaine, he bounded down the stairs. He stopped short when he hit the landing. Sitting in the living room with Jennifer and her folks were his parents. "Mom, Dad, what are you doing here?" Any hint of dread regarding the day vanished and a broad smile formed on his face as he hugged each of them in turn.

"Allison thought since neither of us had seen you in almost a year; we'd share Thanksgiving with you." His mother smiled at him as he stepped away from the bear hug he gave her.

He turned to his in-laws. "Thank you." His throat tightened with emotion. He didn't realize how much he missed his parents until this moment.

Jennifer's father nodded in acknowledgement and accepted his hand in a quick shake.

Jennifer cleared her throat and took Steve by the arm, leading him to the couch.

"Did you know about this?" he whispered in her ear.

She shook her head and turned her focus on the two sets of parents surrounding them. "We have some news."

The room went dead silent, and four pairs of eyes stared expectantly.

"Well?" his father asked when they exchanged a glance.

"We're pregnant," Jennifer announced.

The only grandparent-to-be in the room who didn't jump to his feet with a joker like grin on his face was Joe Curtis. His eyes narrowed a fraction before he put a smile on for appearance's sake and rose to his feet, joining the others.

"I guess this means you're going to stop this undercover nonsense," Joe said, layering the blanket of silence on the room once more. This time, all eyes swiveled in his direction.

Steve shot a glare at his father-in-law. "We'll see." He buffered any further commentary by turning his attention to his mother-in-law and his parents. They returned to the edges of their seats and shot questions all at once.

"When did you find out?"

"When are you due?"

"What names do you have picked out?"

He put his hands up. "Stop firing questions at us at the same time! This isn't an interrogation!" The smile on his face was information enough as to how he felt about the baby.

Jennifer began fielding questions, and he sat back, allowing her to take the limelight. He shot a sideways glance in Joe's direction and got a scowl in return. Instead of letting it get under his skin, he ignored it and returned his attention to the over excited grandparents in the room.

THEY PULLED OUT OF the driveway with both sets of parents waving from the front stoop.

"That was definitely fun," Steve commented as he glanced at Jennifer. "And you really did not know they were inviting my folks over?"

"None whatsoever, but I am so glad, because my father had to behave."

"He got a couple of subtle digs in, but you're right, he was pretty damn amicable."

Jennifer giggled. "Amicable?"

He nodded. "It was a new experience for me." He sent a flash of teeth in her direction. The grin produced those dimples she loved.

"See? My dad can be fun; you just have to have the right crowd there."

"We should always have our parents over together. Avoid the nasty arguments your father and I get into."

"There's an idea!"

As they crossed the border into New York, Steve's smile faded. "Charlie's going to ask how it went." He glanced at Jennifer. "And our stories have to be the same."

"Okay, how did it go?"

"It went pretty well." He offered a shrug. "I got to meet the whole family."

Jennifer's dimples showed. "And my parents loved you, especially my father."

The laughter snorted out of Steve's nose. "Yeah, that's definitely in the land of make-believe."

"Well, since we're blowing smoke up his ass..."

"You know, I really love you. I'm not sure if I've said that lately." He picked up her hand, kissing her palm.

"You haven't said it quite like that, but yes, I know."

Steve watched the road while he drove and held her hand. Their situation seemed to weigh on him the closer he got to the city. "I don't like that you're in as much danger as I am. If Charlie ever gets wind that I'm the mole in his organization, you will be his first target." He glanced at her. "And when I'm not with you, Desiree is. She'd be the one he calls."

"I can take Desiree."

"No, you can't. She might even be able to take me."

"I've bested you before."

His dimples flashed. "Yeah, but I wasn't armed." He gave her a sideways glance. "And I wasn't trying to kill you."

"Desiree likes me. Why would she hurt me?"

"If Charlie gives the order..." He paused and shook his head. "When we execute the sting, I want you in protective custody."

Vengeance
Chapter 35

"WE HAD A LOT of fun. Steve was absolutely charming, as always," Jennifer said. "My family seemed to like him, although they were really disappointed when we told them about the wedding date we settled on."

"Why?"

"Because they're going on a cruise they've been planning for years with some close friends of the family. My mom said they'd throw us a reception in the spring after the baby is born if we wanted. That way, they can have the party for all their friends to celebrate both the marriage and the baby."

Desiree lifted her eyebrows. "Wow."

"Yeah, they like to have their parties," she said as she crossed to the kitchen.

"Are you going to see them for Christmas?"

"No, they'll be on the cruise."

"Then you and Steve will have to come to Charlie's for dinner on Christmas Eve. I'm cooking a roast and I know he was planning on having a few of his associates over."

"I'll have to talk to Steve, but I can't see why he can't join you. I've got a performance that night, so I won't be able to make it." She could see a thousand reasons why not, none of which she could voice to Desiree. It was an intrusion on her life, but her saving grace was her job.

"How much longer are you going to perform?" Her eyes drifted to the small bump that was Jennifer's belly.

Jennifer looked down at her stomach, running her hand along the slight arc. "I don't know. I didn't think you were supposed to pop until after the third month, but," she shrugged. "I keep asking for the costumes to be let out a little in the waist and they keep putting me off." She raised her eyes. "I'm sure once it's clear I'm pregnant from the audience's view, I'm done until after the baby is born." She pulled the toast out of the toaster and ran butter over the bread.

The room disappeared.

The bare arm appeared in her field of view, the tattoo vivid on tanned skin. She stared at the scorpion holding a bloody rose, burning it to memory as the scene opened up. The setting looked familiar, and she gasped.

Blinking, she was back in the apartment, her eyes darting around the room as Desiree shook her shoulder. Jennifer shot to her feet, overturning the chair she'd been sitting in. A wheeze came with every breath as her lungs contracted. "Shit!" She took a shaky step toward the couch and the world swam in front of her.

When she opened her eyes, the view of the ceiling filled her vision and a damp warm cloth lay across her forehead. Desiree's concerned eyes stared down at her with the phone plastered to her ear.

"She's coming to now." Desiree handed the phone to Jennifer.

"Are you okay?" Steve asked.

"Yeah, um, I just, um…" She didn't know how to tell him what she saw. It obviously wasn't something destined to happen in the next couple of months, so she didn't want to burden him with it. The fragment was unnerving enough, the tattoo along with the view out the front window of their cottage in New Hampshire.

"You had another vision?"

"I think so, I'm not sure." She lifted her eyes to Desiree. "I haven't had anything to eat this morning, so it could just be that."

"Do you need me to come take you to the doctor's office?"

"Uh, no, I'm okay." Jennifer got her bearings and sat up. "I need to eat something."

Silence filtered through the line.

"I'm okay, Steve. I just need to get some food," she said. "Just let me go eat the toast I was making. I'm sure I'll feel better." She looked over her shoulder at the table. The plate was still there. "I'll talk to you later." She ended the call and stood on shaky legs, making her way to the kitchen table. She took a seat and began eating without meeting Desiree's gaze.

"You're still pale."

"Remind me to eat first thing in the morning," she said with her mouth full of toast.

Desiree took the seat opposite Jennifer. "Are you sure you're all right? Because your eyes got really weird. It was like looking at a corpse."

Her eyebrows rose at the remark. "I'm sorry, it's just when I don't eat, I get dizzy. The pregnancy, you know." She shrugged and took a sip of her orange juice.

"Bullshit!" Desiree's hand slammed on the table in unison with the expletive. "It wasn't normal!"

Jennifer's eyes narrowed, and she picked up the butter knife, slathering another slice of toast, and then pointed it in Desiree's direction. "Don't take that tone with me!"

Desiree sat back in the chair, her jaw slack and eyes wide.

"It's the pregnancy, that's all," she said.

They both turned toward the sound of the lock clicking and Desiree was on her feet instantly, with her gun drawn and pointing at the door. She pulled the hammer back as the door swung open.

"Whoa, girl, it's only me." Steve put his hands up and stepped into view.

Desiree stood down, flipping the safety on. "You almost got yourself shot."

He shrugged. "I wanted to see how you were," he said to Jennifer and crossed the apartment.

"I'm fine."

Steve turned to Desiree. "I've got her for the rest of the day."

Desiree hesitated until Jennifer nodded.

Once the door closed behind her, Jennifer turned to her husband. "What are you doing?"

He took a seat opposite her. "You had another vision?"

Jennifer tilted her head and took a bite of the toast before she met his gaze. "Yes."

"Well?"

"I saw the tattoo."

Steve grabbed a piece of paper and a pencil off the desk. He handed both to her and sat down. "Draw it for me."

She took the paper and pencil and sketched a likeness of the tattoo from her vision. "Do we have any markers or colored pencils?" she asked without looking up.

Steve stood and rummaged through the desk. The only thing he found was a box of crayons, and he stared at it with curiosity. He brought it to the table. "Will these do?"

Jennifer glanced at the crayons and up at him with the same curiosity. "Crayons?"

"Don't look at me. They were in the desk." He hooked his thumb over his shoulder. "For all I know, they could have been in there for years."

"Ah." She went back to the drawing, doing a fairly accurate job of detailing the scorpion with the rose in the claw and the drops falling from the petals. When she had the outline, she pulled out the yellow, red, blue, green, and brown, and finished the drawing by adding colors, even blending where the blue, green, and brown combined on the scorpion. The rose was yellow, tainted by droplets of blood instead of dew. She put down the red crayon, staring at an identical likeness, and raised her eyes to Steve. "That is on the inside of his right forearm." She handed him the drawing.

HE STARED AT THE first concrete lead they had in the Slasher case after so many deaths. He raised his gaze to her. "What else did you see?"

"It was me."

The heat in his face drained, and Steve's gaze fell to the picture in his hand. "Not on your life, babe." When his gaze found hers again, his jaw tightened. "He won't get the chance." He stopped himself as the urge to crumple the paper overwhelmed him. Instead, he brought the drawing over to his computer and laid it on the scanner, waiting while the machine booted up.

The scan took just a few minutes, and he sent the image off to Jack along with the following message:

This is on the inside of the unsub's right forearm, Jack.

Find the bastard before I do.

Vengeance
Chapter 36

THE WEEK BEFORE CHRISTMAS, Steve sat at the desk, staring at the computer screen. The message in his inbox sent an icy chill through his bones. Charlie wanted him out at the warehouse immediately.

He inhaled, his mind going over the last few weeks, shuffling through everything from Thanksgiving recounts to the side conversation about word of a snitch in the organization. Nothing he said or did could have led Charlie to the truth. Could it? He looked out the window and typed '*On my way*', and locked his computer before he grabbed his coat.

"I'm meeting Charlie for lunch," he said to Linda over his shoulder. He didn't say to keep it under wraps—he just said to get his ass over there now.

The car was waiting for him in the garage. Manny stood by the open passenger door, waving him inside. He went without hesitation, knowing any sign of doubt would be met with a violent end. Steve didn't speak, just gave Manny a nod and kept his hands from fidgeting, making his body relax and his manner as casual as the circumstances would allow.

Manny turned up the radio. A Spanish blend of hip-hop rang through the car, and Steve raised his eyebrow.

"You can walk if you don't like it."

He laughed and returned his gaze to the passing buildings. His heart slammed against his ribs and sweat threatened to douse his shirt. "Charlie didn't mention what the hell's got his shorts in a wad, did he?"

"Nope, he just said to get your ass down there pronto."

Steve gave a nod, wondering if Charlie would give the hit to Manny or if he'd want to tear him limb from limb himself.

His phone buzzed, and he pulled it from his pocket, glancing at the caller ID. *Jesus.* It was Jennifer. He pressed the on button and put the phone to his ear. "Hey, babe."

"Hi." She said nothing more, just sighed.

"What's up?"

"Nothing much. I'm bored."

He burst out laughing. "Where's Des?"

"She's right here, reading a book."

"You still sucking down those spoonfuls of honey?"

"Yeah."

"They helping?"

"Eh." Silence. "Where are you?"

"I'm in the car with Manny, heading to meet Charlie for lunch."

"You have a chauffeur now?"

Steve snorted and glanced at Manny. "I doubt he'd like being referred to as my driver, hon. He was in the area and when our boss calls..."

"We go," Manny finished, glancing toward Steve.

The look in his eyes gave Steve a start. Whatever was at the other end of this trip would not be pleasant, and he kept the smirk on his face for show. "Why don't you have Desiree take you out for a change?"

"Nah, I'm tired." The sounds of the toilet almost drown out her quick warning and what she said chilled him to numbness.

"Then take a nap." He recovered from the sudden shock of her words, rolled his eyes, and pointed at the phone. "I've got to go, hon. I'll catch you after the show, okay?"

"Sure. Love you."

"Love you, too." He folded the phone. "Christ, I never imagined she'd get so fucking clingy."

Manny laughed. "My brother said my sister-in-law became fucking Godzilla when she was pregnant. She ended up looking like him, too, by the end."

"Jenny's more like a ninja demon that sneaks up on you out of the blue. One minute she's fine, then this stealth monster hits, and I don't know what to do with her. I'm used to her fire, you know, I can deal with that, but this clinging shit has got to go." He slid the phone in his pocket. "I didn't sign on for this."

Manny's laughter cranked up a notch. "I feel for you, dude. If I were living in the same apartment with such a volatile chick, I'd never get any sleep. I'd be too afraid she'd smash my head with the closest knick-knack."

Steve grinned at the reference. "Why do you think I sneak out and hang at the office some of the time? It's not because I'm so dedicated to the job that I think I have to work all night—it's to get the hell away from her."

That earned a roar of approval and a slap on the shoulder. Manny pulled up to the curb in front of the warehouse. He gave Steve a nod. "I'll catch you later, and good luck with the ninja demon."

"Take it easy." He slipped out of the car, crossing to the warehouse door and punching in the proper code. He stepped inside and walked up the stairs to Charlie's office, each step a brutal reminder of his undercover status.

The door swung open, and Charlie stepped out, his features hard and unreadable as he waved him inside the dark office.

The lights shot on and Steve stared at a sweaty bound man he had never seen before. Charlie closed the door behind him and crossed to the desk where his gun sat, along with a pair of bloody pliers. Steve's eyes dropped to the man's equally bloody hand. Charlie had yanked the nails off the man's fingers. He turned his attention to Charlie, regaining his composure. "What the fuck?"

Charlie twirled the gun on the desk, staring at Steve. "This little shit's a nark."

Steve's head snapped toward the man, his eyes narrowing. "And?"

"And he said his contact has more than one of them in my organization." Charlie checked the clip on his gun and reloaded it, pointing it in the man's direction. "Unfortunately, he doesn't know who the other informant is." He pulled the hammer back.

Steve waited and when Charlie didn't say more, he turned fully in Charlie's direction and shrugged, gesturing with his hands, silently saying, *what the hell do you want me to do?*

"I want you to find out if this asshole knows more than he's telling me."

Again, he shrugged with his palms facing the ceiling, perplexed.

Charlie tossed the pliers in his direction and Steve caught them easily, blinking as he looked from the pliers back to Charlie. He turned and looked at the balding man. The man was now blubbering incoherently, his eyes wide and glued to the torture mechanism Steve held.

"I'm a lawyer, Charlie," he said, turning back to his boss. "I'm not qualified to do this." The barrel of the gun swung in his direction, and he sighed, cocking his head. "Really?" Exasperation filled his voice, and Charlie nodded, waving him forward.

"Start with the thumb this time."

Steve put the pliers on the edge of the desk and peeled off his overcoat and suit jacket, tossing them on the couch. "I don't want to have to explain blood on my suit to Jennifer." He rolled up his sleeves, trying to think of a way to stall this, to head this off without exacting the torture Charlie insisted upon. "What's his name?"

"Does it matter?"

Steve sent a glare at Charlie. "Yeah, it does. What's his name?"

"Lefty," he answered, waving the gun again.

Steve turned, swiping the pliers off the corner of the desk before he approached the trembling man. "Now Lefty, I think it's time you leveled with us, don't you?"

Lefty nodded, his head moving at a pace that would make a bobble-head doll proud.

"Who are you feeding information to?" He reached down, taking the man's left hand, studying the finely manicured nails. He raised his eyes, meeting Lefty's frightened stare. "Hmmm?"

"I already told Charlie I don't know his real name. He's a city cop, a detective, and if I saw him, I could tell you who he is, but all I know him as is Mr. L." The man's voice wavered and his eyes darted between the pliers and his hand before returning to Steve's, pleading for him to believe.

He took a deep breath and peeled his thumb from under the rest of his fingers. Staring at the thumbnail and the pliers, he tried to figure out how the technique worked. At a loss, he glanced over his shoulder at Charlie.

"Get a good grip on the nail with the pliers and pull up and back toward the knuckle."

With a nod, he pushed the nail between the pliers, actually embedding the needle-nose point into the tender flesh under the nail. Lefty sobbed, pleading again. Steve paused, turning his gaze to Lefty. "You want to elaborate for us?"

"I don't know anything more." Snot rolled from his nose, and he blubbered some more and then the unmistakable acrid scent filled the room. His bladder let go, and he looked back at Charlie, hoping for sympathy, but the cold eyes returning his stare ignored the pleading man and bore into Steve.

He set his teeth together, tightening his jaw in resignation, and did as instructed. The wet ripping sound accompanied by the scream of anguish hit him like a falling brick and he ground his teeth against the burning bile now lining his esophagus. With a final yank, he pulled the nail free, dropping it on the floor with the other five bloody, peeled fingernails.

The deafening roar of gunfire filled the room, and a bullet exploded through Lefty's head, covering Steve with splattered blood. He jumped back, dropping the pliers on the ground, and spun toward Charlie. "What the fuck!"

"I believed him," Charlie said, flipping the safety on the gun and setting it on the desk.

"Then why the hell did you make me do that?"

He shrugged. "I wanted to see what you were made of."

Steve didn't have to fake the fury that coursed through his veins. He was far beyond that and had to bite down on the Miranda Rights swarming through his brain. He didn't have a weapon; he didn't have backup, and Jennifer had warned him on the phone call today. She said if he followed his instincts, he'd end up dead. She told him to do the opposite—to do what was necessary because nothing he could do today would save the poor slob behind him.

"Another fucking test?" He curled his hands into fists and took a step in Charlie's direction. He must have had murder in his eyes, because Charlie flipped the safety off his gun and pointed it at him.

"Cool your jets." He waved the barrel toward the couch and picked up the phone. With a punch of ten numbers, he muttered, "I need a cleaner at the warehouse," before hanging up the receiver.

Steve moved stiffly to the couch and sat down. His eyes kept traveling to the dead snitch and then snapping back to the floor in front of him. With the fade of the adrenaline rush came the shakes, and he clamped his teeth together so they wouldn't clack. He'd missed this

538

aftereffect in Brooksfield. He'd been too amped up and too worried about Jennifer, and he had passed out before the knowledge of killing sank in, but this time, he was in the thick of the impact.

He caught Charlie's interested study of his reaction and snapped, "Stop staring at me."

"You look a bit green." He slid the mirror holding a clump of raw cocaine and a razor blade in his direction.

His gaze fell to the waiting treat, and he nearly jumped to his feet and ran across the room. He prayed the cocaine would numb his anger instead of turning it into a living, breathing beast that begged for revenge. He hoped the blow would calm the storm.

"Your first dead body?" he asked, flipping the safety on the gun and sliding it in the holster under the desk. He snagged a couple of wipes out of the drawer and handed them to Steve.

He stared at the offered sheets and raised his eyes to Charlie's.

"There's blood on your face."

Steve wiped his fingers across his cheek and pulled them away, disgusted at the thick, red smears. He snatched the wipes from Charlie and mopped them across his skin, frantic to get the blood off, his breath now rasping in and out in rapid succession. The room tilted into a spin.

"Head between the legs."

He heard the partial directions Charlie spouted and sat in the chair next to the desk, dropping his head between his legs until the black spots cleared from his vision and the high-pitched whine disappeared. The tapping of the blade against the glass continued and when he raised his head again, Charlie slid the mirror and a straw in his direction.

He took the straw and snorted two lines before switching and inhaling the other two lines. Dropping the straw on the desk, he leaned back in the chair and closed his eyes, waiting for the rush, waiting for his heart to trip into high gear, waiting for the fury to numb.

"I'm impressed."

He laughed and opened his eyes. "You are a crazy motherfucker. You know that, Wisnowski?"

Charlie grinned. "There's a shower downstairs and a change of clothes. Thought you might want to get out of those before you leave."

He dropped his gaze. His suit was ruined, and he couldn't go home like this. Turning toward the corpse, he exhaled. "What about him?"

"I got cleaners coming."

"Ah." He turned back toward Charlie. "Like in the mafia?"

"Can't operate a drug ring without the help of certain business partners, at least not without finding yourself at the bottom of the Hudson with a Columbian necktie."

He emitted another, "Ah." He stood and headed toward the door. The floor shifted under his feet and, for the first time, he noticed the thin layer of plastic covering the carpet.

"Steve."

He stopped and turned, raising his eyebrows.

"Your clothes."

"I thought..."

Charlie chuckled. "Don't worry; shift change isn't for another hour. No one will see you in your skivvies."

He emptied his pockets, tossing his wallet, keys and cell onto his clean blazer and stripped, leaving in only his socks, undershirt and underwear.

The shower was hot, but not enough to warm up his chilled core.

His mind swirled, coaxed by the drugs and the blatant murder. He had the bastard cold, even without a body. Steve's testimony would hold enough weight to put Charlie away for life, but he still had the leverage, the power to make a deal. The client list still hadn't surfaced, and neither had the direct connection to the Bondinos. Steve wasn't sure what to do, but he knew if he didn't play it cool, he'd end up just like Lefty.

With a deep breath, he stepped out of the shower, dried off, and pulled on the clothing left for him. When he stepped into the belly of the warehouse, he met Charlie's cool gaze and crossed the expanse to him.

He handed Steve his wallet, keys, and cell and nodded his head toward the front door. "I'll drop you off at your apartment."

"I can finish the day at the office," Steve said, pocketing his items, thankful he cleared his texts and call history daily. The only ones he left were from Charlie, Desiree, and Jennifer.

Charlie sent a sideways glance in his direction.

"What?"

"You sure?"

"Look, I can deal with blood and guts and violent death. I've done my share of hunting and skinning and prepping venison, so while what you did back there took me by surprise, it didn't wig me out." He met Charlie's stare. "If you want to see me freak out, put me in a room with a stage five cancer victim hours away from death, then you'd see me lose it."

"I'll have to remember that."

"Besides, you did the prep work."

Charlie's eyebrows creased.

"The plastic. You covered your ass pretty good."

He chuckled and changed the subject. "You don't get many calls."

He snapped his gaze to Charlie and shrugged. "So?"

"Just making an observation."

"And what else did you observe?"

"You don't carry any pictures of your family."

"I have pictures of Jennifer. That's all I need. Why are you shuffling through my shit?"

"Insurance."

"Against what?"

"Against you going to the authorities."

"I'm your lawyer."

"Wasn't it you who said if you see something that involves a commission of a crime, that lawyer client confidentiality is compromised?"

"Yeah, so?"

"Well, you just witnessed a murder."

"Okay, I'm going to stop you right there. What I witnessed was an accident. You were teaching us the proper way to load and unload a gun, and it inadvertently went off and scared the shit out of Lefty. The last time we saw him, he was running out of CW FOG's warehouse."

Charlie chuckled.

"I assume you have a gun that is licensed?"

Charlie stopped laughing and nodded.

"Then I suggest you discharge it into the floor of your office at CW FOG after hours."

"Shit, you are good."

"Why the hell did you think I took so long in the shower?"

"I figured you were freaking out or throwing up or both."

It was Steve's turn to laugh. "Ever skin a deer?"

"No."

"It's a hundred times grosser than shooting someone in the head."

Vengeance
Chapter 37

STEVE WALKED INTO THE apartment and dropped his briefcase. He closed the door and crossed into the bathroom, dropping in front of the toilet and finally letting the bile barrel out of his stomach. Shaking, he propped his elbows on the edges of the toilet and held his head.

The day got the best of him, and he spit, flushing the toilet before sliding to the side and leaning his head against the cabinet. Both anger and fear crawled through him, festering in the pit of his stomach.

Shit like today wasn't supposed to happen. He wasn't supposed to bear witness to murder and pretend nothing was wrong. He wasn't supposed to torture innocent men and then grab a light lunch at the office. He wasn't supposed to crave the numbness of drugs, but he did. He did all these things and now his haunted eyes stared back, detesting and accusing.

He didn't know how long he sat glaring at his reflection, but finally his eyes closed, and he stopped shaking, his throat raw and sore and his eyes burned. He stood and crossed to the sink and threw cold water on his face.

The minty toothpaste couldn't quite wipe out the acrid bile, and every time his thoughts twirled around the day, his throat clenched. He had to get a message to Jack, but before he did anything, he'd have to comb through the apartment. Manny had enough time to drop a bug even with the deadbolt and he had to be sure, otherwise it would be his body tossed into the incinerator.

He rummaged around the top shelf of the closet, muttering under his breath until his hand fell on the frequency scanner the FBI gave him after the last sweep. He walked around the apartment scanning everything, and the last item on the list was his phone. Charlie had it long enough and his hunch was right. The scanner beeped its high pitch staccato pulse, and he turned it off.

"Fuck."

His phone was now useless, and he looked around the apartment before crumbling in the chair behind his computer. He stared at the cell phone, unwilling to do a full inspection of the electronic device for fear of tipping Charlie off. Instead, he went back to the closet and rummaged on the shelf again, tucking the scanner away and pulling out the extra disposable phone he had for just this situation. For all he knew, Charlie could even record text messages and keystrokes.

With the television switched on for background noise, he opened his laptop and constructed the details of his day, along with the warning that his phone was compromised, and the secondary precaution was now in place. The reaction was immediate. Both Jerry and Jack insisted he call them right away, and he declined both requests. His fingers flew over the keyboard with his response.

If I call you right now, I'll be in deep shit. I have to act like nothing happened for a couple of days; otherwise, I'm a dead man. He has the tap on my cell phone and I'm sure he's got another tail on me.

I'm aware of the magnitude of what happened today, but I want an airtight case, Jack. I don't want any chance of compromise and right now, I'm afraid it could be. I might not be your best witness, especially after following Charlie's orders today. Any good lawyer could cast reasonable doubt if given all the facts and I don't want that bastard to have any latitude to plea bargain.

Besides, with this under my belt, if I can stay cool, I might get lucky. He mentioned mafia ties. Give me until New Year's. If we don't have more to pin on the fucker, I'll bust him for all the charges we have stacked against him. Okay?

In the meantime, I want to know who the fuck Lefty is and why we didn't know about him. He said there was someone else. Another informant, and we need to find out who before Charlie does, otherwise we'll have another dead body on our hands.

And yeah, I know. That dead body could be mine.

Vengeance
Chapter 38

STEVE GLANCED AT THE calendar on his desk. Two days away from Christmas and nothing had happened since the Lefty incident. In fact, Charlie had left him alone since then, and Steve turned his attention to his window and the falling snow against the darkening city backdrop.

"Want to catch a drink?"

Steve shot a startled glance over his shoulder at Charlie. "I need to hit the gym."

"Where do you work out?"

"Gold's Gym near the apartment."

"Tell you what: we've got a gym in my apartment building. We can work out, and then we can grab a drink."

Steve swiveled the chair around. The last thing he wanted tonight was another Charlie conversation. That usually led to snorting cocaine or having a gun pressed to his forehead, but instead of declining, he nodded.

"Good, cause we need to talk." His casual tone belied the hardness of his stare, and Steve swallowed the sudden lump of fear in his throat.

"About what?" he asked and shut his computer down. Crossing the office, he grabbed his gym bag stashed behind the door and followed a silent Charlie to the elevator.

"Where's the beeamer?" Charlie asked when they stepped out into the garage.

"It sucks in the snow," he answered and slid into the passenger seat of the SUV and tossed his bag on the floor. "What'd you want to discuss?"

Charlie's silence unnerved him, and he watched the downtown buildings transition to mid-town as they navigated the city streets, shooting uptown on Broadway. He pulled into his building, electing not to use the valet. "We can talk after the workout." Charlie stepped out of the car.

The gym encompassed the two floors above the lobby and included state-of-the-art equipment and a sauna. Charlie dropped Steve in the locker room. "I'll be down in a few minutes." He waved to the suit and excused himself.

Steve changed, stowing his suit and bag in a locker the attendant gave him, and stepped into the equipment room. He headed toward the Nautilus weight training stations and took a seat, beginning his weight routine.

Charlie took a seat next to Steve a few minutes later. "How many reps in are you?" he asked.

Steve froze mid-lift, his gaze riveted to the ornate tattoo on the inside of Charlie's right arm. The spitting image of Jennifer's drawing. He had to force himself to finish his repetition and not launch through the distance and beat Charlie to death. His mouth went dry, and his mind raced, filtering through the timings of every attack, including hers. He forced a swallow and raised his eyes to Charlie's. "Just a couple," he answered. His grip tightened on the weight bar, and he finished his repetitions while his mind whirled. "Nice tattoo. When'd you get that?"

Charlie looked at the artwork that graced his arm. "A couple of days before my brother died."

"Ah," he said, wiping his hands on the towel. "Pretty detailed artwork there."

Charlie smiled and went back to his repetitions. "You interested in getting a tattoo?"

He shook his head. "I have a needle phobia. Just can't get my mind around that."

"You said that about your nose as well. You seemed to have gotten over that pretty quickly," he said, and Steve stood to move on to the treadmill.

"Needles are different," he answered and started up the tread, slowly increasing speed until he was jogging at an eight-minute mile clip. He stared at the television set hanging in front of him, but he didn't see the stories unfolding across the screen. Instead, his mind was picking at everything he knew about the crime scenes, every detail of Jennifer's attack.

The only thing that didn't add up was the deliveryman with the dark curly hair. He didn't think it was Charlie in disguise, but he couldn't be sure. He bit the side of his lip, dissecting the memory. The height and build correlated, but the voice didn't. Neither did the dark stubble. His light hair just didn't coincide with the memory, but he hadn't been in the office that morning either, and he showed up awfully damn fast at the hospital.

Steve took a deep breath to calm the fury boiling under his skin. He closed his eyes and forced himself to mentally step back and assess the situation without the emotions.

Did Charlie fit the profile?

Violent. Check.

Objectifies women. Check.

Superiority complex. Check.

Can I account for his whereabouts during any of the attacks?

Steve chewed on the inside of his lip, digging backwards in his memory, and came up empty. No, he couldn't account for Charlie's whereabouts.

But why would he risk all he's built?

Charlie was militant about the business, and that's where the facts fell apart. Steve slowed and shot a glance at Charlie, who had climbed on the treadmill next to him while he did his silent assessment.

"Desiree tells me you and Jennifer are coming by tomorrow night."

"Yep."

"I'm looking forward to it," he said.

"So are we." He stopped the treadmill, shifting his weight from foot to foot for a minute before stepping off and stretching, his mind still grappling with the new information in his arsenal.

"I'm heading for the showers. I'll meet you in the lobby." Steve crossed to the locker room. The steamy shower calmed his jumpy nerves, soothing the anger, nearly bursting every cell in his body.

Could Charlie be the fucking Slasher?

CHARLIE STRAIGHTENED WHEN STEVE stepped out of the glass doors leading to the lobby and led the way to his apartment. Steve's heart pumped faster than normal, fueled by the thoughts swarming in his mind. For the first time, he stepped into Charlie's apartment and looked around, making a silent mental note of the absence of plastic lining the floors. He relaxed as much as his adrenaline would allow and scanned the room with appreciation. The living room donned an eighty-two inch flat-screen mounted above a gas fireplace. Surround sound wireless speakers graced every corner of the room, and he imagined the acoustics would be theater quality. The plush leather couches looked inviting and in the far corner, just before the sliders to the terrace, sat an amply stocked bar.

Charlie pointed to the sofa. "I'll be out in a few. Make yourself comfortable." With that, he disappeared.

Steve stood, scanning the room, memorizing and analyzing. It was pristine, not what he envisioned for a bachelor. Walking through the room, he noted the neatly stacked and arranged magazines. The combination of *Entertainment Weekly* along with *Architectural Digest* surprised him. At least he didn't have *Penthouse* on the coffee table. The mahogany desk opposite the bar piqued his interest, and he gave a quick glance down the hallway where Charlie disappeared and crossed to the desk. He scanned the calendar, fanning the pages back a few months, looking for anything that would clear him.

Nothing. No clandestine meetings noted on the dates. No out-of-town reminders. Nothing. Steve bit the inside of his lip, harnessing the growing ferocity gripping him. Visions of Jennifer lying on the floor of his apartment snapped off in his head, and he inhaled, returning his focus to the desk. Nothing on the desk set off any internal alarms, and he glanced at the drawers, pausing. Pretending to study the architecture of the room, his trained eye breezed right over the hidden camera in the ceiling before falling back on the desk. Charlie was watching. Shit.

He sat in the plush leather desk chair, running his hands over the arms in appreciation. Spinning it around toward the terrace, he looked at the cityscape. With a deep breath, he stood and headed toward the bar, praying he did a convincing job for the camera. Behind the matching mahogany face, he found a refrigerator full of beer. Corona. *At least he has good taste.* He also found already-sliced limes and raised an eyebrow. He grabbed a bottle and a sliced lime and was searching for the bottle opener when Charlie came back into the living room.

"I see you found the alcohol."

"Yeah, but where the hell is the bottle opener?"

Charlie pointed at the back of the bar.

Steve turned and grabbed the gold-plated bottle opener that hung from the back wall. He popped the top of the beer and pushed the lime in before taking a long draw with his back to Charlie. "The guy who attacked Jennifer had a similar tattoo," he said without turning. His gaze landed on the mirrored image of Charlie.

Charlie blinked, and his mouth popped open. His gaze dropped to his covered arm and then back to Steve's reflection. His head cocked to the side and his eyebrows drew together in confusion. After a moment, he closed his mouth.

"And?" he asked once his composure returned.

Steve turned, meeting his gaze. "You wouldn't know anything about it, would you?" he asked and wasn't sure the sudden display of shock on Charlie's face was real.

Shock transitioned to confusion and Steve stared him down, wondering if Charlie really was that good an actor. Doubt wrapped around his gut as he kept Charlie's gaze.

"Did they catch him?" Charlie said, trying to piece together sections of a puzzle he didn't have all the parts to.

"No." He mentally reviewed Charlie's reaction. There were no tells, no concrete signs that gave any indication Charlie was the one who attacked Jennifer and he sighed, pulling his temper back into control. "Sorry," he added. "Your tattoo just set me off. The fact the asshole is still out there burns the hell out of me." Steve took another sip of beer.

"You thought..." Charlie started and stopped, closing his eyes for a moment before continuing. "I guess I'd be the same way if Jennifer was my girl." He leaned on the side of his desk.

The mention of her name almost released the raving beast, and Steve raised an eyebrow. *Easy now.* "I want to be the one to find the bastard," Steve said. "But that's not what you wanted to talk to me about, was it?"

"No." Charlie shifted. "Are you really ready to marry Jennifer?"

"I don't have the same commitment phobia that you do." He pointed the neck of his bottle in Charlie's direction.

"So, you're ready to commit to her forever just because she's pregnant?"

Steve nodded. "It's not just because of the pregnancy, either."

Charlie paused. "In that case." He pulled an envelope out of his pocket and handed it to him.

He opened the card and stared at the enclosed check. All thought ceased—the tattoo, the Slasher, the drugs—all of it drowned by the figure on the check. He blinked and then his eyebrows arched, and his jaw dropped before he shot his gaze to Charlie. "What's this?"

"A wedding gift."

He cleared his throat. "You're giving me a million dollars as a wedding gift?"

Charlie smiled, visibly pleased at the reaction. "Think you can find a way to spend it?" he asked and retrieved a beer for himself.

"I'm sure Jennifer can find half a dozen ways to spend the money." He grinned, and his eyes lowered to the check. *Money can be a pretty seductive bitch,* Jack's words echoed, and he certainly was right. Steve blinked again, his thoughts resuming along with a torrent of doubt.

Does this fit the profile?

"Find a nice house and use that as a down payment. Kids shouldn't grow up in an apartment."

Speechless, he sat down on one of the overstuffed chairs, staring at the check while he drained his beer. "Thanks, Charlie." He looked up at his boss, wondering again if the man was capable of doing the kind of damage he suspected. He looked back at the check, tucked it in the card, and slipped it in his inside suit pocket. "But, why?"

"Because you're the closest thing I have to family." Charlie took a seat. "No one else I know gives me shit like you do." He shrugged it off and stared at his beer. "It's been a long time since I had a friend." He glanced at Steve.

The shock of Charlie's answer wrapped around the flurry in his mind, soothing the fury and forming a chuckle in the back of his throat. "Same here." He tapped his bottle against Charlie's and finished the last of the beer.

Vengeance
Chapter 39

STEVE STOOD IN THE wings of the theater, still dressed in his suit and staring into space, not seeing the chaos surrounding him.

"Earth to Steve," Jennifer said as she approached, watching his eyes focus on her. A hint of a smile form on his lips.

"Hey. You about ready?" he yelled in her ear over the applause.

Jennifer nodded.

Steve was unusually quiet and self-absorbed on the subway ride, and she tilted her head as they stepped off in Brooklyn, a block from the apartment. When he remained quiet in their enclosed apartment, sitting on the edge of the bed and turning an envelope over in his hands, she spoke up. "What's eating you?"

He handed her the envelope.

She pulled the card out, smiling at the sweet sentiment on the front. When she opened it, the check slipped. She caught it and stared at the amount. "Holy shit."

"Our wedding gift."

She sat on the side of the bed next to him. "A million dollars?"

He nodded. "I guess you could say I'm now in his 'inner' circle." He made a quotation gesture with his hands when he said the word *inner*. "Charlie's looking forward to Christmas Eve." He glanced at her. "I'm not."

"This isn't going to be an easy holiday, is it?"

"Not the one I was hoping for." He ran his hand over her stomach. "You've got that ultrasound tomorrow, right?"

"Yes. Do you want to know the sex?"

Steve shook his head. "No. I want to be surprised."

"Mister, *I-want-to-be-prepared-for-everything* doesn't want to know the sex of his child?" she teased without looking away from the check. Her eyes were glued to the amount they would never see a penny of.

"That's right. Some things are worth waiting for." He stood and stripped his jacket off.

"Since when have you waited for anything?" She stood and wrapped her arms around his shoulders, planting a kiss on his lips. "What are you going to do with this?" She waved the check at him.

"Give it to Jack. It'll go into the account where the rest of my paychecks from Charlie go."

Jennifer pulled away. "Where does that go?" She'd always assumed they'd been living off the funds.

"Charity," he said. "I got to choose where I wanted the money to go."

"What'd you choose?"

"St. Jude's Children's Hospital and the New York City Food Pantry and Homeless Shelters."

She smiled at her husband and leaned up, gently kissing his soft lips, inviting the kiss to become more.

Vengeance
Chapter 40

STEVE STARED AT THE images on the ultrasound screen, trying to make out anything familiar as the technician ran the wand over Jennifer's stomach.

"There's one heart." Marney, the ultrasound technician, pointed at a small fluttering blob on the screen. "And over here is the second one." She pointed to another fluttering blob.

"Excuse me?" he interrupted. "Two hearts?"

Marney turned and smiled. "You're having twins," she said. "See?" She pointed the two separate bodies out on the screen.

They exchanged glances, then looked back at the monitor as Marney traced each form for them. Like those three-dimensional picture puzzles, one minute the screen was a bunch of black and white blobs and, with a blink, the screen cleared, and he could make out two distinct forms. "Hot damn, look at that." His lips spread into a dimple-clad grin. "Are they identical?"

Marney glanced at the monitor. "It looks like they each have their own sac, so I don't think so. It looks more like fraternal twins." She pointed out the ghost of a line showing the separate sacs. "Do you want to know the sexes?"

"No," they said in unison.

Marney pressed the print button and handed each of them a printout of the ultrasound. "The doctor will be in to see you in a few minutes."

Steve stared at the printout, seeing the forms of his children. The lump in his throat grew, and he blinked the sudden spring of tears away. Awe filled him, and he traced the outlines with his index finger. "Our kids."

"No wonder I popped early. I've got two babies inside my belly." She ran her hand over the bump. "Merry Christmas, Steve," she said, looking up at him.

The euphoria of the moment faded a fraction. They were heading to Charlie's directly from the doctor's office, and all he wanted to do was hold her in his arms and stare at the ultrasound picture. He leaned in and planted a kiss on her lips. "Thank you."

"I haven't *done* anything yet," she answered. She wiped the goop off her stomach and slid into the burgundy velvet Christmas dress he'd bought her. When she stepped out from behind the curtain, Steve blew out a stream of air. "You look fantastic."

"I can't believe we're having twins," he said. He tossed the bag of street clothes she'd worn to the doctor's office in the trunk, pulled out the elegantly gift-wrapped Glenlivet Single Malt Scotch he'd bought for Charlie, and handed it to Jennifer as he slid into the driver's seat.

"And I can't believe you bought him a thousand-dollar bottle of booze," Jennifer said. She filtered through her purse for the jewelry box containing a pair of earrings for Desiree.

"Yeah, well, with the salary he's paying me and the wedding gift, I couldn't go cheap on him for Christmas."

"Pft," she scoffed. "What'd you get me?"

"A thousand-dollar bottle of scotch." He pulled into the traffic, heading uptown. Jennifer smacked his arm when the dimples appeared in his cheek.

Just for one night, he wanted to pretend their lives were normal, to celebrate the news of twins and the Christmas holiday without his undercover job tainting the celebration. "Look, why don't we pretend these are our friends and set out to have a great night?" He glanced at Jennifer. "And forget about the job for a few hours."

She nodded. "That sounds great to me."

When he pulled up to the front of the building, a valet attendant rushed over to the car.

"Are you here for the Wisnowski party?"

Steve nodded and handed over his keys. He was given a numbered tag that disappeared into his pocket. He escorted Jennifer into the crowded elevator, where they shared a quizzical glance. The elevator stopped at the penthouse floor, and everyone filtered out.

"A small party?" she whispered in Steve's ear.

"I guess." The place was packed.

Desiree stopped with a tray of appetizers. "You're finally here!" She glanced at her watch. "This will wind down around seven and then I've got a fabulous dinner on tap." She smiled and disappeared.

Steve glanced around at the crowd, recognizing almost everyone. The entire CW FOG staff was in attendance and some of the more prevalent Gaby Paper representatives. Charlie entertained a group of women by his desk, and when he caught sight of Steve and Jennifer, he excused himself, filtering through the sea of people.

"How'd it go?" he asked above the noise.

"Twins," Steve grinned.

"No shit!" Charlie pumped his hand and gave Jennifer a bear hug, shocking both of them. He leaned over in Steve's ear before he stepped away. "Party room's that way." He pointed down the hall and winked.

"Where do you want me to put these?" Steve raised the gifts.

"Why don't you go get yourself a drink and I'll show your fiancée where she can put those, along with your coats."

Steve glanced at Jennifer, doubt thundering through his blood.

"Want to grab me a soda?" she asked, putting her hands out for his coat and the gift-wrapped scotch.

He shed his jacket. His eyes flitted to Charlie and back to Jennifer. Handing both the scotch and his jacket over, he watched them disappear into the crowd and then turned and made his way to the bar.

CHARLIE LED JENNIFER TO a nice-sized den where a Christmas tree stood to the side of a breathtaking view of Manhattan. "You can put the gifts under the tree and your coats on the chair."

She crossed the room and the noise of the party disappeared behind the closed door. When she glanced over her shoulder, he was standing in front of the large mahogany entry with his head tilted and his hands clasped behind his back, watching her.

Jennifer turned back to the view, setting the packages under the tree. She took her coat off and jumped as hands helped her. She turned and Charlie was there, peeling the coat off with a peculiar smile on his face. Laughing nervously, she tried to step around him, but there was no graceful way to do that, so she looked up into his gray eyes.

"Are you serious about marrying Steve?"

The question caught her off guard, and nerves jumbled in her stomach. "Yes, why?"

He took a small step back and produced a remote. "Because I'm not sure he's the right man for you."

"Oh, and you know what qualifies as the right man?"

Charlie smiled and pointed the remote at the television.

The screen filled with the view of her apartment, her kitchen, to be specific. She looked at him and narrowed her eyes. "I know what happened, Charlie. Your girlfriend seduced Steve." She took a step toward him, hoping to intimidate him, but he stood his ground.

"Really?" He nodded toward the television, turning up the sound.

Steve was saying he could throw something together if she was hungry. When Desiree stepped into view, Steve's reaction to her was obvious. He licked his lips and scanned her in the same way Jennifer saw him do to her countless times. To his credit, he did say maybe they should go out. Desiree stepped closer, cornering him between the refrigerator and the kitchen sink.

She shot a glare at Charlie and stepped to leave the room.

"You need to see this," he said.

She turned toward the television and the image of Steve said, "Um, my girlfriend." She recognized the lust in his eyes and the familiar scan he gave Desiree. She couldn't see what exactly was happening between them, but seconds later Desiree planted a kiss and he pulled away just as quickly, whispering, "I can't do this." But his words lacked conviction, and he didn't stop whatever she'd started.

The frame skipped.

On the screen, Steve spun her around, his face shrouded by her hair. What he did next was clear as the Christmas tree next to her. With his back to the camera, he stripped her pants and picked her up, setting her on their kitchen counter, spreading her legs wide before burying his face between them.

Jennifer stared at the blue cast poking out from under his sweater, blinking back tears. "Why are you showing me this?" The harsh whisper came from her chest.

His hands descended on her shoulders, and he stepped close behind her, moving her hair away from her neck and planting a kiss. "Because I wanted you to know what type of man you're marrying."

Anger burst in her veins. It was one thing to forgive him for being seduced, but a blowjob and this were worlds apart. Grinding her teeth together, she watched her husband please another woman on the screen.

Charlie's hands wandered, and she didn't stop him. Desiree's moans of pleasure fueled her fury until it became unmanageable. Her heart thundered in her chest, all the memories of him proclaiming he loved her, all his lies on the job. Maybe her father was right, and he was so used to pretending that her marriage was just another one of his facades.

Charlie's fingertips grazed the inside of her thigh, settling between her legs and stroking her through her underwear. "I would never do that to you," he whispered in her ear. His finger slid under the edge of her panties.

Her eyes stayed locked on the television, on the movement of Steve's head insinuating the stroke of his tongue. The knowledge of how good he was with his mouth didn't help. The tape skipped again and the scene she saw in her vision played out on the screen, but something about the video cut struck a chord. Moments after the scene change, Steve pushed Desiree away and stepped out of range, zipping his pants in a hell of a hurry.

"No." The word whispered from her lips and she pushed his hand away. "Charlie, no." She stepped away and turned toward him. "I can't, I can't do this."

"You don't want me?"

Jennifer shook her head.

"You still want to marry that son of a bitch?"

She bit her lip and looked at the empty screen. *For better or worse.* Her vows echoed in her mind, and she nodded, glancing back at Charlie.

Charlie put his hands up in the air and stepped away.

Her eyes locked on the tattoo, inching from under his shirt.

"Okay." He turned and left the room.

Jennifer's heart went into overdrive. *Was that the tattoo?* She wasn't sure, but the hint of yellow and red frazzled her beyond the bizarre encounter. Hand combing her hair and wiping her eyes, she glanced back at the screen and the anger filled the space doubt had occupied a moment ago.

How could you?

She glared at her empty kitchen on the television, her mind's eye centering on her husband in the corner with his eyes closed and his good hand threaded in Desiree's blonde locks. She pressed the off button on the remote and the room dimmed with only lights from the Christmas tree and the downtown Manhattan skyline to accompany her. Her hand drifted over the bump in her belly and the tears came.

"JEN?" STEVE POPPED HIS head into the room, seeing her silhouette against the Manhattan sky. "I've been looking everywhere for you."

"Go away."

He stopped halfway across the room. "Are you crying?"

"Get out of here before I say something I can't take back!"

Ignoring her request, he set the drinks on the end table and turned her toward him. "What's wrong?"

Jennifer wiped the tears away and tried to break out of his grasp.

"Did Charlie hurt you?"

"No, you did." She leaned over and pressed the play button on the remote. What appeared on the screen shocked them both. It wasn't the tape Charlie had shown her, it was her watching something on screen with Charlie's hand between her legs.

Steve's jaw dropped and when the camera view changed, he snapped his jaw shut. There in Technicolor was the scene in their kitchen, Desiree on her knees before him. The side view shot showed the video playing while Charlie fondled his wife.

Jennifer leaned over to turn the video off.

"Let it play." His growl filled the room.

Jennifer glanced at Steve, recoiling at the hatred she saw in his profile. When his eyes swiveled in her direction, she took a step backwards. "Nothing happened." She reached for the remote.

"No, let it play." He grabbed her wrist and yanked her backwards. When it was over, Steve sat on the couch, staring at the blank screen. He wasn't angry with her, but Charlie was a whole other hemisphere. The bastard used the video to get her for himself.

The confusion of layered emotions clouded his judgment, and he looked back at her. "So, does this mean the wedding's off?" It was easier to fall into character than deal with what had really happened here.

"I'm carrying your children. What do you think?"

Steve looked out at the city, staring at his reflection and then at hers. "I fucked up. It happens from time to time." He shrugged. "So you tell me. Is this what you want?" He turned toward her.

"I want the man I fell in love with," she whispered, keeping eye contact.

He closed his eyes and nodded. Right now, he would give anything to be that man again, but he had seen too much, gone too far down the rabbit hole to come back. His eyes softened a little as he looked at her. "I'm right here." He spread his arms out.

"Once we're married, if you do that to me, I'll divorce you so fast your head will spin." Her voice shook.

"If anyone touches you *after* we're married, he's dead," he said, his voice steady and fierce. He found the camera lens in the ceiling and looked straight into it. "You hear me, Charlie? I swear, if you ever touch her again, you are a dead man." Steve grabbed the coats and Jennifer's hand and stormed toward the door.

It swung open, and both Charlie and Desiree stepped into the room.

"I hear you, but if you hadn't noticed, she didn't stop me right away, either."

"Yeah, and I deserved that for being such a jackass with Desiree."

Charlie put his arm around Desiree. "She's a naughty minx sometimes." He swatted her ass lightly and smiled. He pulled a gun out of his waistline and pointed it at Steve, producing a silencer in his other hand, and screwed it to the end of the barrel. "I don't take kindly to threats, Steve."

Jennifer gasped and swiftly moved in front of him, putting herself in the path of a potential bullet. "Please don't."

Charlie tilted his head. "You didn't let me finish, darling." The barrel of the gun swung towards Desiree and Charlie pulled the trigger, killing her instantly with a bullet to the brain.

Steve blinked. His breath locked in his chest as Desiree fell to the floor. What was left of her head bounced and splattered blood against the walls. He snapped his gaze back in Charlie's direction once again, suppressing the urge to read him his rights.

"But what I hate even more is disloyalty." He flipped the safety on and glanced between Steve and Jennifer. "Don't worry, I've got someone else lined up to keep watch over you," he addressed Jennifer. "And she won't be double crossing me, either, or hitting on Steve, for that matter."

He walked into the room and flipped on another feed. It showed Desiree in the kitchen. She was whispering to the caterer, and she passed a piece of paper. "He's a cop. Well, he *was* a cop," Charlie corrected himself. "Desiree was his informant." He glanced over his shoulder.

Jennifer stared at Desiree. The breath wheezed out of her chest.

Steve leaned into her ear. "Breathe, baby," he whispered, still watching the screen, turning her away from the dead woman in the corner. It took all his concentration not to recite the Miranda rights. If he played that hand, neither of them would walk out of the building alive.

"So, she was the mole Lefty mentioned." Steve glanced at Desiree and back at Charlie.

Charlie nodded.

"How can you be so calm?" Jennifer screamed at Steve, her entire frame shook in his arms. "He just..."

"Shit happens. She deserved what she got." Steve glared at her. *Be cool baby, please, dear god, be cool or we won't get out of here.*

Steve turned toward Charlie with the same level of venom. "That was fucking stupid," he snapped. "How many people are still out there?"

He pointed at the door. "And where the hell is the dead cop?"

"It's been taken care of. Just like she will be."

"You have that kind of clout?" he asked. "Because, as your lawyer, I can tell you there isn't an angle that can be used for reasonable doubt here."

"Ever hear of the Bondino family?" Charlie shot back.

Steve stopped, letting his eyes reflect the shock he felt. He just got the mother of all Christmas gifts. "Bondino?"

"He can make this disappear like that." Charlie snapped his fingers.

Jennifer sat on the couch. "I'm not feeling so good."

Steve picked up the soda and handed it to her. "Here, this should help. It's ginger ale." Something else clicked. He needed the recording of this conversation and he glanced at Charlie. "This isn't how I envisioned spending Christmas Eve."

Charlie nodded and glanced at Jennifer. "Will she be okay?"

Steve recognized the doubt in his eyes. "Jennifer will be just fine. We're getting married next week." He tilted his head a fraction, conveying the significance of that to Charlie.

"Even after tonight?"

"She's carrying my kids, so yeah, even after tonight. And I was serious, Charlie." Steve pointed at him, clenching his teeth together, his muscles tightly coiled and ready to spring. "If you *ever* touch her like that again, I'll kill you."

Charlie raised his eyebrows, clearly irked by the threat, but he backed down. "Okay." He walked to the tree and picked up two gifts, handing them to Steve and Jennifer.

Steve looked from the package back to Charlie. He really didn't want to exchange Christmas presents with a dead woman in the room and, from the horrified expression on Jennifer's face, she was seconds away from a full freak out. "Go ahead, open them," Charlie prodded and grabbed the box Jennifer had set under the tree.

"I think we should..." Steve began, but the glare he received from Charlie cut him off and he reached over and squeezed Jennifer's hand, meeting her gaze for an instant before focusing on the box in her lap.

Her hands shook, and she ripped the paper off her gift. Her eyes filled with tears as she opened the deep blue box marked with the Swarovski crystal emblem. Inside was the most elegant crystal eagle he had ever seen, but it didn't cut through the fear in his heart, and he willed her to speak, to say something appropriate to the gift and not the circumstances.

"It's b-beautiful," she stammered and glanced up, with tears still tracking down her cheeks.

Steve drew a breath of relief, turning his focus from her to the box in his lap, and unwrapped the paper from the heavy case. He flipped the lid open. He stared at the present in his lap and picked up the Smith & Wesson .45 caliber gun, turning it over in his hands, studying the scrollwork with a gold eagle inlay. The handle was a rich deep cherry, complementing the rest of the presentation. *I'll bet he killed the cop with this;* he thought and put the gun back in the velvet box. He didn't know what to say and glanced back at Charlie.

"Have you ever shot a handgun?"

Steve nodded. "Yeah. I actually own one," he answered. "But this... this... I can't accept this." He put the box on the table.

"Do you like it?" Charlie asked.

"Hell, yeah, but..." He glanced at Jennifer. He ran his fingers along the cool metal barrel. *And I'll have to have Jack run a match on the bullet signature. Shit.* He looked back at him. "I love it."

Charlie smiled and focused on the gift in his lap. He whistled as he pulled the bottle out. "This cost you a mint." He glanced up at Steve. "Thank you, and I'm sorry about the..." He waved his hand toward the door. "The situation. I didn't mean to ruin your evening." Charlie set the bottle on the table and extended his hand toward Steve.

He stared at Charlie's hand and then back at his boss. "I really should deck you for that stunt earlier."

Charlie dropped his hand and shrugged. "I had to see where her loyalties fell."

Steve wasn't sure how to respond, so he dropped his gaze to the floor before meeting Jennifer's. "I already know where her loyalties lie, Charlie. Your little test was unnecessary." He swung his glare back toward Charlie. "And I was dead serious; I'll pop a cap in your ass if you lay a hand on her again."

Charlie gave a nod and extended his hand.

Steve grasped it and stood. "I think I'll be taking Jennifer home, if you don't mind." He placed his hand on her head.

She closed the box, latching it securely, and stood, meeting Charlie's gaze. "Thank you for the eagle." Her voice quivered.

Charlie leaned forward, placing a light kiss on her cheek. "Thank you for the scotch."

She nodded, but Steve could tell she was barely holding it together. Hell, he was barely holding it together.

"Follow me." Charlie opened the sliding glass doors to the balcony. He led them to the bedroom and then through the thinning crowd to the elevator, helping Jennifer with her coat.

"I'll be in a little late on Monday," he said to Steve. His eyes flicked to Jennifer and back. "In the meantime, I'll be watching."

"I figured that was a given. I'll see you Monday."

STEVE SHOOK HIS HEAD when they pulled out of the garage. He didn't know if the car was bugged, and after the evening they'd just lived through, he didn't want to tempt fate.

"What have you gotten us into?" she asked.

Steve turned toward her. "Don't worry about it, Jen. Charlie will take care of it." The masquerade continued until he was sure the apartment was clear. Steve scanned the room. Nothing new had been added, and he inspected both the eagle and the gun, finding nothing in the way of listening devices. He crossed to the window, and, as promised, Manny was sitting out in the car watching the apartment. Steve sent a wave in his direction and got a nod in response before he pulled the shades closed.

When Steve turned away from the window, Jennifer stepped out of the bathroom, wiping her mouth with the back of her hand, her complexion still peaked and pale. He met her gaze and his guard shattered. "What the hell were you doing with Charlie?"

"Me? You…"

"You knew that happened." He cut her off, pointing toward the kitchen. "You saw it in your vision in October. Why the hell did you let Charlie touch you?"

"I… uh…"

The anger boiled over. "You're my wife, damn it!" He stormed over to the computer and flipped it open without speaking to her.

He completed his full report to Jack and his disposable phone rang minutes after he pressed the send button.

Steve flipped the phone open. "Monday. He'll stop first thing before he heads to Manhattan, and you have to nail the fucker before he sets foot in his office, or you are screwed." He met Jennifer's gaze. "I want Jennifer in protective custody. You can get her from the theater on Sunday and we'll need a decoy coming home with me."

"Are you okay?" Jack asked.

"I'm fine. I'm just pissed. He killed her right in front of me and there wasn't a damn thing I could do, just like with Lefty. One minute the gun was aimed at me, and the next, bam, her brains were all over the wall. Why the hell didn't we know they were informants?"

"I'm glad we didn't because it works both ways and I'm keeping a lid on this until after the sting. Only FBI and DEA will execute on Monday. Stay away from the office. Give any excuse, but do not go to the office or anywhere near the warehouse, you understand?"

"I got it. Just take the fucker down." Steve slammed the phone down and closed the computer, glaring at Jennifer.

She glared back at him. She hadn't moved since he opened the computer and he closed his eyes, putting his head down on his arms.

"You didn't tell me everything, Steve."

He lifted his head. "You're the one who warned me about not going with my instincts at the warehouse."

"I wasn't talking about that." Her voice wavered. "I'm talking about the kitchen. You didn't tell me everything." If fire could sprout from someone's eyes, he would have been toast.

"What are you talking about?" He stood and took a step toward her, but she put her hands up and he stopped.

"Charlie showed me the video, Steve. He showed me what you did to Desiree."

Confused, he tilted his head. "And what was that?"

"You... you..." She pointed toward the corner. "You propped her on the counter and... and..." She couldn't finish her sentence.

"And what?" His face grew hot, flushing with the growing anger burrowing into his skin.

"You went down on her."

Steve's eyebrows rose, and he shook his head. "I don't think so, Jen."

"I saw the video. I saw!"

He pressed his lips together and inhaled through his nose. "I didn't touch her. She remained fully clothed while..." He waved at the corner. "While she did her thing. So, whatever you think you saw, it wasn't me."

"And I'm supposed to believe that?"

"Yes, I told you what happened here."

"That's bullshit. You wouldn't have said a thing if I hadn't had the vision."

Steve chewed on the inside of his lip. She was right. He wouldn't have said a word if she didn't already know. "True. But omission isn't the same as lying outright, and I'm not lying to you."

They stared at each other from across the room. Jennifer's mouth opened and closed, and she studied him. Her eyes narrowed, and she cocked her head. "You didn't?"

"No, Jen, I didn't. I admit I was wrong. I should have never let her start what she did, but I stopped it pretty quickly. There's no way in hell I would have done what you're talking about."

She sat on the edge of the bed, staring at Steve. Her eyes dropped to her hands, they narrowed, and he knew she was reviewing the evening. Her eyes widened, and her gaze shot back to his face, her jaw loosening and falling open.

"Charlie." They both said at the same time. Charlie manufactured that video just for Jennifer's benefit.

"That bastard!" she said.

"I told you..." He stopped and inhaled, crossing to her and taking her hands in his. "Charlie's been interested in you since day one and I knew that. You're just lucky he opted to take this route rather than a more drastic solution to his problem."

Jennifer bit her lip, tears sprouting again, and she met his gaze. "I'm sorry."

"You really didn't do anything, Jen. He manipulated you and took advantage of a moment of weakness." He was glad he would not be near the warehouse on Monday. If he was, he might shoot Charlie on sight.

Vengeance
Chapter 41

THE KNOCK ON THE door echoed through the empty apartment, and Charlie crossed, glancing through the peephole. He raised his eyebrows in surprise and threw the door open. "Damn, I didn't know you moonlighted as a cleaner."

Kyle smiled back and shrugged. "Tony sent me after your call. What the hell did you do?"

"Killed an informant and the cop she was feeding information to." He led Kyle down the hall to the den and opened the door to the mess that once was Desiree.

Kyle let his eyes graze over her perfect form and huffed. "Such a waste." He looked around the room. "You said there were witnesses?"

"My lawyer and his fiancé. They won't talk."

"Why are you so sure they won't talk?"

"He's my lawyer."

"And her?"

"She's marrying my lawyer in a couple of weeks."

He nodded and turned toward the body in the corner. "Where's the trash from the party?"

Charlie shrugged. The servant staff started cleaning after the last person left. He told them this room was fine and left the door locked.

Kyle turned toward Charlie. "Go find out. We want this to go into the incinerator at the same time. Where's the cop?"

"In his car on the street."

"Did you use your gun to kill him?"

Charlie smiled and shook his head. "I used the gun I gave my lawyer for Christmas."

"Sweet. Now go get me a large trash bag."

Charlie left the room and Kyle focused on the broken blonde on the floor. Bending her into a garbage bag might be problematic, but as he looked around the room, the roll of Christmas ribbon that sat on the side table caught his attention. "That just might do," he said aloud and began the tedious task of making her the size of a tight one-hundred-and-forty-pound abdominal ball.

She went in the service elevator to the incinerator with the rest of the garbage and Kyle fed each bag in, watching as all the trash turned to dust. He stripped the mechanical suit and donned a bathrobe he had in the last garbage bag. The last of the evidence burned quickly, and he took the elevator back upstairs. The sunrise was beginning and all over the city, children were waking their parents, excitedly reporting that Santa had come.

Vengeance
Chapter 42

STEVE WOKE AROUND TEN with Jennifer lying on his numb arm. He pushed her off and climbed out of bed, heading into the bathroom to strip off the clothes along with the hideous thoughts and images from the prior night. The warm stream felt good on his skin, and he hung his head, letting the water pulse on his neck. He pulled a deep breath into his lungs and held it for a moment before letting it out.

He stepped out of the shower and dressed. Heading for the kitchen, he whipped up her favorite breakfast: strawberry crepes.

He sat down at the table at the same time she came out of the bathroom, dressed in stretchy jeans and an oversized sweater. She met his gaze, crossing the room and sliding into the seat across from him.

"Merry Christmas." He waited until she took a bite of her crepes. "I need to go out for a little while."

She raised her bloodshot eyes. "On Christmas?" Her chin quivered.

He nodded. "I have to get something from the office, and we can open the gifts when I get back, okay?" He stood up and put his empty dishes in the sink. "I won't be long. Lock the deadbolt behind me."

HE STOOD IN HIS office, scanning the contents with a sigh. There was nothing he wanted to take with him, nothing but the mock wedding gift and the full vial of powder sitting in the top drawer. Unlocking the desk, he opened the lower drawer, pulling out the black velvet box. He flipped it open and sighed at the sparkling diamonds. Diamonds he paid for with some of the unreported, under the table cash Charlie gave him. A nugget of guilt laced his mouth, as bitter as spoiled milk. This wasn't the primary reason for coming to the office, and he knew it.

He slid the top-drawer open and pocketed the vial of cocaine, still staring at the necklace. With a sigh, he snapped the box closed and headed out. "God, I hope this makes Christmas better," he said as the elevator doors closed on the office.

Back home, he unlocked the deadbolt and swung the door open, stepping inside empty handed, the box tucked under his arm out of sight.

Jennifer's reaction was instant irritation. "What was so important at the office? Your last stash of drugs?"

He counted to ten before he turned his back to her and reached under the sweater. The velvet box appeared as if by magic and he set it on the middle of the kitchen table. "This was *supposed* to be your wedding gift, but I figured we both could use a Merry Christmas."

"Oh." Her voice softened, and she looked at the box.

He sat down at the table, and she sat across from him.

Steve offered a smile. "I love you, Jen." He pushed the box toward her.

Her chin quivered, and her hands shook as much as they had in Charlie's den. She reached for the box and gasped when she opened the top. The diamond eternity necklace sparkled on the black velvet. Her hand fluttered to her mouth and her wide green eyes shot up to his. "Oh, Steve, my gift is lame compared to this," she said from behind her hand.

He chuckled, moved around the side of the table, and pulled her into his arms. "I couldn't care less about what you got me for Christmas. I'm just glad you're here with me." He kissed the top of her head.

She looked up at him with a nod, blinking back tears. "When we get home, we can talk about what happened, but for now, I'd like to pretend that neither of us crossed the line. I want our happy marriage back for the next couple of days, okay?"

Steve nodded. For her, he could do that. For her, he would do anything.

Vengeance
Chapter 43

STEVE STOOD INSIDE THE back wing of the theater. His heart hammered in his chest, and he scanned the chaos backstage. "You sure you've got a safe place for Jen?"

"Yes, I'm sure," Jack said. "I'll call when we get there."

"Thank you," he said, but apprehension still bit at the surface of his skin, and he wouldn't settle down until that call came in. He turned to the woman standing next to him. "Are you ready?"

Carson Freeman, a petite brunette who could pass as Jennifer from a distance, nodded. "Yes, sir."

Jennifer, having donned a blonde wig and a flannel jacket, approached them. She stopped in front of Steve with green eyes carved with worry. She tilted her head.

"I know. I'll be careful," he said before she could talk. He leaned in and gave her a soft kiss. "You're in good hands." He glanced at Jack and then back at her.

"When will I see you?"

"In a couple of days."

She nodded and wrapped her arms around him.

Her heart beat so hard he felt it against his chest. "It will be okay, I promise," he whispered in her ear. "I love you, babe."

"I love you, too." She stepped out the door with Jack.

Steve stood in the wings for another twenty minutes, with Carson standing by his side. He neither saw nor heard the surrounding commotion. His mind was with Jennifer, and he hoped his silent prayers would be heard.

"You about ready?" Carson asked, bringing him back to the present.

He nodded and helped put the scarf over her head. He led her out into the alley and to his car that was parked on the road in plain sight of Manny. The familiar tail followed them home and parked outside the building.

"You can sleep on the bed; I'll crash on the couch," he said as they entered the apartment.

Carson changed and snuggled under the covers while he stretched out in his clothes, staring at the ceiling.

"She'll be all right. Jack's with her."

"I know," he said, glancing over at Carson. "Thanks."

"No problem."

He continued to stare at the ceiling, mulling over the scenarios that could happen the next day, from the easiest outcome to the worst. Nothing he imagined could have prepared him for what actually happened on that unseasonably warm December morning.

Vengeance
Chapter 44

JENNIFER STARED AT THE passing scenery in silence, chewing on her lower lip.

"Everything will be fine," Jack said. Her emerald eyes swung his way.

"I'm not sure I know what fine is anymore," she admitted. "Not with everything that's happened."

Jack glanced at her.

Jennifer sighed, and silence filled the car again. She looked out the passenger window. "I wasn't any better than Steve was."

The admission shocked Jack enough that his hands jerked on the wheel. The car followed suit on the road. "Does Steve know?"

"Yeah."

"Someone at the theater?"

"Charlie."

This time, the swerve was more severe, and Jack sent a sideways glance at Jennifer. He almost turned the car around, but he'd promised to get Jennifer to safety. "Change in plans," Jack said as he pulled onto the Mass Turnpike and glanced at her. "Just in case."

She swallowed and nodded. "It was a big mistake. Charlie showed me a video of Steve and Desiree and… and things got out of hand."

Jack listened and drove. *The bastard had a tape? God, Steve, I hope to hell this doesn't blow up in our faces.* "Does Steve know it was Charlie?"

"Yeah. He got the full viewing, just like I did."

"When?"

"Christmas Eve. It all happened Christmas Eve."

Jack blew the air out of his lungs. That was the same night they witnessed Desiree's murder. "Holy shit."

"Made for a really shitty Christmas this year. You have no idea how much I hate Steve's job right now." She glanced at him.

"Steve's the best I have," he said. "The very best. For ten years, we've been trying to take Charlie Wisnowski down. Umpteen agents ended up like that girl. Steve's the only one who's ever gotten this close." He took a breath. "I know you hate what he's done on this case, but it's been necessary."

"So, are you telling me getting a blowjob in my kitchen was necessary?"

Jack glanced in her direction and shrugged. "I wasn't there. I can't say whether it was a screw-up or if he knew about the tape and played a part." He shook his head. "Under normal circumstances, he wouldn't be caught dead crossing the line. The man loves you, so you've got to take that into consideration."

"Can we change the subject?"

"Sure." Jack didn't want to talk about this either. He had an uneasy feeling about the entire operation now. He hoped like hell Steve would heed his orders and stay away, but after the information he was just fed, he doubted that would be the case. A sharp inhale from Jennifer caught his attention, and he glanced her way.

Her pasty skin met his gaze and her eyes, her eyes, were cloudy and distant. She looked like a breathing, muttering corpse, and he shivered. *Jesus, she's having a vision. Steve was right. It is scary as hell.*

WITH A BLINK, THE interior of the car disappeared.

A gurgling wail filled the room as he pressed the blade against her throat. "Oh, yeah," he whispered in her ear. Adrenaline pumped through his veins, her fear and pain fueling him to the point he craved. The knife sliced through the tender flesh of her throat, sending an arc of blood onto the bed. The force of it splattered all the way to the ceiling. The tremors that followed brought him close to release, but then the feeling fizzled, replaced by rage and frustration.

"No!" The roar echoed off the walls. He pulled out of her and plunged the knife into her back, severing the spinal cord. Closing his eyes tight, he stroked his throbbing member, playing a fantasy, a fantasy of the woman who got away, finishing what he started, savoring it, having her every way possible before tearing the life from her piece by piece and relishing her cries for mercy, mercy that would never come.

Jennifer breathed in as if she'd been underwater for the last five minutes. Heat rushed into her face and the car spun. "Pull over," she whispered.

Jack transitioned to the breakdown lane, stopping as the wheels crunched gravel.

As soon as the car stopped, she threw the door open. The vomit splattered on the gravel and speckled the inside of the door. She spit a few times. "Do you have any napkins?"

"In the glove box."

She opened the glove compartment and pulled out a couple of napkins, wiping her mouth before cleaning the door. "I'm sorry." She closed the door.

"Are you all set?"

Jennifer nodded, and Jack pulled the car back on the road.

"Another vision?"

"He's going to kill again tonight."

"I gathered. Can you tell me anything more about him than the tattoo and knife?"

"No, that's all I ever see besides the victim."

"Tell me about her."

"Dark hair, fair skin, almond-shaped blue eyes and she is terrified."

Jack inhaled. "With good reason."

Jennifer closed her eyes. "Yes. He's no longer in control. There is no sense of seduction before he kills them, now it's just fury."

Jack raised his eyebrows, glancing sideways at Jennifer. "What do you mean, *seduction*?"

She opened her eyes and looked at him. "Before, he played with them, was always calm and rational, making them undress themselves and get into the position he wanted on the bed. It was a seduction of sorts and that's part of what fuels him, brings him that high. It isn't there anymore, which means he's much more dangerous and unpredictable."

Jack's jaw hung open, and he blinked, looking out at the thinning traffic. "Your assessment parallels that of the profile we were given early on. You sure you don't want a job as a profiler?"

Jennifer burst out laughing. "Yes, very sure. This insight has nothing to do with studying patterns and ways that he acts out his aggression. I'm partially in the bastard's head and it freaks me out. I can't imagine intentionally putting myself in that space and that's what profilers do, correct?"

"In a manner of speaking, yes." Jack took the exit ramp and turned right onto a suburban area north of Boston. "What do you think triggered the change?"

She was quiet and when he pulled into the driveway of a modest colonial; she glanced at him. "I triggered the change."

Jack considered the possibility and grabbed the suitcase out of the back seat.

"Where are we?"

"My house." He led her inside.

Vengeance
Chapter 45

"WHAT DO YOU MEAN?" Steve held the phone to his ear, staring at Carson. "I'm on my way." He flipped the phone closed. "The shit just hit the fan." He didn't wait for a response, just took off out the door, leaving Carson with the new bodyguard Charlie had sent over.

"Steve!" Carson yelled from the doorway.

He turned toward her. "Stay put, Jen." And with that, he bounded down the stairs and across the street to his car. He slipped his badge and gun out from under the seat, sliding them into his coat pocket, and tore out of the garage, wheels spinning on the wet pavement as he took the turn into the morning fog, heading toward Brooklyn.

A crowd had already formed, blocking the route he wanted to take. "Shit," Steve swore. He pulled into a free parking spot and flipped open his ringing cell phone.

"Whatever you do, do not go into the warehouse!"

He looked at the phone and brought it to his ear. "Jenny?"

"Do not go inside. Please promise me."

Her voice was scratchy and strained, and he thought he heard a slight wheeze to boot. "Jenny, what's wrong?"

"If you go inside, he'll kill you. He knows."

Steve looked up at the crowd in front of him. "Where are you?"

"I'm safe. I'm at Jack's house."

He closed his eyes. He had slept through the call, but Jack had left a message that she was safe and sound. "How does Charlie know?"

"I have no clue—but he does and if you go in there, I'll be a widow."

He exhaled. "I won't go in."

"Promise me!"

"I promise, Jenny, I will not set foot in that warehouse."

The muffled sniffle came through the line. "I love you," her hoarse voice whispered.

"Me, too. I gotta go." He flipped the phone closed and stepped out of his car.

Steve fought his way through the crowd.

An officer stopped him at the barricade and he reached into his inner pocket, pulling out his FBI badge. After an inquiry into his walkie-talkie, the officer waved him through.

Vengeance
Chapter 46

CHARLIE ROCKED IN HIS chair at his desk in his office with the six girls from downstairs sitting on the floor within his field of view. The police had taken out the outside cameras after the explosion rocked the warehouse. The workers panicked, and pandemonium broke out to the point Charlie shut off the secondary defenses.

Under false pretense of safety, he corralled six of the office girls in his control room. With a gun trained on them, he tossed each girl a pair of handcuffs and watched as they clasped one end around their wrists and the other to the exposed heating pipes low on the wall. Littered across his desk were half a dozen handguns, a shotgun, and a large bag of cocaine, and he settled into a long morning of negotiations.

After securing the girls to the radiator, he ventured downstairs and set more explosives on a trip wire near the door in case the police were stupid enough to try again. With that, he grabbed a couple of automatic weapons and headed back to the office, re-engaging the perimeter and the floor panel sensors.

His first call was to Steve. He wanted a lawyer present and while Steve wasn't a criminal lawyer; he was sure he could negotiate a fair deal and maybe even help him walk away from this.

A half hour had passed, and the first contact had already been made by the feds. Charlie told them to go pound sand. If they didn't get him a helicopter out of there, he was going to kill the hostages, one every hour. His cell rang, and he flipped it open.

Pictures. *What the fuck?*

Charlie glanced at the girls and opened the first message. His heart tripped, skipping a beat or two. The screen filled with a picture of Steve handing a badge to the cop at the barricade.

Maybe he asked for the cop's credentials.

He blinked and scrolled to the next picture and his cheeks burned with instant anger.

Steve pocketed his badge and was waved through the barricade.

"Son of a bitch." He flipped through the remaining photos, all of which confirmed that the bastard was a cop. *Fucking MOLE!*

"God damn it!" *If Steve thought he would get away from this unscathed, he was sorely mistaken.*

Charlie punched in a text message to the new bodyguard. "Kill the bitch."

A few minutes later, "Done" appeared in his message box. Charlie smiled and looked up at the girls.

"We've got a long day ahead of us." He poured a small amount from the bag and cut it into lines, snorting them while nervously flicking the hammer back and forth on the gun.

Vengeance
Chapter 47

STEVE CROUCHED BEHIND THE car as the bullets whizzed past him. His heart pounded so hard he could almost hear the rattling against his ribs, and he couldn't produce saliva no matter how hard he tried. Bullets rained down around him, and all he wished for was a simple bottle of water.

He exchanged a glance with Jerry, shaking his head as Charlie's ranting drifted through the cloud of gun smoke. The raging artillery masked the metal clang of the warehouse door.

Steve's ears rang, and quiet descended on the street. He cast a quick glance over the hood. Charlie had retreated into the warehouse with the wounded hostage.

Sitting on the pavement, hidden from view, he leaned his head back against the tire, squinting as the early afternoon sunshine peeked through the skyscrapers. The mixture of rubber, oil, and gun smoke assaulted his nostrils, and he sneezed three times in succession.

His cell phone rang again, and he checked the number. Closing his eyes, he flipped it open.

"What the hell are you doing?" This was the fourth call Charlie had made to him since he'd arrived, and each conversation was the same.

"Get your ass in here," Charlie growled into the phone.

"Look, Charlie, they won't let anyone within a couple of blocks of the building and honestly, I'm not so keen on the idea anymore." He faked exasperation, keeping eye contact with Jerry, who was sitting on the pavement next to him.

"Why aren't you keen on coming in?"

"Look, you've killed hostages. I am not interested in dying today and I have a feeling if I went inside, that's exactly what would happen."

"You don't think you could negotiate your way out of this one?"

Steve looked at his partner and raised his eyebrow. "I'm not a criminal lawyer, Charlie. That's really what you need." He was quiet for a moment. The beginning of a headache had formed behind his right eye, and he pressed his thumb on his temple to quiet the throbbing. The telltale sniff filled the other end of the line, and he closed his eyes. "How many lines have you done?"

A sinister chuckled bled through the line. "Wouldn't you like to know?"

"If you let them go…"

He cut him off. "If I let them go, what? You think I don't know what will happen? You think I'm dumb?"

"I never said that."

"But you must have thought it plenty of times, snowing me like you did."

"What are you talking about?"

Charlie hung up the phone and seconds later, a photo came through on Steve's display.

He was handing his badge to the cop at the barricade. Steve swiveled the display, showing Jerry the photo. Jennifer had been right, yet again. Someone had recognized him in the crowd and now he had no negotiation room. He closed his eyes and rested his forehead on his arm. When the phone rang again, he opened it.

"Let me ask you a question," Charlie began. He chuckled and the sound of more cocaine filtering up his nose came over the line. "How does it feel to know I felt up your girlfriend?"

Steve was silent.

"Was she even your girlfriend?" he asked. "Or was she part of the show?"

"Jenny's my wife." He had no reason to keep up the pretense. "We were married in November of last year."

Charlie snickered. "That's even better." Laughter belted through the line. "And now you're a widower."

"What are you talking about?"

"You're responsible for your wife's death. How does that feel?"

Steve closed his eyes. He had left Carson with one of Charlie's people. "You ordered a hit on my wife?" he growled into the phone, exchanging a glance with Jerry.

"That's right. You've got a mess to go home to."

"Bastard!"

"Why don't you come in and we can snort some blow and see who's a faster draw?"

"Let the hostages go."

The line went dead. Steve stared at the phone in frustration. Charlie hung up on him.

"Get someone over to my apartment." He redialed the phone. Jerry pulled out his cell and made a call.

When Charlie answered the phone, he said, "Charlie, do you really think I'm that stupid?"

"You think I'm bluffing?"

It was his turn to laugh. "I'm betting you're bluffing. You have a thing for my Jenny, don't you?"

"I had a thing for Desiree, too."

The laughter died in his throat and Jerry shook his head, conveying that what Charlie had told him was true with one exception; Carson was the one who was dead, not Jennifer.

"You really think *I'm* that stupid, Charlie?" he asked again.

Charlie was silent.

"You think for a minute I'd leave my wife in the care of one of your psychos?"

More silence.

"It wasn't my wife you killed."

"Fucking cop!"

"Actually, I'm with the FBI and if you don't let the hostages go, you won't be leaving here alive."

Jerry made a frantic cutting motion. This was not the protocol for hostage negotiation.

"I'm going to kill you," Charlie said.

He laughed. "It'll be a cold day in hell before that happens. I outsmarted you at every turn, Charlie, admit it. You got lucky today. Someone recognized me and snapped a picture. Without that, you would have never known it was me. You would have died here today, never knowing who infiltrated your organization. How does that make *you* feel?"

He held the phone away from his ear. Charlie's scream of rage was in stereo, acute and clear through the cell phone and muffled through the closed office window. Steve heard the clang through the receiver and a shot rang out, sending high-pitched feedback through the phone line and cutting off the only connection he had to Charlie.

"Fuck!" He closed his cell phone and leaned back, watching as the officers scrambled around.

"That was a stupid move!" Jerry reloaded his gun and slid it into his holster, peeking around the car.

"Charlie was tipped off," he mumbled, checking his watch. "Someone sent him that photo of me, but I have no fucking clue who's feeding him the information." He sighed and pushed his palms to his eyes. He glanced at his watch again. Fifty-five minutes had passed, and they still hadn't found a way in.

Like clockwork, another body fell out of the small office window on the second floor of the warehouse. It bounced lifelessly on the pavement next to where the last victim had landed, blood splattered from the impact.

Screams filtered out the window, echoing off the buildings. They were abruptly muffled as the windowpane slammed closed.

Steve closed his eyes in frustration. A low grumble rose from his chest. "We have to do something!"

"If we go in there, he'll blow the entire block to bits."

He gritted his teeth and banged the back of his head lightly on the tire. Inaction was driving him batty. He wanted to get up and pace, but that wasn't an option.

"Then let me go in and take him down." The words spit out between his clenched teeth.

"We can't do that," Jerry said.

"We have to do something," he insisted, getting to his feet.

Jerry pulled him back down. "Sit tight," he ordered. "You shouldn't even be here. It's bad enough that Charlie knows who you are. If the news crew gets your face on camera, your undercover career is over." Jerry glared at Steve. Jack had been clear when he found out Steve was on site. Protect his identity. As the day wore on, that was getting increasingly difficult, and Steve refused to leave.

Gunfire erupted inside the warehouse, followed by a muffled shriek. Another burst of gunfire cut off the rogue screams.

The silence on the street was unnerving, and the officers glanced at the building, trying to determine whether any of the hostages were still alive.

Steve peered over the car toward the quiet warehouse and sat back down. His eyes drifted to Charlie's punked-out SUV close to a hundred feet behind them and the police barricade blocking the crowd a few hundred yards beyond the car. They were the only officers guarding Charlie's vehicle. The rest were flanked outside the warehouse entrance, keeping watch in case he made a run for it.

Steve exchanged a glance with Jerry. The futility of the situation was visible in his partner's eyes.

"It's not your fault, Steve. Sometimes the best laid plans turn to shit."

He leaned his head back on the tire and closed his eyes. They snapped open to a ruckus behind them.

What was left of the warehouse door banged open and Charlie charged with guns roaring in both hands.

Steve glanced to his left in time to see a gunshot annihilate an officer's shoulder. The screams broke out as a couple of officers were hit by Charlie's assault. Charlie dodged between containers lining the side of the warehouse, weaving in and out as he sprayed the cops with gunfire. A few bullets hit him, but they were not enough to stop his drug-induced rampage. He headed toward his truck.

"Jesus Christ!" Jerry cried. He jumped to his feet and got a shot off, but it went wide. He let out a yell of frustration. "Fu..."

Jerry didn't get the full syllable out before a bullet ripped the top of his head off. He fell dead on the pavement next to Steve.

Anger filled Steve, and he shot to his feet, swiveling in Charlie's direction with his gun drawn. Their eyes locked.

Charlie shot at him, but the bullet sailed wide. "Son of a bitch!" He roared and took another shot.

Ignorant of the bullet that whizzed through his sleeve, leaving a thin trail of blood where it tore his skin, Steve scrunched his face with fury. He trained his sight between Charlie's eyes and pulled the trigger.

Charlie went down. The bullet penetrated the bridge of his nose right between his eyes and blew a hole the size of a coke bottle out of the back of his head, spattering the side of the warehouse with red and gray matter. He was almost certainly dead before he hit the pavement.

Steve lowered his gun, glancing down at his partner. He blinked back the sudden wave of nausea and leaned down, putting his fingers to Jerry's neck just to make sure there was no pulse. He closed his partner's eyes and let out a long, shaky breath.

He stood, pushing the grief away and shifted into autopilot, drinking in the details around him as his training demanded. He put the gun in his holster and looked at the torn material of his shirt. Blood seeped into the fabric from the flesh wound.

His eyes rose, taking in the crowd of officers gathering around Charlie. The SWAT team and bomb squad enter the warehouse through the same door Charlie had come out of. No further gunshots or explosions greeted them.

Steve closed his eyes and hung his head for a moment as the day's events slammed a mixture of grief and guilt into him. With a shaky breath, he turned in time to see the media sharks capturing his face on camera.

His undercover career was officially over.

"Damn," he whispered, and turned away from the scene.

Vengeance
Chapter 48

STEVE SAT IN THE office at his lakeside cottage, staring at pictures of the latest victim.

Three months.

Three months since the warehouse incident. Three months since Charlie's autopsy confirmed the tattoo on his right forearm matched Jennifer's drawing, and the DNA comparison revealed enough similarities to close the Slasher Case, despite both his and Jennifer's arguments.

Three months of nothing.

Until last week.

Last week, Jennifer had another vision and a couple of days later, a body showed up in Los Angeles with the same M.O. as the early Slasher cases. The kicker, the DNA matched perfectly. This wasn't a copycat. This was the real deal, and the bastard had his sadistic control back.

"Damn it, they should have listened to us," he muttered. Steve closed down his computer and stepped into the living room where Jennifer lounged on the couch watching television. "How're you doing?"

She shrugged, and her eyes landed on the crystal eagle. "Why did you bring that back?"

"Because." He swung his gaze toward the figure. He couldn't articulate why he'd brought it home with the rest of their things. It was a constant reminder of Charlie and the lives lost over the holiday, and it kept him from finishing the last vial of cocaine that sat in his desk drawer.

"Because why?"

He turned toward Jennifer. "It keeps me honest."

Her gaze shifted between him and the eagle. "Really?"

Nodding, he said, "Yeah." Taking a seat next to her on the couch, he focused on picking a hangnail from his thumb. "We never talked about... you know."

"The fact we both screwed up?"

Steve nodded and continued to avoid eye contact.

"I'm sorry."

"I'm not asking for an apology, Jen." He glanced up at her. "I'm trying to understand how..." He trailed off.

"How I could allow Charlie, of all people?"

"Yeah."

"Watching that video was devastating, Steve, and I didn't know it wasn't real."

He snorted. He knew exactly what she was talking about.

"I'm serious."

"I know. I wasn't discounting that. I was agreeing with you. Seeing the video of you and Charlie... I'm surprised I didn't kill him when he came into the room."

Jennifer bit her lip. "Did you have a choice at the warehouse?"

The question ruffled his feathers, but it was a question he asked himself day after day. Yes, Charlie was shooting at him and killed more than a dozen people that day, but was that it?

Was that the only reason he planted a bullet in Charlie's brain?

"If I didn't kill him, he would have killed me." He sighed, feeling the weight of all those deaths on his shoulders.

"Well, I, for one, am glad you won't be doing undercover work anymore."

"Yeah, well." He stopped, knowing she didn't want to hear how much losing that work stung. Profiling wasn't as adrenaline inducing as being in the thick of things where one wrong move could mean life or death. That rush was as addictive as the cocaine, and he missed it. Despite the death toll at the warehouse, the executives in both the FBI and DEA marked it as a monumental accomplishment, but he didn't see it that way. Too many innocent people died, and they died because he screwed up.

"You weren't responsible for what happened," she said, accurately reading the blame in his expression.

He raised his eyes to hers and shrugged. "If I hadn't gone to the scene..."

Jennifer cut him off. "If this, if that; stop with the shoulda-coulda-woulda shit. You did the best you could with how things turned out. Even if Charlie hadn't been sent that picture, those women would have died. And maybe more agents would have bitten it. If someone triggered the explosives when they were running out of the building, the entire block would have vaporized. Please don't do this to yourself."

"But..."

"No, Steve. Don't. You blamed yourself for what happened to me here because you couldn't stop it. I know for months you turned that over in your head, thinking of what you could have done differently. Don't let this eat you up inside, too."

It was a little too late for that. "But I screwed up this one."

"No, you didn't. Charlie called and asked you to come down to the scene as his lawyer. Maybe if you had hung back behind the barricades, things would have been different, and he would have never known you were with the FBI." She reached out and turned his face toward her. "But he still would have killed those people."

"Carson and Jerry would have lived."

"Jerry was still between the warehouse and Charlie's car. You can't take the blame for his death." She kept eye contact with him. "You know, maybe you should have kept those sessions with the psychiatrist."

"I don't need a shrink."

Jennifer lifted her eyebrows.

"I don't!" He stood and crossed to the window, looking out at the dark lake. "What I need is a vacation."

"I hear ya." She crossed the room, taking his hand and placing it on her belly.

Steve's attention shot from the lake to the small thump on his hand, their entire conversation forgotten when he felt one of the baby's kick. She had been complaining that they were getting more active, but this felt like a game-winning field goal. "Damn." He glanced up at her. "I felt that."

Jennifer smiled. "I hope they have your eyes." She leaned up and kissed him.

"I'm partial to green myself."

She blushed and looked down at his hand, stroking her stomach.

His gaze snapped to her face when her sharp inhale broke the hypnotic awe of the tiny kicking figure within her belly. Her eyes glazed over in the opaque film of a vision, what Jack had referred to as the death mask, and he shivered, waiting for the mumbling to begin.

"IT ISN'T YOU HONEY. At one time it was, but now it's all about him."

She shivered despite the heat, and all she could think about was her baby. Fear kept her from fighting, and her gaze fell to the ornate tattoo on his forearm before dropping to the detonator clasped in his fist.

"Jennifer!"

His voice cut through the vision, and she exhaled. "Jesus." She took a shaky step. Then all went black.

Fingers tapped her cheeks, and his worry-laced voice filled her ears.

"Jenny? Wake up, babe."

Blinking, her eyes opened. She focused on the bedroom, and then his haunted blue eyes, and sat up despite her lightheadedness. The mattress creaked from the change in pressure and Steve shifted, cocking his head and waiting for her explanation.

"He finds me here."

"Who?"

"I'm not sure, but he has the same tattoo Charlie had." She shivered, looking at Steve.

"When?"

Jennifer's brow knit. "I'm wearing a summer nightgown, and I'm not pregnant anymore." She caught the nuance of surprise in his eyes, but his face remained neutral. Usually, her visions happened within a week or two from the time she had them. With the Slasher, it was within hours of the kill. The only other time she had something so far into the future was the day she drew the tattoo. "He's hunting us, Steve, and his sole purpose is to see you suffer."

This time, the surprise found its way into his features. His eyes went a little wider and his mouth opened a fraction before he regained composure. "Me?"

"Yes, and I'm just a vehicle in his sick game."

He stood and took a step back. "Why?"

All she could do was shrug.

He took a deep breath, his chest rising with his inhale and lowering with the exhale. "Okay. I just need to figure out who would want me to suffer."

"Is there a long list?"

He gave her a sideways look. "Long enough."

Vengeance
Chapter 49

HIDDEN BY THE THICK woods, Kyle blended into the dark shadows, staring at the house across the lake through his night vision goggles. The target and his wife stood in the living room window, and he hoisted the rifle to his shoulder.

Just as he lined the man up in the sights, recognition set in. Tony had ordered this hit, but never explained whom he was going after. Tony just gave him an address and said to take out everyone in the house. He focused on the sights again, moving the rifle from the man to the woman just as she swayed and passed out, falling out of view.

"Shit!" He lowered the rifle.

That's the bastard who killed Charlie.

He'd tried to find Steve Williams for the better part of two months when this assignment was thrown his way. He laughed aloud in the quiet night at the turn of events.

He took his goggles off and sat down on the muddy shoreline, mulling over what to tell Tony. He had no plans to carry out the hit just yet. He wanted the man across the lake to wish he had never survived to kill Charlie, or better yet, never been born.

He wanted to destroy everything that man cared about, and he needed time to execute his plan. He wanted Steve Williams begging for mercy.

Kyle smiled as he glanced around at the few houses he could see. The only home occupied at this time of year was Steve's. All the others were dark. He'd have to check out his hunch in the morning, but he could tell Tony no one was up here. That would buy him at least a few weeks to start his assault on the Williams homestead.

Vengeance
Chapter 50

THE FIRST SATURDAY IN April, Jennifer's usual nervous energy progressed to restlessness, alternating between cleaning the house and driving Steve nuts. He needed a change of scenery, and dinner out was just what the doctor ordered.

Steve led Jennifer into a quaint French restaurant and the maitre d' hurried over to greet them.

"Monsieur, Madame, welcome to Chez Paris." He pulled two menus from beneath the desk before leading them to their table.

"I'll be right back." She stood, heading toward the restrooms.

Steve reached for his water glass, diverting his eyes for an instant. Steve's gaze flew toward her gasp of shock, bouncing between her wide eyes and the puddle around her feet. It took an instant for the reality of the situation to sink in. He stood and went to her. "Come on." He took her arm and led her toward the front door. When the maitre d' approached, he smiled awkwardly. "We have to go." Steve walked out.

"It's too early," Jennifer sniffled and slid into the passenger seat.

Steve's heart pounded in his chest cavity, and he slid into the driver's seat, swallowing back his own bundled nerves and focusing on her. "Don't worry, babe, it's going to be all right." He turned the ignition and sped out of the parking lot, heading toward Brooksfield General Hospital.

"Holy crap!" Jennifer cried and curled into a ball in the passenger seat.

"Breathe through it, hon," he said calmly. Despite the sudden lurch of adrenaline hammering his pulse, he navigated the car expertly through the town. "Breathe, Jen." Then he panted with her like the Lamaze instructor had taught them. He shot glances in her direction as often as he dared, the high-speed hindering both his attention and his panting.

Her breathing slowed, and she uncurled, leaning into the back of the passenger seat. A light sheen of sweat stood out on her forehead.

"That's it." He took the sharp turn into the hospital parking lot and slammed to a stop, yanked the emergency brake, and turned the car off. He didn't realize he was still panting until he glanced in her direction. Her soft laugh escalated into a hysterical gale.

"Breathe, baby," he reminded her, and got out of the car. She was still laughing when he opened her car door. He leaned over and kissed her. "Stop laughing at me." He grinned and pulled away, guiding her into the hospital.

"You look ridiculous breathing like that," she replied after the nurse situated her in one of the maternity rooms and another contraction abated.

"You don't see me laughing at you," he countered and took a seat to complete the forms. He winked at her and turned his attention to filling out the mundane information. "Are you allergic to anything?" he asked, looking up at her.

"Labor," she replied with a smile, which immediately faded with the next contraction.

Steve put the paperwork down and sat on the side of the bed, breathing with her again. He broke out into a smile as he saw the laughter in her eyes and heard it in her breathing.

"Hurts like hell."

Steve shrugged a little. "We've been through worse."

The humor in Jennifer's eyes died, and a shadow passed over them. She offered a slight nod as her breathing returned to normal.

Steve glanced at his watch. *Damn.* "I'll be right back." He hurried into the hall and grabbed the first nurse he could find. "My wife's contractions are less than three minutes apart." He glanced at his watch and knew she would be hit with another one in no time. "Please, can you send a doctor in to look at her?" He didn't wait for an answer, but shot back to the room, stopping for a moment to take a deep breath and gather himself before he entered. Jennifer didn't need to see the anxiety lacing his blood.

Raspy pants came from the opened door, and he crossed the room.

"Don't leave again," she managed to say between pants.

He sat next to her on the bed and took her hand. "I won't. I was just checking to see when the doctor was coming to take a look at you." As if on cue, their obstetrician walked into the room.

"Good evening, Jennifer." Dr. Schneider flipped open her medical chart.

Jennifer panted through the next contraction. "Early, we're too early," she breathed.

Dr. Schneider looked up. "Twins tend to come early." He stepped next to her and moved the sheets over. "Let's see how far you've progressed," he said as he slipped on a pair of medical gloves. He looked under the sheet between her legs and slid his gloved hand out of view.

Nodding, he pulled his hand out and stripped the glove off, making a notation on the chart. "I'll be back to check on you in a little while."

Before Steve could ask when, Jennifer interrupted with a groan.

Curling into a ball on the bed, she gasped and cried, "Something's not right!"

The doctor did an about face and pulled the strip on the fetal monitor. Concern passed over Dr. Schneider's features, taking his smile and turning it into a grimace. He dropped the end of the bed and positioned himself between Jennifer's legs, examining her further.

Steve caught the look that passed between doctor and nurse, and his already hammering heart jumped into his throat. "Is everything all right?"

When Dr. Schneider removed his gloved hand, a gush of blood poured out of Jennifer, sending the doctor and nursing staff into action. The end of the bed jerked up and the locks on the wheels released. They pushed Jennifer's bed out of the birthing room and down to the operating room, with Steve sprinting alongside her.

The nurse stopped Steve at the entrance. "I'm sorry, Mr. Williams, but you can't be in the operating room."

"Bullshit." He tried to maneuver around the stout nurse. "That's my wife and children in there!" Jennifer's wail of pain came from behind the closed doors, fueling his need to be with her.

The nurse stood her ground. "You will only get in the way and the doctors don't need that kind of distraction right now," she stressed, blocking the operating room like a ferocious guard dog.

Steve shot his eyes from the operating room to the nurse, and what he saw in her face shut him down. He looked between the nurse and the operating room. "She is going to be okay, right?"

The nurse took a deep breath. "Your wife is hemorrhaging, Mr. Williams," she said, gaining his full attention. "Dr. Schneider is one of the best in the region. If anyone can save your wife and children, it's him." She took him back to the birthing room and left him to pace in angst.

Steve sat in the empty room in the maternity ward, staring at the blood on the floor, muttering, *"Please God"* over and over and over. His heart knocked against his ribs in an almost painful rhythm, echoing his less than silent mantra. It wasn't until Nurse Rottweiler walked in that he realized he'd been pleading aloud.

"Mr. Williams, you have a daughter. We have her in our neonatal unit right now." The nurse paused. "Did you have a name picked out?"

Relief washed over him. "Um, yeah, Samantha. Samantha Jayne," he answered. He raised his eyes, and the relief morphed into alarm at the sadness in the nurse's eyes. His mouth went dry, and he croaked out the first question, "What about her twin?"

The nurse shook her head.

The air rushed out of Steve's lungs, and he blinked. "My wife?"

"I will let you know just as soon as I hear anything," she replied. "In the meantime, I'll take you to your daughter."

He followed the nurse into the NICU; his chest hollow like someone had ripped a huge hole in the center of his being. He looked down at the small helpless baby in the crib. The tubes flowing from her nose brought her air. A small tube in her arm fed her nutrients, and wires were taped to her chest to monitor her heart rate. "Hey, Samantha," he whispered, and a tear slipped down his cheek, landing on his daughter's forehead, baptizing her with his pain and fear.

When the nurse walked in an hour later, Steve looked up. Her expression killed all hope. "Please tell me my wife is all right," he said, tears forming again.

"She's out of surgery and has been moved to our intensive care unit." She looked down at the tiny bundle in the crib and back up at him.

"When can I see her?"

"The doctor will be here in a few minutes, and he'll take you to see your wife," she said.

Steve nodded and looked down at his daughter. "Okay." He tried not to lose it in front of the nurse, but the tears rolled down his cheeks against his will.

Dr. Schneider walked in after what seemed like an eternity to find Steve still parked next to the crib, waiting. "I'm sorry, Mr. Williams. I wasn't able to save the second child."

"I know. The nurse told me that earlier." Steve stood, wiping his cheeks. "Can I please see Jen?"

"Mr. Williams, before I take you to your wife, I need to explain the extent of her condition."

Steve sat down again, numbness settling over his limbs as he waited for the worst.

"Your wife was touch and go for a while. She lost a great deal of blood and the only option we had to stop the hemorrhaging was to perform a hysterectomy. We believe she's out of danger now, but will keep a close eye on her for the next twelve hours."

He stared at the doctor, digesting his words, and then his gaze fell on his daughter. "She's the only child we'll have?"

Dr. Schneider nodded. "And I would prefer to wait until Jennifer's out of danger before I tell her the extent of the damage." When Steve nodded agreement, Dr. Schneider led the way to the recovery room in the ICU.

Steve sat next to Jennifer and took her hand. Her face was slack and neutral under the influence of the anesthesia and tubes ran from her arms, bringing her the blood and hydration she needed. He put his head down on her hand. Unmanageable relief flowed through his body, turning his muscles to a mass of trembling flesh.

"Thank God."

JENNIFER'S EYES FLUTTERED OPEN, and she glanced around in confusion until her eyes fell on Steve. He looked like hell, hair disheveled, stubble creating a dark shadow on his cheeks and chin, and puffy bloodshot eyes rimmed with dark circles. The last thing she remembered was hearing him yelling outside the operating room door.

"The babies?" she croaked.

"Samantha's in the neonatal unit." He wiped his eyes.

She nodded, waiting for word on Samantha's twin.

His mouth opened and closed in succession.

"What about Jasmine?"

Steve inhaled. "We lost the second baby."

What did he just say? She scrunched her eyebrows, trying to understand the words he said, but with the drugs still filling her mind with haze, she couldn't grasp it. "What?"

"She didn't make it, honey." His eyes filled with tears, and he blinked, driving them out and down his cheeks.

The depth of sorrow reflecting in his eyes spoke volumes. "We lost a baby?"

"Yes."

The confirmation was potent as a physical blow and her chin trembled, her breath locked in her chest and her vision wobbled. The drug haze dissipated, leaving her hollow and devastated. "I'm so sorry." Tears spilled as fast as they appeared.

"Awe, babe, it's not your fault." He wiped the tears off her cheeks.

"I knew something was wrong. I felt it."

"Sweetheart, there was nothing either of us could have done."

"You need to rest now. Your body has had quite a trauma." Dr. Schneider stepped out of the shadows and picked up her wrist, taking her pulse.

The need to see her daughter, to hold her, to make sure she was real and healthy struck like an eighteen-wheeler plowing through a stray fawn on the highway. "When can I see Samantha?"

"She's in the neonatal unit, in intensive care." Steve said, clarifying his earlier comment.

Fear, more potent than even the attack at the apartment, gripped her heart. "Is she okay?"

"She's got a hell of a fight ahead of her," he answered before the doctor could.

Jennifer nodded and sniffled, bringing fresh oxygen through her nose while she wiped away her tears. "I want to see her. When can I see my daughter?" she asked again. This time, Steve looked up at Doctor Schneider for the answer.

"Hopefully we'll be able to release you from the ICU in the morning, and then you can see her," the doctor answered. "But for now, you need to rest and your husband needs to tend to your daughter."

Steve leaned over and kissed her. "I love you, Jen." He stood and followed the doctor out of the room.

BACK IN THE NICU, Steve sat in the rocking chair and looked at the pleasant colors painted on the walls, countering the depressing sight of his daughter struggling for her life. She was the only child in the NICU. Steve looked at his watch. It was almost five in the morning. Twelve hours had elapsed since Jennifer's water broke and close to eleven hours since he was given news of Samantha and her doomed twin. He pulled out his phone and dialed a familiar number.

"Hey, Jack," he said, his voice reflecting the exhaustion saturating his muscles. "Sorry to wake you." Steve closed his eyes. "We have a daughter."

"Twin girls?" Jack asked groggily.

"No, just one, and she's in the NICU." His answer was met with silence.

"Is Jennifer all right?"

"There were complications." He closed his mouth, pressing his lips together against the sudden quell of emotion. When he finally spoke again, his voice shook. "She almost died, Jack."

"Is she going to make it?"

He looked at the ceiling. "Yes, but she can't have any more kids."

"You want me to call anyone for you, Steve?"

"Thanks, but no. I've got to call the folks."

"If things change, let me know," Jack said.

"I will." He flipped the phone closed and leaned his head back on the soft cushion as the stress of the night bled out of him. His eyelids drooped, and he closed them for just a moment.

Vengeance
Chapter 51

KYLE STUDIED THE HOUSE on the lake. There was no barrier to preventing a water attack, but that might not be the best route in. Too many windows faced the lake and that would offer anyone inside a warning that a stranger was approaching. There were too many turns in the driveway and the distance between the last bend and the house was substantial enough to give warning to the occupants if they were looking in that direction, especially if the vehicle used made a distinct noise like the rundown Chevy Nova he bought for this gig. But the driveway could be effective if he were to enter on a bicycle that could be hidden in the lush woods.

He smiled as he slipped into the car and turned on the ignition. The old clunker roared to life, and he headed toward the house to scope it out. He knew they were still at the hospital, and from his inquiries, he knew it would be at least another day before they came home. Erring on the side of caution, he pulled over to the side of the dirt driveway just beyond the last curve and walked the remainder of the way.

He surveyed the distance between the opening and the wood line where the driveway opened up into the yard. Estimating it was roughly one hundred yards to the front door; he set the timer and sprinted to it. He checked his watch and nodded in satisfaction. It had only taken him twelve seconds to sprint the distance of a football field. When he peered in the side window, he could see all the way to the other side of the house. He tried the door and wasn't surprised to find the knob resistant. He pulled a small kit from his pocket and seconds later; the knob turned easily in his hand. Kyle slipped his shoes off on the front porch and stepped inside.

He took his time walking through the house, memorizing the layout and forming his plan of attack. He stood in the bedroom for ages, looking out at the lake. Turning slowly, he glanced at the bed itself and then to the nightstand at Steve and Jennifer's wedding photo. He walked over and picked up the frame, looking at the photograph. She was as beautiful then as she was in the play last fall. He glanced at the bed again and a sadistic smile spread over his face.

I'll definitely be having a little fun before I kill her.

Slipping on his shoes, he shut the door and walked back to the car. He tossed the keys in the air and caught them, whistling as he went. He had some supplies to pick up. He wanted to catch her there with the babies and work them over before Steve came home. He chuckled, thinking of the bastard's reaction, and slipped behind the wheel of the car.

Vengeance
Chapter 52

"WHAT DO YOU MEAN there won't be any more kids?" Jennifer's gaze shot between the doctor, Steve, and the little bundle in the neonatal crib.

"There were complications," Dr. Schneider began. "You were hemorrhaging and in order to stop the bleeding, we had to perform a hysterectomy."

The room wobbled through the tears filling her eyes and she bit down on her lower lip. Her insides were as unsettled as the air before a thunderstorm. She wanted more than just one child, and this was a curve ball she couldn't deal with. Not right now, not on the heels of losing a child. She needed to focus her energy on the small infant before her and she nodded, sniffling back the tears.

Steve stood. "When can I take them home?"

"You can take Jennifer home in a couple of days, depending on how she does," Dr. Schneider said. "As for Samantha, she will remain here until she can breathe on her own, which may take a few weeks."

"I don't want to leave without my daughter," Jennifer said.

"I understand, but you can't stay in the hospital once you're released. Visiting hours in the neonatal unit are from six in the morning until ten at night."

Jennifer nodded and reached into the crib. She ran her finger along the crown of Samantha's head. "Hi, baby." Her voice wavered. "Mommy's here." Tears cut wet paths down her cheeks.

After the doctor left, Steve wiped her face and gave her a soft, sweet kiss.

Jennifer glanced at the sleeping baby, then back at him. "I wanted more."

"This doesn't mean we can't have more," he said. "We can always adopt." His thumb ran lazy paths back and forth over her wet cheek. "I know that doesn't make the hurt go away." He took her hand, kissing her palm.

Jennifer closed her eyes and bit her lip to stifle the sob in her chest as he pulled her close.

"Look at the upside. You'll never have a period again."

Jennifer let out a small laugh. "You *would* think of that," she said, pulling away and wiping her face.

Vengeance
Chapter 53

KYLE GATHERED THE ELECTRONIC devices he'd brought from New York, putting them in the rental van. Driving to Mirror Lake, he took the road on the opposite side of the lake from Steve and Jennifer's home, looking for a specific lot. He pulled into the driveway and grabbed a clipboard, closing the door to the van that sported the same natural gas logo as the overalls he wore.

He rang the doorbell and waited. Noises from within the house confirmed his suspicion—the snowbirds had returned. He slipped the tazer under the clipboard for easy retrieval, setting it on high.

An elderly woman peered out the window at him. She undid the latch and opened the door. "Hello," she said tentatively, her eyebrows scrunched together.

"Hello, ma'am," he said, sending an innocent smile that smoothed her tight features. "I'm checking all our natural gas customers in the area. Is it all right if I come in and check your connections?"

The old woman smiled and nodded. "Henry?" she yelled over her shoulder as she allowed him to enter. He shut the door behind him and zapped her with the stun gun. The electrical buzz filled the small atrium, and her body fell with a thud.

He hurried to the side, waiting for Henry to come into view. After a moment, the leisurely shuffle turned to a fast patter. The old man came around the corner right into his path. Kyle pressed the trigger, and the stunner launched from the end of the gun, shooting enough wattage to drop him to the ground. He tied them to the banister and retreated to the side garden, where he dug a sizeable hole. It took him an hour to attain the length and depth he needed and when he was done; he stood back and surveyed the surroundings. Nothing stirred.

He went to his van and opened the rear doors. Grabbing the pistol with the silencer, he tucked it in his waistband. He went back inside the house, whistling.

"What do you want?" Henry asked with eyes wide in terror.

Kyle said nothing as he pulled the stun gun out again and zapped both of them, neutralizing any threat of a fight. "I need your house," he explained as he untied and carried one at a time to the hole, dropping them into the muddy ground. "Sorry, but this is necessary," he said, pulling the gun from his belt. He shot both of them between the eyes, killing them instantly, the silencer muffling the sound to a small pop. He stood, staring at the old couple for a moment, the bullet hole reminding him of Charlie and a wave of anger layered his skin. His gaze rose to the house across the water, and he swore vengeance would be his.

He dropped a tarp over them and shoveled the dirt back into the hole, replacing the vibrant spring flowers when he was finished. He stepped back and assessed his work. It didn't look like much had been disturbed.

Smiling, he entered the house again. After a search, he found keys for the car parked in the garage and the house keys. He unpacked the lion's share of electronics, setting them up underneath the living room window where he had a full view of the house across the lake. He glanced at his watch and hurried out of the house, locking it behind him.

After dropping off the rental van and retrieving his car, he headed back to the lake. Digging the hole had taken him longer than he had anticipated and there was a small fraction of time left to complete everything he wanted to do. He pulled into Steve's driveway, this time pulling right up to the house. He grabbed the bag of electronics and ran to the door, pulling on rubber gloves and slipping off his shoes. The doorknob turned easily, and he slid inside, setting up the cameras throughout the house: in the bedroom, living room, kitchen, bathroom and nursery. He set them all wide enough to encompass the entire room. Satisfied, he slipped out and put on his shoes. Reaching into his car, he grabbed the outdoor surveillance camera and the remote signal he would use to pick up the transmissions. He shimmied up a tree, placing the camera where he could see the house, yard, and driveway, but out of view from anyone looking at the woods. He attached the transmitter and slid back down the tree. Jumping into his car, he took a deep breath, calming his frantically beating heart. The prospect of being caught stirred his adrenaline, and he started the vehicle and headed back around the lake.

Settling into the confiscated house, he flipped on the monitors, looking at each of the views with satisfaction. Now all he had to do was watch and wait. He wandered into the kitchen and opened the refrigerator. It was nicely stocked, as if the old couple had gone grocery shopping in the last day or so. He grabbed a beer and took a seat in the comfortable recliner, flipping on the television to pass the time.

He dozed in the chair, waking to noise coming from the monitors. When he opened his eyes, glancing at the bank of monitors, he sat up. His target walked into the nursery.

What Steve did next surprised him.

Vengeance
Chapter 54

STEVE WALKED INTO THE house, dropping the keys on the stand by the door, annoyed. He thought he'd locked the cottage on the way out to dinner, but apparently not. Nothing seemed out of place in the living room. He ran his hand over his face. "I must be tired."

He wandered into the nursery and sighed. Standing side by side were twin cribs and pain seared his heart. He hung his head, clamping his eyes shut and concentrating on the slow inhale-exhale of his breath to steady his emotions.

"Okay." He opened his eyes, glanced at the cribs, and walked out of the nursery.

Snatching his toolbox from the garage, he returned and disassembled one of the cribs. He didn't want Jennifer to come home to this kind of reminder. It was hard enough for him, and she was emotionally shot from the entire ordeal.

When he finished, he brought the parts out to the storage area in the back of the garage. Next, he took the second car seat out of his car, moving it to the back seat of Jennifer's. Fresh tire tracks thicker than his own caught his attention on the return to the house. He stopped and surveyed the yard, catching almost unrecognizable footprints leading up to the front door and back. Between the unlocked door, the tire tracks, and the footprints, his instincts peaked. The hair on the back of his neck rippled with the uncomfortable sense of being watched.

Steve stepped inside the house and flipped the deadbolt, scanning the house again. Nothing seemed out of place. He went to the bedroom, grabbed a change of clothing, and took a shower. A half hour later, he headed back to the hospital in clean, comfortable clothes.

KYLE STARED AT THE monitors, watching as Steve climbed in the car and drove away. "You lost one of the twins." He chuckled at the thought of the despair Steve must be feeling. "That's only the beginning." He looked at the array of weapons laid out at his feet on the living room floor.

Leaning over, he picked up the large hunting knife and the sharpening block. He slowly dragged the blade across the block several times, gritting his teeth at the gravelly high-pitched sound it made.

Each drag of the blade was accompanied by a vision of his revenge. His gaze landed on the hedge shears, and he grinned. Those were sharp enough to slice through skin and bone. And he wanted that bastard's shooting hand. He scanned the rest of his arsenal, zip-ties, screws, drill, and two deadly bomb jackets for the babies.

He put the sharpening stone down and picked up a magazine. The knife cut cleanly through the paper, and he smiled, imagining slicing her throat and covering Steve Williams with his wife's blood.

He slipped the knife back in the case and stared out at the house with a satisfied grin.

Vengeance
Chapter 55

STEVE STOPPED AT THE florist and bought a large bouquet of multi-colored roses for Jennifer, walking into the maternity ward ten minutes later

Jennifer emerged from the bathroom with her hair pulled back in a wet ponytail. "Those are beautiful." She pointed at the bouquet.

"Yeah, well, you deserve it," Steve replied. He placed the flowers on the windowsill. "How are you feeling?"

"I'm still sore, but I feel much better now that I've cleaned up a little," she said. "How 'bout you?" she asked.

"I'm clean." He shrugged. The tasks he'd completed at home took a toll on his emotions, leaving him drained. He leaned over and kissed her cheek. "And hungry," he replied, his stomach growled.

"You look tired."

He shrugged. "It's nothing."

"What's bothering you?"

He took a deep breath. "I took down one of the cribs."

Tears immediately sprang to her eyes, and she nodded. "You didn't have to do that."

"Yes, I did. You didn't need to come home to that kind of blatant reminder." Steve's vision blurred, and he blinked the tears back. He offered her a small smile, drew a deep breath, and put his feelings aside.

"Thank you," Jennifer whispered. Her tears brimmed, slipping down her cheeks.

Steve leaned over and kissed her. "No problem." They shuffled to the NICU.

"She is so tiny." Steve ran his finger gently down the bridge of their baby's nose. The edges of his lips curled into a smile, and he lifted his gaze toward Jennifer.

Jennifer sat on the other side of the crib, holding the tiny hand.

The phone in Steve's pocket vibrated, and he glanced at the display. "I'll be right back." He left the room. "What's up, Jack?"

"Another murder—in Boston this time," Jack said. "How much time are you taking off?"

"How much time do I have?"

"How much do you need?"

He glanced through the glass at Jennifer. "At least a couple of weeks," he replied. "If Jen hasn't been given the go ahead to drive by that point, I may need to revisit this conversation. Okay?"

"I'll give you a week completely off the clock," Jack stated. "I can't give you more than that. I need you to continue your research on this case."

Steve inhaled sharply. "My daughter's still in the NICU, Jack."

"Look, you can give me feedback from home for as long as you need. Fair enough?"

"Fair enough," he agreed and folded the phone, walking back into the NICU.

“I’m tired,” Jennifer said.

He nodded and helped her back to the maternity ward and into her hospital bed. “Do you mind if I crawl under the sheets with you?” He wanted to hold her tonight.

“I’d like that.” Jennifer moved a little to the side. “Just be careful. My stomach is still really tender.”

Steve slipped his shoes off and slid into the bed, gently wrapping his arms around his wife. “This okay?”

“It’s perfect.”

Sleep came fast.

“PLEASE DON’T.” HIS BLUE eyes were full of anger and anguish.

Searing agony gripped her, and a hand grabbed a fistful of her hair, yanking her head back. The sharp edge of a knife pressed against her throat, and then her blood sprayed like a geyser, covering him.

Jennifer sat up in bed, gagging. Her breath came in sharp pants.

Steve peeked out from the bathroom, grabbing a towel for his hands. He hurried to her side. “Jen, are you all right?”

Tremors flowed through her and the bed vibrated with them. “No,” she finally gasped.

“What’s wrong?” Panic crept into his voice.

“Nightmare.”

He reached out and touched her cheek. “Breathe,” he said.

Her eyes held his, and she got a hold of her airway. It was one thing to see all those women die, but seeing her own death rattled her to the core. She was still shaking, but at least her lungs gave way, allowing air to flow freely again. "I died."

His skin broke out in gooseflesh. "Tell me what you saw," he said, his voice raspy and dry.

"We were at home," she began, trying to dissect the dream for him. "You were sitting in a chair in front of the window and I..." She trailed off.

"I was sitting in front of the window," he said, picking up where she had left off.

She nodded. "Facing the living room." She swallowed.

"Where were you?"

"In the living room. Looking at you while..." She stopped and closed her eyes. The dream dissolved.

"While what?"

She opened her eyes. "I remember being terrified, and it wasn't because he was hurting me." She looked back at him. "I was terrified for Samantha." Her chin trembled with the memory and tears sprung from her eyes, blurring Steve's face into a hall of tiny prisms.

He ran his hand over her cheek. "Sweetheart." He kissed her gently.

She tried to smile.

"I won't let anything happen to either of you," he said, slipping under the covers and wrapping his arms around her. "I promise."

Eventually, she drifted to sleep in his arms.

<hr>

STEVE LAY AWAKE LONG after sleep found Jennifer. He pulled his arm out from under her and folded the chair in the corner into the bed it doubled as. Falling face-first on a pillow, he was out in seconds. This time, sleep took hold and didn't let go for six hours.

633

Fragmented memories of the ordeal at Brooksfield University assaulted his dreams, keeping him somewhere between a state of sleep and wakefulness. Claws raked across his back, and he sat bolt upright in the makeshift bed. The blanket Jennifer must have draped on him during the night slipped to his lap. The bright sun streaming through the window made him squint.

Jennifer stepped out of the bathroom, fresh from a shower. "Morning." She flopped into the cushy chair in the corner. She sighed.

"You're thinking about that nightmare."

She met his gaze. "Yes."

"Tell me about it."

"He's holding the knife to my throat while you watch him hurt me."

He shook his head slowly. "Not going to happen, Jen," he said. The muscles in his jaw worked, and he stubbornly stared at her. "Nothing is going to happen." He denied the possibility, refusing to accept it. Something she said triggered his next question. "Why didn't I stop him?"

Jennifer chewed her bottom lip in that familiar way, signaling that she was thinking, and he waited. After a minute, her eyes widened, and her face drained of color. "I, uh, I think you were tied to the chair."

Steve saw the change in her eyes. "What'd you just see?"

"Nothing." Her eyes focused on the pattern on the linoleum.

He crossed his arms, his brow furrowing, and his lips pressed together, waiting.

Jennifer brought her gaze to his before glancing at the door. "You don't want to know."

He tilted his head and raised his eyebrows, silently willing her to continue.

She shook her head and met his gaze. "Why didn't you get up?" Biting her lip, she blinked back tears. "You were tied to the chair." She averted her eyes again, looking at the floor.

"Jen." He reached across the small table and lifted her chin, so she met his glance.

"This was violent, not the bizarre pseudo-seduction he's fallen back into. It was more like the last few killings when we were in New York," she replied.

"What else?"

"He stabbed me in the side."

Steve leaned back in the seat, his throat tightening at the prospect of anyone hurting her. "Why?"

Jennifer's eyes welled up. "I fought back," she replied, almost too low for him to hear.

"What else?"

"I tried to get what he put down. That's when he stabbed me." She trembled a little.

"What did he put down?"

Her eyebrows creased and then her eyes slowly went wide again. "A detonator."

"Where's the bomb?"

Jennifer began to cry.

"Is it under my chair?"

"No, it's on Samantha."

He didn't want to hear any more, but he needed to in order to prevent what she described, what she believed their future held. "What happens next?"

"He slits my throat," she said without looking up at him.

Steve sighed and wiped his face. "Okay. Let's look at this differently. Let's say this is only a nightmare. That makes sense, too."

She tilted her head. "You psychoanalyzing me?"

He shrugged. "Go with it for a sec. Based on everything that has happened in the last few days, it makes perfect sense. It could be your subconscious trying to figure out how to accept the fact that you can't have any more kids and the resulting fear of losing Sam."

"But..."

He put his hand up. "The rest could stem from the combinations of visions, Charlie, and here. Being raped in front of me again as well as dying violently."

Jennifer seemed to reflect on what he was saying. She didn't respond either way immediately. Silence blanketed the room.

"While I'd like to believe it was just a nightmare, you and I both know differently," she finally said.

Steve looked away. He stood and walked to the window. His mind turned over how to change the course of fate. He had changed his fate before because of Jennifer's warnings and he had to find a way to change it again.

"How does he get the drop on us?" he asked.

"I don't know," she whispered.

As he glanced at the bright cloudless sky, questions flurried in his head and one barreled into the forefront of all the others.

How the hell do I stop this?

Vengeance
Chapter 56

COMING HOME WASN'T THE joyous occasion it should have been. Neither Jennifer nor Steve wanted to leave Samantha in the hospital, but now that Jennifer had been released, they needed to abide by the neonatal visiting hours and were shooed out at ten on the mark.

She curled up in the recliner with an ice pack on her chest. "My breasts are killing me."

Steve glanced at her from his position on the couch, raising his eyebrows.

"Shut up."

"I didn't say anything." He turned away from her, his lips pressed together to stop the smile from forming, and he flipped the television on. The drone of the eleven o'clock news followed him into a light doze.

Steve woke up with a start. A rasping sound like rough sandpaper on a tree stump was coming from somewhere on his right, and he turned his head toward the noise. His heart leaped into his throat, and he was up, running into the bathroom, rummaging through the medicine cabinet, his hands shaking. He grabbed the inhaler and ran back into the living room.

Jennifer gasped like a guppy out of the water, her eyes wide and filled with panic. Steve shoved the end of the inhaler in her mouth and pressed down, sending a spray of medicine into her constricted lungs. Jennifer took a breath and nodded for him to spray again. He complied, and this time she was able to get a bigger breath of the medicine into her lungs. She took the inhaler out of his hand and held it.

He took a seat on the couch and ran a shaky hand through his hair. *Jesus, she hasn't sounded like that since we were at Brooksfield U.* That memory triggered a shiver, and he clamped his teeth against it, instead, focusing on her. "You okay?"

She didn't nod, nor did she shake her head, just wheezed. She brought the medicine to her mouth again and shot it down her throat, inhaling as her chest rose with the infusion of oxygen.

She exhaled and dropped her shaking hand to the armrest, the inhaler still clutched in a death grip.

"That bad?"

Tears slipped down her cheeks.

"Shhh." Steve kneeled next to the chair and took her hand. "Just breathe." He kissed her palm. "Breathe, baby," he whispered. He kept his gaze steady, holding eye contact. "That's right, just breathe. We don't have to talk about it now."

Jennifer nodded, tears still making tracks down her cheek. The crease between her eyes smoothed and her glistening eyes reflected relief.

STEVE DROVE JENNIFER TO the hospital the next day and they sat by Samantha's bedside watching her struggle, silently praying their little girl would make it.

"Tell me about your vision last night," Steve asked when he pulled out of the parking lot.

"He makes me hurt you," Jennifer said. "If I don't do what he tells me, he'll blow up our daughter." She took a breath.

"What does he make you do?" He turned toward her.

Jennifer lifted his right hand to her lips, kissing his palm. Tears sprouted from the corner of her eyes. "He makes me cut off this hand."

Shock like a tazer shot rammed Steve's frame, and he tried not to let it show. "Why?" he asked, miraculously keeping the shake from his voice.

"You're right-handed." Her chin quivered. "You'll never shoot anyone again."

Steve pulled over to the side of the road. The only person he ever shot was Charlie. "Did you see him?"

"No, but he's definitely got the same scorpion tattoo Charlie had."

Steve put the car in gear and pulled back on the road, chewing on this new information. *Who would want him to suffer for Charlie's death? Bondino?* He stared at the road, wondering if the biggest mafia boss in the country would go to that kind of extreme.

Would he?

What Jennifer described was a personal vendetta and not a mafia hit. *Who the hell would be angry enough at Charlie's death to come after us with that kind of vitriol?*

Facts swirled in his head, and his mind centered on the anomaly in Charlie's background. There was only one that would make sense, even though it was as farfetched as Jennifer's clairvoyance.

The muscles in his jaw contracted and Jennifer inhaled. "What?"

"Don't worry about it."

"Bullshit! You pushed for the details. Now you're going to tell me what that look on your face is all about."

"I need to do some research," he answered and took a deep breath as they pulled into their driveway.

He had a call to make.

Vengeance
Chapter 57

"KYLE WISNOWSKI," HE SAID into the phone.

"He's dead, Steve."

"What if he's alive?"

Silence was Steve's momentary answer, while Jack mulled the question over. "What's your point?"

"Maybe he has the same tattoo?"

"There are hundreds of people with that kind of tattoo."

"I know," Steve answered and looked out over the dark lake. He knew that better than anyone did. He'd been tracking them down since Jennifer provided the sketch. The list was dwindling fast.

"What are you driving at?"

Steve sighed. "Jenny's been having some visions. The first one happened quite a while ago. But she's telling me someone's hunting us and will eventually attack us. At first, she thought it was the Slasher, but then she switched gears, saying he wants me to suffer. So, I got to thinking, what if Kyle was alive? Charlie's DNA didn't match exactly to that of the Slasher, but it was close enough to be a family member. Hell, it was close enough for them to close the case until the killings started again. It would make perfect sense that he'd come after me since I was the one who killed his brother. And who knows, he might have the same ties to the Bondino's."

"Do you have anything concrete to back the notion?"

"No. I'll do some research, but the car accident that Kyle died in was suspect, anyway. Cars don't just blow up."

"True. Let me know what you uncover."

"Will do." Steve snapped the phone closed and headed into the house.

He tucked Jennifer into bed and gave her a peck on the cheek, retiring to his office to dig through Charlie's history, specifically focusing on finding some interesting tidbits beyond the auto accident when Kyle was sixteen.

The fiery crash had rendered the kid's body unidentifiable, yet his foster parents provided identification by confirming he had driven the car away less than an hour before the accident. No dental match was done, and it peaked Steve's interest more now than it had when he stumbled on it in New York.

He leaned back in his chair, his radar now in overdrive. Leaning forward, he opened the photo file, studying the last school picture. The kid certainly looked like Charlie, even with the punk rock hair. Pouring over the information, he found allegations against his foster parents by the school stating Kyle had been abused, but nothing ever came of the complaint. Steve glanced at the names and searched in the database.

What came up made his blood turn to ice.

He read the news and autopsy reports, and sat back in the chair with his heart hammering in his chest. "Jesus," he muttered and pressed the print button.

He stared at the report and then dropped it on the desk, wiping his face with his hands. It was time to call it a night, and he made a note that he'd have to call Jack tomorrow. He wanted the grave exhumed to verify that Kyle was indeed dead and buried.

Vengeance
Chapter 58

“THE FRONT DOOR IS unlocked again.” Jennifer glanced over her shoulder at Steve and pushed open the door.

“Wait!” His senses snapped into high alert, and he glanced around the yard and back at her. It was dark, and his adrenalin kicked in, turning his blood into octane fuel, throbbing in his veins, pumping hard and fast. He pulled Jennifer back a step and slipped into the car. Reaching under the front seat, he grabbed his revolver.

He passed by her, their eyes meeting for the briefest moment. “Stay here,” he ordered and slid into the house, gun drawn, slowly moving along the wall. His eyes darted through the dark, looking for any sign of an intruder. It took him several minutes to cover the entire house. When he was through, he stood in their bedroom and closed his eyes, taking a deep breath before setting the safety on his gun. He flipped the living room lights and walked to the front door, nodding for Jennifer to come in. “It’s clear.”

“I’m ready for bed,” she announced. The stress created dark circles under her eyes. She headed toward the bedroom.

Steve stood in the living room. The feeling of being watched hung on, and he slowly surveyed the room. It took a second to recognize the camera mounted at the top of the bookshelf.

"Shit!" He crossed the room and pulled the gadget down, flipping it over in his hands before spiking it onto the floor. *How long has that been here?* He turned in a circle, studying anywhere else in the living room that could house a camera before looking at the broken electronics on the floor.

He flipped open the phone. "Jack. I need a crew out here to scan the cottage. I found a camera in our living room."

"I'll have one up there tomorrow."

"I think Bondino is watching." Steve turned the broken equipment over in his hand. It was a pretty advanced camera, the kind of thing only someone with money could afford. He slowly stood and crossed to the garbage, dumping it.

Someone has been in this house.

He glanced at the door and around the room again, and the hairs on the back of his neck prickled. "In the meantime, I'd like Kyle Wisnowski's grave exhumed."

"I'll see what I can do. It may take some time, Steve. I don't know if we can do this without something concrete to give the judge, but I'll give it a go."

Vengeance
Chapter 59

THE MONITOR WENT FUZZY as Steve spiked the camera on the floor. Kyle glared at the cottage and down at the limited number of weapons arranged on the living room floor. Inhaling deeply, Kyle stood and stretched. "It isn't time, yet," he reminded himself. This would freak Steve out for a little while, and that pleased him.

The cell phone in his pocket vibrated. Kyle dug it out. "Hello?"

"It's Tony," his boss announced. "Where the hell are you?"

"I'm taking care of some personal business on the east coast," Kyle replied, turning the volume down on all the monitors.

"I got a job for you."

Kyle looked out at the lake house and didn't say a word.

"Kyle?"

"Where and when?"

"Milan, next week."

Kyle sighed. "How long?"

"If all goes well, you will be back in a couple of weeks."

"When do you expect me to head out?"

"Monday."

Kyle looked out at the cottage. "What hotel in Milan?"

"Hotel Principe di Savoia. I think you'll enjoy this one immensely. I'll send your documents to the usual address."

"I'll be there Sunday night."

"Good," Tony answered. "If you need anything, don't hesitate to call."

"Thanks, Tony. See ya." He flipped the phone closed. "Shit," he said, looking across the lake. He flipped through the remaining working cameras in the cottage. They hadn't brought the baby home yet, so his plans were on hold, anyway.

Vengeance
Chapter 60

THEY STEPPED INTO THE cottage after another exhausting day at the hospital. Jennifer dropped asleep on the bed almost immediately. The staples had been taken out of her abdomen and the drugs they gave her for the discomfort affected her all day. She'd dozed several times in the chair, holding Samantha's hand while Steve read Dr. Seuss books to his daughter.

Steve planted a kiss on her forehead and slipped into the office, taking a seat behind the desk. He closed his eyes for a second before getting down to another night of research.

He stood in the clearing of Paradise Cove as fog drifted up from the ground. Steve heard a noise behind him and twirled around. As he turned, he watched the lush green beauty of Paradise Cove deteriorate, turning brown. The moss under his feet turned black, and he knew what was behind him even as his eyes landed on the beast. It was laughing, and its clawed hand rose in the air and came down fast.

The chair banged into the wall from the force of the push he gave with his legs. His eyes flew open, and he was still in the office. Disoriented, heart pounding, and breath rasping, he glanced around the room and back at the computer.

Just a nightmare.

"Damn." He shook the cobwebs from his mind.

He opened the folder containing the financial research he'd put together from Charlie's ledgers, specifically focusing on the months before and after Kyle had supposedly died.

"Bingo!"

He found the entry he remembered. A seven-figure sum was put into a trust account for K. Winslow, along with a smaller figure going to the shell corporation Steve was familiar with. The cocaine business filtered a percentage off the top to the same corporation.

"Tony Bondino." He found the connection.

"Okay, Charlie got Kyle out of an abusive foster home, faked his death, and sent him to work for Tony." His eyebrows creased.

He pulled up the report of Kyle's foster parents, opting for the full document this time. He read through and looked at the crime scene photos. The killer had taken his time with them, torturing them to a degree Steve had never seen before. The last thing he read struck a chord. Both parents were missing their index fingers. Steve sat back in the chair. His mind whizzed through his own data files. It took a moment, but when the answer he was searching for reared its head, he nearly shot to his feet.

"Holy Shit!"

Kyle was an assassin.

The mark, the index finger, they had seen that in several cases they suspected to be Bondino hits—the last being a judge in New York City in October. Every single wound inflicted on

Kyle's foster parents was a form of torture they'd seen in mafia hits over the last six or seven years, all bundled into one brutal and sadistic session. An application of everything he'd learned wherever the Bondinos had sent him.

It was too late to call Jack, so Steve shot an email his way and shut down the computer for the night. Opening his top desk drawer, he stared at the vial of cocaine, picking it up and rolling it between his thumb and forefinger, debating. He could almost taste the rush. He shook his head and sighed, dropping it back into the drawer and twisting the lock.

He cracked open a bottle of wine instead.

"What are you doing?"

He jumped at the sound of her voice, turning toward his rumpled wife. "Having a drink. You want one?"

Jennifer glanced at the clock. "It's after eleven."

"I know. Do you want a glass?" He held up the bottle of zinfandel.

She nodded, rubbing the sleep out of her eyes, and he poured her a glass.

Steve drained his cup and poured a second.

She raised her eyebrows and took a small sip without taking her eyes off him.

"What?" he asked.

"You're hitting that pretty hard."

"Yeah, well, I don't have to work tomorrow, and it's been a long day." He was not about to divulge the facts he'd uncovered. The idea of going up against a mafia assassin didn't sit well with him.

"So, you're going to get drunk?"

"Precisely! And then I'm going to let you take advantage of me."

She almost spit her wine out with the laughter that exploded. "You think so?"

He nodded and drained the second glass. Drinking was a more palatable choice than snorting the cocaine, and he needed to get sauced. He poured the rest of the bottle into his glass.

Her smile disappeared. "You were serious about getting drunk."

"Yes."

Jennifer set her glass down. "What's wrong?"

Steve took a deep breath and finished his drink.

THE HEAT DRAINED FROM her face as the dark kitchen dissolved to their bright, sun-streaked living room.

She kneeled on the floor in front of the chair Steve was tied to.

"Anchor him to the floor." Her assailant handed her two six-inch galvanized screws.

"I can't."

"Say goodbye to your little angel," he said from behind her.

"Don't kill my little girl," she cried and looked up at Steve, tears blurring her vision. "How?" she finally asked.

"Through his feet," the voice instructed, and he dropped the power drill on the floor next to her.

Jennifer sobbed as she took the drill.

"Jenny!" Steve yelled and shook her.

Jennifer blinked and looked around. Her hand flew to her mouth at the realization of the vision's insinuation. Tears welled in her eyes and the shakes began. "I can't." She looked into Steve's wide blue eyes.

"You can't what?" Steve asked, visibly rattled this time.

Her eyes rolled up in their sockets and she slumped forward.

HE CAUGHT HER AND propped her back on the seat, splashing a little water on her face.

Her eyelids raised, and she glanced around the kitchen, her breath catching in her throat. She threw her arms around Steve, burying her wet face in his shoulder. She clung to him until the shakes subsided.

When she pulled away, he asked, "Are you all right now?"

Jennifer shrugged in response.

Already tipsy from the first bottle of wine, he grabbed another chilled bottle of zinfandel and filled his glass. He really didn't want to know what Jennifer had seen. What she had said while under the spell of the vision was disturbing enough. He just wanted to drink the rest of the bottle in front of him.

"Don't you want to know what I saw?"

"No," he said without looking at her. "I really don't want to know." His words slurred as the wine and stress took their toll.

"Steve?"

He glanced over at her. "What, babe?"

"I'm sorry." She burst into tears.

He picked up his wine and drained the goblet again before he spoke. "Don't apologize," he said, refilling his empty wineglass. "It's not your fault. It's mine." He slammed the drink back like a shot of tequila. "I'm the one who's responsible for this mess." He poured the remainder of the bottle into his glass and looked down at the table.

"How can this be your fault?"

"I killed Charlie," he began and sat back in his seat. "It doesn't matter that he was shooting at me and had already killed a bunch of people. All that matters is that I killed him, and I believe his brother was watching." He took another sip of wine before continuing. "And here's the kicker. Charlie's brother is a mafia assassin." He smiled and finished his glass. Instead of pouring another round, Steve took a swig directly from the bottle.

"Kyle, Charlie's little brother, supposedly died close to ten years ago." He took a deep breath. "Kyle didn't die. Charlie got him out of an abusive home and sent him somewhere. He had enough contacts to pull it off." Steve finished the second bottle. "And Kyle's been trained by some very nasty people. When he came back to New York, he killed his foster parents." Standing, he crossed to the cabinet, pulling out a bottle of cabernet. "Jack's going to get the body exhumed and run dental records. I'm betting my career that the body in the grave isn't Kyle Wisnowski's."

"Holy shit," Jennifer said.

"HOLY SHIT, INDEED!"

Kyle stared at the computer screen in his apartment in New York, his jaw slack and his eyes wide. His blood turned cold at the slurred explanation Steve gave Jennifer.

"How the fuck do you know?" Kyle whispered at the screen.

Kyle sat back and covered his face with his hands, silently thanking God that he was going out of the country in the morning. The exhumation would tell the FBI that Kyle

Wisnowski was not in the grave that bore his name.

"Fuck." He switched the connection off in disgust.

Vengeance
Chapter 61

THE PHONE INTERRUPTED STEVE'S drunken slumber, and he reached for the receiver on the nightstand with a groan of protest. "Hello?" he croaked.

"Steve?" Jack asked.

"What's up?" Steve rolled onto his back, pressing his forearm over his eyes to block the bright sun filtering into the room.

"You sound like shit."

"Hangover. What's up?"

"There's been another murder."

Steve moved his arm and opened his eyes. "Where?"

"New York City. Last night. I'm sending over the photos and preliminary forensics."

"Shit." Steve closed his eyes again. He didn't even know if Jennifer had another vision. He was too drunk last night to remember much.

"I need you to take a look," Jack said.

"Okay. Give me a minute." He slid out of bed and stumbled out of the bedroom into his office, booting up his desktop. Even the thin whirl of the computer hurt his head. "Got it," Steve mumbled as the email archive opened. He scanned the pictures slowly, stopping to look at the very pretty, very dead blonde-haired woman. "It's our guy. Same M.O. The marks on the neck are consistent with the others and there's evidence of sodomy, according to the preliminary notes. The pinkie's missing too. I'll bet the DNA comes back as a match." Steve rubbed his face and leaned back, noticing the quiet pervading the cabin.

"I'm heading down to the crime scene. I'll let you know what I find out," Jack said.

"Thanks. Talk to you later." He hung up the phone and wandered into the living room, looking out at the gazebo, thinking Jennifer must have gone outside.

She wasn't there.

"Jen?" When no answer came, he turned around again, now fully awake. *Where the hell is she?* A thin layer of alarm wrapped around his chest and then his eyes fell on the note that lay in plain sight on the coffee table. Her parents had come, and she took them to the hospital to see Samantha. Slumping on the couch in relief, Steve leaned his head back on the puffy pillows and closed his eyes.

He was still lying on the couch in a semi-conscious state when Jennifer and her parents arrived home. "Hi." He sat up, rubbing his eyes and offering a shrug and smile to his in-laws. "I have to apologize. I had a little too much wine last night."

"It happens," Joe said. "Hope our visit wasn't the cause."

Steve let out a soft laugh. "Not in the least. I was looking forward to seeing you and Allison."

Joe nodded, but pressed his lips together in a skeptical scowl.

"Seriously." Steve glanced at Jennifer for help.

"Give him a break, Dad." Jennifer walked over to Steve and gave him a quick kiss. "You feeling any better?"

Steve shook his head. "But I'll live. How's Sam doing today?"

"She's doing all right. You should head over when you're feeling a little better."

Steve nodded, which his stomach immediately reacted to. He was able to control the flop, swallowing the bile that rose. Time to grab some aspirin.

"Jennifer tells me the stories on the news about you were accurate," Joe said as Steve walked out of the bathroom.

Steve sighed and nodded. He knew damn well Jennifer talked to him shortly after the news hit the airwaves, but it was another cause for Joe to get his digs in. "Yep."

"I don't like the fact that you put my daughter in danger like that again."

Steve took a deep breath and turned, looking out at the lake as the anger engulfed him. He counted to ten silently before he turned back toward his guests. He didn't dignify the jab with an answer. Instead, he glanced at Jennifer and turned. Crossing into his office, he closed the door, but it still didn't shut out the conversation.

"Dad, why do you always do that?"

"You know damn well why! He ruined your life."

"No, he didn't, Dad," Jennifer said.

No one reacted when the office door opened.

"He put you in the middle of his investigation, twice."

"I never intended to put Jennifer in danger," Steve answered, causing everyone to turn toward him.

"The road to hell is paved with good intentions," Joe blurted, which earned him a stern look from his wife.

Steve actually laughed at his father-in-law. "I was working undercover, Joe, and I didn't know what I was up against. I swear if I had any clue, I would have gotten Jennifer as far away from this town as I possibly could, regardless of the ramifications." He glanced at Jennifer. "I didn't want her in New York with me last fall, either." His gaze returned to his father-in-law. "Believe me, that was an ongoing argument between Jennifer and me for months."

Joe scoffed at him. "Bullshit."

Steve raised his eyebrows at Jennifer. "I'm not doing this." He closed the office door again, this time turning the lock so no one could interrupt him. Crossing to the desk, he slid into the seat and unlocked the drawer, pulling the vial out. Without hesitation, he unscrewed the cap and took a hit off the little metal spoon. He wasn't going to deal with her father without help today. Leaning back in the chair, he hoped that between the aspirin and the jolt of cocaine, he'd feel better in a little while.

He turned on his computer and began the search for Kyle Wisnowski, AKA K. Winslow. Steve typed in the name Kyle Winslow and the search results brought back fifty-one entries, of which two were identified under age thirty, and several were not identified by age at all. He sighed and saved the results. He tried K Winslow and some two hundred and fifty-five entries came back, most of which had no age tied to them.

"Let's try our database." He pulled up the FBI database, typing in both versions of the name. Twenty-five names came back within the age parameter between twenty-three and thirty.

Steve crosschecked the lists and took a deep breath. He requested photo identification. Nineteen came back with photos and he paged through them. Only one remotely looked like Charlie. He saved that page and looked at the six that had no photo in their file. One was living in Las Vegas, three were out of New York City, and the other two were slated as living in the Chicago area. He requested social security numbers of the six people and the photo that he had set aside.

His eyebrows rose when the results came back. One of the numbers appeared twice, once in Las Vegas and again in New York City.

"Hmmm." He looked at the results again, looking back to the common social security number.

He did a separate search on only the social security number and three sets of results came back. The first result set was for a man who died close to thirty years before.

Steve smiled.

"I believe I just found Kyle Wisnowski," he said as he saved the results and turned the computer off. The cocaine was already pulsing through his system, denying the hangover any traction.

LATER THAT EVENING, AFTER her parents left, Steve stood in the living room with the phone in his hand, punching Jack's number into the keypad.

Jack's phone dumped into voicemail, and Steve sighed, waiting for the beep. "Jack, Kyle isn't going by the name of Wisnowski, he's under the name Winslow. He has an apartment in New York and a house in Las Vegas. Call me." He snapped the phone shut and turned around.

Jennifer leaned against the bedroom doorframe. "You're going after him."

He nodded. "Yes."

Vengeance
Chapter 62

JENNIFER STOOD IN THE middle of a busy Manhattan city street.

Steve entered the building in front of her with his gun drawn and she hurried, catching up to him in the stairwell. Steve climbed the stairs with the gun in front of him and his badge hanging from his belt, announcing his status as a federal officer to anyone he might encounter.

"Don't do this," she whispered, but he didn't hear her. She was just a ghost to him.

He entered the hallway and slid to the apartment door, holstering his gun and pulling a lock pick set from his pocket.

A shadow moved behind him and Jennifer gasped. A small pop filled the hallway and Steve slumped against the door, his eyes wide and his body limp.

A man still cast in shadows crouched in front of Steve. "I knew you were coming, and I just wanted you to know I'm going to have a field day with your wife and daughter before I kill them."

Steve turned his eyes upward, looking beyond the silenced muzzle of the gun pressed between his eyes.

Another pop echoed, and the back of Steve's head blew all over the door.

Jennifer sat up and hitched her breath in the dark room. "He kills you," she gasped. Steve crossed to her and wrapped his arms around her, cradling her before pulling away and gently running his fingers over her wet cheek.

"Another nightmare?"

Her eyes fluttered open and immediately filled with tears, blurring her vision. "You'll die if you go after him." She swallowed, still stunned by her dream.

"It was just a dream. Besides, you know damn well I have to try."

"He knew you were coming. He was waiting for you."

"Where?"

She pulled away from him and wiped her face. "An apartment building in the city."

"Which city?"

"You already know which city."

"New York."

Jennifer nodded. "You can't go."

"Yes, I can." He shot his gaze back at her, his jaw tight and his eyes hard. "I can stop the son of a bitch. I have to." He stormed out of the house.

STEVE MADE HIS WAY through the woods to Paradise Cove, stomping on roots and old pine needles covering the path, ignoring the painful stabs in his bare feet. He walked onto the moss and glared at the water. Fury, like a caged animal throwing itself against the walls of its prison, built inside him. He'd stop the bastard any way possible.

"I'm a cop. He's a criminal." He screamed at his reflection, trying to justify his murderous thoughts, and came up short.

He could almost hear his grandfather chuckle.

"Justice and vengeance are two very different things, Steven, and we both know justice isn't what you're after."

The air went out of his chest, and he fell to his knees, knowing he'd hit the nail on the head. He didn't want justice; he had no intention of arresting Kyle if he ever found the man. Staring at his reflection, he knew he was on the edge of the abyss and realized if he didn't step back, he'd be no different from Charlie.

Vengeance
Chapter 63

IT WAS A LITTLE after one by the time Kyle arrived at his hotel halfway around the world from Brooksfield. He changed into a pair of jeans before popping his laptop open. With a few keystrokes, he activated the video stream from the cottage just in time to see Steve walk into the bedroom with the phone. He clicked on the bedroom camera view and turned up the volume.

The words that tumbled out of Steve's mouth caused Kyle's heart to drop to his knees and his jaw to follow. *The son of a bitch knows who I am.*

"Jesus Christ," he whispered. "How the hell did you track my name down?"

Perhaps Steve Williams was more of an adversary than he thought. Admiration mixed with irritation, and he slammed the laptop closed. Walking to the window, he stared out over Milan.

"Fuck." In twelve years, no one had ever suspected he was alive, even after his foster parents' brutal death.

He turned, glaring at his computer and, with a deep breath, crossed back to the desk and raised the screen.

"I am going to have such fun tearing your life apart," he said to Steve's image and then dumped out of the feed. He began the tedious task of moving all his bank accounts in a mass exodus from Kyle Winslow to his new identity.

"Shit," he muttered. *This is going to be such a pain in the ass.*

Vengeance
Chapter 64

STEVE STEPPED INTO A quiet house after an evening sitting by Samantha's side. Jennifer looked up from her curled position on the couch, folding the book in her lap and sighing.

"Did you have a nice time with your folks?"

"Yeah. How's Samantha tonight?"

"She seems to be doing a little better." He yawned. "I have to do a little more research for Jack." He caught a quick kiss and headed into the office.

Flipping the computer on, he accessed his email and opened the case notes Jack had sent. The picture of the most recent victim, this one in New York City, stared back at him. He skimmed through the case, flipping back to the picture. She had been sodomized like all the other women and her throat was slit wide open, almost to the spine. Jack confirmed the DNA match. It was the same killer. Steve sighed, closing the file.

He switched gears, pulling up the list of Social Security Numbers again.

He did a separate search in the system for all accounts related to the social security number. The authorization screen appeared, and he plugged in his code, waiting for results. When the screen came back with the information, Steve's breath caught in his throat.

Every single one of Kyle's accounts was closed as of the end of the business day.

"Son of a bitch," he whispered. Their values were all significant enough to put them on the radar of all the monitoring agencies, especially since the money went overseas. He banged another command on the keyboard.

Steve swayed in the chair, looking at the results. "Where did the money go?" He typed more commands on the keyboard.

Tracing the wires to five overseas accounts, he tried to pull the owners of those accounts, but they were only identified by numbers in the database.

"Shit. He flew the coop." The irony of the timing struck a chord. "It's almost like he knew I was onto him." He leaned back in the chair, staring at the computer.

Reaching for the phone, he placed a call. "Jack, did you ever send the sweepers?"

"You weren't there," Jack said.

"Send them now." Steve stood, looking around the office for a camera or microphone.

"Why?"

"Kyle knows we're onto him. All his bank accounts were transferred out today."

"What?"

"Kyle Wisnowski," he said, looking at the computer. "I called you this morning and now all the bank accounts are empty."

Steve heard the tapping of a keyboard. "They'll be there in an hour."

"Thanks."

"Did you find a solid connection?"

"I'm working on it. Can we at least check out the residences in New York and Las Vegas?"

"Not without a warrant, and I need proof to get that," Jack said.

Steve glared at the computer screen and held his tongue. "I'll get you proof. Talk to you later." He hung up before Jack could say anything else.

Flipping through his Rolodex, he came across the name he wanted—an old college buddy from Yale. He stared at the number, drumming his fingers on the desk. He dialed the number.

"Hi, Ted, it's Steve. You still flying?"

"Steve, Jesus, it's been a while. How the hell are you?"

"I'm good, but I need a lift to New York City tomorrow. Are you still flying?"

"You bet your ass, and as luck would have it, I don't have any charters tomorrow. The wife and I were supposed to go pick out tile for the bathroom. I'd do anything to get out of that. You still up in New Hampshire?"

"Yep. Jen and I had a little girl a couple of weeks ago."

"Congratulations. Mine are three and one, both tiny little terrors, too," he laughed. "Want me to pick you up in Wolfeboro?"

"That would be perfect. What time?"

"How does nine sound? We can land in Essex and catch a cab from there."

"Perfect." Steve leaned back. "What time will we get to the city?"

"Around eleven."

"So, what time would you want to head back?" Steve asked, figuring he had a couple of hours at the most.

"I'd want to be airborne by three to be home in time for dinner," Ted answered.

"That's perfect. I'll see you at nine." He hung up the phone. With a deep breath, he stood and headed out of his office.

Jennifer glanced up from her book when the door opened.

"I've got a chance to go flying tomorrow with an old friend from Yale," he said. "Do you mind?"

Jennifer sat back on the couch, looking him over. "Who?"

"Ted Beaumont. He was at Yale when I was there. He's going to be up in the area and wanted to know if I wanted to go for a ride," Steve answered, telling the partial truth. "I'll be back in time to cook dinner."

Jennifer stared at him. "Where are you flying?"

He shrugged. "Around. He wants me to meet him in Wolfeboro at nine."

Jennifer glanced at the paperback in her hand. "Okay." She shrugged.

He allowed a grin to surface. "Thanks, babe." He crossed the room and planted a kiss on her lips.

"You sure you didn't call him to get out of a day with my parents?"

"I'm sure. It just happened to be perfect timing and you'll have a much more relaxing day if your dad and I aren't at each other's throats."

"You're probably right."

"You know I'm right." He headed back to the office. Steve closed the door and leaned against it for a moment, closing his eyes and admonishing himself for lying. He sat down at the computer again, pulling up the exact address of the New York residence. Printing and folding the paper, he slipped it in his wallet. He threw a small locksmith set into a duffle bag, as well as a light jacket and his ankle holster. He wasn't going unarmed or unprepared, especially after Jennifer's dream, although he believed the place would be empty, based on the movement of money and erasing of an identity that was underway.

Grabbing a beer, he wandered outside. The warm spell was still going strong, and the night sky reflected a thousand tiny lights on the still water of the lake. Taking a seat on the dock, he cracked the beer open and took a sip, then stretched out on the wood, looking at the bright stars filling the sky.

Jennifer stood a few feet away, looking down at him. "What aren't you telling me?"

Steve looked backwards at her. "What do you mean?"

"You're holding something back."

"Jack's sending a sweep crew over right now. I think Kyle's watching us," Steve said, keeping eye contact.

Jennifer took a deep breath and shivered.

"And I know where he lives."

"New York?"

"No, Las Vegas. But we can't do anything without proof." He looked back at the stars and then closed his eyes. "He's also in the process of changing identities again."

Jennifer sat on the steps. "How do you know that?"

He sat up and turned toward her. "He liquidated all his accounts today." He looked back at the water. "I traced it overseas." He turned back to her. "I'm not sure how many layers it'll go through or if I can trace it any farther. I don't have a subpoena to hold the money where it is, either." He faced the water again. "So, I'm pretty frustrated."

She approached him, putting her hand on the top of his head.

"Don't worry; I will not put myself in a position where I'll get hurt." He was sure he'd lied convincingly this time. "I'm just following the leads and giving the case information to Jack."

Jennifer kneeled down and planted a kiss on the top of his head. "I'm going back to my book."

"Okay. I won't be much longer. Matt should be here by nine."

HE STOOD WHEN THE car rolled into the driveway, crossing the lawn to greet the sweeper. "Hi, Matt. Thanks for coming so quickly."

"No problem." Matt Banks, the bureau's northeastern technical expert, extended his hand to Steve. He went into the house and began the sweep while they sat in the living room.

Matt sat down, placing four tiny cameras on the coffee table. "Bedroom, kitchen, bathroom, and nursery. Your office is clean. These things are state-of-the-art wide-angle lenses with a hell of an audio range. They were placed in the most optimal spots with full views of each room."

"Add to that the living room and he had a pretty good view of everything." Steve shook his head. Their lives, their privacy, violated. He was pissed and more determined than ever to stop the son of a bitch.

Jennifer crossed her arms and legs. "The bathroom?"

"I'm afraid so."

"Do you have a sense of where they were transmitting to?"

Matt tilted his head slightly. "These aren't long range. I'd say the receiver is within a mile at best."

That gave him an advantage. There weren't many places within a mile of their cottage, and Steve crossed to the window, staring out at the darkness. "Thanks, Matt." He looked at the reflection of the technician.

"For what it's worth, the person who planted these knew what he was doing." Matt stood, collecting the equipment.

Steve showed him out. When he returned, Jennifer was still curled up on the couch.

"In our bathroom? He was watching us?" A thin rash of goose bumps broke out over her arms.

"Yep." He looked around the house before crossing to her, crouching down in front of the couch. "I'm going to stop him, Jen. I promise."

Vengeance
Chapter 65

LEANING AGAINST HIS BMW with his backpack slung over his shoulder, Steve waited. The rumble of the plane caught his attention, and he glanced at his watch. *Like clockwork,* he thought as the Learjet touched down, stopping at the end of the runway near where he parked.

The pilot swung the door open.

Steve smiled and removed his sunglasses, approaching his old friend. "Always spot on." He extended his hand.

"Early as usual." Ted pumped his hand twice. "You ready?" He signaled to the approaching fuel truck.

Steve nodded. "I really appreciate this," he said, and Ted led him onto the tarmac into the plane.

Ted shelled out cash to the fuel attendant and closed the door, swinging the airlock in place. "You remember how to fly?" He pointed to the co-pilot seat.

"Yeah, I remember. Flying's easy. It's the landing part I have issues with."

Ted chuckled. "My father was livid. I think it was about six months before he let me fly again and every time I asked to go solo, he reminded me we almost crashed *his* plane into the runway barriers." He hooked himself into the pilot seat. "When I told him I was meeting you, he reminded me again of the dangers of letting inexperienced folks fly our planes."

Steve glanced around the jet and nodded in appreciation. "This is a step up from that little twin prop we flew."

"Business has been real good." He taxied to the opposite end of the runway and the engines whined when he pushed the throttle forward, accelerating, speeding down the runway, and slowly lifting off. He charted the course in the computer and flipped the autopilot on, turning toward Steve. "What are we really doing in New York?"

"I was wondering how long you were going to take before you asked."

Ted waited expectantly.

"I'm dropping in on an old friend."

"You're packing?"

Steve said nothing and folded his arms across his chest.

Ted raised his eyebrows. "You're on my plane; I've got a right to know if you're carrying firearms."

"Yes, I've got my gun." He turned toward Ted, leveling a hard stare. "But it's not official business. This is personal."

"You're still in the bureau, right?"

"Yes, but they don't know I'm taking this trip."

"I gather from your tone they wouldn't be thrilled."

Steve laughed. "That's an understatement."

Ted looked out the windshield for a while before speaking. Steve could see the wheels turning in his friend's head and wondered if he'd said too much.

With a great exhale, Ted turned toward him. "You saved Heather from that bastard at Yale. I'll never forget that." He chewed on his lip and looked back out the window before shooting a sideways glance in Steve's direction. "It's been a while since I've had an adventure. Do you need backup?"

Chuckling, Steve said, "If you want adventure, let me try to land this plane." He had no intention of letting Ted tag along.

Ted burst out laughing. "Not on your life! Besides, I'm not going to let you get yourself into trouble."

Leaning back, Steve closed his eyes, regretting his decision to involve Ted. "It's dangerous." He opened his eyes and looked at his friend.

"So?"

"Just stay with the plane when we get there."

"Bullshit! I'll turn this puppy around."

Steve gave Ted a sideways glance before he looked out the window. "Fine. But you can't come into the building with me. I don't want that on my conscience, too."

"Fine by me." Ted nodded and flipped the plane off autopilot as they approached their destination. "So, now that you're not undercover, what exactly are you doing for the bureau?"

"Research and profiling," he stated. "Not exactly the adrenaline rush I'm used to."

"I'll bet." He switched his headset on. "Essex Airfield, Flight six-one-two approaching. Request permission to land," Ted said into the mouthpiece.

"Flight six-one-two, affirmative. Field is clear, approach from the Northwest."

Ted adjusted his course as Steve spotted the runway. Ted pulled back on the throttle, slowing the speed of the aircraft for the landing approach. Seconds later, they touched down on the runway. Ted reverse-throttled, slowing the plane to a stop. He taxied off the runway toward a waiting hangar.

"That was so much smoother than the last landing," Steve said as they pulled to a stop.

After he'd powered the jet down and flipped off all the control buttons, Ted unhooked the seatbelt. "I've got a car waiting for us," he said, glancing at his watch. "We've got three hours before we need to head back to the airfield."

"Thanks." Steve hauled his backpack over his shoulder and paused at the door of the plane. "I really wish you'd stay here," he said with his back to Ted.

"What's the worst that could happen?"

He glanced over his shoulder. "We could both get our brains blown out."

Ted's complexion paled, and he stepped back. "You're not kidding, are you?"

"No, I'm not. It's an actual possibility." He leveled his gaze at his friend. Even though he knew it would be better for Ted to stay with the plane, a part of him wanted his old friend to tag along—if only to mitigate the possibility of Jennifer's vision. "You still want to tag along?"

He hesitated.

"Good call." Steve turned to leave.

"I'm still going," Ted answered, following him out of the plane.

"You're just as insane as I am."

"Where to?" he asked as they settled in the back seat of the town-car.

Pulling his wallet out, Steve opened the slip of paper. "Sixteen-ninety-five West Ninety-Sixth Street."

"That's a pretty affluent area."

He shrugged. "Maybe we can grab a bite to eat while we're up there."

Ted nodded, and silence filled the car. Neither of them spoke until the driver pulled up alongside the beautiful brownstone and they tumbled out onto the sidewalk. After the car moved off, Steve turned his attention to the building. The front door operated on an electronic card.

"Shit," he mumbled. Looking at the call buttons on the wall to his right, he pushed the button for the apartment above his destination.

A female voice answered. "Hello?"

"Hi, I'm sorry for buzzing but I live below you, and unfortunately, I left my card key in my apartment. Think you could buzz me in?"

Silence followed.

"My name is Kyle Winslow," he added into the intercom, "Apartment 3B."

More silence followed, and then the door clicked. He opened it and pressed the intercom again. "Thanks, I appreciate it." He slipped inside with Ted in tow.

Steve climbed the stairs with his back to the wall. Pointing his gun at the floor, he scanned the stairwell above and below them until they got to the third-floor landing. Sliding the gun into his holster, he turned to Ted. "Stay here."

Ted looked at the stairwell and back at him. "No way."

With a quick nod, Steve flipped the backpack off his shoulder, digging inside for the locksmith set before approaching apartment 3B. Giving the hallway one final scan, he crouched to eye level with the lock. A few seconds later, he swung the apartment door open and pulled his gun out, stepping inside.

Ted followed and closed the door behind him, staying in place as Steve crossed the living area and slid into the back hallway.

"No one's here," Steve said, returning the gun under his shirt. The sparsely furnished abode definitely wasn't a long-term residence; it looked more like a safe house than an apartment. His scan stopped at the computer desk in the corner, and he stepped toward it. "Take a load off." He pointed to the couch.

"What if he comes in while we're here?" Ted asked, glancing at the door.

Steve looked between the door and his friend. "Then we're screwed." The desk drawer didn't budge when he pulled on it, so he peeled the locksmith set from his pocket, choosing the right instrument for the job. Kneeling, he picked the lock on the drawer, sliding it open.

"Did you learn that in the bureau?"

Nodding, he smiled. "It's one of the areas I excel in." He shuffled through the papers in the drawer, but there was nothing in the obnoxious organization that would implicate the guy for anything, and he really had to concentrate to put it back in the original order. He slid the drawer closed and relocked it.

"What are the other areas?"

Steve paused, looking up at his friend. "Planting a bullet where it needs to go."

Ted whistled and picked up one of the magazines off the table.

The file cabinet was next, and it slid open easily. Shuffling through the files, he stopped, yanking out an itinerary for a trip to Italy. He raised his eyebrow and scanned the document, turning it to see if anything was detailed on the back.

The bastard's in Italy but there's no name, no flight numbers or hotels, just a reference to the Galleria Vittorio Emanuele II and today's date. What the fuck?

He put the itinerary on top of the file cabinet. Nothing else in the cabinet called for his attention.

"I'm going to check the bedroom. Just hang there and don't touch anything else."

Steve searched the nightstand and found nothing out of the ordinary. He rifled through all the drawers in the bureau before focusing on the closet. Nothing but neatly stacked clothing on the shelves above the pristine rack of suits and the shoebox-lined floor. Steve paused and then kneeled, opening every box. He got to the second to last one and stopped when he flipped the lid off.

"Jesus." He pulled out photographs.

He'd hit the mother lode.

Sweet Jesus.

The pretty blonde in the picture was the same one from the case file Jack had sent a few weeks ago. She was naked with a slit throat. He sat down hard, recognizing the photographs as he shuffled through them. Underneath the snapshots was a single Ziploc bag with a decapitated pinky, and he assumed that belonged to the latest victim.

Not only was Charlie's brother a mafia assassin, but he was also a serial killer. The Slasher. The bastard who attacked Jennifer.

"Fuck," he whispered. His nagging hunch had been right all along. Fear seeded in his stomach, taking on a life of its own, and he closed his eyes. "Shit," he muttered, and looked around the bedroom. He'd just compromised their case.

With the box in hand, he walked to the living room, turning on the printer. He slid the photos on the scanner bed and pressed print. There were eight pictures and newspaper clippings. Steve photocopied all the items, including the baggie holding the finger, and placed them back in the shoebox, returning them to their original spot in the closet.

He opened the last box and sat back on the floor, covering his mouth with the back of his hand.

Old bones lay across a scattered stack of pictures and Steve pulled the top photograph, staring at the mutilated couple. His brain fired off a different set of pictures that matched the ones on the top of the pile. As he shuffled through the rest of the prints, his stomach churned with hot acid.

These were Kyle's foster parents. He had captured the progression of torture on film and Steve dropped the snapshots back in the box and scrambled to his feet, making a run for the master bathroom at the other side of the bedroom.

He made the toilet in time. The foul taste burned his tongue and he spit, flushing the toilet and crossing to the sink to rinse his mouth. His hands shook as he wiped them on the perfectly aligned rack of hand towels. He glanced at his reflection one last time before heading to the living room with the box. Ignoring the questioning expression on Ted's face, he photocopied the contents of the box and then returned it to the closet.

On his way back to the printer, he glanced at the small shelf on the living room wall. Diverting his path, he pulled out a framed picture partially obscured by a candle and stared at it. A much younger Charlie stood next to a punk rocker with the same facial features, showing off identical tattoos. The kid's eyes were blue gray, leaning more on the gray side, and much more intense than his older brother's. He brought it to the scanner and made a copy of both the picture and the itinerary before returning them to their rightful places.

Retrieving the papers off the printer, he slid them into his backpack, finally meeting Ted's gaze. "Let's go." He crossed to the door.

"I gather you found what you wanted," Ted said, following him out of the apartment building.

Steve uttered a high-pitched laugh. "You could say that." He shuffled down the street with his head hung, deep in thought.

"Want to grab a bite to eat?"

"Sure," Steve said, although that was the last thing on his mind. "Where?"

"There's a great deli near the museum. We can grab something there and head back." Ted steered Steve in the right direction. A few minutes later, they were standing in the Parkside Deli, ordering lunch. "Are you going to show me what you found?"

"It'll spoil your appetite." He made no move to open the backpack. "What we did was breaking and entering. The evidence that I have is inadmissible in court." He closed his eyes. "Fuck."

"That bad?"

"Oh, yeah," he said as their food arrived. He dug into his meal without further comment.

"You said this was personal. Who is this guy?" He took a bite of his corned beef Rueben.

Steve finished the roast beef sandwich and picked at the French fries on his plate. "He's the brother of someone I killed while on duty, and this guy is a crazy son of a bitch." He popped another French fry in his mouth. "I needed something tangible to bring him down, and I found enough proof to put him away for life. The only problem is how I obtained it. I wasn't authorized to enter the apartment."

Ted sat back. "What about me? I could say I got the information."

Steve considered his comment. "I don't want anyone to get burned by something I did." He knew if the information leaked out, his friend would end up in Kyle's crosshairs.

Ted glanced at his watch. "We should head back." He stood, peeling off enough cash to cover the bill.

"At least let me buy lunch." Steve reached for his wallet.

"No. A government salary doesn't compare to what I bring in. Besides, you can return the favor when we get up in the air by showing me what you have in the backpack."

Steve laughed. "You might wish I'd paid for lunch instead," he said, and they stepped out onto the street.

Vengeance
Chapter 66

JENNIFER SAT UP IN bed. The vision was still vivid, and her breath hitched in her chest.

"Honey, are you all right?" Her mother sat on the edge of the bed, her gaze brimming with concern.

Jennifer nodded. "Just a nightmare." She looked out at the twilight. "Steve isn't back yet?"

Allison shook her head. "Not yet." She wiped the hair out of Jennifer's face. "Are you sure you're okay?"

"Yes, Mom," she answered, swinging her legs over the edge of the bed and looking at the clock. Six. Damn. She smiled reassuringly at her mother and got out of bed, crossing to the bathroom to clean the coppery taste out of her mouth.

This time she saw his face, and he was the spitting image of Charlie.

Her brow knit together as she looked at the sink. The connection hit. Her knees wobbled under her weight and she caught herself on the counter.

Oh my god, Charlie's brother is the Slasher.

Her wide green eyes stared back from the mirror. "God help us."

Vengeance
Chapter 67

KYLE OPENED HIS EMAIL and read the note from his boss. Two words leaped from the page, making him smile. His new identity was now solid. Kyle Winslow would end up dead in a gutter in New York.

"Life is good." Kyle leaned back in the seat and sighed.

He signed into each bank account and began transferring funds to the corporation that would pay employee John Sheridan a grand monthly sum for consulting work until the account was depleted.

He'd have to make a quick stop at the apartment in New York to gather the personal mementos in his closet and make sure there was nothing that could point to John Sheridan as his next identity.

Vengeance
Chapter 68

STEVE ARRIVED HOME A little after seven and smiled awkwardly at Jennifer and her parents. "Sorry I'm late." He crossed the room, deposited the backpack in his office, and closed the door. "I'll get dinner started." He caught a kiss from Jennifer on his way to the kitchen.

"What happened?" Jennifer asked, following him into the kitchen.

"We hit some weather down in southern New Hampshire and had to change our flight path."

"Did you have a good time?"

Steve nodded, but didn't turn around. He focused on getting dinner thrown together, trying to sort out his thoughts and neutralize the fear lacing his arteries. "Yeah." He chopped up the tomatoes and onions, dropping them in the stir fry pan on the stove. "I'm just a little tired." He looked over his shoulder at her and then went back to preparing dinner.

Steve leaned on the stove for a moment, the impact of his adventure finally taking its toll. He understood there would be an attack on his family if he didn't find Kyle first. A brother with a grudge was one thing, but this man was a serial killer, not to mention a trained assassin, and Steve was more terrified now than he'd been when he saw the beast that clawed his chest to hell.

He took a deep breath and realized the conversation had stopped. Steve glanced over his shoulder and caught the three of them gazing in his direction. "What?" he asked, straightening up.

"Are you all right?" Jennifer approached him.

"Yeah, I'm just exhausted," he said. "It was great to see Ted, but flying around in a plane all day kind of takes the wind out of you." He wrapped his arms around her waist. "How was Samantha today?"

"She's doing great. The doctor thinks it might be a few more days before we can bring her home," Jennifer replied.

The timer buzzed, and Steve unclasped his arms, turning back toward the rice. He pushed away the images that kept flashing in his mind, ignoring them for the time being. He needed to feed his family and get his in-laws out of the house before he settled down in his office to analyze what he had gathered.

"Dinner is served," he announced and formed a lackluster smile. It felt foreign on his lips, but he had to keep up the pretenses.

Jennifer tilted her head, her eyes locked with his.

"Do you want some wine?" Steve asked.

"Um, no," Jennifer answered. She waved her parents toward the seats on the far side of the table and then slid into the chair next to Steve. "Thanks for the dinner." She leaned over and kissed his cheek.

"Thanks for letting me take off for the day," he replied. "Joe, Allison, any wine?" He held up the bottle and filled both glasses when they nodded. "Dig in."

"Jen said you flew down to Martha's Vineyard?" Allison asked.

Steve nodded. "The weather was beautiful. Clear skies all the way down. The return trip was a little different. I'm surprised you didn't get any storms up this way."

"Who were you with?" Joe asked, his voice laced with suspicion.

"A friend of mine from Yale." The accusatory undertone in his father-in-law's question didn't go unnoticed.

"Yale?" Joe raised his eyebrow.

Steve sighed and nodded. "My first field case was at Yale. Ted was my roommate while I was there." He glanced at Jennifer and then at her parents.

"Does he know you're with the FBI?"

Steve nodded. "He didn't know while I was his roommate. But he knew before I left Yale."

"It must be tough to lie about who you are all the time," Joe commented.

Steve shrugged, ignoring the dig. "I caught the bad guy."

"So, lying is second nature to you?" Joe pushed.

Steve set his silverware down and stared at his father-in-law. Anger raged, burning through the fear, and setting his pulse on overdrive. "I'm not doing this." He stood up.

Jennifer grabbed his arm. "Please."

Steve looked into her green eyes and slowly sank back into the seat. He turned his attention back to his father-in-law, reaching for his glass, draining it, refilling his goblet, silently daring Joe to make a comment about his drinking.

"Dad, please stop," Jennifer said. "Steve is a good man."

Joe turned toward Jennifer. "He lies for a living."

"He puts criminals behind bars," Jennifer countered.

"You know, I had a long day. I come home and cook this nice dinner for you, and this is the way you thank me?" Steve stood up, this time shaking Jennifer's hand off his arm as she tried to stop him from leaving the kitchen. Steve stormed across the living room and slammed his office door behind him. He stood for a moment. "Fuck it," he muttered and opened the door, stormed back into the kitchen, leaned across the table, and grabbed the full wine bottle and his wineglass. He returned to his office feeling the stares on his back as he closed the door again.

⁃⇒ ⁃⇒ ⁃⇒

"THANKS A LOT, DAD." Jennifer threw her napkin on the table. Her vision blurred with tears. The pleasant day went to hell in less than a half hour because her father just couldn't keep his opinion to himself. "I think you should go."

"Jennifer, he's a time bomb waiting to explode," Joe said. "He's been unstable all his life."

Jennifer laughed. "Bullshit."

"Joe, stop," Allison piped in.

"He freaked out after his sister died, and I heard he freaked out when his fiancé died a few years back," Joe pushed.

"I freaked out when I saw his sister's death, too," Jennifer snapped. "That was the first time I had an asthma attack, and you know who saved my ass back then? The man you just insulted."

688

Jennifer stood and crossed the room, leaving her parents staring after her. She stepped into the office, startling Steve enough that he dropped the stack of papers he was looking at. A couple of pages drifted onto the floor at the side of the desk.

Steve scrambled to collect the copies, but she was faster, reaching down and picking up two of the pages. She froze at the photocopy in her hand. The details burned into her consciousness by her very vivid visions. Her gaze shot to his. "Where did you go today?"

Steve reached down and plucked the copies from her, avoiding eye contact. When he finally met her gaze, she knew.

"You didn't," she gasped, her hand flying up to cover her mouth.

Steve looked down at the mess of paper on his desk and nodded. He raised his eyes but didn't say a word.

The strength left her legs, and she sat down in the chair facing his desk. "But?"

"But what? I'm in the middle of an active investigation, Jen," he snapped and held up the photocopies. "The shit thing is that I may have compromised the entire case." He took a seat behind the desk. "I broke into his apartment and got this without a warrant. It's inadmissible." He threw the paper onto the desk and leaned back, covering his face. "Kyle is the Slasher." He raked his hands down his face.

"I know."

Steve's eyebrows creased, and he leaned forward. "You know? Why the hell didn't you tell me?"

Jennifer leaned away from his angry glare. "I didn't know until today. He killed again, and I saw his face, okay?"

Steve snapped his mouth closed and glanced at the array of photographs on the desk. When he looked back at her, he nodded.

"Was there even a Ted?"

"Yes. Ted was with me," he answered. "He owns a private charter company, and I called him."

Jennifer raised her eyebrows. "How much did that set us back?"

"Nothing."

"You expect me to believe you?"

"I saved his wife from the rapist at Yale."

"Oh." Jennifer blinked and looked down at her hands. Steve didn't call in favors unless he was desperate, and she knew her visions had pushed him into that category. The magnitude of his stunt crashed down on her and she bit her lip, blinking back the mist that covered her eyes.

He could have been killed today. The thought resounded in her head over and over.

The man stalking them was the same one who attacked her in New York, the same one who killed all those women, the same one who made her chop off Steve's arm in her vision.

The depths of his darkness terrified her, and the thought of him actually finding her alone in the cottage just added to her horror.

AFTER HER PARENTS LEFT, Steve walked into the nursery, flipping on the light and staring at the empty crib. A part of him was glad she wasn't home yet. At least he knew his daughter was safe. He took a deep breath and headed out of the nursery toward the bedroom.

Leaning on the doorjamb, Steve watched Jennifer pretend to read. He knew she was angry, but instead of talking with her, he grabbed the wine and headed outside to the gazebo. The last of the light faded behind the mountains and he finished the bottle of wine, rocking gently with his thoughts.

After a while, Jennifer slid into the seat next to him. She didn't speak, she just sat with her hands folded in her lap and let the silence build between them.

Steve reached over and took her hand.

Jennifer pulled it away, glaring at him. "You lied to me," she finally said.

"Yep," Steve agreed. He reached for the bottle, pouring the last few drops into his glass before draining it.

Jennifer stood up to leave, and he grabbed her arm.

"Sit for a while."

"Why?" she asked.

"Because," he answered, blinking the misty film from his eyes.

Jennifer stared at him and the tight muscles in her jaw relaxed. She slowly lowered back onto the seat. "I'm still pissed at you," she said after a few minutes.

"I know." He took her hand.

She allowed him to lace his fingers through hers as they rocked in silence. The slow creak of the swing filled the dusk.

"What if my dream had come true?"

Steve let the air out of his lungs. "That's why I let Ted come with me. I figured it would change the outcome." He paused. "I was right."

"How could you put yourself in danger like that?" she snapped. She attempted to yank her hand from his, but he clamped down.

He finally looked fully in her direction. "It's my job." The words hissed from his chest.

"But you put your friend in danger, too," she pointed out.

Steve closed his mouth, gritting his teeth together. "He knew what he was getting into."

Jennifer tilted her head. "Is he a cop?"

"No, he isn't."

Jennifer shook her head, laughing slightly. "You're still using people to get what you want." She shot a glare in his direction.

"I'm aware of that," he whispered, looking out at the water. A tear cut a hot path down his cheek. "But I've got to know I did everything I could do. Otherwise, I'll go insane." He looked back at her. "If I can't stop him..." he trailed off.

The fear that seeded in his stomach today took over his entire body at the thoughts following that statement. A shadow passed over the lake and he looked away, running his hand through his hair. "If I can't stop him, we'll all end up in Brooksfield Cemetery."

Vengeance
Chapter 69

SHUFFLING THROUGH THE PICTURES in his office, Steve took a deep breath and began matching them to cases in the file, achieving a chronological record of Kyle's transgressions. Kyle didn't have all the pictures of his victims in his closet in New York. Steve was willing to bet a month's salary that pictures of the remaining women from his case file hid in Kyle's Las Vegas homestead.

The case file had twenty victims in the last eight years. He studied the locations of the deaths again and glanced at the itinerary, his brow creasing. He typed in a search request for the same modus operandi against the Interpol database and let out a tuneless whistle when the results came back. Another half dozen cases matched his criteria, spread throughout the major cities of Europe.

He had struck in London, Paris, Barcelona, Rome and most recently Milan. Steve glanced at the itinerary and covered his face with his hands as he pushed the chair away from his desk.

He leaned back and took a deep breath, picking up the photographs of Kyle's foster parents. The whole signature was different. He took his time with them, relishing each atrocity versus the relatively quick deaths of the women Kyle had killed. This was personal, and Steve wondered how they would fare, because Kyle's vendetta against him was definitely personal.

He got lost in the research, his heart hammering in his chest loudly enough to drown the sound of the doorknob turning.

Steve hammered away on the keyboard until she cleared her throat. He looked up to see Jennifer leaning against the doorjamb with her arms folded across her chest. He met her questioning green eyes.

"I'm mapping a correlation between the assassinations we attribute to the Bondinos and the killings in our files." He looked back to the computer screen. He had been cross-referencing items back and forth for the last couple of hours. He glanced back at the doorway. And she wasn't there anymore.

"Shit," he mumbled and saved his research. He stood up and wandered through the house, finding her in the bed, under the covers with her back to the door. He slid under the covers behind her, kissing her shoulder.

JENNIFER DIDN'T RESPOND. SHE took a deep breath, letting it out slowly. She knew her husband had a dark and dangerous side when pushed too far. She was scared to death that when all this passed, he would plummet into that abyss and never return.

Vengeance
Chapter 70

STEVE SMILED DOWN AT Samantha and glanced at Jennifer. "I'm going to grab lunch. Anything you want in particular?"

Jennifer nodded. "A cheeseburger?"

He kissed her and headed toward the cafeteria, pulling his cell out of his pocket. "Morning, Jack," he said when the voice answered.

"Hi, Steve. What's up?"

"Kyle Wisnowski is the Slasher." When his boss sucked the air in between his teeth, Steve waited for Jack to process the information. "We need to search the house in Las Vegas."

"How did you make that connection?"

"I've got proof," he mumbled, knowing he was going to get reamed.

"What did you do?"

Steve placed his order at the counter and took a seat in the wings, waiting with his ticket number. "I took a little trip yesterday," he finally said to Jack.

"What the hell did you do?"

"I pulled some strings and got a lift down to the city," he said. "I paid a visit to our friend and found some interesting photos in a couple of shoe boxes in the closet.”

“You did what?” Jack barreled into the phone.

“He’s the Slasher, Jack. And I found proof leading to his foster parents’ death. And he’s in Italy right now. I found an itinerary there and Jennifer had another vision, and there was a murder in Italy that corresponds to the Slasher case. She saw his face this time, Jack, and said he’s the spitting image of Charlie.”

“You entered a suspect’s house without a warrant?” he growled.

“I’ve got the trail, both in dates and bodies, and there’s a direct correlation with some of the hits we pegged to the Bondinos. It’s enough to get a warrant to search Kyle’s house.”

“You need more than just a hunch, and what you got is inadmissible.”

“God damn it, Jack, this guy is the one who attacked Jennifer in October!” He turned his back to the patrons, who glanced his way, shielding the mouthpiece with his hand. “We both know what this guy is capable of.” His voice rumbled from his chest.

“Steve, you broke the law and compromised our case.”

“I didn’t take anything. I made copies and put things back.”

“If I send someone in there now, will they find your fingerprints?”

Steve closed his eyes and let himself slump into the chair. “Shit,” he said, knowing exactly where his boss was going.

“They’ll say you planted evidence.”

“My fingerprints aren’t in Las Vegas.”

"Can you tie him to any of the crime scenes without the evidence you found?"

Steve was quiet. "I've got the correlations to mafia hits, and we have the DNA profile, which was similar enough to Charlie's that it was written off as him—but it didn't match exactly, which tells me it has to be family and the only living relative is Kyle."

"I've got a marked grave and death certificate that says otherwise. They're exhuming Kyle's body on Monday, but it could take a couple of weeks to get DNA results. In the meantime, I'll start the paperwork to get a warrant for the Las Vegas residence, but you may have fucked up any case we have against the bastard. Get me a tie that would put him at or near the crime scene without compromising the case any further," Jack ordered.

"Okay."

"Steve?"

"Yeah."

"I'm serious. Don't do anything else that will compromise this case," Jack spat through the phone.

"Okay. I'll talk to you later." Steve hung up the phone and closed his eyes. He knew damn well he was lucky to still have his badge. The fact that Jack didn't threaten to pull it was nothing short of a miracle.

Vengeance
Chapter 71

THE PLANE TOUCHED DOWN at JFK airport at a little after five. By the time Kyle strolled into his apartment, it was close to seven-thirty and he was ravenous. He walked over to his desk, picked up the phone to order takeout, and froze. The printer was on. Kyle turned, scanning the apartment for anything else that was out of order. His eyes landed on the couch and coffee table. The pillow was wrong, and the magazine wasn't the way he left it. He put the phone down. Walking to the other side of the desk, he reached under the drawer, pulling out his handgun. He flipped off the safety and slid out of his shoes so he would be soundless as he stalked through the apartment.

He stood in his bedroom with the closet open. His mouth parted as he gazed at the shoeboxes. They weren't lined up perfectly.

"Shit." He crouched down, opening them up. He quashed the urge to throw the boxes across the room. The contents had been disturbed.

"God damn it!" He stood up, pacing across the room and back.

He emptied half of his drawers into a suitcase, closed it, and stormed into the living room, flipped the safety back on the gun, and slammed it on the desk.

He turned on the computer and did a quick search, finding the poor soul who was going to suddenly and violently die in the next couple of days. Same height, same weight, and same tattoo, but that's where the similarities ended. He opened the desk drawer and looked at the slightly disheveled items.

Nothing in the drawer had his picture on it. He leaned back in the seat and looked around.

Whoever had been in the apartment was good, but leaving the copier on was a slip-up. If he wasn't such an obsessive-compulsive person, he would have noticed nothing out of the ordinary. Even the copier could have been overlooked.

His transition plans needed to be executed more quickly than expected. He dragged his suitcase down to the car and returned to the apartment.

Kyle went about the tedious task of cleaning every surface in the apartment, including each picture in the shoeboxes. He swore under his breath as he slid the boxes back in the closet. The mementos of his adventures would need to be left behind. He opened the box that held the pictures of his first kill and he shuffled through them quickly, stopping at the last shot of the carnage. "Fucking asshole." He tossed the picture back in the box, covering it.

It took Kyle close to six hours to scour every surface in the place and then he dropped all the cleaning supplies, including the vacuum bag, into the incinerator on his way out. His last look around the apartment produced a heavy sigh and then he closed the door on that chapter in his life.

Once he'd settled into the house across the lake from his pet project, he'd come back to the city to finish the job of wiping Kyle Winslow off the face of the earth. A quick stop at Grand Central Station procured his identity documents. His normal drop locker contained credit cards and a driver's license in the name of John Sheridan. Whistling, he pocketed the items and returned to his double-parked car, starting the long trek north.

Pulling into the driveway at six-thirty in the morning, he grabbed the suitcase and headed inside, exhausted. He dropped his bags in the foyer and closed the door. Heading to the couch in front of the bay windows, he sprawled on the soft cushions and instantly fell asleep.

Vengeance
Chapter 72

STEVE WAS QUIET ON the drive home. He had been so preoccupied with Jennifer's visions that he hadn't looked into finding the receivers for the cameras. He flipped the phone open and pressed redial. "Jack?"

"I've been trying to call you. The coffin was empty."

He pulled to a stop in front of the garage. "Empty?"

"Yes, empty. You were right. Kyle Wisnowski is not dead—or at least not dead and buried where everyone thought he was."

Steve closed his eyes. Jennifer's gaze bore into him from the passenger seat, and he took a deep breath. "That's not the reason I was calling. I need the houses and hotels within a one-mile radius of the cottage searched, or at least approached."

"Why?"

"That's the radius of the transmitters in the cameras Matt found."

"I'll get the local sheriff's office to help with coverage," he agreed. "By the way, the paperwork's been filed to search the Las Vegas apartment. We're just waiting for the judge."

"Good, then we can get a definitive DNA sample," Steve answered. "I've also got another question." He glanced at Jennifer. "Is it possible to continue working from home for a couple more weeks, or at least until Samantha comes home?" Steve pressed his lips together, waiting for his boss to balk. He wasn't ready to leave yet; he had a feeling that would be inviting disaster.

"Fine. I'll see what I can do," Jack mumbled.

"Thanks."

"Just find a connection to tie him to the hits."

Vengeance
Chapter 73

HE WOKE TO BLINDING sunlight and blinked, disoriented. Glancing at his watch, the time registered after a few blinks—a little after noon, Eastern Time—a stomach rumble followed. The last time he ate was in Italy a little over a day ago. Ravenous and a little light-headed, he looked around the house, the brain fog lifting.

New Hampshire. He squinted out the window at the bright day.

Kyle fumbled around the kitchen, looking for anything that resembled breakfast. Granola bars seemed to be the only thing edible on the menu. The milk in the refrigerator had gone bad during the time he'd been gone, and the orange juice wasn't that far behind. He dumped them down the sink and grabbed one of the bottled waters in the pantry, cracking it open to wash down the granola bars he inhaled.

He flipped the monitors on and stared at the static. The only working monitor was the one showing the outside of the cottage, and it revealed an empty driveway. They weren't home. Standing and looking out the window, he confirmed what was on the television.

Kyle went back out to the car and emptied it, leaving only the registration in the glove compartment. He wiped it down, expunging his fingerprints from the surfaces.

Flipping the phone open, he dialed a familiar number. "Morning, Tony," he said when his boss picked up. "I need one more favor."

"What's that?" Tony Bondino snapped into the phone.

"Torch my place," Kyle said.

The appeal was met with silence, and Kyle waited.

"Why?"

"I got wind that somehow I'm on the feds' radar, and I won't get the chance to clean house before they swarm. I don't want them to get hold of anything that would point to you," he said, knowing Tony would jump on his request if he thought there was any danger of a connection.

Tony swore under his breath. "Fine."

"Thanks, Tony." He hung up.

The next assignment on his list was two-fold: plant more cameras and carry out the assassination of Kyle Winslow.

He disappeared upstairs to clean up.

Kyle came downstairs a half hour later and rummaged through his electronics bag, pulled out five more cameras, added them to his backpack, and headed over to the empty cottage. He slipped inside and planted the small recording devices, setting them to a different frequency—one he would switch on when he got back into town.

He grabbed the last thing in his backpack and stared at it with a smile. Getting down on the floor on his back, he taped the little bomb jacket to the bottom of the crib.

When he left, he made damn sure the door was locked behind him.

His number one priority right now was getting to New York and cleaning up this mess before Tony got wind of it; otherwise, he was in deep shit. He had to make a very public statement with the death of Kyle Winslow. That was the only way he would be afforded the time he needed to finish his side venture.

Vengeance
Chapter 74

THE WALKIE-TALKIE SQUAWKED. "I think I found something!"

Within twenty minutes, the house across the lake was crawling with police and federal officers.

Steve stood in the living room, staring at the monitors. The only one with a live shot was a long view of his yard. That camera was currently being taken down. He turned to the closest officer. "Did you find the elderly couple that lives here?"

"No, sir."

"Keep looking. They have to be on the property somewhere." He walked out of the house, his fists clenching and unclenching. They had been close. There was evidence of a quick getaway, but they hadn't been able to make the car. Without that, they were out of the water.

"Shit!" He slipped into his car and drove the two-minute loop around the lake to his cabin.

"Jack, he was there. They have suitcases full of clothing, and the monitors to the cameras in my house were there. The bastard got away." He swore into the phone, leaning back in the driver's seat. "There wasn't a fucking print anywhere! Just like all the crime scenes, not a goddamned fingerprint on anything."

"We'll set up surveillance to see if he comes back."

Steve closed the cell phone. He didn't think the bastard was coming back, not with the obvious getaway.

LATER THAT EVENING, HIS phone rang. It was Jack.

Steve turned toward the lake, his eyes taking in the scene. "They found the old couple?" Police lights reflected across the surface of the lake. He could make out the pile of dirt in the far corner of the house.

"They were buried in the flower garden. One shot to the head each."

"Damn."

Vengeance
Chapter 75

STEVE WAS STILL IN a foul mood. The couple across the lake didn't deserve to die like that, and it was all because of him that they'd been murdered.

If he hadn't killed Charlie...

He shook the thought out of his head, staring out the window at the lake in back, the plate in his hand momentarily forgotten.

"I think that dish is clean," Jennifer said, interrupting his self-depreciating train of thought.

"Yeah," he said. Sending a half smile in her direction, he finished washing the rest of the dinner dishes.

"You can't keep beating yourself up. It's been two days and you're still sulking."

Before the snide comeback reached his lips, the phone rang. He snatched it off the hook, sending a sideways glance at Jennifer.

"Steve, it's Jack."

"What's up?"

"Winslow's dead."

Steve shut the water off. "Say again." He wiped his hands on a paper towel.

"They found the body of Kyle Winslow in his car. He was murdered."

Steve pulled out the kitchen chair and sat down. "How'd they identify him?"

"Well, his dental records were out—the killer smashed his teeth to hell—but his wallet was in the glove compartment along with the registration. Both carried items with the name Kyle Winslow. And Steve, he had the same tattoo on his right forearm that Charlie had. The one Jennifer drew."

"Scorpion tattoo?"

"Yep, and the house in Las Vegas was torched before we got the search warrant." Jack paused. "Were you able to find a concrete connection to the Bondinos?"

"No, not yet. Did you cross-check the DNA samples?"

"No."

"Can we?"

Jack paused and exhaled through the receiver. "I'll send the request tomorrow, but Steve, this is the guy."

"How do you know it's not just another trick?"

"We found one more thing hidden in the trunk."

"What's that?"

"A knife with remnants of blood on it. It has the same signature as all the local Slasher cases, and I'm sure the blood on the knife will match the most recent victim."

Steve inhaled and let the air slowly blow through his pursed lips.

"He's dead, so you can relax now."

"He's really dead?" The full impact of the information finally sunk in. Jennifer had had some broken dreams over the last few days, but she categorized them as nightmares, not visions.

"Yes," Jack confirmed. "I'll send you the photos and police reports, and I'll expect to see you in the office on Monday."

"I would prefer to wait for the DNA results."

"I need you here."

Steve sighed. Jack's conviction that the body was Kyle's eased some knots in his stomach. "Fine. I'll see you Monday. Thanks for letting me know." Steve turned off the phone. He looked at Jennifer. "They found Kyle Winslow's body."

"Really?" Jennifer searched his eyes, and he nodded. "Are you sure?" she asked, echoing his earlier skepticism.

"Jack is sure." Relief washed through his muscles, releasing the tiny knots of stress in his neck and shoulders, despite the nagging doubt in his stomach. His energy level sparked, giving him hope. Hope that he seemed to have lost since Samantha was born. His lips slowly spread into his signature smile. The one he knew drove Jennifer wild.

"You can't smile at me like that."

Blush rose in her cheeks, and he crossed to her, wrapping his arms around her waist and pulling her close. "Why not?"

"Because it drives me crazy."

A smile played on her lips, her eyes bordering on smoldering, and his body reacted instantly. Sizzling heat, the kind that used to accost him every time he looked at her, burned through his blood. He stole a kiss, letting it linger and morph into the hot pace of passion. Reluctantly, he broke the kiss and stepped away. "Good," he said, flashing the smile again before retreating to the couch and stretching out.

It was the first time in months he felt relaxed. The news, however morbid, meant their life together would be much longer than just this summer.

Vengeance
Chapter 76

KYLE PULLED INTO THE old couple's house around two in the afternoon. He slid the key in the lock and his eyebrows creased when the knob didn't turn. Slowly, he pulled the key out and stepped back.

COMPROMISED!

His heart slammed against the walls of his chest, and he glanced in the window. The monitors were gone. "Shit!" He stepped to the side of the porch, glancing across the lake. Jennifer sat in the gazebo, slowly rocking back and forth. He pulled his handheld transmitter, programming it to the right frequency. The rooms of the house came into view and Steve was inside, talking on the phone.

The muscles in Kyle's jaw contracted and relaxed as he ground his teeth in frustration. He glanced around the yard and then set his hand held to scan for other frequencies. Nothing appeared, and he exhaled. They must have shut surveillance off when the news of his death reached New Hampshire.

Kyle picked the lock and headed inside. The house was spotless, and his clothing was nowhere to be found. He shook his head, looking out at the gazebo. His eyes shifted to the kayak sitting on the boathouse rack. A slow smile appeared on his lips.

Vengeance
Chapter 77

THE SPRING HEAT WAVE kicked into high gear the day they brought Samantha home from the hospital. Jennifer spent the afternoon in the gazebo's shade, enjoying the breeze filtering off the lake. She stared at the tiny baby in her arms and glanced at the cottage where Steve chatted with his folks and whipped up another delectable culinary delight.

She didn't notice the kayak until it drifted into her peripheral vision. Glancing up, she saw a muscular blonde man pulling the oars like a professional rower. The glare of the sun made it difficult to see any details beyond his ripped form and blonde hair.

Jennifer stood up. "Watch out for the reef!" she called out, shading her eyes as she held Samantha to her shoulder.

The rower immediately reversed his stroke, stopping the canoe in place.

"There's a pretty nasty reef under the surface over there." Jennifer pointed to the right, her voice echoing across the water.

KYLE LOOKED IN THE direction he had been rowing and then back at Jennifer, his brows creasing and his heart doing the two-step in his chest.

"If you hit it going as fast as you were, it would rip that kayak to shreds."

"Thanks." He sent his disarming smile her way and waited for any hint of recognition.

"No problem." She settled back in the swing, returning her attention to the bundle in her arms.

No recognition, no interest, nothing, and his heart slowed in disappointment. He scanned the yard and inhaled, just sitting in the kayak, debating.

Not yet, you idiot.

He shook the wanton thoughts from his head and rowed away, keeping his eye on her, hoping she wouldn't look up. He was both impressed and more than a little disappointed when she didn't. While he would prefer time with her and the baby before her husband came home, he also was itching for payback.

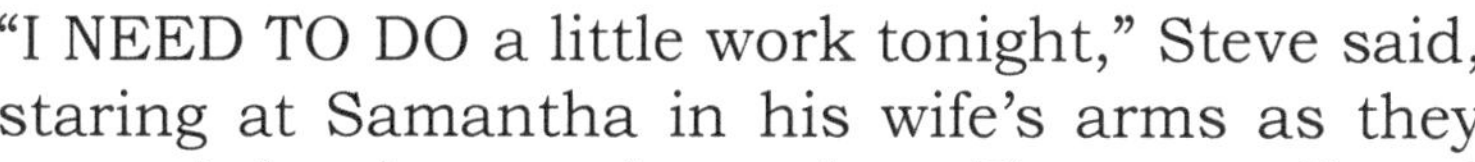

"I NEED TO DO a little work tonight," Steve said, staring at Samantha in his wife's arms as they swayed in the gazebo swing. The sun dipped below the mountains, drawing the heat with it.

"No problem." Jennifer stood when Samantha let out a small cry of discontent. She walked into the cottage to get a bottle for the baby, and he followed.

When Jennifer settled into the recliner and propped the bottle in Samantha's mouth, Steve leaned over and caught a kiss. "I shouldn't be that late." He planted a kiss on Samantha's forehead and crossed to his office, taking a seat and flipping the computer on.

Piecing the links between Kyle and the Bondinos took him a good part of the evening, but when he was done, he sat back and looked at the map of the murdered women with all the suspected mafia hits. The assassinations were in the same general vicinity as the murders. One correlation or even two would have been a coincidence, but there were sixteen consecutive hits in the same vicinity within a day or two of the murders.

"I guess Tony Bondino must have gotten wind of your extracurricular activities." He pulled up the photos of Kyle Winslow. He was killed by a shot to the head and then beaten with his own gun, which shattered all the bones in his face to the point of being unrecognizable. Steve leaned back, his brow furrowed, mulling it over.

He stretched and glanced at the clock. It was close to midnight, and he shut down the computer, dreading the thought of going into the office in the morning.

Vengeance
Chapter 78

STEVE DRAGGED HIMSELF OUT of bed in the dark bedroom and headed into the bathroom, muttering about the early hour.

Kyle smiled at the image on his screen.

"You think you're unhappy now," he said to the monitor. "Wait until you get home tonight."

Steve puttered in the kitchen, fixing himself a cup of coffee for the road, and then walked into the bedroom to kiss his wife goodbye.

Jennifer's eyes fluttered open and a small smile appeared on her lips as she bid her husband a good day and drifted back to sleep.

Setting his plan into motion, he grabbed his clothing, shoved it in the backpack with the rest of his tools, and waited until Steve's car pulled out of the driveway.

Reaching for his handheld monitor, Kyle chuckled. He flipped through the rooms in the house and then back to the bedroom. Steve had fed the baby before he left, and she was still sleeping peacefully in the crib. He didn't think she would wake up for another couple of hours.

The nursery was his target waiting area. He doubted Jennifer would wake before the baby, and even if she did, that would be her first stop.

Grinning, he slung the backpack over his shoulder, walking out of the hotel room. Daylight was still tucked behind the mountains, but the sky had the ambient morning hue signaling that the sun was not far from peeking over the horizon. He rolled the bike out and hopped on, peddling the couple of miles to the house. It took him fifteen minutes to pull into their driveway, and he slowed to a stop before breaching the last bend. Hopping off, he pulled the monitor from his pocket, quickly checking the rooms in the house. Nothing had changed, and he tucked the phone in his pocket and hid the bike in the thick underbrush on the side of the driveway. Sprinting, he made it to the house in just under ten seconds.

One more check on his handheld and then he tried the door. The knob resisted, and he kneeled down, quickly picking the lock. Kyle slipped inside and shut the door behind him, flipping the deadbolt in place. His heart ricocheted against his rib cage, creating a beat that drowned out his footsteps to the nursery. His gaze never left the bedroom doorway, and he swallowed, licking his lips and rubbing his fingers on his palms to calm his hungry nerves.

He turned off the baby monitor and kneeled, peeling the explosives from under the crib. Standing, he glanced down at the sleeping baby, squashing the urge to cover her mouth and nose with his hands. That wouldn't do, no; he needed to keep this child alive as long as possible in order to gain both Jennifer and Steve's cooperation.

Kyle laid the vest on the bedding and gently picked up the baby, putting her down on the deadly fabric, and threaded her arms through the armholes. Samantha jerked a little but did not wake up. Kyle took a deep breath and zipped the jacket. It was a pretty good fit, and he stepped back, satisfied. He flipped the trigger to activate the remote-control detonator. The light on the side of the vest went on.

Retrieving the detonator from his backpack, he flipped the switch on. The trigger was now live. He flipped the baby monitor back on and took a seat in the rocking chair, waiting for sleeping beauty to rise.

Vengeance
Chapter 79

JENNIFER WOKE TO THE soft sounds of her daughter stirring and the bright morning sun shining in her eyes. She stretched and slipped into the bathroom to relieve herself, splash water on her face, and clean her teeth. Just as Samantha woke, she headed into the nursery.

"I'm coming, I'm..." She stepped into the room and all the blood drained from her face, leaving her dizzy and terrified.

"Hello, Jennifer," Kyle Winslow, aka *The Slasher,* smiled from the chair, slowly rocking back and forth. One hand lay on the armrest and the other held the detonator.

The world tilted, and she reached for the wall. Her eyes darted to her daughter. There, wrapped around her little angel, was the bomb. She looked back at him, feeling hollow and naked in her little summer negligee. "You bastard!"

"If you do anything I don't like today, I'll blow her to bits." He held the detonator up so she could see.

Samantha let out an unhappy cry.

"Your daughter needs to be fed." He stood and crossed to the door. His steel-gray eyes bore into her, and he pointed toward the kitchen.

Jennifer slid by him, each step jarring her heart in a painful pattern of panic.

"Have you ever seen what happens to a person when they're blown up?"

Just his tone, alone, left her shivering like someone raked fingernails across a chalkboard and she stopped, giving him a cursory glance over her shoulder.

He held the detonator for her to see. "They become blood mist. It's pretty cool," he smiled. "And I can push the button faster than you can launch a knife at me or faster than your husband can shoot me between the eyes."

"He's pretty fast."

"I know. But he wouldn't gamble with his daughter's life, and neither will you."
Jennifer turned away and grabbed a bottle, preparing it with shaking hands. Her mind raced a thousand miles a minute, trying to figure out how to change the outcome of all her visions. Desperation blinded her, and no magical solutions came to mind. With no other option, she turned and strode through the house toward her screaming daughter. She picked up her child, cringing at the ugly bomb jacket that fit snug around her torso.

"Don't even think about it," he said from the doorway. "The collateral damage will still kill her."

Sitting in the chair he'd originally occupied, she glared at him, her teeth clenched hard enough to create an ache in her jaw. She propped the bottle in Samantha's mouth, silencing her daughter's hungry cries.

Kyle crossed his arms and smiled. "That's a good girl."

"How long have you been watching me?"

"This isn't about you, honey," he said. "At one time it was, but the minute your husband killed my brother, it became all about him."

Anger bloomed through the tornado of emotions, and she snapped, "Your brother didn't back off. That's why he's dead."

His eyebrows rose at the venomous outburst. "Your husband killed him and now he needs to pay," he said with a smile that killed any hope she had.

She pulled the bottle out of Samantha's mouth and leaned the baby's small frame on her shoulder, gently patting her back, taking her time with her daughter. Jennifer's anger succumbed to the pressure of fear as each minute ticked past. Samantha rewarded her with a burp and a small noise as she grasped Jennifer's hair in her flailing hand.

"Put her back in the crib now."

"She needs a diaper change." Jennifer peeled her hair out of Samantha's hand.

"Fine." He allowed her to change the diaper. "In the crib," he reminded after the soiled diaper disappeared into the diaper-genie.

Jennifer reluctantly put Samantha in the crib, knowing her personal hell was just about to begin. She swallowed and ran her finger down Samantha's nose, offering what she hoped was a smile of reassurance, but her heart cried to the heavens.

Kyle grabbed her by the upper arm, dragging her to the living room and tossed her onto the floor. "You know, I saw you in that play last fall. You were good." Kyle glanced around the living room, biting his lower lip.

She blinked, letting the injustice of the situation surface. "I don't give a shit whether you saw my play. I want you out of my house." She rose to her feet.

He backhanded her, sending her to the ground a second time. Her cheek burned where his hand struck.

"I want *you* to move the couch over here facing the TV and put the chair over there." He pointed to the corner near their bedroom.

Anger-laced fear screamed through her, souring the lining of her stomach and kept her pulse high enough for the incision on her belly to throb. She slowly got off the floor and pushed the heavy couch where he directed and dragged the recliner to the spot he indicated. She stood just out of his reach as he surveyed the setup, nodding and bringing his eyes back to her.

"Move the coffee table over there." He pointed toward the window, and she slid it to his specification. The backpack slung over his shoulder came off and he reached inside. Pulling out a DVD and a camera, he set them up on top of the television and tossed the remote on the couch. With a few clicks, he switched the television to the video setting, and then turned his focus to her.

"Come here, now."

She looked at the setup and back at him.

What the hell is he doing?

Memories of his brutality clicked off in her mind, his sense of seduction, what sets his rocks off, all fast-forwarded like a broken video out of control.

When he raised the detonator, she moved to the spot in front of him, each step closer, raising her terror.

He turned her toward the camera sitting on top of the television. "Now, my little actress, I expect you to put on a hell of a show." He ran his fingers down her arm in the all too familiar motion and she gasped.

Charlie. Oh my god, he saw the tape of Charlie.

He chuckled at the look of horror reflected on the blank television screen. "That's right. My brother was a saint to stop, but today, we are going to play that scene through and you're going to convince me that this is what you want."

Trembling, she kept the tears locked up. Her thoughts clouded with the memory of his hand squeezing her throat and the pain in her fingers as she clawed at both his hands and the floor, desperate for escape.

"If you don't, I'll kill your daughter."

His comment cleared the fog and Jennifer looked at the floor to her side, nodding.

The phone rang, making her jump and interrupting his twisted seduction.

"Answer it," he demanded, "but if you give anything away, she'll die."

"Hello?" she said, making her voice sound groggy.

"You still sleeping?" Steve asked.

"Mhm," she answered as a tear slid down her cheek. Her mind sent SOS waves through the phone line, but her mouth clamped shut against the need to scream. He*'s here.* Instead, she inhaled and cleared her throat.

"Are you all right?"

"I'm feeling a little sick this morning," she answered, looking at Kyle.

"You need me to come home?"

She didn't answer right away, just closed her eyes and gritted her teeth together to stop the sob that caught in her throat. "I'll be okay." She opened her eyes. Kyle signaled to end the call. "I think Sam is waking up."

"I've got a couple of things I need to do, but as soon as I'm finished, I'll head out, okay?"

"Okay."

"I love you."

"I love you, too." She listened to the dial tone after he hung up and the tears came in earnest. She glanced at the clock. *Hours.* She had a couple of hours alone in the house with this psycho. She looked back at Kyle and shivered.

"I almost believed you." He approached her and took the phone. "Now, where were we? Oh, yeah." Kyle pointed the remote, pressing play. The television came to life with the video of Steve and Desiree in the kitchen.

She closed her eyes.

"No. Watch the video," he snarled in her ear.

Jennifer's eyes opened. "You know that isn't my husband between her legs, right?" she asked, sending a wicked glare in his direction.

"Yes, I know. It was me."

Jennifer's gaze snapped back to the television set, her mouth askew.

"Charlie asked us to make that little video for him." His free hand drifted over her, and her skin crawled in the path of his fingers. "Now you better start acting... or perhaps you'd like to see me carve up your daughter?"

Jennifer shivered when his lips found the nape of her neck. A hint of peppermint and old spice drifted from him, and he pressed his body against hers, his hand pulling the hem of her nightshirt up enough for his fingers to slip under the waistband of her panties. She tilted her head back, resting on his chest, clamping her mouth against the scream that wanted to surface and taking long, slow breaths through her nose to keep from vomiting.

His violation revolted her as much as his gentleness. He was treating her like a lover and not a prisoner, helpless to fight back without retribution. His slow caress brought shivers to the surface, and her skin broke out in gooseflesh. This was more horrifying that what Bill and his fraternity brothers did to her.

She didn't know if her acting abilities ran deeply enough to make this lunatic believe what he demanded. Her eyes flashed to the nursery, and she steeled her feelings, shoving them aside for the sake of her daughter.

The sob locked in her chest morphed into a moan, sounding much more like ecstasy rather than her raging horror and despair.

"Oh, yes," he whispered, plunging his fingers into her. "Now, let's see if you're as good as Desiree." He stripped her clothes and pushed her onto the couch.

Jennifer covered her chest with her arms, curling her legs, unable to continue the ruse, and her gaze dropped to the knife on his belt.

Kyle grabbed her hair and tilted her head back, his eyes gleeful at the prospect of seeing her squirm. He waved the detonator in front of her, his thumb covering the trigger. "I'm going to count to three. One, two..."

She uncurled, muttering curses and shooting a glare in his direction. Anger was a much easier emotion to manage, and she clung to it like a life raft. When his head lowered into her lap, Jennifer stared at the video, at the expression of pure delight on Desiree's face, trying to tap into the same emotion while Kyle mimicked his actions on the screen. She couldn't react, couldn't reach the same plateau the woman on screen did, especially while convincing herself not to let her roiling stomach purge all over this vile bastard.

He stopped and sent a glare up at her that chilled her beyond the memories of his attack, and she shuddered. He climbed between her legs, pinning her to the couch. "What do you think will piss off your husband more? My face buried in your cunt... or my cock?"

The doctor's warning resounded in her mind and she shook her head. "I can't, not yet. I'm not supposed to yet." She struggled under his weight until he brought the detonator into her line of sight with a sadistic grin.

Fear paralyzed her, and she hardly noticed him shifting to peel off his shorts, but the ripping pain of his penetration brought her back along with a throaty scream.

"I can't." Jennifer cried, tears blurring her vision as she planted her hands on his chest. Pushing him away was as futile as her pushing her stone chimney over.

Kyle smiled down at her and drove his full length inside her harder than his initial penetration. "I don't care whether you can, I am. Now you better start acting." He almost pulled out and then shoved into her again.

She arched, bringing her hips to his with the same ferocity as he did. Pain ripped through her abdomen with each thrust. Her teeth clenched against the screams dying to be freed from her chest.

He stopped, glaring down at her. "I think I'd have more fun carving up your daughter." He pulled away.

Startled and frightened, she yelled, "No!" Wrapping her legs around his waist, she pulled him back into her. "I can do this."

His eyes narrowed. "Prove it."

Closing her eyes, she took a deep breath and exhaled through her mouth. Changing the scene in her mind, pretending this was Steve instead of the twisted killer inside her, she forced the fear and disgust into something she could work with. All her tense muscles relaxed, and she prayed the command reached her face. With another deep breath, she opened her eyes and tilted her head, allowing a smile to form.

He raised an eyebrow and circled his hips in a slow grind.

Even though his motion sent tendrils of sharp pain through her entire frame, she joined him, swiveling her hips in time with his. "Oh, Kyle," she moaned, observing the glossy eyes of passionate domination.

He smiled, and she shivered.

She closed her eyes and arched into each of Kyle's thrusts, repeating his name and *yes* until he groaned, shuddering through his release.

He moved away and pulled up his shorts, inspecting her like a bug after a successful experiment. "That was acceptable."

Jennifer glared at him and curled away, clenching her jaw against the tremble that started in her core. "I hate you, you son of a bitch!" Her stomach rolled, and she shot off the couch, grabbing her discarded nightgown. She barely made it to the toilet before the acid poured into the bowl. She spit, and her stomach lurched again. The hot trail of excretions leaking down her legs was enough to make her dry heave.

"Get up."

"Fuck you!"

"I just did." He laughed at his own wit.

She stood, slipping her nightgown on, and reached for a towel.

"No." Kyle grabbed her arm, dragging her back to the living room. He pressed the reverse arrow to the point on the tape where Desiree took Steve in her mouth. "I want that." He froze the frame.

"You're out of your fucking mind."

He swung his fist toward her face.

Jennifer parried, blocking the punch.

He held up the detonator. "You do that again, and I'll start by cutting off one of your daughter's fingers." He backhanded her across the face with the hand holding the detonator, sending her to her side.

Bright flashes of light filled her vision and her face throbbed. She pressed her hand to the fiery burn on her cheek where his hand connected and blinked away the stars. When her vision cleared, she sent invisible daggers at him, wishing he'd drop dead. Her gaze fell on the knife attached to his belt and she scuttled backwards, getting to her feet with her eyes darting between Samantha's room and the sadistic stranger in front of her.

He shot forward, grabbing a handful of her hair. "I want a blow job."

She clamped her mouth closed, anger filling her, and she brought her knee up.

He blocked her attempt and punched her in the stomach. His blow knocked the air out of her lungs, and she crumpled to the floor.

The knife came out of the sheath, and he kneeled down, putting the tip under her chin, tilting her head up with it, piercing her skin. "I don't think you understand the consequences of your actions." He studied her and flicked his wrist, cutting her chin. "You get to choose which of your daughter's fingers I cut off."

Jennifer gulped. "Please, no, not my daughter, please." Her voice came out in a harsh plea, one she didn't recognize.

"Oh, but you misbehaved and need to be punished."

He slid the knife into its sheath, and she breathed a sigh of relief, but it was short-lived as his hand wrapped around her throat, drawing her near his smiling face.

"Maybe we should finish what I started in New York. You remember that, don't you?" He stood, dragging her to her feet, and slammed his fist into her side. "That's payback for the kick in *my* side."

Pain gagged the cry in her throat, and he didn't stop with just one punch. His fist brutalized her abdomen half a dozen times, cracking bone and bruising muscles with each powerful blow.

He let her go. She crumpled to the ground, each breath excruciating, and tears blurred her vision. She blinked them away in time to see him step into the nursery. "No!" She scrambled to her feet and limped to the door in time to see the knife lower into the crib. "Please, no, you can have one of mine."

He hesitated, looking over his shoulder at her. "What finger?"

"Please don't hurt my baby." Tears sprang, heating her face, and she stepped into the room, fear overpowering every other painful sensation wracking her body and she extended her hands. "Take whatever you want, but don't hurt her."

He turned toward her, pointing the knife in her direction. "I plan on taking whatever I want. Now which finger do you choose, or should I just chop off her entire hand?"

She couldn't speak. His unyielding gaze turned back to the crib and her sleeping child. When the knife moved in Samantha's direction, Jennifer lunged, grabbing his arm.

He smiled and twisted. The fist holding the detonator smashed into her nose.

A crunching sound followed by sharp pain split her face and she fell backwards on her ass, the impact rattling her teeth and ripping a yelp from her chest right before the room faded.

She woke on the living room floor. A shrill, wavering cry coming from the nursery filled the cottage. A cry she knew she couldn't coddle and pain she knew she couldn't take away. Her heart cried in outrage and her gaze shot to the chair where Kyle sat, wishing him the most horrifying, painful death possible. Her gaze dropped to the knife embedded in the coffee table. "You bastard."

"I think you learned your lesson." He pulled the knife out of the table and replaced it on the sheath at his hip before crossing to her. He squatted in front of her. "Next time, I won't reconsider. Instead, I'll take her entire hand."

She looked away toward the nursery and relief flooded every cell. He grabbed a handful of her hair, sitting her up and turning her head toward him.

"Are we clear on the rules?"

Her vision blurred and then cleared. His gray eyes waited for an answer with patience that promised more agony before the day was through. She nodded.

"Good. I think I'll take a rain check on that blowjob. I'm hungry," he announced, pulling her to her feet. "Make me some food and don't burn it,"

Tremors started in her jaw, and she pressed her lips together. *Get a grip.* She took a deep breath, ignoring her daughter's screams and the grinding of bone in her side. "What do you want?"

"Eggs, over easy."

She bit her lower lip. "How about scrambled?"

He shook his head and backhanded her again.

She blinked the tears out of her eyes and pushed herself into a sitting position on the floor. The skin of her cheek felt like a hot iron had been pressed against it, adding to her list of ailments. She shook, locking the sobs in her chest because that's exactly what the bastard wanted.

She climbed to her feet and headed into the kitchen. The act of pulling the fry pan from the cabinet took all her strength. Pain, now diluted to numbness in some parts of her body, prevented her from functioning properly and the pan slipped, falling to the floor with a ringing clatter. She stared at it and closed her eyes before she bent over, picked it up again, and put it on the stove. Images of Kyle screaming from a face full of hot grease crossed her mind, and she opened her eyes at the shuffle behind her.

"I don't want the yolks broken," he announced and sat at the kitchen table.

Anger and fear throbbed inside her, surfacing in the form of tremors. Shaking, she prepared his meal. By some miracle, neither of the egg yolks broke when they landed in the pan and Jennifer let out a sob of relief. Samantha's hand would be safe for another few minutes. Tears blurred her vision while the eggs cooked. She held her breath and flipped them, a squeak escaping when she did it successfully. She grabbed a plate and slid the eggs from the pan, turning and placing the dish on the table.

He stared at the eggs and stood, advancing on her.

Jennifer backed into the corner.

"I didn't want the yolk broken," he said.

Her gaze shot to his plate. A thin yellow line ran from one yolk. "I didn't burn it," she said in desperation.

Cornering her, he dragged the detonator down the front of her nightgown and leaned forward. His teeth sank into her bare shoulder, piercing the skin, and pain flared, yanking a whimper from her chest.

"If you continue to disobey me, your husband won't recognize either of you when he gets home." He pulled the knife out of his belt. With a flick of his wrist, he cut her nipple, drawing blood.

Her sharp inhale filled the room. She focused on the sharp pain, letting it clear some of the numbness from her mind, and her eyes narrowed with the hatred that flared.

Grabbing the plate and a fork, Kyle retreated to the living room and took a seat in the recliner. "Clean up the kitchen."

She limped to the sink and cleaned the dishes while a thin trail of blood flowed from her wound, running slowly down her leg and staining the bright linoleum floor. She looked

out the window at the lake and silently wished
for a miracle.

Vengeance
Chapter 80

STEVE SAT AT HIS desk, shuffling through Kyle's file. He picked up the crime scene photo of the car and the dead man with the smashed face. Something gnawed inside, and he looked up at the clock.

Why now? Why doesn't this make sense?

That deep-seated intuition he relied on bristled and he shook his head, dropping the file on the desk. He stood, crossing to Jack's office while mulling the murder over in his head.

Jack looked up from his computer. "What's eating you?"

"Did you get the DNA results yet?"

"They just came." Jack rifled through the pile of papers in his inbox, pulled out an envelope and tossed it to Steve.

Steve returned to his desk and opened the envelope. He scanned the report and his heart rate tripled. The DNA of the dead man did not match the multiple samples they had of the Slasher.

God damn it! And I left her alone. Shit!

He shot to his feet, dropped the paper on his desk, and walked out of the office. He was running at top speed by the time he reached the parking lot.

Vengeance
Chapter 81

"**B**EDROOM." KYLE POINTED AS she shut off the water.

Jennifer hung her head and closed her eyes. Samantha had finally quieted to an exhausted whimper and all she could think about were her visions.

If he kills me now, I won't have to hurt Steve and maybe, just maybe, Samantha will live.

"Now." He stood up, tossing his plate onto the coffee table.

"Fuck off," the words whispered from her mouth, feeling foreign, like a death sentence, and she met his gaze, bracing herself for the pain he was about to deliver.

He approached her. His free hand clenched into a fist and his eyes narrowed.

She doubled over at the force of the strike to her stomach. He threw another punch, connecting his fist into her lower back and she fell to her knees, her muscles seizing with the pain pulsing through her. He yanked her hair and slammed her into the wall face first, creating dazzling blinking lights in her field of vision. Dazed by his assault, she barely felt the wood floor scraping her knees as he dragged her into the bedroom.

This time, he didn't even use a pretense of gentleness or seduction. This time was meant to be excruciating, demeaning, and brutal. Each thrust ripped her anal path, bringing forth paralyzing pain, stealing her breath. Her screams were muffled by Kyle's hand squeezing her throat, constricting her airway enough to strike terror in her heart, but not enough to kill.

A hundred showers scrubbing her skin raw wouldn't erase this violation.

A litany of prayers repeated in her head, looping between vengeance and pleas for strength. *Oh god, Steve, please come home, please kill the bastard, please... God please, please give me the strength to save my little girl.*

When he finished, he slipped off the bed and dressed. "Go clean your face."

Jennifer stumbled from the bedroom and collapsed on the living room floor, her legs unable to carry her to the bathroom. She crawled the rest of the way, pulling herself up onto the sink. When her gaze landed on her reflection, she bit back the sob. Her nose was crushed into a crooked mess, her cheeks a relief map of black, blue, and purple, her front tooth chipped under the mass of swollen bloody lips. She reached a shaky hand toward the hand towel, wincing at the pain in her abdomen. Drawing cool water from the tap, she wet the washcloth and wiped as much of the blood as she could.

She prayed. For what, she wasn't sure, but she prayed just the same. She limped out of the bathroom, holding the wall for support.

When she stepped out, Kyle pointed to the bouncy seat on the kitchen table. "Bring your daughter out here."

His words didn't quite seep into the haze surrounding her, and Jennifer blinked. "What?"

"I want you to strap your daughter into the seat on the table," he said, enunciating each word like talking to a dimwit.

Jennifer made her way into the nursery and wrapped Samantha in a blanket. Her whimpers continued in shaky starts and then died down to a small whine after Jennifer swaddled her tight and squeezed her in a gentle hug. Jennifer bit her lip, her vision blurred behind the sheen of tears, her physical pain nothing compared to the mental agony of the unknown waiting for them in the living room.

"I'm waiting."

His voice jarred her, and she sucked in a breath, turning and crossing into the room with Samantha against her chest. She strapped Samantha in the bouncy seat just as he instructed. The last thing she wanted to do was cause her daughter any pain, and that is what Kyle's eyes promised if she didn't obey.

Turning toward Kyle, her gaze landed on the hedge sheers now lying across the table.

Jesus.

The image from her vision surfaced, of clamping those things around Steve's forearm and slicing it off. Shivering, her eyes shot to Kyle's, and she pointed a shaky finger at the table. "What's that for?" Her voice sounded distant and detached.

"I've got plans for that. Plans you're going to carry out for me."

Jennifer shook her head. "I don't think so."

He stood and crossed to her, grabbing a handful of her hair. "Do I have to remind you of the rules?"

She shook her head, her gaze drifting toward her daughter and back.

"Okay then, it's time for that blow-job." He dragged her to the recliner and unzipped his shorts.

Jennifer stared at his crotch. The scent drifting from the opening in his shorts was foul, and she gagged at the thought of putting the source of that stench in her mouth. She raised her gaze to his and shook her head. "I can't."

He threaded his hand through her hair and yanked her forward. "Come on, baby, show me what that mouth can do and maybe I'll let your daughter live."

She met his gaze. "Liar."

He grinned. "Maybe, but if you don't open your mouth and suck me dry, your daughter will lose her hand."

Resignation and disgust settled into her bones, and she moved closer and closed her eyes, attempting to breathe out of her open mouth even as he forced the tip of his member between her lips. It tasted like licking dog shit off the ground and her throat closed in a gag.

An insistent beep opened her eyes, and she looked up, with him still filling her mouth.

He looked at a little hand-held monitor and smiled, his gaze flitting from the screen to her. "Showtime, baby, and if you stop for any reason, I will kill your daughter." He waved the detonator in front of her and pocketed the monitor, glancing toward the door.

His gaze lowered, and he raised an eyebrow, challenging her stillness. His thumb caressing the trigger set her in motion, and his hand guided her farther down his shaft with each stroke. "That a girl."

Vengeance
Chapter 82

STEVE RAN TO THE door with his gun drawn. The shade was still down, and the deadbolt stopped him. He slipped the key in, threw the lock, and swung the door open, calling her name as he stepped in, the gun trained in front of him. The sound died in his throat at the sight of Jennifer's head buried in Kyle's lap and the familiar motion of a blowjob in progress.

Acute fury stormed through Steve's frame and the gun trembled. He couldn't rip his gaze from Jennifer, he couldn't pull a breath into his lungs, and he couldn't squeeze the trigger because the bastard had his little girl wired somewhere in the cottage.

"Come on in," Kyle said, waving the detonator, his thumb over the trigger. "If you *so* much as flinch, I will blow your daughter to bits." His other hand was in Jennifer's hair as she serviced him. "Close the door," he ordered.

He swung the door shut and closed his eyes for a moment. Reining in his fury, he got a grip on the fear lacing his stomach with a burn more toxic than battery acid. He steadied the gun in his hands and opened his eyes. His gaze fell to the intricate tattoo on the wrist holding the detonator.

"Put the gun down and have a seat." Kyle pointed toward the chair in front of the window.

Steve moved toward the chair, still gripping his gun, training it on the point between Kyle's eyes, ignoring the sobs coming from Jennifer's full mouth. He glanced toward the kitchen and stopped walking. There on the table strapped into the bouncy seat was his daughter, fully enclosed in a deadly jacket and his gaze shot back to Kyle.

Kyle smiled when Steve's head snapped in his direction. "She gives good head."

Steve ground his teeth so hard his jaw ached, and he squelched the urge to pull the trigger. "Kyle, I presume."

He gave a slight nod in Steve's direction, pulling Jennifer down and thrusting deeper into her mouth. "That's right, suck me, baby." He moved her more fervently, grinning at Steve.

Fury lined his skin, and his trigger finger just itched to yank back, blowing a hole between this bastard's eyes. But he paused, frozen by indecision, his eyes dropping between her bobbing head and the detonator.

Kyle pushed her head farther into his lap, his jaw clenching along with his fist in her hair, and Jennifer gagged. A wet throaty sound Steve remembered from the crypt and the forced fraternity rite he witnessed in Brooksfield. And his soul blackened.

Kyle pushed her away and zipped up his shorts. "Drop the gun and sit your ass down!"

Steve glanced at Jennifer's battered face, and he knew if he put the gun down, they were all dead.

"I'll give you to three, then I press the button. One... Two..."

One look in Steve's direction sent Jennifer scrambling toward the kitchen.

All motion and sound ceased to exist. Steve adjusted the sights on his target and pulled the trigger. The roar of the gun blasted, reverberating in his ears, dulling the sound of the explosion that rocked the cabin a split second later. He had less than a second to register that his shot missed before the explosion lifted him off his feet and sent him careening toward the far wall, his gun knocked from his grip.

Kyle rolled toward the door, shielded from the explosion by the furniture.

Steve's ankle caught on the couch and torqued, ripping the tendons and crunching bones. His right arm snapped as he landed, the ulna ripping through his skin at an odd angle. He blinked, dazed and numb, lifting his ringing head. The front door stood ajar, and he looked toward the kitchen. Blood covered everything.

Blood and bits of the bouncy seat.

Oh, god, what have I done?

His gaze shot to Jennifer, and he crawled to her, pulling her unconscious form into his lap. He rocked, holding her bloody head to his chest, sobbing her name over, and over, and over.

Vengeance
Chapter 83

KYLE SLID OUT THE door, his ears ringing, and his clothing splattered with blood. He paused, looking between the lake and the woods where his bike was stowed, debating. When he ran a hand over his face, that was the deciding factor. It came away covered with a thin sheen of blood and he wondered if it was his or the baby's.

The handheld monitor somehow remained in his pocket, and he pulled it out, scanning the carnage in the cottage, sending the signal to his laptop at the hotel along with the relay code that fed the entire day's events to his computer at his new apartment in Connecticut. Once the feed completed, the signal would be cut and the laptop at the hotel would be rendered useless by a virus. With the sequence of commands sent, he dove off the end of the dock, sneakers and all, and let the electronic device drop to the sandy bottom of the lake after a few powerful strokes toward his compromised safe house. He could use the kayak stored in the boathouse.

The explosion had blown out the kitchen and living room windows and he was unsure whether Steve had the sense to call the cops or not, but he didn't want to take the chance of being anywhere near their side of the lake when first responders got to the scene.

Halfway across the lake, he heard the sirens and the distinct whirl of helicopter blades chopping through the air.

Shit! A fucking helicopter? Was he wired?

The thought chilled him, and he dove underwater, stripping his sneakers and socks before surfacing and taking a deep breath. He plunged and kicked, pulling through the water as fast as he could.

Surfacing less than fifty yards from the shore, he took another deep breath. This time, he was a few feet from where he'd pulled the kayak on the shore the day before. Without hesitation or even a glance over his shoulder, he hoisted himself onto the small dock of the boathouse and quickly launched the kayak into the water, grabbing the oar and rowing toward the far side of the lake where the public beach and hotels resided. He peeled off his shirt, shoved the ball in the small storage space behind him, and continued rowing. He dared a glance toward the cottage, now barely visible through the thick woods.

The trees bent in response to the force of air from the chopper's blades.

Damn, damn, damn.

Bondino will skin me alive if I get caught.

The thought tripped his heart, knocking it in his chest in half-beats to each stroke of his oars. He retraced his steps, from the alias he used at the hotel to the car rental and even to the computer signals. Nothing could be traced back to Kyle Winslow or John Sheridan or, more importantly, to Tony Bondino.

With each foot he gained away from the cottage, confidence edged the hammering fear from his body.

New sirens echoed off the lake. He pegged them as ambulances and his tense muscles relaxed another fraction. With the incremental release of stress came irritation.

His plans thwarted *again.*

The satisfaction of having Jennifer torture Steve at his direction, gone with the sound of Steve's gun. The absolute ecstasy of killing her like he killed all his victims. And delivering the final crushing blow, using Steve's severed hand to detonate the bomb, all robbed from him because of that bastard.

The sweet revenge he dreamed of turned bitter and he pulled on the oars, taking a quick check at the distance from the hotel docks that were now in sight. He estimated a half-mile and then a quick walk to the hotel room.

The oars stopped in the water. Kyle sent a glance toward the cottage and closed his eyes. "Shit."

His hotel key was in his backpack. His backpack was somewhere in the wreckage.

"Fuck."

He turned his attention to rowing. If he could get to his room and get out of the hotel before they figured out the backpack was his, he had a chance, and at least being shirtless, shoeless and wet wasn't a big deal, not at a beach resort.

He docked the kayak, tying it to the mooring before hopping out and approaching the boating attendant. Patting his pockets, he smiled, letting it fade as he pulled out nothing from the recesses of the wet fabric.

"Um." He looked back at the boat. "I seem to have lost my room key." He turned back to the boating attendant.

The attendant just stared at him, his jaw slightly askew and his gaze glued to a spot on Kyle's temple.

He swiped his forehead, bringing back bloody fingers, and uttered a slight laugh. "I must have hit that rock harder than I thought." He raised his gaze from his hand to the blinking attendant. "It's just a minor scratch. I'm fine." His eyes flicked to the attendant's nametag. "Really, Todd, I'm fine. I just need my room key, but I have a feeling it's at the bottom of the lake."

Todd's jaw snapped shut, and he offered a tight-lipped smile before speaking. "They can help you at the front desk." He pointed toward the hotel and Kyle followed his directive, heading toward the hotel without a glance back.

The kid's nervous gaze bore a knot of fire between his shoulder blades, and he grabbed a towel on the way through the pool area, pressing it to his head and offering an embarrassed smile to anyone who looked his way.

The lobby was quiet except for a few stragglers and hotel employees. In his haste, he didn't scan for danger like he normally would. Instead, he walked straight toward the desk. The same clerk who had signed him in the day before raised his eyes from the computer screen and swallowed. Licking his lips, he tried on a smile that didn't work, and before Kyle could turn around, they grabbed him, slamming him against the desk and slapping cuffs around his wrists.

"Kyle Winslow, you have the right to remain silent. Anything you say or do will be used against you in a court of law..."

He turned, glancing at the FBI badge hanging from the agent's pocket and memorizing the name.

Special Agent Jack Murphy.

Another target on his ever-growing hit list.

Vengeance
Chapter 84

STEVE'S EYE OPENED AND his focus wavered. He blinked, glancing around the hospital room. His vision blurred, and he lifted his hand to wipe the crust off his eyelashes. The cast on his right arm prevented him from reaching his face and he stared at it, trying to understand where he was.

Slowly, through the drug-induced stupor, the memories flooded in. He shifted his gaze to the chair next to the bed. His father was sound asleep with a book on his chest.

"Dad?" Steve's voice croaked from his dry throat.

Adam Williams jerked awake. The book slid to the floor. "Steve." His eyes filled with tears.

"They're dead." Steve shook.

"Jennifer's still alive." Adam swallowed and studied his hands. "She's in a coma, Son." Looking into Steve's eyes, he continued, "And it doesn't look good."

"Did they catch him?"

Adam nodded his head. "Yes."

Relief opened the floodgates, and the sobs began. Steve brought his un-bandaged hand to his face, covering his eyes and feeling the fabric of the eye patch for the first time. "I should have killed the bastard when I walked in the door." The words spilled out between sobs.

Adam moved to the edge of the bed and pulled his son into his arms, holding Steve while he cried.

When the tears subsided, Steve pulled away and wiped his face.

Adam sighed and took a seat in the chair again. "You've been in and out of consciousness for a few days."

Steve glanced at the cast, raising his eyebrows.

"You had a green-stick fracture." Adam said. "There was some nerve damage, and they aren't sure how much dexterity you'll have." He took a deep breath. "Your left ankle is broken as well."

"What's with the eye patch?" Steve asked.

"Shrapnel from the explosion pierced your eye. They're not sure if you'll be able to see once the patch comes off." Steve nodded, opening his eye as the information his father fed him sank in. "Jenny's alive?"

Adam nodded.

Steve sat up and threw his legs over the side of the bed, pulling the IV out of his arm. Gritting his teeth, he stood on his throbbing ankle. "I want to see my wife."

Adam shot out of his seat. "Get back in bed," he ordered.

"No. Take me to Jennifer." He took a step toward the door and the dull pain turned sharp. Air hissed between his teeth as the wince caught him off-guard. His father grabbed the wheelchair sitting in the corner and Steve collapsed into the seat when his father pushed it behind him.

"Take me to Jenny. Please, Dad, I need to see her."

With a sharp inhale and a nod, Adam pushed Steve to the Intensive Care Unit, parking the wheelchair next to Jennifer's bed. "I'll be waiting outside," he said before he stepped out of the room.

Jennifer's head was wrapped in bandages, and her face held blue and purple tones. An oxygen tube protruded from her nose and an IV stemmed from her arm, with two bags hanging from the T-bar on the bed. The air in the room held the sterile antiseptic quality that he remembered waking to in the ICU after the Brooksfield incident. Steve closed his eye for a moment, listening to the steady beep of the heart monitor mixed with the inflection of her breathing.

"Jesus, Jenny," he whispered, opening his tear-filled eye.

Steve reached out and took her hand, bringing it to his lips. Scanning her unconscious form, fury overrode all sense of sorrow. "The bastard's going to get the death penalty for what he did to you and Sam," Steve said through a clenched jaw. "I swear."

The pain of his mistakes blurred his vision, and he bit his lip, stifling the sob and swallowing the burning tears. He leaned forward and planted a kiss on her cheek. "I'm so sorry, Jenny." His voice quivered, and he laid his head on her shoulder, gripping her hand as his harsh sobs filled the desolate hospital room.

The End

Continue The Steve Williams Series on the next
page with HUNTING SEASON.

753

Hunting Season
Prologue

"WHAT DO YOU MEAN he escaped?" Steve Williams shot to his feet, the constant whoosh of the breathing apparatus drowned by his sudden, sharp inhale. Pain tremors shot up from his throbbing ankle, the cast providing enough inertia against the tile floor to slide, and he tumbled back in the chair with his heart hammering against his rib cage.

"Kyle escaped during the transfer. A semi sideswiped the police van, rolling it into a ditch on the side of the highway. By the time the cops got there, he was gone," Jack Murphy hissed into the phone, his anger bleeding through the line.

"Where?"

"Just outside of Concord."

"Fuck," Steve muttered. He glanced at his wife. The bruises from Kyle's attack were still visible on her pale skin.

"We've got crews scouring the woods right now. We'll get him."

Steve lacked Jack's confidence, and he balled his hand into a fist around the phone. "You'd better, because if I find him first, I'll kill him."

Hunting Season
Chapter 1

*F*UBAR.

The thought produced a quiet *humph* and Steve studied the falling snow outside the window, waiting. His fingers rose to the eye-patch, grazing the pliable material that covered the hollowness of the socket underneath. A shiver rippled through him, and he clenched his teeth.

He flexed his right hand. After six months of physical therapy, he still did not have the dexterity to shoot straight, and his arm constantly ached where the bone had splintered. His leg screamed whenever a low-pressure-system arrived; making his slight limp more prevalent, and right now, it throbbed in time with his heartbeat. Sighing, he returned his attention to the swirling white flakes.

Dr. Montgomery, the FBI sponsored psychiatrist assigned to his case, slipped into the room and took a seat, opening Steve's file. He adjusted his spectacles before resuming where they left off. "You need to deal with what happened, Steve."

"The son of a bitch is still out there."

Dr. Montgomery leaned forward and folded his arms on his desk.

They had been through this routine a dozen times in the past few months. Dr. Montgomery, always calm and reasonable, and Steve, always falling back to his unimpassioned crime scene analysis, avoiding the trauma he endured.

Steve watched the snowfall for a few minutes before continuing. "I'm an FBI agent. I should be out there looking for him." He attempted to skirt his emotions again.

"And what does the husband and father part feel?"

Steve's jaw clenched. "I'm not sure I want to answer that."

"Why not?"

Steve turned toward Dr. Montgomery. "Because you'll never clear me for active duty."

"Anger is a perfectly normal emotion, Steve."

Steve scoffed and turned, catching his reflection in the glass. A single unwavering azure eye stared back. He ground his teeth so hard they ached before meeting the doctor's gaze. "He blew up my daughter."

"Keep going." Dr. Montgomery said.

"I want to kill him!" Steve closed his eyes, willing the rabid dog inside to stay caged. He drew a deep breath and blew it out slowly, fogging the windowpane in front of him.

Steve turned his head toward the doctor. Fury coursed through his veins. He clenched his jaw and pulled the air in through his nose before he continued. "I should have shot him when I walked in the door."

"Why didn't you?"

That question plagued Steve at least a dozen times a day since the explosion. If he had,

Jennifer wouldn't be lying in a hospital bed with no hope of recovery. Instead, he paused, and that cost him his daughter and his wife. "He had a detonator in his hand, and he said if I didn't put the gun down, he'd blow up Samantha."

Steve's jaw worked overtime, grinding his teeth. Anger pulsed through his body, making the tips of his fingers and toes tingle and his skin burn.

The rage consumed Steve. Raw, unbridled, unstoppable rage.

Rage because he was stupid.

Rage because his baby girl was dead.

Rage because Kyle escaped.

Steve's breath came in short gasps. His jagged nails dug into the soft flesh of his palms, tempering the rage a notch. Slowly, he uncurled his fists, stretching his fingers as he stared at the floor.

"The fucker's still out there. And he isn't done with me yet."

Hunting Season
Chapter 2

STEVE LEFT THE SESSION with Dr. Montgomery and headed over to the hospital. He sat, slipping Jennifer's pallid hand in his.

The steady pulse in her wrist echoed the constant blip of the heart monitor. Both grim reminders, mocking him with a constant cadence of life where they said there was none. He blinked away the sudden mist that formed over his good eye, biting his lower lip to stave off the sorrow. Steve's eyes closed against the vision of his beautiful wife lying there like the shrouded corpse of Snow White. He prayed numbly, his mind playing out a desperate litany to whatever God would hear him.

"I swear, Jenny, if I ever find that bastard, I'm going to rip his heart out with my bare hands."

Six months in the ICU left her nothing more than a skeleton with stretched pale skin amidst the tubes and wires that kept her alive. Despite breathing without a respirator, her brain activity was sporadic at best. The only movement that appeared on the graph coincided with Kyle's murders; otherwise, the line was endlessly straight. The visions continued, even in her catatonic mind, and every time the blip appeared, someone died.

JENNIFER STOOD FROM HER crouched position in the corner and crossed to Steve. Laying her hand on his shoulder, she stifled a sob when it passed through him with a ghost-like quality, and she cursed the wasted body trapping her in this living hell.

"I love you, baby. Please don't give up on me," Jennifer whispered.

She reached for him again, to push his bangs out of his eye, but her hand had as much effect on his black locks as a trail of smoke. Not even a strand moved.

Pain seared her soul, and she crumpled at his feet.

Was this her damnation for not being able to save their daughter?

To spend all eternity near Steve and never be able to touch him, to feel his strong arms wrapped around her, his tender lips on the curve of her neck, his peppermint breath on her tongue?

She had to get back—she had to tell him Samantha's death was not his fault. She had to tell him she loved him, no matter what. She had to tell him about...

The door banged open, interrupting her train of thought.

"Don't do this, Dad, please don't do this again!" Jennifer climbed to her feet, voicing her disdain on deaf ears.

HER FATHER, JOE CURTIS, shoved the door open and glared at Steve like he was a giant insect in need of extermination. Stiffening, Steve prepared himself for whatever bullshit Joe was dishing out this time.

"Aren't you supposed to be in therapy?" Joe slammed his tray down on the table.

"I got out early."

"This is your fault!"

Steve ignored him, the pulse in his temple blinding as anger simmered just below the boiling point. He exhaled. The rush of crushed bones under his fist flashed against his closed eyelids, satisfying the need burning in his skin. The mini-mind-flick contained his anger for the moment.

"She wouldn't be lying here if you hadn't screwed up her life."

He counted to ten silently before he met Joe's glare, but it wasn't enough to calm the beast inside. He shot from his chair, rocketing across the room until he stood toe to toe with Joe. "You want to repeat that?" A satisfied smile formed on his lips when Joe stepped back.

"You screwed up her life," he repeated, stabbing his finger against Steve's chest.

Raw willpower kept him from breaking the finger that poked his chest. The inferno raged, edging his vision with flares of red as he met Joe's brazen glare and pressed forward, crowding him. "Don't you dare!"

"You put her in danger. You're responsible for this!" Joe waved toward the bed. "And you're responsible for my granddaughter's death!"

Steve slammed Joe against the wall, his hand clamped around his father-in-law's throat. "The fucker staged his own death. Had I known he was still alive, I never would have left Jenny alone."

"If you hadn't married her, she'd still be alive!" Joe croaked under the pressure of his strained vocal cords.

Steve let go and stepped away, putting distance between them. "She is alive."

"Her body is, but her mind has been gone for the past six months."

"She's still in there and I'm not pulling the plug." He pointed toward the door. "Now get the hell out of here before I get a restraining order."

Joe stormed out of the room, leaving Steve alone with the steady sound of the machines.

Like a hurricane making landfall, despair decimated him, constricting his lungs, bowing him over. He slumped in the chair, cradling his head in his hands.

Jennifer had to be in there somewhere. She had to be.

He clutched her limp hand and the silent mantra played on. After what seemed like hours, he glanced at his wife, wiping his tear-stained cheeks.

"I need a miracle."

Hunting Season
Chapter 3

STEVE SHOT TO HIS feet at the sudden high-pitched beep on the brain wave monitor, reaching for his gun and blinking the sleep out of his eyes. When his hand fell on nothing but his shirt, he glanced around the room, getting his bearings. The heart monitor bleeped sporadic and fast and Jennifer's eyelids opened. Opaque eyes, covered with the film of clairvoyance. Dead eyes like a corpse.

A tremor started in his toes and slinked its way up his spine, causing the exposed skin on his arms to curl into bumpy knots.

"Shit." He flipped his phone open and hit the speed dial. "Jack, she's having another one."

"How long do we have?"

Steve listened to the staccato beat of her heart, the monitor showing the frantic red lines crossing the screen. The needle on the brain monitor swayed back and forth, covering the entire paper readout, matching the pace of her heart.

He didn't have an answer for Jack.

"How long?"

"I don't know. When she was having them in New York, it was a window of a couple of hours."

"God damn it!" The sound of a palm hitting the desk accompanied the curse.

"Where was the last one?"

"San Francisco." Jack answered. "But that was a couple of months back. He's been quiet lately."

Jennifer's eyelids dropped, settling down again along with her heart rate. The brain monitor returned to the solid unmoving line along the middle of the paper. Whatever vision consuming her ended as abruptly as it began.

Steve inhaled. "Like clockwork. A couple of months and then he has to kill. I wonder how he's controlling the urge between murders." He studied Jennifer. "Any hits correspond with the other murders?"

Jack didn't answer right away.

"Well?"

"Steve, this isn't your case anymore."

Jack's unwillingness to share information brought the blood rushing to his cheeks. "Jack, he killed my daughter."

"You are not active, Steve. And even if you were, I wouldn't discuss the details with you. It is not your case."

"Come on, Jack." Steve's teeth clamped together. Frustration tingled in his fingers as he squeezed the cell phone.

"This is not negotiable. You already know what you're required to do to reactivate."

Steve cut his boss off. "I can't go to Quantico right now."

Silence.

"Jack, I can't, not yet."

More silence.

"God damn it, Jack, tell me what's happening! Tell me what you're doing to find that bastard!"

"We're doing all we can to find him, Steve."

"That's not enough!"

The sharp inhale filled the line. "You know I'm doing everything humanly possible, but he disappeared off the grid again. He has a new identity and the money trail you found last spring went cold. Our subpoena held no weight overseas and without that trail; we can't find him unless he makes a mistake."

Steve hung his head, the phone still to his ear. Jack was right and that burned him, fanning the torch of rage further. Exhaling, his breath whistled through his tight lips. "I get it." He ended the call and sat back in the chair, rubbing his two-day stubble with his palms.

He raised his eyes to the full moon peeking in the window. Someone was going to die tonight and there wasn't a damn thing he could do about it.

Hunting Season
Chapter 4

ANOTHER DEATH. THIS TIME closer to home.

New York City.

Steve sat, angry and bitter, in Dr. Montgomery's office. He wanted to be out there hunting the bastard, but no, Jack insisted on these stupid sessions.

His hands trembled with rage and his gaze snapped from the floor to meet the doctor's. "If I ever find him, he's a dead man," he said through a solid wall of teeth. "Can I go now?"

Dr. Montgomery leaned back in his chair with his hands clasped on the desk. "I think you should join my group therapy sessions."

He laughed.

The doctor cocked his head. "Do you want to remain in the FBI?"

His chuckle stopped as if a light switch tripped. "Fine. When?"

"Monday at Brooksfield Mental Hospital. Nine A.M. sharp."

Steve raised his eyebrows. "You want me to discuss an active case in front of a bunch of crazy lunatics?"

Dr. Montgomery nodded and offered his most sincere a-yup smile.

Steve muttered a ream of curses under his breath. He rose and crossed to the door. "Fine," he shot over his shoulder and slammed the mahogany door, storming away while the wood rattled in its frame.

Hunting Season
Chapter 5

JACK GLANCED THROUGH THE dossiers on the table in front of him. "I need the best we've got, Ron." He looked up at Assistant Director Ron Cleary. "And that's Steve Williams."

"I've got reservations..."

Jack held his hand up, interrupting his superior. "Steve's the best field agent I've ever seen. There hasn't been anyone like him since his grandfather walked these halls. But he's angry, and if we cut him loose, he's got nothing left. He'll go after Winslow." Jack paused and looked out the window at the Quantico campus. "If he's paired up with a partner, he'll be less likely to go rogue on us."

"He's overdue for his refresher," Cleary said.

"If I can get him down here, will you reinstate him?"

"I don't like this. His psychiatric evaluation says he's an unstable risk."

"He's a little hotheaded at times, but I'd stake my career on him." Jack kept Cleary's sharp stare, holding his ground, wondering if he'd be able to deliver on his end of the bargain.

Cleary drummed his fingers on the desk and then turned, pulling another file out of the cabinet. He tossed it to Jack. "Eric Connor. He's the brightest of the new recruits."

Jack opened the file and perused the contents. His eyebrow rose. "You want to pair Williams with this kid?"

"He'll keep your boy in line."

"You're willing to give him up?"

Cleary leaned forward on the desk. "I looked into Agent Williams' file and you're right, his ability to put the facts together is genius and if you're willing to put your career on the line, he must be even better than the paperwork suggests. That kid is the best I have, and he could learn a thing or two from Agent Williams. So, yes, I'll lend him to you, provided you can get Williams down here to run through the refresher course."

"I'd like to speak with him," Jack said, holding up the file.

With a nod, Cleary picked up the phone, punched in a few numbers, and beckoned the young agent. Before he resumed the conversation, a knock interrupted, and Cleary traded a glance with Jack. He crossed to the door and opened it.

Eric Connor stood in the doorway wearing gray sweats and a t-shirt, his hair wet and slicked back. "You called, sir?"

Jack blinked, shocked at the kid's unusual eyes—eyes that would stand out anywhere. They reminded him of a spring storm in New England—grays, greens and blues gave the illusion of raging, rolling clouds.

"Yes. Special Agent Eric Connor, I'd like you to meet Special Agent in Charge Jack Murphy," Cleary said.

Eric stepped forward, extending his hand. "Nice to meet you, sir."

Jack accepted the handshake and nodded. "Likewise. Director Cleary speaks highly of you, young man."

Eric raised an eyebrow and glanced at Cleary before bringing his gaze back to Jack's. "What can I do for you, sir?"

"What do you know about Kyle Winslow?"

Both the kid's eyebrows rose, and he took a deep breath. "Kyle Winslow is wanted by the FBI and Interpol for the murders of twenty some women across the globe in relation to the slasher cases. The FBI believes he is Tony Bondino's personal assassin because nearly all the slasher cases correspond to mafia hits, but they were unable to get concrete evidence to that fact." Eric stopped and shifted his gaze to his commanding officer before continuing. "Last spring, he went after an FBI agent and his family before being arrested. Unfortunately, he escaped and went underground for a couple of months before the killings started again. His latest victim showed up in New York City a few days ago."

Impressed, Jack nodded. "Now tell me what you know about Agent Williams."

The question clearly stunned Eric, and he opened his mouth to speak and then closed it for a second, shifting his weight and staring at the floor. He raised his gaze. "Steve Williams is perhaps the most gifted agent the FBI has ever encountered. His ability to sniff out the truth is as uncanny as..." he trailed off, his lips pressing together like he didn't want to finish the sentence.

"As what?" Jack asked. He had a feeling Eric was going to say as his wife's clairvoyance, but this kid would have no way of knowing about Jennifer's abilities.

"As his aptitude to find trouble."

The answer brought a bark of a laugh from Jack. He studied the young agent. "Why do you say that?"

"With the exception of the rape case at Yale, his career is peppered with as many close calls as collars."

"True," Jack said. He'd been there for some of those narrow escapes. "How would you feel about working with him?"

Eric's eyes widened, and the color bled out of his cheeks. "I, uh," he stumbled and cleared his throat. His gaze dropped to the floor, and he shifted his stance. "I, um, I'm not sure. Didn't his last partner die?"

Jack crossed his arms. "Yes. His partner died in a firefight with Charlie Wisnowski. If Agent Williams hadn't been there, Wisnowski might have gotten away." And his cover wouldn't have been blown and we wouldn't be having this conversation.

Eric chewed on his lip and nodded.

"Let me clarify what SAC Murphy is trying to say," Cleary interrupted. "You are Special Agent Williams' new partner. He will join us in a few days and while he is here, you are to keep him out of trouble."

Even though Eric frowned at the news, he nodded. "Yes, sir."

"I don't want him going after Kyle Winslow half-cocked, understand?" Jack asked.

"Yes, sir," Eric replied.

Hunting Season
Chapter 6

STEVE STOOD IN THE doorway of the community room at Brooksfield Mental Hospital with his arms crossed, observing the dynamics. Patients wearing olive-green scrubs gathered in a circle, waiting for the group therapy session to begin.

"There's a seat for you, too." Dr. Montgomery said as he approached Steve from behind.

Steve grumbled and followed Dr. Montgomery, annoyed at the prospect of discussing his situation with a bunch of crazy strangers. He didn't exactly blend in, not with his jeans and work shirt marred with a hospital issued ID badge slapped on the pocket. Everyone gawked as he slid into the empty seat and crossed his arms.

"We have a new member of the group today. Steve Williams." Dr. Montgomery said. "Mr. Williams, would you like to tell the group why you are here?"

"Not particularly," Steve answered. He let the silence fill the space, unaffected by the dozen pairs of eyes boring into him. He cocked his head, his lips curling into a smirk. *I'm not going to make this easy.*

"I lost my daughter a couple of years ago." A man sitting next to the doctor said, breaking the awkward silence. He was staring at Steve.

Steve turned, and it only took a moment to identify the familiar face. When the name came, so did the circumstances. Little girl, seven years old, killed in the woods here in Brooksfield. The most bizarre case he ever encountered, but at least he met Jennifer. *We almost died that year, too.*

A shiver caressed the back of his neck and Steve uncrossed his arms, shifting in his seat.

"I was too busy trying to put up the stupid tent and when my wife showed up at the campsite, that was when I realized Amy was gone." He took a moment to pick at the hangnail on his thumb. "They found her a couple of days later." He paused, his Adam's apple jiggling. "In pieces." An audible gulp followed.

"Harry, right?" Steve asked, pulling the name out of his memory banks. When the man nodded, Steve continued. "You didn't know what was in those woods."

Harry shrugged. "I should have kept an eye on my daughter. I yelled at her to stay out of the way." He took a deep breath. "That was the last thing I said to her." A tear slid from the corner of his eye.

"You didn't know." Steve sighed, fidgeting restlessly, one ankle tapping the chair leg. Propping his chin on his thumb, he curled his index finger over his lips, sucking in a deep gulp of air. He held it for a moment, letting it seep out like a punctured tire, leaving him empty and hollow. Guarded. His gaze slid away from Harry, calm and unblinking, belying the drumbeat of his pulse roaring in his ears. It amazed him that the rest of the group couldn't hear it. His stare hardened as he aimed it at the doctor. The bastard ambushed him.

"Agent Williams was the one who caught the monster." Harry informed the group.

All eyes swung toward Steve.

Steve acknowledged the statement with a nod.

"Why are you here?" Harry asked.

"My little girl was murdered in April. She was less than a month old."

Harry stared at Steve with parted lips.

"How did that make you feel?" Dr. Montgomery interjected.

He tilted his head, challenging the doctor. Silence filled the space as twelve pairs of eyes bore into him and he shifted in the chair.

"Why don't you tell the group how losing your daughter made you feel?" Dr. Montgomery pressed.

"I felt like someone kicked me in the gut and I'd never be able to take a full breath of air again." He locked eyes with Harry. "Then the anger took over," Steve admitted.

"And now?" Dr. Montgomery asked.

Steve crossed his arms. "Now, I'm going hunting." A deadly smile spread over Steve's lips, creating a collective shiver through the group like the brittle New Hampshire winter stroked their skin.

Dr. Montgomery blinked, unable to hide the shock of Steve's answer quickly enough. He paused and took a sip of water. "What are you hunting?"

Steve's smile widened a fraction. "Another monster."

Hunting Season
Chapter 7

STEVE STEPPED OUT OF the Brooksfield Physical Therapy center, slipping on the sunglasses that hid his eye patch.

"Hi, Steve."

Steve turned and raised his eyebrows. "Jack, what are you doing up this way?"

"You need to get your ass down to Quantico."

"I'm not leaving Jennifer."

Jack dug his hands in his pockets. "Has there been any change?"

"No. There's been no brain activity, not since the last murder, if that's what you're asking," he snapped. "Have you found the son of a bitch?"

Jack shook his head. "We've got nothing." The disgust bled into his voice, and he looked away, taking a deep breath. "You need to go through the refresher course if you want to remain in the FBI."

You are out of your fucking mind! He went to speak but thought better of it; instead, he dug in his pocket and pulled out the keys to his car. "I can't leave her." The bleep-bleep of the car unlocking punctuated his statement, and Steve met Jack's irritated stare.

"I promise, if her status changes, we'll get you back here as fast as we can."

Steve paused, looking out over the rugged, snow-covered landscape. He opened the car door and leaned his arm on it. "Only if you put me on the case."

"You know I can't do that."

Steve cocked his head and shrugged. He went to sit in the car.

"God damn it, Steve!"

He paused and glanced at his boss. "You want me back? You let me track down that son of a bitch."

"And what are you going to do when you find him?" Jack shot the question back, his face red with aggravation.

"You've seen my psych evaluation."

Jack sucked his breath in. Steve had made it clear in his psychotherapy sessions that if he ever found Kyle; he was going to kill him. "Is that what Jenny would want you to do?"

Steve's nostrils flared. "That's low, even for you." He slid into the seat and pulled the door closed.

Jack stopped the door from latching, pulling it open and staring at Steve. "You can't keep her alive if you don't have a job."

Steve closed his eye and hung his head. He turned so he could see Jack with his good eye. "Fine," he growled with white knuckles on the steering wheel. "When?"

Jack reached into his pocket and pulled out a plane ticket. "Today," he said, slipping the paperwork into Steve's hand. "Go pack."

Hunting Season
Chapter 8

WITH HIS BAGS ALREADY packed and in the trunk of the car, he headed up to the third floor ICU. He gave the nurse a nod and slipped into the room, sitting in the vacant seat by the side of the bed and taking her pallid hand in his.

"Jack says I have to go to Quantico." He closed his eyes.

"I don't want to go, but if I don't, I'll lose my job." Steve dipped his head, struggling with the internal war—one side yanking him toward his job, his duty, and the other grounding him to the spot next to Jennifer. He knew Kyle planned to destroy him, and it was more than personal now. Nothing was off limits. Not even his comatose wife.

Steve glanced at his wrist. He had to get moving if he had any hope of catching the plane. He stood and pressed his lips to her forehead. "I promise I'll be here as soon as I can if you wake up. I love you." He turned, leaving the room without a glance back.

JENNIFER JUMPED TO HER feet. "You can't leave me! Please, Steve, don't go. He'll come back. He'll

hurt me, again." Jennifer screamed and lunged, her hands passing right through him. She crumpled to the ground at the entrance to her room, unable to break from her prison.

Hunting Season
Chapter 9

STEVE STRETCHED IN THE balmy Virginia air, stifling a yawn. "I forgot how nice it is down here."

"It's hit or miss this time of year." Jack pointed out, popping the trunk of the Explorer.

Steve glanced at him, grabbing his suitcase. "It's still a far cry from New Hampshire." A sideways smile accompanied the comment. "Where to?"

"This way." Jack led Steve to the third floor of the dormitory. He swung open the fourth door on the right and waved him in.

A student, fresh out of college, sat behind the desk clicking away on his laptop. He closed the computer and stood as they entered the room.

Steve scrunched his eyebrows. The kid looked familiar. Something about his multi-colored eyes triggered his memory, and the information flooded into the forefront of his mind. His eyes widened a fraction and his brow smoothed out. New York City. About five years back. A psycho attacked his family in one of the warehouses on the river. The news stories of that event rivaled his own.

"Eric. Eric Connor." He reached his hand toward Steve.

"Steve Williams. Glad to meet you." Steve swung his suitcase onto the bed before trading handshakes with Eric.

"Thanks. I can take it from here," Eric said to Jack.

Jack nodded and took a step toward the door.

"I don't need a babysitter."

"Yes, you do. He's your new partner." Jack pointed his thumb at Eric. "He's the best to come along since you graced these halls, maybe even better."

Steve scoffed. "I thought *you* were my partner."

"I was never your partner, Steve." Jack turned and left.

Steve sat on the edge of the bed, abandoned. He glanced at Eric. "I don't need a fucking babysitter."

"No, sir."

Steve looked the kid over. "Bet you never thought you'd end up with a crazy freak as a partner," he said after a few minutes.

"Bet you never thought you'd have a smartass kid as one," Eric volleyed back.

Steve chuckled, not expecting such a snappy comeback.

"Seriously, I've seen your file. You're a hell of an agent."

"Bet your ass I am." He unpacked his clothes.

"I was sorry to hear about your daughter," Eric added, shifting uncomfortably. "I know what it's like to lose someone close."

Steve paused, glancing over his shoulder. *Bullshit. Tell me that when you've lost your only child.* He nodded and returned his attention to his half-empty suitcase.

"I guess losing a sister isn't the same as losing a child though... but..." He trailed off and shrugged.

Steve hesitated and went back to unpacking. "So, you really think I'm a crazy freak?" He pushed the last drawer closed.

"No," Eric answered. "You're not a freak," he clarified with a smile.

"You're a smart ass," Steve answered.

He grinned. "Always have been. Drives my parents crazy."

Steve took a seat on the edge of the bed, observing Eric. "What exactly did they tell you about me?"

"I have your file, including the psych evaluation."

Steve remained calm on the exterior, but his heart jumped like a taser shot. *What the fuck happened to doctor-patient confidentiality?*

Eric chuckled.

"What's so funny?"

"Doctor patient-confidentiality, I don't think it applies to FBI sponsored shrinks."

Steve creased his brow, his instinct flaring. *You reading my mind?* The thought leaped into his gut so quickly he trusted it.

"I wouldn't know about that. I've never been considered an unstable risk." Eric made little quotations with his fingers as he said unstable risk, quoting the evaluation.

"Fuck you." Steve stood up and crossed the room to the door. *If you saw the things I've seen...*

"What the fuck do you mean if you saw the things I've seen? You don't know what I've seen, so don't give me that bullshit!"

Steve stopped with his hand on the doorknob. *I didn't say that aloud.* He slowly turned toward his new partner. "Does Jack know?"

"Does Jack know what?" Eric asked with wide eyes.

"That you can read minds."

"That's ridiculous."

Steve smiled. "If you're going to work undercover, you damn well need to lie better than that."

"I don't know what you're talking about?"

Steve changed tactics. "My wife used to be able to tell I was lying a mile away even when no one else could." *I'll have to do some background checks on this one.*

"My background is clean," Eric blurted.

"Yeah, right." Steve studied Eric. The kid shifted restlessly, trying to steady his nervous energy. "So, back to my original question. Does Jack know?"

Eric met Steve's sharp gaze and shook his head. "No one knows."

"I'll be damned." Steve dropped his hand from the doorknob. This could be his golden opportunity to find Kyle, and he raised an eyebrow at the possibilities.

"I won't help you kill anyone."

Steve took in a breath. "You don't have to; you just need to help me find him."

Eric shook his head. "I swore to uphold the law."

He glanced at Eric and his eyes narrowed, his mind flowing over their brief conversation. *What are you hiding?*

"I'm not hiding anything."

Steve's mind went off like prisms of light shooting in several directions, assembling the information he just received into a coherent jumble of thoughts. *If the kid is clean, it must be something else.*

Eric's eyebrows creased.

Family.

The click in his mind was almost audible and Eric's eyes went a fraction wider.

Something about his family. He smiled at the reaction. "So, you might not have background issues, but your family does."

"I need to get to the shooting range." Eric looked at his watch, sidestepping the conversation again. He headed toward the door and Steve grabbed his arm.

Steve found himself slammed face first against the door, his arm protesting with a flare of pain as it twisted behind his back.

"My stepfather is a third-degree black belt and taught me everything he knows," Eric said in his ear. "So, please, don't fuck around with me." He let go and stepped back.

Eric thudded on the floor from the sweep Steve executed.

"I actually *earned* my black belts, so don't ever try that again."

"God damn, you're fast," Eric said, looking up in awe from his vantage point on the floor.

"Why do you want to be my partner?" he asked, looming over Eric.

"I didn't have a choice," he replied. "Agent Murphy ordered me to."

Steve laughed. "Do you do everything you're ordered to?"

"Yeah. Don't you?" Eric replied.

"Not always." Steve shrugged, and the smile faded. He had broken the rules a time or two and skirted by without reprimand. "You realize I'm your senior officer."

It was Eric's turn to laugh. "Not." He headed out of the room.

Hunting Season
Chapter 10

STEVE WALKED OUT OF the bathroom, naked and dripping wet, and crossed to his room, ignoring the stares of his classmates. He swung the door open, glaring at Eric, who was sitting behind the desk with a grin playing on his lips.

"Forget something?" Eric asked, nodding toward the bed where he had tossed Steve's clothes and towel.

"You are such an asshole." The door slammed behind him, and he crossed the room, ripping the towel from its resting place. He dried the water off his body, muttering under his breath, all the while his roommate chuckled from behind the computer.

"Aw, c'mon, you don't find that the least bit amusing?"

Steve shot a glare his way.

"I'm sure the women were digging it," Eric pushed. The floor they were on was co-ed.

Steve scoffed, snorting air through his nose. "Yeah, right," he muttered, pulling his clothes on.

ERIC GLANCED BACK AT the computer, looking over Steve's case file again. Steve was brilliant. He cracked the handful of assigned cases much faster than the norm. Even the case he met his wife on wrapped up within two months of his arrival. Of course, that was as far from a normal case as you could get. Steve claimed the thing stalking Brooksfield wasn't a human and if it hadn't been for Jennifer's testimony, they might have admitted him to the loony bin. The psych file notes stated Steve must have been hallucinating during the ordeal, but Eric knew better. He had seen the thing in Steve's mind, and it was evil.

Eric looked up.

Steve stood over the computer, staring down at him.

"What?"

Steve pointed. "One of these days."

"You just try your best, old man, but I can see you coming a mile away." He leaned back in the chair, grinning.

STEVE CLAMPED HIS TEETH together. "Fuck!" He swung around and stormed out of the room because Eric was dead on. He thwarted all of his attempts at practical jokes, taunting him every time. The kid had even sent their instructor into the room after Steve hung a bucket of water over the door. Needless to say, the instructor didn't take kindly to being doused. The reaming he got for that attempt was infamous.

Steve parked himself on the front steps, scanning the campus and shaking his head, a smirk making a brief appearance. Eric got him good this time. He hadn't even heard him slip into the shower stall and snatch the clothes off the bench, and he was usually so in tune with what was happening around him.

How could he pay him back for this latest stunt?

If I had access to a kitchen... He raised an eyebrow. *Ex-lax brownies might be fun.* The edges of his lips twitched, and he shook his head.

Nah, Eric would know, and I'd probably be the one to end up with the shits. The sigh escaped. *No matter what I dream up, Eric will know.*

"Yep."

He turned, and Eric took a seat next to him. "Yep, what?"

"I would know."

"Get out of my head," Steve whispered, shooting him a glare.

Eric laughed. "C'mon, it's like watching a freak show, disturbing, yet undeniably entertaining."

"Fuck you, Connor."

"Nah, you're not my type."

"How the hell did your parents deal with you for twenty-three years?"

Eric shrugged. "They passed me back and forth whenever they couldn't stand it anymore." He winked.

"Did that bother you?"

Eric glanced sideways. "Sometimes," he answered and inspected his fingernails. "How much do you know about me?"

"I know about New York."

Eric nodded. "Do you know who my mother is?"

Steve's eyebrows creased. The details of the New York case surfaced again, and he scanned the information like it was laid out on paper in front of him. Pictures, police reports, notes, but nothing beyond the fact that Eric's stepfather was filthy rich jumped out. He slowly shook his head.

"She was one of two survivors of the Aris family."

Steve's head snapped in Eric's direction, his eyes pulsing in their sockets. That name carried notoriety. It was also a case analyzed at Quantico. At least it was on his first go round.

"They still do."

Steve raised his eyebrows.

"Study the case," he said before Steve could ask the question.

"Holy shit." A whole brain dump of information came barreling from the recesses of his mind. "You're lucky she's alive."

Eric dipped his head in a nod. "It was really hard when my mom came back. Everyone said she died in that car crash, but I knew better. I knew. But who was going to believe an eight-year-old, especially when the dental records came back saying it *was* my mom?" He surveyed the landscape before he continued. "My dad had already remarried, so her homecoming was pretty entertaining." He let that hang in the air for a few minutes.

"How'd your mom deal with that?" Especially after the physical and psychological torture she endured during captivity.

He shrugged, turning toward Steve. "I'm not sure she could have gone back with my dad after everything, anyway. I guess being locked in a room with Tom Whitman for two months kinda changed her point of view." He offered a hint of a smile. "They ended up hooking until Chris entered the picture."

"Ah." Steve commented, remembering the headlines. Tom Whitman's wife was the one who went ballistic on Eric's family. "So, your mom's been married three times?" *That ordeal must have fucked her up pretty bad.*

"It had nothing to do with the ordeal," Eric answered Steve's train of thought instead of the question. "She never should have married Tom."

"You didn't like him?"

Eric let a laugh escape. "Tom was very cool as a stepfather. Hollywood, stardom, it was fun, but he wasn't around very much. My mom wanted nothing to do with the limelight after the media blitz she endured when she came back from the dead, so Tom bounced between coasts for five years. When he got the lead in that movie, things went south."

Steve let out a whistle. "That must have been hard on her."

"It was, but in a way, it made it easier when Chris came along."

"She obviously doesn't get till death do us part."

Eric stood, glaring down at his partner. "Shut up." He turned and went into the dorm.

Steve stayed on the front steps, mulling over the conversation. His mind shuffled through the new set of facts bombarding his brain, sifting, analyzing. His attention wandered back to the first day in the dorm when he found out Eric could read minds. "Family," he mumbled and stood up, retreating to their room.

Hunting Season
Chapter 11

STEVE SAT AT HIS computer, sifting through the FBI file on Kyle Wisnowski when he came to the pictures of his living room; he paused and closed his eyes.

"What are you doing?" Eric stepped into the room. Steve had blown off morning classes.

Steve raised his eyes, meeting Eric's gaze. He didn't have to speak.

"Jack's going to kill you." Eric had been given access to the case file on Kyle with the instruction not to give Steve the password.

Steve shrugged and took a deep breath, glancing back at the monitor. "Did you ever see the case file?"

"Yes, I've read the file," he said. "How the hell did you get access? The file's password protected."

"I know Jack well enough to figure out his passwords." He glanced up at Eric. "Besides, this is *my* research, *my* life." He sighed, looking at the crime scene photographs. "This is what he did to my family." Steve spun the monitor around so Eric could see the carnage. "The blood you see covering everything. That was my daughter."

Eric lost all color in his face as he took in the scene. There, in vivid color, was Steve, lying with Jennifer in his lap. Bone jutting from his right arm and his foot twisted almost backwards, but the worst of it was the shard of bone sticking from his eye. Bloody vapor covered everything. "Jesus." Eric stumbled backwards.

"I thought you saw the case file."

"I *read* the file. I wasn't given access to the crime scene photos."

Steve chuckled at the pale shock in Eric's expression. "I thought you had seen so much in your life."

Eric snapped his mouth closed and his eyes hardened. "Fuck you."

"Look, are you going to help me catch this bastard or not?"

"What are you going to do if you catch him?"

Steve swiveled the monitor back in his direction, studying the picture on the screen. "I'm going to kill him... slowly." He glanced up.

Eric shook his head. "I'm not going to help you."

Steve couldn't blame him. If the tables were turned, he wouldn't stand by and let his partner kill someone, either. Justice was no longer an option in his mind—it had been replaced by a visceral craving for vengeance. "Then I suggest you stay out of my way."

"No can do. Jack specifically told me to keep you away from that case."

Steve cocked his head and folded his arms, leaning back in the seat. "And how did Jack suggest you do that?"

Eric shrugged. "Jack didn't tell me how to do it, just that I had to."

Steve laughed. "Kid, you have no idea what kind of trouble you're paired up with, do you?"

"You really think you can throw all your training away and kill someone in cold blood?"

Steve inhaled through his nose and glanced at the screen. The blow of seeing the picture in Technicolor pierced the center of his being like a shotgun blast. He raised his gaze to Eric's and nodded. "He took everything from me." Steve blinked the haze away, resolved in his mission.

"That doesn't make it right."

Steve closed his eyes and let out a slight burst of laughter. "That's something Jenny would say."

"Sounds like a very wise woman."

"She was." Steve opened his eyes to the battered form on the screen.

"Maybe you should rethink your plan."

Steve's eyebrows rose. "What's to rethink? He's an animal and I'm going to hunt him down."

"I agree he needs to be stopped, but wouldn't putting him behind bars be more of a punishment than killing him?"

Steve mulled it over. "With this guy's connections, he'd make a deal and probably walk because of it."

It was Eric's turn to raise his eyebrows. "Bondino?"

Steve nodded. "Yeah, he's a bigger fish, and the bureau wants to take him down. I couldn't get the goods on him when I was undercover in Charlie's organization. Nothing more than hearsay anyhow." Steve reflected on the night Charlie killed Desiree. That was the only time he ever indicated a connection to Tony Bondino. He hadn't been able to find the tape with that conversation in Charlie's repertoire and unfortunately, without that, or the money trail, it wasn't solid enough to go after the Bondinos.

Steve logged out and leaned back in the chair. "What'd I miss?"

Eric tossed the mini-recorder to Steve. "I taped it for you."

Suspicion crawled under his skin. Eric never did anything for him, and he studied the recording device and then glanced at Eric. "What are you buttering me up for?"

"My girlfriend is coming up this weekend."

Steve rocked in the chair, not showing a hint of the amusement playing in his mind, even though he was sure Eric got a whiff, especially with the sour pout playing on his partner's lips.

He knew what it was like here, how rare it was to have a moment alone with a girl, but he didn't want to make this easy for Eric. "And?"

"Do I even have to say it?"

Suppressing a smile, Steve raised an eyebrow.

"Fine. I was wondering if you could be scarce on Saturday night."

Steve leaned forward in his chair, narrowing his eyes. "You have to ask me nicely," he said with a passable impression of Jack Nicholson in *A Few Good Men.*

"You're an asshole, you know that?"

"That doesn't qualify as nice." He made parenthesis with his fingers when he said the word nice.

"Are you going to be scarce or not?" Eric wasn't taking the bait and his face grew red with aggravation.

Steve chuckled. "You really suck the fun out of razzing you sometimes."

It was Eric's turn to raise an eyebrow.

"Yeah, I'll find something to do Saturday night," he said. "And thanks for taping the class."

Hunting Season
Chapter 12

SATURDAY ROLLED AROUND, AND Steve found solace in the library while Eric entertained his girl for the night. It was the first time Eric left him alone for more than an hour's time and with no new information on Kyle and no change in Jennifer's condition, Steve focused on his new partner, pilfering through the archives, digging up everything he could on Eric Connor and his family.

He accessed the New York City police department database, pulling up the video of Eric's family under siege at the warehouse incident five years before. After repeated viewings, he concluded that the only ones who should be alive today were Eric and one of his younger brothers.

Besides his sister's death, his younger brother should have bled to death when the crazy bitch raked the knife across his throat, but nothing happened to him, nothing, no mark, no blood, nothing.

Eric was another story—at that same moment, his right hand split open to the bone, as if he somehow put his hand between the knife and his brother's throat, saving the kid's life.

The gunshot wounds Eric's mother sustained should have killed her, but according to the medical reports; she only had one shallow lesion in her shoulder. He re-read that part, switching between the video and the medical notes again, and again, and again.

"No fucking way." He sat back in the seat, wiping his mouth with his hand.

Eric's stepfather was something different entirely. With so much that didn't add up, Steve wondered how they could close the case so quickly. *But then again, having more money than God must have helped.* Filthy rich didn't begin to describe it. Eric's stepfather was one of the wealthiest men in the world.

The shitty quality of the tape didn't diminish the horror of Chris Ryan's beating and the crucifixion that followed. The blood loss alone, three quarts according to the forensic notes, would have killed a normal man. Yet he somehow lived and had the strength to kill the bitch with his own hands.

"Shit." Steve muttered, biting his lower lip and concentrating on a frame-by-frame analysis. Some frames were warped static and he couldn't make out a thing, but the clear ones made him shiver.

Frame by frame, Chris Ryan fell from the cross and just before he disappeared from view, Steve swore he saw the man split in two. He rewound to see it again, printing the frame.

He rubbed his eyes and watched a third time. "Was that a fucking ghost?" Steve leaned back, his jaw slack, and he watched yet again. That meant Eric's stepfather actually died in that warehouse. "Holy shit."

A dozen frames later, Eric's stepfather stepped back into view. Steve froze the frame and stared at the man's back. Bloody, but smooth—not a trace of the raw shredded welts it had been when she finished the flogging.

"Jesus Christ almighty!" He rubbed his sweaty palms on the soft fabric of his jeans, swallowing the rock that formed in his throat. After a deep, calming breath, he rewound to the full frame of the ghost.

His heart lurched in his chest.

The ghost wasn't Eric's stepfather.

This face was familiar for very different reasons and Steve's blood shifted, braised by an arctic wind that attacked his veins, chilling him to the core.

"Ho-ly shit." He pushed his chair, shot to his feet, and paced back and forth, staring at the monitor like it was a cobra ready to strike. "No fucking way."

He took a seat again, pushing the heel of his palm to his good eye, sucking air in to calm his racing pulse. He slammed his index finger on the print button, lifting the color photograph off the printer, studying it. A shiver bit his neck and he shuddered, dropping the photo in his backpack with the others.

He played the rest of the video in slow motion. Slowing to frame by frame as the woman blinded Eric's stepfather with chemical mace. Chemical burns scarred the skin around his eyes in one frame, but in the next, it was gone.

Steve shook his head, rubbed his eyes, and played the scene again. The same results, impossible becoming possible, and Steve exhaled, suddenly aware he had been holding his breath.

Eric's stepfather insisted he killed the woman out of self-defense, and from what Steve saw—it looked valid even with the rest of the inconsistencies on the tape. He burned the video to disk and slid it into his backpack.

Steve picked up the print of the ghost. The case analysis they had done on this one still gave him the creeps. Kidnapping, rape, murder, all for what? Underground porn and snuff videos?

He plugged in a name and the picture that came back was identical to the picture of the ghost in his hand. He tossed the picture in his backpack and brought up the archive of the still open case. The file included ten years' worth of videos, violent and bloody mixed with steamy and hot. Steve pulled up the last one. The one aired on national television after the story broke. He burned it to a disc and went through the gruesome scene frame by frame.

Steve stopped the video when an image in the mirror gave him pause. It was a little boy holding his mother's hand. Not the image of the room. He rewound a few frames and played the tape again.

It wasn't his imagination.

A little boy was holding the woman's hand in a long hallway. Not the horrifying reflection of Ty Aris stretched by chains, like the frame before and after the anomaly.

Steve pushed the chair back. He wiped his face with his hands and glanced up.

ERIC STOOD AT THE head of the stairs, looking down at Steve, his heart hammering in his throat. He had been there long enough to know Steve had figured out his family secret.

Steve didn't move. He just sat in the chair looking up at Eric, his hands frozen halfway down his face. His eye glanced back at the frame in front of him and back up to Eric as a new thought echoed in his mind. *That's you, isn't it?*

"Yes."

Steve winced at the volume of the voice invading his mind.

Leave it alone. Eric's voice boomed again.

"Stop doing that," Steve said aloud.

Eric smiled at Steve's discomfort. *Not until you forget everything you just spent the last twelve hours sorting through.*

"Bullshit!" Steve raised his voice. It echoed through the nearly empty library.

Eric trotted down the stairs and approached the table. He took a seat opposite Steve, his swirling eyes hard and intense.

Steve blinked and looked at the screen, the images converging together in his mind like a storm. His mind grappled with the unimaginable, processing the information he gained from all the reports—the inconsistencies. The miracles.

"Jesus!" The exclamation accompanied a sudden epiphany, and he knew what Eric was hiding. He shook his head, glancing between the screen, his backpack, and Eric. His eyes narrowed as everything slammed into place. "Why are you here?"

"To uphold the law."

Steve laughed. "You've been aiding and abetting a fugitive, for what, fifteen years?"

"You have no idea what you are talking about." Eric sat back.

Steve leaned forward. "Your stepfather is Ty Aris," he whispered.

"His name is Chris Ryan." Eric said. "Ty was his brother."

"Then why did Ty's ghost split off from your stepfather in that warehouse?"

It was Eric's turn to blink. He couldn't cover the surprise fast enough. "You've got no proof."

"That's where you're wrong." Steve pulled the copy paper out of the bag and handed it to Eric.

The picture was a blur. Eric looked at it and handed it back to Steve, the crease between his eyes deepening. "Are you sure you're all right?"

Steve looked at the photograph, and his mouth dropped. He clamped it shut and looked at the screen. Only the reflection of the room was visible in the mirror. He glanced at Eric, filled with both fury and self-doubt. "I know what I saw."

"I'm sure you do," Eric allowed. "But understand this: if you come after my family, you will never get the chance to get the bastard who destroyed yours." He stood and left the library, leaving Steve gaping at him.

STEVE LOOKED BACK AT the computer, and the image was there, blazing on the screen, and burned in his memory.

Hunting Season
Chapter 13

*T*WELVE HOURS. IT TOOK *Steve twelve hours. Jesus, he's good.* Eric sat at the computer, doing some reconnaissance of his own, but there was nothing in the files or news reports to use against his roommate. "You're a fucking boy scout," Eric said, looking up at Steve as he stormed into the dorm room.

"And you're a fucking felon." Steve slammed the door.

"I was eight," Eric admitted. "I didn't know any better. The guy had just saved my mother, so to me he was a saint."

It took a second, a couple of rapid blinks while he processed the words, and then Steve tilted his head. "But?"

"No, I wasn't there, not physically anyway. But I saw most of what happened, and I was the one who fixed him."

Steve scrunched his eyebrows, confused. *What the hell was this kid babbling about?* "Fixed him?"

Eric nodded. "Healed him."

STEVE STEPPED BACK, THE full force of those two words sucked the air out of his chest.

Flashes of the videos he just spent the night watching snapped like a slide show in his mind. From the bowels of his soul came a swell of possibility with Jennifer's name on it. His mouth opened to speak, then closed it as he formulated the question. "What do you mean 'healed him'?"

"He would have bled to death on the floor," Eric said. "He saved my mom. I couldn't let him die." He stood and walked to the window.

"You can heal people?" Again, Jennifer's shrunken form passed through his head.

"No. Not anymore." He glanced back. "I gave it all to him. Any sort of healing powers I had transferred to him that day."

Steve slowly sank into the nearest chair. "Why, in God's name, would you do that?"

"I was eight. I didn't know any better."

"So why didn't you turn him in when he came back into the picture?"

"Do you believe in ghosts?"

Considering what he just saw in the video, Steve laughed.

Eric ignored Steve's laughter. "You know who Frank Aris is, right?"

"He was your uncle."

A bark of a laugh escaped Eric. He had never thought of it that way. "Man, that's fucking twisted." He shook his head, meeting Steve's intense gaze. "But, technically true." An involuntary shiver rippled through him. "He came after us."

"He's dead."

"Yeah, I know," Eric said. "I don't know why I'm telling you this. You're just going to turn around and throw us all in jail."

"That depends." Steve crossed his arms and leaned back in the chair, placing his feet up on

801

the desk. His curiosity flared, creating an itch at the base of his neck that could only be satiated by the full story.

"Depends on what?"

"How good the story is," Steve admitted with a smile.

"The ghost raped my sister," Eric said.

Steve's smile disappeared. The memories of Jennifer's multiple rapes flashed through his mind.

"Jesus," Eric recoiled, paling at the visions.

Steve's eye narrowed. "You saw that?" He walked around the desk and on impulse, Steve grabbed Eric's right wrist with every intention of peeling the clenched fist open to see the knife scar. The instant assault of visions fed from Eric made his breath hitch and his heart hammer fast enough to border heart attack status.

He yanked his hand away. The contact broke, and the panic abated, but he now had the entire history of Eric and his family embedded in his brain. The transfer had taken seconds, but it seemed like years.

Eric sat stunned, blinking up at Steve with wide, scared eyes.

"What the fuck did you just do?" Steve finally asked when he was sure his voice wouldn't shake.

"I, uh, I have no idea. I've never done that before." Eric stared at his hand and the stormy colors in his cornea wavered, swirling, then settled back into place.

"I've got to meet your family," Steve lifted his gaze, looking through a lock of hair that had fallen out of place. "Your mother in particular."

Not on your life.

"I'm not sure you understand. She's the miracle I've been looking for," Steve said. His mind raced a mile a minute, cataloging, scanning the memory dump. Awed.

The powers they possessed were light years beyond Jennifer's haunting clairvoyance. Mind reading and healing were just the tip of the iceberg. He saw everything. Every nuance. Every strength. Every weakness. Everything.

She can't fix your wife. Eric's eyebrows lowered with doubt.

"What do you mean, she can't fix my wife?"

Holy shit. You can read my mind now?

Steve laughed. *I guess so.*

"Can you?" Eric asked. *Shit, I can't hear him anymore.*

Steve stopped laughing. "You can't hear my thoughts anymore?"

FOR THE FIRST TIME since he was born, Eric couldn't hear what others around him were thinking and his mouth went dry. He slowly shook his head. "No." He mopped his face with his hand, his eyes going even wider. "Holy shit." He moved his chair back. "My mom is going to freak." The ramifications of what just occurred hit as fatally as a head on collision at a hundred miles per hour.

He had transferred not only his memories but also his mind reading ability to Steve Williams.

They stared at each other for a moment, and then Eric bolted from the room.

Hunting Season
Chapter 14

ERIC SAT ON THE front steps, watching the stars in the night sky. He took the time to analyze the conglomerate of memories that Steve downloaded. The anger he carried festered, poisoning his judgment and driving him in a direction he couldn't go, a direction that would destroy him if he followed the path of vengeance.

Eric refocused on Steve's brilliance. The man could see connections that others couldn't, and Eric was sure that if anyone else did a frame-by-frame analysis of the video footage, they would not have seen what Steve did.

"Twelve hours," he whispered to the night, shaking his head. Steve did in twelve hours what no one else had done in fifteen years. He closed his eyes, hanging his head and listened to the crickets chirping.

He opened his eyes at the shuffling of fabric next to him.

Steve took a seat on the stairs next to him. "How much of my life did you see?"

"I saw everything."

Steve was quiet.

"What are you going to do?" Eric asked. *Jesus, why did I ever agree to be his partner?*

Steve sighed. "You might want to request another partner, Eric. You don't want to go where I'm going."

Eric studied the shadow of the trees lining the other side of the road. "Are you going after my stepfather?" Eric asked, voicing the thoughts he knew Steve had already heard but ignored.

"It's not right that he's free after everything he's done."

"My little brother won't let you near him."

"CJ? There's an interesting kid."

Eric shot a glare in Steve's direction. "What the hell do you mean by that?"

"I'm just saying he's an interesting kid." Steve studied the patterns of the stars.

He saw the wheels turning in his partner's mind and shifted, uncomfortable without the ability to get into Steve's head, to know what was coming. *What am I going to tell my mother?*

Steve chuckled. "Momma's boy?"

"Shut up!"

After a few minutes of hushed tension, Steve broke the quiet. "I'm sorry. That was out of line," Steve said. "I can be a real shit sometimes, but you already knew that."

Silence filled the space between them, broken only by the sounds of the night.

Eric, still processing Steve's history, focused on Steve's wife. The strongest memories were the inconsequential ones. The line of her neck, her musical laugh, the way she teased him, the way her chin jutted out when she got stubborn. Eric blushed at the more intimate memories, shuffling through them as quickly as possible, especially with his partner sitting next to him, privy to every thought. She was a hot ticket, even when she was pregnant.

Steve surveyed the night sky. "I miss her." He looked down at the wedding band on his left hand, twirling it absently.

"You're lucky."

Steve shot a glance his way.

"I don't think I'm destined to find my soul mate." He leaned back on his elbows, stretching out on the steps.

Steve looked away. "Yeah, well, my soul mate is clinically brain dead in a hospital bed in New Hampshire." He stood and disappeared into the building, leaving Eric to noodle on that for a while.

Hunting Season
Chapter 15

SCREAMING VOICES, LIKE FANS in Fenway Park during a Yankees game, barreled in Steve's head, vaulting him into a sitting position. His hands covered his ears. His eyes darted around the empty room and his breath came in harsh pulls. The thoughts of everyone in the dorm assaulted his mind all at once. "Jesus Christ!" he swore, much louder than he realized.

A soft chuckle breached the darkness, breaking through the sounds in Steve's head.

"How do you shut them up?" Steve yelled the question, trying to hear his own voice above the clatter.

Eric shrugged and rolled, leaving Steve only his back as an answer.

"Fuck," Steve muttered and tried to block out the clamor. Sleep finally overtook the voices as the sky lightened, pushing him into a dark dreamless slumber.

The alarm woke him an hour later. Grumbling at the din still raging in his head, he slid out of bed and slapped Eric on the head. "How do I stop this?"

Eric's sleepy eyes blinked, and he struggled to get his bearings.

"Yes, last night was real. Now, how the fuck do I stop the voices?"

"Concentrate on your own thoughts." Eric muttered and slid out of bed. "Or focus on one person at a time." He left the room to grab a quick shower before their morning regiment began.

The ten-mile jog was enlightening. At first, the noise level was distracting, but by the end of the jog, before they reached the field training obstacle course, Steve was able to control the din to an acceptable level, focusing on specific classmates, and Eric hadn't been kidding. The females in the group had some very interesting ideas of what they wanted to do to him. He blushed and tried to wipe the smirk off his face as he cast a glance in Eric's direction.

Eric laughed aloud.

Steve focused on Eric. The kid wasn't thinking about anything, just a big blank page of paper. Huh, that was strange.

Steve and Eric ran neck and neck through the obstacle course and sprinted to the dorm to clean up before their advanced behavioral science class.

Eric walked into the room ahead of Steve, stepping over a package on the floor. "You've got a package," he said over his shoulder.

Steve picked up the nondescript envelope and opened it. Inside was a computer disc and nothing else. Steve crossed to his computer and took a seat, booting it up as he studied the envelope, twirling it in his hand, looking for any hint of where it came from. He raised his gaze to Eric.

Eric hung back. "You weren't expecting anything?"

Steve shook his head. He popped the disc in, and the screen filled with the inside of his cabin last spring.

"I figured you might want to see what your wife and I did before you came home." Kyle announced from the screen.

His cheeks tingled as the blood rushed into his skin, leaving it as hot as the anger boiling in his veins. Kyle was fucking Jennifer on their couch, and she called out the bastard's name. Their couch. She called out his fucking name on their couch.

If he could have blown the monitor to pieces with his mind, it would have vaporized under the fury that sparked. Steve sent his fist through the glass with a guttural cry that echoed off the concrete walls of the dorm room. Pieces of glass stuck in his knuckles, but he didn't feel the pain that should have accompanied the jagged shards.

The insane contortion on Steve's face was enough to make Eric take a step backwards. He felt for the door and Steve picked up the monitor, spiking it on the floor. "You might want to calm down."

Steve paced back and forth, muttering under his breath, his entire body shaking. He couldn't form the words for the rage overtaking his being. A roar filled the room, and he threw himself face first on the bed.

Eric took a tentative step toward Steve. *He's finally snapped.*

Steve growled with his face in the pillow. "I'm not crazy!" He glanced toward Eric. "I'm pissed!"

"Oh, well, that makes me feel eons better." Eric rolled his eyes.

Steve cracked a smile. "Now's not the time to be a smart ass. Okay?"

Eric nodded and relaxed a fraction.

"He's in town," Steve said, looking at the destroyed monitor.

The window disintegrated. The echo of a rifle shot drifted through the shattered glass. Steve's eyes went wide at the shot's destination.

Catapulted backwards by the force of the gunshot, Eric stared at the blood covering his chest and slowly slid to the ground, leaving a red trail on the door.

Steve rolled off the bed, grabbing his cell phone and crawled to Eric. "God damn it." He stared out the window, hearing the bastard laughing over the dim noise of thoughts.

He rattled off the situation to the 911 operator and grabbed the towel Eric dropped, pressed it to his chest in a futile effort to save his life.

"Jesus, kid." Steve examined the gunshot wound, shaking his head and meeting Eric's frightened stare. He pressed the towel back in place.

Eric grabbed Steve's wrist. "Leave them alone."

Steve raised his eyebrows. "Don't worry about that."

Eric's thoughts centered on his parents and not the current situation. "Promise you won't ruin their lives."

"I promise. Now just hang in there."

You know it's too late. Tell my family I love them. Eric's eyes fluttered closed, and his last breath wheezed out in a shaky rasping gurgle.

"Shit!" Steve dialed the familiar number as the ambulance pulled in. "Jack, the son of a bitch killed the kid." Chaos descended around him and he let the paramedics take over.

"What the hell are you talking about?" Jack asked.

"Kyle." Steve popped the disc from the computer, put it in the sheath it arrived in, and glanced out the window. "Kyle shot and killed Eric Connor!"

Hunting Season
Chapter 16

STEVE SAT IN THE airport, turning the disc over in his bandaged hand. His throat tightened and the boulder sitting on his chest got a fraction heavier. His breath was shallow and painful against the pressure. He forced a deep breath, closed his eyes, and leaned his head back against the seat. The slow exhale seemed to remove the rock cutting off his breath, and he opened his eyes, lowering them to the computer in his lap. He plugged in his headset and slipped the disc in the slot. Gritting his teeth, he pressed play.

This time, he watched the entire disc. The edited scenes switched from one lewd shot to the next and in all of them; Jennifer seemed willing, responding to Kyle like she had with him. Her moans of pleasure made him shiver. He heard that sound for close to three years whenever he made love to her, and his chest tightened again.

The video faded to black, with Kyle's laughter filling the void.

"No," he growled low in his throat. "There's no way she wanted you to touch her," he said without conviction. He closed his eyes and let the assault of thoughts of the strangers around him take over his mind, leaving no room to lament over what he had just seen on the disc.

Steve opened his eyes and stared at the blank screen for a few moments before replaying the disc. This time, instead of concentrating on Jennifer, he was looking for something specific and when he saw the detonator clutched in Kyle's hand; he let out the breath he had been holding. A miniscule amount of relief washed over him. He let his head dip to his chest and shut his eyes, willing the tears to stay below the surface.

His wife put on a first-rate performance to save their daughter's life.

Steve turned the computer off and closed it, tucking it back into his bag. The aimless thought process of strangers still interjected in his head.

How the hell did you deal with this all the time?

He turned and looked around, trying to focus on one person at a time, like Eric suggested. When he focused on one person, all other noise dimmed to a whisper, but that person's thoughts were like a beacon on a dark stormy night.

The boarding announcement for his plane came over the PA system and he picked up his carry-on bag, heading toward the concourse. The direct flight from Washington National to Boston took a little under two hours.

As Steve slid behind the wheel of a rental car, he flipped open his phone.

"Hi, Jack. I just landed. It should take me about an hour to get to the Ryan's house in York."

"I'm almost at the Connor's. I'll catch a bite to eat before I head over," Jack replied.

"Thanks. I'll let you know how it goes." He flipped the phone closed and pulled onto the road. Steve opened up the sporty rental coup, flying at close to a hundred miles an hour, making it to York, Maine, in less than forty minutes, navigating the side roads using Eric's memories.

He pulled up to the gate surrounding the Ryan residence and looked at the keypad. He knew the entry code but pressed the call button instead, opting not to surprise them in that manner.

"Hello?" A little boy's voice came over the intercom.

"Hi, my name is Agent Williams; I'm a friend of Eric's." *How the hell am I going to tell them this?*

"I know who you are." The gate opened.

"Thank you, CJ," Steve answered, already knowing the owner of the young voice.

Steve pulled up the driveway and sat in the car, looking at the house. It was understated and almost quaint. Quite the opposite of what he expected from one of the richest men in the world. His hands shook as he reached for the latch. Both excitement and dread flowed through his veins, and he opened the door, stepping onto the gravel driveway, the crunching sound of his boots filling the still air.

CJ Ryan stepped outside, closing the front door behind him, watching Steve approach with a somber expression. "You're here to tell us Eric died."

Steve blinked, looking at the house and back at the nine-year-old boy. Tall for his age, CJ stood at close to five feet with bright blue eyes that held a blend of sorrow and wisdom, giving him a strange grown-up quality that Steve had never seen in a child. He stopped a few feet from the steps, trying to formulate the words. "It's my fault," he finally said.

CJ tilted his head and Steve felt the thought probe. A strange tingling slid across his scalp. As disconcerting as it was, Steve allowed this boy to see inside his mind.

CJ's chin quivered. "You're here to tell us Eric is dead," he whispered, and the tears came.

Steve hung his head for a moment and nodded, grappling with his own sorrow for an instant before he pushed it aside. "Yes," he said. "Are your parent's home?"

"They're in back." CJ wiped his eyes on his sleeve. He planted his feet, blocking the entrance to the house. He let his eyes drift over the stranger. "You want to take my father away."

Steve sighed. "I promised your brother I wouldn't."

"But you're an FBI agent."

Steve nodded. "But I keep my promises." He took a step closer and extended his hand. "Special Agent Steve Williams," he formally introduced himself.

"CJ Ryan." The boy countered and reached out to take Steve's hand; the moment their skin touched, Steve felt the magnitude of the power the boy possessed. He had no doubt that if this kid put his mind to it, he could change the trajectory of the sun.

Steve yanked his hand away from CJ, breaking out in goose bumps. Interesting wasn't the right word to describe this child, frightening was more appropriate.

CJ's lips curled into a ghost of a smile and then he turned, swinging the door wide, waving

Steve inside. He led the way through the house and had him wait in the family room while he went to the backyard where the family was clearing the pool area.

The first one who came through the door was Chris Ryan, led by his guide dog, his blue eyes staring sightlessly from behind the tinted glasses. "Agent Williams," he said. The dog led him to the spot in front of Steve.

"Sir," Steve acknowledged the older man.

"To what do we owe the pleasure?" Chris asked. His expression guarded, and his German shepherd took a seat next to him.

Steve studied the man in front of him and saw his jaw tense. *He's reading my thoughts.* "I would rather wait until your wife is in the room before I discuss what brings me here," he said. His mind flowed through the remnants of memories from Eric and the research he had done the day before.

Chris turned at the sound of the sliding glass door opening.

Jessica Ryan stepped inside with both Tommy and CJ in tow. "You two head up to the playroom," she said. The boys ran by Steve and up the stairs while she removed her gloves and stepped into full view. "Hi." Unbuttoning her coat, she stepped by her husband's side.

Steve stared at her. She looked identical to what he envisioned Jennifer would look like if she reached forty. "Um." He diverted his eyes to the man in front of him.

Jesus, this is Ty Aris.

Both Jessica and Chris took a step back, their eyes widening a fraction.

Oh Christ, they both can read my mind.

"I'm sorry to inform you that there was an accident down at Quantico."

Accident, it wasn't a fucking accident.

"Eric..." Steve closed his eyes, not knowing how to say what was necessary. "Eric is dead." He finished and opened his eyes.

Chris reached out and put his arm around Jessica at the same moment she passed out, catching her in his strong grasp. He swept her up and placed her on the couch a few steps away.

"What happened?" he asked. His face was pale and his voice not as steady as it was before Steve broke the news.

"He was shot," Steve answered. He didn't want to go into the details.

Chris hung his head. "By whom?" The voice that leaped from his chest made Steve step back. Chris turned his head, his eyes falling accurately where he stood.

Steve shook his head. The words wouldn't form, and he felt the air around him spark.

"Dad, it wasn't him," CJ said.

The air settled, and CJ descended the stairs. "He's Eric's partner."

Steve glanced at the child and back at Chris Ryan. "I know who killed your stepson." He finally found his voice. "I think the shot was meant for me." He knew the shot was meant for Eric. He gathered that much in the seconds after the window shattered before the thoughts were lost in the onslaught of others that accosted him.

Chris stood up. "You're lying to me." He lunged toward Steve, his face scrunched with anger.

"Don't." The voice drifted from the couch, stopping Chris in his tracks and sending shivers up Steve's spine.

She even sounds like Jenny. Steve shot a glance at her as she sat up on the couch.

The tears came. "Don't Chris," she said, her voice shaking. "It's not his fault."

Steve glanced at the stairwell as the second child descended. He looked back at Chris. "I know who you are," he blurted.

"You also know what I can do." Chris took another step toward Steve, homing in on his exact whereabouts. He tilted his head. "Don't you?"

Steve thought CJ was frightening, but this man scared the shit out of him. He took a step back. "Yes, and I need what you can do in order to get the son of a bitch who killed my daughter."

Chris reached out like lightning, his hand clamping down on Steve's neck in an iron hold. "You dare come into my house and threaten me after getting my son killed?"

"Stepson," Steve wheezed under the crushing pressure. He executed a neck thrust and knocked Chris to the floor face first, yanking his arm up to the middle of his back. "You do that again and I don't care what kind of promise I made to Eric. I'll throw your ass in jail for the rest of your life. Understand?" Steve snapped, ignoring the growling German shepherd a few steps away.

Chris nodded his submission.

"Let him go," Jessica said.

Steve turned toward the soft, commanding voice. *God, you sound so much like Jenny.* He released Chris, standing and taking a step back.

"Jenny?" she asked.

"My wife," he answered and straightened himself out. "The same man who killed your son killed my daughter and put my wife in a coma."

Feeding off his thoughts, Jessica approached him. "You want me to fix her?"

He averted his eyes and nodded, allowing a brief flash of his past to escape into her mind. He smiled when she tried to cover the gasp with her hand. "That wasn't the worst of it," he said to her horrified expression.

Chris got to his feet and snapped his fingers. The dog quickly reacted, guiding him around Jessica and he stopped an inch away from Steve, bringing his eyes to where he thought the agent was standing.

Steve shivered at the accuracy of the gaze, forgetting for a moment that the man was blind. This man was responsible for more deaths than Kyle and he couldn't condone his freedom, but the promise he made to Eric ate at the need for justice. Right and wrong crossed and grappled in his mind.

If he followed the law, he'd never get the chance to avenge Jennifer. Hell, he'd never get the chance to see if Jessica's healing powers could work the miracle he'd been praying for. He pushed the Miranda rights from the tip of his tongue and swallowed. "I hate the fact you're not rotting in jail where you belong, but I made a promise to Eric," Steve said. *A deathbed promise at that.*

"I'm trying to figure out why Eric trusted you."

"He didn't. I figured it out on my own," Steve said. "Well, I figured out who you were." He shifted. "The transfer of his abilities took us both by surprise."

"I'll bet," Chris said with a sarcastic laugh.

"Eric wasn't very pleased by that development," Steve said.

"You know Eric?" Tommy asked, turning his head away from the open refrigerator and the can of soda he swiped off the shelf.

"Eric died today," CJ said, reaching beyond his brother for a soda.

Tommy's mouth dropped open, and the soda fell from his hand, bouncing and fizzling onto the floor. Tommy turned in Steve's direction, meeting his gaze, and Steve gave a nod, confirming what CJ said. The boy's chin quivered, and he sat down on the floor right in the growing puddle of soda. The flow of tears began.

Jessica went to Tommy and collected him in her arms, her own fountain of tears streaking her cheeks. She rocked with him, both sobbing at random intervals.

Steve tore his gaze away from Jessica and Tommy, aiming it at Chris. "Why would she ever let you near her after what you did, never mind marry you?" He needed to know. The explanation Eric gave wasn't enough, neither were the memories.

"She loves me."

"That's insane."

Chris shrugged and took a couple of steps away, giving Steve breathing room. "It is what it is."

Steve's cell phone rang, followed by the house phone. Steve flipped open his cell. "Hi, Jack." He glanced around the room. "I'm still with his family," he said, stepping out of the family room. "How do you think they're taking it?"

He slid into the hall by the front door. "They've lost a child."

That simple statement brought forth a rage of emotion, the emptiness of his own losses slamming into him like a battering ram, and he leaned against the wall, helpless against the onslaught. "You're not supposed to outlive your kids," he said, his voice rough with grief. "I'll catch you later." He flipped the phone closed and stood with his head against the wall, desperately trying to stop his own tears from surfacing.

He jumped when the hand touched his arm. Tommy stood next to him, his bay blue eyes glistening with tears.

"I'm sorry about your brother," Steve said.

"Eric told me about you. He said we needed to look after you."

The boy's words knocked the sorrow out of him, replacing it with a shiver that made the hair on the back of his neck stand on end.

"When did you talk to him?"

"A couple of hours ago. He said he was going away for a little while and he told me you'd be visiting and not to be sad."

What are you? A ghost whisperer?

"Do you think he'll be angry because I'm sad?"

The lump returned to his throat, and he shook his head, thinking of years ago when his own sister died. Tommy was about the same age he was, and he knew how hard the death of a sibling was at that age. "No, he won't be angry. It's okay to miss your brother, and it's okay to be sad."

Tommy gave him a hug and then stepped away, disappearing around the corner.

Steve wiped his face and slipped out of the house, closing the front door behind him. Halfway to the car, the door opened.

"Why don't you stay for dinner?" Chris asked.

"Why?" Steve felt like an intruder. He had only known Eric for six weeks and despite their memory exchange, he didn't feel it was appropriate for him to share in their grief. Besides, the idea of breaking bread with Ty Aris wasn't at the top of his to-do list.

"Where else are you going to go?" Chris asked.

"Brooksfield," Steve answered and stepped toward his car. He hadn't seen his wife in six weeks and even though he was itching to see her, he slowed his pace. Leaving now might screw his chances of ever getting Jessica Ryan to spin her magic on Jennifer.

"I'm sorry about your daughter," Chris said. "This must be tough for you."

Steve stopped in his tracks. "It is," Steve said over his shoulder. "We aren't supposed to outlive our kids," he repeated the same words he said to Jack a few minutes ago. "And Eric was a good kid."

"Eric was an exceptional kid," Chris agreed, crossing the distance unaided by the guide dog. He put his hand on Steve's shoulder. "When you find the son of a bitch, call me," he whispered in Steve's ear.

Steve turned his head. "Why?"

"Because I want this bastard as badly as you do."

Something in the way Chris spoke sent a flow of tremors down Steve's spine, and he spun in

Chris's direction. The eerie smile on Chris's face brought the shiver to the surface, and he stepped back.

Angel of Death.

The thought leaped forth before he could stop it.

Chris chuckled. "Tom called me that more than once." His smile faded, and he turned his head toward his family, who were all now standing at the door watching the exchange. He looked back in Steve's direction. "Stay for dinner," he said, and it wasn't a request.

Steve sighed, and curiosity got the best of him. He nodded.

"I'm blind, remember?" Chris pointed out after a few moments of silence.

"Okay," Steve said. He would head over to Brooksfield in the morning. His eyes landed on Jessica. *With you.*

STEVE STOOD IN THE center of the room, shifting his weight from the heels to the balls of his feet while Chris comforted his wife. *I really shouldn't be here.*

"Want to play a video game?" CJ asked, disrupting Steve's awkward thoughts.

Steve shrugged and took a seat on the couch. When CJ handed him the remote, he stared at it as if he had never seen one before. His right hand still had limited dexterity, especially with the new set of stitches, and the compact unit required fine motor skills he doubted he had. "I'm not sure I'll be able to do this."

"Just try." CJ put in an army game where they were enemies, trying to take each other down.

Steve cursed under his breath, maneuvering his army on screen with the skill of a two-year-old. He sucked, and CJ beat him at every turn, wasting his team easily. Frustration built, and he had to remind himself it was just a game before he whipped the remote across the room. Instead, he dropped it on the coffee table and glared at his hand in disgust. "Sorry, kid," he said, glancing in CJ's direction.

"You used to call Eric kid." CJ didn't divert his eyes from the television, continuing to play even though Steve had given up.

"Yep," Steve answered, flexing his hand, wincing at the pull of the sutures. "And he used to call me old man."

⚬⚬⚬

JESSICA WATCHED THE EXCHANGE. Frustration radiated off Steve in waves, and it wasn't just the video game. He blamed himself. For his daughter, his wife, and now Eric. He took their deaths personally, believing if he had been more diligent, more alert, none of it would have happened. Underneath the cool exterior was a man fighting for his life, fighting his guilt and fighting his sensibilities where Chris was concerned. He would like nothing more than putting Chris behind bars, but he made a promise to Eric. A deathbed promise. A promise he'd never break.

She peeled herself out of Chris's arms and crossed into the family room, wiping the tears off her face.

Steve glanced at her as she took a seat on the couch next to him.

"I'm not sure I can fix your eye." She reached for his right hand. She brought his palm to her lips and pressed a kiss to his skin, pushing a small fraction of her healing powers into him.

Pain gripped him. "Shit," he groaned and squeezed his eyes shut. His flesh felt like he'd been doused with gasoline and set on fire. His breath hitched in his chest, the airflow shutting down until the pain gave way to tingling, much like pins and needles after your arm or leg falls asleep. It amplified, starting at his fingertips, racing through his body until it concentrated behind the patch covering his deformed eye. "God damn that hurts," he said, and the world swam in front of him. Blackness descended.

Hunting Season
Chapter 17

STEVE BLINKED, DISORIENTED BY the silence in his mind and the unfamiliar noise around him. A cool cloth lay on his forehead and a ceiling he didn't recognize met his gaze. He inhaled, closing his eyes, and the succulent aroma of roasted tomatoes and garlic filled his nostrils. His mouth watered in response.

"Feeling better?" The boy's voice broke through the cobwebs.

Steve turned, opening his eye. Tommy perched on the edge of the couch, staring at him with red, swollen eyes and a nose to match.

He sat up and looked around.

Jessica and Chris were in the kitchen cooking and CJ sat on the other couch, engrossed in the same video game they were playing when he passed out.

"Yeah," Steve croaked. His mouth was as dry as Phoenix during the summer. He stood on unsteady legs and made his way into the kitchen, clearing the desert sand from his throat.

Jessica turned toward the noise. "You're back with us." Her eyes matched Tommy's, red and puffy.

Steve nodded. "How long was I out?"

"A little over an hour," Jessica said. "I've never had anyone faint before. I'm usually the one that passes out." She moved to the refrigerator and grabbed a beer, popped the cap off, and handed it to Steve.

"Thanks. You're really hooked up here." He pointed the beer at the kitchen. "Reminds me of the apartment my wife had her senior year in college." He took a sip of the Corona.

"Did she cook?" Jessica asked.

Steve burst out laughing, almost spitting the beer across the room. "No. She burned just about everything she touched." He smiled, remembering his wife's lack of culinary skill with fondness. "It just wasn't dinner without the smoke alarm going off."

"How long has it been?" Jessica asked, glancing at him.

"Almost a year now," he said. His smile faded. "Jennifer's still in a coma," he explained. "There's been very little brain activity since the explosion." *Most of which coincide with Kyle's murders.* He took a sip of his beer.

"I'm not sure I can do anything for her."

Steve offered a slight shrug. "I still want you to try. She's all I've got." Steve took a draw on his beer, his eye focusing on the hand holding the bottle. Shock, like a zap of electricity, hit him.

The scar on his right forearm where his bone broke through the skin was gone.

Steve put the bottle down on the table and pulled his sleeve up, taking a closer look. He ripped the bandages off and stared at his unmarred palm. *Completely gone. No way!*

He turned his hand around and flexed it, squeezed it into a fist and then picked up the beer again, draining it.

Chris laughed. "It's the damnedest thing, isn't it?"

"Yes." Steve still marveled at his arm. He touched the eye patch as an afterthought and glanced at Jessica. *My eye?*

"I don't know," she answered his unspoken question.

"It feels different." Steve glanced around.

"Bathroom's that way." CJ pointed to the far side of the kitchen and slid into one of the seats at the table.

"Thanks." Steve messed up CJ's hair as he passed, heading in the direction he pointed.

He stood in the bathroom staring at the mirror. The eye patch fell from his slack fingertips and drifted to the floor. Baby blue irises stared back. Both of them. He covered his right eye, and the room went black. *Blind, but an eye just the same.* He uncovered his eye, staring at the reflection again. *A hell of a lot better than the sunken deflated eye it was a couple of hours ago.* A slightly hysterical laugh escaped.

He leaned closer; the small scar on his cheek was gone too. "Holy Mary, Mother of God!" the muttering mantra continued, and he ripped through the buttons on his shirt. The words fell away, and he stared at his perfect chest, running his fingers over the skin. There wasn't a mark on him. He leaned against the wall and the world tilted again. Slowly, he sank to the floor. Steve didn't know whether to laugh or cry. He jumped at the soft tap on the door and scrambled to his feet as it swung open.

"Are you all right?" Her soft, imploring voice reached his ears.

Steve uttered a high laugh and looked in the mirror. "I haven't been all right since the day my daughter died." He glanced at Jessica when she cracked the door. "Somehow, this makes it worse."

Jessica offered a smile. "Be careful what you wish for."

Steve nodded; thoughts of Jenny filled his mind. "I need to get you to Brooksfield."

Jessica took a deep breath. "Why?"

"I need her." Steve leaned on the sink with his head hung low. "And if you help me, I'll forget everything I know about your family." He tilted his gaze toward her and straightened up.

Her lips thinned into a tight line. "Dinner's ready." She turned, leaving him in the bathroom.

Steve raised his eyes to his perfect, haunted face, her words echoing in his brain. This is what he wished for, to be whole again—but he was as far from whole as he had been before she worked her magic. Taking a deep breath, he headed back into the kitchen and took the empty seat between the two boys.

"Freaky, isn't it?" Chris asked and raised his beer.

Steve glanced at the two boys. Both were staring at him. "A bit," he answered, meeting CJ's gaze.

"I think I stared in the mirror for over an hour when I got to my brother's house," Chris said, taking a bite of the lasagna.

Steve didn't respond, but a deep crease appeared between his eyebrows as he studied Chris.

Jessica cleared her throat, catching his attention. "How long have you been with the FBI?" she asked, pushing the lasagna around with her fork.

"Close to ten years."

Jessica cocked her head, scrunching her eyebrows together. *He couldn't be much older than Eric.*

"I'm twenty-eight. My grandfather was FBI, and he pulled some serious strings to get me in right out of high school." He took a bite of the lasagna. "This is terrific, Mrs. Ryan."

"Thank you," Chris answered. "I made it."

Steve's eyebrows rose, and the boys chuckled. "It's good."

Chris leaned back with a nod, his plate already picked clean. "She actually does a better job, but it was my turn to cook."

"I'm amazed you don't have servants do the cooking and cleaning," Steve said.

"I hate cleaning," Jessica interjected. "We have a maid service that comes in each week." She tasted a bite and put her fork back down.

Chris leaned over. "You need to eat."

"I'm not hungry," she answered and pressed her lips together, tears glossing her eyes and she blinked them back, straightening her back in the seat as if taking a stand against the threatening sorrow.

Chris slung his arm around her and pulled her close, kissing her temple.

"You live pretty modestly considering," Steve continued, waving his fork in a small circle.

"Considering what?"

"Considering you're a billionaire."

"You've done your homework." Chris stood, putting his plate in the sink. He crossed the kitchen, his hand in front of him so he knew when he reached a solid object. He opened the refrigerator door and accurately grabbed two beers. A small whistle sounded from between his teeth and his shepherd shot across the kitchen, its sharp nails clicking on the tile flooring. When he sat at the table, he flipped the caps off the beers and handed one to Steve. "Don't know if you're done yet, but I figured since I was over there..."

"Thanks Mr. Ryan." Steve took the beer from his hand.

"Please, call me Chris."

"I was thinking more along the lines of Ty." Steve finally spoke the name.

"She's the only one that's allowed to call me that." He hooked his thumb toward Jessica. "You can call me Chris." His blind gaze was accurate and sharp as it bore into Steve. "Boys, when you're done with dinner, you need to take a shower and do your homework."

"Awe, Dad!" they whined in unison.

"Don't give me any flak!"

"Yes, Dad," they replied, glancing at each other around Steve.

"Put your dishes in the sink," Chris ordered, and the shuffle of the chairs and clanking dishes in the sink filled the kitchen.

The boys ran through the family room, ascending the stairs with all the gusto of a herd of elephants.

"Showers first!" Chris called after them and waited until the water turned on upstairs before turning his attention back to Steve.

"What exactly do you want from us?"

"I don't know. I thought..."

"You thought because Eric transferred his power to you, we would do the same."

Steve shrugged and took a sip of beer.

"I'm blind Agent Williams."

"Yes. I thought I'd make a trade. Your freedom for your power."

Jessica turned at his comment.

"And then I made a stupid promise to your son." He shifted in the seat. The beer lost its taste with the next swig. "I would love to put you behind bars for all you've done, but I made that fucking promise."

"You're not the first," Chris answered. "But as I've told all those who came before you, you have absolutely no proof." He tilted his head, raised the beer in a salute and took a swig.

"I do now." Steve's gaze transferred from Chris to Jessica. She shut off the water and turned toward the table, wiping her hands on a dishtowel.

"You see, I did a hell of a lot of digging and found some anomalies on the video of both the underground complex and the warehouse a few years back. Then there's the simple fact that several people saw the scars I had. I come here, meet with the two of you and presto, my scars are all gone." He snapped his fingers. "Thanks to your lovely wife here, I can pull a case together that would hold up in a court of law," he finished.

"You ungrateful..." Jessica stepped forward.

Chris put up his hand to stop her. "Jess, go check on the boys." Chris turned his head in her direction. "Go!"

She muttered under her breath and withdrew up the stairs.

832

CHRIS WAITED A FEW minutes before he spoke.

Anger raged through his body, morphing his lasagna into a living and deadly being in the center of his stomach. Chris inhaled, calming the beast clawing at his insides. If he stepped over the line, all hell would break loose.

"How dare you come into my home and threaten me," he said, his voice carrying the resentment filling his form.

"You think you're above the law. It's my job to take people like you down."

Chris chewed the inside of his lip, weighing his response. "I'm not above the law, Agent Williams. I never thought I was. I knew someday everything would catch up to me one way or another. Hell, I should be in a box six feet under right now, but I'm not. God only knows why I was spared, but I was and as much as you detest my existence, you need my help, otherwise you wouldn't have made that promise to Eric."

He sensed volatility in Steve, a blend of darkness and brilliance intertwined in a tight knot. Steve's aura—white with pulses of red—writhed under the fury begging to overtake the man.

When no response came, Chris chuckled. "Truth hurts, doesn't it?"

"Fuck you," Steve snapped.

"Nah, you're not my type."

Steve's sudden laugh filled the kitchen, and Chris cocked his head in a silent question.

"That's Eric's come back. Now I know where he got it."

"Eric could be a smart ass sometimes, but I loved him like he was my own."

"I imagine you would. He's the one who saved your sorry ass."

Chris nodded and sighed. "Yes, he did. More than once." He tipped his beer to his lips, finishing the bottle and setting it on the table. "Look, I understand revenge, but you don't have a clue of the penance you'll pay for crossing that line."

"You don't regret killing your stepbrother."

Chris shook his head. "No, not one bit." He allowed a slow smile to form and felt the quiver that ran up Steve's spine. For a moment, he wished he could see the reaction—the rush he got from intimidating those around him was lost without the view, but the mental shiver amused him just the same.

"Revenge always has a price, though." His smile faded. His stepbrother was waiting in hell for payback and Chris knew someday he'd come face to face with Frank's wrath. The thought was sobering.

Raising his empty beer bottle, he asked, "You want another, or do you want to move onto something harder?"

"What are the alternatives?" Steve asked.

Chris shuffled through Steve's thoughts, wondering what alternatives he was asking about, him or hard liquor. Instead of guessing, he asked, "Are you asking about drinking alternatives?"

Silence filtered through the room, and a sigh escaped from his visitor. "Yeah, something harder wouldn't be a bad idea right about now."

Chris snapped his fingers, and his dog was again by his side, leading him to the bar at the side of the family room. "You might want to come over and see for yourself. I think we have vodka and scotch, but it's been a while and I don't feel like opening the bottles and sniffing."

STEVE STOOD AND CROSSED the room. "What would you like?" he asked, stepping behind the bar and looking at the stock. There was much more than just vodka and scotch. In addition, they had gin, Bacardi, sangria, tequila, and a few bottles of wine. He reached for the tequila. "You wouldn't happen to have lemons?" he asked, looking at the bottle.

"Sure do. Grab the scotch for me." He crossed to the refrigerator with his dog and rummaged around, lifting a bag out of the fruit crisper. "Are these lemons or limes?" he asked, holding them for Steve to see.

"Lemons," Steve said, setting the bottles on the table.

Chris grabbed a cocktail glass and a shot glass, filling the cocktail glass with ice before he headed to the table.

"Knives?"

"In the drawer behind me," Chris said, feeling the bottles.

"Scotch is on the right," Steve said as he opened the silverware drawer and took out a small paring knife. He grabbed the wood cutting board from behind the sink and brought both to the table.

Chris opened the scotch and took a whiff.

"You don't trust me?" Steve asked, taking a seat opposite Chris.

Chris shrugged. "Habit."

"Ah." Steve cut the first lemon. The tangy scent drifted into his sinuses and for a moment, he was transported back to Brooksfield University and the bar where he and Jennifer drank tequila and danced and let loose like he hadn't done since.

A lump formed in his throat, and he cleared it, concentrating on slicing the lemon and not looking at the criminal mentally studying him from the opposite side of the table. Chris had hit a nerve earlier, one that burned just under his skin, along with the promise he made to Eric. It wasn't right, none of this was right.

With four neat slices set out in front of him, he poured his first shot.

Chris pushed the saltshaker in his direction.

"Thanks." He licked the space between his thumb and forefinger, pouring the salt on the wet skin. With everything set up, he licked the salt, downed the shot and followed with a lemon wedge. Jennifer's puckered lips came to mind and the memory, like a sucker punch in the gut, forced his breath from his lungs. He pulled the sour wedge from his mouth and dropped it on his napkin, pouring another round.

"I haven't done a shot of tequila in years," Chris said. He leaned back in the chair, swirling his drink, the ice cubes clinking against the side of the glass with the slow movement.

"I needed that," Steve said, feeling the warmth spread from the pit of his stomach through the rest of his body, numbing the nagging in his conscience. He repeated the process twice more before sitting back and studying Chris.

Awkward silence persisted, and Chris took a sip of his scotch, his expression one of contemplation. His arrogance irked Steve, and he pushed the anger away, taking stock of all that had happened since he arrived at the house.

The man hadn't denied the truth. Hadn't even tried, like most common criminals. He almost huffed at the thought. Ty Aris wasn't a common criminal. His intelligence was off the charts to the point he could give any NASA engineer a run for his money. He'd been a member of Mensa and yet he chose to make porn and snuff videos.

"Why'd you do it?"

"Why'd I do what?"

"Kidnap and kill all those people."

Chris downed his scotch and leaned forward, taking the time to refill his glass before speaking. "I would love to say I didn't have a choice, but I did. I knew it was wrong, but I just didn't care. By that time, I had lost everyone who meant anything to me except my brother, and Frank knew that. He played that card a couple of times when he thought I was getting out of hand or having second thoughts."

"So he blackmailed you into it?"

"Yes, and no. He coerced me into building the complex and snatching our first victims. I thought we were doing something like a catch and release program." He chuckled. "Boy, was I naïve. You see, I've always had a knack with cameras and editing equipment and Frank played on my vanities until I was too far in to back out."

Kyle's video crossed Steve's mind.

"He sent a video?"

Steve nodded.

"Blind." Chris reminded him.

"Yes, it was in the dorm room when we got back from our morning training exercises," Steve said. "It set me off." His phone rang, interrupting the conversation. He dug it out of his pocket and looked at the caller ID. "I need to take this." He flipped the phone open.

"Steve?" The familiar voice was uncharacteristically hesitant.

"Hi, Jack," Steve said, pouring another shot of tequila. "I'm still in Maine."

"Steve, there's been another situation."

Steve paused. Dread poured through the line, and he looked at the shot halfway to his mouth, opting to down it before focusing on the call. Another situation meant something bad, and the way Jack phrased it only meant one thing.

His heart banged in his chest as Jack's fragmented thoughts assaulted him, but only two words made sense—Jennifer and danger. His throat clamped, and he slid the chair back, crossing to the slider.

"What kind of situation?" he asked, stepping into the cool evening air.

"Steve, it's your parents."

Steve felt his blood seep out of his face and hands, leaving both heavy and cold. "What about my parents?"

"Kyle," Jack replied. "And he left a note."

The vision of his parent's bedroom painted in blood flooded the serene ocean scene before him. A steamroller of emotions slammed into Steve, leaving his legs numb and wobbling like a teetering tower of Lego's. He stumbled to the closest lawn chair and collapsed with his breath locked in his lungs, unable to voice the flurry of questions plaguing him.

"Steve?"

"My parents? Why?" He forced the words from his closed throat.

"The note says he wants you to suffer alone." Disgust laced Jack's voice, along with barely controlled anger.

Steve looked around the backyard, not seeing what was in front of him, his mind working overtime until one thought snapped all others out of his head. "Jenny," he whispered. "You think she's in danger?"

"Yes, I do, but don't worry—I ordered full shift coverage on the ICU until further notice. Only existing staff members will be allowed to enter her room. She'll be fine. You've got funeral arrangements to make," Jack said.

Jack's assurances didn't settle his frantic heartbeat. His mind kept returning to the vision of blood dripping down his parent's walls, co-mingled with the memory of the cottage last spring, bathed in his daughter's blood—both rendering him unable to pull enough air into his lungs. His field of vision narrowed, and he dropped his head to his knees before it shrunk to blackness.

"Steve?"

"Yeah," he barely whispered.

"Are you okay?"

Steve didn't answer. He didn't know if he'd ever be okay again. His vision blurred and cleared and the strap constricting his lungs eased, allowing oxygen into the far recesses. He took a few gulps of air before sitting upright, his mind clearing from the emotional fog.

"Steve?"

"He was in Virginia this morning and Connecticut this afternoon. There has to be a record of him on a flight."

"We're looking into it."

"I'm going to hunt that fucker down if it's the last thing I do."

Jack sucked the air in on the other end of the line. "Steve, this isn't your case. You still need to finish your refresher course at Quantico."

Steve stood and walked out to the rock wall, anger pulsing every cell in his skin, his temple throbbing under the current. He gripped the cell phone tightly enough to hear it creak in protest. "What do you mean I'm not on the case?" He glared out over the water. "The bastard killed my family."

"You are too close to the situation to be involved." Jack's tone left no room for negotiation.

"Fuck that!" Steve hung up. He drew his arm back to pitch the cell into the ocean, but the shrill ring broke through his fury, and he dropped his arm, staring at the number before he answered it and brought it to his ear. "I'm not going back to Quantico. I quit." He ended the call and turned to head inside.

Chris stood a few feet away with his guide dog. "So, you won't be able to haul my ass to jail after all."

"Fuck off." Steve stormed past him and was stopped by Chris's iron grip on his upper arm. The volcano churning inside him erupted, and he swung his clenched fist in Chris's direction.

Much to his surprise, Chris blocked the wild swing, further churning the inferno inside him. "The bastard killed my parents," Steve growled and threw another punch.

Chris deflected it again with astonishing speed.

Rage blocked all sensibility, blinding him with a red hue, like a veil of blood sliding over everything. He swung and swung and swung, blocked every time until his arms felt like lead and his throat burned.

Steve dropped to his knees on the ground, frustration ripped sobs from his chest. The red hue turned to the distorted clarity of tears. Waves of wrath and sorrow radiated off him, heating the air. A thin layer of sweat drenched his hair. Each ragged breath singed his lungs, and he closed his eyes, reining in the fury.

"I. Want. Him. Dead!"

"I know." Chris crouched next to Steve and put his hand on his shoulder, offering little consolation.

"He's going to kill anyone I get close to." Steve looked up.

"That depends on who you make alliances with," Chris replied. He stood and extended his hand to help Steve off the ground.

Steve glanced at the hand. "I can get up on my own," he grumbled, wiping his face on his sleeve.

Chris nodded and snapped his fingers. The dog appeared and led Chris inside with Steve in tow. "You shouldn't drive," he said over his shoulder.

"I need to get to Brooksfield." Steve headed past Chris.

"Let me rephrase that. You are not driving."

An invisible wall stopped Steve and frustration filled him. *Who does this jackass think he is?* "I'm fine," Steve said through clenched teeth.

"You are about as fine as my wife is," Chris said.

Steve looked over his shoulder. "I need to stop him."

Chris nodded. "But you no longer have the resources of the FBI," he replied, spreading his arms out. "So, where does that leave you?"

The reality of his rash decision knocked the wind out of Steve. He no longer had access to the FBI's computer network to dig into Kyle's past and peg down his current identity. "I don't know." He looked out the window. "But I need to get to Jenny." He glanced at Chris. "I need your wife to do whatever it is she does to make her better, then I need to get her as far away from Brooksfield as I can."

"You're in no condition to drive, and Jessica isn't willing to go with you right now. Not with the shit you pulled at dinner. Give her a little time to cool down."

"I need to get a hotel room and I'll come back in the morning."

"There's a perfectly good bedroom upstairs."

Steve turned toward Chris. "You're out of your fucking mind."

Chris broke out in a grin. "Perhaps, but you're not exactly sober."

"I've driven shitfaced before." His gaze dropped to the bottle of tequila and thoughts of Jennifer swarmed. "And I'm not even close to drunk."

"But you're not sober either. Look, if you're serious about leaving, I won't stop you once you've had a cup of coffee and cooled down some. If you go barreling after this psycho without a plan, you're libel to get yourself killed."

"Why the fuck do you care?"

Chris inhaled and gnawed on his bottom lip for a minute. "Because."

Steve raised an eyebrow and let a bitter laugh escape. "Because why? Because if I take off, you're afraid I'll send in the cavalry?"

Chris laughed. "No. You know damn well I can stop just about anything that comes for me. I can even stop you, but I won't."

"Why not? As a matter of fact, why am I still alive?"

"You're still alive because you made a promise to Eric and no matter how much you hate me, you don't break promises. That much I gathered from you, from your thoughts. But even if you back peddle, and give in to your loyalty to the law, I won't put up a fight. I won't because you've got a little of my stepson rattling around in your brain and if I take you out, I'll live to regret it."

Steve stared at Chris, at the blooms of anger in his cheeks and the rise and fall of his chest, as the man gained control of the venom that leaked into his voice.

"Besides, if I killed you now, I'd have a hell of a time finding the son of a bitch that killed Eric." Chris headed into the kitchen and ran his hand on the table until he found his drink. "Coffee pot's on the counter." He waved in the general direction of the coffee maker. Chris turned and crossed toward the family room with his hand out in front of him until he reached the couch. "I hope you don't mind, but I'm getting shitfaced." He took a seat.

Steve looked between the empty coffeepot and the tequila on the table and sighed. While he'd like nothing better than to force Jessica in the car and take her to Brooksfield, he knew Chris wouldn't allow that, at least not at this moment. The emotional rollercoaster persisted, dipping between anger and sorrow along with a thin layer of fear for anyone he was close to, and he looked at the door. Jennifer's safety was his top concern.

"Your boss said the FBI has the room guarded."

"Get out of my head."

"Not on your life." Chris raised the tumbler. "I need to know what's coming." He lowered his glasses and swung his gaze in Steve's direction.

"Tell me something. Are you really blind? Because you can level a glare pretty damn accurately for someone who can't see."

"I'm blind as a fucking bat—but you've got some sort of aura that breaks through the darkness."

"You see auras?"

Chris laughed. "Nope. Yours is the first one I've ever seen. Ironic, isn't it?"

Steve let out a nervous laugh. "Ironic wasn't the first word that popped into my head."

"I know, but I'd rather not be called a freak."

Steve chuckled and put his hands on his hips, debating. Chris was right. The FBI was guarding Jennifer. And the hospital room had bulletproof glass—he'd seen to that right after Kyle escaped, so for the time being, she was safe. If he left now, all his emotional demons would attack, and he wanted to keep them at bay as long as he could. Besides, he was finding some entertaining relief in this snappy exchange with Chris Ryan. He looked at the tequila again, wanting the numbing bliss that came along with inebriation.

"Are you going to start that coffee, or do you need my help?"

"I was thinking more along the lines of the tequila and a cab."

"I was serious about the bedroom upstairs."

"I know you were, but I doubt your wife would be pleased with me sleeping under her roof."

"She'll be fine," Chris said.

Steve grunted and headed for the bottle on the table. "Yeah, right, but I might never wake up," he mumbled under his breath.

"She's not the one you have to worry about, but I'm pretty useless when I'm drunk. Bring the scotch on your way over."

"You think she'll let me take her to New Hampshire in the morning?"

"We have to go to Connecticut in the morning to finalize Eric's arrangements."

"I'll have her back before ten—besides, I have to go to Connecticut too."

"Why?"

"My parents live there, and I need to plan their funeral." Any reservation he had about drinking himself into oblivion faded and Steve grabbed the shot glass, the tequila and the scotch. He headed into the family room and took a seat on the couch facing Chris, handing him the bottle of scotch. "Here."

"Thanks."

Steve poured another shot and downed it.

Chris filled his glass, using his finger as a gauge to tell when to stop, and then he set the bottle on the table. "Here's to Eric and your parents." Chris raised his glass.

Steve poured another shot and clinked his glass against Chris's before drinking the hot liquid. Pouring another round, he raised the shot glass. "Here's to my wife and daughter." He slammed the shot down, relishing the burn.

"To hunting season," Chris said.

The clink of glass filled the family room, and both men drained their drinks.

Steve smiled. "To hunting season."

Hunting Season
Chapter 18

STEVE WOKE IN THE unfamiliar room. He opened his eyes to the scuttling of feet in the hallway and turned his head. The explosion of pain caught him off guard and he groaned, covering his head again. The taste of tequila was still present in his mouth.

The soft knock interrupted his stupor.

"What?"

"Time to get moving." A male voice on the other side of the door announced.

"I should have stayed at a fucking hotel," Steve muttered. A laugh sifted in from the hall and Steve rolled out of bed, heading into the adjoining bathroom. He flipped the light switch and stared at his reflection, blinking from the bright light.

Something was different, and he blinked, his gaze locked on his own baby blues.

He covered his right eye and his reflection stared back, startled.

Isn't this the one I'm blind in?

He covered the left eye with his hand just to make sure and again, his reflection stared back. He repeated the process two more times, melting away the disbelief and any notion that it was his alcohol-soaked brain playing tricks.

"Well, I'll be damned."

He peeled off his clothing, marveling at the fact there were no scars anywhere, even the small appendix scar was gone. He stood under the warm stream for ages, shutting off all other thoughts except the exquisite feel of the hot water brushing his skin.

The sweet scent of pancakes drifted up the stairs and he navigated down with his backpack, his head still pounding, and his stomach—decidedly sour—flipped, threatening to empty its contents on the floor. Steve put the back of his fist to his mouth, willing his stomach to settle. After a few deep breaths, it obeyed, and he placed his backpack on the floor, digging in his pocket for the car keys. "Thanks for the hospitality."

Jessica looked up from the fry pan. "Do you want pancakes?"

Steve shook his head; food wasn't an option after the tequila binge.

"Coffee?"

Steve hesitated and nodded. "That would be nice." He approached the table.

"Chris has a hangover, too," she said, pouring a cup for Steve and sliding it across the table. "How late did you two stay up?"

"I have no idea," Steve answered and took a sip of coffee. "I don't remember much of anything after I finished the first bottle of tequila."

"I'm sorry about your parents," Jessica said. She sat and picked at the pancakes in front of her without looking up.

"I'm sorry for being such an ass."

Jessica lifted her gaze, her eyebrows arching in surprise.

He offered her an embarrassed grin and a shrug. "I'd like you to come with me to Brooksfield before you head south."

Jessica stared at him, her eyebrows settling back into the arc of irritation.

She opened her mouth to argue, but Steve held up his hand.

"Please," he whispered.

Jessica studied her plate. "And if I refuse?"

Steve closed his eyes and hung his head, despair raking across his back as acutely as the beast's claws did, brutally scarring his soul. He was half-tempted to say he'd throw Chris in jail, but he couldn't do that. Not with the promise of what Jessica held. "Please. I'll have you back here before ten," Steve said, glancing at the clock. That gave him two and a half hours. "I promise." He set the coffee cup on the table and met her gaze.

"Eric's dead. What assurance do I have that you won't turn around and throw Chris in jail once I heal your wife?"

"I don't make promises I can't keep."

"Even if it means you're breaking the law?"

Boy, she gets right to the point. He pressed his lips together and nodded. "Yeah, even if it means breaking the law."

She leaned forward, her eyes narrowing. "My husband isn't some small-time informant you can lean on anytime you please just because you can dangle jail over his head. I won't let you take advantage of him like that."

Steve stepped back and laughed, shocked by her accusation. *If it gets me what I want...* He bit back the response, but her eyes widened and then her jaw clamped shut. "I keep forgetting you can read minds, too."

She shot him a warning glare and went back to her pancakes.

"Look, I'd do anything for my wife. Anything. And if that means pressuring you and your husband, so be it. I need a miracle and you're it, whether you want to be or not."

"Jess, help the boy," Chris said from the stairwell.

"But?"

"No buts. What would you do if the tables were turned?"

Steve blinked at Chris and then turned his attention to Jessica. Her shoulders went from rigid and squared to curved and tense, matching the progression of her demeanor from defiant to resigned.

She nodded her approval.

STEVE PUT THE EYE patch on the dashboard and slid into the car. "Thank you," he said after he started the engine and pulled out onto the road.

Jessica watched the scenery pass. "I haven't done anything yet."

Steve allowed a brief smile and looked her way, meeting her quick gaze. "But you will try, right?"

She didn't answer right away and kept her gaze on the scenery. "You said you'd do anything for your wife. Well, I'd do anything for Chris. So, here's the deal. Once I fix your wife, you promise to leave us alone."

"Done, but if he crosses the line again in any way, shape or form, I'll be the first one to arrest him."

"He wouldn't."

Steve sent a skeptical look in her direction. "He doesn't have any regard for life."

Jessica's jaw dropped. "Oh, and you do?"

He sent a glare in her direction. "Yes."

"And yet you want to kill the man who murdered my son."

He snapped his gaze from the road. "Don't *you* want him dead?"

"No. I want him behind bars."

"That's not good enough. He needs to be put down like a rabid dog."

"Jesus. What kind of cop are you?"

"I'm a damn good cop," he snapped. "I tracked this fucker down and then he duped me by faking his death." He ground his teeth together at his failure. "We had him behind bars and he escaped."

Steve took a breath to quell the beast raging in his heart. "And I figured out just who you married without any help. Eric said no one in the last fifteen years has uncovered that on their own."

"Danny figured it out."

"Figuring it out and proving it are two different things."

Jessica scoffed and returned her attention to the scenery.

"Why on earth did you marry Ty Aris?"

"Because." She didn't elaborate and shut her mind off from him, leaving only silence in the car.

Steve pressed the gas pedal to the floor in frustration. A quick blurt of a laugh from the passenger seat pulled his gaze in her direction.

"I love driving fast," Jessica said, watching the road speed under them.

Steve raised his eyebrows and glanced at the speedometer. He was going close to ninety in a forty mile an hour zone. He allowed a small grin to play on his lips as he refocused back on navigating the car. "Because why?"

Jessica sighed. "Because it was meant to be."

"Fate?"

"Mmm."

"I don't believe in fate."

Jessica offered a shrug when he looked her way. "I used to be the same way." She tilted her head back. "Eric was the one who said we were meant to be together." Her eyes filled with tears. "He said we balance each other."

Steve rolled his eyes. *That's Eric, all right.*

Jessica shot him a glare.

"So, you're telling me my daughter was destined to die?" His gaze turned to stone, along with his heart. "And Eric was destined to die?"

Jessica looked out the window and let the question hang in the air for a few minutes before she spoke. "I know it doesn't make sense and Chris would be the first to tell you he still doesn't understand it, but I love the man. I have since I first set eyes on him. Believe me, I tried to talk myself out of it time and time again, but it just is." A heavy sigh followed as she looked at Steve. "I love him the way you love your wife."

Steve returned her gaze before concentrating on the road again. He didn't speak for the rest of the ride. Thirty-five minutes later, they pulled into the hospital lot and Steve parked and sat with his hands resting on the steering wheel. He took a deep breath and reached for his eye patch, slipping it on before he glanced at Jessica.

"Explaining that would be hard." Jessica nodded in his direction and stepped out of the car.

Steve's lips formed a smirk, and he nodded, closing the car door behind him.

When they stepped into the room, Joe Curtis turned. His tired eyes grew hard at the sight of his son-in-law.

"Ah, shit," Steve muttered and glanced at Jessica. "Hi, Joe." He returned his attention to his father-in-law.

The muscles in Joe's jaw clenched. "I thought you were in Virginia."

Steve nodded. "I was until Kyle killed my partner." He turned toward Jessica. "This is Jessica Ryan. Jessica, Joe Curtis, Jenny's father."

Jessica extended her slim hand in Joe's direction.

Joe stared at it for a moment before grasping it with a quick shake.

His father-in-law's thoughts assaulted him, ranging from derogatory slurs to where he had been a couple of hours before, and Steve's face grew hot with anger. "A court order? What in God's name did you do?"

Joe turned his attention back to his son-in-law and shifted. "It's not fair to keep her alive. She's brain dead, Steve, and it is time to let her go."

"She is *MY* wife. You don't have a say in her care at all. Get out." Steve pointed at the door.

"Her living will says otherwise." Joe pulled the will out of his pocket. "I filed paperwork in court this morning to stop life support based on the living will the two of you put in place."

"Get out!" Steve yelled, ripping the paper out of his hands and crumbling it. He shoved Joe out of the room and slammed the door. Leaning his weight against it, he met Jessica's gaze. "He can't do this."

The room tilted, and he leaned his head back against the door. Tears squeezed out of the corners of his tightly closed eyes. His chest hitched twice before he regained control. Blinking the rest of the tears back, he glanced at his wife, trying to pry out any thoughts locked deep in her brain. Nothing. It was a complete blank. "Fix her." The order came out in a raspy whisper and tears choked him.

Jessica shot a hesitant glance in Steve's direction.

"Just try." Hope glimmered in his teary eyes.

FIX HER? JENNIFER TURNED her attention to the stranger in the room with Steve, watching as she approached the husk in the bed.

The moment the woman's lips touched Jennifer's forehead, the room spun. "What the hell?" Jennifer reached for the wall to steady herself and the light danced over her skeletal form. It filled the room, and she blinked, feeling the strength being sapped from her spirit, yanking her toward the bed, toward her body.

Spiraling, she fell into a void of darkness.

JESSICA TOOK A SHAKY step backwards.

Steve moved quickly to catch her. Her eyes rolled up in a dead faint, her body limp from the exertion. Steve gently tapped her cheeks, his gaze shifting between Jessica and his wife, clinging to hope like a capsized boat in a storm.

Jennifer's mind still registered like a blank slate, black nothingness.

He closed his eyes as Jessica's fluttered open.

Jessica found her feet, pulling herself out of Steve's grasp. She glanced at Jennifer, noting the change in color in her cheeks, but like Steve, she didn't hear any thoughts resounding from the woman. "I'm sorry." She turned to Steve.

Steve nodded and picked up the paper he had tossed on the ground, unfolding it and reading the terms of the will they had put in place shortly after they got married. The accompanying petition had been filed that morning requesting the removal of Jennifer's feeding tube. She would starve to death in a matter of days. "I need to stop this," he said.

Jessica pulled the paper out of his hands and scanned it, flipping open her cell phone. "Chris?" She paused. "Yeah, we're here. I need you to call Lynn and have her file a motion to stop an injunction. It looks like Steve's in-law's filed a petition to stop life support." She glanced up at Steve and nodded. "Jennifer Williams, Brooksfield Hospital, case number 5329051. Thanks, babe. I'll see you in an hour or so." She ended the call. "That will buy you a little time."

Steve stared at her, wondering why the hell she would do that for him, especially since he treated her like such a heel.

"I did it because you've got a little of my son in you now, and I know he'd want me to do whatever I could for you."

A lump formed in his throat, and he swallowed it, irritated at how fucking emotional he'd become in the last twenty-four hours. He turned toward Jennifer, leaned over, and placed a kiss on her forehead. "Kyle killed my parents," he whispered, and his vision blurred. He blinked back the sudden mist and stared at Jennifer's slack face. "Please, come back to me." He hung his head for a moment, gathering himself.

Abruptly, he turned and crossed to the door, swung it open, and glared at his father-in-law, who was leaning against the far wall, waiting. "You will not stop life support until I get back." He pointed at Joe. "Understand?"

"You have until the end of the week," Joe snapped.

"No, Joe. I have a bit longer than that. My lawyer will be in touch." Steve stormed past Joe.

Joe gripped his arm, yanking him back. "Where the hell do you think you're going?"

Steve glared at his father-in-law. "I'm going to bury my parents. Kyle killed them yesterday."

Joe's face fell, his glare softening. "I'm... I'm sorry," he stuttered.

"Yeah, and you want to take my wife away, too," Steve snarled. "I don't think so." He stormed off, leaving Jessica hurrying behind him.

Steve slid into the car and started it as Jessica hopped into the passenger seat. He sat, gripping the steering wheel. The muscles in his arms and neck tightened into hard knots, and he stared through the windshield.

Jessica reached out, putting her hand on his shoulder.

The tremors gripping Steve cascaded through his body, vibrating his entire frame. "They want to kill Jenny." His throat burned from the pent-up tears. He glanced at Jessica, clenching his jaw, and the tears sprouted. He turned away, leaning his forehead on the steering wheel, cursing at this blatant display of weakness.

Jessica left her hand on his shoulder, aware that the underlying rage still coiled up in his depths could strike out at anyone in his path, including her. "I'm sorry," she whispered when he lifted his head.

Steve sat up, shook her hand off his shoulder and wiped his face with his hands, shaking off the despair and grasping onto the anger like a man to a life raft. "Thank you for trying," he said as he put the car in gear and pulled away from the hospital.

Hunting Season
Chapter 19

THE RADIO PLAYED SOFTLY in the car as Steve flew back to York. His eye patch hung from the rearview mirror, and Steve didn't speak until they pulled into the driveway. "Thank you." He put the car in park.

"I'm sorry."

Steve nodded. "At least you tried." He glanced at the clock on the dashboard. It read 10:18 a.m.

"Do you want a cup of coffee before you go?"

Steve considered the offer and nodded, accompanying her into the house where Chris lay on the couch, listening to the boys argue about who was better at the game they were playing.

"How'd it go?" Chris asked as Jessica walked into the kitchen.

"Not so good," Jessica answered. She pulled the full coffee carafe off the heating pad and poured a cup for Steve, handing it to him before she filled one for herself. "Did you contact Lynn?"

"Yep. That injunction will be tied up in court for a while." Chris rose and shuffled into the kitchen, taking the seat next to Jessica.

Steve stood up, setting the coffee cup on the table. "I need to get moving. Do you know when Eric's funeral is going to be?"

"We're aiming for Friday. His body is supposed to arrive today." Tears sprouted in Jessica's eyes.

"Do you mind if I attend?" Steve asked.

Jessica shook her head, offering a sad smile. "No, he'd want you there."

Steve read between the lines. They were only extending the welcome because he was Eric's partner, not because they actually wanted him at the funeral.

"Why do you do that?" Jessica asked, wiping her eyes.

"Do what?"

"Sell yourself short."

Steve raised an eyebrow.

"You assume you're not welcome."

"I've come into your home, delivered bad news and then had every intention of using you to get my wife back, even threatening your husband. If I were you, I wouldn't welcome someone like me into my home."

"Well, you're not me. Besides, both Chris and I can hear your thoughts and we understand what's going on. You're desperate. We get that, and as far as your wife's concerned, I would do the same thing if I were in your shoes." Jessica glanced toward Chris and then back. "Despite your less than grateful attitude, you are welcome here."

He didn't know how to respond—especially since he was the reason their son was dead. He offered her a nod and turned to leave. "I'll see you Friday."

"Call me when you get back up this way," Chris said as he stood by the kitchen table. "Especially if you were serious about quitting the FBI. I've got a couple of opportunities I'd like to run by you."

Steve paused at the door and looked over his shoulder. "We'll see." He turned the knob and headed out to his car, slipped inside, and pulled out without another glance. He studied his reflection, marveling at the full restoration of his eye, and wondered if there would be a delayed reaction with Jennifer.

Jack's going to have a coronary when he sees this.

Steve tried formulating a reasonable explanation but just ended up shaking his head. There was no reasonable explanation for this kind of miracle.

Hunting Season
Chapter 20

WHEN STEVE CROSSED THE Connecticut state line, he put his earpiece in and pushed Jack's number on his phone. The phone rang, dumping into voicemail. "Jack, call when you get this." He hung up.

He flipped the radio on and sighed. Nickleback's Far Away blared from the speakers. "I miss you, Jenny," he said to the empty car. The tune came softly out of his throat, drifting through the car as he sang the words that his wife loved so much. "I'm going after the son of a bitch."

His stomach growled halfway through the four-hour drive, and he pulled off the highway to grab a bite to eat. As the waiter dropped the check on the table, his phone vibrated, and he glanced at the display. Jack's number flashed on the caller ID, and Steve flipped it open. "It's about time."

"Agent Murphy is a little preoccupied."

Steve's face burned. Heat surrounded him, along with the banging in his chest. He remained silent, standing and peeling off the money for lunch before he exited. "I swear, when

I find you, I will take you apart piece by fucking piece," Steve growled.

"You're not going to beg for your boss's life?"

"It wouldn't do any good."

"You're learning," Kyle purred.

"Where are you?" He closed his eyes.

"Wouldn't you like to know?" Kyle teased.

A muffled cry competed with Oprah blaring from the television in the background. "What hotel?"

"Why do you think we are at a hotel?"

Torrington. The thought was louder than the muffled groan from Jack. There were only seven hotels in Torrington. "Television is too loud to be anywhere else," Steve answered and flipped the phone off.

He hopped into the car and dialed 911. "My name is Steve Williams. I'm with the FBI and I have reason to believe my superior officer is being held hostage by a known felon at one of the seven hotels in Torrington," he said. "The assailant is armed and dangerous. My superior's name is Jack Murphy. Please hurry." He disconnected and scrolled to the prior call, hitting redial and called Jack's cell phone. "I want to speak to Jack," he said when Kyle picked up.

"You called the cops."

Steve heard the silence in the background and knew by the absence of background thoughts—his boss was dead. "What you did to us last summer is nothing compared to the hell I'm going to rain down on you." The words came out in a low snarl.

Kyle laughed and hung up.

Steve let out a roar, flinging the phone across the car and peeling out of the parking lot. When he hit the highway, he was already going ninety and muttering under his breath. Thirty minutes into the ride, going over one hundred and ten miles-per hour, he flew by a police officer.

"God damn it." Steve swore. Lights and sirens filled his rearview mirror. He glanced at the road ahead of him and back at the state trooper. "Fuck!" he yelled and hit the steering wheel—he didn't have time to explain the situation. The more time that went by, the less likely they would pick up a trace of where the bastard went. Steve eased up on the gas and pulled to the side of the highway. He slid the patch over his eye and watched the trooper leisurely stroll to the driver's side window.

"You in a hurry, son?" The trooper asked, leaning toward the window.

"FBI." Steve fished in his coat pocket. "God damn it," he cursed under his breath. He no longer had his badge. He leaned his head back on the seat. "I don't have my badge."

"Please step out of the car, sir," the officer said.

Steve turned full toward the trooper. "I don't have time for this shit," he answered. "I have reason to believe my superior officer was just murdered in Torrington."

"Please step out of the car and place your hands on the hood," the officer repeated, placing his hand on the butt of his gun. *Shit, this guy fits the description. Dark hair, patch over the left eye, posing as an FBI agent. Shit.*

Hearing the officer's thoughts, Steve put his hands up slowly. "Ok, I'm getting out." *Fuck! The bastard set me up for Jack's murder.*

He calmly stepped out, skirting around the open door. He put his hands on the hot hood.

"My name is Steve Williams. I'm an agent with the FBI. Jack Murphy was my superior officer," he said while the cop patted him down. "I believe the same man who murdered my parents yesterday killed Jack Murphy today."

The cop clasped the handcuff on Steve's wrist and pulled it behind his back, securing the cuffs to his other wrist. "You have the right to remain silent. Anything you say or do will be used against you in a court of law." He led Steve to the police car reciting the remainder of the Miranda rights and slipped him into the back. The officer retrieved the car keys out of Steve's car and did a careful inspection of the vehicle, finding only a backpack in the trunk. He returned to the squad car and slid into the front seat, starting the cruiser.

"Look, I need to get to Torrington," Steve said from behind the cage.

The officer glanced in the rearview mirror. "The only place you're going to is jail."

Steve leaned back, realizing he had no one to call. "My boss is dead. My parents were killed yesterday, and the psycho is still out there," he reasoned. "Besides, if I was the one who killed Jack Murphy, why the hell would I be speeding *toward* the crime scene?"

The trooper cocked his head. *Kid has a point.*

Steve tried not to act on the thought. He looked out the window, knowing his opportunity slipped away the moment he pulled his car over. "You didn't find the murder weapon in my car either, and I don't have a trace of blood on me." He continued. "Jack Murphy was killed within the last hour."

How the hell does he know that?

"Son of a bitch called me from Jack's phone and chopped him up while I was on the line." Steve hung his head as the magnitude of what had happened in the last two days hit him full force. "He's killed everyone I care about." The words came out embedded in a harsh rasp. "Everyone," he repeated, too soft for even the officer to hear.

When they arrived at the state police barracks in Litchfield, Steve was led to an observation cell and handcuffed to a table. He stared at the mirror, knowing there were at least two officers on the other side of the glass. Steve heard what they were thinking and while doubt was prevalent, they were sure he was the killer based on an anonymous tip they had received. "I want a lawyer," he said to the reflection.

Moments later, two plain-clothes officers entered the room.

"I want a lawyer," Steve repeated.

The officers looked at each other and sat down. "Do you have a lawyer?" The man on the right asked. His badge said he was Detective Bryce Harrington.

"No," Steve replied.

Detective Harrington nodded to his partner and watched as he left the room. He turned his attention back to Steve. "What's your name?" He already had Steve's wallet and the registration from the rental car.

"Steve Williams." Steve answered. "If you ran my fingerprints, you would already know that." He leaned back as far as the handcuffs allowed. "You would also know that I am with the FBI."

"Where's your badge and gun?" The cop pushed. *FBI, my ass.*

"Jack has them," Steve snapped.

"You had a rental vehicle." The detective pointed out.

"I was in Quantico, Virginia, yesterday morning and flew into Boston. I didn't have my car at the airport, so I rented one," he answered.

"What were you doing in Boston?" Detective Harrington pushed.

"None of your fucking business!" Steve glared.

"What were you doing heading to Torrington?" Detective Harrington asked. *Oh yeah, this guy is capable of slitting someone's throat.*

Steve saw the image of Jack in the detective's mind and closed his eyes. "I was initially heading to Litchfield," he admitted.

"Why?" *This bastard is probably responsible for the murder of that couple, too.*

Steve gritted his teeth and opened his eyes. "You already know why. Now let me out of these handcuffs," he demanded.

"Just one more question." Detective Harrington put up his finger, indicating just a minute. He sat back, letting the silence fill the room before he asked why Steve had killed those people.

"I didn't kill anyone," Steve answered the question before it was asked. "The people in Litchfield were my parents," he growled. "And you just let the son of a bitch get away." He yanked at the cuffs in anger and the desk slid a fraction in his direction. "You let him get away, again!" he bellowed as the fury burst through the surface.

Detective Harrington slid his chair back. "You have the right to a phone call," he said, changing tactics.

"I have no one to call. They're all dead!" Anger and desperation altered, each clamoring to take control, and he fought against the belligerent rage. He didn't want to lose it with the asshole across the table still in the room. His chest heaved, and his breath hitched, and an anxiety attack beat out the fury. Steve lost the battle and put his forehead on the edge of the table as the tears blurred his vision and the room spun, muttering under his breath at his lack of self-control.

Assistant Director Ron Cleary walked into the room. "Agent Williams?"

Steve looked up, his vision still blurred and his cheeks still hot. "Yes, sir." His voice carried the gruff scratchiness he expected from his burning throat.

"Un-cuff him," Cleary ordered.

"But we got a tip," Detective Harrington argued.

"This is one of our most highly decorated agents. Release him now!"

Detective Harrington glared at Steve before leaning over and unlocking each cuff.

Steve rubbed his wrists and took a deep breath. "What are you doing here?"

"Jack called last night. He told me your parents had been killed and said you weren't taking it very well." Cleary took a seat. "He asked that you be reinstated without finishing the course at Quantico."

Steve hung his head. "Jack's dead, sir."

"I know." He glanced at the detective. "What are you doing about that?" he snapped at the officer.

Detective Harrington scrambled to his feet. "We thought we had the perp in custody." He pointed at Steve. "He fit the description right down to the make, model and license plate number of the car."

"Did you trace the call?"

The detective nodded. "It came from the same hotel where we found agent Murphy," he said.

"Did you find the person who called in the information?"

"No. None of the hotel staff or customers admitted to making the call."

Cleary looked at Steve. "Do you know who did this?"

Steve stopped listening after Detective Harrington said the caller knew the make, model, and license number of the car he was driving. *How could he know that?* Steve closed his eyes. *The bastard must have been on the plane with him.* He opened his eyes. *That's not right, I would have known.*

"Agent Williams, do you know who did this?" Cleary's voice cut through Steve's lament.

Steve tilted his head, focusing on his boss. "I'm sorry. What'd you say?"

For the third time, Cleary asked, "Do you know who did this?"

"Yes. Kyle Winslow. I don't know his current identity; he changed it last summer before the attack on my family." He paused, looking at the table. "How did he know what car I was driving?" His eyes met Cleary's.

"Maybe he had someone watching you?" Detective Harrington piped in.

Steve pondered the answer. He'd have to give Chris a heads up. His gaze shot between Detective Harrington and Cleary and his eyes widened. "Jenny."

"We have twenty-four-hour surveillance on her hospital room. No one without authorization will get near her." Cleary assured Steve. "Jack made it clear she was a potential target and after today, I'm inclined to agree." He reached into his pocket and pulled out two items, placing them on the table. "Jack was one of the best in the bureau." *You had better be as good as Jack said.*

Steve saw the muscles working in Cleary's jaw line in conjunction with his thoughts. He waited.

"Jack was also my friend," Cleary said. "He said you were the best field agent he's ever seen, and that's about the highest god damned endorsement there is." He slid the badge and gun across the table. "I expect you to bring the bastard in."

Steve blinked and looked at the items, slowly reaching for them without meeting his superior's gaze. "I'll do my best," he said, pulling the badge and gun toward him.

"You will have any and all resources you need." Cleary stood. "I'll assign you a new partner when I get back to Virginia."

Steve raised his gaze. "Sir, no disrespect, but I'd prefer to work alone on this. The same man killed my partner yesterday morning."

Cleary paused. "Will you bring him in?" *Or will you just hunt him down and kill him?*

Steve kept eye contact. "I don't know," he answered. "But I don't want someone else's death on my conscience. I work alone," he insisted. "Or I don't work for the FBI at all." He took his hand off the badge and gun, leaning back.

Cleary reached down and snatched up the badge and gun. "Jack also said you were a cowboy. I don't need a cowboy on my team." He turned to leave.

"I'm the best agent you've got," Steve said, still sitting with his arms crossed.

Cleary paused. *Arrogant son of a bitch.* He glanced back at Steve. "You *were* the best," he clarified.

"Fine, but I'm going after Winslow and without the badge, I'm not obligated to bring him in."

"If you interfere with the investigation in any way, I will make sure you end up in federal prison for the better part of your life." *I should lock him up right now.*

Steve tilted his head. "Want to bet?" He stood up and stalked past Cleary and Detective Harrington.

Cleary stepped into the hallway. "Williams!"

Steve ignored him; he walked out of the police station and stopped. "Fuck," he muttered. His rental was probably still parked on the highway. He turned and entered the station, walking to the desk. "I need my personal effects," he said to the desk clerk.

Cleary approached him. "You need a lift somewhere?"

Steve glanced at him and nodded. "I need my rental car. It's probably still on Route 8." He followed Cleary to his car and slid into the passenger seat. "You don't like me very much," Steve said as Cleary started the car.

"Not particularly. You're young and arrogant," he replied. "But Jack had a lot of confidence in you, even while you were on leave." He glanced at Steve. "He said you had been through hell and back."

Steve nodded, keeping his focus out the window. "Jack's always been there for me," he said. "He didn't deserve to die like that."

Cleary sighed. "No, he didn't. Jack deserved better."

"You'll need to get off at the next exit and swing around. My car's on the other side over there." Steve pointed to the green sports car parked on the side of the road.

Cleary raised his eyebrows. "A little flashy, isn't it?"

"I wanted something fast." He allowed a smile.

"From what I hear, it is fast." He glanced at Steve and pulled off the exit ramp, swinging onto the northbound ramp.

"Yeah, it is." Steve dug in his pocket for the keys as Cleary pulled up behind the car. "I'm sorry for losing my cool." Steve reached for the door handle.

"Williams, aren't you forgetting something?" He put the badge and the gun on the passenger seat.

Steve looked at the items and back at Cleary, hesitating. "I'm serious about working alone." He maintained eye contact.

Cleary nodded. "I'm serious about bringing him in."

"I don't know if I will be able to do that, sir."

"You took an oath to uphold the law."

Steve nodded and picked up the badge and gun. "I know." He slid the gun into his belt and pocketed the badge. "Jack didn't want me on the case," he added.

"He told me, but considering my best agent is dead in a hotel room." He shrugged. "And it's personal now," he added. *I hope you kill the bastard.*

Steve nodded. "I just wanted you to know, sir."

"I appreciate that." Cleary replied.

Steve moved away from Cleary's car and settled into the driver's seat of the rental before glancing in the rearview mirror. Cleary pulled back on the road. He focused on the highway in front of him and fifteen minutes later; he pulled into Jack's hotel. The forensic team was still there, but Jack's body had been removed. The stench of blood and urine filled the small hotel room.

"Agent Murphy's phone was ringing a few minutes ago." The specialist said to Steve as he walked around the hotel room, observing the blood patterns. He handed Steve a pair of latex gloves.

Steve slipped them on and picked up the phone. "Did you dust this for prints?"

"Yes. We got two separate sets."

Steve flipped the phone open and looked at the last number. It was a Connecticut exchange, and he pressed redial, putting the phone to his ear.

"Agent Murphy?" A male voice asked.

"No, I'm sorry. Agent Murphy isn't available. Who am I speaking to?"

"This is Dan Connor," the voice announced.

"Eric's father?" Steve asked.

"Yes."

"I'm Steve Williams. I was your son's partner at Quantico." He looked around the room.

"Oh." Silence. "Agent Murphy gave me this number to call when I had details of the arrangements for Eric."

Steve closed his eyes and pinched the bridge of his nose. "I can take that information." He opened the desk drawer to pull out a pad. He stared at the notepaper. "Hang on while I get some paper." He covered the speaker and turned to the technician. "Over here." Sitting on the pad of paper in the drawer were three pinkies, and the words scrawled above stated:

Three more for your collection, Stevie-boy.
Regards,
Kyle

"We were wondering where those went," the technician said.

Steve uncovered the phone. "Thanks for holding. You can give me that information now." He grabbed the hotel menu and scribbled the date, time, and location for Eric's funeral. "You don't happen to have the Ryan's cell number, would you?"

"If you need to speak with them, my ex-wife is here."

"Is Chris Ryan available?" Steve asked.

There was silence for a moment on the other end. "He's here."

Steve heard the shuffle of the phone.

"Hello?" Chris's voice came over the receiver.

"My boss is dead," Steve said. *The son of a bitch got him, and he knew the make, model, and license plate of my rental car, so watch your back.*

Chris quietly processed the information. "Will do. What else?"

Is that offer still on the table?

"Yes. Will you make it to Eric's funeral?"

"I'll be there," Steve said. *Your wife's ex doesn't like you.*

"Tell me something I don't know," Chris said, almost laughing.

"I'll see you at the end of the week," Steve said.

"Keep safe." Chris ended the call.

Steve folded the cell phone and ripped the corner of the menu he had written the funeral information on, pocketing the piece of paper. He looked around the room and back at the technician. "It's going to be a hell of a week." Taking one last look at the blood-soaked bed and walls; he turned and left the carnage behind. He had one more murder scene to investigate and funeral arrangements to make.

His cell phone rang as he slid into the car and he flipped it open, turning on the ignition at the same time. The chuckling on the line made his blood run cold. "I'm coming after you," Steve said with a voice low and deadly.

Kyle laughed. "How does it feel to be alone?"

"Fuck you," Steve threw the car in gear, resisting the urge to peel out of the parking lot. He blinked the red flares of anger away, concentrating on the road while his hand gripped the wheel so hard his knuckles were devoid of color.

"Speaking of fucking, did you see the video I made of what your wife did for me?"

"Yep," Steve answered. "However, you conveniently forgot to include the beatings," he shot back.

"Oh, she was more than willing," he teased. "She came for me more than once, or didn't you see that? I had her every way possible, and she called out my name. My name, not yours."

Fury contained Steve's voice, blocking it in his chest while Kyle taunted him. He drove faster, his breath barreling in and out, building the molten lava flowing through his veins, bringing him closer to a catastrophic explosion.

"I understand why Charlie wanted her. She was an incredible fuck, and man, oh man, that mouth of hers, she could suck the cum out of a monk!"

Steve ground his teeth together. "I'm going to kill you." Baritone words rumbled from his chest. The red flares resurfaced, and he had to pull over to the side of the road before he rammed the car in front of him out of frustration.

"Temper, temper," Kyle scolded, clicking his tongue.

"Where are you?" Steve asked, closing his eyes. He saw highway signs for New Haven.

"Wouldn't you like to know?" Kyle laughed.

"New Haven?" Steve asked.

Kyle stared at the sign before passing under it. *How the fuck did he do that?*

Steve chuckled. "Where ever you run, I will find you." He opened his eyes and flipped the phone closed, cutting off the call. He pressed redial, putting the phone to his ear.

"I'm sorry, but your call cannot be connected. Please try again."

'Restricted'. Shit. Steve inhaled. A deep therapeutic breath did nothing to quell the inferno in his heart—lava flowed through his veins, pounding at his temples. Ba-bam, ba-bam, ba-bam of his heart echoed in his ears and he watched the traffic sail by. The anger stroked the flames, keeping it burning, dangerous and unpredictable while he temporarily gained control. He allowed a grim smile to surface, aimed at the reflection in the rearview mirror.

"You think that freaked you out, you just wait." Steve had no intention of allowing Chris Ryan to step in and carry out his vengeance. He wanted the pleasure of seeing Kyle squirm and wished he could resurrect the beast in Black Cove just for the occasion.

Hunting Season
Chapter 21

THE WEEK WENT BY in a blur. His parents' funeral on Wednesday, Jack's the day after and now he stood at the gravesite watching them lower Eric's coffin into the ground. Emotionally shot didn't begin to describe it. He had nothing left, and numbness filled the crevices of his skin. He stood stoically in the back of the crowd with his tinted glasses hiding the patch covering his perfectly good eye.

The day slipped from bad to worse when he got a message from his landlord. His lease in the apartment building next to the hospital expired, and the unit had already been rented to another party. All the hotels in Brooksfield were booked solid this weekend, so his only real option, short of the chair next to Jennifer's hospital bed, was the cottage. And that didn't thrill him.

He checked in with the hospital hoping for some sort of lifeline, but Jennifer's condition hadn't changed and the prospect of seeing her father left him lingering at the Ryan's house longer than he expected. He stood at the rock wall, transfixed by the ocean, while the crowd thinned to only family.

A throat cleared behind him.

Steve turned and slid off his sunglasses.

Dan Connor approached Steve. "Agent Williams?"

Steve nodded and raised the scotch to his lips, taking a sip.

"Agent Murphy wasn't able to make it?"

Of all the questions Dan had rattling around in his head, Steve wasn't prepared when this one popped out his mouth. Remnants of scotch slipped down the wrong pipe and he choked, coughing up the burning liquid while shaking his head. "I'm sorry," he wheezed and coughed a couple more times before the last of the sting dissipated. He cleared his throat and took another sip of the scotch to soothe his irritated throat. "I'm sorry, but Agent Murphy died earlier this week."

Dan's eyes went wide, and his eyelids fluttered, blinking in quick succession at the new information.

"He was killed the day I spoke to you." Steve downed the rest of the amber liquid in his glass.

"Any connection to Eric?" Trepidation made his voice quiver.

Steve nodded, and Dan's carefully preserved façade cracked. Tears filled his eyes and his lips pressed together—his mind shuffled memories as quickly as a Las Vegas blackjack dealer.

"Why did my son die?" Dan blurted as his private slideshow slowed.

Steve turned toward the ocean. "For the same reason Jack died." The tide of emotion rolled, turning the numbness into a ball of despair pressing on his chest. He pitched the glass as far as he could, watching it arch, falling and smashing on the rocks below. For a moment he wondered if he should follow suit, perhaps swan dive into the jagged granite below. He pulled his gaze from the drop, forcing his attention back to Dan. "They both knew me."

The sudden onslaught of anguish choked Steve, and he turned away, pushing the wave back into oblivion. He shoved his hands in his pockets, listening to Dan's stuttering thoughts.

But… but… why?

Steve inhaled through his nose. "Unfortunately, your son was paired with the wrong agent, and because of that, he's dead," Steve turned and leaned on the rocks, offering the slightest of shrugs.

"What the hell did you do?"

"I was just doing my job. The man who killed Eric is the Slasher, and I killed his brother during a botched hostage stand-off, and now he's targeting my family and friends," Steve said.

Dan's eyebrows creased, and he studied Steve, his face scrunched in contemplation. The news stories that hit the airwaves last year came to the forefront of his mind. *Holy shit.*

Steve ignored Dan's mental scan of the newspaper articles and news footage. "I'm sorry Eric got caught in the crossfire. He was an exceptional kid and didn't deserve this." Steve shifted, dropping his gaze back to the ground in front of him, wishing he knew what to say to make Dan's pained expression ease.

"Leave him alone, Dan," Chris approached. "He's had a tough week."

Dan spun on Chris. "And I haven't?"

Chris lifted his hands. "The same fucker that killed Eric killed his parents this week, too."

Steve sent a glare in Chris's direction for airing his personal business and then shifted his gaze to Dan's wide eyes.

"Is that true?"

Steve nodded. "He blew up my month-old daughter last spring and my wife is still in a coma," he said before Chris could spill the rest of his sorry existence.

Dan's eyes hardened, and his jaw tightened—the anger almost palpable in the air. He turned toward Chris and his silent demand brought the hairs at the nape of Steve's neck on end.

If you find the bastard, make him suffer.

Chris nodded. "I intend to."

Dan exchanged a glance with Steve and then walked away, leaving Steve staring at the ocean with Chris by his side.

"He knows who you are?" Steve glanced at Chris, receiving a nod in response. "What about your in-laws?"

Chris burst out laughing. "No, no, they don't. My father-in-law would shoot me."

Steve glanced back at the house. *Why the hell wouldn't Dan turn you in? You turned his life upside down.*

"Lack of proof," Chris answered his train of thought. "That's why no one came forward. Besides, it would have implicated his kids. Both Eric and Emily knew about me."

"I'm still in the FBI," he answered and looked back at the sailboats drifting by.

"I'm aware of that."

Steve surveyed the horizon. "Why are you being so nice to me?"

"I know what it's like to be alone."

"I'll be fine."

"Sure you will," Chris said, his voice mocking. Without waiting for an answer, he turned and walked toward the house with his guide dog leading the way.

Steve stared at the harbor traffic, mesmerized by the soothing sounds emanating from the water. Focusing on the gentle lapping of the tide was enough to block out the thoughts coming from the remaining people, and he sighed—thankful for a few moments of peace.

"My parents are glad you could make it," CJ said from behind Steve, breaking his trance.

Steve glanced in his direction, taking a moment to scan the backyard. Everyone had retired to the house, and he turned, bringing gaze to the child in front of him. "I need something from you."

CJ's eyes narrowed. "No, you don't. You have enough with Eric's powers."

"It isn't enough. What you've got, what you could give me..."

"You want some of my power to kill him, and killing is wrong." His blue eyes grew hard and unyielding, reminding Steve of his father, and Steve squashed the chill that wanted to creep up his spine.

"How old are you, CJ?"

"Nine."

"You're too young to understand."

"No, I'm not. I know. I remember." CJ's mind opened, giving Steve a glimpse at the memory of the warehouse five years ago along with the murderous thoughts that swarmed his four-year-old senses at the sight of his father nailed to a cross above them and his sister dead beside him.

Steve smiled a sad, knowing smile. "But you don't know, CJ. What would you have done if you woke up and everyone else was dead and you were the only one left?"

"Killing is still wrong," he said, but his voice wavered.

"You don't know what it's like to lose everything."

CJ tilted his head and bit the corner of his lip, studying Steve. "I'm still not gonna help you kill someone, no matter how bad he is."

Steve took a deep breath. "But you'd let your dad kill him?"

The complete dissolution of CJ's composure happened before Steve's eyes. CJ's jaw went slack, and his eyes widened with both shock and horror. Steve immediately regretted asking, but he forged on.

"If it isn't me, it will be your father," he said. The turmoil in the boy made Steve feel dirty, slimy, like a used car salesman swindling an old lady. "You want to protect your father?"

CJ nodded. "Yes." The word was barely a whisper.

"Then give me what I want."

CJ opened his mouth to speak when his gaze snapped to the house and the luster faded from his skin, revealing pale fear.

Chris came barreling out of the back door, practically dragging the guide dog in his wake. His face was a mask of anger that made CJ gulp. His Adam's apple bobbed nervously in his throat.

Don't you dare. He sent the thought out with such force that both Steve and CJ winced at the decibels resounding in their heads.

"CJ, get inside."

CJ scrambled away at his father's request.

Chris turned on Steve. "You son of a bitch," he growled. "CJ is just a child." He pointed accurately toward the house, looking squarely at Steve like he could see him.

"He's gifted and has the ability to transfer it," Steve said.

Chris threw a punch, and it connected with Steve's jaw, knocking him to the ground. "You dare come into my home and threaten my son?" The words came out low through Chris's clenched jaw.

Steve scrambled to his feet. "I didn't threaten him. I manipulated him. There's a difference."

Chris reached out and grabbed Steve's shirt, pulling him close. "No," he snarled. "You cannot use my son."

"Perhaps you'd like to spend the rest of your life in jail?" Steve shot back with the same ferocity. He broke Chris's hold and stepped away.

Chris cocked his head to the right, his lips pressed together in disgust.

Steve's airway closed under the clamping of an invisible force, and his hand flew to his neck. The sudden strain of no oxygen bulged his eyes, and he clawed at his tie, loosening it frantically, but the air still didn't flow. Dizziness mixed with panic in his blood, and he took a staggering step backwards.

Chris stepped forward, leaning in close to Steve. "You really want to fuck with me?" He reached up and pulled off his sunglasses, staring accurately into Steve's eyes.

Steve shivered, shaking his head and croaking, "No." No voice escaped the iron hold. *No, I want to kill the son of a bitch!*

Chris released Steve and slid his glasses back on.

Steve sucked large volumes of air into his lungs and leaned over, his hands on his knees, his muscles trembling under the knowledge the man before him could snap him like a twig without lifting a finger. He took some time getting his bearings back and his thoughts in order. "I don't just want to kill him, either. I want him to suffer," he said, standing straight again.

"You don't have a clue of how to make someone suffer," Chris answered. "And you wouldn't have the foggiest idea of how to use this power. It'd probably blow your circuits clean and land you in an asylum."

Steve swung, and his fist stopped inches from Chris's face, hitting an invisible barrier as strong as a granite wall. Steve let out a roar of frustration.

"It's taken me years to get this level of control," Chris said. "And it wasn't easy. Jessica's power was nothing compared to the small infusion CJ gave me." He paused and turned toward the house. "Shit. Dan is watching."

"A lot of people are watching," Steve said. He had already heard the undertones of thought coming from the house, but was concentrating on Chris. He turned toward the ocean. "I would prefer to leave you and your family out of my vendetta."

"You're shit out of luck there, son. He made the mistake of shooting Eric. Now it's a personal crusade of mine."

"Your son thinks killing is wrong."

Chris let out a laugh. "He's nine."

"He's right," Steve said.

"Mhm," Chris responded and snapped his fingers. His German shepherd came to his side, and he rubbed the dog behind the ears for a moment before returning his attention to Steve. "Yet you're willing to cross the line."

Steve scanned the marina, letting his gaze drift to the open ocean. He turned toward Chris. "He needs to pay, and a prison cell just isn't enough."

"You realize if you cross the line like this, you will never see your daughter again."

"What the hell are you babbling about?"

"Heaven."

"You believe in heaven?" Steve laughed.

A bitter smile crossed Chris's lips. "Yeah, but I'll never see it," he answered and shuffled a foot on the grass. "There's a special place in hell just for me."

"I suppose there is," Steve said. "I'm not so sure I believe in God anymore, anyway." He glanced back at the ocean. "Not with the things I've seen."

"You won't have to worry about God or heaven if you do what you're thinking."

He would have never pegged Chris Ryan as a religious man and the contradiction struck him silent. Steve shifted, glancing at his watch. "I have to go. I've got to get my rental back to the airport before the agency closes." *And then I have to figure out how to get home.*

"You want me to get a car service from the airport for you?"

Irritation rushed through his veins. "I hated when Eric got in my head, and I like the idea of you in there even less."

Chris responded with a grin and a shrug. "So, do you need a lift?"

Steve was tempted to take him up on the offer, but thought better of it. "Nah, I'll grab a taxi."

"I've got a bone to pick with you," Jessica said, her voice edged with anger as she walked up behind them.

Both men turned, surprised by the interruption.

Jessica glared at Steve. "I don't appreciate you trying to use my son." She slammed her index finger into his chest.

"I'm sorry, ma'am," Steve replied, the flush in his cheeks immediate and hot.

"Don't call me ma'am. It makes me feel old," she snapped and turned to her husband, dismissing Steve. "And you," she began. "You're as much in the doghouse as he is." She hooked her thumb over her shoulder at Steve. "Danny took CJ and Tommy for the night. I already told him we needed to give Agent Williams a ride." She glanced back at Steve. "That little altercation provoked some interesting questions from my ex-husband."

"I'm sorry, but he pissed me off," Chris said.

Jessica slapped him across the face, sending his glasses flying. "My son is dead, and you decide to create a scene the day of his funeral?"

Chris's hand slowly rose to the cheek she hit. His mouth popped open in shock. "I'm, I'm sorry," he stammered.

"Why would you do that?" Her voice choked with tears and Chris wrapped his arms around her, pulling her close.

"Why? Why did Eric have to die?" she whispered, looking at Steve.

"Because he was my friend," Steve replied, and bitterness filled the space between them. "That's why."

Jessica buried her face in Chris's chest and sobbed.

The sight of another mother grieving formed a lump in his throat and Steve turned away, more determined to catch Kyle and make him pay.

"You can't go after him," Jessica said when the crying ceased.

Steve glanced over his shoulder at Chris but said nothing. He didn't want him tagging along any more than Jessica did.

Chris didn't speak, and his thoughts were unattainable. He leaned over and kissed her forehead. "I have to. Eric saved my life. I owe it to him to hunt the bastard down."

Jessica leaned her forehead on his chest, glancing sideways at Steve.

Her glare said it all and Steve looked at the ground. "I'm aware it's my fault," he said at the same time Chris spoke.

"You can't blame him, Jess. Eric was assigned to be his partner. It's not Steve's fault that our son is dead." He pushed Jessica away, his blue eyes glimmering. "I plan on making that bastard regret the day he was born."

"You can't," Jessica whispered.

"That's where you're wrong, babe. I can. And I will."

Jessica glanced between the two men, and her lips flattened into a thin line.

"He needs to be dealt with," Chris added.

"Then let *him* do it." She pointed at Steve.

Chris shook his head. "No."

"Don't I get a say in this?" Steve asked.

Chris didn't speak at first. "I'm already damned," he said, looking past where Steve stood. "You aren't."

"Chris," Jessica sighed. "This is wrong."

"Maybe," he allowed. "But it's also wrong to let him go barreling after the son of a bitch alone."

"He's got the FBI behind him."

"Eric was killed at Quantico," Chris said. "With the FBI surrounding them."

Jessica nodded and stepped away, heading toward the house without another word.

"Can you see where my glasses went?" Chris asked.

Steve reached down, picked up the glasses, and put them in Chris's outstretched hand. "You can't save me," he said.

Chris smiled and slid the sunglasses on. "I can try." He turned and snapped his fingers. His dog obediently led him into the house.

When Steve stepped in the back door, Chris was sitting on the couch, petting the dog with his eyebrows scrunched together, deep in thought.

Chris's mind was complete static. Steve couldn't get anything from him. "How do you do that?"

"Do what?" Chris answered.

"I know your mind can't just be blank," Steve said. "You're like me, knocking things around in your head all the time, but I can't hear you very often."

"Static," Chris replied. "And you do it pretty good yourself, whether or not you know it."

Steve's eyebrows creased. "Static?"

"Yes, static. When you think of more than one thing at a time, it creates static and we can't read your mind. Not many people can do that. Most are linear in thought.”

Steve let that settle, thinking about the assault of thoughts at the airport and at the funerals over the past week. Jessica came into view in a pair of blue jeans and a white button-up shirt, looking crisp and calm, but underneath, she was still fuming.

“So, you can’t read my thoughts when I’m analyzing a situation?” Steve asked. That was one occasion his mind went off in different directions at once.

“No, but when you come to a conclusion, the thought’s there like a crack of thunder on a clear day.”

“So, you’re constantly thinking of more than one thing?”

“I’ve gotten used to doing it. CJ’s very attuned to our thoughts, and this is the only way to keep him out.” He stood up. “But sometimes even this isn’t enough. CJ can force his way in, unlike either of us.” He pointed in the general direction of where he thought Jessica was and was off by a mile.

“Are you ready?” Jessica asked, looking at the two men.

Steve nodded and headed out the front door while Jessica led Chris to the car.

Steve blared the radio as he drove from York to Concord on Route 4. He glanced in the rearview mirror from time to time to make sure Chris and Jessica were still behind him.

Shock filled his skin like a jolt of electricity. She was riding inches behind his car, close enough that if he tapped his brakes, she would be in his back seat, and he didn’t opt for the insurance on the rental car. He pushed down on the gas, widening the gap.

It's about damn time. Jessica's thought resounded in his head and his lips twitched into his trademark smirk. *Ah, that's right. You're a speed demon.*

A quick glance in the rearview mirror begged a laugh. He grinned at Chris's pale face in the passenger seat and Jessica's intense gaze willing him to go faster.

Steve pressed the pedal to the floor and scaled back when he hit ninety. She was still riding his tail, her eyes focused on the rear window of the rental car.

Chris's voice invaded his mind. *Slow down. I may be blind, but I sure as hell can feel excessive speed.*

What normally was a forty-five-minute ride shortened to a little less than a half hour and they pulled into the rental agency with twenty minutes to spare. Steve settled his bill and grabbed his backpack and laptop. He climbed into the backseat of their car and met Jessica's gaze in the rearview mirror. "You are just as crazy as I am."

"Don't encourage her," Chris grumbled from the front seat.

When Jessica pulled out of the parking lot, Steve observed the death grip Chris had on the passenger seat door and smiled. It matched the grip he had on his door. "Seems you're not comfortable being a passenger, either."

Chris laughed in response.

"He really hates my driving," Jessica said, waving a hand in Chris's direction. "You'd think after five years of chauffeuring him around, he would have gained some level of appreciation."

"I had no choice. You wouldn't let me hire a driver," Chris shot back.

"Ungrateful bastard," Jessica mumbled.

Steve burst out laughing. Watching the dynamics between the two of them reminded him of Jennifer shortly after they were married. The light in Jessica's eyes every time she looked at Chris was enough to make Steve look away. He missed the same gaze from Jennifer. That light filled his soul with need.

"You love me, anyway." Chris patted her leg.

"Yes, I do," she said with a sigh. "Ty," she added in a whisper, glancing sideways at him.

Chris's reaction to his spoken name was visible even to Steve in the back seat. The way he looked in her direction was enough to ignite the upholstery in the car.

Jessica's lips formed a brief smile. "Smoldering."

"Um, hello, there is someone else in the car," Steve reminded them.

Chris took a deep breath. "You shouldn't do that to me," he said under his breath. He leaned his head back on the headrest, closing his eyes.

"Head north on 93." Steve watched the scenery pass. "Brooksfield's southeast of Mount Washington. Take Exit 32 onto 112 East toward Conway."

"The Kancamagus Highway?" Jessica asked, looking into the rearview mirror.

Steve nodded. "From there, you take exit sixteen into Brooksfield."

"Got it," Jessica said. She flipped on the radio and out came Nickleback's Far Away.

Steve sang the words he knew so well, words Jennifer begged him to sing any time the song came on. Words she said she wanted to hear every day of her life. He closed his eyes, willing the tightness in his throat to go away and the emptiness in the center of his chest to disappear.

"You have a lovely voice," Jessica said.

"That's Jenny's favorite song," Steve said after the song ended.

Jessica glanced back, meeting his gaze for a moment.

She pulled off the exit forty-five minutes later. "Which way?"

"Right." Steve answered. "It isn't that far, so keep the speed in check," he said, and Chris guffawed.

Jessica smacked his chest with the back of her hand and followed Steve's direction.

"See that dirt road on the right up there?"

"Yes."

"That's the driveway." He leaned back. He hadn't stepped inside the cottage since the explosion, and he shifted in the seat.

"You'll be all right," Chris croaked and cleared his throat.

Steve didn't hear him. He was too busy squashing the shakes that began when they rounded the last corner, and the cabin came into view.

"Got to face your demons some time," Chris said as the car stopped.

"Easy for you to say," Steve scoffed and swung the door open. The lawn needed care, and he glanced towards the woods, torn between heading to Paradise Cove and going into the cabin to be inundated with memories. He opted for the cove to get his nerves under control and headed around the corner.

Hunting Season
Chapter 22

"WHERE'D HE GO?" CHRIS asked and felt his way around the front of the car.

"The woods," Jessica answered. "Come on." She took Chris's arm.

Chris's feet shuffled through tangles of grass that tickled his ankles, telling him the lawn hadn't been cut since long before the summer ended, and snow flew. The terrain changed from the soft lawn to a hard-packed path surrounded by sharp sticks that dug into his shins. The scent of wet leaves drifted around him, and he tripped on a branch, catching himself before he fell. "You suck as a guide," he mumbled.

"Be nice," Jessica replied.

He swatted her ass. "I'm always nice."

"Wow," her soft awed voice filled the silence.

Chris stepped out of her grasp, and the darkness before him shifted. Steve's aura glowed enough for him to see a form in the center. He blinked and took another step onto the lush green moss before him. *Green. Jesus, I see green.*

A thrill like nothing he'd ever felt filled his core, tingled over his skin, and settled in his eye sockets. His vision righted, and he blinked again, gasping and seeing the vibrant colors of Paradise Cove. He removed his glasses and turned, taking his wife in for the first time in five years. "I can see," he whispered. "Jess, I can see," he repeated, mystified at the development.

Steve shot a glance in Jessica's direction. "You fixed his eyes?"

"Not that I know of," she said.

"You can see?" Steve asked.

Chris nodded without moving his gaze away from his wife. She was even more beautiful than he remembered, beautiful enough for him to forget to breathe. His gaze locked with hers and her cheeks bloomed pink, bringing a smile to his lips.

"I guess your wife can make miracles happen," Steve muttered and crossed to the path. With one last look at the water, he turned and headed back toward the cottage, leaving them standing on the moss in the center of the cove.

Chris lifted his hands to her face, tracing her lips with his fingers. "I can see," he repeated and pulled her close, crushing her lips under his. He pulled away smiling, turning and surveying the lush tropical beauty, an anomaly in New Hampshire, more like a Mediterranean or Caribbean paradise.

"This place is beautiful." Deep green moss surrounded by spring wildflowers in a wealth of colors lined the mirrored surface of the water, the colorful spectrum edging the reflection of the afternoon sky, matching his eyes. "Jesus, Jess. I can see," he marveled. "Did you do something?"

Jessica shook her head. "You know damned well I've tried several times before and it never worked."

"Then, it's this place." He pointed at the ground. Looking at the path to the house, his smile faded, his joy replaced by apprehension. He didn't want to step off the moss and fall back into the world of darkness.

"You won't lose your sight again," the familiar voice rang through the Cove.

Chris and Jessica spun toward the water.

Eric smiled back at them and looked around. "This cove *is* mystical. It's been in Steve's family for generations, dating back before the seventeen hundreds," he said. He looked back at his parents and glided across the surface of the water, stepping onto the soft moss.

Jessica broke Chris's grip and ran to the ghost of her son, throwing her arms around the apparition. "My baby," she cried.

Eric rolled his eyes at Chris, prompting a smile in return. "Mom, let go." He peeled her off and pushed her back. "I don't have a lot of time and I need to talk to Chris." He gave her a kiss on the cheek. "I'm fine. I'm with Em and Tom. Go check on Steve for me." He pointed toward the house, and she nodded, trading a glance with Chris before heading down the wooded path.

Eric focused on Chris. "You can't let Steve do what he wants to do."

Chris's eyebrows arched. "Why not?"

Eric returned Chris's intense stare. "Because Steve is your answer. He's the one who can save you. But you already knew that."

"What the fuck are you talking about?"

Eric crossed his arms. "The document you signed and sealed and gave to your lawyer the day after the shit went down in the warehouse?"

Chris looked over his shoulder and then down at the ground before glancing up at Eric. "What about it?"

"You can redeem yourself by saving Steve."

"I made a deal with the devil, Eric."

Eric smiled. "You've cheated him so far."

Chris glanced at the path. The possibility of circumventing hell was tempting, but he knew nothing was free. Nothing came without a price and a chill ran up his arms, raising goose bumps all over his body. "What will it cost me?" he asked, returning his gaze to Eric.

"Nothing." Eric's smile faded. "Your time's up, Ty. Whether or not you do this, your time is up."

"My time?"

"Yes, your time, and there is quite an uproar about who's going to get your soul."

Chris stepped back, and his eyes went wide. "Why?"

Eric smiled and winked. "Seems you're pretty important to both heaven *and* hell."

Chris couldn't help the laughter that rang through the cove. "Heaven? You mean God? He wants me even with all I've done?"

"God *needs* you. Without your intervention, Steve *will* kill in cold blood, and that just can't happen. You think it was a fluke that he and Jennifer were able to kill that beast?"

Chris stood speechless, his voice on lockdown. He looked toward the house and then back at Eric. "Why is Steve so special?"

"Because you will not be around to keep CJ in line. If Steve commits murder, he won't be either." Eric stared at Chris. "You already know all this. You already made allowances for when the shit hits the fan down the road, so why are you questioning it now?"

Chris already knew the name of his son's savior. His brother had whispered enough to him in that dark plane between life and death for him to take actions that even Jessica didn't know about. His brother had given him glimpses of the possible futures to come, not just of that day in the warehouse. Including what prompted him to write a letter that was sealed and certified at his lawyer's office to stave off a future disaster. A disaster that only his written admissions with a time stamp could stop. He knew Steve was the one that would keep CJ from going dark. There was more at stake than just Chris's soul.

Chris shivered. "I didn't believe it until Steve walked into our house."

Eric's form was opaque now. "He's the one who will keep CJ from reigning terror everywhere he goes. Steve will keep CJ honest, but only if you keep Steve from killing Kyle. That's all you have to do."

"That's a tall order," Chris said, and Eric became a wisp of fog, disappearing before his eyes.

The tendrils of fate tickled his spine, and Chris shivered. He took a deep breath, burying the conversation deep within his mind like the predictions his brother had given him. He shut and locked the door in his subconscious.

Chris stepped off the moss onto the winding path, finding his way back to the cottage. When he stepped onto the lawn, Steve glanced in his direction from his vantage point in front of the picture window.

STEVE STOOD IN THE middle of the lawn with his hands in his pockets, returning his gaze to the cottage. Dread crushed down on his chest, bringing with it an emptiness he couldn't erase. The last time he was inside his home, he was holding Jennifer's unconscious body, and both of them were covered with their daughter's blood.

The sound of the explosion echoed in his ears, and he shifted his weight, glancing back toward Chris. The man's childish expression of awe, jaw hanging askew and eyes darting everywhere—like a kid in the Toy's R Us in Times Square—was enough to thaw the trepidation.

"I can see why you love this place," Chris said, taking the spot next to Steve with his back to the cottage. "Your view is almost as beautiful as our place on Lake Wentworth."

Steve glanced sideways and grunted. *Beautiful? Maybe, but not with the memories haunting me.* "I need my computer." He looked back at the cottage.

"It's only a house. It's not going to bite you."

His words felt like salt poured in a wound, and Steve flinched. "You're a real prick."

"Yeah, well, birds of a feather," Chris said.

Steve chuckled and glanced at his guest. "You don't need to stay." He looked over his shoulder at Jessica. "I imagine you're tired." He scanned the property and looked back at the cottage. "I've got some yard work to do."

"Anything not to set foot inside." Chris looked up at the sky. "I never would have taken you for a wimp."

Anger surged like a newly tapped well and Steve swung.

Chris parried, blocking the punch, and he yanked Steve closer, taking him to the ground in one smooth move with agility and speed that knocked the wind out of Steve. He stood and stepped back with a grin, his bright eyes sparkled with mischief. "Come on, I haven't had a good sparring match in five years." Chris slid his shoes off and stripped his jacket, tossing it to Jessica.

Steve climbed to his feet and peeled his suit jacket off, dropping it to the ground. Next came his tie and shoes and he centered himself, reining in the aggravation, harnessing it in preparation. The thought of besting Chris Ryan appealed to his psyche. He faced Chris, bowing and taking form. "You think you can take me, old man?"

Chris returned the bow with a smile. "I've got a degree on you, son," he taunted, raising an eyebrow in a silent challenge. "I used to teach, too."

"Yeah, I saw." Steve executed a spin kick.

Chris maneuvered out of the way and swept Steve's feet out from under him, knocking Steve on his back. The thud blew the air out of his lungs and his frustration mounted. He hopped to his feet in time to see Chris trade a glance with Jessica. Capitalizing on the opportunity, he knocked Chris on his ass.

"You should never take your eye off your opponent," Steve smiled down at him. He glanced over at Jessica and the sudden swish of air filled his head, and he stared up at the blue sky from the ground. "Shit!"

"You need to follow your own advice," Chris hopped to his feet. He stepped back, watching Steve pull himself to his feet.

Chris was far better than Eric was. Hell, he was better than any of his sparring partners throughout the years and he brushed himself off, trying to squash the seeds of admiration. "I really should throw your ass in jail," Steve said, his eyes never leaving Chris's.

Chris laughed. "You have to catch me first." His eyes twinkled with humor, and he hadn't even broken a sweat.

Steve went on the offensive, throwing every conceivable combination Chris's way and the man countered every move until Steve stepped back, out of breath and unable to control the bloom of respect. "You're good," he admitted aloud.

Chris chuckled, not in the least bit out of breath from the physical exertion. "I'm superb."

"Let's see what you've got." Steve took a defensive posture and waited.

Chris went after Steve, tagging him a few times, each one smarting like the end of a bullwhip, but for the most part, Steve defended against a majority of Chris's maneuvers.

Chris stepped back and bowed. "Your forms are a little rusty, but overall, not bad."

Steve leaned over, propping his hands on his knees as he fought to catch his breath. His muscles protested, gathering in tight knots under the strain. Describing Chris's karate skill as superb was an understatement.

"You should be in better shape than that," Chris said, his breath less labored than Steve's.

"You can kiss my ass." Steve straightened.

Chris smiled.

"I've been in rehab for nine months."

"Excuses, excuses." Chris made the motion of a violin, further infuriating him.

"Stop aggravating the boy," Jessica intervened, handing Chris his suit jacket.

"You're a piece of work," Steve said.

Chris huffed and glanced around before bringing his gaze back to Steve. "Thanks for the eyesight," he said. "It's been a while." He offered a shy, crooked smile of gratitude.

"That wasn't my doing."

Chris shrugged. "You allowed us to bring you here."

"Your wife insisted."

"Will you just accept my gratitude without being such a dick?"

Steve laughed.

"You're just as much of a pain in the ass as Eric could be when he wanted." Chris put his arm around Jessica and led her toward the cars. "I'm driving home."

"Thank you," Steve said.

Chris stopped, plucking the keys out of Jessica's hand and turning toward Steve. "I've got just as many resources as the FBI and I'm a computer genius, to boot. If you want to catch the son of a bitch, let me know."

Steve tilted his head and the history he dug up on Ty Aris came barreling back. The man was a member of Mensa. He could certainly use someone like that on his team right about now. "A computer genius?"

Chris nodded. "How do you think I made all those people disappear?"

The admission caught Steve off guard, and his jaw dropped. He snapped it closed after the pass of a heartbeat but from the amused expression on Chris's face; it wasn't fast enough.

"There isn't a system I can't hack into," Chris bragged.

"Financial databases?"

"Yep." Chris tossed the keys up in the air and caught them. "Call me." He turned toward the driver's side door.

"How much are apartments out your way?" Steve asked.

Chris paused and met his gaze. "No way. I don't want to lead that crazy bastard back to my house in York." He chewed on his lip and traded a glance with Jessica. "I've got a place in the city, if you're interested."

"New York?"

"Is there any other city?" He opened the driver's side door.

Steve looked at the cabin and back at Chris. The alternative was not something he wanted to broach, so he nodded. "That could work."

Chris paused with the door open. "You really don't want to go into that house, do you?"

Steve shook his head. "Not really." *Not alone.* He hadn't meant for them to hear the thought, but the change in Chris's expression told him otherwise.

Chris tossed the keys on the front seat and looked over at Jessica. "You don't have to do it alone," he said to Steve. "I'll hang for a few."

Steve tilted his head. "Why?"

"Because being alone sucks," Chris answered and approached the door. It popped open with a slight tilt of Chris's head. He waltzed into the empty living room without waiting for Steve. He crossed the room to the bay window, looking out at the lake.

"Seriously, why are you doing this?" Steve asked, crossing the expanse to the bedroom, pausing at the door for the answer.

"Self-preservation," Chris answered.

Steve burst out laughing.

Chris didn't crack a smile.

"You're not kidding." Steve let his laughter fizzle out.

"No. I'm not kidding." He let his lips curl into a wisp of a smile. "It's all about me."

Steve kept eye contact and could hear nothing but static in the man's head. His gaze drifted to the kitchen and a sharp pang almost doubled him over. Samantha's last moments, her last experiences in this world, filled with pain that ended when the bomb jacket Kyle outfitted her in blew her to heaven.

Damn him.

He turned and disappeared into the bedroom, grabbed a suitcase out of the closet, and threw clothes in. But no matter how hard he jammed his threads into his bag, it didn't satisfy the burning in his veins.

This time, he wouldn't hesitate.

This time, he wouldn't miss.

This time, he'd get vengeance.

He stopped and closed his eyes, his hands balling into tight fists and then loosening with the calming breaths he forced himself to take. When he had his temper in check, he opened his eyes and reached for the nightstand drawer, hoping his keys were there because if they weren't, he had no clue where Jack put them.

"Shit," he mumbled at the keyless drawer and headed to the office. He threw the door open and stared at the array of documents still scattered on the desk. Jack didn't take a thing from the office. Everything was exactly where he left it last spring when he closed the door the night before his life blew to bits.

He pulled the top drawer, and it didn't budge, still locked. The left-hand drawer slid open, and

Steve closed his eyes, breathing a sigh of relief. The extra set of keys sat on the stack of unopened mail, and he plucked them from the pile, unlocking the top drawer. He sat back, raising his gaze to Chris leaning against the doorjamb, waiting.

"I'm not sure any of the cars will start." Steve grabbed a paper box and dumped the documents into it.

"Which car did you want to take?"

Steve looked up. "The one in the garage," he answered, still shuffling paperwork into the box. "We're going to have to move Jennifer's car to get it out of the garage." Steve said, tossing the keys to Chris. "Think you can handle that?"

"You really are a wiseass." Chris disappeared, his footsteps echoing across the hardwood.

Steve unlocked and slid the top drawer open and stared at the vial of cocaine. Jack hadn't been through the drawer, otherwise it would be gone.

"Don't even think about it."

Steve raised his eyes to Chris, standing back in the doorway. A swarm of excuses filled his brain, none of which reached his tongue before Chris spoke again.

"You aren't a junkie."

"I was hooked for a little while," Steve said, admitting to something even his wife didn't know.

"Leave it here." The command was clear, and Chris's eye bore into him.

Steve pulled a file out and closed the drawer. The lock clicked, engaging without the use of his keys, and his gaze shot to Chris.

"I'll go get the cars moved around for you." Chris left Steve alone in the office.

Hunting Season
Chapter 23

CHRIS STARED AT THE interior of the open garage, a vintage BMW roadster sat, dusty and waiting for the next road trip. It reminded him of the restored Corvette in his garage in York. The fact Steve had done all the work impressed him to no end. He popped the trunk and slung the suitcase inside.

Jessica walked by him with the bags Steve had stowed in their trunk, dropping them in the BMW. "Sweet car." She paused at the garage entrance. "When are we going to New York?" She kept her back to him.

"You and the kids are staying in Maine."

Jessica turned. "I haven't gone a day without you by my side in ten years."

"Sorry, babe. I don't want you and the kids around for this one." He glanced back toward the cottage. "We both know how relentless hit men can be and this is personal on all sides." He sighed and headed out of the garage. "It's going to get really ugly, really quickly, especially between the two of us." He hooked his thumb toward the house. "He will not like me interfering."

"How long?"

Chris glanced at her. "As long as it takes for me to find him."

"You're going to kill him?"

Chris nodded. "Unless Steve backs down, and he hauls the bastard in, but I highly doubt that." He looked at the key ring and the car blocking the garage entrance, trying to figure out which was which. "I might end up in jail when this is all over." He glanced back at her, suppressing the urge to say or worse.

Jessica shook her head. "You can't."

Chris shrugged. "It depends on the FBI." He opened the door to Jennifer's car and pushed the key in the ignition, turning it. Nothing happened, not even a click in the engine. The battery was indeed dead.

He exhaled and climbed out of the car, harnessing the power merged in his cells as he positioned himself between their car and Jennifer's. The adrenaline rush that came with conjuring the magic inside him surged and he smiled, locking his gaze with his wife's.

The dead car slid sideways and what he saw in Jessica's eyes turned his cocky smile into a heat-seeking grin. Awe, he could still inspire awe in her and that, more than the power rush, gave him the determination to make things right—to get a second chance at redemption.

His controlled power created ripples in the air, moving outwards, pushing the vehicle out of the path that Steve needed to get his vintage BMW out of the garage and onto the road.

"Holy shit," Steve said, interrupting Chris's concentration.

When the path was wide enough to bring his car forward, Chris stopped and glanced at Steve, exhausted. "You're going to need a jump for the

Beemer." He tossed the keys to Steve and took a step toward his car, stumbling for a moment as the world tilted. Jessica's yell muffled in his ears as darkness descended.

"Catch him," Jessica yelled.

Steve reacted, catching Chris before he hit his head on Jessica's car. He put him on the ground and looked up at Jessica. "Is this normal?"

"No." Jessica shook her head, kneeled by Chris's side, and pat his cheeks.

Chris's eyes fluttered open, and he glanced up at Jessica and Steve before sitting up. "Damn, that's never happened before."

"You've never moved a car before," Jessica said.

"I've made a car explode," he said as he got to his feet. "Besides, I move things all the time at home."

"You move food and sometimes furniture, but that's it."

Steve glanced between the two of them, listening to the absurd conversation, and chuckled. "Sorry guys, but this is the most bizarre conversation I've ever heard."

Jessica broke out in a grin. "I would imagine it is." She put her hand out for the car keys.

"You're out of your mind, woman. I'm driving home."

"You just passed out," she said.

"I don't care. The only reason I tolerated being a passenger with you for all these years was because I couldn't see."

Jessica stiffened, and her lips pressed together in irritation.

"I love you more than life itself, but I hate the way you drive, babe." Chris went to kiss her cheek.

She stepped out of his reach and crossed her arms, leveling him with a gaze only an unhappy wife can muster.

"Fine, be that way." Chris strode to the car and slid inside, turned the engine over, and pulled it up to the garage, close enough so jumper cables could reach the engine of the BMW. "You have jumper cables?" he asked.

Steve nodded and walked to the back of the garage to retrieve the cables. He stopped, staring at the crib he had taken down while Jennifer was in the hospital. The sudden onslaught of heartache froze him in place and his breath locked in his chest.

"Come on, we don't have all day," Chris said.

"Don't be such an insensitive jackass." Jessica breezed past her husband and put her hand on Steve's shoulder. "Are you okay?"

Steve shook his head, words unable to form under the pressure crushing his soul. His gaze was glued to the crib, to the stark reminder of all he had lost.

Jessica reached out and turned his face toward her. "It never goes away," she said when his eyes found hers. "But it gets easier with every day that passes."

Steve nodded and turned away before the tears found their way down his cheeks. His paralysis broke, and he reached for the jumper cables hanging on the wall, turned away from the unassembled crib, and crossed the garage to the front of his BMW, dropping the cables. He squatted, released the hood, propped it up, and leaned on the car with his chin resting on his chest. Grief burned his throat with hot, unshed tears.

"Go get in the driver's seat. Jess and I can put on the cables," Chris said.

Steve nodded and stepped over the discarded cables. Sliding behind the steering wheel, he waited for further instructions.

Grief morphed into irritation, and he ground his teeth together, willing the turmoil back into Pandora's Box. He knew if he operated on emotion alone; he was a dead man.

Turn her over. Chris's voice echoed in his mind, bringing him out of his reverie.

Steve turned the key, and the engine caught. He let the car idle until Chris closed the hood and backed his car up to make room for the BMW. There were still a few things he needed in the cottage, so he threw the car in neutral, set the parking brake, and headed back into the house.

In the office, he shoved papers and files into a box, muttering at his complete lack of self-control.

"You need to chill a little," Chris said as he leaned against the doorjamb.

Steve glared at him. "He's out there."

"I promise, when I'm through with him, he'll wish he had never been born," Chris said with an evil smile.

Steve shivered at the combination of the smile and the look in Chris's eyes. Fueled by the glimpse of his life, Steve concluded that Ty Aris, a.k.a. Chris Ryan was the most frightening man he'd ever been in contact with.

Chris's gaze bore into Steve. "Are you finished?"

"I'm going as fast as I can," Steve snapped, unnerved by the stark stare.

"I'm not very patient," Chris said, leaving the slightest of smiles on his lips and his eyes danced with amusement.

Steve stood up straight. "I'm glad I amuse you."

"You're going to be quite entertaining over the next few weeks."

"Fuck you."

Chris chuckled. "I seem to bring out the best in everyone I come in contact with."

Steve took a deep breath. "Maybe that's because you're a cold, soulless bastard."

Chris shrugged. "Perhaps."

"I have no idea how your wife deals with you every day," Steve mumbled and finished packing up the last box. He turned his computer on and took a seat.

"Why don't you just bring the whole computer with you? I've got a high speed set up and it'll take no time at all to plug that into my network."

"What's your rush?" Steve glanced up at him.

"I haven't been able to see for five years, and my kids won't be back till morning." He raised his eyebrows. "I'm not heading to New York tonight."

"Then just go," Steve snapped. He didn't want to think about what Chris was insinuating.

"You need the keys and my garage pass to get into the apartment building in New York."

"I can get them in the morning," Steve replied without meeting Chris's stare.

"Just bring the hard drive and peripherals. I've got dual monitors."

Steve shut down the computer and dumped the keyboard and mouse in the last box. He unhooked the hard drive and carried it to the car. The hard drive fit on the passenger floor, with the last of the boxes taking up the passenger seat. "I'll catch up with you tomorrow." Steve turned, extending his hand to Chris.

Chris grasped Steve's hand and pumped once before letting go. "Will do." He turned to his car, halting at the sight of Jessica in the front seat, grinning like a Cheshire cat. He opened the driver's door. "I'm driving."

Steve studied the dynamics between the two. "Good luck with that," he said, sliding into the driver's seat of the BMW and waiting for resolution.

Chris stood with the door open while Jessica shook her head. "I am perfectly capable of driving home," he said, clearly annoyed with his wife.

"I know you are." She smiled up at him. "But this is my car."

"Oh, for Christ's sake!" He rolled his eyes, slammed the door, and shuffled to the passenger side, slumping into the seat in misery.

Steve burst out laughing. Any doubts he had were gone. Mrs. Jessica Ryan was the boss of that family.

Fuck you. Chris's voice swore in his mind.

"You are whipped, my friend," Steve said aloud. Chris cracked a smile as Jessica backed the car into a turn and headed out of the driveway.

Hunting Season
Chapter 24

THE GRAVESTONE WAS GRAY marble, and Steve crouched down, tracing the name with his fingertips. He tried to say her name, but no sound came out of his throat at first.

"Samantha." The word finally squeezed out, wrapped in agony. "I'm sorry I couldn't keep you safe, sweetheart," he whispered. He dropped to his knees on the grave with his hands on his thighs, shaking, as his tears glistened on the grass reeds. He wanted the ground to open up and swallow him. He wanted the pain to stop.

He closed his eyes, hanging his head. "I'm so sorry."

"Steve?"

Steve stiffened, wiping the tears from his face. He glanced to his side. "Harry," he said with a raw voice. "They let you out?" He got to his feet and turned.

Harry stepped back in shock. The flowers he was holding fell out of his grasp.

Steve's hand flew to his left eye, and he laughed. *Shit.* "I had surgery." He floundered for some reasonable explanation. "Cornea transplant."

Harry's brow creased. "I didn't know they were so advanced."

Steve nodded, offering a crooked smile. "Neither did I, but it turned out pretty close to the real deal." He stuffed his hands into his pocket and surveyed the cemetery.

Harry looked down at the gravesite.

"My daughter," Steve said. His gaze fell on the mausoleum he and Jennifer had been imprisoned in three years ago, and a shiver fought its way through him. He glanced back at Harry.

Harry stooped and picked up the flowers. "Amy's grave is over there." He pointed to the right.

Steve nodded. "Take care, Harry." He turned to leave, slipping his tinted glasses on.

"Surgery?" Harry asked, studying Steve.

Steve nodded. "Surgery," he said, leaving Harry staring after him.

STEVE WALKED INTO HER room, relieved that her parents weren't there. He sat down next to Jennifer, taking her hand in his. The monitor's beeps and whoosh of the oxygen machine filled the room, and he ran his thumb over the side of her hand. Her mind was still a black hole, but her cheeks were rosy, and her arms looked fuller, less lethargic than the last time he saw her. Physically, she was regenerating, but the mental blankness still pervaded. A blow upside the head would have had less of an impact than her silence, and Steve opened his mind to the thoughts of the rest of the hospital, the din keeping the devastation at bay.

"I'm going to New York for a while," he announced to her comatose ears.

A blip appeared on the brain wave monitor, but Steve didn't notice. The noise blended in with the rest of the chaos in his head. He took a deep breath and focused his attention back on his wife.

Steve pushed back the seat and lifted her thin hospital issued gown, revealing the perfect skin of her abdomen. The C-section scar was gone, disappeared with Jessica's healing infusion. He lowered the nightgown and returned the sheet. "Please come back to me," he whispered, grazing her cheek with his lips.

Steve stood as the door swung open and Dr. Nevins came in.

"Mr. Williams," he said, flipping the chart in his hand.

"Doc."

Dr. Nevins looked between the woman in the bed and Steve and licked his lips. He opened his mouth to speak and then closed it, glancing at the chart again. "There's been a new development." He stepped to Jennifer's side, pulling the sheet back. "One we can't explain," he continued, pulling the nightgown up as Steve had done a few minutes before.

Steve raised his eyebrows as he looked at her stomach, faking surprise. "Her scar's gone."

"Yes, and that isn't all." Dr. Nevins shook his head. "It's the damndest thing, but all her muscles have lost the atrophy they previously had." He offered Steve a smile.

"What about brain activity?" Steve asked, looking between his wife and the doctor.

Dr. Nevins shook his head. "Physically, she is in better shape than she's been for years." He glanced at the chart. "But there is still no sign of the slightest brain activity." His eyebrows creased, and he raised his eyes to Steve's.

"I've filed an injunction against removing life support," he announced, watching as the doctor's features became guarded.

"I'm aware of that. But even with these physical developments..." Dr. Nevins trailed off and glanced at Jennifer. "The likelihood of a full recovery is still a long shot."

Steve nodded and pulled out a business card that listed his cell phone number. He handed it to Dr. Nevins. "I have to leave town for a couple of weeks. If there are any more changes, please let me know." He glanced at Jennifer, leaned over, and planted a kiss on her lips before he headed out of the room.

Hunting Season
Chapter 25

"STEVE!" JENNIFER YELLED, BUT *her voice dropped flat in the darkness.*

She swore she heard his voice, but now, standing alone in the black landscape, she wasn't sure. Ever since that woman came to the hospital room, she'd been locked in this prison.

This hell.

This was much worse than being a living ghost.

Blind and without sensation was a far greater punishment than seeing him every day. Even now, she'd give anything to see the constant pain in his eyes.

To see him.

To see anything.

Hunting Season
Chapter 26

AN HOUR LATER, STEVE pulled the BMW into the York Harbor Inn and sat in the car looking at the hotel. He took a deep breath and stepped out, popped the trunk, and retrieved his laptop and duffel bag before heading inside to see if they had any rooms available.

A small room greeted him, and he tossed his luggage on the chair. Steve slipped his shoes off and stretched out on the bed, pressing his palms on his eyelids. The grueling week caught up to him, and sleep dragged him into oblivion.

The sunrise spread rays of light through the hotel room, bringing Steve awake as twilight turned to full morning. When he moved, his muscles protested, stiff from lying in the same position all night. He rolled off the bed and stripped off yesterday's suit, creating a clothing trail to the bathroom.

Stopping halfway to the shower, he stared at his unblemished torso in the mirror. The absence of scars still astonished him, and he wondered how long it took Chris to get used to the missing scar on his face. Maybe he'd ask when this was all over.

He stepped into the hot water and let a low groan escape. The water felt like heaven on his tired skin, relaxing the knots in his muscles. He took his time getting dressed and opened his laptop while the coffee was brewing. He hadn't looked at his private email box since he left Quantico and after pouring his coffee; he logged in. Spam emails diluted his account, and he deleted all of them until only a few emails remained. Those were from Jack and his parents.

He opened the first one from his parents. They sent a response to his 'I'm back at Quantico' note, stating they were proud he was getting back on his feet and if he needed anything to let them know. The next email from his parents was sent the day they died. He clicked on the link and the email opened.

Steve shot out of the seat away from the computer and the coffee cup slipped out of his hand, bouncing on the carpet. His screen filled with a still snapshot of his father tied to the bed with his throat slit wide open and his mother's face buried in his lap, her hair drenched with his blood.

Swallowing the sudden taste of bile lining his mouth and throat, he reached for the mouse with hands that shook, scrolling down to the second email. He stared at the timestamp. Fifteen minutes after the first one and he couldn't bring himself to open it, knowing it was a picture of how his mother died.

The next email was from Jack's cell phone, and he opened it.

"Oh, Christ," Steve whispered. His hand flew to his mouth, covering both the shock and the possibility of vomiting.

Jack had multiple stab wounds in his chest and abdomen and both legs and a gaping wound in his neck. His eyes wide with pain and fear stared sightlessly at Steve. Gray duct tape covered his mouth, and his arms were bound to the headboard in the same crucifixion style as his father.

There was one more email sent a couple of days ago from an address he didn't recognize with an empty subject line, and he hesitated before he moved the mouse over the entry. He clicked on it and gritted his teeth at the words that leaped from the screen.

Hope you're having fun. I am. Kyle.

A numbing sensation traveled from his trembling fingers up his arms and into his chest, jump-starting his heart into a rage. Fiery fuel pumped in his veins in pulses he could feel in his temple. Edges of red obstructed his vision and his hands clenched. He turned, walking away from the computer, squashing the temptation to heave the laptop across the room.

"I am going to rip your heart out with my bare hands," Steve said to the ocean view before he sent a glare back at the laptop. Returning his gaze out the window, he reined in his fury.

Once he was sure he had control, he approached the machine, shut it down, slipped it into the bag, and packed the rest of his things. He checked out of the hotel and headed to Chris's house.

At the gate, he punched in the code instead of pressing the buzzer, pulling up to the house. He already telepathically announced his arrival, and the door opened as he strode up the walkway.

CJ wasn't smiling. He put his hand up, stopping Steve in his tracks with an invisible wall. "You're taking my dad away."

"CJ, back off." Chris came from behind. "I'm going because I want to catch this guy just as much as he does." He grabbed CJ by the scruff of the neck and pulled him into the house.

Steve felt the invisible wall dissolve, and he stepped inside, closing the front door behind him. He cloaked his thoughts so none of the family could hear the murderous rage enveloping him. "I need your father," he admitted. *Because you wouldn't give me...* He stopped the angry thought midstream, clenching his jaw and glancing up at Chris.

Chris sent him a warning look that needed no words.

"I'm sorry. I had a bad morning. I need your dad to help me catch the man who killed your brother," Steve said to CJ.

"You don't need him," CJ argued. "I don't want him to go."

Chris squatted and turned CJ toward him. "I need to go, CJ. I love you and Tommy and your mother very much, and I'll miss you just as much as you'll miss me." He put his palm on his son's cheek. "If it wasn't for Agent Williams, I wouldn't be able to see you right now," he added for good measure, and planted a kiss on CJ's forehead.

Steve stood, shifting his weight, trying to calm the anxiety raking his skin. He wanted to start hunting now, and the drive to the city loomed. The sooner they started, the sooner Chris could get back home to his family.

"Daddy, please don't kill anyone," CJ pleaded.

"I'll do my best." Chris exchanged eye contact with Steve. He stood and led CJ into the kitchen.

Steve waited by the door as Chris said his goodbye to his family.

"YOU BE GOOD FOR your mother, understand?"

The two boys nodded in response.

"I want you to tell me you understand," he clarified.

"We will," CJ and Tommy said in unison.

"You'd better, because if I find out you gave her a hard time, there will be some serious punishments. Got it?" He stooped down and gave each boy a hug.

"Dad, please come back," CJ whispered in his ear.

Chris pulled away and looked at his son. "Why wouldn't I?" He touched CJ's face.

CJ shrugged and threw his arms around his father. "I love you, Dad."

"I love you both." He looked at Tommy, who was standing a foot behind CJ. He was watching his father with a serious expression, looking more like his biological father than Chris ever imagined he would. He released CJ and pulled Tommy into his arms. "Watch over your brother," he whispered.

"I always do," Tommy answered, pulling away.

Chris stood and turned to Jessica. He let his gaze scan over her body once more and couldn't help the grin that surfaced. "I'll miss you." He stepped toward her and planted a kiss, running one hand into her hair and the other around her waist, pulling her close. The kiss stripped him of his breath. "I love you," he whispered in her ear and then broke free of her grasp.

"I love you, too," Jessica replied, trying not to cry at his departure.

Walking away from his family was the hardest thing Chris had ever done, and he locked his emotions away, letting his thoughts drift over the years they'd had together. The good, the bad, the laughter and the tears mingled in a frantic slide show, rendering his mind a complete blank to those around him.

The best years of his life were here, and he knew he wasn't coming back. His soul screamed for him to turn around, to stay, to hold on to a life he knew was over. But the promise of eternity Eric laid at his feet kept him walking. He was not at all eager to go to hell.

He pulled the already packed vintage candy apple red Corvette out into the bright morning sunshine and stopped parallel to Steve's BMW.

"Nice wheels."

Chris gave a nod and glanced in the rearview mirror at Jessica and the kids standing on the front stoop. They were crying, and his heart tugged. "Try to keep up," Chris called to Steve and pulled out, leading the way to New York.

Hunting Season
Chapter 27

CHRIS PULLED THE CORVETTE into the garage, with Steve following. He smiled at the familiar attendant. "Jason, I thought you'd be off running some corporate conglomerate by now," he said.

Jason approached the corvette with a matching grin. "I'm getting my masters," he answered. "And this job pays damn well."

Chris nodded. "I've got a friend following me; you'll like his car just as much as this one." He peeled off a couple of hundred-dollar bills from his wallet and handed them to Jason. "We'll take them up ourselves."

"Where's your wife?" Jason asked, pocketing the cash.

"She's in Maine. The kids are still in school," Chris said.

"How long are you staying?"

Chris shrugged. "We've got a job to do, so it could be a while." He thought about the last time he had been in New York and peeled off a couple more bills. "Keep your eyes and ears open for me. Okay?" He handed the money to Jason.

Jason stared at the cash and back at Chris, remembering the last time as well.

"The guy in the car behind me is with the FBI. I'm helping him with a case."

Jason took the bills and nodded. "Will do." He waved him on.

Chris pulled into one of the spots reserved for the penthouse, and Steve pulled in next to him. He popped the trunk and retrieved the two suitcases he packed. One had clothing, the other had electronics and his camera equipment. He pushed the elevator button and waited as Steve stepped beside him with two suitcases and a duffel bag slung over his shoulder. "You had a bad morning?"

Steve huffed. "Yep."

Chris glanced sideways at him. "You can tell me about it after we get all your shit upstairs."

Steve whistled when he walked into the penthouse. "Nice." He glanced around at the luxurious surroundings. It was warm and welcoming, quite the opposite of what Steve thought of his host.

Chris chuckled. "Not what you expected?" he asked, brushing past Steve to the master bedroom. He dropped his suitcases and showed Steve to the other bedroom. "Eric and the boys were the last ones to stay in here." He swung the door open. He waited while Steve put his suitcases down and they went to collect the rest of Steve's possessions.

"Are you hungry?" Chris asked as he put the last of the boxes down in the living room.

<hr>

"YES." STEVE ANSWERED, PLACING the hard drive on the coffee table. He opened the doors to the balcony and stepped out. The view of Central Park and the city south of where he stood was breathtaking. "So, this is how the other half lives." He glanced over his shoulder at Chris.

Chris shifted and shrugged. "Money isn't everything."

Steve laughed. "This, coming from the billionaire."

Chris smiled. "Chinese?"

"Sure."

Chris disappeared, and Steve returned his gaze to the incredible view. It was eons nicer than Charlie's view and that had been stellar. *Blood money.* Chris's thought invaded his mind. He turned, meeting Chris's stark stare.

"That's how I got all this," he said. "Food will be here in about twenty minutes." He turned and disappeared from the doorway and the sound of papers rustling caught his attention. Chris was digging through his research.

His audacity irked Steve. "What do you think you're doing?" He crossed the room, reaching for the documents in Chris's hand.

Chris glanced at him, stopping him in his tracks. "I need to see how far you got." He made no move to put the papers down. He leaned back on the couch and assessed Steve. "Are you going to tell me what got you in such an uproar this morning?"

Steve went to the room they had deposited his stuff in and came back with his laptop. With a few keystrokes from Chris, he had access to the wireless network in the apartment and he logged into his email, turning the laptop toward Chris. "The last four emails," he said.

Chris started with the latest one and went down, studying the pictures. "All from their phones, except this last one," he said. Chris ran a trace on the email address and his brow furrowed. The URL it came from was non-existent. "This guy knows his way around the cyber world," Chris said.

The doorbell interrupted the conversation, and he handed the laptop back to Steve.

"Sir, your food." The doorman handed Chris the bag of Chinese food.

"Thank you, Fred."

"How's the Mrs.?"

"She's doing well. She's back in Maine with the kids until school lets out."

"Well, you have a nice evening."

"You too, Fred."

Chris stepped back into the living room with the bag and headed toward the small galley kitchen. Steve walked in as Chris pulled the boxes out of the bag and set them on the table. Chris grabbed two plates and set them down. He sat, scooping half of the containers onto his plate, and grabbed a pair of chopsticks.

Steve took the seat opposite Chris, emptying the contents onto the second plate, looking around. He glanced up at Chris. "Any silverware?"

Chris tossed a pair of chopsticks to Steve.

"No, I mean silverware," Steve said.

"I want to see how lame you actually are with those things." Chris picked up a lump of rice, plopping it in his mouth.

"Come on."

"It's a sin to eat Chinese food in New York with silverware. If you can shoot a bull's eye at a hundred yards, you can do this."

"Jenny tried to teach me more than once, and it didn't go well." He went to stand, and an invisible hand pushed him back into the seat.

"Chopsticks or go hungry," Chris said. "And don't even think about using your hands."

"Asshole," Steve grumbled and put the chopsticks in his hand. He couldn't control the sticks with his awkward hold.

"First, you're doing it completely wrong," Chris said. "The bottom stick always stays still. Use the index and middle fingers to move the top stick like this." He demonstrated by picking up a piece of chicken and popping it in his mouth. He looked at Steve and dipped his head.

Steve's jaw dropped when his hand formed the proper hold and picked up a piece of chicken, bringing it to his lips. He stared at Chris as the piece of chicken dropped into his open mouth. None of the motions he executed were of his own free will.

Chris offered a sly smile and released Steve. "Think you can handle it from here?"

Steve slowly repeated the movement, his muscles remembering the motion, and he picked up another piece of chicken. "I'll be damned," he whispered as he chewed the second piece and successfully scooped up some rice.

"Let's hope that isn't the case," Chris mumbled, catching Steve's attention.

Steve narrowed his eyes, studying his host. He continued eating, attempting to analyze Chris Ryan. He combed through Eric's memories, singling in on the turning points in Chris's life. "Your father was a cop?"

Chris nodded.

Steve mulled over the catalog of events, and it kept coming back to one thing. "How many people died because of you?" Steve asked.

"I'm not disclosing that to you. You are with the FBI." He pointed the chopsticks at Steve.

"And anything you say or do could be used against you in a court of law?"

"Something like that." He met Steve's inquisitive gaze. "I'm not the same person I was back then."

"Yes, you are. You're hiding behind the guise of husband and father, but there is definitely darkness still embedded in your soul."

Chris considered the comment. "You may be right. But isn't that why you brought me along for the ride?"

Steve looked down at his food. He didn't want to admit anything to the man across the table. The promise he made to Eric weighed heavily on his mind.

CHRIS FELT THE CONFLICT in Steve. He finished his meal and put the dishes in the sink, retreating into the living room to set up Steve's hard drive. The right half of the living room consisted of a desk and computer equipment. He brought the hard drive over and hooked up the wires to one of the dual monitors he had in place, and booted it up. He stopped when he heard the water in the sink go on.

"You don't have to do that," Chris said as he stood in the doorway of the kitchen. "I've got a cleaning lady who comes in once a week."

"I'm just rinsing them and putting them in the dishwasher," Steve said, dropping the last plate into the bottom rack and closing the dishwasher door.

Chris returned to the living room, taking a seat at the desk. He hooked up the network to Steve's computer and flipped the monitor around so Steve could pull up a chair on the other side of the desk. He set up the keyboard and mouse for Steve, as well. "You're all set."

Steve raised his eyebrows. "That was fast."

Chris glanced in his direction. "That's nothing." He pointed his chin at the laptop. "Bring that over here." He directed.

Steve retrieved the laptop and put it on the desk.

Chris accessed the DOS prompt and typed in a few commands. He closed the prompt and accessed Steve's email, adding an undetectable tracer to his email account. He turned the computer to Steve. "Reply to the email," he directed.

"What?"

"I put tracers on all your outbound emails. If he retrieves the email, I can tell when the bastard reads it and the protocol for hacking into the computer that he accessed it from."

"No shit?" He glanced at his computer and back.

"Yes. Now reply to the email. Tell him to drop dead."

Steve pressed the reply button, typing Drop Dead Asshole in the email's text. He glanced at Chris again and pressed the send button.

"That may take a while. Show me the financials you had," Chris barked the request and logged onto his own computer.

Steve pulled up the information from files he'd saved on his computer, turning the monitor toward Chris. He stood and got the cardboard box that sat open on the coffee table and brought it over to the desk, rifling through the papers until he came up with the prints of the accounts he had found, handing them to Chris.

Chris's fingers flew over the keyboard, pinpointing the major account Steve had found. It was in the name of a shell corporation and the distribution of funds went to over a dozen accounts worldwide. He whistled, studying the distribution, suppressing the admiration cropping up. "This guy is really good at laundering money," he said.

"Can you track it?"

Chris shot him a cross look. "What do you think?"

Steve put his hands in the air. "Sorry." He stood up. "You have anything to drink here?"

Chris pointed to the bar in the far corner.

Steve found a couple of bottles of scotch covered with a layer of dust and he sighed, settling into an overstuffed chair without a drink in hand.

Chris glanced at his watch. It was almost time for the Yankees game. "You a Red Sox fan?" he asked, knowing the answer already.

"Yeah."

Chris smiled and rolled the chair back, standing and crossing the room. "I know a great place where we can watch the Yankees pummel the Red Sox tonight." He picked up the keys and opened the front door. "They don't have Corona, though." He closed the door and locked it after Steve followed him out.

"Shouldn't you do whatever you were doing?"

"I have to wait for responses, and I doubt they'll come in tonight."

"Responses?"

"Audit information confirming the transfers made to and from that account over the last three years," Chris said. "They're all listed and in a couple of cases, the account numbers are transposed, and the dollar figures are off, so they'll give us the corrections. It looks like an internal request initiated by a client complaint and when they reply with the information, I will get a copy."

"You did all that in a half hour?" Steve gawked, and they stepped into the elevator.

"I told you I was a genius."

"Jesus, the FBI could use someone like you."

Chris burst out laughing. "I didn't exactly request the information through legal means."

"Still." What he had done in such a short time span impressed Steve.

"I'd be the biggest nightmare if I was in the FBI."

They stepped into the lobby.

"Good evening, Mr. Ryan. Can I get you a cab?" The doorman held the door open for them.

"Thank you, Fred." Chris waited while he flagged down a cab. He tipped the doorman, and they slid into the cab. "15 East 7th street."

"Everyone who knows you here seems to like you," Steve said.

"Don't act so shocked." Chris glanced in his direction. "I tip well."

"It has nothing to do with money, Chris," he said. "They actually like you because you treat them with respect."

"I remember what it was like not having money. Besides, not everyone who knows me likes me." He glanced at Steve.

"The jury is still out," Steve replied.

"I'm not talking about you," Chris replied. "Jessica's father tolerates me, and her ex-husband hates me." He sighed. "Tom hated me too."

"Can you blame them?" Steve laughed. "You ruined both their marriages."

Chris smiled. "I see your point with both her exes but her father. That's another story. He doesn't like me because I remind him too much of Ty. Ironic, isn't it?" He glanced out the window.

"Smart man."

Chris didn't reply. He watched uptown transition to midtown. He peeled off a fifty and handed it to the cab driver when they pulled up in front of the bar.

"McSorely's?" Steve asked, reading the banner over the door announcing the name of the bar.

"Best Irish pub in the city and the hot mustard will grow hair on y'er chest if y'er brave enough to try it," Chris drawled in an impeccable Irish accent and entered the crowded bar.

One barstool sat free, and Chris slid in. He glanced at the drunken fool next to him, willing the inebriated man to leave the bar. The man stumbled away, leaving the chair open for Steve.

Steve took the seat as the bartender cleared the spot in front of them, wiping down the bar.

"It's been a long time. What can I get you, Mr. Ryan?" The bartender smiled at Chris.

"I wasn't sure if you'd recognize me." Chris returned the smile. "It's been almost ten years."

"I never forget a big tipper." The bartender grinned. "And you were the biggest."

Chris's cheeks heated, and he traded a glance with Steve. "We will start off with a dozen darks and a cheese platter." He glanced up at the television. It was the bottom of the first inning and the Red Sox were already leading two to nothing. He glanced in Steve's direction. "Wipe that smile off y'er face, boy. This is Yankee country." The Irish drawl persisted.

"Who's whooping who?" Steve asked as twelve ten-ounce beers were set on the counter between them.

"I could announce that we have a Red Sox fan in our midst," Chris said.

"Bring it on." Steve grinned. "Isn't your wife a Red Sox fan?"

Chris grumbled. "Her one flaw."

"I thought her driving was flawed as well," he needled Chris.

"No, that's just scary as hell." He downed the first beer, his eyes riveted on the television.

THE GRUMBLING IN THE bar got more prevalent as the Red Sox expanded their lead to five to nothing. Steve sat with a grin on his face, matching Chris beer for beer. He reached out, dipping a cracker in the hot mustard and slid it in his mouth, following it with a piece of cheese. Fire enveloped his mouth and his eyes watered as the mustard blazed its way through his throat. He downed the rest of the beer to quench the burn that seeped into his esophagus. "Holy shit," he breathed.

Chris chuckled. "I told you that would put hair on your chest," he said, glancing in Steve's direction.

"More like burn a hole through the lining of your stomach," he said, still hoarse from the hot mustard. He drained another beer and the cooling sensation returned to his sinuses. He grabbed another cracker and piece of cheese, opting to stay away from the mustard at all costs.

Chris glanced at his watch and slid out of the seat. "I'll be right back," he said. "Save my seat." He held up the cell phone. "I need to say good night to the boys."

Steve nodded and felt a twinge of envy. He squelched it and focused on the game, putting his feet up on the chair reserving it for Chris's return.

"Do you mind?" A female voice cut through his concentration.

Steve turned and looked at a perky blonde trying to slide into Chris's seat.

"Move your feet," she ordered.

"My friend is sitting there."

"He ain't here now." She shoved his feet off, sliding into the seat before he could object. "You gonna buy me a drink?"

"No," Steve spat out, appalled at her audacity.

She shrugged and took one of their beers.

"Hey, that's ours." He plucked the drink out of her hand.

"Didn't your momma teach you to share?" She grabbed the beer back from his hand.

Flabbergasted, Steve just stared at her and when she reached out to take a cracker off the platter, he slapped her hand away.

She reached into her pocket and pulled out a police shield. "I can take anything I want." She reached for the crackers again.

Steve grabbed her wrist and pulled out his badge. "I don't think so. Mine trumps yours."

"Fucking FBI?" She swung her chair toward him. "Think you're better than a city cop?"

"At least I have manners."

Chris tentatively approached the now explosive situation. "Excuse me."

"What?" Both Steve and the blonde snapped in his direction.

Chris put his hands in the air. "I was sitting there."

"You ain't now," she shot back. "You another FBI agent?"

"No."

"She's a cop," Steve mocked. "Thinks she owns the city and can take anything she wants." He still had her wrist in his grasp.

"Dirty?" Chris tilted his head, looking her over.

"Fuck you, man," she snapped and yanked her wrist out of Steve's hand. She turned her attention back to the television, but both Chris and Steve heard her explosive thoughts. "I ain't dirty." She finally shot back in their direction.

"Could have fooled me," Steve said. He reached out and stopped the punch she threw without taking his eyes off the television. He yanked her close to his face. "Cut the shit or I'll haul your ass in," he growled. "Assaulting a federal officer is a felony."

She blinked at the venom in his words and pried her hand out of his grip, turning back to the television. "Sorry." She glanced at him sideways. "I'm just pissy 'cause the Yanks are losing."

Steve acknowledged her apology with a nod. He wasn't about to tell her he was a Red Sox fan. "What's your name?"

"Sarah, Sarah Connelly. I'm a detective in the seventh precinct."

"Steve Williams." He put out his hand.

She looked at it and then up at him, tentatively taking it. She returned her attention to the television. *I'd love a taste of that.*

"Should I just leave now?" Chris asked from behind Steve.

Steve shook his head and glanced back. *Are you kidding? She's an absolute bitch.*

Yeah, but I bet she's hellfire in bed. Chris grinned, keeping his gaze on the television.

I'm married, jackass. Steve glanced at her again. She was the exact opposite of Jennifer—blonde, abrasive, and controlling. He shrugged and glanced back at Chris.

Ok, but if you change your mind.

I won't. Steve went back to watching the game, aware she was stealing glances his way and when he pushed a beer in her direction, she accepted it with a nod of acknowledgement.

"You're married," she said, observing the ring on his left hand.

"His wife is in a coma," Chris said with his eyes still on the television.

Steve shot a glare in his direction.

"I'm so sorry." Her entire demeanor softened.

Steve nodded and focused on the television. *You are such a son of a bitch.* He heard Chris choke on the beer, trying to stifle his laughter.

On the television, Big Papi hit a grand slam.

"Yeah!" Steve reacted.

The bar suddenly got quiet. All eyes focused on Steve and the grin on his face.

"You're a Red Sox fan?" Sarah gawked.

"Yessiree." He raised his beer and winked at her. "Born and raised in the Red Sox Nation."

"What the fuck are you doing here?"

"I brought him here," Chris interjected. He peeled off a couple of hundred-dollar bills and handed them to the bartender. "Time to go," he said.

"I'm just beginning to enjoy this." Steve smiled.

"You're going to get your ass kicked."

Steve chuckled—the alcohol affected his judgment. "Bring it on." He lifted the beer to his lips, draining the glass. He could hear both Sarah and Chris swearing under their breath, both for very different reasons.

He leaned over and whispered in Sarah's ear. "How'd you like to screw a member of the Red Sox nation?" He wasn't quick enough to get out of the way of her swing. Her fist connected with his cheek and knocked him off the chair. He laughed as he caught himself before he lost his balance completely. "I'll take that as a no."

"Smooth, Williams." Chris grabbed him by the arm, hauling him out of the bar.

Steve broke the grip and swung, the anger surfacing again.

Chris blocked his swing and grabbed him in a headlock. "Cut the shit," he growled.

Steve twisted out of Chris's grip, slamming him into the side of the building with his arm pinned to his back. "You're not my father."

"I'm not trying to be." Chris glared over his shoulder at Steve.

The mental shove made Steve stumble backwards and land on his ass in the street.

Chris turned toward him, straightening out his shirt and jacket before he met Steve's glowering eyes. He crouched down. "If I was, I would have kicked your ass by now. I don't give a shit how many people you've lost. Suck it up. Life goes on." He stood up and walked away.

"And you wouldn't freak out if you lost your boys?" Steve asked, scrambling to his feet.

Chris stopped. His mind wandering back to the close calls he had in the past.

"I lost my daughter," Steve yelled.

Chris's head dropped, and he turned. "Life goes on," he answered. "Whether you like it or not."

"He's right." The voice came from the doorway. Sarah leaned on the doorjamb, watching the exchange between the two men.

Steve spun, his blue eyes shining in the streetlights. "This is none of your business," he snapped and sauntered away, breezing by Chris without another look.

Chris shrugged and followed Steve. "You see, that's where we differ. At your age, I wouldn't have passed on an opportunity like that," Chris said, matching strides with Steve.

"At my age, you were kidnapping and killing people."

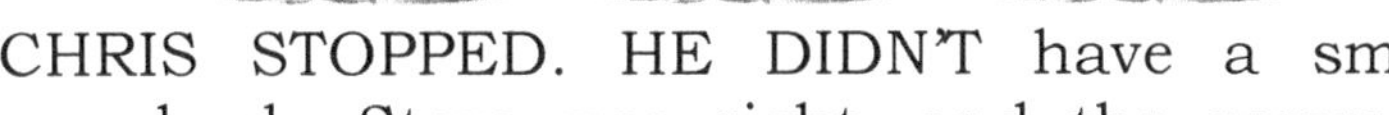

CHRIS STOPPED. HE DIDN'T have a smart comeback. Steve was right, and the comment stung more than he expected. His demons surfaced again, biting at the edges of his heels and the memories flooded in.

Hell and Frank were waiting for him and his only shot at grace just stormed off in the wrong direction.

The amount of anger living within Steve's skin reminded Chris of his own hatred for Frank, and he knew there was no stopping that train once it left the station.

Hunting Season
Chapter 28

STEVE STUMBLED AND SWORE under his breath. He knew Chris turned in the other direction a while back, leaving him to his own devices.

The unmarked car pulled to the curb a few feet ahead of Steve. "Want a lift?"

He stopped and glanced in her direction. "Are you following me?"

Sarah smiled. "No, but I saw your partner catch a cab going in the opposite direction."

"He's not my partner," Steve said.

"Your friend," she corrected. "Do you need a lift?"

Steve looked both ways on the street and then at her and shrugged. He opened the car door and slid inside.

"Where you headed?"

"Uptown." He glanced sideways as she laughed.

"You were headed in the wrong direction."

"I needed some space," he mumbled.

"Are you always this ornery?"

"Are you always such an overbearing bitch?" He shot back, and she stopped dead in the middle of the street. The sudden stop jerked him against the seatbelt.

"Get out!" she ordered.

Steve nearly got clipped by a cab zooming in the right lane when he stepped onto the pavement. He trotted across the road and continued walking in the downtown direction.

Too bad all the hot guys turn out to be cold-hearted bastards.

She zoomed away, leaving Steve watching after her with her last thought.

He huffed and continued walking with his head down and his hands shoved in his pockets.

"I'm a cop, that's why."

He jumped at the sound of her voice, his head snapping up and his gaze falling on her, leaning on the side of her parked car. "That doesn't give you the right to be a bitch," he said, but stopped walking.

"Do you know how hard it is for a woman to become a homicide detective in this city?" she asked with her arms crossed.

"You know, I really don't give a damn." Steve walked away. He stopped a few paces away, turning back toward her. "Using that as an excuse to be abrasive and crude is pretty pathetic."

"Staying stuck in the past is just as pathetic." She stood, dropping her arms to her side.

"You know nothing about me," he growled and turned away.

"You lost your wife and daughter."

Steve glared over his shoulder at her.

"And now you have a chip on your shoulder as big as mine."

Steve couldn't help the smile that surfaced. "What'd you lose?"

"My sister," she answered.

Steve shrugged. He had been there before, too. "It isn't the same." He turned away and began walking.

"How do you know?" She shot back.

Steve stopped. "Because I've been there as well." He turned back. "My little sister died when I was eleven." He took a few backward steps.

"Was she murdered?" Sarah asked.

Steve shook his head. "But my daughter, my parents, and both my partners were." Her jaw went slack. "And my wife is clinically brain dead because of the same bastard." He turned and continued walking.

"Wait."

"Look, I don't want your pity," he snapped, turning on her. "All I want is to find the son of a bitch and kill him myself. And I don't need any distractions along the way."

She took an involuntary step backward.

Steve advanced on her, taking advantage of the fact he scared her.

"You're not FBI are you?" She took another step back. *Bondino, oh shit, he's one of them.*

Steve tilted his head. "Bondino? Tony Bondino?"

Sarah's jaw fell, and she scrambled away.

Steve grabbed her arm and pulled her toward him. "What do you know about Tony Bondino?" He slammed her against the wall, his weight holding her in place.

Oh fuck, my gun's in the car. How stupid can I be? "Nothing. I don't know who that is," she shot back, the fear clear in her features. *Oh shit. I'm going to die.*

"I'm not going to kill you," Steve said. "And I am with the FBI." He let her go and stepped back.

"You don't act like it." She straightened her shirt and glared at him.

"I'm not your typical agent. I was undercover for years before I got married."

"What, in grade school?"

"Right out of high school until a couple of years ago. Having your face splashed all across the television kills an undercover career."

Her eyes went wide. "Oh, my God!" She remembered his face and the news story that accompanied it.

"Now, talk to me about the Bondino's." Steve stood with his arms crossed.

Sarah looked around and back at him. "Not here." She started back toward her car.

Steve followed and slid into the passenger seat, letting her take him wherever she wanted.

She pulled up in front of a little brownstone in Brooklyn twenty minutes later. "My place," she said, blushing.

Steve got out of the car and followed her inside, watching as the brazen obnoxious cop turned into a shy, tempered woman.

"Can I get you anything?" she asked as she stripped her jacket off.

"You wouldn't happen to have a Corona?" he asked, thinking it was a one in a million shot.

She smiled. "With lime?"

Steve raised his eyebrows, hiding the surprise convincingly. "Is there any other way?"

He walked around the small living room, picking up the trinkets on the side tables, inspecting and replacing as he took in his surroundings. He turned back toward her when she came into the room. She had taken off her boots and was now looking up at him from a height of roughly five two at the most. In an unsettling way, she reminded him of a combination of Tracy and Desiree, except her eyes were the shade of milk chocolate. "Thanks," he replied when she handed him the beer. "Have you had this place swept?"

"Pardon?"

"If you're going after the mafia, you better damn well sweep your place from time to time to make sure they haven't bugged it or put in cameras."

Her face went pale, and she glanced around the small abode.

"I'm talking from experience." He took a sip of the beer. "Don't make the same mistake I did of thinking your home can't be compromised."

Sarah nodded.

"Show me what you've got." Steve sat on the couch and looked at her expectantly.

She looked over her shoulder at the dining room and back. "Um, my files are over there." She pointed to the dining room.

He drank her in from the top of her blonde head to her crimson painted toenails. He allowed a slow smile to form and tipped the beer to his lips, draining half of the bottle. His gaze locked with hers. He put the bottle on the table in front of him and stood, heading toward the dining room.

She cut him off, putting her hand on his chest.

He stared down into her chocolate eyes, hearing the carnal thoughts running through her mind and he smiled his famous smile, the one that Tracy once said caused women to swoon, the one that brought bright color to Sarah's cheeks, the one that could charm the pants off Mother Teresa.

When her hand drifted lower, his smile faded, and he shook his head, raised his left hand, and wiggled his fingers. "I'm still married."

Sarah lowered her eyes to his hand and then returned her gaze to his face, stepping closer. "But you want me."

Steve felt the dimples form and his cheeks heat. "You are very attractive, but that doesn't matter." His eyes fell to the ring on his hand, and he inhaled a deep breath before returning his gaze to her.

She backed away, shaken by the rejection.

Steve crossed to the dining room, turning the light on. He flipped open the folder and fanned through the contents, stopping at a crime scene picture. He sat down hard in the chair, and the blood drained from his face, leaving it cold in the warm air of her apartment. He pulled the photograph out of the shuffled papers.

"That's my sister," Sarah said.

Steve's jaw hung open when he looked at Sarah, and the irony of the situation hit him full force. He laughed, still pale as a ghost, his haunted eyes moving between the photograph and the woman in the room.

"What the hell is wrong with you?" Sarah asked, snatching the picture out of his hand. She dropped it on the table.

Steve shook his head, trying to find the syllables to form words. "Kyle." The word finally escaped, and he stared at the photograph. "We're after the same person," he said when he regained his composure. He ran his hands through his hair.

Steve stopped and turned his head toward her, his eyes narrowing. It was all too convenient for chance, and yet, he knew that's exactly what it was. His skin broke out in goose bumps.

"How do you know?"

"Because I have a picture of your sister that was taken by the killer." Steve picked up the file and scanned her notes. "It came from his apartment. His name originally was Kyle Wisnowski. Then it was Kyle Winslow and I don't know what it is right now." He turned and leaned on the table.

She wore a curious expression.

"I know, of all the people in New York City, how the hell did we end up here together?" He offered her a crooked smile and a shrug.

"That's not what I was thinking," she said.

"I know." Steve replied. "You were thinking the same thing I was earlier. That it is too much of a coincidence." His smile faded. "I'm not connected to the Bondino family. The name came up in my research. Every murder like this also coincided with a suspected mafia hit." He let the picture fall to the table again. "I uncovered that last spring and then Kyle Winslow ended up dead." He let a bitter smile find his lips. "Or so I thought."

Her eyes widened.

"He showed up at my house the day I went back to work." He turned his back. "Blew up my little girl. My wife got caught in the explosion and hasn't regained consciousness since." He looked at the array of paper she had on her dining room table. "I almost lost my eye in the explosion."

"You don't have any scars," she whispered.

Steve let a puff of airflow out of his nose. "Plastic surgery." He offered without turning. "My doctor was a miracle worker." He glanced back at Sarah, smiling at the partial truth in that statement.

"Where does the guy you were with at the bar fit in to all this?"

"He's the father of my last partner," Steve said, turning to face her. "Kyle killed him with a high-powered rifle, and Chris is helping me find the bastard."

"The FBI allows you to work with freelancers?"

Steve shook his head. "No. I gotta go." He started for the door, reaching for his jacket. He fished in his pocket and pulled out his cell phone. "What's the address here?"

"1521 Brooklyn Avenue."

Steve punched in Chris's phone number. "Can you send a car?"

"Where?" Chris asked.

"1521 Brooklyn Avenue."

"It will be there in a half-hour."

Steve flipped the phone closed and picked up his half-empty beer, draining it. "I've got a half-hour to kill."

"What is he, your sugar daddy?"

"Does the name Chris Ryan ring a bell?" he asked, passing her and picking up her notes again.

"Oh, my God! I was a rookie right out of the police academy and that was my first homicide. I'd never seen so much blood." She paused and drew a breath. "I was told it was a miracle he was alive, never mind that he had the strength to walk out of that warehouse." Her head lilted to the side. "I thought he was blind."

Shock made him freeze in place. "He was for a while. I guess it was psychological and not a physical thing," he bluffed. *Another coincidence?* He shivered and turned toward her. "If I didn't know better..." He trailed off, shaking the thoughts out of his head.

"That this all was meant to be?" Sarah said, and her arms broke out in a rash of goose bumps.

Steve laughed. "The intersection of our lives?" He shook his head. "That all those people were meant to die? Bullshit." The anger flared again. "We control our fate," he added, and passed by her, grabbed his jacket, and slipped it on. "We make the choices that end in disaster. It isn't a divine plan." He snapped, pulling the words from her thoughts. "Meant to be? My ass!" He stormed out the door and walked to the curb, pacing. "What kind of monster are you?" He looked up at the sky, addressing God.

She opened the door and walked to the sidewalk. "Whether it was fate or chance, I'm glad we got past..." She waved her hand and trailed off.

"Your abrasive nature?" Steve filled in the blank.

Her hands went to her hips. "Your insults."

"You leave that house, and the bitch is back."

She turned on her heels and stormed back inside, slamming the door.

Steve stopped pacing. He turned his back on the house and felt a twinge of guilt. That was downright mean, and he knew it. He hung his head and took a deep breath. "Ah, shit!" He walked back to the house, ringing the doorbell.

Sarah opened the door enough to look out between the chain lock.

"I'm sorry." He shuffled and looked at his feet. "That was uncalled for."

"Damn right." She slammed the door.

"You deserved that," he whispered, admonishing himself. He headed to the curb, relieved to see the approaching town car. He slid inside and gave a quick glance at the house. Sarah was standing in the dark living room, watching him, torn between hating him and wanting him.

"Better you hate me," he mumbled as the car pulled away.

Hunting Season
Chapter 29

STEVE WALKED INTO THE penthouse and flopped on the couch.

Chris sat at the computer and barely acknowledged his entrance.

"She was one of the cops who had to secure the warehouse while the forensic team did their thing," Steve said, reaching for the remote on the coffee table in front of him.

Chris grunted; he was busy mapping the money trail and only half listening to Steve.

"Kyle killed her sister," Steve added.

This statement caught Chris's attention, and he raised his eyes to Steve. "Did you sleep with her?"

"No." Steve turned on the television, flipping through the channels. He closed his mind to Chris. "She's got some interesting research, though." He glanced over his shoulder. "She came to the same conclusion I had about a mafia connection."

Chris paused. "Sounds like she's smart."

"Smart ass is more like it," Steve muttered. He stopped at the opening credits of a movie he had seen a few years back, uttering a laugh; he tossed the remote onto the coffee table.

Chris glanced up, catching the title on-screen. "Tom won an Oscar for that." He went back to his research as the movie title *Survival Games* flashed off the screen. "Unfortunately, he didn't live to see that, but at least he had the chance to meet his son before he died."

Steve turned. "You liked him?"

Chris smiled. "I respected him." He glanced at the screen. "He always had the most honorable intentions, and he loved Jessie as much as I do." He pushed away from the computer and stretched. "He should have made me out to be a monster, but he didn't." The laugh that escaped Chris made Steve shiver. "He actually said I was a hero at some level. Me. Can you believe that?" He stood and disappeared into the kitchen, coming out a few minutes later with two Coronas, crossing the room and handing one to Steve. He retreated to the computer.

Steve watched the movie with a whole different perspective than the first time, impressed by the acting job Tom Whitman did, especially with the arsenal of information Eric had downloaded into his mind. He couldn't fathom how Tom could make Chris anything but a cold-blooded killer with what he knew.

CHRIS DIDN'T COMMENT ON Steve's train of thought and, as the closing credits were rolling, he hit a button and the printer whirled into action. He got up and wandered out to the balcony, leaning on the railing and looking over the city.

Steve stepped out and joined him. "At least you feel remorse," he said after a few minutes of silence.

Chris nodded. "For most, but not all." Frank and Sharon passed through his mind. "If I had killed her when I wanted to, Emily would still be alive." He tipped the beer to his lips. "You would have liked Emily. She was as beautiful as Jess and feisty as hell. She had the same sense of justice you have. It was hard for her to accept that I was free, even though she liked who I had become."

"If I had killed that son of a bitch the second I walked into the cottage, Jenny wouldn't be in a coma right now."

Chris nodded. "Maybe, maybe not. And you have to stop blaming yourself for what happened." He straightened and turned toward Steve. "The alternative could have been far worse. Think of what would have happened if you put your gun down instead." He turned and disappeared inside the apartment.

STEVE THOUGHT OF ALL the nasty things Jennifer saw in her visions and shivered. He followed Chris inside.

"Still."

"If you had shot him when you walked in, you wouldn't be with her right now," Chris said.

Steve raised his eyebrows.

"She would never have forgiven you."

Steve started to say something and closed his mouth. He knew Chris was right. "How did Jessica ever forgive you for making the choice in the warehouse?"

"The alternative." Chris sent the vision of all of them brutally tortured before they were killed. "That's what would have happened if I hadn't made the deal."

"She never knew you had the choice of offering her up instead, did she?"

Chris shot a warning glance in his direction.

Steve put his hands up in the air. "I get it." He backed off.

Chris hung his head. "No, you don't get it." He said with his eyes closed. "Eric used to say we balance each other. We were meant to be together because it was written in the stars." He let out a laugh. "I can't survive without her." He glanced at Steve. "She is literally my heart and soul, my conscience." He looked out the window over the city. "I had none before she came into my life."

Steve raised his eyebrows. "Huh?"

"I had no heart, soul or conscience before I kidnapped Jessica," he admitted. "I lost that the day I killed my stepfather."

"Careful, you just admitted to a crime in the presence of a federal officer," Steve warned. He cracked a smile.

Chris shook his head and let a smile grace his lips. "You impressed the hell out of Eric." He glanced at Steve.

Steve was taken aback by the comment. "Why?"

"Your integrity impressed him and frankly, it impresses me, too."

"If I had an ounce of integrity, I'd lock you up."

"The fact you stuck by your promise to my stepson exhibits a pretty strong sense of honor." Chris pulled the prints off, handing them to Steve.

He shuffled through the papers and glanced up at Chris.

"It isn't admissible in a court of law."

"You found the money."

Chris indeed found the holding corporation with all the funds from Kyle Winslow's disparate accounts. It had close to ten million dollars in it, and some transfers originated from a trust account held by none other than Tony Bondino.

"The question is, what do you want me to do with it?"

"What do you mean?"

"We can't, in good conscience, leave the money in that account, can we?"

Steve pondered the possibilities. "Can you make it look like the Bondino's took the money?"

Chris's grin got wider. "You are truly evil. Yes, I can do that. But where do you want the money to end up?"

Steve shrugged.

Chris chuckled. *Honest to the end.* "Do *you* want the money?"

"No!"

"Ok, then I'll take it." Chris turned and took his seat behind the desk.

"You can't do that, either," Steve said.

Chris waited.

"Victim's fund?" Steve raised an eyebrow.

"I'll set up a trust. We have the victim's names, right?"

"Yes." Steve went over to the box and brought out the names he mapped the victim's pictures to and handed the list to Chris.

"I still haven't been able to get the payroll list for the shell corporation," Chris said, and he banged commands on the keyboard. "So, we don't have everything. Yet." He smiled. "When the next transfer fails, we'll get that information." He activated a series of transfers first into the Bondino's account, then out to a numbered Swiss account held in trust that he'd set up earlier with his banker. The money moved through four different shell corporations into a trust fund in New York for victims he added to the charter based on Steve's list. The transfers happened instantaneously and the only ones that triggered federal review were those out of Kyle's shell corporation and into the Bondino account. There was a transaction for moving the money out, but it didn't have the destination account information.

The destination accounts immediately closed after the money left their hosts and the transfer account record erased, leaving no financial trail outside of funds in and out, making it look like an error at the bank. Chris looked up after a few hours of executing commands and erasing history. "I left him a hundred dollars and we've got roughly ten million dollars to distribute to the families of his victims."

Steve grinned. "I have a feeling there's going to be a bloodbath in Vegas this week."

Hunting Season
Chapter 30

STEVE FELL SOUND ASLEEP as soon as he hit the bed. Waking to the sound of his phone ringing, he grabbed it off the nightstand and flipped it open without looking at the number.

"Hello?" He opened one eye to look at the clock. It was only eight in the morning, and he felt like shit.

"Drop dead asshole? That's the best you can come up with?" Kyle's voice mocked.

Steve catapulted out of bed, fully awake, and charged with fury.

Keep your fucking mouth shut! Chris's voice penetrated his mind just before the bedroom door opened.

"Cat got your tongue?" Kyle persisted. "Did you enjoy the pictures? Your mother was an exceptional fuck. Not as good as your wife. But, hey, I got my rocks off," he taunted.

Chris shook his head. *Don't react.*

"I promise I will find you," Steve said.

"Ooo, I'm scared," Kyle laughed.

"You'd better be," Steve said through clenched teeth.

Cut the call. Now.

Steve pushed the off button. "What the fuck was that all about?"

"He's tracking the call trying to find out where you are," Chris answered. He ran his hand through his hair. "He now knows you're in the city. If he calls again, only stay on for fifteen seconds at a time until I can reverse engineer the trace." He wandered away, leaving Steve alone in the bedroom.

Steve threw on a pair of jeans and wandered out to the living room, finding Chris at the computer controls, madly typing commands. He hacked into the Federal Reserve database and was wiping out all traces of the transfers he did the prior evening.

"Did you find him?"

"I need to finish what I started last night. The trace is running," he said, glancing at the other screen attached to Steve's laptop. Chris exited the site, leaving only a ghost trail. "I couldn't do that last night. They don't allow access over night while the system is backing up." He now focused on the laptop. "Shit." He swore under his breath.

"What?" Steve crossed the room and stepped behind Chris, looking at the computer.

"He doesn't have a landline," Chris mumbled. "Wireless encryption," he clarified. "It's harder to hack into hardware with wireless encryption."

"I thought it would be easier."

Chris looked up at him. "Hacking into the wireless service is easy; cracking wireless encryption is harder, especially if he's pirating the connection."

"Oh, so you can't get into his computer?"

"I never said that. I just said it's going to be harder." He went back to typing commands.

Steve disappeared into the kitchen and opened the refrigerator. He raised his eyebrows at the full contents. Chris had gone shopping.

He pulled out the fixings to make strawberry crêpes. The only missing ingredient was whipped cream and Steve improvised, sprinkling confectionary sugar on the rolled treats instead. He walked back into the living room, putting the plate on the edge of the desk, surprising Chris. He took a seat on the couch, flipped on the local news, and began to eat.

Chris looked at the breakfast. "I didn't realize when you said you did the cooking that you meant you were a gourmet chef," he commented after he took the first bite.

"This is Jenny's favorite," he said without turning.

"I can see why." Chris finished what was on the plate. "Is there any more?"

Steve pointed to the kitchen.

Chris got up and snagged four more crêpes, leaving the last two for Steve. He wolfed them down and dropped the plate into the sink. He glanced at the computers as he passed, heading to his bedroom to change.

Steve got up and wandered over to the desk.

"Don't touch," Chris yelled from down the hall.

"Don't touch," Steve mimicked, irritated at the prospect of hanging out in the apartment all day. He wandered out to the balcony. The New York skyline did nothing to improve his mood.

"You don't have to hang here all day," Chris said from the balcony doors. "I'm going running. I'll be back in a while." He turned. "If he calls again, remember what I told you," he added and left Steve staring after him.

Steve turned back to the view, letting his mind wander back to the prior evening. "Stupid," he muttered and retreated into the apartment, changing into his workout clothes. He locked up the apartment with the set of keys Chris gave him and took the elevator down.

"Sir," the doorman acknowledged and held the door open.

Steve offered an uncomfortable smile and a nod. "Thanks," he mumbled, not used to anyone holding a door for him. He crossed the street and broke out into a moderate jog, traversing the paths throughout Central Park.

Hunting Season
Chapter 31

CENTRAL PARK WAS ONE of her favorite places to jog and on a warm spring day like today, Sarah particularly enjoyed her stride until she looked up to see Chris Ryan heading her way.

His gaze locked with hers, and he slowed down to acknowledge her. She followed suit, stopping as he approached.

"Officer Connelly," Chris said.

"Detective Connelly," she corrected.

"Detective," he repeated. "I understand you were a part of the investigation of my stepdaughter's death."

Heat flushed her cheeks. "I helped secure the building." She shuffled her feet. "I thought you were blind?" she blurted, while thinking of something intelligent to say. Chris Ryan was an exceptionally good-looking man with an intense gaze that made her feel like he could see inside her soul.

Chris chuckled and shrugged. "I was for a while. Guess it was a psychological thing after all." He shifted and glanced around. "But I'm damn glad to have my sight back." He smiled and found her gaze again. "Hear you gave my boy a hard time?"

"Your boy is an asshole."

Chris laughed. "Yeah, he certainly can be."

"What's he got on you?"

"Nothing. Why?"

"I'm trying to figure out what a billionaire is doing with an FBI agent with a chip on his shoulder the size of Staten Island," she said, shifting her weight and looking him over.

Chris took his sunglasses off. "My son was shot and killed by the man he is trying to find, and I've got more resources than the FBI." His eyes bore into her.

"Don't you mean stepson?"

Chris slid his sunglasses back on. "That's just semantics. I considered him my son." He jogged away, leaving her staring after him.

Hunting Season
Chapter 32

STEVE STOPPED IN HIS tracks when he saw Chris talking to Sarah and knew Chris was not happy when he jogged away.

"You seem to have a knack for pissing people off." Steve approached her from behind.

Sarah's head jerked in his direction. Her ponytail whipped around, hitting her cheek. Her brown eyes widened with shock behind the sunglasses. "Fuck off, Williams," she said as she regained her composure.

Steve started laughing. "Always a lady." He jogged away.

"Asshole!" she called after him.

"Bitch." He smiled back at her and promptly tripped on the curb. Steve pin-wheeled onto the grass, losing his balance, he fell on his ass.

Sarah burst into hysterics at both the lack of grace and the wide-eyed, gaping mouthed expression on his face. She couldn't stop. His glare just made the gales of laughter louder.

Steve's face heated as he picked himself off the ground. He turned away as her laughter infected him. He glanced back at her, the humor finally reaching through his embarrassment, and he chuckled. "Call me grace."

Sarah fell to her knees, holding her stomach. Every now and then, a squeak or a snort of a sound would come out, but for the most part, she was laughing so hard that it was silent.

"It wasn't that funny," Steve said, stepping in her direction.

All she could do was nod. "Your face," she sputtered, wiping the tears from her eyes.

Steve smiled and shrugged. He held his hand out to help her up. "Come on, I'll buy you a coffee."

Sarah's laughter wound down. "Oh, man, I needed that today." She smiled as she took his hand and stood.

"Why's that?"

"Because I met a real prick last night, and he put me in a foul mood." She grinned as they walked in the direction Chris went.

"Mhm," Steve replied. "Perhaps you should kick his ass." He smiled and glanced sideways at her.

"The sidewalk did a good job of that for me."

"Ah." Steve tilted his head, picking up her thoughts—her dirty thoughts. "Sorry about that." Steve said, surveying the landscape and trying not to blush at the innuendos playing behind those tinted glasses.

Sarah shrugged, giving the impression she couldn't care less. "I let you see my case notes. I'd say quid pro quo is in order."

Her audacious comment irked Steve, and he stepped in front of her, blocking her forward progress. "The FBI doesn't do quid pro quo with a renegade city cop."

"It's my case," Sarah snapped. "Stay out of my way."

His expression shifted, his eyes holding a fraction of the fire fueling his rage. He shook his head and pointed at her. "If you get in my way, I'll make sure you're sitting at a desk for the rest of your career."

Sarah's lips pressed together as she glared back at him. "Arrogant son of a bitch." She stepped around him.

Steve stepped in front of her, and on impulse, grabbed her arms and pulled her to him as he glared down at her. Before he could issue another threat, her knee connected with his groin and pain exploded.

Steve slowly lowered to the ground, holding his throbbing balls, and looked up at her in shock. Her thoughts were not centered on hurting him, they were centered on fucking his brains out, so this—this came out of nowhere.

She left him kneeling on the sidewalk, trying to catch his breath.

Hunting Season
Chapter 33

STEVE STUMBLED INTO THE empty apartment twenty minutes later, still in pain. His pride wounded more than his groin, and he was glad Chris wasn't back yet to razz him about this. He knew that would come later, but for now, he headed into the bathroom to clean up, hoping that would dull the tormented ache between his legs.

Under the warm spray, his thoughts turned to Sarah. *Feisty bitch.* He chuckled at the understatement, but feisty or not, she was a smart cookie. She'd come to the same conclusion he had last summer—the connection to Tony Bondino.

Regardless of her deductive reasoning skills, he did not intend to share information with her. Although Chris's continued prodding about sleeping with her didn't seem as far-fetched now as it had the night before. Especially with the very lewd thoughts that had run through her mind in the park.

He shook the thought out of his head and focused back on Kyle. A slow smile found his lips as he thought of the chaos Chris created.

Damn, he wished he could be a fly on the wall to see Kyle's reaction.

He turned off the shower and headed to the bedroom wrapped in one of the plush green towels and flipped open his phone, calling into the hospital. "Dr. Nevins, ICU," he said when the operator picked up. He waited, pacing.

"Hello, this is Dr. Nevins."

"Morning doctor. It's Steve Williams. How's Jenny?"

"Your wife's muscle tone has improved, but there is still no sign of brain activity," he said. "I received the injunction from your lawyer, and I assure you, we will not be following through on the request to remove the feeding tube until the courts resolve the issue."

"Thank you." Steve took a deep breath. "I'll check back tomorrow."

"I have your number. If anything changes, I'll call you."

"Thanks." Steve flipped the phone closed and pulled on a clean pair of jeans. He headed into the living room, stopping at the sight of her.

"You took long enough in the god damn shower," Sarah said with her hands on her hips.

Chris came out of the kitchen, handing Sarah a glass of water. "She followed you home." He walked past Steve. *Get rid of her.*

Steve caught Chris's thought as he walked by and turned his attention back to Sarah. "I'm not sharing information with you."

Sarah tried not to stare, but to Steve's amusement, she couldn't help it.

He almost chuckled at the rosy hue of her cheeks and the fact she couldn't concentrate enough to form words. Steve approached her. "Cat got your tongue?" He cocked his head and stopped a few paces away, playing on her attraction.

She blinked and shook her head. "No, I just, um." She stumbled on the words.

The edges of Steve's lips curled upward. He raised an eyebrow. "You um, what?"

"I don't want you messing with my case," she spit the words out and stood a little straighter, getting her mind out of the gutter and projecting the tough bitch of a cop image she wanted him to believe.

The trace of a smile disappeared, and with it, any humor that had surfaced and he stepped closer. "It's not your case," he warned.

She stepped away. "I've been working on this case for three years and lost my sister in the process," she snapped. "I'm close to catching the son of a bitch."

Steve laughed. "Do you know how long it took me to figure out who Kyle was and his connection to Bondinos?" He stepped closer, cornering her. "Six months," he growled. "I even found where he lived and paid a visit. And I've seen his face." His voice shook with the anger throbbing in his veins.

"He killed my sister." She placed her hands on his abdomen, trying to push him away, but he was as solid and unyielding as a brick wall.

"He killed everyone who ever mattered to me." Steve trumped her loss in spades. The ring of his cell phone interrupted the escalating hostilities. He dug into his pocket and put it to his ear.

"New York," Kyle's voice taunted.

Heat enveloped his face, turning his anger into a boiling rage. "Yeah, come find me, you son of a bitch," he growled, keeping eye contact with Sarah. He ended the call and held it up for her to see. "And the fucker seems to think it's funny to taunt me." He turned and stormed out to the veranda, throwing the phone on the couch as he passed.

He paced back and forth in the morning sun, trying to get a handle on the fury. Spinning on his heels, he walked back into the apartment. "That bastard is mine," he said through clenched teeth. "And if you get in my way, I'll run you over." He turned and continued his pacing, muttering under his breath.

The click of the front door stopped his mad pacing, and he shot to the door, whipping it open. "I'm sorry," he said.

Sarah turned toward his voice. "If you kill him, I'll throw you in jail." She stepped into the waiting elevator.

Steve bolted, shooting his hand between the closing doors, triggering the sensors that opened them back up. "He blew up my month-old daughter."

The hard lines in her face softened. "Still, if you kill him without provocation..."

"If I find him..." Steve began and looked down, leaning on the elevator door. He closed his eyes, shaking his head slowly. "If I find him, I don't know what I'll do." He looked back at her.

Steve stepped away from the elevator, watching the doors close on her questioning eyes. He sighed and let the small smile find his lips as he stepped back into the apartment. "It really isn't fair to know what others are thinking," he said as Chris came back into the living room.

Chris shrugged. "You drive that cop insane." He chuckled as he slid behind the computers.

"He called." Steve switched gears on Chris, wandering to the balcony, taking a seat in one of the lounge chairs. He didn't want to discuss Sarah Connelly.

Hunting Season
Chapter 34

STEVE SWORE UNDER HIS breath as he looked out over the city. Both the morning incident with Sarah and the call irked him. He couldn't concentrate. His mind kept alternating between Kyle, Jennifer, Sarah, and the injustice of allowing the man inside to walk free. His promise to Eric weighed on his conscience and Chris's clickety-clack on the keyboard was driving him crazy. He stood up and wandered in.

"No, I don't have anything yet." Chris glanced up at Steve for a fraction of a second.

Steve scoffed.

"Go fuck that girl and get it over with." Chris leaned back and stretched.

"Crude son of a bitch," Steve muttered.

Chris shrugged. "Then stop thinking about it."

"Fuck you," Steve said.

"Please, just go out for a little while," Chris sighed. "Your bouncing thoughts are distracting. And I'm not going to jail when this is all over." He leveled his gaze at Steve.

Steve sighed, keeping eye contact. He nodded and headed out, flagging a cab, spouting out her address as he settled in the seat.

When the cab pulled into the driveway of the brownstone in Brooklyn, the curtain moved aside in the upstairs window. Steve formed a rim with his hand as he glanced up, squinting from the sun. He paid the cab driver and approached the house.

The door opened as he went to knock.

"What are you doing here?" she asked, wrapped in a terry bathrobe with dripping hair.

Steve pulled off his sunglasses. "I was a little harsh this morning." He studied her toenails before he raised his eyes, taking in the milky white legs, scanning her until his eyes reached hers. A hunger there made his lips curl into a smile. "Can I come in?"

Sarah hesitated. "I'm not sure that's such a good idea." She scanned him quickly before her eyes returned to his. She clutched the front of her bathrobe.

Steve looked up at the building and back down into her eyes. He knew she wanted him to come in, but he didn't trust her thoughts. The last time he acted on them, she kneed him in the balls. "Okay." He turned away.

"Wait." Sarah sighed as she stepped aside, waving him in the house again.

When the door closed, he was already standing in the living room. He turned toward Sarah, not really understanding why he had come. "My wife," he started, "she's been in a coma for almost a year." He dug his hands into his pockets and glanced around the room.

"Please, sit," Sarah said, still clutching the bathrobe closed.

Steve took a seat in one of the wing-backed chairs and studied his fingernails. "I, uh." He stopped and closed his eyes. When he opened them, Sarah was standing in front of him, and her hands had dropped to her sides, letting the bathrobe slide open. His eyes scanned her skin and then returned his gaze to her face. He shook his head. "I'm..."

"How long has it been?" Her voice was soft, and she made no move to cover herself.

Steve's eyes wandered again, and he forced them to focus on his hands. "Over a year."

Sarah reached down, took his hand, and moved it to the curve of her hip.

Her silky skin met his fingertips, and he took a deep breath. "Is this what you really want?" he asked, looking up into her fawn-colored eyes.

She nodded.

"I don't want to put you in the line of fire."

Sarah tilted her head. "What line of fire?"

"Kyle's." Steve pulled his hand away from her skin and leaned back in the chair. His need fueled his fear. He didn't want to have any weaknesses when he faced Kyle, and she was fast becoming just that, a weakness.

Sarah smiled. "I'm a cop," she said. "Being in the line of fire doesn't scare me."

Steve let out a small laugh. "He killed my partner at Quantico and grabbed my boss near a crime scene. You should be scared. Being associated with me..." He trailed off and studied the patterns on her carpet. "Being associated with me is a death sentence."

Sarah took a step closer. "I'll be just fine." The words were soft and sultry; the bitchy cop had disappeared again. "I want you," she added as his gaze found hers.

Steve tilted his head, drawing a deep breath. "I'm married."

With that, Sarah stepped back and pulled her robe together. "Then why are you here?" The bitchy cop was back as she slumped onto the corner of the couch, curling her legs underneath her.

Steve shrugged. "You know, I really don't know." He stood to leave.

Sarah audibly sighed. "Sit down." The words came out with her exhale.

Steve hesitated and then sat back in the chair. "I guess I needed someone to talk to." He admitted, running his hand through his thick, dark hair. "My wife is clinically brain dead."

Sarah offered him a shrug.

"I don't know if she'll ever recover." He tilted his head a fraction and offered Sarah a wisp of a smile before looking away. "I should go." He went to stand, and Sarah moved like a cat, blocking his path and pulling him to her lips.

A hint of cinnamon permeated his mouth as her tongue swept across his teeth. He gave in, inviting the kiss as he wrapped his arms around her waist. Her fingers ran down his chest, unbuttoning his shirt as they went. She found the clasp on his belt and his hand stopped her.

Pushing her away, Steve drew in a deep breath. "I fucked up once before and I'd rather not have to lie to my wife if she regains consciousness." He scanned her again. "You're a beautiful woman and while I'd love to..." He licked his lips and closed his eyes. "I can't, not while she's still alive."

Her eyes narrowed, and a crease appeared between her eyes. "What?"

Buttoning up his shirt, he headed toward the door. "I'm sorry. I didn't mean to..." He waved toward the living room and turned away, reaching for the door handle.

"Don't leave."

Steve hesitated at the sound of her soft and soothing voice. When he glanced back at her, his stomach clenched at the pleading in her eyes.

"I have to, because if I stay, I'll do something both of us will regret."

He walked out of the house and turned in the direction the cab had come, not really knowing where he was heading. Coming upon a subway station, he headed uptown and got off at the Brooklyn Bridge and grab a bite at the Seaport. Turning his mind away from Sarah, he watched the ferries come and go and mulled over what he would do with Chris. He couldn't let the man just walk free, could he?

He drained the beer and pulled out the cash for the meal, heading uptown, opting to walk instead of taking the subway. His mind worked overtime during the slow progression, blocking the thoughts of the pedestrians. The promise to Eric clouded his judgment, overshadowing what he knew was wrong. He stopped in front of the building, looking up at the posh apartment complex lining the park.

Sighing, he stepped inside with no actual answer.

Hunting Season
Chapter 35

CHRIS PICKED UP THE phone and placed a call home after he finished cleaning up the accounts and doing a little more research online.

"Hey, babe, are the kids at school?" he asked.

"You know they are," Jessica said.

The transition took a couple of seconds, and he crossed the room, taking her in his arms. "I missed you last night." Chris planted a kiss on her lips, tasting her usual afternoon citrus smoothie. "You were sleeping peacefully when I popped in."

"I hated going to sleep without you here, and waking up was worse. How long are you going to be down there?"

Chris raised his eyebrows. "Are you whining?"

Jessica glanced up into his eyes. "A little." Her lips curved into a smile, and he ran his hands down her still sculpted back.

Her warmth radiated through the silk shirt, and he grinned. His gaze traveled to the bed and back in a quick, suggestive flicker.

She leaned up and kissed him, scraping her teeth along his lower lip in a way that drove him wild.

"Chris?" The familiar voice broke through his trance.

His smile disappeared, and he blinked. Chris looked across his living room at Steve, annoyed at the interruption.

WHEN HE WALKED INTO the apartment, Chris was still sitting at the computer with the phone to his ear, just staring into space, his eyes half closed and his face in frozen animation. The glazed look reminded him of Jennifer when she had her visions. "Chris?"

The animation returned to his face, and Chris glowered at Steve. "I have to go, babe," he said into the receiver. "I love you." He hit the button to end the call. "Don't you fucking knock?" He stood and retreated into the kitchen.

Steve stared after him, not understanding what set off his host. He heard the refrigerator bang shut and a tink on the floor that he assumed was a bottle top. He pushed the kitchen door open. Chris drained a beer.

He glared over the bottle at Steve.

"What'd I do?" Steve asked.

Chris pulled the empty bottle away from his lips and let out a hefty burp. "You came back earlier than I expected," he answered, turning and slamming the bottle on the counter. "I was having a moment with my wife." He pulled out another beer and popped the cap off.

Steve's eyebrows scrunched to the point they almost touched, and he tilted his head. "Huh?"

Chris dipped his head to the side without losing eye contact, conveying his meaning silently.

Steve's eyes went wide. "Projecting?" He stepped back. "Wow." He took another step away, filtering through the memories Eric had downloaded into his mind. "Shit, that's real?" He blinked and let a laugh escape. "Sorry man." He turned and walked out onto the balcony, not knowing what else to say.

Chris followed and handed him a beer as he took the lounge chair next to Steve. "You should have seen my face the first time I did it," he said with a sigh. "I transitioned from New York to California and caught Jessica when she fainted." Shaking his head at the memory, he tipped the beer to his lips.

"Do you have any clue how bizarre this all is?"

He laughed and nodded. "Yes. I actually had to explain it to my lawyer once and saying it all out loud sounds certifiable." He tipped his beer in Steve's direction. "A lot like explaining all the shit that lead up to seeing that monster in Black Cove."

Steve allowed a smile and a shrug. "Bleeding notebooks, off the wall hazing rituals and a monster." He laughed, clicking the neck of his bottle to Chris's.

"Don't forget your wife's visions."

Steve's smile evaporated, and he stood up, crossing to the balcony wall. He surveyed the cityscape before he turned, thinking about his encounter with Sarah. Guilt bit him.

Chris raised his eyebrows. "You screwed the cop?"

Steve shook his head and turned back to the cityscape.

Chris took a sip of beer, debating on whether to razz Steve or just let it be. He sighed. He would have done the same if the tables were reversed.

Silence overtook the balcony.

"Jenny's the reason I pegged Kyle so quickly." Steve broke the silence after a few minutes.

"She wasn't with you when you figured out who I was. Fifteen years and no one else came close." He took a sip of beer and pointed at Steve. "You have moments of brilliance." One side of his mouth curled up as he took another sip of beer.

"And moments of idiocy."

Beer spewed from Chris's mouth, the laughter catching—sending liquid down the wrong pipe and his cough sputtered until he forced his airway clear and released a colossal burp. "Don't we all?"

Steve grinned and raised his beer. He was beginning to really like this man.

Chris got up, wiping the front of his shirt with his hand. He drained the beer. "I've got to run out for a bit. When I get back, I'll take you to Uncle Jack's for a steak."

"Uncle Jack's?"

"Best steakhouse in the city." Chris smiled.

"You trying to bribe a federal officer?"

Chris laughed. "Absolutely!"

Steve watched him leave and shook his head. Chris Ryan was definitely a character.

Hunting Season
Chapter 36

CHRIS WALKED INTO HIS lawyer's office, extending his hand as Lynn Trueman stood behind the desk.

"To what do I owe the pleasure?" Lynn smiled at her client.

"I need to do some updates to my will, and I need to set up a trust fund." He sat down and rattled off the instructions for both the trust fund and the will.

"Are you sure?" Lynn asked before she began typing up the addendum.

"Yes, I'm sure." Chris waited while Lynn drafted up the addendum and trust documents. He gave her the bank account number that Kyle's ten million had been siphoned to and made the call to transfer some funds of his own. He signed the paperwork and handed over an envelope. "This is to be delivered to Mr. Williams with the amount discussed if something should happen to me."

Lynn took the envelope and stared up at Chris as he stood. "Are you in trouble?" she asked as she gazed at the signed documents and the new instructions in front of her.

Chris smiled and shook his head. "No, this kid is very special to the family, and I want him taken care of."

Nodding, Lynn took the documents and filed them in her briefcase to bring to court for submission in the morning. "How's the family?" she asked as she stood up and came around from behind the desk.

"Getting along." Chris answered. Lynn had been at Eric's funeral. "Steve was Eric's partner." He put his hands in his pockets and looked down at his mousy lawyer.

Lynn nodded. "I remember him from the funeral." She cocked her head. "Nice looking." The blush crept into her cheeks as she smiled up at Chris.

"I suppose." Chris took a deep breath. His affairs were now in order. "Thanks for fitting me in at the last minute," he added and opened the door.

"Anytime." She smiled.

Chris walked out with one less thing on his mind. Jessica would eventually understand, and so would his kids.

Hunting Season
Chapter 37

STEVE WAS STILL LOUNGING on the balcony when Chris arrived back at the apartment. He checked the computer programs and smiled.

The transfer failed today and with it came the money trail. He joined Steve on the balcony after a few inquiry searches panned out. Stretching on the lounge chair, he put his hands behind his head and grinned at Steve. "I got a name."

Steve sat up, staring at him with wide eyes, waiting.

"And I know where the money is going."

"What's the name?" Steve asked, his voice a low, gruff growl.

"John Sheridan."

Steve settled back in the seat. "Where is he?"

"I'm working on that, but first I'm draining all his accounts through the same channel."

"Can you max his credit cards, too?"

"Sure."

Steve shot a glance in his direction. "Really?"

Chris nodded. "Just as soon as I get the social security number that he's using." He stood up and retreated into the apartment, checking on the progress of his programs.

Satisfied, he crossed to the balcony door. "I'm ready whenever you are."

Hunting Season
Chapter 38

UNCLE JACK'S WAS CROWDED for a weeknight, so they opted to grab a seat in the bar. The second of a three-game series between the Red Sox and Yankees was on the monitor above the bar. They exchanged a glance.

"You root out loud and I won't pick up the tab," Chris warned.

"Go Red Sox." Steve grinned as the first beer slid across the bar top.

"You are just as much of a pain in the ass as Eric was," he muttered.

"Why, thank you." Steve raised his beer.

"That wasn't a compliment, shithead." Chris glanced at the monitor. Boston was ahead by three in the sixth inning. *God damn it, now I'll never hear the end of it!*

Steve chuckled, hearing Chris's thought process. "Yeah, yeah." He took a sip of beer and returned his gaze to the television.

Chris lowered his head when the Yankees had bases loaded and two outs. The count was two strikes and one ball. "Home run," he whispered as the pitcher drew back. He closed his eyes and sent a pulse, and his eyes flew open at the crack of the bat. The ball sailed out of the park and the Yankees were now ahead by one.

"That's cheating." Steve glared at Chris.

Chris shrugged. *I didn't want to hear your smug comments all night.* He directed the thought to Steve and sipped his beer around the grin on his face. He put the beer down and the room tilted. "Whoa," he said, gripping the edge of the bar.

Steve glanced in his direction, grabbing Chris's arm as he swayed in the seat.

Chris shook the fog out of his head. He didn't pass out this time, but the wave of dizziness threw him off balance. "Shit." He glanced at his reflection. A small tear escaped the corner of his eye, tracking a hot path down the side of his nose, and he reached for a napkin to wipe it off.

"Are you okay?" Steve's concern was genuine, and Chris stared at the smear of blood on the napkin.

Chris nodded. "I will be," he said, without looking at Steve. "Just give me a second." He took a deep breath and glanced at Steve, cloaking his thoughts and wondering whether it would be Steve or a stroke that killed him. "I'm just hungry," he said, although he was still a little unsteady.

The bartender returned with their food. Both plates had a T-bone steak with sides of baked potatoes and green beans.

The Yankees pulled out the win as they finished their meals.

"You should have that checked," Steve said as they strolled from mid-town toward the apartment building.

Chris pressed his lips together before he shook his head. "I'll be fine," he said, even though the restaurant bathroom mirror had said otherwise. He knew the corner of his right eye was blood red, like he had popped a vessel.

"You don't look fine," Steve said, and his thoughts echoed the fact that Chris still hadn't gotten all the color back in his face.

"All I need is a decent night's sleep," Chris mumbled.

"Getting old, there?"

Chris allowed the edges of his lips to curl into a smile at the dig. What he really needed was another fifteen years with Jessica. "I just have a few more things to do on the computer tonight."

Steve nodded. He wanted to know where Kyle was, too.

Hunting Season
Chapter 39

SARAH SAT AT THE computer looking at Steven Williams' dossier, her eyes wide with wonder as she scanned report after report of his heroics.

"Jesus," she whispered as the pictures from the college fraternity case came up. The sinkhole in the woods filled with the dead in various stages of decay. She flipped to the next shot in the FBI report and was equally appalled. It was the inside of a crypt and the number of used condoms by the stone altar told more of a story than the police report did. The pentagram on the floor had smeared bloodstains as well. She flipped to the next shot and actually gasped. It was a picture of Steve on the lawn passed out over a woman. His back was in shreds and the notes said he had walked for over a mile carrying the woman and nearly died from loss of blood.

She flipped to the next file, reading the entire report that accounted for his daughter's death. His actions caused the killer to trigger the bomb. His shot missed.

Sarah sat back, wondering if the shot hadn't missed. Would his family be alive? The crime scene photographs attached showed Steve holding his wife, his face bloody and cut, a bone jutting out of his arm and his ankle twisted almost backwards. His wife lay in his arms with a piece of metal sticking out of her abdomen. The report said her head was bleeding, but with all the blood covering both of them, she couldn't tell.

Her glance moved back to Steve's devastated face and his single blue eye staring at the camera. Sarah leaned back, staring at the photograph. Two things occurred to her; Steve Williams was an extraordinary man, and he had no trace of scars on his body from either ordeal.

Click.

"Oh, my God." She saved the bookmark to his file.

She sifted through the police archives and pulled up the file for Chris Ryan and his family's ordeal in the city five years ago, scanning through the report until she found what she was looking for. The video showed him being whipped. She looked at the counter and opened the video, finding the particular spot and pressing play. She watched the video, cringing with each crack of the whip. She fast-forwarded to where his attacker sprayed mace in his eyes, blinding him. She froze the frame and zoomed in on his face, seeing evidence of a chemical burn around his eyes. She pressed play, stopping the tape as he turned his back to the camera. Again, she zoomed in. Smeared blood, but she could not make out a single cut. She went frame by frame until she got a side view of his face again. "Jesus." She whispered. The chemical burns were gone.

Sarah flipped back to the picture of Steve, feeling like she was missing something.

She flipped back to the video of Chris, opening the report again, this time reading it all. When she was done, she looked back at the video in awe. The report said he was brought into the hospital with a twelve-inch butcher knife embedded in his back roughly an hour and a half before he showed up on the scene at the warehouse. "That's got to be wrong."

Sliding the chair back, she stood and stretched, glancing at her watch. Sarah picked up the phone. "I need a couple of days off," she said to the sergeant. "It's personal," she added when she heard his breath suck in. The case she'd been on had gone cold and all she was doing lately was desk work.

Sarah packed a bag and flipped open her checkbook, sighing at the meager balance. She flipped the checkbook closed and headed out, climbing into her car and heading north. Five hours and several phone calls later, she pulled into Brooksfield Mental Hospital and was met at the door by Dr. Montgomery.

"Thank you for taking the time to talk to me," Sarah said as she flipped her badge open, handing it to him.

Dr. Montgomery took the badge, studied it, and handed it back as they entered his office. "What can I do for you, Detective Connelly?"

"I'm investigating a murder and I believe the FBI agent whom I read about a few months ago was attacked by the same man. Is there any way I could speak with him?" she asked.

Dr. Montgomery's eyebrows creased.
"Steve Williams?"

"He was never a patient here." Dr. Montgomery answered.

"Oh." Sarah blinked and glanced at her notebook. "Can you tell me where I can find him?" She looked back up at the doctor with a sweet smile.

"I believe he's probably finishing up at Quantico by now."

Sarah raised her eyebrows. "Quantico?"

"He was required to go through training again," he clarified.

"Ah." She flipped open her notes, scribbling a couple of sentences, and closed the notebook. "Just a few more questions and I'll get out of your hair. Do you know if Agent Williams had plastic surgery while under your care?" she asked, looking up at Dr. Montgomery.

A line appeared between Dr. Montgomery's eyebrows, and he shook his head slowly. "No." He answered.

"Then am I to assume Agent Williams has distinctive scars?" she probed.

Dr. Montgomery nodded.

"Can you elaborate?"

Dr. Montgomery took a deep breath. "I'm not at liberty to say, Detective."

Sarah smiled. "Well, thank you for your time." She flipped the notebook closed and stood, offering the doctor her extended hand.

Dr. Montgomery grasped her hand as he stood.

"I can find my way out." Sarah smiled and walked out of his office.

Hunting Season
Chapter 40

SARAH SAT IN HER car looking at the cemetery. She took note of the mausoleum and refocused on Samantha Williams' grave. She stepped out of the car and approached it tentatively, sighing as she read the dates on the gravestone.

"Are you a friend of Steve's?" The voice made her jump. She turned and took in a gentleman wearing a pair of shorts and a tee shirt.

"A friend of the family," she said. "You?"

The man nodded. "Harry Wagner." He stuck his hand out.

"Sarah Connelly," she replied. "Where do you know Steve from?" Her eyes narrowed.

Harry shuffled his feet and looked around. He finally looked back at her. "He was on the case that caught my daughter's killer."

Sarah glanced back at the grave. "Was Steve really as bad off as they say?" She shot him a sideways gaze.

Harry snorted. "Yes. He was."

She turned toward him. "How bad?"

Harry sighed. "Bad, but the last time I saw him, he looked pretty good. The transplant was impressive."

Sarah tilted her head.

"Cornea transplant. He lost his eye last summer." Harry shivered.

"Ah." Sarah looked at the grave and then back at Harry. "It was nice to meet you."

"You, too. Give my best to Steve when you see him," Harry said.

Sarah smiled and nodded, watching Harry turn and head in the opposite direction. She sighed and gave the gravestone a last look before heading back to her car.

Sarah sat behind the wheel and punched the address in the navigation system. She pulled out, following the instructions, and found the driveway almost hidden by the overgrown brush. Slowly, she navigated the twisting driveway until she pulled into the open gravel path that led to the charming lake cottage.

"This is beautiful." She looked out at the lake and the mountains beyond, stepping out of her car. She focused back on the cottage, approaching and trying the door. It was locked.

Sarah wandered around to the front bay window and peered inside. The living room was void of furniture. She stepped back, glancing around, and her eyes landed on the path leading into the woods. Crossing the lawn, she hesitated at the opening of the path that wound out of sight. Sarah reached her toe out and tentatively stepped onto the leaf-lined path, following the trodden soil to the lush green barrier of moss that swept over the forest floor by the inlet of water.

The beauty of the cove struck Sarah as something you would see in those horrible fairy tales where everything was too good to be true. It was lush and vibrant, and the water reflected the trees and clouds beyond like a perfect mirror. She stepped to the edge of the water and squatted, dipped her fingers in, and created a ripple effect in the mirror. The water was cool to the touch and for an instant, she could see the minnows scatter before the surface cleared, falling back to the reflection of the sky.

Standing, she glanced around again, taking notice of a small stream that cut through the edge of the moss and headed deeper into the woods. Sarah paused, studying the thick brush and decided against following the stream. She turned and headed back toward the cottage.

Sarah stepped onto the grass and turned to the gazebo at the edge of the water, sitting on the wooden swing and studying the cottage. The slow creak of the swing grated on her nerves, and she stopped its lazy progress by planting her feet on the floorboards. With a last look at the peaceful setting, she got up, crossed to her car, and got in without further lament.

"Why don't you have any scars?" she whispered as the sunset danced on the lake and she turned her car around.

Hunting Season
Chapter 41

STEVE PACED THE APARTMENT floor as Chris typed commands into the computer. "Where is he?"

Chris glared up at Steve. "Chill," he replied. He knew the general area where John Sheridan was, but nothing specific. "I've finished moving the money." He stretched his arms in the air. "Including wiping out the trail."

"That took long enough."

"I also maxed all the cards in his name." Chris stood, stretching the remainder of his body. His back throbbed from hunching over the computer.

"So, where is he?"

"In Connecticut, but I haven't been able to get much outside of a few post office boxes throughout Fairfield county. The residential address he gave is bogus and I haven't been able to find his cell number," he reported. "On the upside, he only has a couple of hundred dollars to his name and no back up credit." Chris smiled. "I've planted a virus on his computer and once it's triggered, his computer will be just a piece of expensive shit."

Steve raised his eyebrows. "Really?"

Chris nodded. "With toilet sound effects and all." Chris ignored the chuckling and took a seat again, typing commands into his computer.

Hunting Season
Chapter 42

“WHAT DO YOU MEAN the money’s gone?” Kyle yelled into the phone. “Where the fuck did it go?”

“I, um, I’ll have to run a check on that for you, Mr. Sheridan.” The branch manager stuttered banging on the keyboard as fast as he could. His client’s ten-million-dollar corporate account was now registering a meager one hundred dollars.

“I want an answer NOW!” Kyle barked.

“The system shows that you authorized the transfer to an account held in Las Vegas, sir.” He repeated the information displayed on the screen.

Kyle was quiet. “Las Vegas?” he asked.

“Yes sir. Would you like me to report this to Interpol?”

Kyle sighed. “No. I’m sorry.” He shuffled papers, so it sounded like he was looking for something. “I thought the transfer was scheduled for next month. I opened the subsidiary account in Nevada and was transferring the business state side,” he said, covering his tracks. He would get his money back, or his boss would wear a wide gap across his throat. "Did you already request the reversal?"

"Yes, sir, unfortunately the request came back denied. It looks as if that account is closed."

"Can you give me the bank and account number the transfer went to?" Kyle asked. "As well as the name, so I can check my records for verification of the account number I have?"

"Yes sir. Nevada National Bank, account number 986455623. The name on the account is Bondino Enterprises, LLC."

"Thank you, that is what I was expecting," Kyle said. "I apologize for my reaction. As I said, I wasn't expecting the transfer until next month. Have a nice day." Kyle added and hung up the phone. He paced the length of the apartment, looking out over Long Island Sound as he got a grip on his anger. He flipped open his laptop and connected to the internet looking for flights to Las Vegas. He found one for a reasonable rate and plugged in his credit card.

"Order denied? What the fuck?" He plugged in the card number again, receiving the same results. He tried a second card with the same results, and a third. He stood, letting a guttural cry of anger peel from his throat. "I am going to kill that bastard!" He screamed at the empty room.

Kyle picked up the phone and dialed his boss. "I need to speak to Tony," he said to the child that answered. He heard the shuffle as the phone was handed off.

"Tony here."

"What did you do?" Kyle growled.

"Kyle?" Tony asked.

"Yes. What did you do with all my money?" Kyle repeated.

"What the fuck are you talking about?" Tony said.

"Every dime went into your Nevada National Bondino Enterprises, LLC account. And then it was all moved out," Kyle explained. "And all my credit cards are being denied. What did you do?"

"Nothing." Tony answered. "I have no idea what you're talking about."

"You're leaving me out to dry?" Kyle asked.

"I got you out of lockup. Why would I fuck with you like this?" Tony replied.

Kyle looked at the computer and back out the window as he thought about the question. He had enough to bring Tony Bondino to his knees, but the reverse was true as well. "If I find out you had anything to do with this, Tony, you are a dead man." He hung up the phone, leaving his boss sweating halfway across the country.

Kyle sat down at his computer and ran the spyware program he had installed. Watching as it detected the normal items. He opted to delete each one manually and when he came across one he didn't recognize; he skipped it, letting the computer continue to detect and request actions. An hour later, he had two programs that were installed that he didn't delete. One was a monitoring program. When he requested more information, his screen went blank.

"Fuck." Kyle swore. He pressed the escape button, and the screen started swirling in a water pattern. He recognized the sound that went with the video. It was a toilet, and his computer was crashing. Everything was being sucked down the drain. The word that appeared on his screen made his blood boil. BUSTED!

Kyle slammed the escape button again and the entire computer died. He heaved it across the room and paced, going over who could have done this to him. He looked at the computer again. "No fucking way," he whispered.

Hunting Season
Chapter 43

SARAH PULLED INTO BROOKSFIELD Hospital and parked her car. She flipped open her notebook and glanced at the notes she made before heading inside.

The ICU department was quiet. The guard outside Jennifer Williams' door requested to see her badge, and she had to wait as he requested a verification of her identification.

"All set Detective Connelly." Agent Bartholomew Shays handed the badge back to Sarah and waved her into the room.

Sarah entered, finding Steve's unconscious wife in the bed, hooked up to monitors and intravenous bags. Her chest rose and fell in consistent intervals, the beep of the heart monitor steady as well. Her color was high, and she didn't look the least bit atrophied like a comatose patient should after close to a year.

"Huh?" Sarah huffed as she crossed to the bed. Jennifer Williams was stunning, and Sarah sighed. "So, you're the reason he wouldn't sleep with me."

A beep sounded on the brainwave monitor as Sarah spoke.

Sarah shook her head. "It figures." She glanced around the room once more and then headed out. She had to find a hotel. It had been a long day, and she had more to look into in the morning.

Hunting Season
Chapter 44

CHRIS WATCHED THE UPLOAD of data as his Trojan horse was activated by the spyware program on Kyle's machine. He actually chuckled before he took a sip of his morning coffee, thinking of the reaction of his adversary.

Steve was out for his morning jog when the discarded cell phone rang. Chris walked over to the couch and picked it up, flipping it open.

"I want my money," Kyle seethed.

"You aren't going to get it," Chris answered, knowing full well who was on the phone and that his means of tracing the call had been destroyed with the computer.

"Who the fuck is this?" Kyle demanded.

"Your worst fucking nightmare," Chris laughed at the confusion and frustration coming through the phone line, feeling a level of glee he hadn't experienced in years.

"Where is Steve Williams?" Kyle asked.

"Out," Chris answered.

Silence on the phone.

"Your tracer is disabled now," Chris answered cheerfully.

"Fucking FBI."

"No. I'm not with the FBI. I'm freelancing."

Kyle met this reply with silence. "I am going to rain a world of hurt on you."

Chris chuckled into the phone. He was enjoying this a bit too much. "I've dealt with your kind before," he said.

"My kind?" Kyle asked.

"Twisted, psychopathic serial killer assassins," Chris summed it up. "Kyle." He smiled. "Or should I be calling you John right now?"

Kyle didn't speak.

Chris smiled at the shock filtering through the line. "I'm coming after you," he said.

"Who are you?" Kyle whispered, his voice carrying the first thread of fear.

"Ty Aris." Chris hung up the phone.

Hunting Season
Chapter 45

KYLE LOOKED AT THE phone. The name meant nothing to him, but that would soon be eradicated as he headed out of his apartment to the local library.

Kyle sat down at the computer bank and Googled Ty Aris. What came back made him break out in goose bumps. The guy was a serial killer all right, but according to the story, he went out with a bang.

His body was never found and if the voice on the phone was indeed Ty Aris, Kyle was in trouble. The guy had been a member of Mensa, a technological genius and a psychopath, the likes of which the state of New York hadn't seen in years.

He combed through all the stories, reading the details and wishing he had access to more than what was available in the public archives. The only piece of information he had that he could use was that Ty's brother was still alive.

He Googled Christopher Aris and his eyes nearly popped out of his head. This guy was a billionaire. He leaned back and took a deep breath, his next steps beginning to formulate.

He continued his research on the billionaire, stumbling over the story of the warehouse that had occurred five years before. His gaze stopped on a name, Eric Connor, Steve's partner at Quantico.

"Jesus." The kid was connected to the voice on the phone.

Kyle leaned back in the chair and then searched on Eric Connor in the news archives. He came up with quite a few articles. He cruised through them, finding one about his mother marrying an actor, the public divorce a few years later and the warehouse incident. The last article was what he was looking for. It was his obituary and gave the information about surviving parents and the towns they lived in.

Kyle smiled and stood up.

Plan B was now in effect, and there was more than one acquisition on his list. He needed funds to carry out his plan, but in the wake of the credit card denials online; he decided on a different direction and headed back to his apartment. He pulled out the transfer instructions, tucked them into his back pocket, and then began rummaging through his drawers. Finally, he found what he was looking for.

Credit card checks.

They took time to clear, and that's exactly what he needed. Kyle wrote out a check and headed to the bank. The teller at the local branch gladly took the check, peeling off the amount as he flirted with her. He whistled as he pulled away from the bank with a pocket full of cash.

The unmarked van with removable ambulance lights was a little more difficult to get, but Kyle called in a list of favors and within a couple of hours, he was heading north. He arrived in Brooksfield at a little after four.

He slipped into the private uniform, donning a fake mustache and a pair of horn-rimmed glasses before he stepped into the hospital, looking for the Administrator's office. He walked in and gave a winning smile to the receptionist.

"Hello, ma'am." He tipped his hat and handed her the bogus transfer request. Jennifer Williams was being moved to Mount Sinai Hospital in Manhattan by request of her husband and a Dr. Horowitz. The receptionist typed commands into the computer and waited. She smiled at Kyle as he waited patiently in the seat. The confirmation beeped on the computer, and she picked up the phone requesting the patient be brought to the emergency bay for transfer.

Kyle returned to the make-shift ambulance, pulling it up to the emergency bay and taking out the gurney. He waited and a few minutes later, an orderly wheeled Jennifer out. He helped transfer her to the waiting gurney along with the IV bags and loaded her into the ambulance, securing the bed so it wouldn't roll during the ride. Kyle nodded and slid into the driver's seat, pulling out moments later.

He held his breath until he crossed the state line, and then the muscles knotting his neck and back relaxed. *One down, one to go.*

Hunting Season
Chapter 46

SARAH PULLED OVER AT a hotel across from the beach in York, Maine. She checked in and fell into the bed, exhausted. Her mind raced, trying to wrap around all she had read and the encounters with the doctor and the man at the gravesite to the point sleep evaded her tired body.

"God damn it," she muttered and threw on a pair of sweats. Pocketing the hotel key, she left the hotel room and crossed the road to the beach. Meandering down the stretch of sand, she watched the waves lick the shore in a steady, soothing pattern. The moon was not quite full, and its reflection shimmered on the surface, periodically broken by a white cap or two.

The dull ache of exhaustion crept into her legs, and she turned to head back. A man sat on the steps leading to the road, taking sips from a steaming cup, and his gaze found hers. Her heart skipped a beat and her palms broke out in a sweat. Something about the way he studied her was unnerving.

He was easy on the eyes. Not like Steve Williams, but enough so that the knot in her stomach eased. Blonde hair, athletic build and a comfortable smile greeted her, and she couldn't help but smile as she climbed the steps.

"Nice night," he said.

"Yes, it is."

"Would you like to join me?" he asked as she stepped onto the stair next to him.

Sarah paused and looked down at him. "I've got a long day tomorrow."

He nodded and looked back out at the ocean.

Sarah took a few more steps and stopped. Her mind was still racing and perhaps some light conversation with a stranger would be helpful. "I guess a few minutes wouldn't kill me." She plopped herself next to him on the steps. "My name's Sarah." She extended her hand.

"John," the man introduced himself. "What brings you to the coast of Maine?"

"Business. You?"

"A mixture of business and pleasure." He smiled and took a sip of coffee. "You from the city?"

Sarah smiled. "Brooklyn, born and raised."

"Ah, I thought I recognized the accent," he replied.

"Where are you from?" She couldn't quite pin down the accent.

"Connecticut. I've never been up this way and figured it might be interesting." He shrugged, looking around. "It certainly isn't nearly as busy as New York." His eyes drifted back to her.

"What do you do?"

He took a sip of coffee. "A little of this, a little of that." He evaded the question. "How about you?"

"I'm a homicide detective." She watched his reaction.

He laughed. "A little thing like you? I don't believe it."

Offended, Sarah said, "I am a good cop."

He put his hand up in an apologetic gesture. "I didn't mean to upset you. It's just you don't look like your average homicide detective."

"What do you mean?"

"You're beautiful." He commented and looked down at his coffee and back. "I just never would have guessed. Sorry if I offended you."

Sarah relaxed a little and nodded.

"Are you on a case?" he asked, looking at her sideways.

Sarah sighed. "Sort of," she said. "I'm looking for answers," she clarified. "And hopefully I'll find them here."

"I hope you do, too." He raised the coffee cup and took the last sip. "Thank you for spending a little time with me." He stood and helped her to her feet. "It was a pleasure meeting you, and perhaps our paths will cross again someday." He smiled and shook her hand.

Sarah watched him cross the street and head to the opposite end of the hotel.

KYLE WALKED AWAY, EACH step a disappointment. His initial thoughts about having fun with her died when she said she was a cop. If he killed her here, there'd be no way he'd be able to get out of town with his next acquisition.

He took a last glance back with an iota of regret because she certainly was a fine piece of ass.

Hunting Season
Chapter 47

CHRIS NEGLETED TO TELL Steve about the phone call. He didn't want Steve to know he was narrowing down the location, either. He knew if Steve got a whiff of where Kyle was; it was over. Both of their souls would be damned.

Steve paced all day, driving him bat shit.

"You have anything yet?" Steve asked again for the millionth time.

Chris glared at him over the computer. "Get out." He pointed at the door.

Steve stopped pacing and his eyebrows rose.

"You are worse than my kids. Just get out, go for a walk, go to the museum, go see that cop, just get the hell out of here and out of my hair for a while." Chris spat the words out from between tight lips. His patience was gone.

"No. I want to know where he is, Ty." Steve pressed, knowing using his real name would provoke a reaction.

Chris leveled his gaze at Steve, sending a silent command for Steve to sit and shut up.

Steve obediently sat on the couch, his eyes wide at first, but anger flowed into them seconds later, aimed straight at Chris.

Chris focused back on his computer, but the edges of his vision slipped to black, and he blinked. The swoon hit him like the full force of a nor'easter barreling in over the Atlantic and he muttered, "Shit."

Darkness descended, pulling him down into the swirl.

THE IRON GRIP RELEASED, and Steve turned his head at the thump. Chris was no longer sitting in the computer chair. He stood, crossing the room, and stared down at Chris, unconscious on the floor.

"Jesus," he whispered at the thin trails of blood leaking from the corners of Chris's eyes. He crouched and pressed his fingers to Chris's neck, breathing a sigh of relief at the strong pulse.

Chris's eyes blinked open, looking up at him in confusion, both eyes now red, like the blood vessels had declared a mutiny.

"You passed out again," Steve said, helping Chris to his feet. He left him for a moment, retreating into the kitchen to grab some paper towels before returning and handing them to Chris. "You really should have that checked out."

Chris grabbed the paper towels out of his hand and wiped his face, muttering under his breath. "Penance sucks," he said

"What'd you say?"

"Nothing." He closed his eyes, suddenly looking every bit of his forty-five years and then some. "I think I'll call it a night." He opened his eyes, raising them to Steve.

Steve glanced at his watch. "It's only eight. You sure you're okay?"

"Yes, I'm fine, and don't worry. I'm not going to die before we find that bastard," Chris snapped. He locked the computer and headed into the bedroom without further word.

Steve watched him, surprised at the outburst. He glanced down the hall and then at the computer, itching to know where Kyle was.

"Don't even think about it."

Steve looked up at Chris standing in the hallway and he pressed his lips together, clamping down on the nasty comment that came to mind.

"Look, I need sleep. Don't fuck with the computer. Let the program run and I'll look at it first thing in the morning," Chris said.

Steve gave the computer a last glance and nodded, settling on the couch for the evening.

CHRIS TURNED, LEAVING STEVE to his own devices. In the bedroom, he picked up the phone and dialed his residence in Maine.

"Hi, Jess," Chris said.

"Hey, sweetheart. You sound tired."

He took a deep breath, cloaking his thoughts. "I am. I found the money trail for Steve. Now we're just waiting for a confirmation of an address." He closed his eyes, falling back on the bed. "I miss you."

"I miss you, too." She whispered. "Can you cross over?"

"I'm way too tired, babe," he said with a sigh. If she saw his eyes, there would be nothing to stop her from coming down to New York and hauling his ass home. "Can I say good night to the kids?"

"Sure."

The shuffle of the phone being handed off filled his world, and then Tommy's voice came through the line. "Daddy, when are you coming home?"

Chris opened his eyes and swallowed the bitter taste of tears. Home. He didn't think he'd ever see home again. "Soon," he lied.

"I miss you," Tommy replied.

"I know. I miss you, too," Chris said. "You be good for your mother."

"I will. I love you, Daddy," Tommy said, and the phone shuffled.

"Hi, Dad," CJ said, with no enthusiasm in his voice. The words sounded so grown up and filled with bitterness, like he knew his father was never coming home.

Chris bit his quivering lip. "Hey," he said when he had control. "Are you being good for your mom?"

Silence met him.

"CJ?" Chris sat up.

"Yes. I'm being good," he answered.

"I miss you, kiddo."

"Then come back," CJ pushed.

Chris hung his head. "I love you, CJ," he explained, "but I can't come home just yet."

A heavy sigh filled the line and after two beats, CJ spoke, his voice softer, more resigned. "I love you, too, Dad. Here's Mom."

"You're blocking me from your thoughts on purpose. What's going on, Chris?" Jessica asked, her voice carrying the weight of her worry.

"I just miss all of you," Chris answered, but his voice cracked, belying the deep sadness that took seed in his gut. "I love you, Jess. Now, I need some sleep."

"I've never heard you this tired."

"Steve's been running me ragged. I've only had a couple of hours of sleep each night and it's getting to me." Chris stretched out on the bed. "I wish you were here with me," he whispered.

"I wish I was too, sweetheart. Get a good night's sleep."

"Mhm." He was already fading. "Love you."

"Love you, too. Good night."

Hunting Season
Chapter 48

CHRIS WOKE A LITTLE before eight the next morning and checked his computer. Bingo, he had an address. He scribbled a note saying nothing had come back from his searches and he was going out to run some errands. Before he took off, he changed the password to something Steve would never figure out and headed out, leaving Steve snoring in the guest room.

He took Interstate 95 into Branford and stopped in front of the address. The street was quiet, and he slipped across the road to the door. With a quick look up and down the street, he turned his attention to the door, willing the lock to unhitch. The telltale click made him smile, and he commanded the door to open, stepping inside without touching the door. Another tilt of his head and the door shut behind him.

Chris stood in the entry with his eyes closed, scanning the apartment and within seconds he knew it was empty, but he didn't trust his intuition with all the hokey stuff going on lately, so he quickly searched room by room, making sure his sixth sense hadn't deserted him completely. He hoped he was wrong. The opportunity to hurt the son of a bitch who killed Eric sent his blood racing, but unfortunately, that would have to wait. Kyle definitely wasn't there.

Chris took a seat and closed his eyes, wishing he was home and felt the transition. His eyes snapped open to his own living room in Maine and he shivered. He'd never transitioned on a wish before. Usually, he had to have some sort of connection with his destination, either a mirror, which always seemed to act as a portal, or on the phone, and he didn't remember a mirror in the living room of the empty apartment. "Damn," he whispered at his empty house.

"Jess?" he called. When no one answered, he sighed. She was probably shopping while the kids were in school. He closed his eyes and felt the magnetic pull yanking his soul back to his body.

He opened his eyes to the strange apartment again, glancing around.

Nope. No mirrors.

"Shit." It was like his powers were short-circuiting, and now they were as unreliable as the outcome of his current situation.

Hunting Season
Chapter 49

SARAH PULLED UP TO the gate and looked at her watch. It was seven forty-five. She rang the buzzer, hoping Mrs. Ryan was awake, especially with two young boys who had to get ready for school.

"Hello?" a woman's voice asked.

"Mrs. Ryan. My name is Sarah Connelly, and I am a detective in the seventeenth precinct in New York. I need to speak with you for a moment, if you wouldn't mind." She waited, and the gate slid open for her to enter. As she pulled up, a woman stepped out of the front door, her face etched with worry.

"What can I do for you?"

Sarah noted that the worry lines smoothed out as she approached, and Mrs. Ryan's gaze shifted from worry to mistrust. "I, uh," she began, formulating the bizarre questions floating through her mind.

Mrs. Ryan gave Sarah the once over, crossing her arms. "What is it you need to discuss?"

Sarah realized she didn't quite know how to ask the questions that plagued her. "It's about your husband."

"Can it wait until my boys are on the bus?" she asked, glancing at her watch. "It should be here in about ten minutes."

"Of course, Mrs. Ryan." Sarah offered a smile she hoped would disarm the woman.

"Please, call me Jessica," The smile obviously worked because Mrs. Ryan waved her into the house.

"Would you like a cup of coffee?"

"That would be great." Sarah smiled.

The two boys finished their breakfast at the table. One eyed her suspiciously and the other boy gave her only a glance before returning his attention to the cereal in front of him.

"Boys, say hello to Detective Connelly. She is a police officer in New York City." Jessica said. "This is CJ and Tommy," she said to Sarah.

"Pleased to meetcha," Tommy said with a mouthful and a nod.

CJ acknowledged her with a nod. He was a spitting image of his father with the hard-blue eyes that made her feel as if he was seeing into her soul.

"My pleasure," Sarah replied and turned her attention to Jessica Ryan, a beautiful woman with thick, dark hair that fell just beyond her shoulder blades and the most intriguing eyes. Her eyes defied characterization. They were a conglomerate of blues, greens, lavenders and grays surrounded by a thin border of brown. Her eyes looked like the sky at sunset. Beautiful and haunting.

Jessica smiled. "What do you take in your coffee?" she asked, crossing to the refrigerator. She grabbed both the creamer and the orange juice, setting them both on the table as the boys got up. "Make sure you have your homework," she called after them, clearing the morning mess. She poured a cup of coffee and set it on the table. "If you will excuse me a moment." She waved toward the boys.

"Of course." Sarah poured the cream into the cup.

JESSICA COLLECTED THE BOYS and walked with them to the open gate as the bus pulled around the corner.

"Mom?" CJ said before the bus pulled up. His gaze traveled to the front door where Sarah stood with her cup of coffee, watching them.

"It'll be fine, CJ." Jessica smiled at her son, kissing both of them on the cheek. "Have a good day. Remember, your grandparents will be here this afternoon when you get home." After the call last night, she had decided to surprise Chris for the weekend.

CJ nodded and climbed the stairs, casting a glance over his shoulder at his mother. Tommy blew a kiss and disappeared into the seat with his brother.

Jessica waved at the driver and watched the bus disappear up the road. She waited until it was out of sight before she turned and headed back toward the house. She was not looking forward to this conversation. The questions swarming in the detective's head were too close to home. She couldn't let this city cop uncover the truth.

Halfway up the driveway, a sudden sting bit at the back of her neck and within a blink, she was on the ground, unable to move. Her body completely shut down, but the panic made her skin burn and she wondered if she had just died.

The sound of the coffee cup smashing on concrete followed by the same 'oof' of another body crumpling to the ground reached her ears and confusion overrode her senses. *What the hell is going on?*

A van backed down the driveway, stopping a few feet from Jessica, and the driver got out. His footsteps crunching the driveway approached her, stepped beyond her, and then she heard the scraping and clinking of porcelain. *The bastard's cleaning up the broken cup? Why can't I move or speak for that matter?*

"We wouldn't want to set off any alarms." The back of the van opened, and the man put the broken cup in the corner. He picked up Jessica's limp body and tossed her into the back.

Jessica stared at the gurney and the almost empty intravenous bag that hung dripping on the floor because it was no longer hooked to the gurney's occupant. The silhouette looked familiar. *Oh, Jesus, that's Steve's wife!*

Outside the van, she heard him speak to the detective.

He chuckled. "Hey, beautiful. My name isn't really John, and I know why you looked so familiar to me." He laughed as he threw her into the van.

Whistling, the man pulled out of the driveway. "We are going to have such fun today." He laughed and turned on the radio, singing off tune to the raunchy rock and roll lyrics.

Four hours later, the van pulled off the smooth highway, stopping and starting until it turned onto uneven pavement, bumping to a stop. Jessica strained to listen, to figure out just where they were, but the busy street traffic and the driver's thoughts kept intruding.

She thought Frank Aris was bad, but compared to this psycho, Frank was a pussycat. This was the man who killed her son, and his plans for the three of them included some pretty sick torture techniques. Jessica prayed for some dexterity before he got them to their destination.

The van doors opened, and he stared, his gaze bouncing between her and the officer lying next to her, and he licked his lips. Grabbing the bag stored under the gurney, he reached inside and pulled out a full syringe.

Jessica flinched, her fear of needles prickling under her numb skin and her mouth went dry. She tried to swallow as he grabbed her arm.

"Hope you don't mind sharing." He stabbed her with the needle, compressing the shot halfway.

It took a couple of blinks before blackness pulled her under.

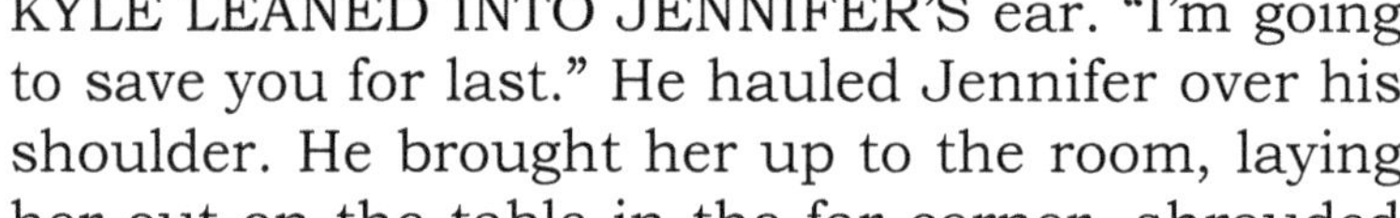

KYLE LEANED INTO JENNIFER'S ear. "I'm going to save you for last." He hauled Jennifer over his shoulder. He brought her up to the room, laying her out on the table in the far corner, shrouded by the shadows, not bothering to bind her in any way.

He strolled over to Sarah, running his hands over her torso before ripping her shirt open, stripping it off. He crouched over her, taking in her athletic and shapely familiar form. A slow smile formed on his lips. "You must be a wild one in bed. Just like your sister was." Her pants came off next, and he picked her up, carrying her to the table in the middle of the room. He stretched her out face down, feeling her skin with his hands. He leaned over and licked her from her shoulder down her back to her ass, where he took a bite, breaking the skin. *Out cold.* Disappointment laced his mouth; he would have preferred some sort of whimper rather than the limp non-reaction. *Later, when I have an audience.*

The thought sent a burst of sexual energy through him as he looked at the large wooden cross hanging from the rafters.

An audience of at least one.

He stood, wiping his mouth before he went about the task of tying her face down with her legs spread wide and her ankles tied to the bottom of the table legs.

Turning, he let his gaze drift over Jessica.

His ten-million-dollar prize.

He crossed to her and wiped the hair out of her face. "You and I are going to get acquainted today," he purred, running his hand under the sweater and finding a silky camisole under the thick cotton. He pulled the sweater off, leaving the silky fabric on her. He ran his hands over her chest; he pushed the fabric up and ripped the bra off, smiling at her full breasts, taking them in his hands and squeezing until his fingernails embedded in her flesh, leaving little red crescent moons behind.

"I am so going to fuck you every way I can until I get my money back," he said to her unconscious form and pulled away. He stripped the jeans and underwear off her and left her in the camisole. He picked her up and slid her into a chair.

From memory, he tied her to the chair in the same way that Aris guy had bound her. Her wrists clamped to the arms and her legs threaded through the sides with her ankles bound to the lower rear rung of the chair. He knew the psychology of the position itself, as well as this place, would breed terror.

⚬══ ══ ══

THE HORRID STENCH OF smelling salts assaulted her senses, and Jessica twisted her head away from the burning smell. Her eyes batted open, and she coughed. When she tried to move her arm, the sensation of rope binding her wrist in place snapped her eyes into focus.

The cop was bound half on and half off a table; her legs spread wide and still unconscious. She couldn't see where he brought Steve's wife, but when her eyes drifted toward the rafters, her heart hit triple time, feeling as if someone had reached in and ripped it out.

The cross. Oh my God, that's the cross.

She knew where they were. Chris had died on that cross five years ago, and her gaze snapped back to her captor's face.

"I thought this was a pretty slick set up." Kyle looked around the room and back at her. "The building's condemned, but I've got this little generator here that will give me all the light and power I need, and this room is pretty well blocked off from any windows and doors. I certainly understand why that woman chose this place." He ran his fingers up the inside of her thigh. "It's a great place for me to take all the time I need with you and your friends."

Jessica struggled against the binds. "You son of a bitch!"

"It took me a little while to figure out just who Ty Aris was and then I ran across the news articles about your husband, and I'll bet he'll pay ten times what your brother-in-law stole from me just to get you back." He pulled his hand away and stood, flipping the phone open.

Hunting Season
Chapter 50

STEVE'S PHONE RANG AS he walked out of the kitchen with a sandwich in his hand. He grabbed the phone and flipped it open without looking at the number. "Williams here."

"What the fuck did you do with my daughter?" Joe swore through the phone line.

Steve cocked his head. "Excuse me?"

"Jenny. She's gone. They said you had her transferred."

Steve's legs gave way, and he sat on the couch. "When?" The question came out in a harsh whisper.

"Don't give me that shit! Where is she?"

"I don't know." Steve swallowed the sudden lump in his throat and turned, looking out over the city.

Joe was silent. "You don't know?" Fear crept into his voice.

"No." Steve answered. The second line beeped, and Steve looked at the caller ID. It was a restricted caller. "I need to take this." He cut off Joe's angry protest.

"You better tell your friend I want my money back or else I'll kill Jessica Ryan," Kyle growled.

Steve froze in place, his eyebrows furrowed, and he clenched his teeth. "What did you do with my wife?"

"I've got Jessica Ryan, and I'm holding her for ransom." Kyle ignored the question.

"What the fuck did you do with my wife?" Steve bellowed. He closed his eyes.

Kyle chuckled.

"Where are you?" Steve concentrated. The image he received could only be from Jessica, and his eyes shot open.

"Somewhere near and dear to Mrs. Ryan's heart. Let me talk to Ty Aris?" Kyle demanded.

"Ty Aris is dead," Steve answered. His mouth went dry, and his heart felt dislodged, like it was bouncing around his chest.

"He answered your phone yesterday," Kyle said, frustration filling his voice.

"Bullshit." He paused. "I know where you are." Steve ended the call and grabbed his gun before he bolted out of the apartment. The elevator took forever, and he moved from foot to foot, unable to contain the impatience while he watched the floor counters descend to the garage. Wasting no time, he hopped into his car and peeled out of the garage.

Hunting Season
Chapter 51

*H*IS VOICE BROKE THROUGH *the darkness and Jennifer shivered, clamping her eyes shut. A frightening thought gripped her and turned her insides to liquid.*

What if all this was a dream and Kyle still had her at the house?

What if she woke with him standing over her with that knife, carving patterns in her skin?

What if her daughter was alive?

The last thought brought her to the brink of breaking the surface, and then his evil chuckle filled her ears.

Jennifer plunged back into the black abyss, welcoming the silent depths.

Hunting Season
Chapter 52

STEVE MADE IT TO the warehouse within twenty minutes and ran inside, stopping and getting his head together before he climbed the stairwell. His heart thundered in his chest and the adrenaline pumped oxygen in and out of his lungs in quick succession as he stood, closing his eyes and counting to ten.

Easy. He told himself and opened his eyes, taking the first step and flipping the safety off his gun. The stairwell was narrow, and the drywall crumbled in some areas, revealing the metal studs underneath. The dust tickled his nose, and he stopped, squashing the urge to sneeze.

He slid into the third-floor hallway, glancing at the gaping hole to his right for a fraction of a second.

A sudden sting bit at his chest and Steve looked down. A dart poked out from his shirt. "Fuck," he uttered, and his body shut down, crumpling to the ground.

Laughter rolled down the hallway.

Kyle turned him over and pulled the tranquilizer dart out of his chest. "Hello, Stevie boy." He grabbed the collar of Steve's shirt and dragged him into the room, dropped him to the ground, and left to retrieve the gun.

Steve couldn't move, staring at the joists of the high ceiling. Helpless, he closed his eyes. *Stupid jackass. You should have called Chris first.*

Where's Chris? Jessica's voice invaded his mind, and he opened his eyes.

I don't know. Where's Jenny?

I'm not sure. I haven't seen her since we arrived.

Kyle came back into the room, closed the door behind him, and pushed a button on the wall.

The large wooden cross lowered to the floor and Steve felt the numbness turn cold at the sight of the stained wood.

Oh, Christ. Steve knew what he had in store. He didn't need to hear Kyle's gleeful thoughts to confirm his intentions. He was going to be crucified today and there wasn't a thing he could do about it.

Kyle stripped Steve's shirt, shoes and socks before dragging him to the cross and balancing him on the thick stud, with his arms laid out on the crossbar. He stepped out of Steve's line of sight, coming back seconds later with a power drill and screws, waving them in front of Steve's face.

"You may not be able to move, but you will feel everything." He smiled and lined the first screw in the middle of Steve's wrist. He pushed the drill into the bit and turned it on, keeping it in line as he pushed the screw through Steve's flesh and bone and deep into the wood.

Steve couldn't react to the crippling pain—the most he could conjure up was a low groan from the wells of his chest. The tranquilizer rendered him helpless. Tears sprouted in the corner of his eyes, blurring his vision and his stomach clenched. The second screw produced the same guttural sound of agony.

Kyle stepped back, grinning down at Steve. "This is much more fun than last summer. You'll die slowly and painfully, while I fuck the life out of the three of them waiting for my ransom money." He pointed behind him and checked Steve's pockets, pulling out the cell phone and slipped it into his pocket before he continued.

Three? Who else is here?

Kyle reached down and pulled off the patch. He stepped back, his eyebrows arching in shock at the sight of a perfectly good eye staring back at him.

Steve was able to make his lips curl a fraction at Kyle's reaction, and he made a point of following Kyle's movements with both his eyes.

"Leave him alone," a female voice with a thick Brooklyn accent said from behind Kyle.

Steve's eyebrows arched despite the tranquilizer. *Sarah?*

"You know Detective Connelly? My, oh my, this is going to be so much more fun than I thought." Kyle placed Steve's right foot on top of his left on the small jut of wood at the base of the cross and lined up the largest screw, pushing it through both Steve's feet with the help of the power drill until the head of the screw touched the top of his foot.

The wrists weren't nearly as bad as the feet, and the room swirled for a moment. Steve blinked to keep conscious, his throat convulsing, threatening to allow the sudden burning acid to erupt from his stomach. "Bastard," the hissing word formed on his lips.

Kyle left his field of vision, and a low hum filled the room. The chains holding the cross moved, and the wood rose slowly off the floor, each jerk sending debilitating pain through Steve. His head lolled, and he had a view of the warehouse floor. Sarah lay face down and naked on the table, her arms and legs spreadeagled. Jessica was tied to a chair, her lower half stripped, and the silk camisole barely covered her.

The cross jerked to a stop close to seven feet above the floor and his vision doubled, then tripled as the burning, brutal pain gripped his arms and shoulders. His head leaned back against the wood, and he closed his eyes.

Please God, please don't let him get away with this.

He opened his eyes, willing them to focus, and lowered his glance. His heart stopped for a moment. Jennifer was there in the far corner of the room, still wearing the hospital gown. He hitched his breath in and the power of the bellow that came from his chest filled the room. "Son of a bitch!"

Kyle laughed and walked over to the table where Jennifer was. "Transfer orders signed by you." He smiled, waving the bogus forms at Steve. "I'm saving her for last." He ran his hand over Jennifer's body, sliding it under the hospital gown between her legs, chuckling.

"I am going to kill you." Steve's head lolled on his neck, and tears spilled from his eyelashes.

Kyle pointed to the screen he had hung on the opposite wall and pressed a button. "I've been fucking your wife for months, and I figure you can watch my adventures over and over until you die."

Jennifer's hospital room filled the screen and Steve roared, finding the strength to struggle against the metal holding him to the wood. The momentary rush fizzled and his body sagged. Again, a prisoner of the tranquilizer Kyle shot him with.

On the display, his greatest enemy violated Jennifer's comatose form.

Tears sprouted, and Steve could not tear his eyes away from the screen. Pain and fury mixed in his blood and kept him from drawing a breath. The thought of Kyle raping Jennifer night after night while he slept less than two hundred yards from the building made him physically ill and he swallowed the bile burning his throat.

The video switched between vile scenes in the hospital to the scenes at their cottage a year ago, alternating from one sick violation to the next, and Steve leaned his head back against the wood and screamed a wordless roar of fury.

JESSICA GROUND HER TEETH together. She couldn't see the video, but the agony etched into Steve's features was enough. She didn't need to be a mind reader to understand what was playing on the screen behind her, but she needed his attention, needed him to be in the present, to be smart and aware because things were only going to get worse.

Where is my husband? She silently sent the thought, gaining Steve's attention, bringing him back to the present situation, his gaze shifting to hers.

I don't know. He left a note this morning.

Kyle approached Jessica. He stepped behind the chair and yanked her head back, running his knife over her cheek and drawing a thin line of blood. "Did you know she's worth billions?"

Steve tightened the muscles in his jaw and blinked back the tears that made his vision warble. "Her husband will tear you to pieces." The words growled from his throat, and he kept eye contact with Jessica. *Can you call him?*

I've tried, but I can't reach him.

Steve closed his eyes and Kyle chuckled, rounding the front of her chair, his gray eyes intense and focused on Jessica's. "I've never fucked a billionaire." He ran the knife over her camisole, moving his gaze over her.

"My husband will kill you."

Kyle planted the knife in the chair between her legs and laughed at her sudden jerk.

"Do you know what my husband did to the last man who raped me?" Jessica asked, tilting her head.

Kyle backhanded her. "Do you know what I did to the last woman I fucked?" he asked, ignoring her question. "Not counting coma girl over there." He pointed toward the table in the far corner. "The last conscious woman I fucked, I had the pleasure of slitting her throat wide open while I came." He yanked the knife out of the chair. "I'm looking forward to doing that to you once I get my money." He nicked her chin and smiled. "Your brother-in-law needs to be taught a lesson," he added. "No one fucks with me."

Jessica tilted her head, glancing beyond him at Steve and then back at Kyle. "Ty Aris is dead."

"He stole ten million dollars from me with the help of the FBI." He pointed his knife at Steve.

Jessica chuckled.

"What are you laughing at?" Kyle snapped.

"You. You're pathetic and I can't wait to watch my husband tear you limb from limb." She spat back at Kyle.

Kyle lashed out with the knife, cutting through the fabric of her camisole and into the tender skin across her chest. "You're going to be sorely disappointed when I kill him."

Jessica belted out the laughter, which earned her a punch square in the nose. Her head slammed against the wooden backdrop of the chair, dazing her.

KYLE STEPPED BACK, LOOKING between the two remaining women, and headed in Jennifer's direction with the knife in his hand.

Steve willed the words to form and come out of his mouth. "I'm going to kill you," he said clearly from his post on the cross. The pain dulled to a slight roar from the scream it had been, but it was becoming increasingly hard to breathe and he still didn't have control of his muscles to push himself up the fraction to ease his breath.

Kyle glanced back at Steve and stopped, turning fully toward where the cross hung. "I hate to disappoint you, but I think you're going to die today, along with these lovely women." He pointed the knife at Jessica and Sarah.

Kyle diverted to the table behind him, bypassing Jennifer, and traded the knife for a cigar cutter. He crossed to Jessica and slipped the cutter over her pinky, threading it through the hole and snapping the cutters closed.

Kyle smiled at her sharp inhale, her first real reaction. "It's going to be fun to break you down." He waved the pinky in front of her and plopped it into a box along with a hand-written note for ransom.

"Fuck you!"

Kyle ignored the slur and turned his attention to the cop tied to the table. He stepped into the center of the room, running his fingers down Sarah's back, staring up at Steve's cobalt eyes. He saw the nuance of change in Steve's expression. "Pretty little thing, isn't she?" He stepped closer.

"Get away from me," Sarah snapped. She raised her eyes to Steve.

Threads of blood flowed out of his wrists and slid down his arms. Thin red trails of life seeped out of him, making Kyle grin.

Kyle moved between her legs and ran his hands over her back and around the front, squeezing her breasts. "Have you fucked her?"

Steve pressed his lips together.

"Get away from me." She struggled against the bonds holding her firmly to the table.

"I'm going to have more fun with you than I did with your sister."

Sarah screamed, struggling against the restraints. His fingers slid over her back and ass, all the way to the back of her knees, and he pressed his body against her.

"Stop!" Steve yelled, but it was futile.

Steve's reaction was exactly what Kyle wanted. "Where can I find Ty Aris?" he asked, running his hands up the insides of Sarah's thighs.

Steve closed his eyes. "I don't know," he said. "But you might be able to find his brother at the Park View Condos. He owns the penthouse." He opened his eyes, meeting Kyle's gaze.

Kyle ran his finger inside Sarah, and she renewed her struggle.

The muscles in Steve's jaw clenched. "I told you what you wanted. Now leave her alone!"

The anguish on Steve's face made him giddy. Tilting his head to the side and keeping eye contact with Steve, he moved his fingers roughly inside the cop while she sobbed, struggling against his assault. "Don't worry, doll, I've got plans for you when I get back." He pulled his fingers out and swatted her ass.

Steve let out a guttural cry and then slumped again. "I swear to God, I am going to kill you," he bellowed. "Even if I have to rise from the dead to do it."

Kyle laughed and looked up at Steve. "I'm sure your wife will like the things I have in store for her when I'm through with these two." He smiled and left the room with the box in his hand. Steve's roar followed him out.

Hunting Season
Chapter 53

CHRIS'S STOMACH GROWLED AGAIN. He had raided Kyle's refrigerator earlier, but now he paced, still hungry and getting more uncomfortable as the day wore on. Something wasn't right. He felt the tickle of a voice in his head and looked around.

It was after four and Kyle hadn't returned home yet. Chris took another walk through the apartment, shuffling through the papers on the table. A nagging feeling gripped his stomach.

"He isn't coming back," Chris said to the empty room. Silence was his answer. He turned and left, grabbing a hamburger, fries and a milkshake at the McDonald's before the highway entrance, and headed back to Manhattan.

Hunting Season
Chapter 54

KYLE DROVE TO THE address and walked in with the box wrapped in brown delivery paper.

"Excuse me." The desk attendant stopped him.

"I have a package for Mr. Ryan." He held the box out for the attendant to see.

The attendant smiled at Kyle. "You may leave the package here. I'll see that Mr. Ryan receives it."

Kyle nodded and handed the package over.

"Can I tell Mr. Ryan who it is from?"

"Tell him Kyle stopped by." He smiled and headed out.

Hunting Season
Chapter 55

"JENNY." STEVE SAID AFTER the door shut and the footfalls fell silent. He looked at his unconscious wife and let his head hang. Random visions of what happened ten months ago filled his head and, just like then, he was helpless to stop what Kyle had planned.

There was nothing he could do to protect any of them.

He tipped his head back and let out another roar of frustration.

Sarah's entire body shook, rattling the table with silent sobs. Her fear, like Jessica's, radiated in his mind, clouding his own thoughts. He clenched his teeth together, grinding them to control his temper, his despair, and his pain.

"You don't know where Chris is?"

"He doesn't have Chris," Steve answered her fears, tilting his head against the wood. He found he could support himself for small amounts of time by his feet before the pain became too overwhelming. He focused on Sarah again. "Sarah," he said, gaining her attention.

Sarah slowly turned her head in his direction. "He's going to kill me."

Steve shook his head. "Not if I can help it."

She actually laughed. "You're screwed to a cross."

Steve glanced over at Jessica. "Yeah, well." He glanced back at Sarah. "I'll figure something out."

Sarah started sobbing again.

The video looped, replaying the hospital rape and a rape that looked like it happened in the back of the ambulance, followed by those scenes at the cottage that Kyle sent on the disc. Steve's hatred flared.

Killing Kyle was the number one to do on his list and he'd see to it that the bastard suffered.

Steve tore his eyes away from the screen, glancing toward Jenny, his eyes glossing over with tears. It looked like Jennifer had shifted on the gurney and he blinked the tears back.

"Jenny?" He shot a glance toward Jessica. She was looking over her shoulder at his wife with the same perplexed gaze—she turned her head toward Steve.

"Stop crying, Sarah," Steve said, annoyance now rode his pain riddled body. Acute agony in his wrists and shoulders wore on his patience. "That only makes him get off more." He sagged again, his legs giving way. A low groan escaped. "Does anyone know how long it takes for someone to die from crucifixion?" he asked, looking at the ceiling. His chest felt like a thousand-pound boulder had fallen on it, constricting to the point of crushing.

"Chris was only up there for an hour," Jessica said. "But he died from blood loss, not the crucifixion itself."

Sarah turned her head and stared at Jessica. "He walked out of here without a scratch."

Jessica shot her gaze in Sarah's direction. "I'm aware of that."

"I hope he gets here soon," Steve said, trying to prop himself back up and diverting the conversation as much as he could.

Because we don't have Tommy or CJ here this time. And if he doesn't get here soon, I'm toast.

Jessica bit her lower lip and her eyes welled with tears. The front she had put up crumbled at the mention of her children and she leaned her head back, letting the tears flow.

"Shit." Steve swore. Now he had two women in the room crying. "Get yourselves together, girls," he said, clenching his teeth against the pain.

He propped himself up with his feet. He flexed his right arm, straining against the screw that held him in place. A roar of pain filled the room, and he pulled with all his might. The screw didn't budge, and blood seeped from the wound, tickling as it followed the line of his arm and trickled down his side. He slumped again, closed his eyes, and leaned his head back.

"Why are you here?" he finally asked, looking down at Sarah.

Sarah turned her head away.

"You were investigating me?"

Sarah snapped her head back in his direction. "I never said that." Her eyes alternated between fear and confusion.

"I know, but you thought it," he replied. "And I can read your mind."

Sarah raised her eyebrows. She didn't know whether to be pissed or awed.

He laughed a little and then his own tears began as he looked at his wife. "I wish you knew her." He clenched his jaw, shifting his weight.

Steve?

Jenny's voice invaded his head, and he shot a quick glance at Jessica.

"Jenny?" No response and he wondered if he were hallucinating.

The door swung open, and Kyle stepped inside. "Looks like I'll just have to wait a little while for my money." He crossed the room and dropped a brown paper bag on the chair next to Jessica. "I bought a toy." He smiled and pulled out a riding crop. "I figured I'd have some fun with you girls while I wait." He glanced back at Steve. "Any preference who I fuck?"

"Yourself." Steve breathed the word.

Kyle laughed and picked up the riding crop and his knife. He crossed the room to Sarah, planted the knife in the table and ran the crop down her back.

"No," she whined pitifully as he began his horrific violation.

"Oh, yes. And you're going to cum for me." He turned on the handle of the crop and pulled his fingers away, replacing them with the vibrating metal, rubbing it in slow circles. She struggled in the bindings holding her to the table.

Kyle laughed, glancing up at Steve. "I bet you're wishing you had the chance to fuck her," he teased.

"Son of a bitch." He shifted his weight to his feet, feeling a little relief from the pain in his wrists and shoulders.

Kyle shrugged. "She'll still cum, just like your wife did."

The mention of Jenny made Steve see red. His jaws clenched, and he tried to pull the screw out of the wood again, bellowing with anger and frustration when the pain overwhelmed him. Again, the screw didn't budge.

Kyle laughed and focused his attention on Sarah. "Sweet fuck, it's too bad you won't live to see nightfall." He unzipped his pants.

"No!" she screamed and renewed her struggles.

Steve closed his eyes. Hearing her cry was enough, seeing the assault just made the anger unbearable. There wasn't a thing he could do to stop this bastard.

Sarah's cries increased, mixed with swear-laden sobs.

"I hate you!" she screamed.

Kyle laughed and reached for the knife.

Steve's eyes flew open. He knew what Kyle was going to do. "No." He spread his right hand wide.

Kyle grabbed a handful of Sarah's hair and jerked her head back. She cried out in pain and fear. The knife disappeared from view under her chin.

Oh, my God, I'm going to die!

The thought flashed through her mind and the metal blade bit into his hand and not her throat. Steve concentrated with everything he had, envisioning his hand between her throat and the knife, despite the searing pain.

Steve cried out as the flesh of his hand split open at the same time Kyle raked the knife across Sarah's throat. He prayed Kyle saw the vision of blood spreading over the table, courtesy of Jessica and her silent command.

Kyle pumped a couple more times and pulled out, satisfied. He zipped up and wiped the bloody knife on his pant leg.

Steve closed his hand into a fist, ignoring the pain and keeping eye contact with Sarah. *Don't move and don't breathe.* He sent the thought to her, praying she would hear him. Warm blood dripped from his fist.

Sarah blinked when his voice filled her mind. She took the smallest of breaths and her eyes filled with doubt. *This isn't going to work.*

Kyle turned, focusing on Jessica. He walked back to her, waving the crop in front of her face.

Jessica looked between the riding crop and his face without speaking.

Steve gave her credit—her face never gave away the screams locked in her mind.

He kneeled and slid it inside her, flipping the switch to maximum vibration. "You're pretty hot for an old lady."

Jessica spit in his face.

Kyle wiped the spit off and continued to fuck her with the vibrating handle. "I want you to cum for me." He smiled at her, wiping his hand on his jeans.

"Ain't gonna happen."

Kyle's smile faded. She wasn't as much fun as the sobbing cop. He stood and grabbed a fistful of her hair, pulling her toward his crotch, unzipping his pants.

"The last time a man tried to force his dick in my mouth, I bit a chunk off. Care to take that kind of a gamble?" she said through clenched teeth.

Even Steve shivered at the thought, his family jewels shrinking away, trying to retreat into his body.

Kyle faltered and let go of her hair. He stepped away, ignoring the labored chuckling coming from Steve. He picked up the knife, sliding it between her breasts. The blade sliced into her skin. "I don't like you." He grasped the riding crop and slammed the full length inside her.

Jessica gasped and clenched her teeth again, blinking back the sheen of tears the pain produced.

The phone rang, interrupting Kyle's assault.

Hunting Season
Chapter 56

CHRIS PULLED INTO THE garage at close to seven. The sun dipped behind the tall skyscrapers. He waved to the valet and drove to his parking spot, glancing at the empty slot where Steve's car had been, wondering if he had gone to find that hot little number after all. He stepped into the elevator and rubbed his face.

The message light on the phone blinked when he stepped into the apartment, and he pressed the button.

"Mr. Ryan, there's a package at the front desk for you." The telltale beep followed, signifying that was the only message.

Chris picked up the phone and dialed the front desk. "Hello, it's Chris Ryan. I understand there's a package down there for me?"

"Yes, there is. Would you like me to bring it up, sir?"

"Yes, that would be helpful."

Chris opened the door a few minutes later. He took the package from the attendant and forked over a hefty tip. "Did they leave a name?"

"The man said his name was Kyle."

"Thank you." Chris held the frozen smile on his face until the door closed and then tore open the box. The world swam in front of him, and he read the note. His eyes returned to the severed finger as each word penetrated him like a gunshot.

"Jesus Christ." He found his way to the couch and grabbed the phone, dialing his home in Maine.

"Hello?"

"Mom?" Chris asked in surprise.

"Hi, Chris, has Jessie gotten there yet?" Jessica's mother replied.

"Oh, yeah, I just wanted to make sure the kids got home okay," Chris answered quickly.

"They're playing outside. Do you want me to call them inside?"

"No, just making sure. I'll call before bedtime. Thanks, Mom." He hung up the phone. His gaze swiveled back to the box, trying to put two and two together in his mind.

He picked up the note and read it slowly, trying to comprehend what had gone wrong. Chris stared at the box on the table in front of him again, his stomach in knots and his heart pounded too hard in his chest. Pulling his cell from his pocket, he dialed Steve's cell number.

"I was wondering how long it would take for you to call," Kyle purred in the phone. "Your wife is going to be such a good fuck."

Jessica's scream barreled through his brain like an F-15 breaking the sound barrier, and Chris jumped to his feet. The last time he heard that volume from Jessica was when Frank raped her in the hallway of the complex fifteen years before. He closed his eyes, containing the anger inside. The image she sent, along with the mental scream, made his eyes snap wide again.

He knew exactly where they were.

"You really have no clue, do you?" Chris growled. It was the same low tone of voice he used earlier.

"Your brother stole my money and I want it back. I will give you an hour and then you will get another piece of your wife."

"My brother is dead, you stupid fuck," he said, grabbing the box and left the apartment. "I stole your money." He stabbed his finger on the down button.

"Well, then, I guess I've got the upper hand here. I have your wife and your FBI boy here and we've been having a ball. If I don't have my money back in my account along with another hundred million in the next hour, I'll start chopping her up."

"I'll see what I can do," Chris snapped and stepped onto the elevator, closing the phone. "I'm coming, babe," he said aloud and ran into the garage, sliding into his car.

Hunting Season
Chapter 57

KYLE FLIPPED THE PHONE closed, smiling at Jessica. "He's going to see what he can do." He kneeled back down on the ground in front of her, moving the handle again. "In the meantime..." He slammed the crop into her. "I need to teach you a lesson."

Jessica threw herself forward, connecting her forehead to his nose and sending him back on the floor. She sat back, glaring at him.

Jessica calculated how long it would take her husband to cross Manhattan and prayed he'd get there before this man lost it. What she saw in his eyes planted doubt in her soul, and she braced herself.

"Bitch!" he snapped, holding his bloody nose. He grabbed the knife off the floor and buried it in her side, spearing layers of her intestines. He yanked the blade out and put the tip to her throat.

White spots of pain flared in her line of sight, and her breath locked in her throat. A scream trapped by the lack of air pressed against her chest and she clamped her teeth together. A red spot spread across her camisole, and she concentrated on mending the wound. Searing pain engulfed her, and a gasp escaped, the skin binding at her direction. "If you kill me, you can kiss the money goodbye," she hissed.

Kyle's lips twitched, and his murderous glare dulled. He pulled the knife away, setting it carefully down on the floor like it could turn on him at any moment.

When he returned his gaze to her, she knew she was in trouble.

He wiped his bloody nose on his sleeve and grabbed hold of the crop, slamming its length inside her again. "But I can hurt you as much as I want until I get paid."

"YOU BASTARD, LEAVE HER alone," Steve wheezed, the effort draining what little strength he had left.

His vision doubled and then tripled. He snapped his head back and forth, trying to shake himself into full consciousness, but he kept slipping into the dark. His chest burned under the pressure, each breath a fight to sustain life.

Hanging on the cross for seven hours left his muscles cramping and unable to support his weight any longer.

Stay with me! Chris is on his way. His eyes fluttered open as Jessica's voice barreled through his brain and he groaned.

Hunting Season
Chapter 58

GOOSEBUMPS COVERED HER SKIN, and she shivered. A crease appeared between her eyes. Jennifer Williams blinked her eyes open for the first time in close to a year, staring at the bare rafters above her. Confusion overwhelmed her, and she tilted her head, inspecting her surroundings.

The wall to her left was not that of the cabin. It was metal and brick and she blinked, lowering her eyes to the light hospital gown she wore.

This certainly wasn't a hospital either.

She closed her eyes and her last memory of the cottage surfaced—running toward her daughter and the sound of her world ripping apart. Her eyes snapped open, and she focused on the room beyond the table.

Her surroundings made no sense, and she sat up, swaying from the sudden light-headedness. Voices registered, but the sight of a man who looked frighteningly like her husband nailed to a cross brought her hand to her mouth.

It couldn't be him. There are no scars. "Steve?"

His eyes swiveled to hers and widened a fraction.

Jennifer stared at him and swung her legs over the side of the table. Her eyes darted toward the movement on her right and her gaze fell on Kyle. A sudden pain ripped through her at the sight of him. Her eyes jumped from him to Steve and back when he stood and started in her direction.

"Run." The word hissed from Steve's chest and her eyes found his again.

The command registered in her brain, mingling with the memory in the glade outside of Black Cove with the same tone and urgency in his voice. Jennifer reacted, darting toward the door.

Kyle was faster, intercepting her and reaching for her arm. Jennifer sidestepped him, and fury filled her. Memories like a sick slide show snapped off in her mind: the cabin, the hospital, her daughter, everything; and rage took over.

She spun away, executing a sidekick that connected with his groin, and instead of running, she went into attack mode.

"Jenny, RUN!" Steve bellowed.

This time, she ignored him.

"You killed my daughter!" The words hissed from her dry throat. Venom spit from her mouth along with a string of curses that did nothing to ease the raw rage rattling through her veins, giving her an inhuman strength.

Her next kick connected with Kyle's face, and he rolled away, still clutching the knife. He shot to his feet, and she swung her fist, hell bent on smashing his nose, but he blocked the wild swing, whipping her around and letting go.

Jennifer tripped, sprawling to the ground, and her anger transitioned to fear. She tried to roll away, but Kyle was already on top of her, pinning her with his knees. He swung his fist, connecting with her nose and slamming her head into the hard floor, dazing her.

STEVE WAS NOW FULLY lucid. His labored heart pounded in his chest.

"Bitch!" Kyle raised the knife in the air

The roar that escaped Steve echoed against the brick walls and the knife arched toward Jennifer's chest. It stopped a few feet above her and blood slid down the suspended blade.

Searing pain tore the flesh of Steve's chest, puncturing his lung, and his breath hitched.

For the second time that day, he put himself between the blade and someone he cared about, but this time, it wasn't just his hand. His already taxed lungs seized with agony and the world swam as he drowned in his own blood.

Hunting Season
Chapter 59

CHRIS SLID INTO THE parking lot in less than fifteen minutes. He hopped out of the car and sprinted inside, vaulting up the stairs two at a time.

Steve's roar filled the hallway and Chris blew the door off the hinges, stepping inside as Kyle turned his head toward the door. The knife hung in the air above Jennifer, dripping with blood and Chris knew without looking that Steve had blocked it just like Eric did so many years ago.

Kyle pivoted, scrambling to his feet with the knife. He crossed the room, reaching Jessica and Chris took another step into the room.

Chris raised his eyes to the back of the cross, the anger sparking to fury inside him. The screws holding Steve in place exploded out of the wood, catapulted across the room, and embedded head first into the brick façade.

Steve fell, and when his feet hit the floor, he collapsed with a yelp of pain. He choked on blood, trying to suck large quantities of oxygen into his starving lungs. Pain caused him to see dark spots, and he struggled not to suffocate on the blood filling his lung. He rolled onto his stomach, maneuvering to his knees with the palms of his hands on the floor, the air gurgling through the wound in his chest.

Kyle pressed the knife against Jessica's throat, staring into the eyes of the man who interrupted his killing spree.

"Took you long enough." Jessica tried to smile at her husband.

Chris nodded, and his eyes lowered to the riding crop sticking out from beneath her camisole. Raw rage filled his form, flaring his power into a roaring beast. His eyes returned to meet Kyle's. "You just fucked with the wrong person."

The knife ripped out of Kyle's hand and flew to the far wall. At the same time, the riding crop dislodged from Jessica, falling to the floor.

Chris mentally shoved Kyle, and he fell backwards, landing on his ass with a thud. Kyle's gaze darted toward both the gun on the far chair and the knife to his left, the indecision etched into his features.

With a twitch of Chris's head, the bindings holding Jessica and Sarah evaporated, freeing them, and he tossed Jessica the box with her finger in it and then pointed toward Steve. "Help him, Jess," he ordered and stepped into the center of the room.

Sarah rolled off the table, and Kyle's jaw dropped. His eyes nearly bugged out of his head. "But..."

Chris chuckled. "But what?"

Kyle's head snapped back toward Chris, his shock transitioning to fear. Fear Chris could feel pulsing through the bastard's veins.

"Who are you?" Kyle asked, his voice hardly a whisper.

With a dismissive hand gesture, the furniture between them flew in opposite directions, crashing against the far walls, clearing a wide path and Chris smiled. "I am your worst fucking nightmare."

Kyle lunged for Steve's gun.

"I don't think so," Chris said, willing the gun across the room. It landed behind him next to the door.

Kyle shook, sweat breaking out on his upper lip, and his eyes widened. "What are you?"

Chris chuckled and spread his arms wide. "I'm the angel of death, boy, and I've come to drag you to hell."

JESSICA CROSSED THE ROOM, sliding next to Steve and leaned forward, planting a healing kiss on his forehead. Light spread over his body and patched the knife wounds and the holes in his wrists and feet.

Steve drew in a hissing breath. "Jenny." He looked up at his wife before his eyes rolled up in his head and he passed out.

"What did you do to him?" Jennifer gasped, falling to her knees in front of him. Her jaw dropped when the last of the wounds on his wrists disappeared, erasing any remnant of a scar, leaving the skin perfect and unbroken. She scanned his perfect back before turning toward Jessica.

Jessica met her gaze for an instant as her own agony flared as she mended her pinkie back in place. She ignored the awe tattooed on Jennifer's face and turned her attention to Chris. Her fear of Kyle wasn't in the same vicinity as what raked through her slight form at the sight of Chris's eyes. His blue irises stood out against a blood-red backdrop, making him look more demon than human. Thin streams of blood leaked from the corner of his eyes, marring his perfect profile, reminding her of the scars her son erased.

"Ty," Jessica whispered, calling Chris's attention. She shook her head. "Don't."

Chris took a deep breath, tearing his gaze away from Jessica, focusing back on the man who had hurt her today. "Sorry, babe." He stepped dead center, squaring himself toward Kyle.

"Let's see what you've got." Chris waved Kyle in, curling his hands into fists.

Hunting Season
Chapter 60

STEVE GROANED, RAISED HIS head from the floor, and blinked up at his wife. "Jenny," his voice hitched and in one motion, he had her in his arms, clinging to her as the pain subsided.

For a moment, the world was right. Her scent, her soft skin, even the concern in her voice as she said his name flooded his senses and he squeezed his eyes shut, controlling the onslaught of emotion.

Chris's voice brought him out of his silent reverie and back to the current situation. He turned his attention to the center of the room, dislodging himself from Jennifer.

"He's mine." Steve stood.

"No, Steve." Chris diverted his eyes from Kyle, meeting his gaze. "You can't." He mentally pushed Steve back on his ass, holding him there with an invisible grip as unyielding as the screws that had held him to the cross.

Chris turned toward Kyle in time to see the knife hurtling through the air toward him. He spun to the side, striking the knife with his forearm, sending it sailing away and leaving a bloody welt in his arm.

Kyle's eyes went wide.

Chris studied his forearm and glanced up at Kyle. He took form again, allowing a small smile to find his lips.

Kyle's brow creased. "You're Ty Aris, aren't you?" He remembered the picture he saw of Ty and the icy stare was the same.

Chris let the smile disappear and glared at Kyle. "Perhaps."

Kyle shivered. "This is a little unfair, don't you think?" His voice shook.

Chris shrugged. "Tying a bomb to an infant is a little unfair. At least *I* didn't hurt kids."

They circled each other, keeping a good five feet between them. Finally, Chris stopped.

"Come on, do something," he demanded. He spread his arms wide. "I'll even give you the first shot for free."

Kyle took the bait and stepped in, throwing a right hook.

Chris pivoted and stepped back, throwing a punch that connected with Kyle's kidney as he sailed by. "Pathetic attempt. I thought a big, badass assassin would have cleaner moves than that. You're nothing but a common punk."

Kyle caught his balance. Spinning toward Chris, he roared and lunged.

Chris spun out of the way and swept Kyle's feet out from under him.

Kyle sprawled on the floor. "Fuck!" Cursing, he scrambled to his feet.

"Stop playing games, Chris, kill the bastard," Steve said, straining against the mental grip enough to get to his feet.

"Sit your ass down!" Chris yelled and pointed in his direction.

Steve sat on the floor obediently, the invisible hand back and holding him in place. "God damn it, Chris, he killed my little girl!"

"Don't worry, Steve. He won't leave this warehouse alive," Chris said, while keeping sight of Kyle and blinking back the blood red film covering his eyes. He offered a cold smile. "You killed my son," he said, addressing Kyle.

Kyle smiled. "He was such an easy shot, bullet tore right through his heart."

The fury took over and Chris stepped forward, throwing a hard right, connecting with Kyle's chest, sending him flying off his feet onto his back and into the wall. Chris was on him seconds later, yanking him to his feet and he slammed him into the hard bricks. He never saw the knife until the pain flashed in his side.

Kyle smiled and pulled the blade out of Chris's stomach, plunging it a second time before Chris could react.

This time, the knife sliced Chris's liver in half. Adrenaline rushed, and Chris picked Kyle up and threw him across the room with a roar. He looked down at the blood spreading across the lower half of his shirt and down the front of his pants. "Shit," he said, falling to his knee in a swoon. He shook his head clear and struggled to his feet, facing Kyle.

Kyle charged.

Chris snarled, lashing a fraction of the power in Kyle's direction, focusing in on his face.

Kyle's eyes exploded, and he screamed. His hands flew to his face with the knife still clutched in his fist.

The gunshot rang through the room. The deafening boom made Steve wince and within a blink, a wall of raw power slammed into him, knocking him back on his ass. The impact of Chris's power filled his skin and nearly stopped his heart. With it came the knowledge of why Steve couldn't kill Kyle, and his breath caught in his throat.

Chris's passing from this world to the next overwhelmed him and his gaze snapped to his body. Blood pooled around his head on the wooden floor and Chris stared at the ceiling with one eye. The other eye was gone, taken out by chance, by a ricocheted bullet.

Tears sprang to Steve's eyes. "Jesus, no," he whispered. The invisible hand that held him in place was gone, and he stood.

"No!" Jessica's scream diminished under the sound of the second gunshot.

A bullet tore through Kyle's groin, and he fell to his knees. His scream was louder than Jessica's.

Steve spun toward the gunshot.

Sarah had the gun trained on Kyle with her face twisted into a mask of fury. She squeezed the trigger again, and Kyle's screams drowned out Jessica's pleading sobs.

Steve stepped between Sarah and what was left of Kyle, blocking her line of fire. "Enough, Sarah," he said, and her eyes met his.

He wanted to say he understood.

He wanted to say he wanted Kyle dead, too.

He wanted to say he was sorry, but the words wouldn't come. Instead, he put his hand out for the gun.

"Get out of the way."

Steve shook his head. "Give me the gun," he said, wishing it to be so. When she complied, placing the pistol in his hand, he was sure his expression matched her wide-eyed shock.

He slid the pistol into his waistband and turned to Jennifer. "Call 9-1-1."

Jennifer nodded, scrambling to the discarded cell phone on the floor, and called for help. "Where are we?"

Steve rattled off the address of the warehouse and approached the husk of a man moaning in the center of the room. His hand itched to pull the gun and plant a bullet in his brain, but the responsibility Chris laid at his feet stopped him. He finally understood the burden of having this much power. It took a life of its own within him, making him shake at the thought of trying to contain and control it.

He clenched his fists and closed his eyes, feeling the power snake through his veins, reining it into a tightly controlled coil.

Opening his eyes, he fell back on police procedure, reciting the Miranda rights to Kyle through a tightly clenched jaw, keeping his desire to lash out in check. He had the power to eviscerate the beast, to turn him to dust, but that wasn't good enough. The man needed to suffer.

"You're not dying today," Steve growled low in Kyle's ear. "I'm going to make sure you live a solitary, miserable life on death row until the day comes when I'll watch you die." He allowed a fraction of a smile, his eyes meeting Jennifer's across the room. "And I *will* make sure it isn't a painless death."

Hunting Season
Chapter 61

STEVE PULLED THE BMW up to the cottage and sat staring at the little house with the warm sun on his tired face. He glanced at Jennifer, took her hand, and brought it to his lips.

Jennifer glanced at the cottage and back at Steve. "What happened?"

Steve took a deep breath. "You've been in a coma for the last year, and they said you were brain dead."

Jennifer raised her eyebrows.

"Jessica, um, fixed you." He let his lips curl a fraction. "She's a miracle worker." Steve got out of the car and leaned on the side, looking out at the lake as she got out, coming around to his side.

"What now?" Jennifer asked.

"I don't know," Steve said, his eyes still glued on the path to Paradise Cove. "I'll be right back." He crossed the lawn, disappearing into the thick spring woods. When he stepped onto the soft moss, he sighed, slipped his shoes off, and sat on the lily pad shaped rock, lowering his feet into the cool water before closing his eyes.

"Thank you, God," he whispered. Water seeped up his legs, his pants acted like a sponge, sucking the wetness through the fabric. Steve leaned back, supporting himself with his palms, and let the sun wash over his face.

The air shifted. "Why'd you do it?" he asked without opening his eyes.

"Do what?"

Steve opened his eyes and glanced toward the voice. Chris Ryan sat with his legs in the water, leaning with his hands back on the moss, mirroring Steve.

"Trade your life for mine," Steve said.

The ghost of Chris Ryan laughed. "I didn't."

Steve raised his eyebrows.

"I was sent to make sure you didn't slip to the dark side," he said, his imitation of Darth Vader impeccable, followed by musical laughter. He hopped to his feet and looked around the cove. When his eyes fell back on Steve, they were serious. "I owe you a lot more than you realize," he said, looking up at the sky as a cloud passed over, blocking the sun. He returned his unearthly blue eyes to Steve and let the beautiful ebony wings embedded in his back spread wide. They spanned almost to that of the clearing.

Steve yanked his legs out of the water and scrambled to his feet. He shivered at the sight of a winged man.

Angel of Death.

Her voice leaped into his mind, and he shot his eyes to the path in the woods.

Jennifer stared, her jaw slack and eyes wide.

Chris smiled at her. "Angel of Death is close enough." He returned his focus to Steve and his mighty wings beat, lifting him in the air and creating ripples across the surface of the cove. A ray of sunshine broke through the clouds and enveloped Chris, turning the black wings to pristine white before he faded into the sunlight.

The End

Continue The Steve Williams Series Books 4—6

Check out an excerpt from Georgia Reign, the next book in the Steve Williams Series on the next page.

Excerpt from Georgia Reign

STEVE WILLIAMS SAT ON the stairs of the dock, looking out over the lake. Gravel crunching under tires interrupted his fragmented thoughts, and he turned to see a Cadillac sedan pull to a stop behind his roadster. A small, mousy woman slid out of the car with an attaché case in her hand.

"Mr. Steven Williams?" she asked, pushing her glasses higher on the bridge of her nose as she approached the dock.

Steve nodded.

"Lynn Trueman. I'm Mr. Ryan's attorney," she began, extending her hand.

He shook her hand, pulling information from her thoughts. His brow creased. "Chris put me in his will?"

"Mr. Ryan came to see me at the beginning of last week to set up the trust fund for the victims of Kyle Winslow." She rummaged in her bag for the documents, pulling out an envelope and a couple of legal forms. "He said if anything should happen to him, you were to become the executor of that trust." Her lips spread in a ghost of a smile.

"But that wasn't all he requested, was it?"

"No, sir." Lynn handed the envelope to Steve. "He asked that I give you this."

He glanced between the document and the lawyer in front of him. Sliding his finger under the seal, he ripped open the envelope. The handwritten letter contained a check made out to Steven Williams in the same graceful long hand.

The amount leaped out at him, and he took a step back on rubbery legs. If he had been a cartoon character, his eyes would have shot out of his head with a grand AYEOOOGA, sound effects and all.

Somehow, he remained standing and shot his gaze back to hers. "Fifty million?"

She nodded. "Yes, that's your settlement from the trust."

Steve sat down hard on the lawn and stared at the letter. The script was wide and looping, slanting across the page. *Chris must have gotten straight A's in penmanship,* he thought.

Steve,

I'm assuming that you're probably sitting on your ass on the lawn just staring between the check and this letter right about now. I'm also assuming you believe you're responsible for my death. Get over it. You aren't. It was my time.

I knew it was coming, but I didn't know there would be a chance at redemption by saving your sorry ass. If I've done the job right, you're still breathing with a little extra juice you hadn't bargained for.

Now, for the favor. Keep an eye on my son. This whole thing is going to push him close to the edge, and I'm not sure Tommy can keep him from going over this time. He needs someone who can keep him in line. You've now got a significant piece of his father flowing through your veins, so he'll listen. Eventually.

As a side note, watch the temper. That's when you'll find the juice gets away from you. Otherwise, relax, it's your time in the sun, kid, enjoy it.

Best Regards,
Chris Ryan

If you would like to purchase the second installment of The Steve Williams Series: The Steve Williams Series II in hardcover, please visit her website store here: https://books.JETaylor75.com.

ABOUT J.E. TAYLOR

J.E. Taylor is a USA Today bestselling author, a publisher, an editor, a manuscript formatter, a mother, a wife, a business analyst, and a Supernatural fangirl. Not necessarily in that order. She first sat down to seriously write in February of 2007 after her daughter asked:

"Mom, if you could do anything, what would you do?"
From that moment on, she hasn't looked back.

Besides being co-owner of Novel Concept Publishing, Ms. Taylor also moonlights as a Senior Editor of Allegory E-zine, an online venue for Science Fiction, Fantasy and Horror, and co-host of the popular YouTube talk show Spilling Ink.

She lives in New Hampshire with her husband and during the summer months enjoys her weekends on the shore in southern Maine.

Visit her at www.jetaylor75.com to check out her other titles and sign up for her newsletter for early previews of her upcoming books, release announcements, and special opportunities for free swag!